LLOYD C. DOUGLAS

The
Robe

INTERNATIONAL COLLECTORS LIBRARY
AMERICAN HEADQUARTERS
Garden City, New York

PRINTED IN THE U.S.A.

Dedicated with appreciation

to

Hazel McCann

who wondered what became of

The Robe

Chapter I

BECAUSE she was only fifteen and busy with her growing up, Lucia's periods of reflection were brief and infrequent; but this morning she felt weighted with responsibility.

Last night her mother, who rarely talked to her about anything more perplexing than the advantages of clean hands and a pure heart, had privately discussed the possible outcome of Father's reckless remarks yesterday in the Senate; and Lucia, flattered by this confidence, had declared maturely that Prince Gaius wasn't in a position to do anything about it.

But after she had gone to bed, Lucia began to fret. Gaius might indeed overlook her father's heated comments about the extravagances and mismanagement of his government, if he had had no previous occasion for grievance against the Gallio family. There was, however, another grievance that no one knew about except herself—and Diana. They would all have to be careful now or they might get into serious trouble.

The birds had awakened her early. She was not yet used to their flutterings and twitterings, for they had returned much sooner than usual, Spring having arrived and unpacked before February's lease was up. Lucia roused to a consciousness of the fret that she had taken to bed with her. It was still there, like a toothache.

Dressing quietly so as not to disturb Tertia, who was soundly sleeping in the alcove—and would be alarmed when she roused to find her mistress's couch vacant—Lucia slipped her sandals softly over the exquisitely wrought mosaics that led from her bedchamber and through her parlor into the long corridor and down the wide stairway to the spacious hall and out into the vast peristyle where she paused, shielding her eyes against the sun.

For the past year or more, Lucia had been acutely conscious of her increasing height and rapid development into womanhood; but here on this expanse of tessellated tiling she always felt very insignificant. Everything in this immense peristyle dwarfed her; the tall marble columns that supported the vaulted roofs, the stately statues standing in their silent dignity on the close-clipped lawn, the high silver spray of the fountain. No matter how old she became, she would be ever a child here.

Nor did it make her feel any more mature when, proceeding along

the patterned pavement, she passed Servius whose face had been as
bronzed and deep-lined when Lucia was a mere toddler. Acknowledging with twinkling fingers and a smile the old slave's grave salute,
as he brought the shaft of his spear to his wrinkled forehead, she
moved on to the vine-covered pergola at the far end of the rectangle.

There, with her folded arms resting on the marble balustrade that
overlooked the terraced gardens, the arbors, the tiled pool, and commanded a breath-taking view of the city and the river, Lucia tried
to decide whether to tell Marcellus. He would be terrifically angry,
of course, and if he did anything about it at all he might make matters
worse; but—somebody in the family must be informed where we
stood in the opinion of Gaius before any more risks were taken. It
was unlikely, thought Lucia, that she would have an opportunity to
talk alone with her brother until later in the day; for Marcellus had
been out—probably all night—at the Military Tribunes' Banquet, and
wouldn't be up before noon; but she must resolve at once upon a
course of action. She wished now that she had told Marcellus last
summer, when it had happened.

The soft whisper of sandal-straps made her turn about. Decimus
the butler was approaching, followed by the Macedonian twins bearing silver trays aloft on their outspread palms. Would his mistress,
inquired Decimus with a deep bow, desire her breakfast served here?

'Why not?' said Lucia, absently.

Decimus barked at the twins and they made haste to prepare the
table while Lucia watched their graceful movements with amused
curiosity, as if observing the antics of a pair of playful terriers. Pretty
things, they were; a little older than she, though not so tall; agile and
shapely, and as nearly alike as two peas. It was the first time that
Lucia had seen them in action, for they had been purchased only a
week ago. Apparently Decimus, who had been training them, thought
they were ready now for active duty. It would be interesting to see
how they performed, for Father said they had been brought up in a
home of refinement and were probably having their first experience
of serving a table. Without risking an inquiring glance at the young
woman who stood watching them, they proceeded swiftly but quietly
with their task. They were both very white, observed Lucia, doubtless
from confinement in some prisonship.

One of Father's hobbies, and his chief extravagance, was the possession of valuable slaves. The Gallio family did not own very many,
for Father considered it a vulgar, dangerous, and ruinously expensive
vanity to have swarms of them about with little to do but eat, sulk,
and conspire. He selected his slaves with the same discriminating care
that he exercised when purchasing beautiful statuary and other art
objects. He had no interest in public sales. Upon the return of a
military expedition from some civilized country, the commanding
officers would notify a few of their well-to-do acquaintances that a

limited number of high-grade captives were available; and Father would go down, the day before the sale, and look them over, learn their history, sound them out, and if he found anything he wanted to add to his household staff he would bid. He never told anyone in the family how much he had paid for their slaves, but it was generally felt that he had never practiced economy in acquiring such merchandise.

Most of the people they knew were in a constant dither about their slaves; buying and selling and exchanging. It wasn't often that Father disposed of one; and when, rarely, he had done so, it was because the slave had mistreated another over whom he had some small authority. They had lost an excellent cook that way, about a year ago. Minna had grown crusty and cruel toward the kitchen crew, scolding them loudly and knocking them about. She had been warned a few times. Then, one day, Minna had slapped Tertia. Lucia wondered, briefly, where Minna was now. She certainly did know how to bake honey cakes.

You had to say this for Father: he was a good judge of people. Of course, slaves weren't people, exactly; but some of them were almost people. There was Demetrius, for example, who was at this moment marching through the colonnade with long, measured strides. Father had bought Demetrius six years ago and presented him to Marcellus on his seventeenth birthday. What a wonderful day that was, with all their good friends assembled in the Forum to see Marcellus—clean-shaven for the first time in his life—step forward to receive his white toga. Cornelius Capito and Father had made speeches, and then they had put the white toga on Marcellus. Lucia had been so proud and happy that her heart had pounded and her throat had hurt, though she was only nine then, and couldn't know much about the ceremony except that Marcellus was expected to act like a man now—though sometimes he forgot to, when Demetrius wasn't about.

Lucia pursed her full lips and grinned as she thought of their relationship; Demetrius, two years older than Marcellus, always so seriously respectful, never relaxing for an instant from his position as a slave; Marcellus, stern and dignified, but occasionally forgetting to be the master and slipping absurdly into the rôle of intimate friend. Very funny it was, sometimes. Lucia loved to watch them together at such moments. Of course she had about the same relation to Tertia; but that seemed different.

Demetrius had come from Corinth, where his father—a wealthy shipowner—had taken a too conspicuous part in defensive politics. Everything had happened at once in Demetrius' family. His father had been executed, his two elder brothers had been given to the new Legate of Achaea, his patrician mother had committed suicide; and Demetrius—tall, handsome, athletic—had been brought to Rome under heavy guard, for he was not only valuable but violent.

Lucia remembered when, a week before Marcellus' coming of age, she had heard Father telling Mother about his purchase of the Corinthian slave, only an hour earlier. She had been much impressed—and a little frightened, too.

'He will require careful handling for a while,' Father was saying. 'He has seen some rough treatment. His keeper told me I had better sleep with a dagger under my pillow until the Corinthian cooled down. It seems he had badly beaten up one of his guards. Ordinarily, of course, they would have dealt with him briefly and decisively; but they were under orders to deliver him uninjured. They were quite relieved to get him off their hands.'

'But is this not dangerous?' Mother had inquired anxiously. 'What might he not do to our son?'

'That,' Father had replied, 'will be up to Marcellus. He will have to win the fellow's loyalty. And he can do it, I think. All that Demetrius needs is an assurance of fair play. He will not expect to be petted. He is a slave, and he knows it—and hates it; but he will respond to decent discipline.' And then Father had gone on to say that after he had paid the money and signed the documents, he had himself led Demetrius out of the narrow cell; and, when they were in the open plaza, had unlocked his chains; very carefully, too, for his wrists were raw and bleeding. 'Then I walked on ahead of him,' Father had continued, 'without turning to see whether he was following me. Aulus had driven me down and was waiting in the chariot at the Appian Gate, a few yards away. I had planned to bring the Corinthian back with me. But, as we neared the chariot, I decided to give him instructions about how to reach our villa on foot.'

'Alone?' Mother had exclaimed. 'Was that not very risky?'

'Yes,' Father had agreed, 'but not quite so risky as to have brought him here as a shackled prisoner. He was free to run away. I wanted him to be in a position to decide whether he would rather take a chance with us than gamble on some other fate. I could see that my gestures of confidence had surprised and mellowed him a little. He said—in beautiful Greek, for he had been well educated, "What shall I do, sir, when I arrive at your villa?" I told him to inquire for Marcipor, who would advise him. He nodded, and stood fumbling with the rusty chains that I had loosed from his hands. "Throw them away," I said. Then I mounted the chariot, and drove home.'

'I wonder if you will ever see him again,' Mother had said; and, in answer to her question, Marcipor appeared in the doorway.

'A young Corinthian has arrived, Master,' said Marcipor, a Corinthian himself. 'He says he belongs to us.'

'That is true,' Father said, pleased with the news. 'I bought him this morning. He will attend my son, though Marcellus is to know nothing of this for the present. Feed him well. And provide him with a bath and clean clothing. He has been imprisoned for a long time.'

'The Greek has already bathed, Master,' replied Marcipor.

'Quite right,' approved Father. 'That was thoughtful of you.'

'I had not yet thought of it,' admitted Marcipor. 'I was in the sunken garden, supervising the building of the new rose arbor, when this Greek appeared. Having told me his name, and that he belonged here, he caught sight of the pool—'

'You mean'—expostulated Mother—'that he dared to use our pool?'

'I am sorry,' Marcipor replied. 'It happened so quickly I was unable to thwart it. The Greek ran swiftly, tossing aside his garments, and dived in. I regret the incident. The pool will be drained immediately, and thoroughly cleansed.'

'Very good, Marcipor,' said Father. 'And do not rebuke him; though he should be advised not to do that again.' And Father had laughed, after Marcipor had left the room. Mother said, 'The fellow should have known better than that.' 'Doubtless he did,' Father had replied. 'But I cannot blame him. He must have been immensely dirty. The sight of that much water probably drove him temporarily insane.'

One could be sure, reflected Lucia, that Marcipor hadn't been too hard on poor Demetrius; for, from that day, he had treated him as if he were his own son. Indeed, the attachment was so close that slaves more recently acquired often asked if Marcipor and Demetrius were not somehow related.

* * * * * *

Demetrius had reappeared from the house now, and was advancing over the tiled pavement on his way to the pergola. Lucia wondered what errand was bringing him. Presently he was standing before her, waiting for a signal to speak.

'Yes, Demetrius?' she drawled.

'The Tribune,' he announced, with dignity, 'presents his good wishes for his sister's health and happiness, and requests that he be permitted to join her at breakfast.'

Lucia brightened momentarily; then sobered, and replied, 'Inform your master that his sister will be much pleased—and tell him,' she added, in a tone somewhat less formal, 'that breakfast will be served here in the pergola.'

After Denetrius had bowed deeply and was turning to go, Lucia sauntered past him and proceeded along the pavement for several yards. He followed her at a discreet distance. When they were out of earshot, she paused and confronted him.

'How does he happen to be up so early?' she asked, in a tone that was neither perpendicular nor oblique, but frankly horizontal. 'Didn't he go to the banquet?'

'The Tribune attended the banquet,' replied Demetrius, respectfully. 'It is of that, perhaps, that he is impatient to speak.'

'Now don't tell me that he got into some sort of mess, Demetrius.' She tried to invade his eyes, but the bridge was up.

'If so,' he replied, prudently, 'the Tribune may wish to report it without the assistance of his slave. Shall I go now?'

'You were there, of course, attending my brother,' pursued Lucia. And when Demetrius bowed an affirmative, she asked, 'Was Prince Gaius there?' Demetrius bowed again, and she went on, uncertainly, 'Did you—was he—had you an opportunity to notice whether the Prince was in good humor?'

'Very,' replied Demetrius—'until he went to sleep.'

'Drunk?' Lucia wrinkled her nose.

'It is possible,' deliberated Demetrius, 'but it is not for me to say.'

'Did the Prince seem friendly—toward my brother?' persisted Lucia.

'No more than usual.' Demetrius shifted his weight and glanced toward the house.

Lucia sighed significantly, shook her black curls, and pouted.

'You can be very trying sometimes, Demetrius.'

'I know,' he admitted ruefully. 'May I go now? My master—'

'By all means!' snapped Lucia. 'And swiftly!' She turned and marched back with clipped steps to the pergola. Something had gone wrong last night, or Demetrius wouldn't have taken that frozen attitude.

Decimus, whose instinct advised him that his young mistress was displeased, retreated to a safe distance. The twins, who had now finished laying the table, were standing side by side awaiting orders. Lucia advanced on them.

'What are you called?' she demanded, her tone still laced with annoyance.

'I am Helen,' squeaked one of them, nervously. 'My sister is Nesta.'

'Can't she talk?'

'Please—she is frightened.'

Their long-lashed eyes widened with apprehension as Lucia drew closer, but they did not flinch. Cupping her hands softly under their round chins, she drew up their faces, smiled a little, and said, 'Don't be afraid. I won't bite you.' Then—as if caressing a doll—she toyed with the tight little curls that had escaped from Helen's cap. Turning to Nesta, she untied and painstakingly retied her broad sash. Both girls' eyes were swimming. Nesta stopped a big tear with the back of her hand.

'Now, now,' soothed Lucia, 'don't cry. No one is going to hurt you here.' She impulsively abandoned the lullaby, drew herself erect, and declared proudly: 'You belong to Senator Marcus Lucan Gallio! He paid a great price for you—because you are valuable; and—because you are valuable—you will not be mistreated. . . . Decimus'—she called, over her shoulder—'see that these pretty children have new tunics; white ones—with coral trimmings.' She picked up their hands, one by one, and examined them critically. 'Clean,' she remarked, half aloud—'and beautiful, too. That is good.' Facing Decimus, she said: 'You may go now. Take the twins. Have them bring the food. My brother will have breakfast with me here. You need not come back.'

Lucia had never liked Decimus very well; not that there was any particular ground for complaint, for he was a perfect servant; almost too deferential, a chilling deference that lacked only a little of being sulkiness. It had been Lucia's observation that imported slaves were more comfortable to live with than the natives. Decimus had been born in Rome and had been in their family for almost as long a Lucia could remember. He had a responsible position; attended to all the purchasing of supplies for their tables, personally interviewed the merchants, visited the markets, met the foreign caravans that brought spices and other exotics from afar; a very competent person indeed, who minded his own business, kept his own counsel, and carried himself with dignity. But he was a stranger.

One never could feel toward Decimus as one did toward good old Marcipor who was always so gentle—and trustworthy too. Marcipor had managed the business affairs of the family for so long that he probably knew more about their estate than Father did.

Decimus bowed gravely now, as Lucia dismissed him, and started toward the house, his stiff back registering disapproval of this episode that had flouted the discipline he believed in and firmly exercised. The Macedonians, their small even teeth flashing an ecstatic smile, scampered away, hand in hand, without waiting for formal permission. Lucia stopped them in their tracks with a stern command.

'Come back here!' she called severely. They obeyed with spiritless feet and stood dejectedly before her. 'Take it easy,' drawled Lucia. 'You shouldn't romp when you're on duty. Decimus does not like it.'

They looked up shyly from under their long lashes, and Lucia's lips curled into a sympathetic grin that relighted their eyes.

'You may go now,' she said, abruptly resuming a tone of command. Lounging onto the long marble seat beside the table, she watched the twins as they marched a few paces behind Decimus, their spines straight and stiff as arrows, accenting each determined step with jerks of their heads from side to side, in a quite too faithful imitation of the crusty butler. Lucia chuckled. 'The little rascals,' she muttered. 'They deserve to be spanked for that.' Then she suddenly sobered and sat studiously frowning at the rhythmic flexion of her sandaled toes. Marcellus would be here in a moment. How much—if anything—should she tell her adored brother about her unpleasant experience with Gaius? But first, of course, she must discover what dreadful thing had happened last night at the Tribunes' Banquet.

* * * * * *

'Good morning, sweet child!' Marcellus tipped back his sister's head, noisily kissed her between the eyes, and tousled her hair, while Bambo, his big black sheep-dog, snuggled his grinning muzzle under her arm and wagged amiably.

'Down! Both of you!' commanded Lucia. 'You're uncommonly bright this morning, Tribune Marcellus Lucan Gallio. I thought you were going to a party at the Club.'

'Ah—my infant sister—but what a party!' Marcellus gingerly touched his finely moulded, close-cropped, curly head in several ailing areas, and winced. 'You may well be glad that you are not—and can never be—a Tribune. It was indeed a long, stormy night.'

'A wet one, at any rate, to judge from your puffy eyes. Tell me about it—or as much as you can remember.' Lucia scooped Bambo off the marble lectus with her foot, and her brother eased himself onto the seat beside her. He laughed, reminiscently, painfully.

'I fear I disgraced the family. Only the dear gods know what may come of it. His Highness was too far gone to understand, but someone will be sure to tell him before the day is over.'

Lucia leaned forward anxiously, laid a hand on his knee, and searched his cloudy eyes.

'Gaius?' she asked, in a frightened whisper. 'What happened, Marcellus?'

'A poem,' he muttered, 'an ode; a long, tiresome, incredibly stupid ode, wrought for the occasion by old Senator Tuscus, who, having reached that ripeness of senescence where Time and Eternity are mistaken for each other—'

'Sounds as if you'd arrived there, too,' broke in Lucia. 'Can't you speed it up a little?'

'Don't hurry me, impatient youth,' sighed Marcellus. 'I am very frail. As I was saying, this interminable ode, conceived by the ancient Tuscus to improve his rating, was read by his son Antonius, also in need of royal favor; a grandiloquent eulogy to our glorious Prince.'

'He must have loved the flattery,' observed Lucia, 'and of course you all applauded it. You and Tullus, especially.'

'I was just coming to that,' said Marcellus, thickly. 'For hours there had been a succession of rich foods and many beverages; also a plentitude of metal music interspersed with Greek choruses—pretty good—and an exhibition of magic—pretty bad; and some perfunctory speeches, of great length and thickness. A wrestling-match, too, I believe. The night was far advanced. Long before Antonius rose, my sister, if any man among us had been free to consult his own desire, we would all have stretched out on our comfortable couches and slept. The gallant Tullus, of whose good health you are ever unaccountably solicitous, sat across from me, frankly asleep like a little child.'

'And then you had the ode,' encouraged Lucia, crisply.

'Yes—we then had the ode. And as Antonius droned on—and on—

he seemed to recede farther and farther; his features became dimmer and dimmer; and the measured noise he was making sounded fainter and fainter, as my tortured eyes grew hotter and heavier—'

'Marcellus!' shouted Lucia. 'In the name of every immortal god! Get on with it!'

'Be calm, impetuous child. I do not think rapidly today. Never again shall I be anything but tiresome. That ode did something to me, I fear. Well—after it had been inching along for leagues and decades, I suddenly roused, pulled myself together, and gazed about upon the distinguished company. Almost everyone had peacefully passed away, except a few at the high table whose frozen smiles were held with clenched teeth; and Antonius' insufferable young brother, Quintus, who was purple with anger. I can't stomach that arrogant pup and he knows I despise him.'

'Gaius!' barked Lucia, in her brother's face, so savagely that Bambo growled. 'I want to know what you did to offend Gaius!'

Marcellus laughed whimperingly, for it hurt; then burst into hysterical guffaws.

'If the Glorious One had been merely asleep, quietly, decently, with his fat chins on his bosom—as were his devoted subjects—your unfortunate brother might have borne it. But our Prince had allowed his head to tip far back. His mouth—by no means a thing of beauty, at best—was open. The tongue protruded unprettily and the bulbous nose twitched at each resounding inhalation. Our banquet-hall was deathly quiet, but for Antonius and Gaius, who shared the floor.'

'Revolting!' muttered Lucia.

'A feeble word, my sister. You should give more heed to your diction. Well—at that fateful moment Antonius had reached the climax of his father's ode with an apostrophe to our Prince that must have caused a storm on Mount Parnassus. Gaius was a Fountain of Knowledge! The eyes of Gaius glowed with Divine Light! When the lips of Gaius moved, Wisdom flowed and Justice smiled! . . . Precious child,' went on Marcellus, taking her hand, 'I felt my tragic mishap coming on, not unlike an unbeatable sneeze. I suddenly burst out laughing! No—I do not mean that I chuckled furtively into my hands: I threw back my head and roared! Howled! Long, lusty yells of insane laughter!' Reliving the experience, Marcellus went off again into an abandon of undisciplined mirth. 'Believe me—I woke everybody up—but Gaius.'

'Marcellus!'

Suddenly sobered by the tone of alarm in his sister's voice, he looked into her pale, unsmiling face.

'What is it, Lucia?' he demanded. 'Are you ill?'

'I'm—afraid!' she whispered, weakly.

He put his arm about her and she pressed her forehead against his shoulder.

'There, there!' he murmured. 'We've nothing to fear, Lucia. I was
foolish to have upset you. I thought you would be amused. Gaius will
be angry, of course, when he learns of it; but he will not venture
to punish the son of Marcus Lucan Gallio.'

'But—you see—' stammered Lucia, 'it was only yesterday that Father
openly criticized him in the Senate. Had you not heard?'

'Of course; but the Pater's strong enough to take care of himself,'
declared Marcellus, almost too confidently to be convincing. There
was a considerable pause before his sister spoke. He felt her body
trembling.

'If it were just that one thing,' she said, slowly, 'perhaps it might
be overlooked. But—now you have offended him. And he was already
angry at me.'

'You!' Marcellus took her by the shoulders and stared into her
worried eyes. 'And why should Gaius be angry at you?'

'Do you remember, last summer, when Diana and her mother and
I were guests at the Palace on Capri—and Gaius came to visit the
Emperor?'

'Well? Go on!' demanded Marcellus. 'What of it? What did he
say? What did he do?'

'He tried to make love to me.'

'That loathsome beast!' roared Marcellus, leaping to his feet. 'I'll
tear his dirty tongue out! I'll gouge his eyes out with my thumbs! Why
haven't you told me this before?'

'You have given the reason,' said Lucia, dejectedly. 'I was afraid of
the tongue-tearing—and eye-gouging. Had my brother been a puny,
timid man, I might have told him at once. But my brother is strong
and brave—and reckless. Now that I have told him, he will kill Gaius;
and my brother, whom I so dearly love, will be put to death, and my
father, too, I suppose. And my mother will be banished or imprisoned,
and—'

'What did Mother think about this?' broke in Marcellus.

'I did not tell her.'

'Why not? You should have done so—instantly!'

'Then she would have told Father. That would have been as dangerous as telling my brother.'

'You should have told the Emperor!' spluttered Marcellus. 'Tiberius
is no monument to virtue, but he would have done something about
that! He's not so very fond of Gaius.'

'Don't be foolish! That half-crazy old man? He would probably have
gone into one of his towering tantrums, and scolded Gaius in the
presence of everybody; and then he would have cooled off and forgotten all about it. But Gaius wouldn't have forgotten! No—I decided to ignore it. Nobody knows—but Diana.'

'Diana! If you thought you had such a dangerous secret, why should
you tell that romping infant Diana?'

'Because she was afraid of him, too, and understood my reasons for not wanting to be left alone with him. But Diana is not a baby, Marcellus. She is nearly sixteen. And—if you'll pardon my saying so—I think you should stop mussing her hair, and tickling her under the chin, when she comes here to visit me—as if she were five, and you a hundred.'

'Sorry! It hadn't occurred to me that she would resent my playful caresses. I never thought of her except as a child—like yourself.'

'Well—it's time you realized that Diana is a young woman. If she resents your playful caresses, it is not because they are caresses but because they are playful.' Lucia hesitated; then continued softly, her eyes intent on her brother's gloomy face. 'She might even like your caresses—if they meant anything. I think it hurts her, Marcellus, when you call her "Sweetheart."'

'I had not realized that Diana was so sensitive,' mumbled Marcellus. 'She is certainly stormy enough when anything displeases her. She was audacious enough to demand that her name be changed.'

'She hated to be called Asinia, Marcellus,' said Lucia, loyally. 'Diana is prettier, don't you think?'

'Perhaps,' shrugged Marcellus. 'Name of a silly goddess. The name of the Asinius stock is noble; means something!'

'Don't be tiresome, Marcellus!' snapped Lucia. 'What I am saying is: Diana would probably enjoy having you call her "Sweetheart"—if—'

Marcellus, who had been restlessly panthering about, drew up to inspect his sister with sudden interest.

'Are you trying to imply that this youngster thinks she is fond of me?'

'Of course! And I think you're pretty dumb, not to have noticed it! Come and sit down—and compose yourself. Our breakfast is on the way.'

Marcellus glanced casually in the direction of the house; then stared frowningly; then rubbed his eyes with his fists, and stared again. Lucia's lips puckered into a reluctant grin.

'In truth, my sister,' he groaned, 'I am in much worse condition than I had supposed.'

'You're all right, Tribune,' she drawled. 'There really are two of them.'

'Thanks! I am relieved. Are they as bright as they are beautiful?' he asked, as the twins neared.

'It is too early to tell. This is their first day on duty. Don't frighten them, Marcellus. They're already scared half out of their wits. They have never worked before . . . No, no, Bambo! Come here!'

Rosy with embarrassment, the Macedonians began unburdening their silver trays, fussily pretending they were not under observation.

'Cute little things; aren't they?' chirped Marcellus. 'Where did Father pick them up?'

'Don't!' whispered Lucia. She rose and walked to the balustrade, her brother sauntering after her. They turned their faces toward the city. 'What did Tullus think of what you did?' she asked, irrelevantly.

'Tell me'—Marcellus ignored her query—'is there anything peculiar about these slaves that makes you so extraordinarily considerate?'

Lucia shook her head, without looking up—and sighed.

'I was just thinking,' she said, at length, 'how I might feel if I were in their place.' Her troubled eyes lifted to meet his look of inquiry. 'It is not impossible, Marcellus, that I may soon find myself in some such predicament. . . . You wouldn't like that. Would you?'

'Nonsense!' he growled, out of the corner of his mouth. 'You're making too great a disaster of this! Nothing's going to happen. I'll see to that.'

'How?' demanded Lucia. 'How are you going to see to it?'

'Well'—temporized Marcellus—'what do you think I should do—short of going to that ugly reptile with an apology?'

Lucia brightened a little and laid her hand on his arm.

'Do that!' she pleaded. 'Today! Make peace with him, Marcellus! Tell him you were drunk. You were; weren't you?'

'I'd rather be flogged—in the market-place!'

'Yes—I know. And perhaps you will be. Gaius is dangerous!'

'Ah—what could he do? Tiberius would not permit his half-witted stepson to punish a member of the Gallio family. It's common knowledge that the old man despises him.'

'Yes—but Tiberius consented to his regency because Julia demanded it. And Julia still has to be reckoned with. If it came to a decision whether that worn-out old man should stand up for the Gallio family—against Gaius—with his shrewish wife screaming in his ears, I doubt that he would trouble himself. Julia would stop at nothing!'

'The vindictive old—' Marcellus paused on the edge of a kennel word.

'Think it over.' Lucia's tone was brighter, as if she felt herself gaining ground. 'Come—let us eat our breakfast. Then you will go to Gaius, and take your medicine. Praise him! Flatter him! He can stand any amount of it. Tell him he is beautiful! Tell him there's nobody in the whole Empire as wise as he is. Tell him he is divine! But—be sure you keep your face straight. Gaius already knows you have a keen sense of humor.'

*   *   *   *   *   *

Having decided to accept his sister's counsel, Marcellus was anxious to perform his unpleasant duty and be done with it. Prudence suggested that he seek an interview through the formal channels and await the convenience of the Prince; but, increasingly impressed by the gravity of his position, he resolved to ignore the customary court procedure and take a chance of seeing Gaius without an appointment. By appearing at the Palace shortly before noon, he might even be lucky enough to have a few minutes alone with the Prince before anyone had informed him about last night's mishap.

At ten, rejuvenated by a hot bath, a vigorous massage by Demetrius, and a plunge in the pool, the Tribune returned to his rooms, dressed with care, and sauntered downstairs. Observing that the library door was ajar, he paused to greet his father, whom he had not seen since yesterday. The handsome, white-haired Senator was seated at his desk, writing. He glanced up, nodded, smiled briefly, and invited Marcellus to come in.

'If you are at liberty today, my son, I should be pleased to have you go with me to inspect a span of matched Hispanian mares.'

'I should like to, sir; but might tomorrow serve as well? I have an important errand to do; something that cannot be put off.' There was a note of anxiety in the Tribune's voice that narrowed the wise old eyes.

'Nothing serious, I trust.' Gallio pointed to a vacant seat.

'I hope not, sir.' Marcellus sat tentatively on the broad arm of the chair as a fair compromise between candid reticence and complete explanation.

'Your manner,' observed his father, pointedly, 'suggests that you are worried. I have no wish to intrude upon your private perplexities, but is there anything I might do for you?'

'I'm afraid not, sir; thank you.' After a moment of indecision, Marcellus slowly slid into the chair and regarded his distinguished parent with a sober face. 'If you have the time, I will tell you.'

Gallio nodded, put down his stylus, and leaned forward on his folded arms encouragingly. It was quite a long narrative. Marcellus did not spare himself. He told it all. At one juncture, he was half-disposed to introduce Lucia's dilemma as relevant to his own; but decided against it, feeling that their pater was getting about all he could take for one session. He concluded, at length, with the declaration that he was going at once to apologize. Gallio, who had listened attentively but without comment, now shook his leonine head and shouted 'No!' He straightened and shook his head again. 'No!—No, no!'

Amazed by his father's outburst, for he had anticipated his full approval, Marcellus asked, 'Why not, sir?'

'The most dangerous implement a man can use for the repair of a damaged relationship is an abject apology.' Gallio pushed back his huge chair and rose to his full height as if preparing to deliver an address. 'Even in the most favorable circumstances, as when placating an injured friend, a self-abasing apology may do much harm. If the friend is contented with nothing less, he should not be served with

it at all; for his friendship is not worth its upkeep. In the case of
Gaius, an apology would be a fatality; for you are not dealing here
with a gentleman, but with a congenital scoundrel. Your apology will
imply that you expect Gaius to be generous. Generosity, in his opinion,
is a sign of weakness. By imputing it to him, you will have given
him further offense. Gaius has reasons to be sensitive about his power.
Never put yourself on the defensive with a man who is fretting about
his own insecurity. Here, he says, is at least one opportunity to demon-
strate my strength.'

'Perhaps you are right, sir,' conceded Marcellus.

'Perhaps? Of course, I am right!' The Senator walked to the door,
closed it softly, and resumed his seat. 'And that is not all,' he went
on. 'Let me refresh your mind about the peculiar relations in the
imperial family which explain why Gaius is a man to be watched and
feared. There is old Tiberius, alternately raging and rotting in his
fifty-room villa on Capri; a pathetic and disgusting figure, mooning
over his necromancies and chattering to his gods—My son,' Gallio
interrupted himself, 'there is always something fundamentally wrong
with a rich man or a king who pretends to be religious. Let the poor
and helpless invoke the gods. That is what the gods are for—to distract the attention of the weak from their otherwise intolerable mis-
eries. When an emperor makes much ado about religion, he is either
cracked or crooked. Tiberius is not crooked. If he is cracked, the cause
is not far to seek. For a score of years he has nursed a bitter grudge
against his mother for demanding that he divorce Vipsania—the only
creature he ever loved—'

'I think he is fond of Diana,' interjected Marcellus.

'Right! And why? He is fond of the child because she is Vipsania's
granddaughter. Let us remember that he was not a bad ruler in his
earlier days. Rome had never known such prosperity; not even under
Julius. As you know, when Vipsania passed out of his life, Tiberius
went to pieces; lost all interest in the Empire; surrounded himself
with soothsayers, mountebanks, priests, and astrologers. Presently his
mind was so deranged by all this nonsense that he consented to marry
Julia, whom he had despised from childhood.' The Senator chuckled,
not very pleasantly, and remarked: 'Perhaps that was why he wished
to be relieved of all his administrative duties. He found that to hate
Julia as adequately as she deserved to be hated, he had to make it
a full-time occupation. So—there was the vixenish Julia, together with
the obnoxious offspring she had whelped before he married her. And
he has not only hated Julia: he has been deathly afraid of her—and
with good reason—for she has the morbid mind of an assassin—and
the courage, too."

'Lucia says the old gentleman never touches his wine, at table,
until the Empress has tasted it,' put in Marcellus, 'but she thought
that was just a little family joke.'

'We will not disturb your young sister with any other interpretation,' advised the Senator, 'but it is no joke; nor is Tiberius merely trying to be playful when he stations a dozen Numidian gladiators at the doors and windows of his bedchamber. . . . Now, these facts are, I suspect, never absent very long from Gaius' mind. He knows that the Emperor is half-insane; that his mother lives precariously; and that if anything should happen to her his regency would last no longer than it takes a galley to clear for Crete with a deposed prince on board.'

'Were that to happen,' broke in Marcellus, 'who would succeed Gaius?'

'Well—' Gallio slighted the query with a shrug. 'It will not happen. If anyone dies, down there, it won't be Julia. You can depend on that.'

'But—just supposing—' persisted Marcellus. 'If, for any reason—accident, illness, or forthright murder—Julia should be eliminated—and Gaius, too, in consequence—do you think Tiberius might put Asinius Gallus on the throne?'

'It is possible,' said Gallio. 'The Emperor might feel that he was making tardy amends to Vipsania by honoring her son. And Gallus would be no mean choice. No Roman has ever commanded more respect than Pollio, his learned sire. Gallus would have the full support of our legions—both at home and abroad. However'—he added, half to himself—'a brave soldier does not inevitably make a wise monarch. Your military commander has only a foreign foe to fight. All that he requires is tactics and bravery. An emperor is forever at war with a jealous court, an obstreperous Senate, and a swarm of avaricious landholders. What he needs is a keen scent for conspiracy, a mind crafty enough to outmaneuver treachery, a natural talent for duplicity—and the hide of an alligator.'

'Thick enough to turn the point of a stiletto,' assisted Marcellus.

'It is a hazardous occupation,' nodded Gallio, 'but I do not think our excellent friend Gallus will ever be exposed to its dangers.'

'I wonder how Diana would like being a princess,' remarked Marcellus, absently. He glanced up to find his father's eyes alight with curiosity.

'We are quite far afield, aren't we; discussing Diana?' observed Gallio, slyly. 'Are you interested in her?'

'Not any more than Lucia is,' replied Marcellus, elaborately casual. 'They are, as you know, inseparable. Naturally, I see Diana almost every day.'

'A beautiful and amazingly vivacious child,' commented the Senator.

'Beautiful and vivacious,' agreed Marcellus—'but not a child. Diana is nearly sixteen, you know.'

'Old enough to be married: is that what you are trying to say? You could hardly do better—if she can be tamed. Diana has fine blood. Sixteen, eh? It is a wonder Gaius has not noticed. He might do himself much good in the esteem of the Emperor—and he certainly is in need of it—if he should win Diana's favor.'

'She loathes him!'

'Indeed? Then she has talked with you about it?'

'No, sir. Lucia told me.'

There was a considerable interval of silence before Gallio spoke again, slowly measuring his words.

'In your present strained relation to Gaius, my son, you would show discretion, I think, if you made your attentions to Diana as inconspicuous as possible.'

'I never see her anywhere else than here, sir.'

'Even so: treat her casually. Gaius has spies everywhere.'

'Here—in our house?' Marcellus frowned incredulously.

'Why not? Do you think that Gaius, the son of Agrippa, who never had an honest thought in his life, and of Julia, who was born with both ears shaped like keyholes, would be too honorable for that?' Gallio deftly rolled up the scroll that lay at his elbow, indicating that he was ready to put aside his work for the day. 'We have discussed this fully enough, I think. As for what occurred last night, the Prince's friends may advise him to let the matter drop. Your best course is to do nothing, say nothing—and wait developments.' He rose and straightened the lines of his toga. 'Come! Let us ride to Ismael's camp and look at the Hispanians. You will like them; milk-white, highspirited, intelligent—and undoubtedly expensive. Ismael, the old rascal, knows I am interested in them, unfortunately for my purse.'

Marcellus responded eagerly to his father's elevated mood. It was almost as if the shrewd Marcus Lucan Gallio had firmly settled the unhappy affair with Gaius. He opened the door for the Senator to precede him. In the atrium, leaning against a column, lounged Demetrius. Coming smartly to attention he saluted with his spear and followed a few paces behind the two men as they strolled through the vasty rooms and out to the spacious western portico.

'Rather unusual for Demetrius to be loitering in the atrium,' remarked Marcellus in a guarded undertone.

'Perhaps he was standing there,' surmised Gallio, 'to discourage anyone else from loitering by the door.'

'Do you think he may have had a special reason for taking that precaution?'

'Possibly. He was with you at the banquet; knows that you gave offense to Gaius; concludes that you are in disfavor; and, by adding it all up, thinks it is time to be vigilant.'

'Shall I ask him if he suspects that there are spies in the house?' suggested Marcellus.

Gallio shook his head.

'If he observes anything irregular, he will tell you, my son.'

'I wonder who this is coming.' Marcellus nodded toward a uniformed Equestrian Knight who had just turned in from the Via Aurelia. 'We're to be honored,' he growled. 'It is Quintus, the younger Tuscus. The Prince has been seeing much of him lately, I hear.'

The youthful Tribune, followed by a well-mounted aide, rode briskly toward them; and, neglecting to salute, drew a gilded scroll from the belt of his tunic.

'I am ordered by His Highness, Prince Gaius, to deliver this message into the hands of Tribune Marcellus Lucan Gallio,' he barked, haughtily. The aide, who had dismounted, carried the scroll up the steps and handed it over.

'His Highness might do well to employ messengers with better manners,' drawled Marcellus. 'Are you to await an answer?'

'Imperial commands require obedience; not replies!' shouted Quintus. He pulled his horse about savagely, dug in his spurs, and made off, pursued by his obsequious aide.

'Gaius is prompt,' commented the Senator. There was satisfaction on his face as he watched his son's steady hands, and the cool deliberateness with which he drew his dagger and thrust the point of it through the wax. Unrolling the ostentatious document, Marcellus held it at an angle where his father might share its contents. Gallio read it aloud, in a rasping undertone.

Prince Gaius Drusus Agrippa to Trib. Marcellus Lucan Gallio:
> Greeting:
> The courage of a Military Tribune should not be squandered in banquet-halls. It should be serving the Empire in positions where reckless audacity is honorable and valorous. Tribune Marcellus Lucan Gallio is commanded to report, before sunset, at the Praetorium of Chief Legate M. Cornelius Capito, and receive his commission.

Marcellus rolled up the scroll, tossed it negligently to Demetrius, who thrust it into the breast of his tunic; and, turning to his father, remarked, 'We have plenty of time to go out and see Ismael's horses.'

The Senator proudly drew himself erect, gave his son a respectful bow, strutted down the marble steps; and, taking the bridle reins, mounted his mettlesome black gelding. Marcellus beckoned to Demetrius.

'You heard that message?' he queried, abruptly.

'Not if it was private, sir,' countered Demetrius.

'Sounds a bit malicious,' observed Marcellus. 'The Prince evidently wishes to dispose of me.'

'Yes, sir,' agreed Demetrius.

'Well—I brought this upon myself,' said Marcellus. 'I shall not order you to risk your life. You are at liberty to decide whether—'

'I shall go with you, sir.'

'Very good. Inspect my equipment—and look over your own tackle, too.' Marcellus started down the steps, and turned to say, soberly, 'You're going to your death, you know.'

'Yes, sir,' said Demetrius. 'You will need some heavier sandals, sir. Shall I get them?'

'Yes—and several pairs for yourself. Ask Marcipor for the money.'

After a lively tussle with the bay, who was impatient to overtake her stable-mate, Marcellus drew up beside the Senator, and they slowed their horses to a trot.

'I tarried for a word with Demetrius. I shall take him with me.'

'Of course.'

'I told him he might decide.'

'That was quite proper.'

'I told him he might never come back alive.'

'Probably not,' said the Senator, grimly, 'but you can be assured that he will never come back alone.'

'Demetrius is a very sound fellow—for a slave,' observed Marcellus.

The Senator made no immediate rejoinder, but his stern face and flexed jaw indicated that his reflections were weighty.

'My son,' he said at length, staring moodily down the road, 'we could use a few men in the Roman Senate with the brains and bravery of your slave, Demetrius.' He pulled his horse down to a walk. ' "Demetrius is a sound fellow—for a slave"; eh? Well—his being a slave does not mean that what he thinks, what he says, and what he does are unimportant. One of these days the slaves are going to take over this rotted Government! They could do it tomorrow if they were organized. You might say that their common desire for liberty should unite them, but that is not enough. All men want more liberty than they have. What the Roman slaves lack is leadership. In time, that will come. You shall see!' The Senator paused so long, after this amazing declaration, that Marcellus felt some response was in order.

'I never heard you express that opinion before, sir. Do you think there will be an uprising—among the slaves?'

'It lacks form,' replied Gallio. 'It lacks cohesion. But some day it will take shape; it will be integrated; it will develop a leader, a cause, a slogan, a banner. Three-fourths of this city's inhabitants either have been or are slaves. Daily our expeditionary forces arrive with new shiploads of them. It would require a very shrewd and powerful Government to keep in subjugation a force three times its size and strength. But—look at our Government! A mere hollow shell! It has no moral fiber! Content with its luxury, indolence, and profligacy, its extravagant pageants in honor of its silly gods; ruled by an insane dotard and a drunken nonentity! So, my son, Rome is doomed! I do not venture to predict when or how Nemesis will arrive—but it is on its way. The Roman Empire is too weak and wicked to survive!'

Chapter II

CORNELIUS CAPITO was not in when Marcellus called at three to learn what Gaius had planned for him. This was surprising and a bit ominous too. The conspicuous absence of the Chief Legate, and his deputizing of a young understrapper to handle the case, clearly meant that Capito had no relish for an unpleasant interview with the son of his lifelong friend.

The Gallios had walked their horses for the last two miles of the journey in from Ismael's camp where the Senator had declined to purchase the Hispanian mares at the exorbitant price demanded by the avaricious old Syrian, though it was plain to see that the day's events had dulled his interest in the negotiation.

The Senator's mind was fully occupied now with speculations about Cornelius. If anybody in Rome could temper the punitive assignment which Gaius intended for his son, it would be the Commander of the Praetorian Guard and Chief of the Legates who wielded an enormous power in the making of appointments.

Slipping into a reminiscent—and candidly pessimistic—mood, the elder Gallio had recited the deplorable story they both knew by heart, the dismal epic of the Praetorian Guard. Marcellus had been brought up on it. As if his son had never heard the tale before, the Senator began away back in the time when Julius Caesar had created this organization for his own security. Picked men they were, with notable records for daring deeds. As the years rolled on, the traditions of the Praetorian Guard became richer. A magnificent armory was built to house its battle trophies, and in its spacious atrium were erected bronze and marble tablets certifying to the memorable careers of its heroes. To be a member of the Praetorian Guard in those great—long since outmoded—days when courage and integrity were valuable property, was the highest honor the Empire could bestow.

Then, Gallio had continued gloomily, Augustus—whose vanity had swollen into a monstrous, stinking, cancerous growth—had begun to confer honorary memberships upon his favorites; upon Senators who slavishly approved his mistakes and weren't above softening the royal sandal-straps with their saliva; upon certain rich men who had fattened on manipulations in foreign loot; upon wealthy slave-brokers, dealers in stolen sculpture; upon provincial revenue-collectors; upon almost anybody indeed who could minister to the diseased Augustan ego, or pour ointment on his itching avarice. And thus had passed away the glory and distinction of the Praetorian Guard. Its memberships were for sale.

For a little while, Tiberius had tried to arrest its accelerating descent into hell. Cornelius Capito, who had so often led his legion into suicidal forays that a legend had taken shape about him—for were not the gods directing a man whose life was so cheaply held and so miraculously preserved?—was summoned home to be Commander of the Praetorian Guard. Capito had not wanted the office, but had obeyed the command. With the same kind of recklessness that had won him honors on many a battle-field, he had begun to clean up the discredited institution. But it hadn't been long until hard pressure on Tiberius made it necessary for the Emperor to caution the uncompromising warrior about his honest zeal. He mustn't go too far in this business of cleansing the Praetorian Guard.

'It was then,' declaimed Gallio, 'that brave old Capito discovered, to his dismay, why Tiberius had called him to be the Commander; simply to use his name as a deodorant!'

Marcellus had realized, at this juncture of his father's painful reflections, that the remainder of the story would be somewhat embarrassing; for it concerned the Military Tribunes.

'If Augustus had only been content'—the Senator was proceeding according to schedule—'with his destruction of the Praetorian Guard! Perhaps, had he foreseen the result of his policy there, not even his rapacious greed could have induced him to work the same havoc with the Order of Tribunes. But you know what happened, my son.'

Yes—Marcellus knew. The Order of Tribunes had been honorable too. You had to be a Tribune, in deed and in truth, if you wanted to wear its insignia. Like the Praetorian Guard, it too was handsomely quartered. Tribunes, home on furlough or recovering from injuries or awaiting orders, took advantage of the library, the baths, the commissary that the Empire had provided for them. Then Augustus had decided to expand the Order of Tribunes to include all sons of Senators and influential taxpayers. You needn't ever have shouted an order or spent a night in a tent. If your father had enough money and political weight, you could wear the uniform and receive the salute.

Marcellus liked to think that his own case was not quite so indefensible as most of them. He had not been a mere playboy. At the Academy he had given his full devotion to the history of military campaigns, strategy, and tactics. He was an accomplished athlete, expert with the javelin, a winner of many prizes for marksmanship with the bow. He handled a dueling sword with the skill of a professional gladiator.

Nor had his recreations been profitless. Aristocratic youths, eligible to the hierarchy of public offices, disdained any actual practice of the fine arts. They affected to be critics and connoisseurs of painting and sculpture, but would have experienced much embarrassment had they been caught with a brush or chisel in hand. Independent of this taboo, Marcellus had taken a serious interest in sculpture, much to the delight of his father, who—upon observing that he had a natural genius for it—had provided him with competent tutors.

But—sometimes he had been appropriately sensitive about his status as a Military Tribune when, as happened infrequently, some *real* Tribune showed up at the ornate clubhouse, bronzed and battered and bandaged, after grueling months on active duty.

However—Marcellus said to himself—it wasn't as if he had no qualifications for military service. He was abundantly prepared to accept a commission if required to do so. Occasionally he had wished that an opportunity for such service might arise. He had never been asked to take a command. And a man would be a fool, indeed, to seek a commission. War was a swinish business, intended for bullies who liked to strut their medals and yell obscenities at their inferiors and go for weeks without a bath. He could do all this if he had to. He didn't have to; but he had never been honestly proud of his title. Sometimes when Decimus addressed him as 'Tribune'—which was the surly fellow's custom on such occasions as serving him his late break-fast in bed—Marcellus was tempted to slap him, and he would have done so had he a better case.

They had ridden in silence for a little time, after the Senator had aired his favorite grievances.

'Once in a while,' continued Gallio, meditatively, 'crusty Capito —like blind Samson of the Hebrew myth—rouses to have his way. I am hopeful that he may intervene in your behalf, my son. If it is an honorable post, we will not lament even though it involves peril. I am prepared to hand you over to danger—but not to disgrace. I cannot believe that my trusted friend will fail to do his utmost for you, today. I bid you to approach him with that expectation!'

His father had seemed so confident of this outcome that the re-mainder of their ride had been almost enjoyable. Assured that the gruff but loyal old warrior, who had helped him into his first white toga, would see to it that no indignities were practiced on him by a petulant and vengeful Prince, Marcellus set off light-heartedly to the impressive headquarters of the Chief Legate.

Accompanied by Demetrius, who was himself a striking figure in the saddle, he rode through the increasingly crowded streets on the way to the huge circular plaza, around half of which were grouped the impressive marble buildings serving the Praetorian Guard and ranking officials of the army. To the left stretched a vast parade-ground, now literally filled with loaded camel caravans and hundreds of pack-asses.

An expedition was mobilizing, ready for departure on the long trip to Gaul. The plaza was a stirring scene! Banners fluttered. The young officers were smart in their field uniforms. The legionaries were alert, spirited, apparently eager to be on their way. Maybe an experience of this sort would be stimulating, thought Marcellus.

Unable to ride into the plaza, because of the congestion, they dismounted in the street, Marcellus handing his reins to Demetrius, and proceeding through the narrow lane toward the Praetorium. The broad corridors were filled with Centurions awaiting orders. Many of them he knew. They smiled recognition and saluted. Perhaps they surmised that he was here on some such business as their own, and it gave him a little thrill of pride. You could think what you liked about the brutishness and griminess of war, it was no small honor to be a Roman soldier—whatever your rank! He shouldered his way to the open door leading into Capito's offices.

'The Commander is not in,' rasped the busy deputy. 'He ordered me to deliver this commission to you.'

Marcellus took the heavily sealed scroll from the fellow's hand, hesitated a moment, half-inclined to inquire whether Capito expected to return presently, decided against it; turned, and went out, down the broad steps and across the densely packed plaza. Demetrius, seeing him coming, led the horses forward and handed his master the bay mare's bridle-reins. Their eyes met. After all, thought Marcellus, Demetrius had a right to know where we stood in this business.

'I have not opened it yet,' he said, tapping the scroll. 'Let us go home.'

* * * * * *

The Senator was waiting for him in the library.

'Well—what did our friend Capito have for you?' he asked, making no attempt to disguise his uneasiness.

'He was not there. A deputy served me.' Marcellus laid the scroll on the desk and sat down to wait while his father impatiently thrust his knife through the heavy seals. For what seemed a very long time the narrowed eyes raced the length of the pompous manifesto. Then Gallio cleared his throat, and faced his son with troubled eyes.

'You are ordered to take command of the garrison at Minoa,' he muttered.

'Where's Minoa?'

'Minoa is a villainously dirty little port city in southern Palestine.'

'I never heard of it,' said Marcellus. 'I know about our forts at Caesarea and Joppa; but—what have we at this Minoa?'

'It is the point of departure for the old trail that leads to the Dead Sea. Most of our salt comes from there, as you probably know. The duty of our garrison at Minoa is to make that road safe for our caravans.'

'Doesn't sound like a very interesting job,' commented Marcellus. 'I was anticipating something dangerous.'

'Well—you will not be disappointed. It is dangerous enough. The Bedouins who menace that salt trail are notoriously brutal savages. But because they are independent gangs of bandits, with hideouts in that rocky desert region, we have never undertaken a campaign to crush them. It would have required five legions.' The Senator was speaking as if he were very well informed about Minoa, and Marcellus was listening with full attention.

'You mean these desert brigands steal the salt from our caravans?'

'No—not the salt. They plunder the caravans on the way in, for they have to carry supplies and money to hire laborers at the salt deposits. Many of the caravans that set out over that trail are never heard from again. But that isn't quite all,' the Senator continued. 'We have not been wasting very good men in the fort at Minoa. The garrison is composed of a tough lot of rascals. More than half of them were once commissioned officers who, for rank insubordination or other irregularities, are in disfavor with the Government. The lesser half is made up of an assortment of brawlers whose politics bred discontent.'

'I thought the Empire had a more prompt and less expensive method of dealing with objectionable people.'

'There are some cases,' explained the Senator, 'in which a public trial or a private assassination might stir up a protest. In these instances, it is as effective—and more practical—to send the offender to Minoa.'

'Why, sir—this is equivalent to exile!' Marcellus rose, bent forward over his father's desk, and leaned his weight on his white-knuckled fists. 'Do you know anything more about this dreadful place?'

Gallio slowly nodded his head.

'I know all about it, my son. For many years, one of my special duties in the Senate—together with four of my colleagues—has been the supervision of that fort.' He paused, and began slowly rising to his feet, his deep-lined face livid with anger. 'I believe that was why Gaius Drusus Agrippa—' The Senator savagely ground the hated name to bits with his teeth. 'He planned this for my son—because he knew— that I would know—what you were going into.' Raising his arms high, and shaking his fists in rage, Gallio shouted, 'Now I would that I were religious! I would beseech some god to damn his soul!'

* * * * * *

Cornelia Vipsania Gallio, who always slightly accented her middle name—though she was only a stepdaughter to the divorced spouse of Emperor Tiberius—might have been socially important had she made the necessary effort.

If mere wishing on Cornelia's part could have induced her husband to ingratiate himself with the Crown, Marcus Lucan Gallio could have belonged to the inner circle, and any favor he desired for himself or his family might have been granted; or if Cornelia herself had gone to the bother of fawning upon the insufferable old Julia, the Gallio household might have reached that happy elevation by this shorter route. But Cornelia lacked the necessary energy.

She was an exquisite creature, even in her middle forties; a person of considerable culture, a gracious hostess, an affectionate wife, an indulgent mother, and probably the laziest woman in the whole Roman Empire. It was said that sometimes slaves would serve the Gallio establishment for months before discovering that their mistress was not an invalid.

Cornelia had her breakfast in bed at noon, lounged in her rooms or in the sunny garden all afternoon, drowsed over the classics, apathetically swept her slim fingers across the strings of her pandura; and was waited on, hand and foot, by everybody in the house. And everybody loved her, too, for she was kind and easy to please. Moreover, she never gave orders—except for her personal comfort. The slaves—under the competent and loyal supervision of Marcipor; and the diligent, if somewhat surly, dictatorship of Decimus in the culinary department—managed the institution unaided by her counsel and untroubled by her criticism. She was by nature an optimist, possibly because fretting was laborious. On rare occasions, she was briefly baffled by unhappy events, and at such times she wept quietly—and recovered.

Yesterday, however, something had seriously disturbed her habitual tranquillity. The Senator had made a speech. Paula Gallus, calling in the late afternoon, had told her. Paula had been considerably upset.

Cornelia was not surprised by the report that her famous husband was pessimistic in regard to the current administration of Roman government, for he was accustomed to walking the floor of her bedchamber while delivering opinions of this nature; but she was shocked to learn that Marcus had given the Senate the full benefit of his accumulated dissatisfactions. Cornelia had no need to ask Paula why she was so concerned. Paula didn't want Senator Gallio to get himself into trouble with the Crown. In the first place, it would be awkward for Diana to continue her close friendship with Lucia if the latter's eminent parent persisted in baiting Prince Gaius. And, too, was there not a long-standing conspiracy between Paula and Cornelia to encourage an alliance of their houses whenever Diana and Marcellus should become romantically aware of each other?

Paula had not hinted at these considerations when informing Cornelia that the Senator was cutting an impressive figure on some pretty thin ice, but she had gone so far as to remind her long-time friend that Prince Gaius—while notably unskillful at everything else—was amazingly resourceful and ingenious when it came to devising reprisals for his critics.

'But what can I do about it?' Cornelia had moaned languidly. 'Surely you're not hoping that I will rebuke him. My husband would not like to have people telling him what he may say in the Senate.'

'Not even his wife?' Paula arched her patrician brows.

'Especially his wife,' rejoined Cornelia. 'We have a tacit understanding that Marcus is to attend to his profession without my assistance. My responsibility is to manage his home.'

Paula had grinned dryly; and, shortly after, had taken her departure, leaving behind her a distressing dilemma. Cornelia wished that the Senator could be a little less candid. He was such an amiable man when he wanted to be. Of course, Gaius was a waster and a fool; but—after all—he was the Prince Regent, and you didn't have to call him names in public assemblies. First thing you knew, they'd all be blacklisted. Paula Gallus was far too prudent to let Diana become involved in their scrapes. If the situation became serious, they wouldn't be seeing much more of Diana. That would be a great grief to Lucia. And it might affect the future of Marcellus, too. It was precious little attention he had paid to the high-spirited young Diana, but Cornelia was still hopeful.

Sometimes she worried, for a moment or two, about Marcellus. One of her most enjoyable dreams posed her son on a beautiful white horse, leading a victorious army through the streets, dignifiedly acknowledging the plaudits of a multitude no man could number. To be sure, you didn't head that sort of parade unless you had risked some perils; but Marcellus had never been a coward. All he needed was a chance to show what kind of stuff he was made of. He would probably never get that chance now. Cornelia cried bitterly; and because there was no one else to talk to about it, she bared her heart to Lucia. And Lucia, shocked by her mother's unprecedented display of emotion, had tried to console her.

But today, Cornelia had quite disposed of her anxiety; not because the reason for it had been in any way relieved, but because she was temperamentally incapable of concentrating diligently upon anything—not even upon a threatened catastrophe.

* * * * * *

About four o'clock (Cornelia was in her luxurious sitting-room, gently combing her shaggy terrier) the Senator entered and without speaking dropped wearily into a chair, frowning darkly.

'Tired?' asked Cornelia, tenderly. 'Of course you are. That long ride. And you were disappointed with the Hispanian horses, I think. What was the matter with them?'

'Marcellus has been ordered into service,' growled Gallio, abruptly.

Cornelia pushed the dog off her lap and leaned forward interestedly.

'But that is as it should be, don't you think? We had expected that it might happen some day. Perhaps we should be glad. Will it take him far away?'

'Yes.' The Senator nodded impressively. 'Far away. He has been ordered to command the fort at Minoa.'

'Command! How very nice for him! Minoa! Our son is to be the commander—of the Roman fort—at Minoa! We shall be proud!'

'No!' Gallio shook his white head. 'No! We shall not be proud! Minoa, my dear, is where we send men to be well rid of them. They have little to do there but quarrel. They are a mob of mutinous cutthroats. We frequently have to appoint a new commander.' He paused for a long, moody moment. 'This time the Senate Committee on affairs at Minoa was not consulted about the appointment. Our son had his orders directly from Gaius.'

This was too much even for the well-balanced Cornelia. She broke into a storm of weeping; noisily hysterical weeping; her fingers digging frantically into the glossy black hair that had tumbled about her shapely shoulders; moaning painful and incoherent reproaches that gradually became intelligible. Racked with sobs, Cornelia amazed them both by crying out, 'Why did you do it, Marcus? Oh—why did you have to bring this tragedy upon our son? Was it so important that you should denounce Gaius—at such a cost to Marcellus—and all of us? Oh—I wish I could have died before this day!'

Gallio bowed his head in his hands and made no effort to share the blame with Marcellus. His son was in plenty of trouble without the added burden of a rebuke from his overwrought mother.

'Where is he?' she asked, thickly, trying to compose herself. 'I must see him.'

'Packing his kit, I think,' muttered Gallio. 'He is ordered to leave at once. A galley will take him to Ostia where a ship sails tomorrow.'

'A ship? What ship? If he must go, why cannot he travel in a manner consistent with his rank? Surely he can charter or buy a vessel, and sail in comfort as becomes a Tribune.'

'There is no time for that, my dear. They are leaving tonight.'

'They? Marcellus—and who else?'

'Demetrius.'

'Well—the gods be thanked for that much!' Cornelia broke out again into tempestuous weeping. 'Why doesn't Marcellus come to see me?' she sobbed.

'He will, in a little while,' said Gallio. 'He wanted me to tell you about it first. And I hope you will meet him in the spirit of a courageous Roman matron.' The Senator's tone was almost severe now. 'Our son has received some very unhappy tidings. He is bearing them manfully, calmly, according to our best traditions. But I do not think he could bear to see his mother destroy herself in his presence.'

'Destroy myself!' Cornelia, stunned by the words, faced him with anguished eyes. 'You know I could never do a thing like that—no matter what happened to us!'

'One does not have to swallow poison or hug a dagger, my dear, to commit suicide. One can kill oneself and remain alive physically.' Gallio rose, took her hand, and drew Cornelia to her feet. 'Dry your tears now, my love,' he said gently. 'When Marcellus comes, let him continue to be proud of you. There may be some trying days ahead for our son. Perhaps the memory of an intrepid mother will rearm him when he is low in spirit.'

'I shall try, Marcus.' Cornelia clung to him hungrily. It had been a long time since they had needed each other so urgently.

* * * * * *

After Marcellus had spent a half-hour alone with his mother—an ordeal he had dreaded—his next engagement was with his sister. Father had informed Lucia, and she had sent word by Tertia that she would be waiting for him in the pergola whenever it was convenient for him to come.

But first he must return to his rooms with the silk pillow his mother had insisted on giving him. It would be one more thing for Demetrius to add to their already cumbersome impedimenta, but it seemed heartless to refuse the present, particularly in view of the fine fortitude with which she had accepted their mutual misfortune. She had been tearful, but there had been no painful break-up of her emotional discipline.

Marcellus found the luggage packed and strapped for the journey, but Demetrius was nowhere to be found. Marcipor, who had appeared in the doorway to see if he might be of service, was queried; and replied, with some reluctance and obvious perplexity, that he had seen Demetrius on his horse, galloping furiously down the driveway, fully an hour ago. Marcellus accepted this information without betraying his amazement. It was quite possible that the Greek had belatedly discovered the lack of some equipment necessary to their trip, and had set off for it minus the permission to do so. It was inconceivable that Demetrius would take advantage of this opportunity to make a dash for freedom. No, decided Marcellus, it wouldn't be that. But the incident needed explanation, for if Demetrius had gone for additional supplies he would not have strapped the luggage until his return.

Lucia was leaning against the balustrade, gazing toward the Tiber where little sails reflected final flashes of almost horizontal sunshine, and galleys moved so sluggishly they would have seemed not to be in motion at all but for the rhythmic dip of the long oars. One galley, a little larger than the others, was headed toward a wharf.

Lucia cupped her hands about her eyes and was so intent upon the
sinister black hulk that she did not hear Marcellus coming.

He joined her without words, and circled her girlish waist tenderly.
She slipped her arm about him, but did not turn her head.

'Might that be your galley?' she asked, pointing. 'It has three banks,
I think, and a very high prow. Isn't that the kind that meets ships
at Ostia?'

'That's the kind, agreed Marcellus, pleased that the conversation
promised to be dispassionate. 'Perhaps that is the boat.'

Lucia slowly turned about in his arms and affectionately patted
his cheeks with her soft palms. She looked up, smiling resolutely, her
lips quivering a little; but she was doing very well, her brother thought.
He hoped his eyes were assuring her of his approval.

'I am so glad you are taking Demetrius,' she said, steadily. 'He
wanted to go?'

'Yes,' replied Marcellus, adding after a pause, 'Yes—he quite wanted
to go.' They stood in silence for a little while, her fingers gently
toying with the knotted silk cord at the throat of his tunic.

'All packed up?' Lucia was certainly doing a good job, they both
felt. Her voice was well under control.

'Yes.' Marcellus nodded with a smile that meant everything was
proceeding normally, just as if they were leaving on a hunting excursion. 'Yes, dear—all ready to go.' There was another longer interval
of silence.

'Of course, you don't know—yet'—said Lucia—'when you will be
coming home.'

'No,' said Marcellus. After a momentary hesitation he added, 'Not
yet.'

Suddenly Lucia drew a long, agonized 'Oh!'—wrapped her arms
tightly around her brother's neck, buried her face against his breast,
and shook with stifled sobs. Marcellus held her trembling body close.

'No, no,' he whispered. 'Let's see it through, precious child. It's
not easy; but—well—we must behave like Romans, you know.'

Lucia stiffened, flung back her head, and faced him with streaming
eyes aflame with anger.

'Like Romans!' she mocked. 'Behave like Romans! And what does
a Roman ever get for being brave—and pretending it is fine—and
noble—to give up everything—and make-believe it is glorious—glorious
to suffer—and die—for Rome! For Rome! I hate Rome! Look what
Rome has done to you—and all of us! Why can't we live in peace?
The Roman Empire—Bah! What is the Roman Empire? A great
swarm of slaves! I don't mean slaves like Tertia and Demetrius; I
mean slaves like you and me—all our lives bowing and scraping and
flattering; our legions looting and murdering—and for what? To make
Rome the capital of the world, they say! But why should the whole

world be ruled by a lunatic like old Tiberius and a drunken bully like Gaius? I hate Rome! I hate it all!'

Marcellus made no effort to arrest the torrent, thinking it more practical to let his sister wear her passion out—and have done with it. She hung limp in his arms now, her heart pounding hard.

'Feel better?' he asked, sympathetically. She slowly nodded against his breast. Instinctively glancing about, Marcellus saw Demetrius standing a few yards away with his face averted from them. 'I must see what he wants,' he murmured, relaxing his embrace. Lucia slipped from his arms and stared again at the river, unwilling to let the imperturbable Greek see her so nearly broken.

'The daughter of Legate Gallus is here, sir,' announced Demetrius.

'I can't see Diana now, Marcellus,' put in Lucia, thickly. 'I'll go down through the gardens, and you talk to her.' She raised her voice a little. 'Bring Diana to the pergola, Demetrius.' Without waiting for her brother's approval, she walked rapidly toward the circular marble stairway that led to the arbors and the pool. Assuming that his master's silence confirmed the order, Demetrius was setting off on his errand. Marcellus recalled him with a quiet word and he retraced his steps.

'Do you suppose she knows?' asked Marcellus, frowning.

'Yes, sir.'

'What makes you think so?'

'The daughter of Legate Gallus appears to have been weeping, sir.' Marcellus winced and shook his head.

'I hardly know what to say to her,' he confided, mostly to himself, a dilemma that Demetrius made no attempt to solve. 'But'—Marcellus sighed—'I suppose I must see her.'

'Yes, sir,' said Demetrius, departing on his errand.

Turning toward the balustrade, Marcellus watched his sister's dejected figure moving slowly through the arbors, and his heart was suffused with pity. He had never seen Lucia so forlorn and undone. It was not much wonder if she had a reluctance to meet Diana in her present state of collapse. Something told him that this impending interview with Diana was likely to be difficult. He had not often been alone with her, even for a moment. This time they would not only be alone, but in circumstances extremely trying. He was uncertain what attitude he should take toward her.

She was coming now, out through the peristyle, walking with her usual effortless grace, but lacking animation. It was unlike Demetrius to send a guest to the pergola unattended, even though well aware that Diana knew the way. Damn Demetrius!—he was behaving very strangely this afternoon. Greeting Diana might be much more natural and unconstrained if he were present. Marcellus sauntered along the pavement to meet her. It was true, as Lucia had said; Diana was growing up—and she was lovelier in this pensiveness than he had ever seen her. Perhaps the bad news had taken all the adolescent bounce out of her. But, whatever might account for it, Diana had magically matured. His heart speeded a little. The elder-brotherly smile with which he was preparing to welcome her seemed inappropriate if not insincere, and as Diana neared him, his eyes were no less sober then hers.

She gave him both hands, at his unspoken invitation, and looked up from under her long lashes, winking back the tears and trying to smile. Marcellus had never faced her like this before, and the intimate contact stirred him. As he looked deeply into her dark eyes, it was almost as if he were discovering her; aware, for the first time, of her womanly contours, her finely sculptured brows, the firm but piquant chin, and the full lips—now parted with painful anxiety— disclosing even white teeth, tensely locked.

'I am glad you came, Diana.' Marcellus had wanted this to sound fraternal, but it didn't. He was intending to add, 'Lucia will want to see you presently'—but he didn't; nor did he release her hands. It mystified him that she could stand still that long.

'Are you really going—tonight?' she asked, in a husky whisper.

Marcellus stared into her uplifted eyes, marveling that the tempestuous, teasing, unpredictable Diana had suddenly became so winsome.

'How did you know?' he queried. 'Who could have told you so soon? I learned about it myself not more than three hours ago.'

'Does it matter—how I found out?' She hesitated, as if debating what next to say. 'I had to come, Marcellus,' she went on, bravely. 'I knew you would have no time—to come to me—and say good-bye.'

'It was very—' He stopped on the verge of 'kind,' which, he felt, would be too coolly casual, and saw Diana's eyes swimming with tears. 'It was very dear of you,' he said, tenderly. Marcellus clasped her hands more firmly and drew her closer. She responded, after a momentary reluctance.

'I wouldn't have done it, of course,' she said, rather breathlessly— 'if the time hadn't been so short. We're all going to miss you.' Then, a little unsteadily, she asked, 'Will I hear from you, Marcellus?' And when he did not immediately find words to express his happy surprise, she shook her head and murmured, 'I shouldn't have said that, I think. You will have more than enough to do. We can learn about each other through Lucia.'

'But I shall want to write to you, dear,' declared Marcellus, 'and you will write to me—often—I hope. Promise!'

Diana smiled mistily, and Marcellus watched her dimples deepen —and disappear. His heart skipped a beat when she whispered, 'You will write to me tonight? And send it back from Ostia—on the galley?'

'Yes—Diana!'

'Where is Lucia?' she asked, impetuously reclaiming her hands.

'Down in the arbors,' said Marcellus.

Before he realized her intention, Diana had run away. At the top
of the stairs she paused to wave to him. He was on the point of
calling to her—to wait a moment—that he had something more to
say; but the utter hopelessness of his predicament kept him silent.
What more, he asked himself, did he want to say to Diana? What
promise could he make to her—or exact of her? No—it was better
to let this be their leave-taking. He waved her a kiss—and she vanished
down the stairway. It was quite possible—quite probable indeed—that
he would never see Diana again.

Moodily, he started toward the house; then abruptly turned back to
the pergola. The girls had met and were strolling, arm in arm, through
the rose arbor. Perhaps he was having a final glimpse of his lovable
young sister, too. There was no good reason why he should put Lucia
to the additional pain of another farewell.

It surprised him to see Demetrius ascending the stairway. What
errand could have taken him down to the gardens, wondered Marcellus. Perhaps he would explain without being queried. His loyal
Corinthian was not acting normally today. Presently he appeared at
the top of the stairs and approached with the long, military stride
that Marcellus had often found difficult to match when they were
out on hunting trips. Demetrius seemed very well pleased about something; better than merely pleased. He was exultant! Marcellus had
never seen such an expression on his slave's face.

'Shall I have the dunnage taken down to the galley now, sir?'
asked Demetrius, in a voice that betrayed recent excitement.

'Yes—if it is ready.' Marcellus was organizing a question, but found
it difficult, and decided not to pry. 'You may wait for me at the
wharf,' he added.

'You will have had dinner, sir?'

Marcellus nodded; then suddenly changed his mind. He had taken
leave of his family, one by one. They had all borne up magnificently.
It was too much to ask of them—and him—that they should undergo
a repetition of this distress in one another's presence.

'No,' he said, shortly. 'I shall have my dinner on the galley. You
may arrange for it.'

'Yes, sir.' Demetrius' tone indicated that he quite approved of this
decision.

Marcellus followed slowly toward the house. There were plenty of
things he would have liked to do, if he had been given one more
day. There was Tullus, for one. He must leave a note for Tullus.

*   *   *   *   *   *

Upon meeting in the arbor, Lucia and Diana had both wept, word-
lessly. Then they had talked in broken sentences about the possibilities
of Marcellus' return, his sister fearing the worst, Diana wondering
whether some pressure might be brought to bear on Gaius.

'You mean'—Lucia queried—'that perhaps my father might—'

'No.' Diana shook her head decisively. 'Not your father. It would have to be done some other way.' Her eyes narrowed thoughtfully.

'Maybe your father could do something about it,' suggested Lucia.

'I don't know. Perhaps he might, if he were here. But his business in Marseilles may keep him stationed there until next winter.'

'You said good-bye to Marcellus?' asked Lucia, after they had walked on a little way in silence. She questioned Diana's eyes and smiled pensively as she watched the color creeping up her cheeks. Diana nodded and pressed Lucia's arm affectionately, but made no other response.

'How did Demetrius get down here so fast?' she asked, impulsively. 'He came for me, you know, telling me Marcellus was leaving and wanted to see me. Just now I passed him. Don't tell me that slave was saying good-bye—like an equal?'

'It was rather strange,' admitted Lucia. 'Demetrius had never spoken to me in his life, except to acknowledge an order. I hardly knew what to make of it, Diana. He came out here, saluted with his usual formality, and delivered a little speech that sounded as if he had carefully rehearsed it. He said, "I am going away with the Tribune. I may never return. I wish to bid farewell to the sister of my master and thank her for being kind to her brother's slave. I shall remember her goodness." Then he took this ring out of his wallet—'

'Ring?' echoed Diana, incredulously. 'Hold still. Let me look at it,' she breathed. Lucia held up her hand, with fingers outspread, for a closer inspection in the waning light. 'Pretty; isn't it?' commented Diana. 'What is that device—a ship?'

'Demetrius said,' continued Lucia, ' "I should like to leave this with my master's sister. If I come back, she may return it to me. If I do not come back, it shall be hers. My father gave it to my mother. It is the only possession I was able to save." '

'But—how queer!' murmured Diana. 'What did you say to him?'

'Well—what could I say?' Lucia's tone was self-defensive. 'After all—he is going away with my brother—at the risk of his own life. He's human; isn't he?'

'Yes—he's human,' agreed Diana, impatiently. 'Go on! What did you say?'

'I thanked him,' said Lucia, exasperatingly deliberate, 'and told him I thought it was wonderful of him—and I do think it was, Diana—to let me keep his precious ring; and—and—I said I hoped they would both come home safely—and I promised to take good care of his keepsake.'

'That was all right, I suppose,' nodded Diana, judicially. 'And—then what?' They had stopped on the tiled path, and Lucia seemed a little confused.

'Well,' she stammered, 'he was still standing there—and I gave him my hand.'

'You didn't!' exclaimed Diana. 'To a slave?'

'To shake, you know,' defended Lucia. 'Why shouldn't I have been willing to shake hands with Demetrius? He's as clean as we are; certainly a lot cleaner than Bambo, who is always pawing me.'

'That's not the point, Lucia, whether Demetrius' hands are cleaner than Bambo's feet—and you know it. He is a slave, and we can't be too careful.' Diana's tone was distinctly stern, until her curiosity overwhelmed her indignation. 'So—then'—she went on, a little more gently—'he shook hands with you.'

'No—it was ever so much worse than that.' Lucia grinned at the sight of Diana's shocked eyes. 'Demetrius took my hand, and put the ring on my finger—and then he kissed my hand—and—well—after all, Diana—he's going away with Marcellus—maybe to die for him! What should I have done? Slap him?'

Diana laid her hands on Lucia's shoulders and looked her squarely in the eyes.

'So—then—after that—what happened?'

'Wasn't that enough?' parried Lucia, flinching a little from Diana's insistent search.

'Quite!' After a pause, she said, 'You're not expecting to wear that ring; are you, Lucia?'

'No. There's no reason why I should. It might get lost. And I don't want to hurt Tertia.'

'Is Tertia in love with Demetrius?'

'Mad about him! She has been crying her eyes out, this afternoon, the poor dear.'

'Does Demetrius know?'

'I don't see how he could help it.'

'And he doesn't care for her?'

'Not that way. I made him promise he would say good-bye to her.'

'Lucia—had it ever occurred to you that Demetrius has been secretly in love with you—maybe for a long time?'

'He has never given me any reason to think so,' replied Lucia, rather vaguely.

'Until today, you mean,' persisted Diana.

Lucia meditated an answer for a long moment.

'Diana,' she said soberly, 'Demetrius is a slave. That is true. That is his misfortune. He was gently bred, in a home of refinement, and brought here in chains by ruffians who weren't fit to tie his sandals!' Her voice trembled with suppressed anger. 'Of course'—she went on, bitterly ironical—'their being Romans made all the difference! Just so you're a Roman, you don't have to know anything—but pillage and bloodshed! Don't you realize, Diana, that everything in the Roman Empire today that's worth a second thought on the part of any decent person was stolen from Greece? Tell me!—how does it happen that we speak Greek, in preference to Latin? It's because the Greeks are leagues ahead of us, mentally. There's only one thing we do better: we're better butchers!'

Diana frowned darkly.

With her lips close to Lucia's ear, she said guardedly, 'You are a fool to say such things—even to me! It's too dangerous! Isn't your family in enough trouble? Do you want to see all of us banished—or in prison?'

* * * * * *

Marcellus stood alone at the rail of the afterdeck. He had not arrived at the wharf until a few minutes before the galley's departure; and, going up to the cramped and stuffy cabin to make sure his heavy luggage had been safely stowed, was hardly aware that they were out in the river until he came down and looked about. Already the long warehouse and the docks had retreated into the gloom, and the voices sounded far away.

High up on an exclusive residential hillside, two small points of light flickered. He identified them as the brasiers at the eastern corners of the pergola. Perhaps his father was standing there at the balustrade.

Now they had passed the bend and the lights had disappeared. It was as if the first scroll of his life had now been written, read, and sealed. The pink glow that was Rome had faded and the stars were brightening. Marcellus viewed them with a strange interest. They seemed like so many unresponsive spectators; not so dull-eyed and apathetic as the Sphinx, but calmly observant, winking occasionally to relieve the strain and clear their vision. He wondered whether they were ever moved to sympathy or admiration; or if they cared, at all.

After a while he became conscious of the inexorable rasp of sixty oars methodically swinging with one obedience to the metallic blows of the boatswain's hammers as he measured their slavery on his huge anvil. . . . Click! Clack! Click! Clack!

Home—and Life—and Love made a final, urgent tug at his spirit. He wished he might have had an hour with Tullus, his closest friend. Tullus hadn't even heard what had happened to him. He wished he had gone back once more to see his mother. He wished he had kissed Diana. He wished he had not witnessed the devastating grief of his sister. . . . Click! Clack! Click! Clack!

He turned about and noticed Demetrius standing in the shadows near the ladder leading to the cabins. It was a comfort to sense the presence of his loyal slave. Marcellus decided to engage him in conversation; for the steady hammer-blows, down deep in the galley's hull, were beginning to pound hard in his temples. He beckoned. Demetrius approached and stood at attention. Marcellus made the impatient little gesture with both hands and a shake of the head which, by long custom, had come to mean, 'Be at ease! Be a friend!' Demetrius relaxed his stiff posture and drifted over to the rail beside Marcellus where he silently and without obvious curiosity waited his master's pleasure.

'Demetrius'—Marcellus swept the sky with an all-inclusive arm—'do you ever believe in the gods?'

'If it is my master's wish, I do,' replied Demetrius, perfunctorily.

'No, no,' said Marcellus, testily, 'be honest. Never mind what I believe. Tell me what you think about the gods. Do you ever pray to them?'

'When I was a small boy, sir,' complied Demetrius, 'my mother taught us to invoke the gods. She was quite religious. There was a pretty statue of Priapus in our flower garden. I can still remember my mother kneeling there, on a fine spring day, with a little trowel in one hand and a basket of plants in the other. She believed that Priapus made things grow. . . . And my mother prayed to Athene every morning when my brothers and I followed the teacher into our schoolroom.' He was silent for a while; and then, prodded by an encouraging nod from Marcellus, he continued: 'My father offered libations to the gods on their feast-days, but I think that was to please my mother.'

'This is most interesting—and touching, too,' observed Marcellus. 'But you haven't quite answered my question, Demetrius. Do you believe in the gods—now?'

'No, sir.'

'Do you mean that you don't believe they render any service to men? Or do you doubt that the gods exist, at all?'

'I think it better for the mind, sir, to disbelieve in their existence. The last time I prayed—it was on the day that our home was broken up. As my father was led away in chains, I knelt by my mother and we prayed to Zeus—the Father of gods and men—to protect his life. But Zeus either did not hear us; or, hearing us, had no power to aid us; or, having power to aid us, refused to do so. It is better, I think, to believe that he did not hear us than to believe that he was unable or unwilling to give aid. . . . That afternoon my mother went away—upon her own invitation—because she could bear no more sorrow. . . . I have not prayed to the gods since that day, sir. I have cursed and reviled them, on occasions; but with very little hope that they might resent my blasphemies. Cursing the gods is foolish and futile, I think.'

Marcellus chuckled grimly. This fine quality of contempt for the gods surpassed any profanity he had ever heard. Demetrius had spoken without heat. He had so little interest in the gods that he even felt it was silly to curse them.

'You don't believe there is any sort of supernatural intelligence in charge of the universe?' queried Marcellus, gazing up into the sky.

'I have no clear thought about that, sir,' replied Demetrius, deliberately. 'It is difficult to account for the world without believing in a Creator, but I do not want to think that the acts of men are inspired by superhuman beings. It is better, I feel, to believe that men have devised their brutish deeds without divine assistance.'

'I am inclined to agree with you, Demetrius. It would be a great comfort, though, if—especially in an hour of bewilderment—one could nourish a reasonable hope that a benevolent Power existed—somewhere—and might be invoked.'

'Yes, sir,' conceded Demetrius, looking upward. 'The stars pursue an orderly plan. I believe they are honest and sensible. I believe in the Tiber, and in the mountains, and in the sheep and cattle and horses. If there are gods in charge of them, such gods are honest and sound of mind. But if there are gods on Mount Olympus, directing human affairs, they are vicious and insane.' Apparently feeling that he had been talking too much, Demetrius stiffened, drew himself erect, and gave the usual evidences that he was preparing to get back on his leash. But Marcellus wasn't quite ready to let him do so.

'Perhaps you think,' he persisted, 'that all humanity is crazy.'

'I would not know, sir,' replied Demetrius, very formally, pretending not to have observed his master's sardonic grin.

'Well'—hectored Marcellus—'let's narrow it down to the Roman Empire. Do you think the Roman Empire is an insane thing?'

'Your slave, sir,' answered Demetrius, stiffly, 'believes whatever his master thinks about that.'

It was clear to Marcellus that the philosophical discussion was ended. By experience he had learned that once Demetrius resolved to crawl back into his slave status, no amount of coaxing would hale him forth. They both stood silently now, looking at the dark water swirling about the stern.

The Greek is right, thought Marcellus. That's what ails the Roman Empire: it is mad! That's what ails the whole world of men. *Mad!* If there is any Supreme Power in charge, He is *mad!* The stars are honest and sensible. But humanity is *insane!* . . . Click! Clack! Click! Clack!

Chapter III

AFTER the tipsy little ship had staggered down past the Lapari Islands in the foulest weather of the year, and had tacked gingerly through the perilous Strait of Messina, a smooth sea and a favorable breeze so eased Captain Manius' vigilance that he was available for a leisurely chat.

'Tell me something about Minoa,' urged Marcellus, after Manius had talked at considerable length about his many voyages: Ostia to Palermo and back, Ostia to Crete, to Alexandria, to Joppa.

Manius laughed, down deep in his whiskers.

'You'll find, sir, that there is no such place as Minoa.' And when Marcellus' stare invited an explanation, the swarthy navigator gave his passenger a lesson in history, some little of which he already knew.

Fifty years ago, the legions of Augustus had laid siege to the ancient city of Gaza, and had subdued it after a long and bitter campaign that had cost more than the conquest was worth.

'It would have been cheaper,' observed Manius, 'to have paid the high toll they demanded for travel on the salt trail.'

'But how about the Bedouins?' Marcellus wondered.

'Yes—and the Emperor could have bought off the Bedouins, too, for less than that war cost. We lost twenty-three thousand men, taking Gaza.'

Manius went on with the story. Old Augustus had been beside himself with rage over the stubborn resistance of the defense—composed of a conglomeration of Egyptians, Syrians, and Jews, none of whom were a bit squeamish at the sight of blood, and never took prisoners and were notoriously ingenious in the arts of torture. Their attitude, he felt, in willfully defying the might of the Empire demanded that the old pest-hole Gaza should be cleaned up. Henceforth, declared Augustus, it was to be known as the Roman city of Minoa; and it was to be hoped that the inhabitants thereof, rejoicing in the benefits conferred upon them by a civilized state, would forget that there had ever been a municipality so dirty, unhealthy, quarrelsome, and altogether nasty as Gaza.

'But Gaza,' continued Manius, 'had been Gaza for seventeen centuries, and it would have taken more than an edict by Augustus to change its name.'

'Or its manners, either, I daresay,' commented Marcellus.

'Or its smell,' added Manius, dryly. 'You know, sir,' he went on, 'the crusty white shore of that old Dead Sea is like a salt lick beside a water-hole in the jungle where animals of all breeds and sizes gather and fight. This has been going on longer than any nation's history can remember. Occasionally some animal bigger than the others has shown up, driving all the rest of them away. Sometimes they have ganged on the big fellow and chased him off, after which the little ones have gone to fighting again among themselves. Well—that's Gaza for you!'

'But the salt lick,' put in Marcellus, 'is not at Gaza; but at the Dead Sea.'

'Quite true,' agreed Manius, 'but you don't get to the Dead Sea for a lick at the salt unless Gaza lets you. For a long time the lion of Judah kept all the other animals away, after he had scared off the Philistine hyenas. Then the big elephant Egypt frightened away the lion. Then Alexander the tiger jumped onto the elephant. Always after a battle the little fellows would come sneaking back, and claw the hides off one another while the big ones were licking their wounds.'

'And what animal came after the tiger?' prodded Marcellus, though he knew the answer.

'The Roman eagle,' replied Manius. 'Flocks and swarms of Roman eagles, thinking to pick the bones; but there were plenty of survivors not ready to have their bones picked. That,' he interrupted himself to remark, 'was how we lost three-and-twenty thousand Romans—to get possession of the old salt lick.'

'A most interesting story,' mused Marcellus, who had never heard it told just that way.

'Yes,' nodded Manius, 'an interesting story; but the most curious part of it is the effect that these long battles had upon the old city of Gaza. After every invasion, a remnant of these foreign armies would remain; deserters and men too badly crippled to travel home. They stayed in Gaza—a score of different breeds—to continue their feuds.' The Captain shook his head and made a wry face. 'Many will tell you of the constant quarreling and fighting in port cities such as Rhodes and Alexandria where there is a mixed population composed of every known tint and tongue. Some say the worst inferno on any coast of our sea is Joppa. But I'll vote for Gaza as the last place in the world where a sane man would want to live.'

'Perhaps Rome should clean up Gaza again,' remarked Marcellus.

'Quite impossible! And what is true of old Gaza is equally true of all that country, up as far as Damascus. The Emperor could send in all the legions that Rome has under arms, and put on such a campaign of slaughter as the world has never seen; but it wouldn't be a permanent victory. You can't defeat a Syrian. And as for the Jews!—you can kill a Jew, and bury him, but he'll climb out alive!' Noting Marcellus' amusement, Manius grinningly elaborated, 'Yes, sir

—he will climb right up the spade-handle and sell you the rug he'd died in!'

'But'—queried Marcellus, anxious to know more about his own job—'doesn't our fort at Minoa—or Gaza, rather—keep order in the city?'

'Not at all! Hasn't anything to do with the city. Isn't located in the city, but away to the east in a most desolate strip of desert sand, rocks, and scratchy vegetation. You will find only about five hundred officers and men—though the garrison is called a legion. They are there to make the marauding Bedouins a bit cautious. Armed detachments from the fort go along with the caravans, so that the brigands will not molest them. Oh, occasionally'—Manius yawned widely—'not very often—a caravan starts across and never comes back.'

'How often?' asked Marcellus, hoping the question would sound as if he were just making conversation.

'Well—let's see,' mumbled Manius, squinting one eye shut and counting on his battered fingers. 'I've heard of only four, this past year.'

'Only four,' repeated Marcellus, thoughtfully. 'I suppose that on these occasions the detachment from the fort is captured too.'

'Of course,' drawled Manius.

'And put into slavery, maybe?'

'No—not likely. The Bedouins don't need slaves; wouldn't be bothered with them. Your Bedouin, sir, is a wild man; wild as a fox and sneaking as a jackal. When he strikes, he slips up on you from the rear and lets you have it between your shoulder blades.'

'But—doesn't the garrison avenge these murders?' exclaimed Marcellus.

Manius shook his head and drew a crooked grin.

'That garrison, sir, does not amount to much, if you'll excuse my saying so. None of them care. They're poorly disciplined, poorly commanded, and haven't the slightest interest in the fort. Ever so often they have a mutiny and somebody gets killed. You can't expect much of a fort that sheds most of its blood on the drill-ground.'

*   *   *   *   *   *

That night Marcellus felt he should confide his recent information to Demetrius. In a quiet voice, as they lay in their adjacent bunks, he gave his Corinthian a sketch of the conditions in which they were presently to find themselves, speaking his thoughts as freely as if his slave were jointly responsible for whatever policy might be pursued.

Demetrius had listened in silence throughout the dismaying recital, and when Marcellus had concluded he ventured to remark laconically, 'My master must command the fort.'

'Obviously!' responded Marcellus. 'That's what I am commissioned

to do! What else—indeed?' And as there was no immediate reply
from the other bunk, he added, testily, 'What do you mean?'

'I mean, sir—if the garrison is unruly and disorderly, my master
will exact obedience. It is not for his slave to suggest how this may
be accomplished; but it will be safer for my master if he takes full
command of the fort instantly—and firmly!'

Marcellus raised up on one elbow and searched the Greek's eyes
in the gloom of the stuffy cabin.

'I see what you have in mind, Demetrius. Now that we know the
temper of this place, you think the new Legate should not bother
about making himself agreeable, but should swagger in and crack a
few heads without waiting for formal introductions.'

'Something like that,' approved Demetrius.

'Give them some strong medicine; eh? Is that your idea?'

'When one picks up a nettle, sir, one should not grasp it gently.
Perhaps these idle men would be pleased to obey a commander as
well-favored and fearless as my master.'

'Your words are gracious, Demetrius.'

'Almost any man, sir, values justice and courage. My master is
just—and my master is also bold.'

'That's how your master got into this predicament, Demetrius,'
chuckled Marcellus ironically—'by being bold.'

Apparently unwilling to discuss that unhappy circumstance, but
wanting to support his end of the conversation, Demetrius said, 'Yes,
sir,' so soberly that Marcellus laughed. Afterward there was such a long
hiatus that it was probable the Corinthian had dropped off to sleep,
for the lazy roll of the little ship was an urgent sedative. Marcellus
lay awake for an hour, consolidating the plan suggested by his shrewd
and loyal Greek. Demetrius, he reflected, is right. If I am to command
this fort at all, I must command it from the moment of my arrival.
If they strike me down, my exit will be at least honorable.

*   *   *   *   *   *

It was well past mid-afternoon on the eighth day of March when
Captain Manius maneuvered his unwieldy little tub through the busy
roadstead of Gaza, and warped her flank against a vacant wharf. His
duties at the moment were pressing, but he found time to say good-bye
to the young Tribune with something of the somber solicitude of the
next of kin bidding farewell to the dying.

Demetrius had been among the early ones over the rail. After a
while he returned with five husky Syrians to whom he pointed out
the burdens to be carried. There were no uniforms on the dirty wharf,
but Marcellus was not disappointed. He had not expected to be met.
The garrison had not been advised of his arrival. He would be obliged
to appear at the fort unheralded.

Gaza was in no hurry, probably because of her great age and many

infirmities. It was a full hour before enough pack-asses were found to
carry the baggage. Some more time was consumed in loading them.
Another hour was spent moving at tortoise speed through the narrow,
rough-cobbled, filthy streets, occasionally blocked by shrieking contestants for the right of way.

The Syrians had divined the Tribune's destination when they saw
his uniform, and gave him a surly obedience. At length they were
out on a busy, dusty highway, Marcellus heading the procession on a
venerable, half-shed camel, led by the reeking Syrian with whom Demetrius—by pantomime—had haggled over the price of the expedition. This bargaining had amused Marcellus; for Demetrius, habitually
quiet and reserved, had shouted and gesticulated with the best of
them. Knowing nothing about the money of Gaza, or the rates for
the service he sought, the Corinthian had fiercely objected to the
Syrian's first three proposals, and had finally come to terms with savage mutters and scowls. It was difficult to recognize Demetrius in
this new rôle.

Far ahead, viewed through the billowing clouds of yellow dust,
appeared an immensely ugly twelve-acre square bounded by a high
wall built of sun-baked brick, its corners dignified by tall towers. As
they drew nearer, a limp Roman banner was identified, pendent from
an oblique pole at the corner.

An indolent, untidy sentry detached himself from a villainous group
of unkempt legionaries squatting on the ground, slouched to the big
gate, and swung it open without challenging the party. Perhaps,
thought Marcellus, the lazy lout had mistaken their little parade for
a caravan that wanted to be convoyed. After they had filed through
into the barren, sunblistered courtyard, another sentry ambled down
the steps of the praetorium and stood waiting until the Tribune's
grunting camel had folded up her creaking joints. Demetrius, who had
brought up the rear of the procession, dismounted from his donkey
and marched forward to stand at his master's elbow. The sentry, whose
curiosity had been stirred by the sight of the Tribune's insignia, saluted clumsily with a tarnished sword in a dirty hand.

'I am Tribune Marcellus Gallio!' the words were clipped and harsh.
'I am commissioned to take command of this fort. Conduct me to
the officer in charge.'

'Centurion Paulus is not here, sir.'

'Where is he?'

'In the city, sir.'

'And when Centurion Paulus goes to the city, is there no one in
command?'

'Centurion Sextus, sir; but he is resting, and has given orders not to
be disturbed.'

Marcellus advanced a step and stared into the sulky eyes.

'I am not accustomed to waiting for men to finish their naps,' he growled. 'Obey me—instantly! And wash your dirty face before you let me see it again! What is this—a Roman fort—or a pigsty?'

Blinking a little, the sentry backed away for a few steps; and, turning, disappeared through the heavy doors. Marcellus strode heavily to and fro before the entrance, his impatience mounting. After waiting for a few minutes, he marched up the steps, closely followed by Demetrius, and stalked through the gloomy hall. Another sentry appeared.

'Conduct me to Centurion Sextus!' shouted Marcellus.

'By whose orders?' demanded the sentry, gruffly.

'By the orders of Tribune Marcellus Gallio, who has taken command of this fort. Lead on—and be quick about it!'

At that moment a near-by door opened and a burly, bearded figure emerged wearing an ill-conditioned uniform with a black eagle woven into the right sleeve of his red tunic. Marcellus brushed the sentry aside and confronted him.

'You are Centurion Sextus?' asked Marcellus; and when Sextus had nodded dully, he went on, 'I am ordered by Prince Gaius to command this fort. Have your men bring in my equipment.'

'Well—not so fast, not so fast,' drawled Sextus. 'Let's have a look at that commission.'

'Certainly,' Marcellus handed him the scroll; and Sextus, lazily unrolling it, held it close to his face in the waning light.

'I suggest, Centurion Sextus,' rasped Marcellus, 'that we repair to the Legate's quarters for this examination. In the country of which I am a citizen, there are certain courtesies—'

Sextus grinned unpleasantly and shrugged.

'You're in Gaza now,' he remarked, half-contemptuously. 'In Gaza, you will find, we do things the easy way, and are more patient than our better-dressed equals in Rome. Incidentally,' added Sextus, dryly, as he led the way down the hall, 'I too am a Roman citizen.'

'How long has Centurion Paulus been in command here?' asked Marcellus, glancing about the large room into which Sextus had shown him.

'Since December. He took over, temporarily, after the death of Legate Vitelius.'

'What did Vitelius die of?'

'I don't know, sir.'

'Not of wounds, then,' guessed Marcellus.

'No, sir. He had been ailing. It was a fever.'

'It's a wonder you're not all sick,' observed Marcellus, dusting his hands, distastefully. Turning to Demetrius he advised him to go out and stand guard over their equipment until it was called for.

Sextus mumbled some instructions to the sentry, who drifted away.

'I'll show you the quarters you may occupy until Commander Paulus returns,' he said, moving toward the door. Marcellus followed. The room into which he was shown contained a bunk, a table, and two chairs. Otherwise it was bare and grim as a prison cell. A door led into a smaller unfurnished cubicle.

'Order another bunk for this kennel,' growled Marcellus. 'My slave will sleep here.'

'Slaves do not sleep in the officers' row, sir,' replied Sextus, firmly. 'My slave does!'

'But it's against orders, sir!'

'There are no orders at this fort—but mine!' barked Marcellus.

Sextus nodded his head, and a knowing grin twisted his shaggy lips as he left the room.

* * * * * *

It was a memorable evening at the fort. For years afterward the story was retold until it had the flavor of a legend.

Marcellus, accompanied by his orderly, had entered the big mess-hall to find the junior officers seated. They did not rise, but there were no evidences of hostility in the inquisitive glances they turned in his direction as he made his way to the round table in the center of the room. A superficial survey of the surrounding tables informed Marcellus that he was the youngest man present. Demetrius went directly to the kitchen to oversee his master's service.

After a while, Centurion Paulus arrived, followed by Sextus who had apparently waited to advise his chief of recent events. There was something of a stir when they came striding across the room to the center table. Sextus mumbled an ungracious introduction. Marcellus rose and was ready to offer his hand, but Paulus did not see it; merely bowed, drew out his chair, and sat. He was not drunk, but it was evident that he had been drinking. His lean face, stubbly with a three-days' beard, was unhealthily ruddy; and his hands, when he began to gobble his food, were shaky. They were also dirty. And yet, in spite of his general appearance, Paulus bore marks of a discarded refinement. This man, thought Marcellus, may have been somebody, once upon a time.

'The new Legate; eh?' drawled Paulus, with his mouth full. 'We have had no word of his appointment. However'—he waved a negligent hand, and helped himself to another large portion from the messy bowl of stewed meat—'we can go into that later; tomorrow, perhaps.' For some minutes he wolfed his rations, washing down the greasy meat with noisy gulps of a sharp native wine.

Having finished, Paulus folded his hairy arms on the table and stared insolently into the face of the young interloper. Marcellus met his cloudy eyes steadily. Each knew that the other was taking his measure, not only as to height and weight—in which dimensions they were approximately matched, with Paulus a few pounds heavier, perhaps, and a few years older—but, more particularly, appraising each other's timber and temper. Paulus drew an unpleasant grin.

'Important name—Gallio,' he remarked, with mock deference. 'Any relation to the rich Senator?'

'My father,' replied Marcellus, coolly.

'Oh-ho!' chuckled Paulus. 'Then you must be one of these club-house Tribunes.' He glanced about, as conversations at the adjoining tables were throttled down. 'One would think Prince Gaius could have found a more attractive post for the son of Senator Gallio,' he went on, raising his voice for the benefit of the staff. 'By Jove—I have it!' he shouted, hilariously, slapping Sextus on the shoulder. 'The son of Marcus Lucan Gallio has been a bad boy!' He turned again to Marcellus. 'I'll wager this is your first command, Tribune.'

'It is,' replied Marcellus. The room was deathly still now.

'Never gave an order in your life; eh?' sneered Paulus.

Marcellus pushed back his chair and rose, conscious that three score of interested eyes were studying his serious face.

'I am about to give an order now!' he said, steadily. 'Centurion Paulus, you will stand and apologize for conduct unbecoming an officer!'

Paulus hooked an arm over the back of his chair, and grinned.

'You gave the wrong order, my boy,' he snarled. Then, as he watched Marcellus deliberately unsheathing his broadsword, Paulus overturned his chair as he sprang to his feet. Drawing his sword, he muttered, 'You'd better put that down, youngster!'

'Clear the room!' commanded Marcellus.

There was no doubt in anyone's mind now as to the young Tribune's intention. He and Paulus had gone into this business too far to retreat. The tables were quickly pushed back against the wall. Chairs were dragged out of the way. And the battle was on.

At the beginning of the engagement, it appeared to the audience that Paulus had decided to make it a brief and decisive affair. His command of the fort was insecurely held, for he was of erratic temper and dissolute habits. Obviously he had resolved upon a quick conquest as an object lesson to his staff. As for the consequences, Paulus had little to lose. Communication with Rome was slow. The tenure of a commander's office was unstable and brief. Nobody in Rome cared much what happened in the fort at Minoa. True—it was risky to kill the son of a Senator, but the staff would bear witness that the Tribune had drawn first.

Paulus immediately forced the fight with flailing blows, any one of which would have split his young adversary in twain had it landed elsewhere than on Marcellus' parrying sword. Entirely willing to be on the defensive for a while, Marcellus allowed himself to be rushed backward until they had almost reached the end of the long mess-hall. The faces of the junior officers, ranged around the wall, were tense.

Demetrius stood with clenched fists and anxious eyes as he saw his master being crowded back toward a corner.

Step by step, Paulus marched into his retreating antagonist, raining blow after blow upon the defensive sword until, encouraged by his success, he saw his quarry backing into a quite hopeless position. He laughed—as he decreased the tempo of his strokes, assured now of his victory. But Marcellus believed there was a note of anxiety in the tone of that guttural laugh; believed also that the decreased fury of the blows was not due to the heavier man's assurance—but because of a much more serious matter. Paulus was getting tired. There was a strained look on his face as he raised his sword-arm. It was probably beginning to ache. Paulus was out of training. Life at Minoa had slowed him up. We take things easy in Gaza.

As they neared the critical corner, Paulus raised his arm woodenly to strike a mighty blow; and, this time, Marcellus did not wait for it to descend, but slashed his sword laterally so close to Paulus' throat that he instinctively threw back his head, and the blow went wild. In that instant, Marcellus wheeled about quickly. It was Paulus now who was defending the corner.

Marcellus did not violently press his advantage. Wearied by his unaccustomed exercise, Paulus was breathing heavily and his contorted mouth showed a mounting alarm. He had left off flailing now; and, changing his tactics for a better strategy, seemed to be remembering his training. And he was no mean swordsman, Marcellus discovered: at least, there had been a time, no doubt, when Paulus might have given a good account of himself in the arena.

Marcellus caught sight of Demetrius again, and noted that his slave's face was eased of its strain. We were on familiar ground now, doing battle with skill rather than brute strength. This was ever so much better. Up till this moment, Marcellus had never been engaged in a dueling-match where his adversary had tried to hew him down with a weapon handled as an axe is swung. Paulus was fighting like a Roman Centurion now; not like a common butcher cleaving a beef.

For a brief period, while their swords rang with short, sharp, angry clashes, Marcellus gradually advanced. Once, Paulus cast his eyes about to see how much room was left to him; and Marcellus obligingly retreated a few steps. It was quite clear to every watcher that he had voluntarily donated Paulus a better chance to take care of himself. There was a half-audible ejaculation. This maneuver of the new Legate might not be in keeping with the dulled spirit of Minoa, but it stirred a memory of the manner in which brave men dealt with one another in Rome. The eyes of Demetrius shone with pride! His master was indeed a thoroughbred. 'Eugenos!' he exclaimed.

But Paulus was in no mood to accept favors. He came along swiftly, with as much audacity as if he had earned this more stable footing, and endeavored to spar Marcellus into a further retreat. But on that spot the battle was permanently located. Paulus tried everything he could recall, weaving, crouching, feinting—and all the time growing more and more fatigued. Now his guard was becoming sluggish and increasingly vulnerable. On two occasions, the spectators noted, it would have been simple enough for the Tribune to have ended the affair.

And now—with a deft maneuver—Marcellus brought the engagement to a dramatic close. Studying his opportunity, he thrust the tip of his broadsword into the hilt-housing of Paulus' wearied weapon, and tore it out of his hand. It fell with a clatter to the stone floor. Then there was a moment of absolute silence. Paulus stood waiting. His posture did him credit, they all thought; for, though his face showed the shock of this stunning surprise, it was not the face of a coward. Paulus was decisively defeated, but he had better stuff in him than any of them had thought.

Marcellus stooped and picked up the fallen broadsword by its tip, drew back his arm with the slow precision of a careful aim, and sent it swiftly—end over end over end through the mess-hall—to the massive wooden door where it drove its weight deep into the timber with a resounding thud. Nobody broke the stillness that followed. Marcellus then reversed his own sword in his hand, again took a deliberate aim, and sent the heavy weapon hurtling through the air toward the same target. It thudded deep into the door close beside the sword of Paulus.

The two men faced each other silently. Then Marcellus spoke; firmly but not arrogantly.

'Centurion Paulus,' he said, 'you will now apologize for conduct unbecoming an officer.'

Paulus shifted his weight and drew a long breath; half-turned to face the tightening ring of spectators; then straightened defiantly, folded his arms, and sneered.

Marcellus deliberately drew his dagger from his belt, and stepped forward. Paulus did not move.

'You had better defend yourself, Centurion,' warned Marcellus. 'You have a dagger; have you not? I advise you to draw it!' He advanced another step. 'Because—if you do not obey my order—I intend to kill you!'

It wasn't easy for Paulus, but he managed to do it adequately. Demetrius remarked afterward that it was plain to be seen Centurion Paulus was not an accomplished orator, which Marcellus thought was a very droll comment.

After Paulus had stammered through his glum, impromptu speech, Marcellus responded, 'Your apology is accepted, Centurion. Now perhaps there is something else that you might think it timely to say to your fellow officers. I have not yet been officially presented to them.

As the retiring Commander, it is, I feel, your right to extend this courtesy.'

Paulus fully found his voice this time, and his announcement was made in a firm tone.

'I am introducing Tribune Marcellus Gallio, the Legate of this legion, and Commander of this fort.'

There was a concerted clatter of swords drawn in salute—all but the sword of paunchy old Sextus, who pretended to be adjusting his harness.

'Centurion Sextus!' called Marcellus, sharply. 'Bring me my sword!'

All eyes watched Sextus plod awkwardly over to the big door and tug the sword out of the thick planking.

'Bring the sword of Centurion Paulus, also!' commanded Marcellus.

Sextus worked the second broadsword out of the timber, and came with heavy feet and a dogged air. Marcellus took the heavy weapons, handed Paulus his, and waited to receive Sextus' salute. The hint was taken without further delay. Paulus also saluted before sheathing his sword.

'We will now finish our dinner,' said Marcellus, coolly. 'You will restore the tables to their places. Breakfast will be served to the staff tomorrow morning at five. All officers will be smooth-shaven. There will be an inspection on the parade-ground at six, conducted by Lieutenant-Commander Paulus. That will do.'

Paulus had asked, respectfully enough, to be excused as they returned to their table, and Marcellus had given him permission to go. Sextus was trailing along after him, without asking leave; and upon being sharply asked if he had not forgotten something, mumbled that he had finished his dinner.

'Then you will have time,' said Marcellus, 'to clear the Commander's quarters, so that I may occupy those rooms tonight.'

Sextus acknowledged the order and tramped heavily to the door. Appetites were not keen, but the staff made a show of finishing dinner. Marcellus lingered at his table. At length, when he rose, they all stood in their places. He bowed and left the room, followed by Demetrius. As they passed the open door of the Commander's rooms, on their way to the quarters which had been assigned them earlier, it was observed that a dozen slaves were busily engaged in making the place ready for occupancy.

After a few minutes, the men came and transferred their various gear to the Commander's quarters. When they were alone, Marcellus sat down behind the big desk. Demetrius stood at attention before him.

'Well, Demetrius?' Marcellus raised his brows inquiringly. 'What is on your mind?'

Demetrius brought the shaft of his spear to his forehead in salute.

'I wish to say, sir, that I am much honored to be the slave of the Commander of Minoa.'

'Thanks, Demetrius,' smiled Marcellus, wearily. 'We will have to wait—and see—who commands Minoa. This is a tough outfit. The preliminary skirmish was satisfactory; but—making peace is always more difficult than making war.'

For the next few days the nerves of the legion were tense. The new Legate had demonstrated his determination to be in full authority, but it was by no means clear whether that authority would be maintained on any other terms than a relentless coercion.

Paulus had suffered a severe loss of prestige, but his influence was still to be reckoned with. He was obeying orders respectfully, but with such grim taciturnity that no one was able to guess what was going on in his mind. Whether he was not yet fully convalescent from the wounds dealt to his pride, or was sullenly deliberating some overt act of revenge, remained to be seen. Marcellus had formed no clear opinion about this. Demetrius planted his bunk directly inside the door, every night, and slept with his dagger in his hand.

After a week, the tension began to relax a little as the garrison became accustomed to the new discipline. Marcellus issued crisp orders and insisted upon absolute obedience; not the sluggish compliance that had been good enough for Gaza, but a prompt and vigorous response that marched with clipped steps and made no tarrying to ask foolish questions or offer lame excuses.

It had seemed wise to the new Commander to let his more personal relations with the staff develop naturally without too much cultivation. He showed no favoritism, preserved his official dignity, and in his dealings with his fellow officers wasted no words. He was just, considerate, and approachable; but very firm. Presently the whole organization was feeling the effect of the tighter regulations, but without apparent resentment. The men marched with a fresh vigor and seemed to take pride in keeping their equipment in order. The appearance and morale of the officers had vastly improved.

Every morning, Paulus, now second in command, came to the office of Marcellus for instructions. Not a word had passed between them, relative to their dramatic introduction. Their conversations were conducted with icy formality and the stiffest kind of official courtesy. Paulus, faultlessly dressed, would appear at the door and ask to see the Commander. The sentry would convey the request. The Commander would instruct the sentry to admit the Centurion. Paulus would enter and stand straight as an arrow before the official desk. Salutes would be exchanged.

'It is necessary to replace six camels, sir.'

'Why?' The query would snap like a bowstring.

'One is lame. Two are sick. Three are too old for service.'

'Replace them!'

'Yes, sir,'

Then Paulus would salute and stalk out. Sometimes Marcellus wondered whether this frosty relationship was to continue forever. He hoped not. He was getting lonesome in the remote altitude to which he had climbed for sake of maintaining discipline. Paulus was, he felt, an excellent fellow; embittered by this exile, and morally disintegrated by the boredom and futility of his desert life. Marcellus had resolved that if Paulus showed the slightest inclination to be friendly, he would meet the overture halfway; but not a step further. Nor would he take the initiative.

As for Sextus, Marcellus had very little direct contact with him, for Sextus received his orders through Paulus. The big, gruff fellow had been punctilious in his obedience, but very glum. At the mess-table he had nothing to say; ate his rations with a scowl, and asked to be excused.

One evening, after ten days had passed, Marcellus noticed that Sextus' chair was vacant.

'Where is he?' demanded the Commander, nodding toward the unoccupied place.

'Broke his leg, sir,' answered Paulus.

'When?'

'This afternoon, sir.'

'How?'

'Stockade gate fell on him, sir.'

Marcellus immediately rose and left the table. After a moment, Paulus followed and overtook him on the way to Sextus' quarters. They fell into step, and marched side by side with long strides.

'Bad break?

'Clean break. Upper leg. Not much mangled.'

Sextus was stretched out on his back, beads of sweat on his fore-head. He glanced up and made an awkward gesture of greeting.

'Much pain?' inquired Marcellus.

'No, sir.' Sextus gritted his teeth.

'Gallant liar!' snapped Marcellus. 'Typical Roman lie! You wouldn't admit you were in pain if you'd been chopped to mincemeat! That bunk is bad; sags like a hammock. We will find a better one. Have you had your dinner?'

Sextus shook his head; said he didn't want anything to eat.

'Well—we'll see about that!' said Marcellus, gruffly.

By inspection hour, next morning, the story had spread through the acres of brown tents that the new Commander—who had had them all on the jump and had strutted about through the camp with long legs and a dark frown—had gone to the kitchen of the officers' mess and had concocted a nourishing broth for old Sextus; had moved him to airier quarters; had supervised the making of a special bed for him.

That day Marcellus became the Commander of the fort at Minoa.

That night Demetrius did not take his dagger to bed with him; he
didn't even bother to lock the door.

* * * * * *

The next morning, Paulus pushed the sentry aside at the Commander's quarters and entered without more ceremony than a casual
salute. Marcellus pointed to a vacant chair and Paulus accepted it.

'Hot day, Centurion Paulus,' remarked Marcellus.

'Gaza does not believe in pleasant weather, sir. The climate suits
the temper of the people. It's either hot or cold.' Paulus tipped back
his chair and thrust his thumbs under his belt. 'The Jews have an
important festival, sir. They observe it for a week when the moon is
full in the month they call Nisan. Perhaps you know about it.'

'No—never heard of it,' admitted Marcellus. 'Is it any of our business?'

'It's their annual Passover Week,' explained Paulus, 'celebrating
their flight from Egypt.'

'What have they been doing down in Egypt?' asked Marcellus
indifferently.

'Nothing—lately,' grinned Paulus. 'This happened fifteen centuries
ago.'

'Oh—that! Do they still remember?'

'The Jews never forgot anything, sir. Every year at this season, all
the Jews who can possibly get there go to Jerusalem to "eat the
Passover," as their saying is; but most of them are quite as much
interested in family reunions, games, sports, auctions, and all manner
of shows. Caravans of merchandise come from afar to market their
wares. Thousands crowd the city and camp in the surrounding hills.
It is a lively spectacle, sir.'

'You have been there, it seems.'

'On each of the eleven years since I was sent to this fort, sir,'
nodded Paulus. 'The Procurator in Jerusalem—I think you know that
his office outranks all of the other Palestinian establishments—expects
detachments from the forts at Capernaum, Caesarea, Joppa, and
Minoa to come and help keep order.'

'An unruly crowd, then?' surmised Marcellus.

'Not very, sir. But always, when that many Jews assemble, there is
the usual talk of revolution. They wail sad chants and prattle about
their lost heritage. So far as I know, this unrest has never amounted
to anything more alarming than a few street brawls. But the Procurator thinks it is a good thing, on these occasions, to have a conspicuous display of Roman uniforms—and a bit of drill-work in the vicinity
of the Temple.' Paulus chuckled, reminiscently.

'Do we get a formal notice?'

'No, sir. The Procurator does not trouble himself to send a courier.
He takes it for granted that a detachment from Minoa will show up.'

'Very well, Paulus. How many men do we send, and when do they go?'

'A company, sir; a full hundred. It is a three-day journey. We should start the day after tomorrow.'

'You may arrange for it then, Paulus. Would you like to command the detachment, or have you had enough of it?'

'Enough of it! By no means, sir! This expedition is the only bright event of the year! And if I may venture to suggest, Tribune, you yourself might find this a most refreshing diversion.'

'On your recommendation, I shall go. What is the nature of the equipment?'

'It is not very burdensome, sir. Because it is a gala occasion, we carry our best uniforms. You will be proud of your command, I think; for it is a reward of merit here to be chosen for this duty, and the men are diligent in polishing their weapons. Otherwise we pack nothing but provisions for tenting and meals on the way. We are put up in commodious barracks in Jerusalem, and the food is of an uncommonly fine quality, furnished by certain rich men of the city.'

'What?' Marcellus screwed up his face in surprise. 'Do they not resent Roman rule in Jerusalem?'

Paulus laughed ironically.

'It is the common people who feel the weight of the Roman yoke, sir. As for the rich, many of whom collect the tribute for Tiberius —and keep a quarter of it for themselves—they are quite content. Oh—publicly, of course, the nabobs have to make a show of lamenting the loss of their kingdom; but these fat old merchants and money-lenders would be quite upset if a real revolution got started. You will find that the city fathers and the Procurator are thick as thieves, though they pretend to be at odds.'

'But this is amazing, Paulus! I had always supposed that the Jews were passionately patriotic, and uncompromising in their bitter hatred of the Empire.'

'That is quite true, sir, of the common people. Very zealous, indeed! They keep hoping for their old independence. Doubtless you have heard of their ancient myth about a Messiah.'

'No. What's a Messiah?'

'The Messiah is their deliverer, sir. According to their prophets, he will appear, one day, and organize the people to accomplish their freedom.'

'I never heard of it,' admitted Marcellus, indifferently. 'But small wonder. I haven't had much interest in religious superstitions.'

'Nor I!' protested Paulus. 'But one hears quite a little about this Messiah business during Passover Week.' He laughed at the recollection. 'Why, sir—you should see them! Sleek, paunchy old fellows, swathed from their whiskers to their sandals in voluminous black robes, stalking through the streets, with their heads thrown back and their eyes closed, beating their breasts and bleating about their lost kingdom and bellowing for their Messiah! Pouf! They don't want any other kingdom than the one that stuffs their wallets and their bellies. They don't want a Messiah—and if they thought there was the slightest likelihood of a revolution against Roman domination they would be the first to stamp it out.'

'They must be a precious lot of hypocrites!' growled Marcellus.

'Yes, sir,' agreed Paulus, 'but they set a fine table!'

For a little while, the Tribune sat silently shaking his head in glum disgust.

'I know the world is full of rascality, Paulus, but this beats anything I ever heard of!'

'It is rather sickening, sir,' conceded Paulus. 'The sight that always makes me want to slip a knife under one of those pious arms, upraised in prayer, is the long procession of the poor and sick and blind and crippled trailing along after one of these villainous old frauds, under the impression that their holy cause is in good hands.' He interrupted himself to lean over the arm of his chair for a better view of the doorway, and caught sight of Demetrius standing in the hall within sound of their voices. Marcellus' eyes followed.

'My Greek slave keeps his own counsel, Centurion,' he said, in a confidential tone. 'You need not fear that he will betray any private conversation.'

'What I was going to say, sir,' continued Paulus, lowering his voice—'this political situation in Jerusalem, revolting as it sounds, is not unusual.' He leaned halfway across the desk, and went on in a guarded whisper, 'Commander—that's what holds the Empire together! If it were not for the rich men in all of our subjugated provinces—men whose avarice is greater than their local patriotism—the Roman Empire would collapse!'

'Steady, Paulus!' warned Marcellus. 'That's a dangerous theory to expound! You might get into trouble—saying such things.'

Paulus stiffened with sudden wrath.

'Trouble!' he snarled, bitterly. 'I did get into trouble, sir, that way! I was fool enough to be honest in the presence of Germanicus! That' —he added, only half audibly—'was how I—a Legate—earned my passage to Minoa to become a Centurion! But—by the Gods—what I said was true! The Roman Empire was consolidated, and is now supported, by the treachery of rich provincials, willing to sell out their own people! This strategy is not original with us, of course! Rome learned the trick from Alexander. He learned it from the Persians, who had learned it in Egypt. Buy up the big men of a little country— and—pouf!—you can have the rest of them for nothing!' Paulus' face was flushed with anger, and after his seditious speech he sat with clenched hands, flexing the muscles of his jaw. Then he faced Marcellus squarely, and muttered: 'Valor of Rome! Bah! I spit on the

valor of Rome! Valor of treachery! Valor of gold! Valor of hurling
the poor at one another on the battle-field, while the big ones are
off in a corner selling them out! The great and proud Roman Empire!' Paulus brought his fist down with a bang on the desk. 'I spit
on the Roman Empire!'

'You are very indiscreet, Paulus,' said Marcellus, seriously. 'For remarks of that sort, you could have your pelt pulled off. I hope you do
not often let yourself go like that.'

Paulus rose and hitched up his broad belt.

'I had no fear of speaking my mind to you, sir,' he said.

'What makes you think I wouldn't give you away?' asked Marcellus.

'Because'—replied Paulus, confidently—'you believe in real valor—
the kind that demands courage!'

Marcellus drew an appreciative smile.

'It is a wonder, Paulus,' he said, thoughtfully, 'that the ordinary
rank and file do not take things into their own hands.'

'Pouf! What can they do?' scoffed Paulus, with a shrug. 'They're
nothing but sheep, with no shepherd! Take these Jews, for example:
now and then, some fiery fellow goes howling mad over the raw injustice, and gets up on a cart, and lets out a few shrieks—but they
dispose of him in a hurry!'

'Who shuts him up? The rich men?'

'Well—not directly. We're always called in to do the dirty work.
It's obvious that Rome can't permit such uprisings; but it is the rich
and greedy provincials who nip revolutions in the bud.'

'Damned scoundrels!' exclaimed Marcellus.

'Yes, sir,' assented Paulus, his gusty storm having blown out—'but
you will find that these damned scoundrels in Jerusalem know good
wine when they see it, and aren't mean about sharing it with the
Roman legions. That'—he added, with cool mockery—'is to encourage
us to be on the lookout for any foolhardy patriot who squeaks about
the lost kingdom!'

Chapter IV

THE first day's journey, from Gaza to Ascalon, was intolerably tedious, for the deep-rutted highway was crowded with creeping caravans and filthy with dust.

'It will be better tomorrow,' promised Melas, amused by the grotesque appearance of Demetrius who had rewound his turban about his face until only his eyes were visible.

'Let us hope so!' grumbled the Corinthian, tugging at the lead-donkey that was setting off toward a clump of thistles. 'But how will it be better? These snails are all crawling to Jerusalem; are they not?'

'Yes—but we leave the highway at Ascalon,' explained Melas, 'and take a shorter road through the hills. The caravans do not travel it. They're afraid of the Bedouins.'

'And we aren't?'

'We're too many for them. They wouldn't risk it.'

Centurion Paulus' stocky, bow-legged, red-headed Thracian was enjoying himself. Not often was Melas in a position to inform his betters; and, observing that the status of Demetrius was enviable compared to his own, it had made him quite expansive to be on such friendly terms with the new Legate's well-spoken slave.

'It isn't the camels that stir up the dust,' advised Melas, out of his long experience. 'Your camel lifts his big, padded paws and lays them down on top of the soft dirt. It's the asses that drag their feet. But I hate camels!'

'I am not very well acquainted with camels,' admitted Demetrius, willing to show some interest in his education.

'Nobody is,' declared Melas. 'You can live with a camel for years and treat him as your brother, but you can never trust him. See that?' He tapped a badly disfigured nose. 'I got that up in Gaul, a dozen years ago. The fleas and flies were driving my master's old Menepthah crazy. I spent the better part of two days rubbing olive oil into his mangy hide. And he stood like a rock, and purred like a cat; because he liked it. When I was all through, he turned around and kicked me in the face.'

Demetrius laughed, as was expected, and inquired what sort of revenge Melas had considered appropriate, a query that delighted him, for there was more of the story.

'I was so blind mad,' continued Melas, 'that I did the same thing to him—only Menepthah saw it coming and grabbed my foot. Ever have a camel bite you? Now—an ass,' he expounded, 'or a dog, will snap and nip and nibble at you; but if he is going to bite, he tells you. Your camel never lets you into the secret. When he bites, nobody knows what is in his mind—but himself. I was laid up for two weeks, the time Menepthah bit my foot. I don't like camels,' he added, reasonably enough, his new friend thought.

'They can't be blamed much for wanting to get even,' observed Demetrius. 'It's a pretty rough life, I suppose.'

Melas seemed to be weighing this bland comment on his not very sensitive scales as they trudged along, and presently gave Demetrius a long, appraising look out of the tail of his eye. His lip curled in a sour grin. At length he ventured to give his thoughts an airing; having a care, however, to keep them in leash.

'It doesn't do much good—trying to get even. Take your slave, now: he can't get anywhere that way. Camels and asses and slaves are better off minding their masters.' And when Demetrius did not comment, Melas added, encouragingly, 'Or—don't you think so?'

Demetrius nodded, without interest. He had no desire to discuss this matter.

'If you're going to serve another man, at all,' he remarked casually, 'it's only good sense to serve him well.'

'That's what I always say,' approved Melas, with such exaggerated innocence that Demetrius wondered whether the fellow was making a smug pretense of lily-white loyalty—or recklessly toying with a piece of crude irony. He thought it might be interesting to find out.

'Of course, slavery is a bit different from the employment of freed-men,' experimented Demetrius. 'If a freedman finds his work dis-tasteful, he can leave it, which is ever so much better than keeping on at it—and shirking it. The slave does not have this choice.'

Melas chuckled a little.

'Some slaves,' he remarked, 'are like asses. They snap at their masters, and get slapped for it. They sit down and balk, and get themselves whipped and kicked. There's no sense in that. And then there are some slaves that behave like camels; just keep going on, and taking it, no matter how they're used'—Melas' tone was getting noticeably metallic, to match his heavy scowl—'and, one day—when the master is drunk, maybe—the poor beast pays him off.'

'And then what?' demanded Demetrius.

Melas shrugged, sullenly.

'Then he'd better run away,' he concluded. Presently he muttered an afterthought: 'Not much chance for a camel. Once in a while a slave gets away. Three years ago'—Melas lowered his voice, though there was no need of this precaution as they were far at the rear of the procession, and the furtive quality of the Thracian's tone hinted at a conspiratorial confidence. 'It was on this same trip—three years ago. Commander Vitelius' slave, as cheerful and obedient as anybody you ever met—Sevenus, by name—managed to lose himself the next to the last day in Jerusalem. Nobody knows what became of him.' Melas stepped nearer and muttered out of the corner of his mouth: 'Nobody but me. Sevenus left for Damascus. Wanted me to go along. Sometimes I've wished I had taken him up. It's easy enough. We're more or less on our own in Jerusalem. The officers have themselves a good time. Don't want the slaves hanging about. Bad for discipline.' Melas winked significantly. 'The Centurions like to play a little.'

Demetrius listened without comment to this lengthy speech; and Melas, a bit anxious, searched his eyes for advice as to the safety of proceeding farther.

'Of course, it's no secret,' he proclaimed, doffing his air of mystery. 'Everybody at Minoa knows about it—all but what I just told you.'

Demetrius knew he was making a mistake when he asked the question that implied a personal interest in this matter, but the story had stirred his curiosity.

'What made this fellow Sevenus think he had a chance of freedom in Damascus?'

Melas' eyes relighted.

'Why—Damascus is Syrian. Those people up there hate Rome like poison! The old city's full of Roman slaves, they say; living right out in the open, too; making no attempt to hide. Once you get there, you're safe as a bug in a donkey's ear.'

* * * * * *

Early next morning, their caravan broke camp and moved off through the bare hills over a winding road which narrowed frequently, in long ravines and deep wadies, to a mere bridlepath that raveled out yesterday's compact pilgrimage into a single thread.

It was a desolate country, practically uninhabited. Small herds of wild goats, almost indistinguishable from the jagged brown rocks on the treeless hillsides, grouped to stare an absurd defiance of any attempted trespass upon their domain. In the valleys, the spring rains had fraudulently invited an occasional tuft of vegetation to believe it had a chance of survival. Beside a blistered water-hole a brave little clump of violets drooped with thirst.

Demetrius was finding pleasure in this stage of the journey. The landscape was uninspiring, but it refreshed his spirit to be out in the open and at a comfortable distance from the uncouth Melas whose favorite topic had become disquieting. There was little doubt but the Thracian was building up toward a proposal of escape; either that, or was harboring an even more sinister design to engage him in a conspiracy and then expose him. Of course, this suspicion might be quite unfair to the fellow; but it would be dangerous to take any risks. No matter what he, himself, might say to Melas, on this touchy matter, it could easily become a weapon in the garrulous Thracian's hand, in the event he were to be miffed about something or made envious of the unusual privileges accorded to the Commander's more fortunate slave. Demetrius had resolved to be painstakingly prudent in any conversation with Melas, and—as much as possible—avoid being alone with him. Besides, there was much to think about, left over from a discussion between Marcellus and Paulus, last night; a most provocative—and highly amusing—survey of the gods, conducted by two men who had no piety at all. A good deal of it had been shockingly irreverent, but undeniably entertaining.

Late yesterday afternoon, when the company had halted near a spring—on city property, a mile northeast of Ascalon—Demetrius had been happy to receive a summons to attend his master, for he had begun to feel lonesome and degraded. He was amazed at the smart appearance of the camp. Almost by magic the brown tents had risen in four precise rows, the commissary had unpacked and set up its field equipment, chairs and tables and bunks had been unfolded and put in order. Banners were flying. Sentries were posted. The local Roman representative—a seedy, unprepossessing old fellow, with the bright pink nose of a seasoned winebibber, accompanied by three obsequious Jewish merchants—came out to read and present an illuminated scroll which eloquently (and untruthfully) certified to Ascalon's delight that the famed Legion of Minoa had deigned to accept the city's poor but cheerful hospitality. They had brought with them four huge wineskins bulging with the best of the native product, and were invited to remain for supper, after the Commander had formally replied—with his staff ranged stiffly to the rear of him—that Minoa was fully as glad to be in Ascalon as Ascalon was to entertain Minoa, which his slave considered deliciously droll.

After the evening meal had been disposed of, and his immediate duties performed, Demetrius had stretched out on the ground in the shadow of the Commander's tent—a quite imposing tent, it was, larger than the others, trimmed with red flouncing, red silk curtains at the entrance, and a canopy over the doorway supported by slanting spear-shafts. With his fingers interlaced behind his head, Demetrius lay gazing up at the stars, marveling at their uncommon brightness, and effortlessly listening to the subdued voices of his master and Paulus, lounging in camp-chairs under the gaudy canopy. Apparently the visitation of the local dignitaries, who had now left for home, accounted for the conversation. Paulus was holding forth with the leisurely drawl of an amateur philospher—benign, tolerant, and a little bit tight. Demetrius cocked an ear. Occasionally, in such circumstances, a man imprudently spoke his honest convictions about something; and, if Paulus had any convictions, it might be interesting to learn what they were.

'The Jews,' Paulus was saying, 'are a queer people. They admit it themselves; brag about it, in fact; no other people like them in the whole world. For one thing, they're under a special divine protection. Their god, Jehovah—they have only one, you know—isn't interested in anybody else but the Jews. Of course, there would be nothing positively immoral about that belief, if it weren't for the fact that their Jehovah created the world and all its inhabitants; but has no use for any of the other people; says the Jews are his children. Presumably the rest of the world can look out for itself. If they'd just admit that Jehovah was a sort of local deity—'

'Oh—but we do the same thing, Paulus; don't we?' rejoined Marcellus. 'Isn't Jupiter a sort of general superintendent of the universe, with unlimited jurisdiction?'

'Not at all; not at all, sir,' protested Paulus, lazily. 'Jupiter hasn't any interests in the Egyptians, but he doesn't claim he made them what they are, and then despised them for being no better. And he never said that the Syrians are a lousy lot, for not lighting bonfires on his feast-day. And Jupiter never said he was going to see that the Romans had the best of it—all the time.'

'Did Jehovah say that to the Jews?'

Demetrius laughed silently. He had suspected that Marcellus wasn't very well informed about the various religions, but his master's almost complete ignorance on the subject was ludicrous.

'Why—certainly!' Paulus was orating. 'Started them off in a garden where he had grown a fruit they were forbidden to eat. Of course they ate it, not to satisfy their hunger but their curiosity.'

'One would think Jehovah might have been delighted over their curiosity,' put in Marcellus, 'seeing that every good thing we have was discovered through someone's inquisitiveness.'

'Yes—but this made Jehovah angry,' explained Paulus, 'so he pitched them out into the desert, and let them get tricked into slavery. Then he told them how to escape, and turned them loose in a wilderness. Then he promised them a land of their own—'

'And this is it!' laughed Marcellus. 'What a promised land!'

'There isn't a more worthless strip of country in the world!' declared Paulus. 'And now the Jews have lost control of it. You'd think that after about fifteen hundred years of hard knocks, poverty, and slavery, these specially favored children of Jehovah would begin to wonder whether they might not be better off without so much divine attention.'

'Perhaps that accounts for this Messiah business that you spoke about, the other day. Maybe they've given up hope that Jehovah will take care of them, and think the Messiah might improve their fortunes when he comes. Do you suppose that's what they have in mind? It's not unreasonable. I daresay that's the way we and the Greeks accumulated so many gods, Paulus. When one god gets weary and impotent, another fresher god takes over. Didn't old Zeus retire once in favor of his son Apollo?'

'Not for long,' remembered Paulus. 'Aparently the weather hadn't been very good, so young Apollo decided he would manage the sun; and ran amuck with it. Old Zeus had to straighten out the tangle for the boy. Now—there's sense in a religion like that, Tribune. Our gods behave the way we do, naturally, because we made them the way we are. Everybody gets tired of the dictatorial old man, and eventually he gets tired too; decides to let his son run the business— whether it's growing gourds or managing the planets; but he never thinks the young fellow is competent, so he keeps on interfering until presently there is a row. That's why our religion is such a comfort to us,' Paulus continued, elaborately ironical.

'I'm afraid you're not very pious,' commented Marcellus. 'If the gods hear what you are saying, they may not like it. They might think you doubted their reality.'

'Not at all, sir! It's men like me who really believe in their reality. They're authentic—the gods! Some of them want war, some want peace, some of them don't know what they want—except an annual feast-day and a big parade. Some give you rest and sleep, some drive you insane. Some you are expected to admire, and some you are expected to hate, and all of them are never quite happy unless they are frightening you and assured that you are afraid. This is sensible. This is the way life is! . . . But these Jews! There they are, with only one god; and he is perpetually right, perpetually good, wise, loving. Of course he is stubborn, because they are stubborn; doesn't approve of pleasure, because they never learned how to play; never makes any mistakes, because the Jew never makes any mistakes. Tribune, Jehovah can't help being a pessimist. The Jews are a pessimistic people.'

'Maybe Jehovah thinks it is a good thing for his children to endure hardship,' speculated Marcellus; 'toughens their fiber, knocks off their surplus fat, keeps them in fighting trim. I believe he has a good idea there, Paulus. Sometimes I've thought that Rome would be better off if we patricians had to scratch for a living, and stole less from the neighbors.'

There was a considerable pause at this point in the sacrilegious discussion, and Demetrius had wondered whether they hadn't about exhausted themselves and their subject. But not quite.

'Rome will have that problem solved for her, one of these days,' Paulus was muttering, ominously. 'The scepter is passed around, Commander. Egypt has her day in the sunshine. Darius tramps about, scaring everybody for an hour or two. Alexander sobs because there's no one left to be subdued. The Caesars drive their chariots over Alexander's world; so drunk with power that they can't even bear to let these poor Hebrews own a few acres of weeds and snakes. . . . Ho-hum!'

Demetrius had yawned, too, and wished they would go to bed.

'But it will be somebody else's turn—soon,' said Paulus.

'When?' asked Marcellus, exactly as Demetrius thought he might.

'Well—if justice were served to crazy old Tiberius and his addled stepchild,' deliberated Paulus, 'I should think it might be someone else's turn tomorrow—or by the end of next week, at the latest. . . . How about a little more wine, Tribune?'

Demetrius had sat up, ready for the summons. It came instantly, and he presented himself.

'Fill Centurion Paulus' cup,' ordered Marcellus. 'No—none for me.'

And then Demetrius had gone back into the shadow of the tent to resume his waiting. The conversation had taken a queer turn now.

'Paulus,' his master was saying, 'you believe that the gods are manufactured by men. If it isn't an impertinent question—did you ever try to make one?'

Demetrius, sauntering today along through a narrow ravine, almost oblivious of the long procession single-filing on ahead, laughed as he recalled that extraordinary question and its absurd answer.

'No,' Paulus had replied, 'but it isn't too late. Shall I make one for you now?'

'By all means!' chuckled Marcellus. 'I assume that when you have him completed he will closely resemble yourself.'

'Well—not too closely; for this god I'm going to invent is good. He doesn't just pretend to be good. He really is good! He takes a few bright men into his confidence—not necessarily Romans or Greeks or Gauls; just so they're honest and intelligent—and entrusts them with some important tasks. He tells one man how to cure leprosy, and others how to restore sight to the blind and hearing to the deaf. He confides the secrets of light and fire; how to store up summer heat for use in winter; how to capture the light of day and save it to illumine the night; how to pour idle lakes onto arid land.' Paulus had paused, probably to take another drink.

'Very good, Centurion,' Marcellus had commented, thoughtfully. 'If you'll set up your god somewhere, and get him to producing these effects, he can have all my trade.'

'Perhaps you might like to assist in his creation, sir,' suggested Paulus, companionably.

Demetrius had not expected the quite serious speech that followed. As it proceeded, he raised up on one elbow and listened intently.

'It occurs to me, Paulus,' Marcellus was saying, soberly, 'that this god of yours, who seems a very fine fellow indeed, might well consider a revision of the present plan for removing men from this world. What happens to us is something like this: a man spends his active life striving to accomplish a few useful deeds, and eventually arrives at the top of his powers; honored—we will say—and a good example

to his community. Then he begins to go into a decline; loses his
teeth and his hair; his step slows, his eyes grow dim, his hearing is
dulled. This disintegration frets him, and he becomes gusty and irascible, like an old dog. Now he retires to a sunny corner of the garden
with a woolen cap and a rug around his legs, and sits there in everybody's way until it is time for him to take to his bed with grievous
aches and pains which twist him into revolting postures. When no
dignity is left to him, nor any longer deserved, he opens his sunken
mouth and snores for a few days, unaware of his inglorious end. Now
—I think your new god should do something about this, Paulus.'

'We will take it up with him, sir,' promised Paulus, agreeably. 'How
would you like to have the matter handled?'

Apparently this required a bit of concentration, for the reply was
delayed a little while. When it came, Marcellus' tone had abandoned
all trace of persiflage and was deeply sincere.

'When a Roman of our sort comes of age, Paulus, there is an impressive ceremony by which we are inducted into manhood. Doubtless you felt, as I did, that this was one of the high moments of life.
Well do I remember—the thrill of it abides with me still—how all
of our relatives and friends assembled, that day, in the stately Forum
Julium. My father made an address, welcoming me into Roman
citizenship. It was as if I had never lived until that hour. I was so
deeply stirred, Paulus, that my eyes swam with tears. And then good
old Cornelius Capito made a speech, a very serious one, about Rome's
right to my loyalty, my courage, and my strength. I knew that tough
old Capito had a right to talk of such matters, and I was proud that
he was there! They beckoned to me, and I stepped forward. Capito
and my father put the white toga on me—and life had begun!'

There was an interval of silence here. Demetrius, much moved by
this recital, had strained to hear above his own accented heartbeats,
for the reminiscence had been spoken in a tone so low that it was
almost as if Marcellus were talking to himself.

'Now—I think your god should ordain that at the crowning moment of a mature man's career; at the apex; when his strength has
reached its zenith; when his best contribution has been made; let
your god ordain that another assembly be held, with all present who
know and revere this worthy man. And who among us would not
strive to be worthy, with such a consummation in prospect? Let
there be a great assembly of the people. Let there be an accounting
of this man's deeds; and, if he has earned a lofty eulogy, let it be
spoken with eloquence.'

'And then?' demanded Paulus. 'A valedictory, perhaps?'

'No,' Marcellus had decided, after a pause. 'Let the man keep
silent. He will have no need to explain his deeds, if they were worth
emulation. He will arise, and his peers will remove his toga; and it
will be treasured; perhaps conferred upon another, some day, for

courageous action. It would be a great responsibility to wear such a garment, Paulus.' There was another long pause.

'I think the god should prescribe that this event occur in the waning of a golden afternoon in springtime. There should be a great chorus, singing an elegiac ode. And while the triumphant music fills the air—with the vast assembly standing reverently—let the honored man march erectly and with firm step from the rostrum—and out—to face the sunset! Then—let him vanish! And be seen no more!'

After he had gone to bed, last night, and the camp was quiet, except for the footfalls and jangling side-arms of the sentries, Demetrius had pondered long and deeply over this strange conceit—the making of a better god!

This morning, as he marched through the barren hills, towing a file of stupid donkeys who had as much control over their destiny as had he over his own, Demetrius wondered what he might have said if they had invited him to add a desirable attribute to their imaginary deity. Doubtless the world would be a more comfortable place to live in if, as Paulus had suggested, some plan were arrived at for a better distribution of light and heat. And perhaps it would bring a man's days to a more dramatic conclusion if, as his master had so beautifully visioned, the human career might close with music and pageantry instead of a tedious glissade into helpless senility; though, as things stood, a man's lack of honor at the end of his life seemed quite compatible with his absurd plight at life's beginning. If Marcellus proposed to add dignity to a man's departure from the world, he should also pray for a more dignified arrival.

No—such idle speculations were a mere waste of opportunity if one had a chance to mend the world. There were other needs of far greater import. Surely, this amazingly honest deity whom Marcellus and Paulus had invoked would want to do something about the cruel injustice of men in their dealings, one with another. With hot indignation, Demetrius reconstructed the painful scene of that day when Roman ruffians forced the doors, and threw his beautiful mother aside as they stalked into his honored father's library to bind him and carry him away to his death.

This nobler god—if he had any interest in justice, at all—would appear, at such a tragic moment, and sternly declare, 'You can't *do* that!'

Demetrius repeated the words aloud—over and over—louder and louder—until the high-walled ravine believed in them, and said so.

'*You can't do that!*' he shouted, so loudly that Melas—far on ahead—turned to look back inquiringly.

*   *   *   *   *   *

They had all but reached the end of their journey now. For the past hour their caravan had been plodding up a long hill. At its crest, a very impressive spectacle had confronted them. They were gazing down upon Jerusalem, whose turrets and domes were aglow with the smouldering fire of sunset.

'Gorgeous!' Marcellus had murmured.

All day, Demetrius had marched beside his master's tall camel, happy to be relieved of his unpleasant duties at the rear. Early in the forenoon, they had come to the junction of the lonesome valley road and a highway running up from Hebron. All along the thorough-fare were encampments of caravans, making no sign of preparation for travel.

'Is this not strange, Paulus?' Marcellus had inquired, 'Why aren't they on the road?'

'It's the Sabbath day, sir,' answered Paulus. 'Jews can't travel on the last day of the week. It's against their law.'

'Can't move at all, eh?'

'Oh—practically not. They may proceed a little way—what they call a Sabbath day's journey—two thousand cubits. Look, sir.' Paulus pointed down the road. 'Two thousand of their cubits would take them to that group of olive trees. That's as far as a Jew can go from his residence on the Sabbath.'

'Quite inconvenient,' observed Marcellus, idly.

'For the poor people—yes,' Paulus laughed. 'The rich, as usual, have their own way of circumventing the law.'

'How's that?'

'Well, sir; in their interpretation of this statute, any place where a man has a possession is considered his residence. If a rich man wants to visit somebody ten miles away, on the Sabbath, he sends his servants on ahead, a day earlier, and they deposit along the road —at two-thousand-cubit intervals—such trifling articles as an old sandal, a cracked pot, a worn-out rug, a scroll-spool; and thus pre-pare the way for their law-abiding lord.'

'Do you mean that—seriously?' inquired Marcellus.

'Yes—and so do they. I tell you, sir, these rich Jews will go to more bother about the external appearance of their religion than any peo-ple on earth. And they do it with straight faces, too. It is a great mistake to be playful with them about it. They've deceived them-selves so long that they really think they're honest. Of course,' he added, dryly, 'the opulent Jew has no monopoly on self-deception. All our rich and influential men, whatever their race or country, are subject to this unhappy malady. It must be a tragic condition to possess great wealth and a sensitive conscience. I never thought much about this before,' he rambled on, 'but I doubt not the sophists could prove self-deception to rate high among the cardinal virtues. None but the noble would heap upon himself so much sham and shame in the cause of righteousness.'

'Paulus, you're a cynic—and an uncommonly bitter one,' drawled

Marcellus. 'By the way—what must these people, along the roadside, think of our disregard of their holy Sabbath?'

'Pouf! They expect nothing better of us. And I'm not sure they'd like it if we laid up for the day in honor of their beliefs. In their opinion, we could defile their religion worse by recognizing it than by ignoring it. They don't want anything from us—not even our respect. They can't be blamed, of course,' Paulus added. 'No man should be asked to think highly of a master who has robbed him of his liberty.'

Demetrius had turned his face away, at that speech, pretending an interest in a tented caravan resting on a neighboring slope. He wondered whether his master thought this remark of the Centurion's was injudicious; wondered whether he wished his slave had not overheard it.

* * * * * *

Early the next morning, the militia from Minoa broke camp and prepared to complete the journey into the city. Demetrius had been glad to see the sunrise. It was the first night, since he had been the slave of Marcellus, that he had slept beyond the sound of his master's call. After the encampment had been made, late yesterday afternoon, the Legate and four of the senior staff officers had decided to ride on into Jerusalem. None of the slaves, except the Syrian camel-boys, had been taken along. Demetrius, left to guard Marcellus' effects, had slept in the ornate tent alone.

Rousing at dawn, he had drawn the curtains aside, and was amazed at the tide of traffic already on the highway; processions of heavily laden camels, rhythmically lifting their haughty noses at every step; long trains of pack-asses, weighted with clumsy burdens; men, women, children, slaves—all carrying bundles and baskets and boxes of every shape and size. The pestilential dust rolled high.

With the speed and skill of long experience, the contingent from Minoa leveled their camp, rolled up the tents, packed the stores, and took to the road. Proudly the uniformed company marched down the highway, the pilgrims scurrying to the stone fences at the trumpet's strident command. But the pack-train did not fare so well. The laden asses from Minoa, not carrying the banners or blowing trumpets or wearing the Roman uniform, were considered by the travelers as of no more importance than a similar number of pack-asses from anywhere else.

Melas, ever anxious to display large knowledge to the newcomer, seemed highly amused by Demetrius' efforts to keep his string of donkeys in hand. It was quite apparent that the unkempt Thracian was enjoying the Corinthian's dilemma. At a disadvantage in Demetrius' company, the odds were all in his favor now. He wasn't as cultured as the Legate's slave, but when it came to managing pack-asses in a dense crowd of uncivil travelers, Melas was in a position to offer counsel. He looked back and grinned patronizingly.

It was a peculiar crowd! In Rome, on a feast-day, there was plenty of rough jostling and all manner of rudeness. Arrogant charioteers thought nothing of driving their broad iron wheels over the bare feet of little children. People on foot treated one another with almost incredible discourtesy. One favorite method of making one's way through a crowd was to dive in with both hands full of mud and filth scooped up from the street. Few cared to debate the right of way with persons thus armed. No—Rome had won no prizes for the politeness of her gala-day multitudes. But, in spite of her forthright brutality, Rome—on such occasions—was hilarious. Her crowds sang, cheered, laughed! They were mischievous, merciless, vulgar—but they were merry!

There was no laughter in this pilgrim throng that crowded the widening avenue today. This was a tense, impassioned, fanatical multitude; its voice a guttural murmur as if each man canted his own distresses, indifferent to the mumbled yearnings of his neighbors. On these strained faces was an expression of an almost terrifying earnestness and a quality of pietistic zeal that seemed ready to burst forth into wild hysteria; faces that fascinated Demetrius by the very ugliness of their unabashed contortions. Not for all the wealth of the world would he have so bared his private griefs and longings to the cool stare of the public. But apparently the Jews didn't care who read their minds. All this, thought the Corinthian, was what the sight of their holy city had done to their emotions.

Suddenly, for no reason at all that Demetrius could observe, there was a wave of excitement. It swept down over the sluggish swollen stream of zealots like a sharp breeze. Men all about him were breaking loose from their families, tossing their packs into the arms of their overburdened children, and racing forward toward some urgent attraction. Far up ahead the shouts were increasing in volume, spontaneously organizing into a concerted reiterated cry; a single, magic word that drove the multitude into a frenzy.

Unable to keep his footing in this onrushing tide, Demetrius dragged and pushed his stubborn charges to the roadside where Melas stood savagely battering his tangled donkeys over their heads with his heavy cudgel.

'Crack them on the nose!' yelled Melas.

'I have no club,' shouted Demetrius. 'You take them!'

Melas, pleased to have his competency appealed to, grasped the lead-strap to the other string of donkeys and began laying on the discipline with a practiced hand. While he was thus engaged, Demetrius set off after the hurrying crowd, forcing his way with the others until the congestion was too dense for further progress. Wedged tight against his arm, and grinning up into his face, was another Greek, older but smaller than himself; a slave, easily recognizable as such by the slit in his ear-lobe. Impudently the ill-scented little fellow bent about for a glimpse of Demetrius' ear; and, having assured himself of their social equality, laughed fraternally.

'Athens,' he announced, by way of introduction.

'Corinth,' returned Demetrius, crisply. 'Do you know what is going on?'

'They're yelling something about a king. That's all I can make of it.'

'Understand their language?'

'A little. Just what I've picked up on these trips. We come up every year with a load of spices.'

'You think they've got somebody up front who wants to be their king? Is that it?'

'Looks like it. They keep howling another word that I don't know —Messiah. The man's name, maybe.'

Demetrius impulsively turned about, thrust a shoulder into the steaming mass, and began pushing through to the side of the road, followed closely—to his distaste—by his diminutive countryman. All along the way, men were recklessly tearing branches from the palms that bordered the residential thoroughfare, indifferent to the violent protests of property-owners. Running swiftly among the half-crazed vandals, the Greeks arrived at the front of the procession and jammed their way into it.

Standing on tiptoe for an instant in the swaying crowd, Demetrius caught a fleeting glimpse of the obvious center of interest, a brown-haired, bareheaded, well-favored Jew. A tight little circle had been left open for the slow advance of the shaggy white donkey on which he rode. It instantly occurred to Demetrius that this coronation project was an impromptu affair for which no preparation had been made. Certainly there had been no effort to bedeck the pretender with any royal regalia. He was clad in a simple brown mantle with no decorations of any kind, and the handful of men—his intimate friends, no doubt—who tried to shield him from the pressure of the throng, wore the commonest sort of country garb.

The huzzas of the crowd were deafening. It was evident that these passionate zealots had all gone stark, raving mad! Paulus had drawn a very clear picture of the Jew's mood on these occasions of the holy festival commemorative of an ancient flight from bondage.

Again Demetrius, regaining his lost balance, stretched to full height for another look at the man who had somehow evoked all this wild adulation. It was difficult to believe that this was the sort of person who could be expected to inflame a mob into some audacious action. Instead of receiving the applause with an air of triumph—or even of satisfaction—the unresponsive man on the white donkey seemed sad about the whole affair. He looked as if he would gladly have had none of it.

'Can you see him?' called the little Athenian, who had stuck fast in the sticky-hot pack an arm's length away.

Demetrius nodded without turning his head.

'Old man?'

'No—not very,' answered Demetrius, candidly remote.

'What does he look like?' shouted the Athenian, impatiently.

Demetrius shook his head—and his hand, too—signaling that he couldn't be bothered now, especially with questions as hard to answer as this one.

'Look like a king?' yelled the little Greek, guffawing boisterously.

Demetrius did not reply. Tugging at his impounded garments, he crushed his way forward. The surging mass, pushing hard from the rear, now carried him on until he was borne almost into the very hub of the procession that edged along, step by step, keeping pace with the plodding donkey.

Conspicious in the inner circle, as if they constituted the mysterious man's retinue, were the dozen or more who seemed stunned by the event that obviously had taken them by surprise. They too were shouting, erratically, but they wore puzzled faces, and appeared anxious that their honored friend would measure up a little more heroically to the demands of this great occasion.

It was quite clear now to Demetrius that the incident was accidental. It was quite understandable, in the light of Paulus' irreverent comments on the Passover celebration. All these proud, poverty-cursed, subjugated pilgrims, pressing toward their ancient shrine, would be on the alert for any movement that savored of revolt against their rapacious foe. It needed only the shout—'Messiah!'—and they would spring into action without pausing to ask questions. That explained it, believed Demetrius. In any case, whoever had started this wild pandemonium, it was apparent that it lacked the hero's approbation.

The face of the enigmatic Jew seemed weighted with an almost insupportable burden of anxiety. The eyes, narrowed as if in resigned acceptance of some inevitable catastrophe, stared straight ahead toward Jerusalem. Perhaps the man, intent upon larger responsibilities far removed from this pitiable little coronation farce, wasn't really hearing the racket at all.

So deeply absorbed had Demetrius become, in his wide-eyed study of the young Jew's face, that he too was beginning to be unmindful of the general clamor and confusion. He moved along with inching steps, slanting his body against the weight of the pressing crowd, so close now to the preoccupied rider that with one stride he could have touched him.

Now there was a temporary blocking of the way, and the noisy procession came to a complete stop. The man on the white donkey straightened, as if roused from a reverie, drew a deep sigh, and slowly turned his head. Demetrius watched, with parted lips and a pounding heart.

The meditative eyes, drifting about over the excited multitude, seemed to carry a sort of wistful compassion for these helpless victims of an aggression for which they thought he had a remedy. Everyone was shouting, shouting—all but the Corinthian slave, whose throat was so dry he couldn't have shouted, who had no inclination to shout, who wished they would all be quiet, quiet! It wasn't the time or place for shouting. Quiet! This man wasn't the sort of person one shouted at, or shouted for. Quiet! That was what this moment called for—Quiet!

Gradually the brooding eyes moved over the crowd until they came to rest on the strained, bewildered face of Demetrius. Perhaps, he wondered, the man's gaze halted there because he alone—in all this welter of hysteria—refrained from shouting. His silence singled him out. The eyes calmly appraised Demetrius. They neither widened nor smiled; but, in some indefinable manner, they held Demetrius in a grip so firm it was almost a physical compulsion. The message they communicated was something other than sympathy, something more vital than friendly concern; a sort of stabilizing power that swept away all such negations as slavery, poverty, or any other afflicting circumstance. Demetrius was suffused with the glow of this curious kinship. Blind with sudden tears, he elbowed through the throng and reached the roadside. The uncouth Athenian, bursting with curiosity, inopportunely accosted him.

'See him—close up?' he asked.

Demetrius nodded; and, turning away, began to retrace his steps toward his abandoned duty.

'Crazy?' persisted the Athenian, trudging alongside.

'No.'

'King?'

'No,' muttered Demetrius, soberly—'not a king.'

'What is he, then?' demanded the Athenian, piqued by the Corinthian's aloofness.

'I don't know,' mumbled Demetrius, in a puzzled voice, 'but—he is something more important than a king.'

Chapter V

AFTER the camp had been set up near the suburban village of Bethany, Marcellus and his staff continued down the long hill into the city. There was very little traffic on the streets, for the people were keeping the Sabbath.

Though Paulus had not exaggerated Jerusalem's provision for the representatives of her Roman Emperor, the young Legate of Minoa was not prepared for his first sight of the majestic Insula of the Procurator.

As they halted their weary camels at twilight before the imposing façade of Rome's provincial seat, Marcellus sat in speechless admiration. No one needed to inform a stranger that this massive structure was of foreign origin, for it fairly shouted that it had no relation whatever to its mean environment.

Apparently the architects, sculptors, and landscape artists had been advised that expense was the least of their problems. Seeing the Jews had it to pay for, explained Paulus, the Emperor had not been parsimonious, and when Herod—the first Procurator—had professed a grandiose ambition 'to rebuild this brick city in marble,' Augustus had told him to go as far as he liked.

'And you can see that he did,' added Paulus, with an inclusive gesture made as proudly as if he had done it himself.

True, Jerusalem wasn't all marble. The greater part of it was decidedly shabby, dirty, and in need of repair. But Herod the Great had rebuilt the Temple on a magnificent scale and then had erected this Insula on a commanding elevation far enough away from the holy precincts to avoid an unhappy competition.

It was a huge quadrangle stronghold, dominating the very heart of Jerusalem. Three spacious levels of finely wrought mosaic pavement, united by marble steps and balustrades with pedestals bearing the exquisitely sculptured busts of eminent Romans, terraced up from the avenue to the colonnaded portal of the Praetorium. On either side of the paved area sloped an exotic garden of flowers and ornamental shrubbery watered from marble basins in which lavish fountains played.

'These fountains,' said Paulus, in a discreet undertone, 'were an afterthought. They were installed only seven years ago, when Pilate came. And they caused an uprising that brought all the available troops to the new Procurator's rescue.'

'Were you in it, too, Paulus?' asked Marcellus.

'Indeed—yes! We were all here, and a merry time it was. The Jew has his little imperfections, but he is no coward. He whines when he trades, but he is no whimperer in battle. He hates war and will go to any length to preserve the peace; but—and this was something Pontius Pilate didn't know—there is a point where you'd better stop imposing on a Jew.'

'Well, go on then about the fountains,' urged Marcellus, for the sight of the water had made him impatient for a bath.

'Pilate's wife was responsible for it. They had been down in Crete for many years where Pontius had been the Prefect. You can grow anything in Crete, and the lady was dismayed to find herself in such an arid country as Judea. She begged for gardens. Gardens must have water. To have that much water there must be an aqueduct. Aqueducts are expensive. There was no appropriation to cover this item. So—the new Procurator helped himself to some funds from the Temple treasury, and—'

'And the battle was on,' surmised Marcellus.

'You have said it, sir,' declared Paulus, fervently. 'And it stayed on for seven exciting months. Pilate nearly lost his post. Two thousand Jews were killed, and nearly half that many Romans. It would have been better, I suppose, if Tiberius had transferred Pilate to another position. The Jews will never respect him; not if he stays here a thousand years. He makes every effort to humor them, remembering what they can do to him if they wish. He is here to keep the peace. And he knows that the next time there is a riot, his term of office will expire.'

'It's a wonder the Jews do not raise a general clamor for his removal,' speculated Marcellus.

'Ah—but they don't want him removed,' laughed Paulus. 'These rich and wily old merchants and money-lenders, who pay the bulk of the taxes and exercise a great deal of influence, know that Pilate is not in a position to dictate harsh terms to them. They hate him, of course, but they wouldn't like to see him go. I'll wager that if the Emperor appointed another man to the office of Procurator, the Sanhedrin would protest.'

'What's the Sanhedrin?' inquired Marcellus.

'The Jewish legislative body. It isn't supposed to deal with any matters except religious observances; but—well—when the Sanhedrin growls, Pontius Pilate listens!' Paulus shouted to the squatting camel-boys, and the apathetic beasts plodded on. 'But I do not wish to convey the idea, sir,' continued the Centurion, 'that Pilate is a nobody. He is in a very unfortunate predicament here. You will like him, I think. He is a genial fellow, and deserves a more comfortable Prefecture.'

They had moved on then, around the corner, to the section of the vast barracks assigned to the garrison from Minoa. Three sides of the great quadrangle had been equipped for the accommodation of troops, the local constabulary occupying less than a third of it. Now the entire structure was filled almost to capacity. The whole institution was alive. The immense parade-ground, bounded by the two-story stone buildings, was gay with the uniforms of the legions arriving from the subordinate Palestinian forts. The banners of Caesarea, Joppa, and Capernaum, topped by the imperial ensign, added bright color to the teeming courtyard.

Marcellus was delighted with the appointments of the suite into which he was shown. They compared favorably with the comforts to be had at the Tribunes' Club in Rome. It was the first time he had been entirely at ease since the night he had left home.

After a while Paulus came in to see if his young Commander had everything he wanted.

'I am writing some letters,' he said. 'The Vestris should arrive at Joppa by tomorrow or next day, and will probably sail for home before the end of the week. You remember, sir, she was just coming into the harbor at Gaza as we passed through.'

'Thanks, Paulus, for reminding me,' said Marcellus. 'It is a good suggestion.'

* * * * * *

He had not written to Diana since the night of his departure on the galley to Ostia. That had been a difficult letter to compose. He was very deeply depressed. After several unsatisfactory attempts to tell her how sorry he was to leave her and with what impatience he would await their next meeting—in the face of his serious doubt that he should ever see her again—his letter had turned out to be a fond little note of farewell, containing neither fatuous promises nor grim forebodings. The lovely Diana would be cherished in his thoughts, he wrote, and she was not to worry about him.

Many times, on the long voyage to Gaza, he had begun letters that were never finished. There was so little to say. He would wait until there was something of interest to report. On the last day before making port, he had written a letter to his family, dry as the little ship's log, promising to do better next time.

The early days at Minoa had been eventful enough to furnish material for a letter, but his new duties had kept him occupied. To-night he would write to Diana. He could tell her honestly that things were ever so much better than he had expected. He would explain how he happened to be in Jerusalem. He would tell her that he was handsomely quartered, and describe the appointments of the Insula.

It would need no gilding. Marcellus' dignity, sadly battered by the punitive assignment to discredited Minoa, had been immeasurably restored. He was almost proud of his Roman citizenship. He could write Diana now with some self-confidence.

For two hours, under the light of the three large stone lamps bracketed on the wall beside his desk, he reviewed the important events of his life at Minoa. He didn't say how arid, how desolate, how altogether unlovely was the old fort and its environs; nor did he exhaust the details of his first day's experience there.

'The acting Commander,' he wrote, 'was a bit inclined to be surly, and he did not overdo his hospitality when I arrived; but a little later he decided to co-operate, and we are now the best of friends. I quite like this Centurion Paulus. Indeed I hardly know what I should do without him, for he knows all the traditions of the fort; what things must be done, and the right time and way to do them.'

Marcellus was enjoying his work on the letter. It gave him a glow of pleasure to inform Diana of these things which now made up his life. It was almost as if they belonged to each other; almost as an absent husband might write to his wife.

The scroll, when he should paste the sheets of papyrus end to end, would be a bulky one. Before it quite outgrew its spindle-rims, he must bring it to a close with something from his heart. This was not quite so easy to do.

For a long time he sat deliberating what should be his proper attitude. Should he obey his feelings and tell Diana, without reserve, how much she had been in his thoughts, how dear she was to him, and how ardently he wished their separation was over? Would that be fair? Diana was young, so full of life. Was it right to encourage her in the hope that he might be coming home some day to claim her? Was it right to let Diana believe that he entertained that hope himself? Might it not be more honest to tell her frankly that there was no likelihood of his return for a long time; years, perhaps? Of course Diana already knew the circumstances. And he had casually mentioned of Paulus that he had been sent to Minoa eleven years ago; and had not been home since his appointment. She could draw her own dismaying conclusions. At length, Marcellus finished his letter almost to his satisfaction.

'You know, Diana, what things I would be saying to you if we were together. At the far distance which separates us—in miles, and who can tell how much of time?—it is enough to say that your happiness will always be mine. Whatever things make you sad, dear girl, sadden me also. A ship—*The Vestris*—is reported to be arriving at Joppa. She called at Gaza. I am impatient to return to the fort, for I may find a letter from you there. I fondly hope so. Demetrius will come in tomorrow morning and deliver this scroll to the Insula's courier who meets *The Vestris*. She sails soon. Would I were a passenger!'

* * * * * *

Demetrius had never been so restless. Of course, whenever he had paused to contemplate his hopeless position in the scheme of things, his life held out no promise. But gradually he had become inured to his fate. He was a slave, and nothing could be done about it. Comparing himself to a free man, his lot was wretched indeed; but when he contrasted the terms of his slavery with the cruel conditions imposed upon most of the people in bondage, he was fortunate.

In the house of Gallio, he had been treated with every consideration due a servant. And his life had become so inextricably related to the life of Marcellus that his freedom—even if it were offered him—might cost him more in companionship than it was worth in liberty of action. As for his deep affection for Lucia, it was, he knew, wholly unrequited. He couldn't have had Lucia, if he had been as free as a sea-gull. Such common-sense reflections as these had saved his mind and reconciled him to his destiny.

Now his bland little philosophy had ceased to comfort him. Not only was his small world in disarray, but the whole institution of human existence had become utterly futile, meaningless, empty, a mere mockery of something that had had sublime possibilities, perhaps, but had been thrown away; lost beyond recovery!

He had tried to analyze his topsy-turvy mind and find reasons for his heavy depression. For one thing, he was lonely. Marcellus had not willfully ignored him, since their arrival in Jerusalem, but it was apparent that slaves were not welcome in the officers' quarters except when actually on duty. When their service was performed, they were to clear out. Demetrius had not been accustomed to such treatment. He had been his master's shadow for so long that this new attitude of indifference was as painful as a physical wound.

Again and again, he said to himself that Marcellus probably felt unhappy too, and maybe deplored the necessity to exclude him from his friendship. Demetrius had been made to feel his slavery as he had never felt it before, not since the day that he had been sold to Senator Gallio.

But there was another cause of Demetrius' mental distress. It was the haunting memory of the beseeching eyes into which he had gazed momentarily on the road into the city. Afterward, he had sat for hours, in a brown study, trying to define those eyes, and had arrived at the conclusion that they were chiefly distinguished by their loneliness. It was so apparent that the little group of men, who had tried to keep the crowd from pressing too hard, were disappointed. Whatever it was that the noisy fanatics wanted him to do, it was the wrong thing. You could see that, at a glance. It was a wonder they couldn't see it them-

selves. Everybody there had urged him to lead a cause in which—it
was so obvious!—he had no interest. He was a lonely man. The eyes
hungered for an understanding friend. And the loneliness of this mysterious man had somehow communicated with the loneliness of
Demetrius. It was a loneliness that plainly said, 'You could all do something about this unhappy world, if you would; but you won't.'

Three days had passed now, singularly alike in program. Melas had
been almost too attentive in his capacity of uninvited guide to the
sights of the city. It was inevitable that they should be thrown into
each other's company. Their duties were light and briefly accomplished.
As Melas had foreseen, you looked after your master at mealtime,
polished his equipment, helped him into his complicated military
harness in the morning and out of it at night. The rest of the time was
yours.

Breakfast was served at dawn, after which the troops turned out on
the parade-ground for routine inspection. Then a small detachment
of each contingent returned to their respective barracks to be on call
while the main bodies—commanded by junior officers and led by the
larger, but no more splendidly accoutered, Legion of the Procurator—
marched smartly into the street.

It was a stirring sight and Demetrius—his tasks completed for the
morning—liked to watch the impressive parade as, four abreast, the
gaily uniformed soldiers strutted around the corner, stood like statues
while the colors were dipped before the proud portals of the Praetorium, and proceeded down the avenue to the Temple, passing in
their march the quite pretentious marble residence of Caiaphas, the
High Priest. Caiaphas did not rate a salute; neither did the Temple.

On two occasions, Demetrius, attended by Melas as voluntary com-
mentator, trailed along at the rear of the procession. On an equivalent
occasion in Rome, hundreds would have followed such a parade; but
not here. Perhaps the people were too sullen, perhaps they hated Rome
too much. Perhaps, again, they lacked the vitality to pick up their heels
and keep pace with the long steps of the soldiers. Demetrius had seen
plenty of rags and tatters and blind beggars and hopeless cripples, but
never in such numbers or in such dire distress. His own native Corinth
had its share of misery, but its wretchedness was on display mostly in
the port area. Athens—he had been there once with his father and
brothers when he was twelve—had plenty of poverty, but it also had
beautiful parks and exquisite works of art. This Jerusalem—that called
itself a holy city—was horrible; its streets crowded with disease and
deformities and verminous mendicants. Other cities had their faults;
hateful ones, too. But Jerusalem? Not much wonder the strange man
on the white donkey had been lonely!

The return of the troops to the Insula was made by a circuitous
route which bisected the center of the market district where hucksters
and customers scrambled to give the legionaries plenty of room as

they went striding arrogantly down the narrow street, their manner saying that Emperor Tiberius mustn't be detained even at the cost of a few trampled toes. If a recumbent camel, indifferent to the dignity of the Empire, remained seated in the middle of the road, Rome did not debate the right of way, but opened the formation and pretended that the sullen beast was an island. Occasionally a balky pack-ass was similarly deferred to by the armed forces of Tiberius. Everybody else sought the protection of doorways and alleys.

This rambling route included the Roman Consulates, a not very imposing group of official residences, where brief pauses were made to salute the imperial arms rather than the imperial representatives of Samaria, Decapolis, and Galilee.

'You watch them,' advised Melas, 'when they stop to salute Herod's house. It's funny.'

And it was funny. Herod, who handled Rome's diplomatic dealings with Galilee, which were reputed to be trivial and infrequent, had made himself very well-to-do, but the homage paid to his establishment was perfunctory enough to constitute a forthright insult.

'I've heard them say,' Melas had explained, 'that this Herod fellow would like to be the Procurator. That's why Pilate's Legion begins the salute with the thumb to the nose. Maybe that's orders: I don't know.'

Back at the parade-ground, the companies were dismissed for the day. By twos and threes the men swaggered down into the congested business zone, capitalizing the privileges of their resplendent garb and glittering weapons, rejoicing alike in the shy admiration of the olive-tinted girls and the candid hatred of the merchants whose wares they impudently pawed and pilfered.

In the afternoon, the majority of the troops strolled out to the small arena, south of the city, and watched the games—foot races, discus-hurling, javelin-throwing, wrestling—tame sports, but better than none. No gladiatorial combats were permitted, nor any other amusing bloodshed. Immediately outside of the arena but within its compound, every conceivable type of imposture flourished. Many of the mounte-banks were from far distances. There were magicians from India, pygmies from Africa, Syrian fortune-tellers. Patently crooked gambling wheels and other games of chance beguiled many a hard-earned shekel. Innumerable booths dispensed lukewarm, sickeningly sweet beverages of doubtful origin, flyblown figs, and dirty confections.

To the Romans, accustomed at home to more exciting events on their festal days, the arena and its accessories had but little charm. To the country people, it was a stupendous show, especially for the younger ones. Most of their elders, mightily concerned with the sale of pottery, rugs, shawls, assorted homespun, sandals, saddles, bracelets, bangles, and ornamental trifles in leather, wood, and silver, remained downtown in the thick of serious trade.

As for Marcellus and his staff, and the ranking officers of the other garrisons, their chief diversion—aside from lounging in the baths—was gambling. After the first day, spent in making ceremonious calls upon the Procurator and the Consuls, and a bit of sight-seeing, the staff members idled in their sumptuous quarters.

There seemed to be an unlimited supply of wine, and it was apparent that the officers were making abundant use of it. On two occasions, Centurion Paulus had not appeared at the evening dinner, and many another place was vacant at the well-provided tables in the ornate mess-hall. Demetrius had been pleased to note that his master was exercising a little more discretion than some of the others, but it was evident that he too was relieving his boredom by the only available method. It was to be hoped that the week could be brought to an end without a row. The materials for quarrels were all at hand; the wine, the dice, the idleness. It had never taken very much liquor to make Marcellus reckless. Paulus, when drunk, was surly and sensitive. Demetrius had begun to count the hours until it would be time to take to the road. Minoa had its disadvantages, but it was a safer and more attractive place than Jerusalem.

He wished he could find out what had become of the man who didn't want to be king of this country. One day he had broached the subject to the Thracian; but Melas, who knew everything, knew nothing about this; had quite forgotten the little furor on the hill.

'The patrol probably scared him back to the country,' surmised Melas.

'Perhaps they put him in prison,' wondered Demetrius.

'He'd be lucky,' laughed Melas. 'Men who gather up big crowds around them are better off in jail, this week, than on the street.'

'Do you know where the prison is?' Demetrius had inquired, suddenly inspired with an idea.

Melas gave him a quizzical glance. No, he didn't know where the prison was and didn't want to know. Prisons were fine places to stay away from. Any man was a fool to visit a friend in prison. First thing you knew, they'd gobble you up, too. No, sir! Melas had had enough of prisons to last him the rest of his life.

One afternoon—it was their fourth day in Jerusalem—Demetrius went out alone over the road on which they had come into the city, and on up the long hill until he reached the place where he had seen the lonely man with the beseeching eyes. He easily recognized the spot: there were dusty and broken palm branches scattered along the roadside, poor shreds of a brief and doubtful glory.

Retracing his steps slowly to the brow of the hill, he turned aside into a public park where well-worn paths wound through a grove of ancient olive trees, gnarled and twisted as if they had shared with the hapless Jews a long, stubborn withstanding of persecution. He sat there in the shade for an hour looking down over Jerusalem. You'd think a city thirty-five centuries old would have a little more to show for its experience. For that matter, the whole world seemed incapable of learning anything useful. Jerusalem wanted her freedom. What would she do with freedom if she had it? Everybody in the world wanted more freedom; freedom to do and be what?

Suppose—it was inconceivable—but suppose the Jews contrived to drive the Romans out? Then what? Would they then leave off quarreling among themselves, and forget their old party differences, and work together for the good of their country? Would the rich landlords and money-lenders ease up on the poor? If they disposed of the Romans, would they feed the hungry and care for the sick and clean the streets? Why—they could do all that now, if they wished. The Romans wouldn't stop them. The Romans would be glad enough to see such improvements, for some of them had to live there too.

What was the nature of this bondage that Jerusalem so bitterly resented? That noisy pack of fanatics on the road, the other day, thought their trouble was with the Roman Government. If they could find a leader strong enough to free them from Rome, they would set up a kingdom of their own. That, they seemed to think, would make everything right. But would it? How would a revolution help the mass of the people? Once a new Government was in the saddle, a small group of greedy men would promptly impose upon the public. Maybe this lonely man from the country knew that. This tatterdemalion throng wanted him to be their king; wanted him to live at the Insula, instead of Pilate. Then the few, who had helped him into power, would begin to make themselves great. But Jerusalem would continue to be what she was now. A change of masters wouldn't help the people.

Demetrius rose and sauntered back to the main thoroughfare, surprised to see that so few travelers were on the road. It still lacked two hours of sunset. Something important must be going on to have drawn the traffic off the highway; yet the city seemed unusually quiet.

He walked slowly down the hill, his thoughtful mood persisting. What kind of government would solve the world's problems? As matters stood, all governments were rapacious. People everywhere endured their rulers until they had gained strength enough to throw them off and take on another load of tyranny. The real trouble wasn't located at the capital, but in the immediate neighborhood, in the tribe, in the family, in themselves. Demetrius wished he might talk with the lonely man from the country, and learn what he thought of government; how, in his opinion, a better freedom might be found.

It suddenly occurred to him that the impudent little Athenian might know what had become of the man who didn't want to be a king. He quickened his steps, resolved to make inquiries for a caravan with spices to sell.

Down in the city, nearly all of the usual activity had ceased. What had become of everybody? Even in the market area, there were very few traders about. Accosting a bearded old Greek, who was laboriously folding a bundle of rugs, Demetrius inquired what was up; where were the people? The tired old man shrugged and grinned, without making a reply. It was evident that he thought the young fellow was trying to be playful.

'Has anything happened?' persisted Demetrius, soberly.

The old man tied his bundle and sat on it, puffing from his exertion. Presently he regarded his fellow countryman with fresh interest.

'You trying to say,' he exclaimed, 'that you honestly don't know what's happening? My boy, this is the night of the Jewish Passover. All the Jews are in their houses. And those who haven't houses have crawled in somewhere under shelter.'

'For how long?'

'Until morning. Tomorrow they will be out early, for it is the last day of Passover Week, and there will be much business. But—where have you been, that you didn't know?'

Demetrius was amused at the old man's comments on his ignorance. 'I've never been here before,' he said. 'I know nothing about the Jews' customs. For the past two hours I've been out on the hill. There's an olive grove.'

'I know.' The old man nodded. 'They call it the Garden of Gethsemane. Not much there to see. Ever on Mars' Hill—in Athens?'

'Yes; beautiful!'

'These people can't make any statues. It's against their religion. Can't carve anything.'

'There's a lot of carving on the Temple,' said Demetrius.

'Yes—but they didn't do it.' The old man rose and shouldered his burden.

'I wonder if you know where I might find a caravan from Athens that deals in spices,' asked Demetrius.

'Oh, yes. You mean Popygos. He's down by the old tower. You passed his place when you came in from the hill. Popygos. Better keep your hand on your wallet.'

'Would he rob a fellow Greek?'

'Popygos would rob his grandmother.'

Demetrius grinned and bade the grizzled old merchant good-bye. He started toward the Insula. It was too late to go back looking for the spice caravan. He would find it tomorrow. People were very much alike, wherever you found them. The Jews hated their government. So did the Greeks. But a change of government wouldn't help. That wasn't the trouble. The trouble was that the people couldn't change each other or themselves. The rug merchant discredited the spice merchant. Popygos would rob his grandmother. But that wasn't Tiberius Caesar's fault. Tiberius was a bad Emperor, no doubt; but under any other government the grandmother of Popygos would be no more safe than she was now. The lonely man from the country probably knew that. He didn't want to be a king. No matter who was king, you'd better keep your hand on your wallet. The world was in serious need of something—but it wasn't something that a new king could furnish.

* * * * * *

Demetrius did not wait to watch the early morning inspection. As soon as he had finished serving his master's breakfast, he made off alone. Already the streets were crowded. You had to pick your way carefully through the market district or you might tramp on some reckless huckster sitting cross-legged on the narrow sidewalk surrounded by his pitiful little stock of merchandise; a few crude earthenware jugs, perhaps. Here sat a shapeless bundle of rags that turned out to be an old woman with three eggs and a melon for sale. The roadway was choked with pack-animals unloading into the little bazaars. Everywhere emaciated arms stretched out for a penny. Loathsome sores were unwrapped and put on display accompanied progressively by a wheedle, a whine, a hiss, and a curse. A hollow-chested old man with empty, fly-infested eye-sockets apathetically blew a plaintive squawk from a decrepit flageolet. Now the street narrowed into a dark, pestilential cavern that declined over a series of broad stone steps, slippery with refuse, swarming with beggars and mangy, half-starved dogs. According to Centurion Paulus, the Jews believed that they were created in the image of their god. Demetrius held his nose and hurried through this assortment of divine reproductions, having a care not to brush against them.

The caravan was not hard to find. Near the old tower, overlooking the little Kedron River, there was an open plaza where the road to the west began. A pungent aroma—distinctly refreshing after a trip through the market—guided Demetrius to his destination. A welcoming voice hailed him.

'Ho, adelphos!' shouted the garrulous little Athenian. Demetrius was honestly glad to see him, though at any other time or place he wouldn't have liked to be hailed as brother by this intrusive fellow. They shook hands. 'I was hoping to see you again. My name is Zenos. I don't think I told you.'

'I am Demetrius. You have a pleasant location here.'

'Right! Plenty of room, and we see everything. You should have been here last night. Much excitement! They arrested this Nazarene, you know. Found him up there in the old park.'

'Nazarene? I hadn't heard. What had he done?' asked Demetrius, without interest.

'Why—you know! The man we saw on the white donkey, the other day.'

Demetrius came alive and pressed a flock of inquiries. Zenos was delighted to have so much information to dispense. Troops from the Insula had been on the lookout for this Jesus ever since Sunday noon.

Last night they had captured him; brought him, and his little band of
friends, back into the city.

'But what had he done?' demanded Demetrius, impatiently.

'Well—they arrested him for stirring up the people, and for wanting
to be a king. Popygos says if they convict him of treason, it will go
hard with him.'

'Treason! But that's nonsense!' exclaimed Demetrius, hotly. 'That
man doesn't want to upset the Government; doesn't want to have
anything to do with the Government; neither this Government
nor any other. Treason? They're all crazy!'

'No—they're not crazy,' objected Zenos. 'The people who run the
Temple have got to dispose of him somehow, or he'll ruin their
business. Haven't you heard what he did over there—same day we saw
him?'

'Not a word. What happened?'

'What happened! Plenty! You see—the Temple is where the
people make sacrifices; buy animals and burn them; nasty mess, bad
smell; but their god likes the idea. So—the loggia—or whatever they
may call it—is crowded full of animals for sale. The people bring their
money, and the money-changers—just inside the door—convert it into
Temple money'—Zenos laughed heartily. 'And everybody says that
these bankers make a fat thing of it, too.'

'Do you mean to say that they sell animals inside of that beautiful
Temple?' asked Demetrius, incredulously.

'In an arcaded court done in marble!' declared Zenos, solemnly
nodding his head. 'In a court with gorgeous tiled paving; walls and
ceiling in the finest mosaic you ever saw; nothing nicer in Athens.
And they have it full of calves and sheep and pigeons. You can imagine
how it looks—but you can't imagine how it stinks! You've got to go
there and smell it! Well—this Jesus came in from the country—away
up in Galilee some place—and went into the Temple—and didn't like
it; said it was not the place to sell animals. And he must have caught
on to the thievery, too, for he made short work of the money-changers.'

'What?' doubted Demetrius.

Zenos laughed delightedly over his friend's bewilderment.

'Yes, sir! If you'll believe it—he didn't look like a man who would
risk it—this Jesus picked up a whip and began slashing about'—Zenos
elaborately cracked an imaginary whip a dozen times in swift succession. 'Just as if he owned the whole establishment! Crack! Zip! Lash!
Crash! Slash!—and out they came. It was wonderful! Out galloped the
calves and the priests and the sheep and the bankers and the air was
full of pigeons and feathers. And Jesus upset the money-tables. It
poured out over the floor—shekels and drachmas and denarii—big
money, little money, good money, bad money; swarms of pilgrims
down on their hands and knees fighting for it. Thrilling sight! I
wouldn't have missed it!' Zenos glanced over his shoulder and mut-

tered, 'Here comes the old man. He's sore today. His best customers
are all busy attending to this Jesus.'

The door of the largest tent had been drawn aside and a paunchy
old fellow with graying hair and beard had stepped out and was
waddling toward them. It had been a long time since Demetrius had
seen anyone so barbarously festooned with jewelry; heavy silver chains
around his neck and depending to his middle, rings on his fingers,
rings in his ears, bracelets, anklets. He paused to regard Demetrius
with an appraising scowl.

'He's from Corinth.' Zenos pointed with his thumb. 'We got
acquainted on the road.'

'I see you wear a Roman tunic,' observed Popygos, crossly.

'My master,' explained Demetrius, respectfully, 'commands the fort
at Minoa.'

'It would have been well,' said Popygos, 'if the Roman guard had
let the Jews settle their own quarrels today. Everybody in Jerusalem
who has so much as two shekels to rub together is mixed up with the
case of this man from Nazareth. Now that the Government is in
it, the affair will go on all day. And tomorrow is the Jews' Sabbath.'

'And they can't do business on the Sabbath,' remarked Demetrius,
for something to say.

Old Popygos stroked his whiskers reflectively.

'I have been making this trip for three-and-twenty years,' he said,
'and we have sold fewer goods this time than ever before. It gets
worse and worse. Always some big squabble, Passover Week, to keep
my best customers from coming for their cloves and cinnamon.'
Popygos upended a reed basket and sat down, jingling. 'I can remember a time,' he went on, deliberately, 'when they didn't have so many
rackets. Now you take this thing that happened down here at the
Temple, last Sunday. A few years ago, they were quite peaceful. The
country people came in to do the Passover business and a little trading.
Always brought a dove in a cage, if they were very poor, or a lamb
or a calf, if they could afford it. That was for the Temple. The priests
burned the offering—or said they did. They must have, from the way it
reeked down around there. Then these Temple people got a little
smarter. A man from the country would bring a lamb and the priests
would examine it and find a wart on its belly—or some small blemish.
So that lamb wouldn't do. But they could take his damaged lamb
and give him a good one for it, if he would pay a cash difference. Then
the blemished lamb was ready to sell to the next customer.'

'Rather dirty trading,' commented Demetrius. 'Not much wonder
this Nazarene objected.'

'Well—it won't do any good,' drawled Popygos. 'At least, it hasn't
done him any good.'

'What will they do to him?' wondered Demetrius. 'Put him in
prison?'

'Hardly! I understand they took him last night to the High Priest's house and tried him for making a disturbance in the Temple. Defiling the Temple—that was what they charged him with.' Popygos broke into bitter laughter. 'As if anybody could defile a Temple that had been turned into a stable. Of course they had enough people on their side to convict him, so they all rushed over to the Insula and got Pilate out of bed to hear the case. He told them that they had better settle it among themselves, if it was just another Temple brawl. But the rich old fellows wouldn't let the Procurator off so easily as that. They said this Jesus was trying to make himself a king. Pilate didn't take any stock in that, of course. So he suggested that they whip him and let him go.'

'And did they whip him?' asked Demetrius, anxiously.

'That they did! And quite heavily, too. Then somebody in the crowd yelled, "Kill the Galilean!" Pilate pricked up his ears, at that. "If this man is a Galilean," he said, "try him before Herod. He handles all Galilean matters." '

'Did they take him there?' asked Demetrius.

'Took him there,' nodded Popygos, 'and Herod had a good time tormenting him, thinking that would please the Temple crowd and the fat money-lenders. He had the soldiers whip Jesus again; then dressed him in some old scarlet regalia, and pretended to do homage to him. Some drunken lout rolled up a thornbush and put it on his head for a crown. But the money-bags were not satisfied with the show. They wanted this Jesus put to death—'

'To death!' shouted Demetrius.

'Yes. And they knew that nobody could give that order but Pilate. So—they all went back to the Insula.'

'And then what happened?' demanded Demetrius.

Popygos shook his head and twitched a shoulder.

'That's all I know,' he said. 'Diophanos the goldsmith, who was there and told me this, had to come back to his bazaar.'

'Perhaps the trial is still going on at the Insula,' said Demetrius, restlessly.

'You'd better keep away from there,' warned Popygos. 'No good comes from mixing into business like that.'

'But my master may need me,' said Demetrius. 'I must go. I hope you have a safe journey home, sir. Good-bye, Zenos.'

* * * * * *

While still some distance away, Demetrius, who had quickened his pace until he was almost running, saw a compact crowd gathered about the main entrance to the Praetorium. He hurried up the steps and stood at the edge of the tensely occupied audience, receiving dark glances from his well-dressed Jewish neighbors as he appeared beside them. There were no poor people present.

The Procurator was standing within the colonnade, surrounded
by a detachment of palace guards. On the highest level of the terraced flagging, a company of troops, four ranks deep, stood stiffly
at attention. In front of them, standing alone, was the captive.
Questions were being asked and answered in a language Demetrius
could not understand. He concluded it was Aramaic, for that was
the tongue spoken by the tempestuous crowd on the road. He left his
place and edged around until he was at the extreme right. Now
he could see the profile of the lonely man. Yes—he was wearing
the crown of thorns that Popygos had reported. The blood had run
down from his forehead until his face was streaked with it. His hands
were tied. His coat had been pulled back off his bare shoulders, showing livid whip-welts. Some of them were bleeding. But he seemed
not to be conscious of his injuries. The Procurator's interrogations
—whatever they were—proceeded quietly, the prisoner, with uplifted
face, as quietly answering them in a respectful but self-confident
tone. Occasionally a low dissenting mutter ran through the sullen
crowd that stood with eyes squinted and mouths open to hear the
testimony.

So intently had Demetrius been watching the victim's face that
he had barely glanced about. It now occurred to him to look for
Marcellus. The front rank was composed of officers representing the
various forts. Paulus was among them, resolutely erect, but swaying
rhythmically. Immediately behind him stood a single line of troops
from Minoa. Marcellus was not to be seen.

Now the Procurator was speaking in a louder voice. It brought
an instant, concerted, angry roar from the civilian audience. Demetrius maneuvered to a position where he could get a better view of
the judge. Now he saw Marcellus, standing with the other Legates
at the immediate left of the Procurator. He wondered whether his
master really knew what was going on. Unless someone was at hand
to act as interpreter, Marcellus probably had no notion what all this
was about. Demetrius knew the exact meaning of the slightest expression on his master's face. At the moment, it conveyed a good
deal of bewilderment, and about the same amount of boredom. It
was evident that Marcellus wished he were somewhere else.

Procurator Pilate seemed quite confused. The hostile attitude of
his influential audience had rattled him. He turned aside and gave
an order to one of the guards, who retired within the wide doorway. Presently he was back with a huge silver basin. Pilate dipped
his hands in it, and flicked water from his fingers. The crowd roared
again, but this time it was a cry of vengeful triumph. It was clear
that a decision had been made; equally apparent that the decision
had satisfied the prosecution. Now Demetrius understood what was
meant by the pantomime with the basin. Pilate was washing his hands
of the case. The people were to have their way, but they were to

consider themselves responsible for the judgment. As for the Procurator, he didn't care to have the prisoner's blood on his hands. Demetrius felt that his master would undoubtedly understand. Even if he knew nothing about the case, he would know that Pilate had made a decision against his own inclinations.

Now Pilate had turned to Marcellus, who had stepped forward saluting. There was a brief, inaudible colloquy. Marcellus bowed in acknowledgment of an order, saluted again; and, descending the steps, approached Paulus and gave him some instructions. Paulus barked a command, and the Minoa contingent advanced, formed a line by twos, and executed a smart right-about. Led by Marcellus, with Paulus to the immediate rear of him, the troops marched through the crowd that opened a passage for them. One soldier of the final pair paused to grasp the dangling rope that bound the condemned man's hands. It was a rough and apparently unanticipated jerk, for it nearly drew the prisoner off his feet. The legionaries were marching with long strides.

Not many of the crowd fell in behind the procession. Most of them coagulated into muttering little groups, wagging their beards in sour satisfaction. Demetrius wondered what was to be the fate of this Jesus. He had received the death penalty; no question about that. Nothing less would have appeased the people. He would probably be taken to the courtyard of some prison to face a detachment of archers. On the other side of the street, a small company of pale-faced, poorly dressed, badly frightened men from the country seemed trying to decide whether to follow. After a moment, a few of them did; but they were in no hurry to catch up. These people were undoubtedly Jesus' friends. It was a pity, Demetrius thought, that they had shown up so meanly. The man surely deserved a more loyal support.

Undecided whether to trail along after the procession or wait at the barracks for his master's return, Demetrius stood for some time irresolute. Presently Melas joined him, grinning feebly.

'What are they going to do with him?' inquired Demetrius, unsteadily.

'Crucify him,' said Melas.

'Crucify him!' Demetrius' voice was husky. 'Why—he hasn't done anything to deserve a death like that!'

'Maybe not,' agreed Melas, 'but that's the order. My guess is that the Procurator didn't want to have it done, and thinks it may stir up some trouble for him. That's why he gave Minoa the job; didn't want his own legion mixed up in it. Minoa's pretty far away, and a tough outfit.' Melas chuckled. He was glad to belong to a tough outfit. Minoa didn't mind a little brutality.

'Are you going along?' asked Demetrius.

Melas scowled and shook his head.

'No—nothing for me to do there. Had you thought of going? It's not a very pretty business: I can tell you that! I saw it done—once—over in Gaul. Soldier stabbed his Centurion. They nailed him up for that. It took all day. You could hear him cry for half a league. The big black birds came before he died and—'

Demetrius shook his head, made an overhand protest, and swallowed convulsively. Melas grinned and spat awkwardly. Then he turned and started ambling slowly back toward the barracks, leaving Demetrius standing there debating with himself what to do.

After a while he moved along woodenly after Melas. Reaching his master's silent and empty quarters, he sat down and tried to compose himself. His heart was beating so hard it made his head ache.

Then he rose and found a drink of water. It occurred to him that Marcellus too might want a drink before this dreadful business was over. He filled a small jug, and started; walking slowly, for he didn't want to go.

Ever since he had looked into this Jesus' eyes, Demetrius had thought of him as the lonely man whom nobody understood; not even his close friends. Today he would be a lonely man indeed.

Chapter VI

ONE of the Insula's ten companies was absent from inspection. Marcellus noticed the diminished strength of the Procurator's Legion, but thought little of it. Whatever might be the nature of the business that had called out these troops so early in the day, it was of no concern to Minoa.

But when Julian, the Capernaum Commander who was taking his turn as officer of the day, glumly announced that the customary parade was canceled and that all the legionaries would return to their barracks to await further orders, Marcellus' curiosity was stirred. Returning to his quarters, he sent for Paulus, confident that this ever-active fountain of gossip could explain the mystery.

After a considerable delay, the Centurion drifted in unsteadily with flushed cheeks and bloodshot eyes. His Commander regarded him with unconcealed distaste and pointed to a chair into which the dazed and untidy Paulus eased himself gently.

'Do you know what's up?' inquired Marcellus.

'The Procurator,' mumbled Paulus, 'has had a bad night.'

'So have you, from all appearances,' observed Marcellus, frostily. 'What has been going on—if it isn't a secret?'

'Pilate is in trouble.' Paulus' tongue was clumsy, and he chewed out his words slowly. 'He is in trouble with everybody. He is even in trouble with good old Julian, who says that if the man is a Galilean, Capernaum should have been detailed to police the trial at Herod's court.'

'Would you be good enough to tell me what you are talking about?' rasped Marcellus. 'What man? What trial? Begin at the beginning, and pretend I don't know anything about it.'

Paulus yawned prodigiously, scrubbed his watery eyes with shaky fingers, and began to spin a long, involved yarn about last night's experiences. An imprudent carpenter from somewhere up in Galilee had been tried for disturbing the peace and exciting the people to revolt. A few days ago, he had become violent in the Temple, chasing the sacrificial animals out into the street, upsetting the money-tills, and loudly condemning the holy place as a den of robbers. 'A true statement, no doubt,' commented Paulus, 'but not very polite.'

'The fellow must be crazy,' remarked Marcellus.

Paulus pursed his swollen lips judicially and shook his head.

'Something peculiar about this man,' he muttered. 'They arrested him last night. They've had him up before old Annas, who used to be the High Priest; and Caiaphas, the present High Priest; and Pilate —and Herod—and—'

'You seem to know a lot about it,' broke in Marcellus.

Paulus grinned sheepishly.

'A few of us were seeing the holy city by moonlight,' he confessed. 'Shortly after midnight we ran into this mob and tagged along. It was the only entertainment to be had. We were a bit tight, sir, if you'll believe it.'

'I believe it,' said Marcellus. 'Go on, please, with whatever you can remember.'

'Well—we went to the trials. As I have said, we were not in prime condition to understand what was going on, and most of the testimony was shrieked in Aramaic. But it was clear enough that the Temple crowd and the merchants were trying to have the man put to death.'

'For what happened at the Temple?'

'Yes—for that, and for going about through the country gathering up big crowds to hear him talk.'

'About what?'

'A new religion. I was talking with one of Pilate's legionaries who understands the language. He said this Jesus was urging the country people to adopt a religion that doesn't have much to do with the Temple. Some of the testimony was rubbish. One fellow swore the Galilean had said that if the Temple were torn down he could put it up again in three days. Stuff like that! Of course, all they want is a conviction. Any sort of testimony is good enough.'

'Where does the matter stand now?' asked Marcellus.

'I got a plenty of it at Herod's court, and came back before daybreak; dead on my feet. They had just decided to have another trial before Pilate, directly after breakfast. They are probably at the Insula now. Pilate will have to give them what they want—and'—Paulus hesitated, and then continued grimly—'what they want is a crucifixion. I heard them talking about it.'

'Shall we go over?' queried Marcellus.

'I've had enough sir, if you'll excuse me.' Paulus rose with an effort and ambled uncertainly across the room. In the doorway he confronted a sentinel, garbed in the Insula uniform, who saluted stiffly.

'The Procurator's compliments,' he barked, in a metallic tone. 'The ranking officers and a detachment of twenty men from the Minoa Legion will attend immediately in the Procurator's court.' With another ceremonious salute, he backed out and strutted down the corridor without waiting for a reply.

'I wonder what Pilate wants of us,' reflected Marcellus, uneasily, searching the Centurion's apprehensive eyes.

'I think I can guess,' growled Paulus. 'Pilate doesn't confer honors on Minoa. He's going to detail us to do something too dirty and dangerous for the local troops; doesn't want his precious legion mixed up in it. The Minoa contingent will be leaving tomorrow. If any trouble results, we will be out of reach.' He hitched up his belt and left the room. Marcellus stood irresolute for a moment and followed, intending to ask Paulus to order out the detachment. Through the half-open door to the Centurion's quarters, he saw him greedily gulping from an enormous cup. He strode angrily into the room.

'If I were you, Paulus,' he said, sternly, 'I shouldn't drink any more at present. You've already had much too much!'

'If I were you,' retorted Paulus, recklessly, 'I would take as much of this as I could hold!' He took a couple of uncertain steps toward Marcellus, and faced him with brazen audacity. 'You're going to crucify a man today!' he muttered. 'Ever see that done?'

'No.' Marcellus shook his head. 'I don't even know how it is done. You'll have to tell me.'

Paulus carefully picked his way back to the table where the grotesquely shaped wineskin sat. Refilling the big cup, he handed it, dripping, to his Commander.

'I'll show you—when we get there,' he said, huskily. 'Drink that! All of it! If you don't, you'll wish you had. What we're going to do is not a job for a sober man.'

Marcellus, unprotesting, took the cup and drank.

'It isn't just that the thing is sickeningly cruel,' continued Paulus. 'There's something strange about this man. I'd rather not have anything to do with it!'

'Afraid he'll haunt you?' Marcellus paused at the middle of the cup, and drew an unconvincing grin.

'Well—you wait—and see what you think!' murmured Paulus, wagging his head mysteriously. 'The witnesses said he acted, at the Temple, as if it were his own personal property. And that didn't sound as silly as you might think, sir. At old man Annas' house, I'm bound if he didn't act as if he owned the place. At Caiaphas' palace, everybody was on trial—but this Jesus! He was the only cool man in the crowd at the Insula. He owns that, too. Pilate felt it, I think. One of the witnesses testified that Jesus had professed to be a king. Pilate leaned forward, looked him squarely in the face, and said, "Are you?" Mind, sir, Pilate didn't ask him, "Did you say you were a king?" He said, "Are you?" And he wasn't trying to be sarcastic, either.'

'But that's nonsense, Paulus! Your wine-soaked imagination was playing tricks on you!' Marcellus walked across to the table and poured himself another cupful. 'You get out the troops,' he ordered, resolutely. 'I hope you'll be able to stand straight, over at the Insula. You're definitely drunk, you know.' He took another long drink, and wiped his mouth on the back of his hand. 'So—what did the Galilean say to that—when Pilate asked him if he was a king?'

'Said he had a kingdom—but not in the world,' muttered Paulus, with a vague, upward-spiraling gesture.

'You're worse than drunk,' accused Marcellus, disgustedly. 'You're losing your mind. I think you'd better go to bed. I'll report you sick.'

'No—I'm not going to leave you in the lurch, Marcellus.' It was the first time Paulus had ever addressed the Commander by his given name.

'You're goo-fellow, Paulus,' declared Marcellus, giving him his hand. He retraced his way to the wineskin. Paulus followed and took the cup from his hand.

'You have had just the right amount, sir,' he advised. 'I suggest that you go now. Pilate will not like it if we are tardy. He has endured about all the annoyance he can take, for one morning's dose. I shall order out the detachment, and meet you over there.'

* * * * * *

With a purposely belated start, and after experiencing much difficulty in learning the way to the place of execution—an outlying field where the city's refuse was burned—Demetrius did not expect to arrive in time to witness the initial phase of the crucifixion.

Tardy as he was, he proceeded with reluctant steps; very low in spirit, weighted with a dejection he had not known since the day of his enslavement. The years had healed the chain-scars on his wrists: fair treatment at the hands of the Gallio family had done much to mend his heart: but today it seemed that the world was totally unfit for a civilized man to live in. Every human institution was loaded with lies. The courts were corrupt. Justice was not to be had. All rulers, big and little, were purchasable. Even the temples were full of deceit. You could call the roll of all the supposed reliances that laid claim to the people's respect and reverence, and there wasn't one of them that hadn't earned the bitter contempt of decent men!

Though accustomed to walk with long strides and clipped steps, Demetrius slogged along through the dirty streets with the shambling gait of a hopeless, faithless, worthless vagabond. At times his scornful thoughts almost became articulate as he passionately reviled every tribunal and judiciary, every crown and consistory in the whole, wide, wicked world. Patriotism! How the poets and minstrels loved to babble about the high honor of shedding one's blood. Maybe they, too, had been bought up. Old Horace: maybe Augustus had just sent him a new coat and a cask of wine when he was inspired to write, 'How sweet and glorious to die for one's country!' Nonsense! Why should any sane man think it pleasant or noble to give up his life to save the world? It wasn't fit to live in; much less die for! And it was never going to be any better. Here was this foolhardy Galilean,

so thoroughly enraged over the pollution of a holy place that he had
impulsively made an ineffective little gesture of protest. Doubtless
nineteen out of every twenty men in this barren, beaten, beggared
land would inwardly applaud this poor man's reckless courage; but,
when it came to the test, these downtrodden, poverty-cursed nobodies
would let this Jesus stand alone—without one friend—before the
official representatives of a crooked Temple and a crooked Empire.

Loyalty? Why should any man bother himself to be loyal? Let
him go out on his own, and protect himself the best he can. Why
should you spend your life following at the heels of a Roman master, who alternately confided in you and humiliated you? What had
you to lose, in self-respect, by abandoning this aristocrat? It wasn't
hard to make one's way to Damascus.

It was a dark day for Demetrius. Even the sky was overcast with
leaden, sullen clouds. The sun had shone brightly at dawn. For the
past half-hour, an almost sinister gloom had been thickening.

As he neared the disreputable field, identifiable for some distance
by the noisome smoke that drifted from its smouldering corruptions,
he met many men walking rapidly back to the city. Most of them
were well-fed, well-dressed, pompous, preoccupied; men of middle
age or older, strutting along in single file, as if each had come alone.
These people, surmised Demetrius, were responsible for the day's
crime. It relieved him to feel that the worst of it was over. They
had seen the public assassination to a successful conclusion, and were
now free to return to their banks and bazaars. Some, doubtless, would
go to the Temple and say their prayers.

After the last straggling group of mud hovels had been passed,
the loathsome, garbage-littered field lay before him. He was amazed
to see how much pollution had been conveyed to this place, for the
city's streets had not shown so huge a loss of filth. A fairly clean,
narrow path led toward a little knoll that seemed to have been protected. Demetrius stopped—and looked. On the green knoll, three
tall crosses stood in a row. Perhaps it had been decided, as an afterthought, to execute a couple of the Galilean's friends. Could it be
possible that two among them, crazed by their leader's impending
torture, had attempted to defend him? Hardly: they didn't have it
in them: not the ones he had seen that day on the road: not the
ones he had seen, this morning.

Forcing his unwilling feet, he advanced slowly to within less than
a stadium of the gruesome scene. There he came to a stop. The
two unidentified men were writhing on their crosses. The lonely man
on the central cross was still as a statue. His head hung forward.
Perhaps he was dead, or at least unconscious. Demetrius hoped so.

For a long time he stood there, contemplating this tragic sight.
The hot anger that had almost suffocated him was measurably cooled
now. The lonely man had thrown his life away. There was nothing

to show for his audacious courage. The Temple would continue to cheat the country people who came in to offer a lamb. Herod would continue to bully and whip the poor if they inconvenienced the rich. Caiaphas would continue to condemn the blasphemies of men who didn't want the gods fetched to market. Pilate would deal out injustice—and wash his dirty hands in a silver bowl. This lonely man had paid a high price for his brief and fruitless war on wickedness. But —he had spoken: he had acted. By tomorrow, nobody would remember that he had risked everything—and lost his life—in the cause of honesty. But—perhaps a man was better off dead than in a world where such an event as this could happen. Demetrius felt very lonely too.

There was not as large a crowd as he had expected to see. There was no disorder, probably because the legionaries were scattered about among the people. It was apparent, from the negligence of the soldiers' posture, as they stood leaning on their lances, that no rioting had occurred or was anticipated.

Demetrius moved closer in and joined the outer rim of spectators. Not many of the well-to-do, who had been conspicuous at the Insula, were present. Most of the civilians were poorly dressed. Many of them were weeping. There were several women, heavily veiled and huddled in little groups, in attitudes of silent, hopeless grief. A large circle had been left unoccupied below the crosses.

Edging his way slowly forward, occasionally rising on tiptoe to search for his master, Demetrius paused beside one of the legionaries who, recognizing him with a brief nod, replied to his low-voiced inquiry. The Commander and several other officers were on the other side of the knoll, at the rear of the crosses, he said.

'I brought him some water,' explained Demetrius, holding up the jug. The soldier showed how many of his teeth were missing.

'That's good,' he said. 'He can wash his hands. They're not drinking water today. The Procurator sent out a wineskin.'

'Is the man dead?' asked Demetrius.

'No—he said something awhile ago.'

'What did he say? Could you hear?'

'Said he was thirsty.'

'Did they give him water?'

'No—they filled a sponge with vinegar that had some sort of balm in it, and raised it to his mouth; but he wouldn't have it. I don't rightly understand what he is up there for—but he's no coward.' The legionary shifted his position, pointed to the darkening sky, remarked that there was going to be a storm, and moved on through the crowd.

Demetrius did not look at the lonely man again. He edged out into the open and made a wide détour around to the other side of the knoll. Marcellus, Paulus, and four or five others were lounging in a small circle on the ground. A leather dice-cup was being shaken negligently, and passed from hand to hand. At first sight of it, Demetrius was hotly indignant. It wasn't like Marcellus to be so brutally unfeeling. A decent man would have to be very drunk indeed to exhibit such callous unconcern in this circumstance.

Now that he was here, Demetrius thought he should inquire whether there was anything he could do for his master. He slowly approached the group of preoccupied officers. After a while, Marcellus glanced up dully and beckoned to him. The others gave him a brief glance and resumed their play.

'Anything you want to tell me?' asked Marcellus, thickly.

'I brought you some water, sir.'

'Very good. Put it down there. I'll have a drink presently.' It was his turn to play. He shook the cup languidly and tossed out the dice.

'Your lucky day!' growled Paulus. 'That finishes me.' He stretched his long arms and laced his fingers behind his head. 'Demetrius,' he said, nodding toward a rumpled brown mantle that lay near the foot of the central cross, 'hand me that coat. I want to look at it.'

Demetrius picked up the garment and gave it to him. Paulus examined it with idle interest.

'Not a bad robe,' he remarked, holding it up at arm's length. 'Woven in the country; dyed with walnut juice. He'll not be needing it any more. I think I'll say it's mine. How about it, Tribune?'

'Why should it be yours?' asked Marcellus, indifferently. 'If it's worth anything, let us toss for it.' He handed Paulus the dice-cup. 'High number wins. It's your turn.'

There was a low mutter of thunder in the north and a savage tongue of flame leaped through the black cloud. Paulus tossed a pair of threes, and stared apprehensively at the sky.

'Not hard to beat,' said Vinitius, who sat next him. He took the cup and poured out a five and a four. The cup made the circle without bettering this cast until it arrived at Marcellus.

'Double six!' he called. 'Demetrius, you take care of the robe.' Paulus handed up the garment.

'Shall I wait here for you, sir?' asked Demetrius.

'No—nothing you can do. Go back to the Insula. Begin packing up. We want to be off to an early start in the morning.' Marcellus looked up at the sky. 'Paulus, go around and see how they are doing. There's going to be a hard storm.' He rose heavily to his feet, and stood swaying. Demetrius wanted to take his arm and steady him, but felt that any solicitude would be resented. His indignation had cooled now. It was evident that Marcellus had been drinking because he couldn't bear to do this shameful work in his right mind. There was a deafening, stunning thunderclap that fairly shook the ground on which they stood. Marcellus put out a hand and steadied himself against the central cross. There was blood on his hand when he regained his balance. He wiped it off on his toga.

A fat man, expensively dressed in a black robe, waddled out of the crowd and confronted Marcellus with surly arrogance.

'Rebuke these people!' he shouted, angrily. 'They are saying that the storm is a judgment on us!'

There was another gigantic crash of thunder.

'Maybe it is!' yelled Marcellus, recklessly.

The fat man waved a menacing fist.

'It is your duty to keep order here!' he shrieked.

'Do you want me to stop the storm?' demanded Marcellus.

'Stop the blasphemy! These people are crying out that this Galilean is the Son of God!'

'Maybe he *is!*' shouted Marcellus. '*You* wouldn't know!' He was fumbling with the hilt of his sword. The fat man backed away, howling that the Procurator should hear of this.

Circling the knoll, Demetrius paused for a final look at the lonely man on the central cross. He had raised his face and was gazing up into the black sky. Suddenly he burst forth with a resonant call, as if crying to a distant friend for aid.

A poorly dressed, bearded man of middle age, apparently one of the Galilean's friends from the country, rushed out of the crowd and ran down the slope weeping aloud in an abandon of grief. Demetrius grasped him by the sleeve as he stumbled past.

'What did he say?'

The man made no reply, tore himself loose, and ran on shouting his unintelligible lamentations.

Now the dying Galilean was looking down upon the crowd below him. His lips moved. His eyes surveyed the people with the same sorrow they had expressed on the road when the multitude had hailed him as their king. There was another savage burst of thunder. The darkness deepened.

Demetrius rolled up the Robe and thrust it inside his tunic, pressing it tightly under his arm. The intimate touch of the garment relieved his feeling of desolation. He wondered if Marcellus might not let him keep the Robe. It would be a comfort to own something that this courageous man had worn. He would cherish it as a priceless inheritance. It would have been a great experience, he felt, to have known this man; to have learned the nature of his mind. Now that there would be no opportunity to share his friendship, it would be an enduring consolation to possess his Robe.

Turning about, with swimming eyes, he started down the hill. It was growing so dark now that the narrow path was indistinct. He flung a backward look over his shoulder, but the descending gloom had swallowed up the knoll.

By the time he reached the city streets, night had fallen on Jerusalem, though it was only mid-afternoon. Lights flickered in the windows. Pedestrians moved slowly, carrying torches. Frightened voices called to one another. Demetrius could not understand what they were saying, but their tone was apprehensive, as if they were wondering about the cause of this strange darkness. He wondered, too, but felt no sense of depression or alarm. The sensation of being alone and unwanted in an unfriendly world had left him. He was not lonely now. He hugged the Robe close to his side as if it contained some inexplicable remedy for heartache.

Melas was standing in the corridor, in front of Paulus' door, when he arrived at the barracks. Demetrius was in no mood to talk, and proceeded to his master's quarters, Melas following with his torch. 'So—you went out there; eh?' said the Thracian, grimly. 'How did you like it?' They entered the room and Melas applied his torch to the big stone lamps. Receiving no answer to his rough query, he asked, 'What do you think this is; an eclipse?'

'I don't know,' replied Demetrius. 'Never heard of an eclipse lasting so long.'

'Maybe it's the end of the world,' said Melas, forcing an uncouth laugh.

'That will be all right with me,' said Demetrius.

'Think this Jesus has had anything to do with it?' asked Melas, half in earnest.

'No,' said Demetrius, 'I shouldn't think so.'

Melas moved closer and took Demetrius by the arm.

'Thought any more about Damascus?' he whispered.

Demetrius shook his head indifferently.

'Have you?' he asked.

'I'm going—tonight,' said Melas. 'The Procurator always gives a dinner to the officers on the last night. When it is over, and I have put the Centurion to bed—he'll be tight as a tambourine—I'm leaving. Better come with me. You'll wait a long time for another chance as good as this one.'

'No—I'm not going,' said Demetrius firmly.

'You'll not tell on me, will you?'

'Certainly not.'

'If you change your mind, give me a wink at the banquet.' Melas sauntered toward the door. Demetrius, thinking he had gone, drew out the Robe and unfolded it under the light.

'What have you there?' queried Melas, from the doorway.

'His Robe,' said Demetrius, without turning.

Melas came back and regarded the blood-stained garment with silent interest.

'How do you happen to have it?' he asked, in an awed tone.

'It belongs to the Legate. The officers tossed for it. He won it.'

'I shouldn't think he'd want it,' remarked Melas. 'I'm sure I wouldn't. It will probably bring him bad luck.'

'Why *bad* luck?' demanded Demetrius. 'It belonged to a brave man.'

* * * * * *

Marcellus came in, dazed, drunk, and thoroughly exhausted. Unbuckling his sword-belt, he handed it to Demetrius, and sank wearily into a chair.

'Get me some wine,' he ordered, huskily.

Demetrius obeyed; and, on one knee, unlaced his master's dusty sandals while he drank.

'You will feel better after a cold bath, sir,' he said, encouragingly.

Marcellus widened his heavy eyes with an effort and surveyed his slave with curiosity.

'Were you out there?' he asked, thickly. 'Oh, yes; I remember now. You were there. You brought j-jug water.'

'And brought back his Robe,' prompted Demetrius.

Marcellus passed his hand awkwardly across his brow and tried to dismiss the recollection with a shuddering shrug.

'You will be going to the dinner, sir?' asked Demetrius.

'Have to!' grumbled Marcellus. 'Can't have off-cers laughing at us. We're tough—at Minoa. Can't have ossifers—orfficers—chortling that sight of blood makes Minoa Legate sick.'

'Quite true, sir,' approved Demetrius. 'A shower and a rubdown will put you in order. I have laid out fresh clothing for you.'

'Very good,' labored Marcellus. 'Commanner Minoa never this dirty before. Wha's that?' He raked his fingers across a dark wet smudge on the skirt of his toga. 'Blood!' he muttered. 'Great Roman Empire does big brave deed! Wins bloody battle!' The drunken monologue trailed off into foggy incoherences. Marcellus' head sank lower and lower on his chest. Demetrius unfastened the toga, soaked a towel in cold water, and vigorously applied it to his master's puffed face and beating throat.

'Up you come, sir!' he ordered, tugging Marcellus to his feet. 'One more hard battle to fight, sir. Then you can sleep it off.'

Marcellus slowly pulled himself together and rested both hands heavily on his slave's shoulders while being stripped of his soiled clothing.

'I'm dirty,' he mumbled to himself. 'I'm dirty—outside and inside. I'm dirty—and ashamed. Unnerstand—Demetrius? I'm dirty and ashamed.'

'You were only obeying orders, sir,' consoled Demetrius.

'Were you out there?' Marcellus tried to focus his eyes.

'Yes, sir. A very sorry affair.'

'What did you think of him?'

'Very courageous. It was too bad you had it to do, sir.'

'I wouldn't do it again,' declared Marcellus, truculently—'no matter who ordered it! Were you there when he called on his god to forgive us?'

'No—but I couldn't have understood his language.'

'Nor I—but they told me. He looked directly at me after he had said it. I'm afraid I'm going to have a hard time forgetting that look.'

Demetrius put his arm around Marcellus to steady him. It was the first time he had ever seen tears in his master's eyes.

* * * * * *

The Insula's beautiful banquet-hall had been gaily decorated for the occasion with many ensigns, banners, and huge vases of flowers. An orchestra, sequestered in an alcove, played stirring military marches. Great stone lamps on marble pillars brightly lighted the spacious room. At the head table, a little higher than the others, sat the Procurator with Marcellus and Julian on either side and the Commanders from Caesarea and Joppa flanking them. Everyone knew why Marcellus and Julian were given seats of honor. Minoa had been assigned a difficult task and Capernaum had a grievance. Pilate was glum, moody, and distraught.

The household slaves served the elaborate dinner. The officers' orderlies stood ranged against the walls, in readiness to be of aid to their masters, for the Procurator's guests—according to a long-established custom—had come here to get drunk, and not many of them had very far to go.

The representatives of Minoa were more noisy and reckless than any of the others, but it was generally conceded that much latitude should be extended in their case, for they had had a hard day. Paulus had arrived late. Melas had done what he could to straighten him up, but the Centurion was dull and dizzy—and surly. The gaiety of his table companions annoyed him. For some time he sat glumly regarding them with distaste, occasionally jerked out of his lethargy by a painful hiccough. After a while his fellow officers took him in hand, plying him with a particularly heady wine which had the effect of whipping his jaded spirits into fresh activity. He tried to be merry; sang and shouted; but no one could understand anything he said. Presently he upset his tall wine-cup, and laughed uproariously. Paulus was drunk.

It pleased Demetrius to observe that Marcellus was holding his own with dignity. He was having little to say, but Pilate's taciturnity easily accounted for that. Old Julian, quite sober, was eating his dinner with relish, making no effort to engage the Procurator in conversation. The other tables were growing louder and more disorderly as the evening advanced. There was much boisterous laughter; many rude practical jokes; an occasional unexplained quarrel.

The huge silver salvers, piled high with roasted meats and exotic fruits, came and went; exquisitely carved silver flagons poured rare wines into enormous silver goblets. Now and then a flushed Centurion rose from the couch on which he lounged beside his table, his servant skipping swiftly across the marble floor to assist him. After a while they would return. The officer, apparently much improved in health, would strut back to his couch and resume where he had left off. Many of the guests slept, to the chagrin of their slaves. So long as your master was able to stagger out of the room and unburden his stomach, you had no cause for humiliation; but if he went to sleep, your fellow slaves winked at you and grinned.

Demetrius stood at attention, against the wall, immediately behind his master's couch. He noted with satisfaction that Marcellus was merely toying with his food, which showed that he still had some sense left. He wished, however, that the Commander would exhibit a little more interest in the party. It would be unfortunate if anyone surmised that he was brooding over the day's events.

Presently the Procurator sat up and leaned toward Marcellus, who turned his face inquiringly. Demetrius moved a step forward and listened.

'You are not eating your dinner, Legate,' observed Pilate. 'Perhaps there is something else you would prefer.'

'Thank you; no sir,' replied Marcellus. 'I am not hungry.'

'Perhaps your task, this afternoon, dulled your appetite,' suggested Pilate, idly.

Marcellus scowled.

'That would be a good enough reason, sir, for one's not being hungry,' he retorted.

'A painful business, I'm sure,' commented Pilate. 'I did not enjoy my necessity to order it.'

'Necessity?' Marcellus sat up and faced his host with cool impudence. 'This man was not guilty of a crime, as the Procurator himself admitted.'

Pilate frowned darkly at this impertinence.

'Am I to understand that the Legate of Minoa disputes the justice of the court's decision?'

'Of course!' snapped Marcellus. 'Justice? No one knows better than the Procurator that this Galilean was unjustly treated!'

'You are forgetting yourself, Legate!' said Pilate, sternly.

'I did not initiate this conversation, sir,' rejoined Marcellus, 'but if my candor annoys you, we can talk about something else.'

Pilate's face cleared a little.

'You have a right to your opinions, Legate Marcellus Gallio,' he conceded, 'though you certainly know it is unusual for a man to criticize his superior quite so freely as you have done.'

'I know that, sir,' nodded Marcellus, respectfully. 'It is unusual to criticize one's superior. But this is an unusual case.' He paused, and looked Pilate squarely in the eyes. 'It was an unusual trial, an unusual decision, an unusual punishment—and the convict was an unusual man!'

'A strange person, indeed,' agreed Pilate. 'What did you make of him?' he asked, lowering his voice confidentially.

Marcellus shook his head.

'I don't know, sir,' he replied, after an interval.

'He was a fanatic!' said Pilate.

'Doubtless. So was Socrates. So was Plato.'

Pilate shrugged.

'You're not implying that this Galilean was of the same timber as Socrates and Plato!'

The conversation was interrupted before Marcellus had an opportunity to reply. Paulus had risen and was shouting at him drunkenly, incoherently. Pilate scowled, as if this were a bit too much, even for a party that had lost all respect for the dignity of the Insula. Marcellus shook his head and signed to Paulus with his hand that he was quite out of order. Undeterred. Paulus staggered to the head table, leaned far across it on one unstable elbow, and muttered something that Demetrius could not hear. Marcellus tried to dissuade him, but he was obdurate and growing quarrelsome. Obviously much perplexed, the Commander turned and beckoned to Demetrius.

'Centurion Paulus wants to see that Robe,' he muttered. 'Bring it here.'

Demetrius hesitated so long that Pilate regarded him with sour amazement.

'Go—instantly—and get it!' barked Marcellus, angrily.

Regretting that he had put his master to shame, in the presence of the Procurator, Demetrius tried to atone for his reluctant obedience by moving swiftly. His heart pounded hard as he ran down the corridor to the Legate's suite. There was no accounting for the caprice of a man as drunk as Paulus. Almost anything could happen, but Paulus would have to be humored.

Folding the blood-stained, torn-rent Robe over his arm, Demetrius returned to the banquet-hall. He felt like a traitor, assisting in the mockery of a cherished friend. Surely this Jesus deserved a better fate than to be abandoned—even in death—to the whims of a drunken soldier. Once, on the way, Demetrius came to a full stop and debated seriously whether to obey, or take the advice of Melas and run.

Marcellus glanced at the Robe, but did not touch it.

'Take it to Centurion Paulus,' he said.

Paulus, who had returned to his seat, rose unsteadily; and, holding up the Robe by its shoulders, picked his way carefully to the head table. The room grew suddenly quiet, as he stood directly before Pilate.

'Trophy!' shouted Paulus.

Pilate drew a reproachful smile and glanced toward Marcellus as if to hint that the Legate of Minoa might well advise his Centurion to mend his manners.

'Trophy!' repeated Paulus. 'Minoa presents trophy to the Insula.' He waved an expansive arm toward the banners that hung above the Procurator's table.

Pilate shook his head crossly and disclaimed all interest in the drunken farce with a gesture of annoyance. Undaunted by his rebuff, Paulus edged over a few steps and addressed Marcellus.

'Insula doesn't want trophy!' he prattled idiotically. 'Very well! Minoa keep trophy! Legate Marcellus wear trophy back to Minoa! Put it on, Legate!'

'Please, Paulus!' begged Marcellus. 'That's enough.'

'Put it on!' shouted Paulus. 'Here, Demetrius; hold the Robe for the Legate!' He thrust it into Demetrius' hands.

Someone yelled, 'Put it on!' And the rest of them took up the shout, pounding the tables with their goblets. 'Put it on!'

Feeling that the short way out of the dilemma was to humor the drunken crowd, Marcellus rose and reached for the Robe. Demetrius stood clutching it in his arms, seemingly unable to release it. Marcellus was pale with anger.

'Give it to me!' he commanded, severely. All eyes were attentive, and the place grew quiet. Demetrius drew himself erect, with the Robe held tightly in his folded arms. Marcellus waited a long moment, breathing heavily. Then suddenly drawing back his arm he slapped Demetrius in the face with his open hand. It was the first time he had ever ventured to punish him.

Demetrius slowly bowed his head and handed Marcellus the Robe; then stood with slumped shoulders while his master tugged it on over the sleeves of his toga. A gale of appreciative laughter went up, and there was tumultuous applause. Marcellus did not smile. His face was drawn and haggard. The room grew still again. As a man in a dream, he fumbled woodenly with the neck of the garment, trying to pull it off his shoulder. His hands were shaking.

'Shall I help you, sir?' asked Demetrius, anxiously.

Marcellus nodded; and when Demetrius had relieved him of the Robe, he sank into his seat as if his knees had suddenly buckled under him.

'Take that out into the courtyard,' he muttered, hoarsely, 'and burn it!'

Demetrius saluted and walked rapidly across the hall. Melas was standing near the doorway. He moved in closer as Demetrius passed.

'Meet me—at midnight—at the Sheep Gate,' he whispered.

'I'll be there,' flung back Demetrius, as he hurried on.

* * * * * *

'You seem much shaken.' Pilate's tone was coolly derisive. 'Perhaps you are superstitious.'

Marcellus made no reply. It was as if he had not heard the sardonic comment. He took up his wine-cup in a trembling hand and drank. The other tables, now that the unexpected little drama had been played out, resumed their banter and laughter.

'I suspect that you have had about enough for one day,' added the Procurator, more considerately. 'If you wish to go, you may be excused.'

'Thank you, sir,' replied Marcellus, remotely. He half-rose from his couch, but finding that his knees were still weak, sank down again. Too much attention had already been focused on him: he would not take the risk of an unfortunate exit. Doubtless his sudden enfeeblement would soon pass. He tried to analyze this curious enervation. He had been drinking far too much today. He had been under a terrific emotional strain. But even in his present state of mental confusion, he could still think straight enough to know that it wasn't the wine or the day's tragic task. This seizure of unaccountable inertia had come upon him when he thrust his arms into the sleeves of that Robe! Pilate had taunted him about his superstition. Nothing could be farther from the truth: he was not superstitious. Nobody had less interest in or respect for a belief in supernatural persons or powers. That being true, he had not himself invested this Robe with some imagined magic.

He realized that Pilate was looking him over with contemptuous curiosity. His situation was becoming quite embarrassing. Sooner or later he would be obliged to stand up. He wondered if he could.

A palace guard was crossing the room, on his way to the head table. He came to a halt as he faced the Procurator, saluted stiffly, and announced that the Captain of *The Vestris* had arrived and wished to deliver a letter to Legate Marcellus Lucan Gallio.

'Bring it here,' said Pilate.

'Captain Fulvius wishes to deliver it with his own hands, sir,' said the guard.

'Nonsense!' retorted Pilate. 'Tell him to give you the letter. See that the Captain has his dinner and plenty of wine. I shall have a word with him in the morning.'

'The letter, sir,' said the guard, impressively, 'is from the Emperor!'

Marcellus, who had listened with scant interest, now leaned forward and looked at the Procurator inquisitively.

'Very well,' nodded Pilate. 'Tell him to come in.'

The few minutes of waiting seemed long. A letter from the Emperor! What manner of message would be coming from crazy old Tiberius? Presently the bronzed, bearded, bow-legged sailor ambled through the room, in tow of the guard. Pilate greeted him coolly and signed for him to hand the scroll to Marcellus. The Captain waited, and the Procurator watched out of the tail of his eye, while the seals were broken. Marcellus thrust a shaky dagger through the heavy wax, slowly unrolled the papyrus, and ran his eye over the brief message. Then he rolled up the scroll and impassively addressed the Captain.

'When are you sailing?' There was nothing in Marcellus' tone to indicate whether the letter from Emperor Tiberius bore good tidings or bad. Whatever the message was, it had not stirred him out of his strange apathy.

'Tomorrow night, sir. Soon as we get back to Joppa.'

'Very good,' said Marcellus, casually. 'I shall be ready.'

'We should leave here an hour before dawn, sir,' said the Captain. 'I have made all arrangements for your journey to the port. The ship will call at Gaza to pick up whatever you may wish to take with you to Rome.'

'How did you happen to deliver this letter to Legate Marcellus Gallio in Jerusalem?' inquired Pilate, idly.

'I went to the Minoa fort, sir, and they told me he was here.' The Captain bobbed an awkward leave-taking and followed the guard from the hall. Pilate, unable to restrain his curiosity any longer, turned to Marcellus with inquiring eyes.

'If congratulations are in order,' he said, almost deferentially, 'may I be the first to offer them?'

'Thank you,' said Marcellus, evasively. 'If it is agreeable with you, sir, I shall go now.'

'By all means,' approved Pilate, stiffening. 'Perhaps you need some assistance,' he added, as he observed Marcellus' struggle to rise. 'Shall I send for your servant?'

Clutching the table for support, Marcellus contrived to get to his feet. For a moment, as he steadied himself, he was unsure whether his legs would bear his weight until he had crossed the banquet-hall. Clenching his hands, he massed his will into a determined effort to walk. With short, infirm steps, he began the long journey to the door, so intent upon it that he had failed to give his distinguished host so much as a farewell glance. He was immeasurably relieved when, having passed through the door and into the broad corridor, he could brace a hand against the wall. After he had proceeded for some distance down the hall, he came to an arched doorway that opened upon the spacious courtyard. Feeling himself quite unable to go farther, he picked his way—with the caution of an old man—down the steps. On the lower step, he sat down heavily, in the darkness that enveloped the deserted parade-ground, wondering whether he would ever regain his strength.

Occasionally, during the next hour, he made tentative efforts to rise; but they were ineffectual. It struck him oddly that he was not more alarmed over his condition. Indeed, this lethargy that had attacked him physically had similarly disqualified his mind.

The fact that his exile, which had threatened to ruin his life, was now ended, did not exult his spirit. He said, over and over to himself, 'Marcellus, wake up! You are free! You are going home! You are going back to your family! You are going back to Diana! The ship is waiting! You are to sail tomorrow! What ails you, Marcellus?'

Once he roused to brief attention as the figure of a man with a pack on his shoulder neared his darkened doorway. The fellow was keeping close to the wall, proceeding with stealthy steps. It was Paulus' slave. He had the furtive air of a fugitive. As he passed Marcellus, he gave a sudden start at the sight of him sitting there; and, taking to his heels, vanished like a frightened antelope. Marcellus thought this faintly amusing, but did not smile. So—Melas was running away. Well—what of it? The question arrived and departed with no more significance than the fitful flicker in the masses of exotic shrubbery where the fireflies played.

After what seemed like a very long time, there came the sound of sandals scraping along the marble corridor, and thick, tired voices. The banquet was over. Marcellus wondered dully whether he should make his presence known to them as they passed, but felt powerless to come to a decision. Presently the footsteps and voices grew fainter and fainter, down the corridor. After that, the night seemed more dark. But Marcellus did not have a sense of desolation. His mind was inert. He laboriously edged his way over to the marble pillar at the right of the arch; and, leaning against it, dreamlessly slept.

*   *   *   *   *   *

Demetrius had spent a busy hour in the Legate's suite, packing his master's clothing and other equipment for the journey he would be making, in the morning, back to Minoa. He had very few misgivings about escaping from his slavery, but the habit of waiting on Marcellus was not easy to throw off. He would perform this final service, and be on his way to liberty. He might be captured, or he might experience much hardship; but he would be free! Marcellus, when he sobered, would probably regret the incident in the banquethall; might even feel that his slave had a just cause for running away.

He hadn't accomplished his freedom yet, but he was beginning to experience the sense of it. After he had strapped the bulky baggage, Demetrius quietly left the room and returned to his own small cubicle at the far end of the barracks occupied by the contingent from Minoa, where he gathered up his few belongings and stowed them into his bag. Carefully folding the Galilean's Robe, he tucked it in last after packing everything else.

It was, he admitted, a very irrational idea, but the softness of the finely woven, homespun Robe had a curious quality. The touch of it had for him a strangely calming effect, as if it were a new reliance. He remembered a legend from his childhood, about a ring that bore the insignia of a prince. And the prince had given the ring to some poor legionary who had pushed him out of an arrow's path. And, years afterward, when in great need, the soldier had turned the ring to good account in seeking an audience with the prince. Demetrius could not remember all the details of the story, but this Robe seemed to have much the same properties as the prince's ring. It was in the nature of a surety, a defense.

It was a long way to the Sheep Gate, but he had visited it before on one of his solitary excursions, lured there by Melas' information that it was now rarely used except by persons coming into the city from the villages to the north. If a man were heading for the Damascus road, and wished to avoid a challenge, the Sheep Gate offered the best promise. Demetrius had been full of curiosity to see it. He had no intention of running away; but thought it might be interesting to have a glimpse of a road to freedom. Melas had said it was easy.

The gate was unguarded; deserted, indeed. Melas had not yet arrived, but his tardiness gave Demetrius no concern. Perhaps he himself was early. He lounged on the parched grass by the roadside, in the shadow of the crumbling limestone bastion, and waited.

At length he heard the rhythmic lisps of sandal-straps, and stepped out into the road.

'Anyone see you go?' asked Melas, puffing a little as he put down his pack for a momentary rest.

'No. Everything was quiet. How about you?'

'The Legate saw me leave.' Melas chuckled. 'He gave me a fright. I was sneaking along the barracks wall, in the courtyard, and came upon him.'

'What was he doing there?' demanded Demetrius, sharply.

'Just sitting there—by himself—in a doorway.'

'He recognized you?'

'Yes—I feel sure he did; but he didn't speak. Come! Let's not stand here any longer. We must see how far we can travel before sunrise.' Melas led the way through the dilapidated gate.

'Did the Legate appear to be drunk?' asked Demetrius.

'N-no—not very drunk,' said Melas, uncertainly. 'He left the hall before any of the others; seemed dizzy and half out of his head. I was going to wait and put my mean old drunkard to bed, but they kept on at it so long that I decided to leave. He probably won't miss me. I never saw the Centurion that drunk before.'

They plodded on through the dark, keeping to the road with difficulty. Melas stumbled over a rock and cursed eloquently.

'You say he seemed out of his head?' said Demetrius, anxiously.

'Yes—dazed—as if something had hit him. And out there in that archway, he had a sort of empty look in his face. Maybe he didn't even know where he was.'

Demetrius' steps slowed to a stop.

'Melas,' he said, hoarsely, 'I'm sorry—but I've got to go back to him.'

'Why—you—' The Thracian was at a loss for a strong enough epithet. 'I always thought you were soft! Afraid to run away from a fellow who strikes you in the face before a crowd of officers; just to show them how brave he is! Very well! You go back to him and be his slave forever! It will be tough! He has lost his mind!'

Demetrius had turned and was walking away.

'Good luck to you, Melas,' he called, soberly.

'Better get rid of that Robe!' shouted Melas, his voice shrill with anger. 'That's what drove your smart young Marcellus out of his mind! He began to go crazy the minute he put it on! Let him be. He is accursed! The Galilean has had his revenge!'

Demetrius stumbled on through the darkness, Melas' raging imprecations following him as far as the old gate.

'Accursed!' he yelled. 'Accursed!'

Chapter VII

ALTHOUGH winter was usually brief on the Island of Capri there was plenty of it while it lasted—according to Tiberius Caesar who detested it. The murky sky depressed his spirit. The raw dampness made his creaking joints ache. The most forlorn spot, he declared, in the Roman Empire.

The old man's favorite recreation, since committing most of his administrative responsibilities to Prince Gaius, was residential architecture. He was forever building huge, ornate villas on the lofty skyline of Capri; for what purpose not even the gods knew.

All day long through spring, summer, and autumn, he would sit in the sun—or under an awning if it grew too hot—and watch his stonemasons at work on yet another villa. And his builders had respect for these constructions too, for the Emperor was an architect of no mean ability. Nor did he allow his aesthetic taste to run away with his common sense. The great cisterns required for water conservation on a mountaintop were planned with the practical skill of an experienced plumber and concealed with the artistry of an idealistic sculptor.

There were nine of these exquisite villas now, ranged in an impressive row on the highest terrain, isolated from one another by spacious gardens, their architectural genre admitting that they had been derived from the mind and purse of the jaded, restless, irascible old Caesar who lived in the Villa Jovis which dominated them all— a fact further illuminated by the towering pharos rising majestically from the center of its vast, echoing atrium.

Tiberius hated winter because he could not sit in the sun and watch his elaborate fancies take on form and substance. He hadn't very long to live, and it enraged him to see the few remaining days slipping through his bony fingers like fine sand through an hourglass.

When the first wind and rain scurried across the bay to rattle the doors and pelt the windows of his fifty-room palace, the Emperor went into complete and embittered seclusion. No guests were welcome. Relatives were barred from his sumptuous suite. No deputations were received from Rome; no state business was transacted.

Prince Gaius, whom he despised, quite enjoyed this bad weather, for while the Emperor was in hibernation he felt free to exercise all the powers entrusted to him—and sometimes a little more. Tiberius, aware of this, fumed and snuffled, but he had arrived at that stage of senescence where he hadn't the energy to sustain his varied indignations. They burned white-hot for an hour—and expired.

Through the short winter, no one was allowed to see the decaying monarch but his personal attendants and a corps of bored physicians who packed his old bones in hot fomentations of spiced vinegar and listened obsequiously to his profane abuse.

But the first ray of earnest sunshine always made another man of him. When its brightness spread across his bed and dazzled his rheumy eyes, Tiberius kicked off his compresses and his doctors, yelled for his tunic, his toga, his sandals, his cap, his stick, his piper, his chief gardener, and staggered out into the peristyle. He shouted orders, thick and fast; and things began to hum. The Emperor had never been gifted with much patience, and nobody expected that he would miraculously develop this talent at eighty-two. Now that spring had been officially opened with terrifying shrieks and reckless cane-waving, the Villa Jovis came to life with a suddenness that must have shocked the conservative old god for whom the place had been named. The Macedonian musicians and Indian magicians and Ionian minstrels and Rhodesian astrologers and Egyptian dancing girls were violently shelled out of their comfortable winter sloth to line up before his fuming majesty and explain why—at the expense of a tax-harried, poverty-cursed Empire—they had been living in such disgusting indolence.

For the sake of appearances, a servant would then be dispatched to the Villa Dionysus—the name of his aged wife's palace had been chosen with an ironical chuckle—to inquire about the health of the Empress, which was the least of the old man's anxieties. It would not have upset him very much to learn that Julia wasn't so well. Indeed, he had once arranged for the old lady's assassination, an event which had failed to come off only because the Empress, privily advised of the engagement planned for her, had disapproved of it.

This season, spring had arrived much earlier than usual, blasting everything into bloom in a day. The sky was full of birds, the gardens were full of flowers, the flowers were full of bees, and Tiberius was full of joy. He wanted somebody to share it with him; somebody young enough to respond with exultation to all this beauty: who but Diana!

So—that afternoon a courier, ferrying across to Neapolis, set forth on a fast horse, followed an hour later by the most commodious of the royal carriages—stuffed with eider-down pillows as a hint that the return journey from Rome to Capri, albeit hard to take, should be made with dispatch; for the distinguished host was not good at waiting. His letter, addressed to Paula Gallus, was brief and urgent.

Tiberius did not ask whether it would be convenient for her to bring Diana to Capri; and, if so, he would send for them. He simply advised her that the carriage was on the way at full gallop, and that they were to be prepared to take it immediately upon its arrival.

* * * * * *

At dusk on the third day of their hard travel, Paula and Diana had stepped out of the imperial barge onto the Capri wharf; and, climbing wearily into the luxurious litters awaiting them, had been borne swiftly up the precipitous path to the Villa Jovis. There the old Emperor had met them with a pathetic eagerness, and had mercifully suggested that they retire at once to their baths and beds, adding that they were to rest undisturbed until tomorrow noon. This inspired announcement Paula Gallus received with an almost tearful gratitude and made haste to avail herself of its benefits.

Diana, whose physical resources had not been so thoroughly depleted, lingered, much to the old man's delight; slipped her hand through his arm and allowed herself to be led to his private parlor, where, when he had sunk into a comfortable chair, she drew up a stool; sat, with her shapely arms folded on his emaciated knee, and looked up into his deep-lined face with a tender affection that made the Emperor clear his throat and wipe his hawk-like nose.

It was so good of him, and so like him, she said, to want her to come. And how well he was looking! How glad he must be to see spring come again. Now he would be out in the sunshine, every day, probably supervising some new building. What was it going to be, this season: another villa, maybe? Diana smiled into his eyes.

'Yes,' he replied, gently, 'another villa. A truly beautiful villa.' He paused, narrowing his averted eyes thoughtfully. 'The most beautiful of them all, I hope. This one'—Tiberius gave her an enigmatic smile —'this one is for the sweet and lovely Diana.' He did not add that this idea had just now occurred to him. He made it sound as if he were confiding a plan that had been long nurtured in secret.

Diana's eyes swam and sparkled. She patted the brown old hand tenderly. With a husky voice she murmured that he was the very dearest grandfather anyone ever had.

'And you are to help me plan the villa, child,' said Tiberius, warmly.

'Was that why you sent for me?' asked Diana.

The old man pursed his wrinkled lips into a sly smile and lied benevolently with slow nods of his shaggy white head.

'We will talk about it tomorrow,' he promised.

'Then I should get to bed at once,' she decided, springing to her feet. 'May I have breakfast with you, Grandfather?'

Tiberius chuckled amiably.

'That's too much to ask of you, my sweet,' he protested. 'You must be very tired. And I have my breakfast at dawn.'

'I'll be with you!' announced Diana. She softly patted him on the head. 'Good night, Your Majesty.' Dropping to one knee, she bowed ceremoniously and rising retreated—still facing him—until she reached the door where she paused, puckered her smiling lips, and panto-mimed a kiss.

The aged Emperor of Rome was much pleased.

* * * * * *

It was high noon and the day was bright. Not for a long time had Tiberius enjoyed himself so fully. This high-spirited girl was renewing his interest in life. She had matured beyond belief since he had last seen her. He responded to her radiant vitality with an almost adoles-cent yearning. Had Diana hinted that she would like to have the Island of Capri, Tiberius would have handed it to her without pausing to deliberate.

After breakfast they had walked to the far east end of the en-chantingly lovely mall, Diana ecstatic, the Emperor bumbling along with short steps and shorter breaths, scraping the mosaic pavement with his sandal-heels. Yes, he panted, there was plenty of room at the far end of the row for a magnificent villa. Nothing, he declared, could ever obstruct this splendid view. He stopped, clutched at Diana's arm for steadiness, and pointed toward the northeast with a shaky cane. There would always be old Vesuvius to greet you in the morn-ing. 'And do you not see the sunlight glinting from the white roofs of Pompeii and Herculaneum? And across there, close at hand, is sleepy little Surrentum. You can sit at your window and see every-thing that is going on in Surrentum.'

Observing that the old man's legs were getting wobbly, Diana had suggested that they turn aside here and rest in the arbor that marked the eastern boundary of the new—and still unoccupied—Villa Quiri-nus. The Emperor slumped heavily into a rustic chair and mopped his perspiring brow, his thin, mottled hand trembling as if palsied. For some time they sat in silence, waiting for the old man to recuper-ate. His lean face was contorted and his jaw chopped convulsively.

'You have grown to be a beautiful woman, Diana!' he remarked, in a thin treble, after blandly invoicing her charms with the privileged eyes of eighty-two. 'You will probably be married one of these days.'

Diana's bright smile slowly faded and her heavy lashes fell. She shook her curly, blue-black head and drew what seemed a painful little sob through locked teeth. Tiberius snorted impatiently and pounded the pavement with his cane.

'Now what's the trouble?' he demanded. 'In love with the wrong man?'

'Yes.' Diana's face was sober and her reply was a mere whisper. 'I don't mind telling you, Grandfather,' she went on, with over-flowing eyes, 'I'm in love with Marcellus.'

'Well—why not? What's the matter with Marcellus?' The old man leaned forward to peer into her unhappy eyes. 'It would be a most excellent alliance,' he went on. 'There isn't a more honorable man in the Empire than Gallio. And you are fond of Lucia. By all means—marry Marcellus! What's to hinder?'

'Marcellus,' murmured Diana, hopelessly, 'has been sent far away—to be gone for years, perhaps. He has been put in command of the fort at Minoa.'

'Minoa!' yelled Tiberius, straightening his sagging spine with an indignant jerk. 'Minoa!' he shrilled—'that dirty, dried-up, pestilential, old rat-hole? Who ordered him to do that, I'd like to know?'

'Prince Gaius,' exploded Diana, swept with sudden anger.

'Gaius!' The Emperor pried himself up by his elbows, struggled to his feet, and slashed the air with his cane. His leaky old eyes were boiling. 'Gaius!' he shrieked. 'The misbegotten, drunken, dangerous fool! And what made him think he could do that to the son of Marcus Lucan Gallio? To Minoa—indeed! Well!—we'll see about that!' He clawed at Diana's arm. 'Come! Let us return to the villa! Gaius will hear from his Emperor!'

Leaning heavily on her, and wasting his waning strength on savage screams of anger, Tiberius shuffled along toward the Villa Jovis, pausing occasionally to shout long vituperations composed of such ingenious sacrileges and obscenities that Diana was more astounded than embarrassed. On several occasions she had witnessed the old man's grumpiness when annoyed. This was the first time she had seen him in one of his celebrated rages. It was commonly believed that the Emperor, thoroughly roused, went temporarily insane. There was a rumor—probably slanderous—that he had been known to bark like a dog; and bite, too.

Deaf to Diana's urgent entreaty that he should rest a little while before dictating the message to Gaius, the old man began howling for his chief scrivener while they were still trudging through the peristyle. A dozen dignified servants approached from all directions, making as if they would be of service, but keeping a discreet distance. Diana finally got the fuming Emperor as far as the atrium, where she dumped him onto a couch and into the solicitous hands of the Chamberlain; then scurried away to her room, where she flung herself down on her bed, with her face buried in the pillow, and laughed hysterically until she cried.

After a while, she repaired her face at the mirrow; and, slipping across the corridor, tapped gently at her mother's door. She pushed it open and peeped in. Paula Gallus stirred and sleepily opened one eye.

'Mother!' Diana crossed the room and sat down on the edge of the bed. 'What do you think?' she whispered, dramatically. 'He's going to bring Marcellus home!'

'Well,' said Paula, from a considerable distance, 'that's what you had planned to make him do; wasn't it?'

'Yes—but isn't it wonderful?' insisted Diana.

'It will be, when he has done it,' drawled Paula. 'You'd better stand over him—and see that he doesn't forget all about it.'

'Oh—he wouldn't forget! Not this time! Never was anyone so angry! Mother—you should have seen him! He was terrific!'

'I know,' yawned Paula. 'I've seen him.'

'Well—in spite of everything,' declared Diana, 'I think he's an old darling!'

'He's an old lunatic!' mumbled Paula.

Diana pressed her cheek against her mother's heart.

'Marcellus is coming back,' she murmured ecstatically. 'Gaius will be very angry to have his orders flouted—but he won't be able to do a thing about it; will he?' And when Paula did not immediately reply, Diana added, anxiously, 'Will he, Mother?'

'Not at present—no.' Paula's tone carried a hint of warning. 'But we must keep it in mind that Tiberius is a very old man, my dear. He shouts and stamps and slobbers on himself—and forgets, in an hour or two, what it was that had upset him. Besides, he is going to die, one of these days.'

'And then Gaius will be the Emperor?' Diana's voice was full of trouble.

'Nobody knows, dear.'

'But he hates Gaius! You should have heard him!'

'Yes—but that's not imperial power: that's just an angry old man's noise. Julia and her little clique will appoint the next Emperor. It may not be Gaius. They quarrel frequently.'

'I've often wondered whether Tiberius might not appoint Father. I know he likes him.'

'Not a chance in a thousand.' Paula waved aside the suggestion with a lanquid hand.

'But Father is a great man!' declared Diana, loyally.

Paula nodded and her lips curled into a grim smile.

'Great men do not become Emperors, Diana,' she remarked, bitterly. 'It's against the rules. Your father is not eligible. He has no talent for treachery. He is brave and just. And—besides—he is not epileptic. . . . Now—you had better run along and see that the letter gets safely started on its way.'

Diana took a few steps; and, returning slowly, sat down on the bed again. She smiled mysteriously.

'Let's have it,' encouraged Paula. 'It seems to be a secret—yes?'

'Mother—he is going to build a great villa for me!'

Paula grinned.

'Nonsense!' she muttered. 'By noon he won't remember that he

ever said such a thing. At least I sincerely hope he doesn't. Imagine
your living here!'

'Marcellus, too,' said Diana. 'He wants Marcellus to live here, I
think.'

'And do what?'

'We didn't talk about that.'

Paula ran her fingers gently over Diana's hand.

'Well—be sure you don't introduce the subject. Let him talk.
Promise him anything. He'll forget. You don't want a villa on Capri.
You don't want Marcellus living here in this hateful atmosphere. Hot-
headed as he is, you would be a widow in a week! Go, now, child!
Make him write that letter!'

*   *   *   *   *   *

Lucia's intuition told her that Marcellus was on board this galley.
For an hour—ever since its black prow had nosed around the bend,
and the three banks of long oars had pushed the heavy hull into full
view—she had been standing here alone in the pergola, leaning against
the balustrade, intently watching.

If *The Vestris* had experienced no delays, she could have arrived
in Ostia as early as the day before yesterday. Father had cautioned
them to be patient. Watched pots were slow to boil. It was a long
voyage from Joppa, and *The Vestris* had several ports to make on
the way home. But even Father, in spite of his sensible advice, was
restless as a caged fox; you could tell from the way he invented time-
killing errands for himself.

The whole villa was on edge with impatience to have Marcellus
safely home. Tertia was in a flutter of excitement for two good reasons:
she was eager for the return of Marcellus, of course; and she was
beside herself with anxiety to see Demetrius. It was a pity, thought
Lucia, that Demetrius had been so casual in his attitude toward Tertia.
Marcipor drifted about from room to room, making sure that everything was in first-class order. Mother had ordered gay new draperies
for Marcellus' suite. The only self-possessed person in the household
was Mother. She had wept happily when Diana came to tell them
what had happened; but was content to wait calmly.

As for Lucia, she had abandoned all pretence of patience. All yesterday afternoon, and again today, she had waited in the pergola, watching the river. Sometimes she would leave her post and try to stroll in
the rose arbors—now in their full June glory—but in a few minutes
her feet would turn back, of their own accord, to the observation
point at the east end of the pergola.

As the galley crept up the river, veering toward the docks, Lucia's
excitement increased. She knew now that her brother was one of the
passengers, probably fidgeting to be off. If her guess were correct, it
would not be long now until they would see him. He would hire a

carriage at the wharf and come fast. Wouldn't Father be surprised? He wasn't expecting Marcellus today; had gone over beyond the Aventine to look at a new riding horse: it was to be a homecoming present. Maybe Marcellus would be here when Father returned.

It was going to be a great pity that Diana would not be at home to welcome him. Tiresome old Tiberius had sent for her again, and there was nothing she could do but obey him.

'Will he keep on pestering her like that?' Lucia had wondered.

'She must not offend him,' Father had said, seriously. 'The old man is malicious enough to hand Marcellus over to the Prince, if Diana fails to humor him.' After a moment of bitter reflection, he had muttered, 'I am afraid the child is in an awkward—if not dangerous—position. And while we are not directly responsible for it, her predicament worries me.'

'But—the Emperor wouldn't harm Diana!' she had exclaimed. 'That old man?'

Father had growled deep in his throat.

'A Caesar,' he had snarled, contemptuously, 'is capable of great wickedness—up to and including his last gasp—though he should live a thousand years!'

'I don't believe you like the Emperor,' she had said, impishly, to cool him off, as she made for the door. He had grunted crossly—and grinned.

You could just see the hinder part of the galley now, as it slipped into its berth. Lucia had been on this tension for so long that she was ready to fly into bits. She couldn't wait here another instant! The servants might think it strange if she went alone to the entrance gate. But this was a special occasion. Returning to the house, she ran on through to the imposing portico, down the marble steps, and set off briskly on the long, shaded driveway that wound through the acacias and acanthuses and masses of flowering shrubbery. A few slaves, ending their day's work in the formal gardens, raised their eyes inquisitively. At a little distance from the ornate bronze gates, Lucia, flushed and nervous, sat down on a stone bench, resolved to hold herself together until the great moment.

After what seemed a very long time, a battered old public chariot, drawn by two well-lathered horses, turned in from the busy avenue. Beside the driver stood Demetrius, tall, tanned, and lean. He sighted her instantly, clutched the driver's arm, handed him a coin and dismissed him. Stepping down, he walked quickly toward her, and Lucia ran to meet him. His face, she observed, was grave, though his eyes had lighted as she impulsively gave him her hands.

'Demetrius!' she cried. 'Is anything wrong? Where is Marcellus?'

'There was no carriage at the wharf,' he explained. 'I came for a better conveyance.'

'Is my brother not well?' Still holding his hands, Lucia searched his eyes anxiously. He flinched a little from this inquisition, and his reply was evasive.

'No—my master is not—my master did not have a pleasant voyage.'

'Oh—that!' She smiled her relief. 'I thought my brother was a better sailor. Was he sick all the way?'

Demetrius nodded non-committally. It was plain to see he was holding something back. Lucia's eyes were troubled.

'Tell me, Demetrius!' she pleaded, huskily. 'What ails my brother?' There was a disturbingly long silence.

'The Tribune had a very unhappy experience, the day before we sailed.' Demetrius was speaking slowly, measuring his words. 'It is too long a story to tell you now, for my master is at the wharf awaiting me. He has been deeply depressed and is not yet fully recovered. He did not sleep well on the ship.'

'Stormy weather?' suggested Lucia.

'A smooth sea,' went on Demetrius, evenly. 'But my master did not sleep well; and he ate but little.'

'Was the food palatable?'

'No worse than food is on ships, but my master did not eat; and therefore he suffers of weakness. . . . May I go quickly now—and get the large carriage for him?'

'Demetrius—you are trying to spare me, I think.' Lucia challenged his eyes with a demand for the whole truth.

'Your brother,' said Demetrius, deliberately, 'is moody. He prefers not to talk much, but does not like to be left alone.'

'But he did want to come home; didn't he?' asked Lucia, wistfully.

'Your brother,' replied Demetrius, gloomily, 'does not want *anything.*' He glanced up the driveway, restlessly. 'Shall I go now?'

Lucia nodded, and Demetrius, saluting with his spear, turned to go. She moved forward and fell into step with him. He lagged to walk behind her. She slowed her pace. He stopped.

'Please precede me,' he suggested, gently. 'It is not well that a slave should walk beside his master's sister.'

'It is a stupid rule!' flushed Lucia.

'But—a *rule!*' Demetrius' impatience had sharpened his tone. Instantly he saw that he had offended her. Her cheeks were aflame and her eyes were swimming. 'I am sorry,' he murmured, contritely. 'I did not mean to hurt you.'

'It was my fault,' she admitted. Turning abruptly, she led the way with long, determined steps. After they had proceeded for a little way in silence, Lucia—her eyes straight ahead—declared bitterly, 'I hate this whole business of slavery!'

'I don't care much for it myself,' rejoined Demetrius, dryly.

It was the first time he had been amused for nearly two months. Half-turning suddenly, Lucia caught him wearing a broad grin. Her lips curved into a fleeting, reluctant smile. Squaring her shapely

shoulders, she quickened her swinging stride and marched on, Demetrius lengthening his steps as he followed, stirred by the rhythm
of her graceful carriage.

She paused where the driveway divided to serve the great house
and the stables. Demetrius stood at attention.

'Tell me truly,' she begged, in a tone that disposed of his slavery,
'is Marcellus' mind affected?'

Demetrius accepted his temporary freedom and spoke without constraint.

'Marcellus has had a severe shock. Perhaps he will improve, now
that he is back home. He will make an effort to show his interest,
I think. He has promised me that much. But you must not be startled
if he stops talking—in the middle of a remark—and seems to forget
what you were talking about. And then—after a long wait—he will
suddenly ask you a question—always the same question—' Demetrius
averted his eyes, and seemed unwilling to proceed further.

'What is the question?' insisted Lucia.

'He will say, "Were you out there?" '

'Out where?' she asked, frowning mystifiedly.

Demetrius shook his head and winced.

'I shall not try to explain that,' he said. 'But when he asks you if
you were out there, you are to say, "No!" Don't ask him, "Where?"
Just say, "No!" And then he will recover quickly, and seem relieved.
At least, that was the way the conversation went when we were on
The Vestris. Sometimes he would talk quite freely with the Captain
—almost as if nothing was the matter. Then he would suddenly lose
interest and retreat inside himself. Then he would inquire, "Where
you out there?" And Captain Fulvius would say, "No." Then Marcellus would be pleased, and say, "Of course—you weren't there. That
is good. You should be glad." '

'Did the Captain know what he was talking about?' inquired Lucia.

Demetrius nodded, rather grudgingly, she thought.

'Why can't you tell me?' Her tone was almost intimate.

'It's—it's a long story,' he stammered. 'Perhaps I may tell you—
sometime.'

She took a step nearer, and lowering her voice almost to a whisper,
asked, 'Were *you* "out there"?' He nodded reluctantly, avoiding her
eyes. Then, impetuously abandoning the last shred of reserve, he spoke
on terms of equality.

'Don't question him, Lucia. Treat him exactly as you have always
done. Talk to him about anything—but Jerusalem. Be careful not to
touch this sore spot. Maybe it will heal. I don't know. It's very deep—
and painful—this mental wound.'

Her cheeks had flushed a little. Demetrius had made full use of
the liberty she had given him: he had spoken her name. Well—why

not? Who had a better right? They all owed much to this devoted
slave.

'Thanks, Demetrius,' she said, gently. 'It was good of you to tell me
what to do.'

At that, he abruptly terminated his brief parole, snapped to a stiff,
military posture; looked through her without seeing her as he made a
ceremonious salute; turned—and marched away. Lucia stood for a
moment, indecisively, watching his dignified retreat with softened
eyes.

*   *   *   *   *   *

For the first hour after his arrival, it was difficult to reconcile Marcellus' behavior and his slave's warning. Parting from Demetrius, Lucia
had hurried upstairs with the appalling news, and before she had
finished devastating her mother with these sad tidings of her brother's
predicament, her father had returned. There was little to be said. They
were awed, stunned. It was as if they had learned of Marcellus'
death, and were waiting for his body to be brought home.

It was a happy surprise, therefore, when he breezed in with unusually affectionate greetings. True, he was alarmingly thin and his
face was haggard; but good food and plenty of rest (boomed Father,
confidently) would quickly restore him to full weight and vitality.
As for his mental condition, Demetrius' report had been wholly incorrect. What, indeed, had ailed the fellow—to frighten them with
the announcement that his master was moody and depressed? Quite
to the contrary, Marcellus had never been so animated!

Without pausing to change after his journey he had seemed de-
lightfully eager to talk. In Mother's private parlor, they had drawn
their chairs close together, at his suggestion; though Marcellus had
not sat down himself. He had paced about, like a caged animal, talking
rapidly with an almost boisterous exuberance, pausing to toy with
trifles on his mother's table, halting to peer out at the window, but
continuing to chatter about the ship, the ports of call, the aridity of
Gaza, the crude life at Minoa. Under normal conditions, the family
might have surmised that he had had too much wine. It wasn't like
Marcellus to talk so incessantly, or so fast. But they were glad enough
that it wasn't the other thing! He was excited over his homecoming;
that was all. They listened attentively, their eyes shining. They laughed
gaily at his occasional drolleries and cheered him on!

'Do sit down, boy!' Mother had urged, tenderly, at his first full
stop. 'You're tired. Don't wear yourself out.'

So—Marcellus had sat down, in the very middle of a stirring story
about the bandits who infested the old salt trail, and his voice had
become less strident. He continued talking, but more slowly, pausing
to grope for the right word. Presently his forced gaiety acknowledged
his fatigue, and he stopped—quite suddenly, too, as if he had been
interrupted. For an instant his widened eyes and concentrated ex-

pression made him appear to have seen or heard something that had
commanded his full attention. They watched him with silent curiosity,
their hearts beating hard.

'What is it, Marcellus?' asked Mother, trying to steady her voice.
'Would you like a drink of water?'

He tried unsuccessfully to smile, and almost imperceptibly shook
his head, as the brightness faded from his eyes. The room was very
quiet.

'Perhaps you had better lie down, my son,' suggested Father, trying hard to sound casual.

Marcellus seemed not to have heard that. For a little while his
breathing was laborious. His hands twitched, and he slowly clenched
them until the thin knuckles whitened. Then the seizure passed,
leaving him sagged and spiritless. He nervously rubbed his forehead
with the back of his hand. Then he slowly turned his pathetically
sad face toward his father, stared at him curiously, and drew a long,
shuddering sigh.

'Were you—were you—out there—sir?' he asked, weakly.

'No—my son.' It was the thin voice of an old, old man.

Marcellus made a self-deprecating little chuckle, and shook his head,
as if decrying his own foolishness. He glanced about with an attempted smile, vaguely questing their eyes for an opinion of his strange
behavior. He swallowed noisily.

'Of course, you weren't,' he said, disgusted with himself. 'You have
been here—all the time; haven't you?' Then he added, in a tired
voice, 'I think I should go to bed now, Mother.'

'I think so too,' said Mother, softly. She had made an earnest effort
not to let him see how seriously she had been affected, but at the
sight of his drooping head, she put both hands over her eyes and
sobbed. Marcellus looked toward her pleadingly, and sighed.

'Will you call Demetrius, Lucia?' he asked, wearily.

She stepped to the door, thinking to send Tertia, but it was unnecessary. Demetrius, who obviously had been waiting in the corridor,
just outside the door, entered noiselessly and assisted his master to
his feet.

'I'll see you—all—in the morning,' mumbled Marcellus. He leaned
heavily on his slave as they left the room. Lucia made a little moan
and slipped away quietly. The Senator bowed his head in his hands,
and was silent.

* * * * * *

Marcus Lucan Gallio had not made a quick and easy decision when
he resolved to have a confidential, man-to-man conference with Demetrius. The Senator punctiliously practiced the same sort of justice
in dealing with his slaves that he had ever proudly observed in his
relations with freedmen; but he also believed in firm discipline for
them. Sometimes it annoyed him when he observed a little gesture

of affection—almost a caress, indeed!—in Lucia's attitude toward
Tertia; and on a couple of occasions (though this was a long time
ago) he had had to remind his son that the way to have a good slave
was to help him keep his place.

Gallio had an immense respect for Marcellus' handsome and loyal
Corinthian. He would have trusted him anywhere and with anything,
but he had never broken over the inexorable line which he felt should
be drawn, straight and candid, between master and slave. It had now
come to pass that he must invite Demetrius to step across that social
boundary; for how else could he hope to get the full truth about the
circumstances which had made such sad havoc of his son's mind?

Two days had passed, Marcellus remaining in his room. Gallio had
gone up several times to see him, and had been warmly but shyly
welcomed. A disturbing constraint on Marcellus' part, a forced amiability, an involuntary shrinking away from a compassionate contact
less it inadvertently touch some painfully sensitive lesion—these
strange retreats, in pathetic combination with an obvious wish to
show a filial affection, constituted a baffling situation. Gallio didn't
know how to talk with Marcellus about it; feared he might say the
wrong thing. No—Demetrius had the key to it. He must make Demetrius talk. In the middle of the afternoon, he sent for him to come
to the library.

Demetrius entered and stood at attention before Gallio's desk.

'I wish to have a serious talk with you, Demetrius, about my son.
I am greatly disturbed. I shall be grateful to you for a full account
of whatever it is that distresses him.' The Senator pointed to the
chair opposite his desk. 'You may sit down, if you like. Perhaps you
will be more comfortable.'

'Thank you, sir,' said Demetrius, respectfully. 'I shall be more comfortable standing, if you please, sir.'

'As you choose,' said Gallio, a bit curtly. 'It occurred to me that
you might be able to speak more freely—more naturally—if you sat.'

'No, sir, thank you,' said Demetrius. 'I am not accustomed to sitting
in the presence of my betters. I can speak more naturally on my feet.'

'Sit down!' snapped Gallio. 'I don't want you towering over me,
answering questions in stiff monosyllables. This is a life-and-death
matter! I want you to tell me everything I ought to know—without
reserve!'

Demetrius laid his heavy, metal-studded, leather shield on the floor,
stood his spear against a pillar, and sat down.

'Now, then!' said Gallio. 'Let's have it! What ails my son?'

'My master was ordered to bring a detachment of legionaries to
Jerusalem. It was a custom, during the annual festival of the Jews,
for representations from the various Palestinian forts to assemble at
the Procurator's Insula, presumably to keep order, for the city was
crowded with all sorts.'

'Pontius Pilate is the Prefect of Jerusalem: is that not true?'

'Yes, sir. He is called the Procurator. There is another provincial governor residing in Jerusalem.'

'Ah—I remember. A vain fellow—Herod. A rascal!'

'Doubtless,' murmured Demetrius.

'Jealous of Pilate, I am told.'

'No one should be jealous of Pilate, sir. He permits the Temple to dictate to him. At least he did, in the case I must speak of.'

'The one that concerns my son?' Gallio leaned forward on his folded arms and prepared to listen attentively.

'May I inquire, sir, whether you ever heard of the Messiah?'

'No—what is that?'

'For hundreds of years the Jews have been expecting a great hero to arise and liberate them. He is their promised Messiah. On these yearly feast-weeks, the more fanatical among them are on the alert, thinking he may appear. Occasionally they have thought they had found the right man—but nothing much ever came of it. This time—' Demetrius paused, thoughtfully, stared out at the open window, and neglected to finish the sentence.

'There was a Jew from the Province of Galilee'—he continued— 'about my own age, I should think, though he was such an unusual person that he appeared almost independent of age—or time—'

'You saw him, then?'

'A great crowd of country people tried to persuade him that he was the Messiah; that he was their King. I saw that, sir. It happened the day we arrived.'

' "Tried to persuade him" you say.'

'He had no interest in it, at all, sir. It appears that he had been preaching, mostly in his own province, to vast throngs of people; a simple, harmless appeal for common honesty and kindness. He was not interested in the Government.'

'Probably advised them that the Government was bad,' surmised Gallio.

'I do not know, sir; but I think he could have done so without violating the truth.'

The crow's-feet about Gallio's eyes deepened a little.

'I gather that you thought the Government was bad, Demetrius.'

'Yes, sir.'

'Perhaps you think all governments are bad.'

'I am not acquainted with all of them, sir,' parried Demetrius.

'Well,' observed Gallio, 'they're all alike.'

'That is regrettable,' said Demetrius, soberly.

'So—then—the young Galilean repudiated kingship—and got into trouble, I suppose, with his admirers—'

'And the Government, too. The rich Jews, fearing his influence in the country, insisted on having him tried for treason. Pilate, knowing he had done no wrong, made an effort to acquit him. But they would have him condemned. Against his will, Pilate sentenced him to death.' Demetrius hesitated. 'Sentenced him to be crucified,' he went on, in a low tone. 'The Commander of the fort at Minoa was ordered to conduct the execution.'

'Marcellus? Horrible!'

'Yes, sir. He fortunately was blind drunk when he did it. A seasoned Centurion, of the Minoa staff, had seen to that. But he was clear enough to realize that he was crucifying an innocent man—and—well, as you see, sir, he didn't get over it. He dismisses it from his mind for a while—and then it all sweeps over him again, like a bad dream. He sees the whole thing—so vividly that it amounts to acute pain! It is so real to him, sir, that he thinks everybody else must have known something about it; and he asks them if they do—and then he is ashamed that he asked.'

Gallio's eyes widened with sudden understanding.

'Ah!' he exclaimed. ' "Were you out there?" So—that's it!'

'That is it, sir; but not quite all.' Demetrius' eyes traveled to the window and for a moment he sat tapping his finger-tips together as if uncertain how to proceed. Then he faced the Senator squarely and went on. 'Before I tell you the rest of it, sir, I should like to say that I am not a superstitious person. I have not believed in miracles. I am aware that you have no faith in such things, and you may find it very hard to accept what I must now tell you.'

'Say on, Demetrius!' said Gallio, thumping his desk impatiently.

'This Jesus of Galilee wore a simple, brown, homespun Robe to the cross. They stripped if off and flung it on the ground. While he hung there, dying, my master and a few other officers sat near-by playing with dice. One took up this Robe and they cast for it. My master won it. Later in the evening, there was a banquet at the Insula. Everyone had been drinking to excess. A Centurion urged my master to put on the Robe.'

'Shocking idea!' grumbled Gallio. 'Did he do it?'

'He did it—quite unwillingly. He had been very far gone in wine, in the afternoon, but was now steadied. I think he might have recovered from the crucifixion horror if it had not been for the Robe. He put it on—*and he has never been the same since!*'

'You think the Robe is haunted, I suppose.' Gallio's tone was almost contemptuous.

'I think something happened to my master when he put it on. He tore it off quickly, and ordered me to destroy it.'

'Very sensible! A poor keepsake!'

'I still have it, sir.'

'You disobeyed him?'

Demetrius nodded.

'My master was not himself when he gave that order. I have occasionally disobeyed him when I felt that the command was not to his best interest. And now I am glad I kept the Robe. If it was the cause of his derangement, it might become the instrument of his recovery.'

'Absurd!' expostulated Gallio. 'I forbid you to let him see it again!'

Demetrius sat silent while Gallio, rising angrily, paced the floor. Presently he stopped short, rubbed his jaw reflectively, and inquired:

'Just *how* do you think this Robe might be used to restore my son's mind?'

'I do not know, sir,' Demetrius confessed. 'I have thought about it a great deal. No plan has suggested itself.' He rose to his feet and met the Senator's eyes directly. 'It has occurred to me that we might go away for a while. If we were alone, an occasion might arise. He is quite on the defensive here. He is confused and ashamed of his mental condition. Besides—there is something else weighing heavily on his mind. The daughter of Legate Gallus will return soon. She will expect my master to call on her, and he is worrying about this meeting. He does not want her to see him in his present state.'

'I can understand that,' said Gallio. 'Perhaps you are right. Where do you think he should go?'

'Is it not customary for a cultured young man to spend some time in Athens? Should he decide to go there—either to attend lectures or practice some of their arts—no questions would be asked. Your son has always been interested in sculpture. My belief is that it will be difficult to do very much for him while he remains here. He should not be confined to the house; yet he knows he is in no condition to see his friends. The word may get about that something is wrong. This would be an embarrassment for him—and the family. If it is your wish, sir, I shall try to persuade him to go to Athens. I do not think it will require much urging. He is very unhappy.'

'Yes—I know,' muttered Gallio, half to himself.

'He is so unhappy'—Demetrius lowered his voice to a tone of intimate confidence—'that I fear for his safety. If he remains here, Diana may not find him alive when she returns.'

'You mean—Marcellus might destroy himself rather than face her?'

'Why not? It's a serious matter with him.'

'Have you any reason to believe that he has been contemplating suicide?'

Demetrius was slow about replying. Drawing a silver-handled dagger from the breast of his tunic, he tapped its keen blade against the palm of his hand. Gallio recognized the weapon as the property of Marcellus.

'I think he has been toying with the idea, sir,' said Demetrius.

'You took this from him?'

Demetrius nodded.

'He thinks he lost it on the boat.'

Gallio sighed deeply; and, returning to his desk, he sat down, drew out a sheet of papyrus and a stylus, and began writing rapidly in large letters. Finishing, he affixed his seal.

'Take my son to Athens, Demetrius, and help him recover his mind. But no man should ask a slave to accept such a responsibility.' He handed the document to Demetrius. 'This is your certificate of manumission. You are a free man.'

Demetrius stared at the writing in silence. It was hard for him to realize its full significance. Free! Free as Gallio! He was his own man! Now he could speak—even to Lucia—as a freedman! He was conscious of Gallio's eyes studying him with interest as if attempting to read his thoughts. After a long moment, he slowly shook his head and returned the document to the Senator.

'I appreciate your generosity, sir,' he said, in an unsteady voice. 'In any other circumstance, I should be overjoyed to accept it. Liberty means a great deal to any man. But I think we would be making a mistake to alter the relationship between my master and his slave.'

'Would you throw away your chance to be free'—demanded Gallio, huskily—'in order to help my son?'

'My freedom, sir, would be worthless to me—if I accepted it at the peril of Marcellus' recovery.'

'You are a brave fellow!' Gallio rose and walked across the room to his huge bronze strong-box. Opening a drawer, he deposited the certificate of Demetrius' release from bondage. 'Whenever you ask for it,' he declared, 'it will be here, waiting for you.' He was extending his hand; but Demetrius, pretending not to have seen the gesture, quickly raised his spear-shaft to his forehead in a stiff salute.

'May I go now, sir?' he asked, in the customary tone of servitude. Gallio bowed respectfully—as to a social equal.

* * * * * *

No one in the household had been more distressed than Marcipor, who did not feel at liberty to ask questions of anybody but Demetrius, and Demetrius' time had been fully occupied. All day he had paced about restlessly, wondering what manner of tragedy had befallen Marcellus whom he idolized.

When the door of the library opened, after the lengthy interview, Marcipor, waiting impatiently in the atrium, came forward to meet Demetrius. They clasped hands silently and moved away together into an alcove.

'What is it all about, Demetrius?' asked Marcipor, in a guarded tone. 'Is it something you can't tell me?'

Demetrius laid a hand on the older Corinthian's shoulder and drew him closer.

'It is something I *must* tell you,' he murmured. 'Come to my room at midnight. I cannot tarry now. I must go back to him.'

After the villa was quiet and Demetrius was assured that Marcellus was asleep, he retired to his adjacent bedchamber. Presently there was a light tap on the door, and Marcipor entered. They drew their chairs close and talked in hushed voices until the birds began to stir in the pale blue light of the oncoming dawn. It was a long, strange story that Demetrius had to tell. Marcipor wanted to see the Robe. Demetrius handed it to him, and he examined it curiously.

'But *you* don't believe there is some peculiar power in this garment; do you?' asked Marcipor.

'I don't know,' admitted Demetrius. 'If I said, "Yes—I do believe that," you would think I was going crazy; and if I feared I was crazy, I wouldn't be a fit person to look after Marcellus, who unquestionably *is* crazy—and needs my care. So—I think I had better say that there's nothing in this Robe that you don't put into it yourself—out of your own imagination. As for me—I saw this man, and—well—that makes all the difference. He was not an ordinary person, Marcipor. I could be easily persuaded that he was divine.'

'That seems an odd thing for you to say, Demetrius,' disapproved Marcipor, studying his face anxiously. 'You're the last man I would have picked for it.' He stood up, and held the Robe out at arm's length. 'Do you care if I put it on?'

'No—he wouldn't care—if you put it on,' said Demetrius.

'Who do you mean—wouldn't care?' Marcipor's face was puzzled. 'Marcellus?'

'No—the man who owned it. He didn't object to my having it, and you are as honest as I am.'

'By the gods, Demetrius,' muttered Marcipor. 'I believe you *are* a bit touched by all this grim business. How do you know he didn't object to your having his Robe? That's foolish talk!'

'Well—be it foolish or not—when I touch this Robe it—it does something to me,' stammered Demetrius. 'If I am tired, it rests me. If I am dejected, it revives my spirits. If I am rebellious over my slavery, it reconciles me. I suppose that is because—when I handle his Robe—I remember his strength—and courage. Put it on—if you want to, Marcipor. Here—let me hold it for you.'

Marcipor slipped his long arms into the sleeves, and sat down.

'It *is* strangely warm,' he said. 'My imagination, I suppose. You have told me of his deep concern for the welfare of all other people; and—quite naturally—his—Robe—' Marcipor's groping words slowed to a stop, and he gave Demetrius a perplexed wisp of a smile.

'I'm not as crazy as I look; eh?' grinned Demetrius.

'What *is* it?' asked Marcipor, in a husky whisper.

'Well—whatever it *is*,' said Demetrius, it's *there!*'

'Peace?' queried Marcipor, half to himself.

'And confidence,' added Demetrius.

'And—one need not worry—for everything—will come out—all right.'

Chapter VIII

AT SUNSET on the last day of the month which Julius Caesar—revising the calendar—had named for himself, Marcellus and his slave sighted the Parthenon from a decrepit vehicle that rated a place in the Athenian Museum of Antiquities. It was with mingled feelings that Demetrius renewed acquaintance with his native land.

Had his business in the Grecian capital been more urgent, and had he been of normal mind, the erstwhile Legate of the Legion at Minoa might have fretted over the inexcusable tedium of their voyage.

He and Demetrius had embarked on the Greek ship *Clytia* for the sole reason that they wanted to leave Rome without delay and *The Clytia's* sailing was immediate. In no other respect was this boat to be recommended. Primarily a cargo vessel built expressly for wheat shipments to the Imperial City, the battered old hulk usually returned to Greece in ballast, except for certain trivial consignments of furniture and other household gear for Roman envoys in the provinces.

There were no private accommodations for passengers. All nine of them shared the same cabin. There was only one deck. At the stern a primitive kitchen, open to the sky, was at the disposal of fare-paying voyagers who were expected to cook their own meals. *The Clytia* had the raw materials for sale at a nice profit.

Almost too handy to the kitchen and adjacent dining-table a half-dozen not very tidy pens confined a number of unhappy calves and sheep, and a large crate of dilapidated fowls. Upon embarkation there had also been a few pigs, but a Jewish merchant from Cytherea had bought them, on the second day out, and had unceremoniously offered them to Neptune—with his unflattering compliments, for he was not a good sailor.

Amidship in the vicinity of *The Clytia's* solitary mast a constricted area of deck space, bounded by a square of inhospitable wooden benches, served as promenade and recreation center. Beside the mast a narrow hatchway descended steeply into the common cabin which was lighted and ventilated by six diminutive ports. Upon the slightest hint of a fresh breeze these prudent little ports were closed. *The Clytia* made no attempt to pamper her passengers. Indeed, it was doubtful whether any other craft plying between Ostia and Piraeus was equipped to offer so comprehensive an assortment of discomforts.

The grimy old ship's only grace was her love of leisure. She called everywhere and taried long; three days and nights, for example, in unimportant Corfu where she had only to unload a bin of silica and take on a bale of camel's-hair shawls; four whole days in Argostoli where she replenished her water-casks, discharged a grateful passenger, and bought a crate of lemons. She even ambled all the way down to Crete, for no better cause than to leave three blocks of Carrara marble and acquire a case of reeking bull-hides for conversion into shields. While in port, one of her frowsy old hawsers parted, permitting *The Clytia* to stave a galley that lay alongside; and another week had passed before everybody was satisfied about that and clearance was ordered for the next lap of the interminable cruise.

Had Marcellus been mentally well, he would surely have found these delays and discomforts insupportable. In his present mood of apathetic detachment, he endured his experiences with such effortless fortitude that Demetrius' anxiety about him mounted to alarm. Marcellus had no natural talent for bearing calmly with annoyances, however trivial; and it worried the Corinthian to see his high-spirited master growing daily more and more insensitive to his wretched environment. As for himself, Demetrius was so exasperated by all this boredom and drudgery that he was ready to jump out of his skin.

Vainly he tried to kindle a spark of interest in the wool-gathering mind of Marcellus. The Senator had provided his son with a small but carefully selected library; classics, mostly, and Demetrius had tactfully endeavored to make him read; but without success.

For the better part of every fair day, Marcellus would sit silently staring at the water. Immediately after breakfast he would pick his way forward through the clutter that littered the deck; and, seating himself on a coil of anchor-cable near the prow, would remain immobile with his elbows on his knees and his chin in his hands, gazing dully out to sea. Demetrius would give him time to get himself located, and then he too would saunter forward with a few scrolls under his arm and sprawl at full length on a battened hatch close by. Sometimes he would read a paragraph or two aloud and ask a question. On these occasions, Marcellus would sluggishly return from a remote distance to make a laconic reply, but it was obvious that he preferred not to be molested.

Although Demetrius' chief concern was to beguile his master's roving mind, he himself was finding food for reflection. Never before had he found opportunity for so much uninterrupted reading. He was particularly absorbed by the writings of Lucretius. Here, he thought, was a wise man.

'Ever read Lucretius, sir?' he asked, one afternoon, after an hour's silence between them.

Marcellus slowly turned his head and deliberated the question.

'Indifferently,' he replied, at length.

'Lucretius thinks it is the fear of death that makes men miserable,' went on Demetrius. 'He's for abolishing that fear.'

'A good idea,' agreed Marcellus, languidly. After a long wait, he queried, 'How does he propose to do it?'

'By assuming that there is no future life,' explained Demetrius.

'That would do it,' drawled Marcellus—'provided the assumption would stay where you had put it.'

'You mean, sir, that the assumption might drag its anchor in a gale?'

Marcellus smiled wanly at the seagoing metaphor, and nodded. After a meditative interval, he said:

'For some men, Demetrius, the fear of death might be palliated by the belief that nothing more dreadful could possibly happen to them than had already happened—in their present existence. Perhaps Lucretius has no warrant for saying that all men fear death. Some have even sought death. As for me—I am not conscious of that fear; let death bring what it will. . . . But does Lucretius have aught to say to the man who fears life?'

Demetrius was sorry he had introduced the conversation, but he felt he should not abandon it abruptly; assuredly not at this dismaying juncture.

'Lucretius concedes that all life is difficult, but becoming less so as men evolve from savagery to civilization.' Demetrius tried to make this observation sound optimistic. Marcellus chuckled bitterly.

'"As men evolve from savagery," eh! What makes him think men are evolving from savagery?' He had an impatient gesture, throwing the idea away with a toss of his hand. 'Lucretius knew very little about what was going on in the world. Lived like a mole in a burrow. Lived on his own fat like a bear in winter. Went wrong in his head at forty, and died. "Evolving from savagery"? Nonsense! Nothing that ever went on in the jungle can compare with bestiality of our life today!' Marcellus' voice had mounted from a monologic mutter to a high-tensioned harangue. '"Evolving from savagery"!' he shouted. 'You know better than that! *You were out there!*'

Demetrius nodded soberly.

'It was very sad,' he said, 'but I think you have reproached yourself too much, sir. You had no alternative.'

Marcellus had retreated into his accustomed lethargy, but he suddenly roused, clenching his fists.

'That's a lie, Demetrius, and you know it! There *was* an alternative! I could have set the Galilean free! I had enough of those tough fellows from Minoa with me to have dispersed that mob!'

'Pilate would have court-martialed you, sir. It might have cost you your life!'

'My life!' shouted Marcellus. 'It *did* cost me my life! Far better to have lost it honorably!'

'Well,' soothed Demetrius, gently, 'we should try to forget about it now. In Athens you can divert your mind, sir. Are you not looking forward with some pleasure to your studies there?'

There was no reply. Marcellus had turned his back and was again staring at the sea.

On another day, Demetrius—imprudently, he felt afterward—ventured to engage his moody master again in serious talk.

'Lucretius says here that our belief that the gods are concerned with our human affairs has been the source of nothing but unhappiness to mankind.'

'Of course,' muttered Marcellus—'and he was a fool for believing that the gods exist, at all,' After *The Clytia* had swayed to and fro sleepily for a couple of stadia, he mumbled, 'Lucretius was crazy. He knew too much about the unknowable. He sat alone—and thought—and thought—until he lost his mind. . . . That's what I'm doing, Demetrius.'

*　　*　　*　　*　　*　　*

In a less perturbed state of mind, Marcellus—thoroughly fatigued by the long journey—would have been gaily excited over the welcome he received at the hands of his Athenian host, though this warm reception was not altogether unexpected.

When Marcus Lucan Gallio was in his early twenties, he had spent a summer in Athens, studying at the famous old Academy of Hipparchus, and lodging in the exclusive House of Eupolis which had been conducted by one family for five generations. Old Georgias Eupolis, his host, treated the patrons of his establishment as personal guests. You had to be properly vouched for if you sought accommodations there; but having been reliably introduced, nothing was too good for you.

The cool hauteur of the House of Eupolis in its attitude toward applicants was not mere snobbery. Athens was always filled with strangers. The city had more than a hundred inns, and all but a half-dozen of them were notorious. The typical tavern-keeper was a panderer, a thief, and an all-around rascal; and, for the most part, his clients were of the same feather. The Athenian inn that hoped to maintain a reputation for decency had to be critical of its registrants.

Apparently young Gallio had made a favorable impression, for when he left the House of Eupolis old Georgias had broken a silver drachma in two; and, handing one half to Marcus, had attached a little tablet of memoranda to the other which he had put away for safe-keeping.

'Whoever presents your piece of that drachma, my son,' Georgias had said, 'will be welcome here. You will not lose it, please.'

Arriving now at dusk in the shaded courtyard of the fine old hostelry, Marcellus had silently handed the broken coin to the churlish porter who had stepped out of the shadow to question them. Immediately the slave's behavior had changed from surly challenge to alert deference. Bowing and scraping he had made haste to carry the little talisman to his master. In a few moments the genial proprietor—a well-groomed man of forty—had come down the stone steps of the vine-clad portico, offering a smile and outstretched hands. Marcellus had stepped out of the antiquated chariot, announcing that he was the son of Gallio.

'And how are you addressed, sir?' asked the innkeeper.

'I am a Tribune. My name is Marcellus.'

'Your father is well remembered here, Tribune Marcellus. I hope he is alive and well.'

'He is, thank you. Senator Gallio sends his greetings to your house. Though it was a very long time ago, my father hopes his message of affection for Georgias may still be delivered.'

'Alas! My venerable father has been gone these ten years. But in his name, I give you welcome. My name is Dion. The House of Eupolis is yours. Come in! I can see you are weary.'

He turned to Demetrius.

'The porter will help you with your burdens, and show you where you are to sleep.'

'I wish my slave to share my own quarters,' put in Marcellus.

'It is not customary with us,' said Dion, a bit coolly.

'It is with me,' said Marcellus. 'I have been subjected lately to considerable hardship,' he explained, 'and I am not well. I do not wish to be alone. Demetrius will lodge with me.'

Dion, after a momentary debate with himself, gave a shrug of reluctant consent, and signed to Marcellus to precede him into the house.

'You will be responsible for his conduct,' he said, crisply, as they mounted the steps.

'Dion,' said Marcellus, pausing at the doorway, 'had this Corinthian his freedom, he would appear at an advantage in any well-bred company. He has been gently brought up; is a person of culture, and brave withal. The House of Eupolis will come to no dishonor on his account.'

The well-worn appointments of the spacious andronitis, into which entrance was had directly from the front door, offered a substantial, homelike comfort.

'If you will be seated, Marcellus,' advised Dion, recovering his geniality, 'I shall find the other members of my family. Then—because you are tired—I shall show you to your rooms. Will you be with us long?'

Marcellus lifted an indecisive hand.

'For some time, I think,' he said. 'Three months; four; six: I do not know. I want quiet. Two bedchambers, a small parlor, and a studio. I might want to amuse myself with some modeling.' Dion said he understood, and would be able to provide a suitable suite.

'And you will face the garden,' he said, as he moved toward the stairs. 'We have some exceptionally fine roses, this year.'

Demetrius entered as Dion disappeared and came to the chair where Marcellus sat.

'Have you learned, sir, where we are to go?' he asked.

'He will tell us. Remain here until he comes,' said Marcellus, wearily.

Presently they appeared, and he rose to meet them; Dion's comely wife, Phoebe, who, having learned the identity of their guest, was genuinely cordial; and Ino, Dion's widowed elder sister, who thought she saw in Marcellus a strong resemblance to the young man she had admired so much.

'Once we thought,' said Dion, with a teasing smile for his sister, 'that something might come of it.'

'But we Greeks are never comfortable anywhere else,' explained Ino, which made Marcellus wonder if their friendship hadn't been serious.

No one had paid any attention to Demetrius, which was entirely natural, for Dion had probably advised the family that Marcellus was accompanied by his slave.

At the first pause in the conversation, Ino turned to him inquiring if he wasn't a Greek. Demetrius bowed a respectful affirmative.

'Where?' inquired Ino.

'Corinth.'

'You have been in Athens before?'

'Once.'

'Do you read?'

'Sometimes.'

Ino laughed a little. Glancing toward her brother, she was aware that he disapproved of this talk. So did Marcellus, she noticed. Demetrius retreated a step and straightened to a sentry's posture. There was a momentary constraint before general conversation was resumed.

While they talked, a tall, strikingly beautiful girl sauntered in through the front door, apparently having just arrived from without the grounds, for she wore an elaborately fringed and tasseled pink himation, drawn about her so tightly that it accented her graceful figure. Her mother reached out an affectionate hand as she came into the circle.

'Our daughter, Theodosia,' she said. 'My child, our guest is Marcellus, the son of Marcus Gallio, of whom you have often heard your father speak.'

Theodosia gave him a bright smile. Then her dark, appraising eyes drifted over his shoulder and surveyed Demetrius with interest. He met her look of inquiry with what was meant to be a frown. This only added to Theodosia's curiosity. Obviously she was wondering why no one was inclined to introduce him.

It was an awkward moment. Marcellus did not want to hurt Demetrius. He felt it would be cruel to remark, casually, 'That man is my slave.' He heartily wished afterward that he had done so, instead of merely trying to be humane.

'This is Demetrius,' he said.

Theodosia took a step forward, looked up into Demetrius' face, and gave him a slow smile that approved of him first with her candid eyes and then with pouting lips. Demetrius gravely bowed with stiff dignity. Theodosia's eyes were puzzled. Then, after a little hesitation— for unmarried women were not accustomed to shaking hands with men, unless they were close relatives—she offered him her hand. Demetrius stared straight ahead and pretended not to see it.

'He's a slave,' muttered her father.

'Oh,' said Theodosia. 'I didn't know.' Then she looked up into Demetrius' eyes again. He met her look, this time, curiously. 'I'm sorry,' she murmured. After an instant she stammered in a tone that was almost intimate, 'It is too bad—that we have to—to be this way— I think. I hope we have not—I didn't mean—' She floundered to a stop as Demetrius, with an understanding smile, nodded that it was all right, and she wasn't to fret about it.

'We will show you to your suite now,' said Dion, abruptly.

Marcellus bowed to the women and followed his host, Demetrius marching stiffly behind him. Theodosia stared after them until they disappeared. Then she gave a quick little sigh and turned a self-defensive smile on her aunt.

'Forget it, child,' murmured Ino, sensibly. 'How could you know he was a slave; certainly wasn't dressed like one; certainly didn't look like one. And we don't have slaves standing about in here.'

'Well—it shouldn't have happened,' said Phoebe, crossly. 'You'll have to be careful now. If he takes any advantage of this, you must snub him—properly!'

'Wasn't he snubbed—properly?' wondered Theodosia.

'With words, perhaps,' remarked Aunt Ino, with a knowing grin.

* * * * * *

After a week, Demetrius, who had counted heavily upon this sojourn in Athens to relieve his master's deep dejection, began to lose heart.

Upon their arrival at the House of Eupolis, Marcellus had been welcomed so warmly—and had responded to these amenities so gratefully—that Demetrius felt they had already gone a long way toward solving the distressing problem.

The new environment was perfect. Their sunny rooms on the ground floor looked out upon a gay flower-garden. In their stone-flagged little peristyle, comfortable chairs extended an invitation to quiet reading. Surely no one at all interested in sculpture could have asked for a better opportunity than the studio afforded.

But it was of no use. Marcellus' melancholy was too heavy to be lifted. He was not interested in Demetrius' suggestion that they visit the Acropolis or Mars' Hill or some of the celebrated galleries.

'How about strolling down to the agora?' Demetrius had pleaded, on the second morning. 'It's always interesting to see the country people marketing their produce.'

'Why don't you go?' countered Marcellus.

'I do not like to leave you alone, sir.'

'That's true,' nodded Marcellus. 'I dislike being alone.'

He wouldn't even go to see the Temple of Heracles, directly across the street, within a boy's arrow of where he sat slowly examining his fingers. Demetrius expected that he would surely want to show some civility to the Eupolis family. Dion had called twice, frankly perplexed to find his guest so preoccupied and taciturn. Theodosia had appeared, one morning, at the far end of the garden; and Marcellus, observing her, had come in from the peristyle, apparently to avoid speaking to her.

Demetrius thought he knew what was keeping Marcellus away from the Eupolis family. He never could tell when one of these mysterious seizures would arrive to grip him until the sweat streamed down his face, in the midst of which he would stun somebody with the incomprehensible query, 'Were you out there?' Not much wonder he didn't care to have a friendly chat with Theodosia.

True, it was not absolutely necessary for Marcellus to make further connections with his host's family. Meals were sent over to their suite. Household slaves kept their rooms in order. Demetrius had practically nothing to do but wait—and keep a watchful but not too solicitous eye on his master. It was very trying, and he was bored almost to death.

On the morning of the eighth day, he resolved to do something about it.

'If you are not quite ready to do any modeling, sir,' he began, 'would you object if I amused myself with some experiments in clay?'

'Not at all,' mumbled Marcellus. 'I know this must be very tiresome for you. By all means, get the clay.'

So—that afternoon, Demetrius dragged the tall, stout modeling-table into the center of the studio and began some awkward attempts to mould a little statuette. After a while, Marcellus came in from his perpetual stupor in the peristyle and sat down in the corner to watch. Presently he chuckled. It was not a pleasantly mirthful chuckle, but ever so much better than none. Realizing that his early adventure in modeling was at least affording some wholesome entertainment, Demetrius persisted soberly in the production of a bust that would have made a dog laugh.

'Let me show you.' Marcellus came over to the table and took up the clay. 'To begin with, it's too dry,' he said, with something like critical interest. 'Get some water. If you're going to do this at all, you may as well give yourself a chance.'

Now, thought Demetrius, we have solved our problem! He was so happy he could hardly keep his joy out of his face, but he knew that Marcellus would resent any felicitations. All afternoon they worked together; rather, Marcellus worked, and Demetrius watched. That evening Marcellus ate his supper with relish and went early to bed.

After breakfast the next morning, it delighted Demetrius to see his master stroll into the studio. He thought he would leave him alone. Perhaps it would be better for him to work without any distraction.

In a half-hour, Marcellus trudged out to the peristyly and sat down. He was pale. His forehead was beaded with perspiration. His hands were trembling. Demetrius turned away with a deep sigh. That night he decided to do the thing he had resolved to do if all other expedients failed. It would be drastic treatment. In Marcellus' mental condition, it might indeed be the one tragic move that would put him definitely over the border line. But he couldn't go on this way! It was worth a trial.

After Marcellus had retired, Demetrius went over to the kitchen and asked Glycon, the steward, whether he could tell him the name of a first-class weaver: he wanted to have a garment mended for his master. Glycon was prompt with the information. Of course! A skillful weaver? Who but old Benjamin? That would be down near the Theater of Dionysus. Anybody could tell you, once you got to the theater.

'Benjamin sounds like a Jew,' remarked Demetrius.

'So he is,' nodded Glycon, 'and a fine old man; a scholar, they say.' Glycon laughed. 'There's one Jew not interested in getting rich. I've heard it said that if Benjamin doesn't like your looks he won't do business with you.'

'Perhaps he wouldn't care to talk with a slave,' wondered Demetrius.

'Oh—that wouldn't matter to Benjamin,' Glycon declared. 'Why should it? Haven't his own people rattled plenty of chains?'

*   *   *   *   *   *

All the next day until mid-afternoon, Marcellus sat slumped in his big chair outside the doorway, staring dully at the garden. In the adjacent studio, Demetrius disinterestedly toyed with the soft clay, listening for any movement in the little peristyle. Twice he had gone out, with an assumption of cheerfulness, to ask questions which he thought might stir his moody master's curiosity about his absurd attempts at modeling; but there was no response.

The situation had now become so desperate that Demetrius felt it was high time to make the dangerous experiment which—if everything else failed—he had resolved to try. His heart beat rapidly as he turned away from the table and went to his own room, and his hands were trembling as he reached into the depths of the large sail-cloth bag in which the cherished Galilean garment had been stowed.

It had been many weeks since he had seen it himself. He had had no privacy on *The Clytia*, and the enchanted Robe that had so profoundly affected Marcellus' mind had not been unpacked since they had left Rome.

Sitting down on the edge of his couch, Demetrius reverently unfolded it across his kness. Again he had this strange sensation of tranquillity that had come to him when he had handled the Robe in Jerusalem. It was a peculiar sort of calmness; not the calmness of inertia or indifference, but the calmness of self-containment. He was stilled—but strengthened.

There had never been any room in his mind for superstition. He had always disdained the thought that any sort of power could be resident in an inanimate object. People who believed in the magical qualities of insensate things were either out-and-out fools, or had got themselves into an emotional state where they were the easy victims of their own inflamed imagination. He had no patience with otherwise sensible men who carried lucky stones in their pockets. It had comforted him to feel that although he was a slave his mind was not in bondage.

Well—be all that as it might—the solid fact remained that when he laid his hands upon the Galilean's Robe, his agitation ceased. His nervous anxiety vanished. After the previous occasion when he had sensed this, he had told himself that the extraordinary experience could be accounted for on the most practical, common-sense terms. This Robe had been worn by a man of immense courage; effortless, inherent, built-in, automatic courage! Demetrius had seen this Jesus on trial, serene and self-assured with the whole world arrayed against him, with death staring him in the face, and not one protesting friend in sight. Was it not natural that his Robe should become a symbol of fortitude?

With far too much time on his hands during these recent weeks, Demetrius had deliberated upon this phenomenon until he had arrived at the reasonable explanation of his own attitude toward the thorn-torn garment: it was a symbol of moral strength, just as his mother's ring was a symbol of her tender affection.

But now!—with the Robe in his suddenly steadied hands—he wasn't so sure about the soundness of his theory. There was a power clinging to this homespun Galilean Robe which no cool rational argument was fit to cope with. Indeed, it seemed rather impudent to attempt an analysis of its claims upon his emotions.

Folding the Robe across his arm, Demetrius walked confidently to the open door. Marcellus slowly turned his head with a listless expression of inquiry. Then his eyes gradually widened with terror, his face a contorted mask of amazement and alarm. He swallowed convulsively and slowly bent backward over the broad arm of his chair, recoiling from the thing that had destroyed his peace.

'I have learned of a good weaver, sir,' said Demetrius, calmly. 'If you have no objections, I shall have him mend this Robe.'

'I told you'—Marcellus' dry throat drained the life out of his husky tone—'I ordered you—to destroy—that thing!' His voice rose, thin and shrill. 'Take it away! Burn it! Bury the ashes!' Pulling himself to his feet, he staggered to the corner of the peristyle, with the feeble steps of an invalid; and, hooking an arm around the pillar, he cried: 'I had not thought this of you, Demetrius! You have known the nature of my distress! And now—you come coolly confronting me with this torturing reminder; this haunted thing! I tell you—you have gone too far with your callous disobedience! I had always treated you as a friend—you who were my slave. I am finished with you! I shall sell you—in the market-place!' Thoroughly spent with rage, Marcellus slumped down upon the stone bench. 'Leave me,' he muttered, hoarsely. 'I can bear no more! Please go away!'

Demetrius slowly and silently withdrew into the house, shaking his head. His experiment had failed. It had been exactly the wrong thing to do. The patient, wearisome game of restoring Marcellus was now lost. Indeed, he was ever so much worse off; quite out of reach.

Returning to his own small bedchamber, Demetrius sat down, with the Robe still clutched tightly in his arms, and wondered what should be the next step to take. Curiously enough, Marcellus' complete breakdown had not upset him: he was unspeakably sorry, but self-controlled. The hysterical threat of being sold in the agora did not disturb him. Marcellus would not do that. Nor was he going to permit himself to be offended by the savagery of his master's rebuke. If ever Marcellus needed him, it was now.

Clearly the next thing to be done was to do nothing. Marcellus must be given time to compose himself. There would be no sense in trying to reason with him in his present state. It would be equally futile to plead for pardon. Marcellus had far better be left alone for a while.

Laying the folded Robe across the top of the capacious gunny-bag, Demetrius slipped quietly out through the front door and strolled through the cypress grove toward the street. Deeply preoccupied, he did not see Theodosia—in the swing—until he was too close to retreat unobserved. She straightened from her lounging posture, put down the trifle of needlework beside her, and beckoned to him. He was quite lonesome enough to have welcomed her friendly gesture, but he disliked the idea of compromising her. Theodosia was evidently a very willful girl, accustomed to treating the conventions with saucy indifference.

With undisguised reluctance, he walked toward the swing; and, at a little distance, drew up erectly to listen to whatever she might want to say. He was far from pleased by the prospect of getting them both into trouble, but there was no denying that Theodosia made a very pretty picture in the graceful white peplos girdled with a wide belt of paneled silver, a scarlet ribbon about her head that accented the whiteness of her brow, and gaily beaded sandals much too fragile for actual service.

'Why is it,' she demanded, with a comradely smile, 'that we see nothing of your master? Have we offended him? Does he disapprove of us? Tell me, please. I am dying of curiosity.'

'My master has not been well,' replied Demetrius, soberly.

'Ah—but there's more to it than that.' Theodosia's dark eyes were narrowed knowingly as she slowly nodded her blue-black head. 'You're troubled too, my friend. Needn't tell me you're not. You are worried about him. Is that not so?'

It was evident that this girl was used to having her own way with people. She was so radiant with vitality that even her impudence was forgivable. Demetrius suddenly surprised them both with a candid confession.

'It is true,' he admitted. 'I am worried—beyond the telling!'

'Is there anything that we can do?' Theodosia's eager eyes were sincerely sympathetic.

'No,' said Demetrius, hopelessly.

'He has puzzled me,' persisted Theodosia. 'When you arrived the other night, Marcellus struck me as a person who was trying to get away from something. He didn't really want to talk to us. You know that. He was polite enough—but very anxious to be off. I can't think it was because he did not like us. He had the air of one wanting to escape. It's clear enough that he is not hiding from the law; for surely this is no place for a fugitive.'

Demetrius did not immediately reply, though Theodosia had paused several times to give him a chance to say something. He had been busy thinking. As he stood listening to this bright girl's intuitive speculations, it occurred to him that she might be able to offer some sensible advice, if she knew what the problem was. Indeed, it would be better for her to know the facts than to harbor a suspicion that Marcellus was a rascal. He knew that Theodosia was reading in his perplexed eyes a half-formed inclination to be frank. She gave him an encouraging smile.

'Let's have it, Demetrius,' she murmured, intimately. 'I won't tell.'

'It is a long story,' he said, moodily. 'And it would be most imprudent for the daughter of Eupolis to be seen in an extended conversation with a slave.' He lowered his voice confidentially. 'Your father is already annoyed, you know, because you made the mistake of treating me cordially.'

Theodosia's pretty lips puckered thoughtfully.

'I do not think anyone is watching us,' she said, glancing cautiously toward the house. 'If you will walk briskly down the street, as if setting out on an errand, and turn to the right at the first corner —and again to the right, at the next one—you will come to a high-walled garden to the rear of that old temple over there.'

Demetrius shook his head doubtfully.

'Priests are notorious spies,' he said. 'At least they are in Rome, and it was true of them in Corinth. Doubtless it is the same here in Athens. I should think a temple would be about the last place that people would go for a private talk. We might find ourselves under suspicion of discussing a plot.'

Theodosia flushed a little—and gave him a mischievous smile.

'We will not be suspected of sedition,' she promised. 'I shall see to that. Two very good friends will have come to the garden—not to arrange for poisoning the Prefect's porridge—but to exchange pleasant compliments.'

Demetrius' heart quickened, but he frowned.

'Don't you think,' he asked, prudently, 'that you are taking a good deal for granted by trusting quite so much in the honesty of a slave?'

'Yes,' admitted Theodosia. 'Go quickly now. I'll join you presently.'

Deeply stirred by the anticipation of this private interview, but obliged to view it with some anxiety, Demetrius obeyed. Theodosia's almost masculine directness assured him that she was quite beyond a cheap flirtation, but there was no denying her winsome regard for him. Well—we would know, pretty soon, whether she was really concerned about Marcellus, or enlivening a dull afternoon with a bit of adventure. It was conceivable, of course, that both of these things might be true.

As he neared the old wall, Demetrius firmly pressed his gray bandeau down over the ear that denied him a right to talk on terms of equality with a free woman. It gave him a rather rakish appearance which, he felt, might not be altogether inappropriate if this meeting was to be staged as a rendezvous. Sauntering in through the open gate, he strolled to the far end of the arbor and sat down on the commodious marble lectus. A well-nourished priest, in a dirty brown cassock, gave him an indifferent nod, and resumed his hoeing.

He did not have long to wait. She was coming out of the temple, into the cloister, swinging along with her independent head held high. Demetrius stood to wait for her. It was hard to break an old habit, and his posture was stiffly conventional.

'Sit down!' she whispered. 'And don't look so serious.'

He did not have to dissemble a smile as he obeyed her, for her command had been amusing enough. She dropped down close beside him on the stone seat and gave him both hands. The priest leaned on his hoe and sanctioned their meeting with an informed leer. Then he looked a bit puzzled. Presently he dropped the hoe, deliberately cut a large red rose, and waddled toward them, his shifty little eyes alive with inquiry. Drawing an almost sinister smile, he presented the rose to Theodosia. She thanked him prettily and raising it to her face inhaled luxuriously. The priest, with his curiosity about them still unsatisfied, was backing away.

'Put your arm around me,' she muttered, deep in the rose, 'and hold me tight—as if you meant it.'

Demetrius complied, so gently, yet so competently, that the priest wagged his shaggy head and ambled back to his weeds. Then, apparently deciding that he had done enough work for one day, he negligently trailed the hoe behind him as he plodded away to disappear within the cloister, leaving them in sole possession of the quiet garden.

Reluctantly withdrawing his arm as Theodosia straightened, Demetrius remarked, with a twinkle, 'Do you suppose that holy beast might still be watching us—through some private peek-hole?'

'Quite unlikely,' doubted Theodosia, with a gently reproving smile.

'Perhaps we should take no risks,' he cautioned, drawing her closer. She leaned back in his arm without protest.

'Now'—she said, expectantly—'begin at the beginning and tell me all about it. The Tribune is afraid of something—or somebody. Who is it? What is it?'

Demetrius was finding it difficult to launch upon his narrative. Theodosia's persuasive warmth was distracting his mind.

'You are very kind to me,' he said, softly.

'I should have had a brother,' she murmured. 'Let's pretend you are. You know—I feel that way about you—as if we'd known each other a long time.'

Resolutely pulling himself together, Demetrius began his story, not at the beginning but at the end.

'Marcellus,' he declared soberly, 'is afraid of a certain Robe—a brown, homespun, blood-stained Robe—that was worn by a man he was commanded to crucify. The man was innocent—and Marcellus knows it.'

'And the Robe?' queried Theodosia.

It was—as he had threatened—a long story; but Demetrius told it all, beginning with Minoa—and the journey to Jerusalem. Frequently Theodosia detained him with a question.

'But—Demetrius,' she interrupted, turning to look up into his face, 'what was there about this Jesus then that made him seem to you such a great man? You say he was so lonely and disappointed, that morning, when the crowd wanted him as their king: but what had he done to make so many people admire him so much?'

Demetrius had to admit he didn't know.

'It is hard to explain,' he stammered. 'You had a feeling that he was sorry for all of these people. This may sound very foolish,

Theodosia; but it was as if they were homeless little children crying for something, and—'

'Something he couldn't give them?' she wondered, thoughtfully.

'There you have it!' declared Demetrius. 'It was something he couldn't give them, because they were too little and inexperienced to understand what they needed. Maybe this will seem a crazy thing to say: it was almost as if this Galilean had come from some far-away country where people were habitually honest and friendly and did not quarrel; some place where the streets were clean and no one was greedy, and there were no beggars, no thieves, no fights, no courts, no prisons, no soldiers; no rich, no poor.'

'You know there's no place like that,' sighed Theodosia.

'They asked him, at his trial—I'll tell you about that presently—whether he was a king; and he said he had a kingdom—but—it was not in the world.'

Theodosia glanced up, a bit startled, and studied his eyes.

'Now don't tell me you believe anything like that,' she murmured, disappointedly. 'You don't look like a person who would—'

'I'm not!' he protested. 'I don't know what I believe about this Jesus. I never saw anyone like him: that's as far as I can go.'

'That's far enough,' she sighed. 'I was afraid you were going to tell me he was one of the gods.'

'I take it you don't believe in the gods,' grinned Demetrius.

'Of course not! But do go on with your story. I shouldn't have interrupted.'

Demetrius continued. Sometimes it was almost as if he were talking to himself, as he reviewed the tragic events of that sorry day. He relived his strange emotions as the darkness settled over Jerusalem at mid-afternoon. Theodosia was very quiet, but her heart was beating hard and her eyes were misty.

'And he didn't try to defend himself—at all?' she asked, huskily; and Demetrius, shaking his head, went on to tell her of the gambling for the Robe, and what had happened that night at the Insula when Marcellus had been forced to put it on.

When he had finished his strange story, the sun was low. Theodosia rose slowly, and they walked arm in arm toward the cloister.

'Poor Marcellus,' she murmured. 'It would have to be something very exciting indeed—to divert his mind.'

'Well—I've tried everything I can think of,' sighed Demetrius. 'And now I'm afraid he has completely lost confidence in me.'

'He thinks the Robe is—haunted?'

Demetrius made no answer to that; and Theodosia, tugging at his arm, impulsively brought him to a stop. She invaded his eyes, one at a time, bewildered.

'But—*you* don't believe that! Do you?' she demanded.

'For my unhappy master, Theodosia, the Robe is haunted. He is convinced of it—and that make it so—for him.'

'And what do *you* think? Is it haunted for *you?*'

He avoided her eyes for a moment.

'What I am going to say may sound silly. When I was a very little boy, and had fallen down and hurt myself, I would run into the house and find my mother. She would not bother to ask me what in the world I had been doing to bruise myself that way; or scold me for not being more careful. She would take me in her arms and hold me until I was through with my weeping, and everything was all right again. Perhaps my skinned knee still hurt, but I could bear it now.' He looked down tenderly into Theodosia's soft eyes. 'You see —my mother was always definitely on my side—no matter how I came by my mishaps.'

'Go on,' she said. 'I'm following you.'

'Often I have thought—' He interrupted himself to interpolate, 'Slaves get very lonesome, my friend!—Often I have thought there should be—for grown-up people—some place where they could go— when badly hurt—and find the same kind of assurance that a little child experiences in his mother's arms. Now—this Robe—it isn't haunted—for me—but—'

'I think I understand, Demetrius.'

After a moment's silence, they separated, leaving as they had arrived. Demetrius went out through the gate in the old wall. His complete review of the mysterious story had had a peculiar effect on him. Everything seemed unreal, as if he had spent an hour in a dream-world.

The clatter of the busy street, when he had turned the corner, jangled him out of his reverie. It occurred to him—and he couldn't help smiling—that he had spent a long time with his arm around the highly desirable Theodosia, almost oblivious of her physical charms. And he knew she had not been piqued by his fraternal attitude toward her. The story of Jesus—inadequately as Demetrius had related it out of his limited information—was of an emotional quality that had completely eclipsed their natural interest in each other's affections. Apparently the Galilean epic, even when imperfectly understood, had the capacity for lifting a friendship up to very high ground.

* * * * * *

It was quite clear now to Marcellus that the time for decisive action had arrived. Life, under these humiliating conditions, was no longer to be endured.

He had not fully shared his father's earnest hope that a sojourn in Athens—with plenty of leisure and no embarrassing social responsibilities—would relieve his mental strain. He knew that he would be carrying his burden along with him.

It was possible, of course, that time might dim the tragic picture that filled his mind. He would pursue a few distracting studies, give his restless hands some entertaining employments, and try to resume command of his thoughts.

But it was hopeless. He had no interest in anything! Since his arrival in Athens—far from experiencing any easing of the painful nervous tension—he had been losing ground. The dread of meeting people and having to talk with them had deepened into a relentless obsession. He was afraid to stir from the house. He even shunned the gardeners.

And now—he had gone to pieces. In an utter abandonment of all emotional control, he had made a sorry spectacle of himself in the sight of his loyal slave. Demetrius could hardly be expected to maintain his patience or respect much longer.

This afternoon, Marcellus had been noisy with his threats and recriminations. At the rate he was breaking up, by tomorrow afternoon he might commit some deed of violence. It was better to have done with this dreadful business before he brought harm to anyone else.

His people at home would be grieved when they learned the sad tidings, but bereavement was ever so much easier to bear than disgrace. As he sat there in the peristyle, with his head in his hands, Marcellus made a mental leave-taking of those he had loved best. He saw Lucia, in the shaded pergola, her slim legs folded under her as she sat quietly reading. He briefly visited his distinguished father in his library. He didn't worry so much about his father's reception of the bad news. Senator Gallio would not be surprised: he would be relieved to know that the matter was settled. Marcellus went up to his mother's room, and was glad to find her quietly sleeping. He was thankful that his imagination had at least spared him the anguish of a tearful parting.

He bade good-bye to Diana. They were together in the pergola, as on that night when he had left for Minoa. He had taken her in his arms, but rather diffidently, for he felt he would not be coming back; and it wasn't quite honest to make promises. This time he held Diana tightly—and kissed her.

Demetrius had unquestionably deceived him about the dagger he had bought in Corfu. It had been believed that the silver-handled dagger he had carried for years had been lost somehow on *The Vestris*. Marcellus had doubted that. Demetrius, alarmed over his melancholy state, had taken the weapon from him. However—the theft had been well enough meant. Marcellus had not pressed the matter; had even consented unprotestingly to the theory that the dagger was lost. At Corfu, he had found another. It was less ornamental than serviceable.

Next day after leaving Corfu, it was missing. Marcellus had thought it unlikely that any of his fellow passengers would steal a dagger of such insignificant value. Demetrius had it: there was no question about that. Very likely, if he searched his slave's gunny-sack, he would find both of them.

Of course, it was possible that Demetrius might have thrown the weapons overboard, but he was so scrupulously honest that this seemed improbable. Demetrius would hold them against the arrival of a day when he thought it safe to restore them.

Unbuckling the belt of his tunic and casting it aside, Marcellus entered the Corinthian's small bedchamber, and saw the gunny-sack on his couch. His hands were trembling as he moved forward toward it; for it was no light matter to be that close to death.

Now he stopped! There it was—the *Thing!* He slowly retreated and leaned against the wall. Ah!—so the ingenious Demetrius had anticipated his decision! He was going to defend his stolen daggers with the Robe! Marcellus clenched his hands and growled. He would have it out with this Thing!

Resolutely forcing his feet to obey, he moved slowly to the couch and stretched out a shaking hand. The sweat was pouring down his face and his legs were so weak he could hardly stand. Suddenly he brought his hand down with a violent movement as if he were capturing a living thing.

For a long moment Marcellus stood transfixed, his fingers buried in the long-feared and hated garment. Then he sat down on the edge of the couch and slowly drew the Robe toward him. He stared at it uncomprehendingly; held it up to the light; rubbed it softly against his bare arm. He couldn't analyze his peculiar sensations, but something very strange had happened to him. His agitation was stilled. Rising, as if from a dream, he laid the Robe over his arm and went out into the peristyle. He sat down and draped it across the broad arms of his chair. He smoothed it gently with his hand. He felt a curious elation; an indefinable sense of relief—relief from everything! A great load had been lifted! He wasn't afraid anymore! Hot tears gathered in his eyes and overflowed.

After a while he rose and carried the Robe back to Demetrius' room, placing it where he had found it. Unaccustomed to his new sense of well-being, he was puzzled about what to do next. He went into the studio and laughed at Demetrius' poor little statuette. The house wasn't quite large enough to hold him; so, donning his toga, he went out into the garden.

It was there that his slave found him.

Demetrius had approached the house with a feeling of dread. He knew Marcellus well enough to surmise that he wasn't going to be able to endure much more humiliation.

Entering the house quietly, he looked into his master's bedcham-

ber and into the studio. Then he went out to the peristyle. His heart
sank.

Then he saw Marcellus sauntering in the garden. He walked toward
him eagerly, realizing that a great change had come over him.

'You are feeling better, sir! Are you not?' said Demetrius, staring
into his face incredulously.

Marcellus' lips twitched as he smiled.

'I have been away from you a long time, Demetrius,' he said, unsteadily.

'Yes, sir. I need not tell you how glad I am that you have returned. Is there anything I can do for you?'

'Did you tell me that you had learned of a good weaver; one who
might mend that Robe?'

Enlightenment shone in Demetrius' eyes.

'Yes, sir!'

'After we have had our supper,' said Marcellus, 'we will try to find
him.' He sauntered slowly toward the house, Demetrius following
him, his heart almost bursting with exultation. When they reached
the peristyle, Demetrius could no longer keep silent.

'May I ask you, sir, what happened?' he queried. 'Did you touch
it?'

Marcellus nodded and drew a bewildered smile.

'I was hoping you would, sir,' said Demetrius.

'Why? Have you had any strange experiences with it?'

'Yes, sir.'

'What did it do to you?'

'I can't quite define it, sir,' stammered Demetrius. 'There's a queer
energy—belonging to it—clinging to it—somehow.'

'Don't you know that's a very crazy thing to say?' demanded Marcellus.

'Yes, sir. I have tried to account for it. I saw him die, you know.
He was very brave. Perhaps I invested this Robe with my own admiration for his courage. When I look at it, I am ashamed of my
own troubles, and I want to behave with fortitude, and——'

He paused, uncertain how to proceed.

'And that explains it, you think?' persisted Marcellus.

'Y-yes, sir,' stammered Demetrius. 'I suppose so.'

'There's more to it than that, Demetrius, and you know it!'

'Yes, sir.'

Chapter IX

WAKING at dawn, Marcellus was ecstatic to find himself unencumbered by the weight that so long had oppressed him. It was the first time he had ever realized the full meaning of freedom.

Pausing at Demetrius' open door he noted with satisfaction that his loyal slave, whose anxiety had been as painful as his own, was still soundly sleeping. That was good. Demetrius deserved a rest—and a forthright apology, too.

Not since that summer when, at fifteen, Marcellus was slowly convalescing from a serious illness, had he experienced so keen an awareness of life's elemental properties. The wasting fever had left him weak and emaciated; but through those days of his recovery his senses had been abnormally alert. Especially in the early morning: all colors were luminous, all sounds were intensified, all scents were heady concentrates of familiar fragrances.

Until then, the birds chirped and whistled, each species shrieking its own identifying cry; but it was silly to say that they sang. Now the birds sang, their songs melodious and choral. The dawn breeze was saturated with a subtle blend of newmown clover and sweetish honeysuckle, of jasmine and narcissus, welcoming him back to life's brightness and goodness. An occasional cool wisp of dank leaf-mould and fresh-spaded earth momentarily sobered him; and then he would rejoice that he had escaped their more intimate acquaintance.

For those few days, as a youth, Marcellus had been impressed by his kinship with all created things. It stilled and steadied his spirit to find himself so closely integrated with Nature. Then, as he regained his bodily vigor, this peculiar sensitivity gradually ceased to function. He still enjoyed the colors and perfumes of the flowers, the liquid calls of the birds, and the insistent hum of little winged creatures; but his brief understanding of their language was lost in the confusion of ordinary work and play. Nor did he expect ever to reclaim that transient rapture. Perhaps it could be experienced only when one's physical resources had ebbed to low tide, and one's fragility had made common cause with such other fragile things as hummingbirds and heliotrope.

This morning, to his happy amazement, that higher awareness had returned, filling him with a mystifying exaltation. He had somehow recaptured that indefinable ecstasy.

It had rained softly in the night, bathing the tall sycamores until their gaily fluttering leaves reflected glints of gold. The air was heavy with the scent of refreshed roses. Perhaps it was on such a morning, mused Marcellus, that Aristophanes had composed his famous apostrophe to the Birds of Athens.

Doubtless it was inevitable that yesterday afternoon's strange experience should have produced a sequence of varied reactions. The immediate effect of his dealings with the Robe had been a feeling of awe and bewilderment, quickly followed by an exhilaration bordering on hysteria. But the protracted neural strain had been so relentless, and had taken such a heavy toll, that this sudden release of tension had produced an almost paralyzing fatigue. Marcellus had gone supperless to bed and had slept like a little child.

Rousing, wide-awake, with an exultant sense of complete cleansing and renewal, he had wished he could lift his eyes and hands in gratitude to some kindly spirit who might be credited with this ineffable gift. As he sat there in the rose-arbor, he mentally called the roll of the classic gods and goddesses, questing a name worthy of homage; but he could think of none who deserved his intellectual respect; much less his reverence. He had been singularly blest; but the gift was anonymous. For the first time in his life, Marcellus envied all naïve souls who believed in the gods. As for himself, he was incapable of belief in them.

But this amazing experience with the Robe was something that could not be dismissed with a mere 'I do not understand; so—let it be considered a closed incident.'

No—it was a problem that had to be dealt with, somehow. Marcellus gave himself to serious reflection. First of all, the Robe had symbolized that whole shameful affair at Jerusalem. The man who wore it had been innocent of any crime. He had been unfairly tried, unjustly sentenced, and dishonorably put to death. He had borne his pain with admirable fortitude. Was 'fortitude' the word? No— murmured Marcellus—the Galilean had something else besides that. The best that 'fortitude' could accomplish was courageous endurance. This Jesus had not merely endured. It was rather as if he had confronted his tragedy!—*had gone to meet it!*

And then—that night at the Insula—dully sobering from a whole day's drunkenness, Marcellus had gradually roused to a realization that he—in the face of this incredible bravery—had carried out his brutal work as if the victim were an ordinary criminal. The utter perfidy of his behavior had suddenly swept over him like a storm, that night at Pilate's banquet. It was not enough that he had joined hands with cowards and scoundrels to crucify this Jesus. He had consented to ridicule the dead hero by putting on his blood-stained Robe

for the entertainment of a drunken crowd. Not much wonder that
the torturing memory of his own part in the crime had festered—and
burned—and poisoned his spirit! Yes—that part of it was understandable. And because the Robe had been the instrument of his torture,
it was natural, he thought, that he should have developed an almost
insane abhorrence of it!

Yesterday afternoon, its touch had healed his wounded mind. How
was he to evaluate this astonishing fact? Perhaps it was more simple
than it seemed: perhaps he was making it all too difficult. He had
shrunk from this Robe because it symbolized his great mistake and
misfortune. Now—compelled by a desperate circumstance to lay his
hands upon the Robe—his obsession had vanished! Was this effect
purely subjective—or was the Robe actually possessed of magical
power?

This latter suggestion was absurd! It was preposterous! It offended
every principle he had lived by! To admit of such a theory, he would
have to toss overboard all his reasonable beliefs in an impersonal,
law-abiding universe—and become a confessed victim of superstition.

No—he could not and would not do that! There was no magic
in this Robe! It was a mere tool of his imagination. For many weeks
it had symbolized his crime and punishment. Now it symbolized
his release. His remorse had run its full measure through the hourglass
and the time had come for him to put his crime behind him. The
touch of the Robe in his hands had simply marked the moment for
the expiration of his mental punishment. He was not going to admit
that the Robe was invested with power.

Today he would find that weaver and have the Robe repaired.
He would at least show it that much honor and respect. It was nothing more than a garment—but it deserved to be handled with gratitude
—and reverence! Yes—he would go that far! He could honestly say
that he reverenced this Robe!

Demetrius had joined him now, apologetic for tardiness.

'I am glad you could sleep,' smiled Marcellus. 'You have had much
worry—on my account. In my unhappiness, I have been rough with
you. You have been quite understanding, Demetrius, and immensely
patient. I am sorry for the way I have treated you; especially yesterday.
That was too bad!'

'Please, sir!' pleaded Demetrius. 'I am so glad you are well again!'

'I think we will try to find your weaver, today, and see if he can
mend the Robe.'

'Yes, sir. Shall I order your breakfast now?'

'In a moment. Demetrius—in your honest opinion—is that Robe
haunted?'

'It is very mysterious, sir.' Demetrius was spacing his words deliberately. 'I had hoped that you might be able to throw a little light
on it. May I ask what conclusion you have come to?'

Marcellus sighed and shook his head.

'The more I think about it,' he said, slowly, 'the more bewildering it is!' He rose, and moved toward the house.

'Well, sir,' volunteered Demetrius, at his elbow, 'it isn't as if we were *required* to comprehend it. There are plenty of things that we are not expected to understand. This may be one of them.'

* * * * * *

Across the street from the main entrance to the sprawling, open-air Theater of Dionysus, there was a huddle of small bazaars dealing in such trifles as the playgoers might pick up on their way in; sweetmeats, fans, and cushions. At the end of the row stood Benjamin's little shop, somewhat aloof from its frivolous neighbors. There was nothing on the door to indicate the nature of Benjamin's business; nothing but his name, burned into a cypress plank, and that not plainly legible; dryly implying that if you didn't know Benjamin was a weaver—and the oldest and most skillful weaver in Athens—you weren't likely to be a desirable client.

Within, the shop was suffocatingly stuffy. Not a spacious room to begin with, it contained—besides the two looms, one of them the largest Marcellus had ever seen—an ungainly spinning-wheel, a huge carding device, and bulky stores of raw materials; reed baskets heaped high with silk cocoons, big bales of cotton, bulging bags of wool.

Most of the remaining floor space was occupied by the commodious worktable on which Benjamin sat, cross-legged, deeply absorbed in the fine hem he was stitching around the flowing sleeve of an exquisitely wrought chiton. He was shockingly lean and stooped, and his bald head seemed much too large for his frail body. A long white beard covered his breast. His shabby robe was obviously not worn as a specimen of his handicraft. Behind him, against the wall and below the window-ledge, there was a long shelf well filled with scrolls whose glossy spools showed much handling.

Benjamin did not look up until he had reached the end of his thread; then, straightening with a painful grimace, he peered at his new clients with a challenge that wrinkled his long nose and uptipped his lip, after the manner of an overloaded, protesting camel. Except for the beady brightness of his deeply caverned eyes, Benjamin was as old as Jehovah—and as cross, too, if his scowl told the truth about his disposition.

Marcellus advanced confidently with Demetrius at his elbow.

'This garment,' he began, holding it up, 'needs mending.'

Benjamin puckered his leathery old mouth unpleasantly, sniffed, licked his thumb, and twisted a fresh thread to a sharp point.

'I have better things to do,' he declaimed, gutturally, 'than darn holes in old coats.' He raised his needle to the light, and squintingly probed for its eye. 'Go to a sailmaker,' he added, somewhat less gruffly.

'Perhaps I should not have bothered you with so small a matter,' admitted Marcellus, unruffled. 'I am aware that this garment is of little practical value, but it is a keepsake, and I had hoped to have it put in order by someone who knows how.'

'Keepsake, eh!' Old Benjamin reached for the Robe with a pathetically thin hand and pawed over it with well-informed fingers. 'A keepsake,' he mumbled. 'And how did this get to be a keepsake?' He frowned darkly at Marcellus. 'You are a Roman; are you not? This Robe is as Jewish as the Ten Commandments.'

'True!' conceded Marcellus, patiently. 'I am a Roman, and the Robe belonged to a Jew.'

'Friend of yours, I suppose.' Benjamin's tone was bitterly ironical.

'Not exactly a friend—no. But he was a brave Jew and well esteemed by all who knew him. His Robe came into my hands, and I wish to have it treated with respect.' Marcellus leaned closer to watch as the old man scratched lightly at a dark stain with his yellow fingernail.

'Died fighting—maybe,' muttered Benjamin.

'It was a violent death,' said Marcellus, 'but he was not fighting. He was a man of peace—set upon by enemies.'

'You seem to know all about it,' growled Benjamin. 'However—it is naught to me how you came by this garment. It is clear enough that you had no hand in harming the Jew, or you would not think so highly of his old Robe.' Thawing slightly, he added, 'I shall mend it for you. It will cost you nothing.'

'Thanks,' said Marcellus, coolly. 'I prefer to pay for it. When shall I call?'

Benjamin wasn't listening. With his deep-lined old face upturned toward the window he was inspecting the Robe against the light. Over his thin shoulder he beckoned Marcellus to draw closer.

'Observe, please. It is woven without a seam; all in one portion. There is only one locality where they do that. It is up in the neighborhood of the Lake Gennesaret, in Galilee.' Benjamin waggled his beard thoughtfully. 'I have not seen a piece of Galilean homespun for years. This is from up around Capernaum somewhere, I'd say.'

'You are acquainted with that country?' inquired Marcellus.

'Yes, yes; my people are Samaritans, a little way to the south; almost on the border.' Benjamin chuckled grimly. 'The Samaritans and the Galileans never had much use for one another. The Galileans were great Temple people, spending much time in their synagogues, and forever leaving their flocks and crops to look after themselves while they journeyed to Jerusalem for the ceremonies. They kept themselves poor with their pilgrimages and sacrifices. We Samaritans didn't hold with the Temple.'

'Why was that?' wondered Marcellus.

Benjamin swung his thin legs over the edge of the table and sat up prepared to launch upon an extended lecture.

'Of course,' he began, 'you have heard the story of Elijah.'

Marcellus shook his head, and Benjamin regarded him with withering pity; then, apparently deciding not to waste any more time, he drew up his legs again, folded them comfortably, and resumed his rethreading of the needle.

'Was this Elijah one of the gods of Samaria?' Marcellus had the misfortune to inquire.

The old man slowly put down his work and seared his young customer with a contemptuous stare.

'I find it difficult to believe,' he declared, 'that even a Roman could have accumulated so much ignorance. To the Jew—be he Samaritan, Galilean, Judean, or of the dispersed—there is but one God! Elijah was a great prophet. Elisha, who inherited his mantle, was also a great prophet. They lived in the mountains of Samaria, long before the big temples and all the holy fuss of the lazy priests. We Samaritans have always worshiped on the hilltops, in the groves.'

'That sounds quite sensible to me,' approved Marcellus, brightly.

'Well,' grunted the old man, 'that's no compliment to our belief; though I suppose you intended your remark to be polite.'

Marcellus spontaneously laughed outright, and Benjamin, rubbing his long nose, grinned dryly.

'You are of a mild temper, young man,' he observed.

'That depends, sir, upon the nature of the provocation,' said Marcellus, not wishing to be thought weak. 'You are my senior—by many, many years.'

'Ah—so—and you think an old man has a right to be rude?'

'Apparently we share the same opinion on that matter,' drawled Marcellus, complacently.

Benjamin bent low over his work, chuckling deep in his whiskers.

'What is your name, young man?' he asked, after a while, without looking up; and when Marcellus had told him, he inquired, 'How long are you to be in Athens?'

The query was of immense interest to Demetrius. Now that conditions had changed, Marcellus might be contemplating an early return to Rome. He had not yet indicated what his intentions were, or whether he had given the matter any thought at all.

'I do not know,' replied Marcellus. 'Several weeks, perhaps. There are many things I wish to see.'

'How long have you been here?' asked Benjamin.

Marcellus turned an inquiring glance toward Demetrius, who supplied the information.

'Been on Mars' Hill?' queried the old man.

'No,' replied Marcellus, reluctantly.

'Acropolis?'

'Not yet.'

'You have not been in the Parthenon?'

'No—not yet.'

'Humph! What have you been doing with yourself?'

'Resting,' said Marcellus. 'I've recently been on two long voyages.'

'A healthy young fellow like you doesn't need any rest,' scoffed Benjamin. 'Two voyages, eh? You're quite a traveler. Where were you?'

Marcellus frowned. There seemed no limit to the old man's inquisitiveness.

'We came here from Rome,' he said, hoping that might be sufficient.

'That's one voyage,' encouraged Benjamin.

'And—before that—we sailed to Rome from Joppa.'

'Ah—from Joppa!' Benjamin continued his precise stitching, his eyes intent upon it, but his voice was vibrant with sudden interest. 'Then you were in Jerusalem. And how long ago was that?'

Marcellus made a mental calculation, and told him.

'Indeed!' commented Benjamin. 'Then you were there during the week of the Passover. I am told there were some strange happenings.'

Demetrius started; restlessly shifted his weight, and regarded his master with anxiety. Benjamin's darting glance, from under shaggy eyebrows, noted it.

'Doubtless,' replied Marcellus, evasively. 'The city was packed with all sorts. Anything could have happened.' He hitched at his belt, and retreated a step. 'I shall not interfere with your work any longer.'

'Come tomorrow—a little before sunset,' said Benjamin. 'The Robe will be ready for you. We will have a glass of wine together—if you will accept the hospitality of my humble house.'

Marcellus hesitated for a moment before replying, and exchanged glances with Demetrius who almost imperceptibly shook his head as if saying we had better not risk a review of the tragedy.

'You are most kind,' said Marcellus. 'I am not sure—what I may be doing—tomorrow. But—if I do not come, I shall send for the Robe. May I pay you now?' He reached into the breast of his tunic.

Benjamin continued stitching, as if he had not heard. After a long minute, he searched Marcellus' eyes.

'I think,' he said slowly, patting the Robe with gentle fingers, 'I think you do not want to talk—about this Jew.'

Marcellus was plainly uncomfortable, and anxious to be off.

'It is a painful story,' he said, shortly.

'All stories about Jews are painful,' said Benjamin. 'May I expect you tomorrow?'

'Y-yes,' agreed Marcellus, indecisively.

'That is good,' mumbled Benjamin. He held up his bony hand. 'Peace be upon you!'

'Er—thank you,' stammered Marcellus, uncertain whether he, in turn, was expected to confer peace upon the old Jew. Maybe that would be a social error. 'Farewell,' he said, finally, feeling he would be safe to leave it at that.

Outside the shop, Marcellus and Demetrius traded looks of mutual inquiry and sauntered across the road to the empty theater.

'Odd old creature,' remarked Marcellus. 'I'm not sure that I want to see any more of him. Do you think he is crazy?'

'No,' said Demetrius—'far from it. He is a very wise old man.'

'I think you feel that I should be making a mistake to come back here tomorrow.'

'Yes, sir. Better forget all about that now.'

'But—I wouldn't have to talk about that wretched affair in Jerusalem,' protested Marcellus. 'I can simply say that I do not want to discuss it.' His tone sounded as if he were rehearsing the speech he intended to make on that occasion. 'And that,' he finished, 'ought to settle it, I think.'

'Yes, sir; that ought to settle it,' agreed Demetrius—'but it won't. Benjamin will not be easily put off.'

They strolled down the long grass-grown aisle toward the deserted stage.

'Do you know anything about the customs and manners of the Jews, Demetrius?' queried Marcellus, idly.

'Very little, sir, about their customs.'

'When old Benjamin said, "Peace be upon you," what should I have replied? Is there a formulated answer to that?'

' "Farewell" is correct usage, sir, I think,' said Demetrius.

'But I did say that!' retorted Marcellus, returning with a bound from some faraway mental excursion.

'Yes, sir,' agreed Demetrius. He hoped they were not already slipping back into that pool of painful reflection.

They retraced their steps to the theater entrance.

'I wonder how much the old man knows about Galilee,' mused Marcellus.

'He will tell you tomorrow.'

'But—I'm not going back tomorrow! I don't want to have this matter reopened. I intend to put the whole thing out of my mind!'

'That is a wise decision, sir,' approved Demetrius, soberly.

* * * * * *

It was immediately apparent that this firm resolution was to be enforced. Leaving the Theater of Dionysus, they strolled through the agora where Marcellus paused before the market booths to exchange a bit of banter with rosy-cheeked country girls and slip copper denarii into the grimy incredulous hands of their little brothers and sisters.

Then they went up on Mars' Hill and spent an hour in the sacred grove where the great of the Greeks had turned to stone.

Turning aside from the main path, Marcellus sat down on a marble bench, Demetrius standing a little way distant. Both were silently reflective. After an interval, Marcellus waved an arm toward the stately row of mutilated busts.

'Demetrius, it has just occurred to me that there isn't a warrior in the lot! You Greeks are hard fighters, when you're put to it; but the heroes who live forever in your public gardens are men of peace. Remember the Forum? Sulla, Antony, Scipio, Camillus, Julius, Augustus —all tricked out in swords and helmets! But look at this procession of Greeks, marching up the hill! Socrates, Epicurus, Herodotus, Solon, Aristotle, Polybius! Not a fighter among them!'

'But—they all look as if they'd been to war, sir,' jested Demetrius.

'Ah, yes—*we* did that!' said Marcellus, scornfully. 'Our gallant Roman legions; our brave illiterates!' He sat scowling for a moment; then went on, with unaccustomed heat: 'Demetrius—I say damn all men who make war on monuments! The present may belong to the Roman Empire by force of conquest; but, by all the gods, the past does not! A nation is surely of contemptible and cowardly mind that goes to battle against another nation's history! It didn't take much courage to come up here and hack the ears off old Pericles! I daresay the unwashed, drunken vandal who nicked his broadsword on the nose of Hippocrates could neither read nor write! There's not much dignity left in a nation that has no respect for the words and works of geniuses who gave the world whatever wisdom and beauty it owns!'

Deeply stirred to indignation, he rose and strode across the path, and faced the bust of Plato.

'That man!—for example—*he* has no nationality! *He* has no fatherland! *He* has no race! No kingdom—in this world—can claim him— or destroy him!' Abruptly, Marcellus stopped in the midst of what promised to be an oration. He stood silent, for a moment; then walked slowly toward Demetrius, and stared into his eyes.

'Do you know, Demetrius—that is what the Galilean said of himself!'

'I remember,' nodded Demetrius. 'He said his kingdom was not of the world—and nobody knew what he meant.'

'I wonder'—Marcellus' voice was dreamy. 'Perhaps—some day—he'll have a monument—like Plato's. . . . Come—let us go! We had decided to be merry, today; and here we've been owling it like old philosophers.'

It was late in the afternoon before they reached the inn. When they were drawing within sight of it, Marcellus remarked casually that he must call on the Eupolis family.

'I should have done so earlier,' he added, casually. 'Upon my word, I don't believe I've seen any of them since the night we arrived!'

'They will be glad to see you, sir,' said Demetrius. 'They have inquired about you frequently.'

'I shall stop and see them now,' decided Marcellus, impulsively. 'You may return to our suite. I'll be back presently.'

After they had separated, Demetrius reflected with some amusement that this renewal of acquaintance, after so strange a lapse, would be of much interest to the Eupolis household. Perhaps Theodosia would want to tell him about it.

Then he fell to wondering what she would think about himself in this connection. Had he not been so alarmed over his master's condition that he had confided his distress to her? And here was Marcellus—supposedly mired in an incurable despair—drifting in to call, as jauntily as if he had never fretted about anything in his life! Would Theodosia think he had fabricated the whole story? But she couldn't think that! Nobody could invent such a tale!

After a while one of the kitchen slaves came to announce that the Tribune would be dining with the family. Demetrius grinned broadly as he sauntered out alone to the peristyle. He wondered what they would talk about at dinner. The occasion would call for a bit of tact, he felt.

*   *   *   *   *   *

Early the next morning Marcellus donned a coarse tunic and set to work at his modeling-table with the air of a professional sculptor. Demetrius hovered about, waiting to be of service, until it became evident that nothing was desired of him today but his silence, perhaps his absence. He asked if he might take a walk.

Theodosia had set up a gaily colored target near the front wall that bounded the grounds and was shooting at it from a stadium's distance. She made a pretty picture in the short-sleeved white chiton, a fringe of black curls escaping her scarlet bandeau. As Demetrius neared, he was surprised to see that she was using a man's bow, and although she was not drawing it quite to top torsion her arrows struck with a clipped, metallic ping that represented an unusual strength, for a girl. And the shots were well placed, too. Demetrius reflected that if Theodosia wanted to, she could do a lot of damage with one of those long, bone-tipped arrows.

She smiled and inquired whether he had any suggestions for her. He interpreted this as an invitation to join her; but, reluctant, as before, to compromise them both by appearing in conversation together, he did not turn aside from the graveled driveway.

'I think your marksmanship is very good,' he halted to say. 'You surely need no instruction.'

She flushed a little, and drew another arrow from the quiver that leaned against the stone lectus. Demetrius could see that she felt rebuffed as she turned away. Regardless of consequences, he sauntered toward her.

'Are you too busy for a quiet talk?' she asked, without looking at him.

'I was hoping you might suggest it,' said Demetrius. 'But we can't talk here, you know.'

'Ssss—*ping!*' went the arrow.

'Very well,' said Theodosia. 'I'll meet you—over there.'

Walking quickly away, Demetrius made the circuitous trip to the Temple garden. Apparently the priests were occupied with their holy employments, whatever they were, for no one was in sight. His heart speeded a little when he saw Theodosia coming. It was a new experience to be treated on terms of equality, and he was not quite sure how this amenity should be viewed. He needed and wanted Theodosia's friendship—but how was he to interpret the freedom with which she offered it? Should she not have some compunctions about private interviews with a slave? It was a debatable question whether this friendship was honoring him, or merely demoting her.

Theodosia sat down by him, without a greeting, and regarded him soberly, at such short range that he noted the little flecks of gold in her dark eyes.

'Tell me about the dinner-party,' said Demetrius, wanting to get it over with.

'Very strange; is it not?' There was nothing ironical in her tone. 'He is entirely recovered.'

Demetrius nodded.

'I was afraid you might think I had misrepresented the facts,' he said. 'I could not have blamed you.'

'No—I believed what you told me, Demetrius, and I believe it still. Something happened. Something very important happened.'

'That is true. He found the Robe, while I was absent, and came by an entirely different attitude toward it. Once he had touched it, his horror of it suddenly left him. Last night he slept. Today he has been his usual self. I think his obsession has been cured. I don't pretend to understand it!'

'Naturally—I have thought of nothing else all day,' confessed Theodosia. 'If it was the Robe that had tormented Marcellus, it must have been a new view of the Robe that restored him. Maybe it's something like this: I keep a diary, Demetrius. Every night, I write a few things I wish to remember. If someone who does not know me should read a page where I am happy and life is good, he might have quite a different impression of me than if he read the other side of the papyrus where I am a cynic, a stoic; cold and bitter. Now—you and Marcellus recorded many different thoughts on that Galilean Robe. Yours were sad, mostly, but they did not chide you. Marcellus recorded memories on it—and they afflicted him.'

She paused, her eyes asking whether this analogy had any merit at all. Demetrius signed to her to go on.

'You told me that this Jesus forgave them all, and that Marcellus had been much moved by it. Maybe, when he touched the Robe again, this impression came back to him so strongly that it relieved his remorse. Does that sound reasonable?'

'Yes—but wouldn't you think, Theodosia, that after having had an experience like that—a sort of illumination, setting him free of his phobias—Marcellus would be in a great state of exaltation? True—he was ecstatic, for a while; but his high moment was brief. And for the most of the day, yesterday, he acted almost as if nothing had happened to him.'

'My guess is that he is concealing his emotions,' ventured Theodosia. 'Maybe he feels this more deeply than you think.'

'There is no reason for his being reticent with me. He was so stirred by his experience, the night before last, that he was half-indignant because I tried to regard it rationally.'

'Perhaps that is why he doesn't want to discuss it further. He thinks the problem is too big for either of you, so he's resolved not to talk about it. You say he had a high moment—and then proceeded as if the experience had been of no consequence. Well—that's natural; isn't it? We can't live on mountain-tops.' Theodosia's eyes had a faraway look, and her voice was wistful.

'My Aunt Ino,' she continued, 'once said to me, when I was desperately lonely and blue, that our life is like a land journey, too even and easy and dull over long distances across the plains, too hard and painful up the steep grades; but, on the summits of the mountain, you have a magnificent view—and feel exalted—and your eyes are full of happy tears—and you want to sing—and wish you had wings! And then—you can't stay there, but must continue your journey —you begin climbing down the other side, so busy with your footholds that your summit experience is forgotten.'

'You have a pretty mind, Theodosia,' said Demetrius, gently.

'That was my Aunt Ino's mind I was talking about.'

'I am sorry you were lonely and depressed, Theodosia.' Absently he rubbed his finger-tips over the small white scar on his ear. 'I shouldn't have thought you were ever sad. Want to talk about it?'

Her eyes had followed his hand with frank interest.

'Not all slaves have had their ears marked,' she said, pensively. 'Your position is tragic. I know that. There is something very wrong with a world in which a man like you must go through life as a slave. But— really—is there much to choose between your social condition and mine? I am the daughter of an innkeeper. In your case, Demetrius, it makes no difference that you were brought up in a home of refinement and well endowed with a good mind: wicked men put you into slavery—and there you are! And where am I? It makes no difference that my father, Dion, is a man of integrity, well versed in the classics, acquainted with the arts, and bearing himself honorably before the men of Athens, as did his father Georgias. He is an innkeeper. Perhaps it would have been better for me if I had not been taught to love things beyond my social station.'

'But—Theodosia, your advantages have made your life rich,' said Demetrius, consolingly. 'You have so much to make you happy; your books, your music, your boundless vitality, your beautiful clothes——'

'I have no place to wear my nice clothes,' she countered, bitterly, 'and I have no use for my vitality. If the daughter of an innkeeper wants to be happy, she should conform to the traditions. She should be noisy, pert, and not above petty larcenies. Then she could have friends—of her own class.' Her eyes suddenly flooded. 'Demetrius,' she said, huskily, 'sometimes I think I can't bear it!'

He slipped his arm about her, and they sat for a long moment in silence. Then she straightened, and regarded him soberly.

'Why don't you run away?' she demanded, in a whisper. 'I would —if I were a man.'

'Where would you go?' he asked, with an indulgent grin.

Theodosia indicated with a negligent gesture that the question was of secondary importance.

'Anywhere,' she murmured vaguely. 'Sicily—maybe. They say it is lovely—in Sicily.'

'It's a land of thieves and cutthroats,' declared Demetrius. 'It is in the lovely lands that life is most difficult, Theodosia. The only places where one may live in peace—so far as I know—are arid desolations where nothing grows and nothing is covetable.'

'Why not Damascus? You thought of that once, you know.'

'I should die of loneliness up there.'

'You could take me along.' She laughed lightly, as she spoke, to assure him the remark was intended playfully, but they quickly fell silent. Rousing from her reverie, Theodosia sat up, patted her bandeau, and said she must go.

Demetrius rose and watched her as she drifted gracefully away; then resumed his seat and unleashed his thoughts. He was becoming much too fond of Theodosia, and she was being too recklessly generous with her friendship. Perhaps it would be better to avoid any more private talks with her, if he could do so without hurting her feelings. She was very desirable and her tenderness was endearing. The freedom with which she confided in him and the artless candor of her attitude— sometimes but little short of a caress—had stirred him deeply. Until now, whatever devotion he had to offer a woman was silently, hopelessly given to Lucia. As he reflected upon his feeling for her now, Lucia was in the nature of a shrine. Theodosia was real! But he was not going to take advantage of her loneliness. There was nothing he could ever do for her. They were both unhappy enough without exchanging unsecured promises. He was a slave—but not a thief.

The day was still young and at his disposal; for Marcellus did not want him about. Perhaps that was because he wished to be undistracted while he made experiments with his modeling-clay; perhaps, again, he needed solitude for a reshaping of his preconceived theories about supernatural phenomena.

Strolling out of the Temple garden, Demetrius proceeded down the street which grew noisier and more crowded as he neared the agora. He aimlessly sauntered through the vasty market-place, savoring the blended aromas of ground spices, ripe melons, roasted nuts, and fried leeks; enjoying the polyglot confusion. Emerging, he lounged into a circle gathered about a blind lute-player and his loyal dog; drifted across the cobbled street to listen to a white-bearded soothsayer haranguing a small, apathetic company from the portico of an abandoned theater; was jostled off the pavement by a shabby legionary who needed much room for his cruise with a cargo of wine. Time was beginning to hang heavy on his hands.

It now occurred to him that he might trump up some excuse to have a talk with Benjamin. Purchasing a small basket of ripe figs, he proceeded to the weaver's house; and, entering, presented himself before the old man's worktable.

'So—he decided not to come; eh?' observed Benjamin, glancing up sourly and returning immediately to his stitches. 'Well—you're much too early. I have not finished. As you see, I am at work on it now.'

'I did not come for the Robe, sir.' Demetrius held out his gift. 'It was a long day, and I had no employment. I have been strolling about. Would you like some figs?'

Benjamin motioned to have the basket put down on the table beside him; and, taking one of the figs, slowly munched it, without looking up from his work. After a while, he had cleared his mouth enough to be articulate.

'Did you say to yourself, "I must take that cross old Jew some of these nice figs"?—or did you say, "I want to ask Benjamin some questions, and I'll take the figs along, so he'll think I just dropped in to be friendly"?'

'They're quite good figs, sir,' said Demetrius.

'So they are.' Benjamin reached for another. 'Have one yourself,' he mumbled, with difficulty. 'Why did you not want him to come back and see me today? You were afraid I might press him to talk about that poor, dead Jew? Well—and why not? Surely a proud young Roman need not shrink from the questions of an old weaver—an old Jewish weaver—in subjugated Athens!'

'Perhaps I should let my master speak for himself. He has not instructed me to discuss this matter.'

'I daresay you are telling the truth; albeit frugally,' grinned Benjamin. 'You would never be mistaken for a sieve. But why may we not do a little honest trading? You came to ask questions. Very well; ask them. Then—I shall ask questions of you. We will put all of the questions on the table, and bargain for answers. Is that not fair enough?'

'I'm afraid I don't quite understand,' parried Demetrius.

'Well—for one thing—I noticed yesterday that you were surprised and troubled when I showed knowledge of strange doings in Jerusalem, last Passover Week; and I think you would like to ask me how much I know about that. Now—I shall be glad to tell you, if you will first answer some questions of mine.' Benjamin glanced up with a sly, conspiratorial smile. 'I shall give you an easy one first. Doubtless you were in Jerusalem with your master: did you happen to see the Galilean whom they crucified?'

'Yes, sir,' replied Demetrius, promptly.

'Very good. What manner of man was he?' Benjamin put down his work, and leaned forward with eager interest. 'You are a bright fellow, for a slave—and a heathen. Was there anything—anything peculiar—about this Galilean? How close did you get to him? Did you hear him speak?'

'My first sight of the Galilean was on the morning of our entrance into Jerusalem. There was a great crowd accompanying him into the city. Not knowing the language, I did not fully understand the event; but learned that this large multitude of country people wanted to crown him king. They were shouting "Messiah!" I was told that these people were always looking for a great leader to deliver them from political bondage; he would be the "Messiah." So—the crowd shouted "Messiah!"—and waved palms before him, as if he were a king.'

Benjamin's eyes were alert and his shrunken mouth was open, the puckered lips trembling.

'Go on!' he demanded, gutturally, when Demetrius paused.

'I forced my way into the pack until I was almost close enough to have touched him. He was indeed an impressive man, sir, albeit simply clad——'

'In this?' Benjamin caught up the Robe in his shaking hands and pushed it toward Demetrius, who nodded—and went on.

'It was quite evident that the man was not enjoying the honor. His eyes were brooding; full of sadness; full of loneliness.'

'Ah!—wait a moment, my friend!' Benjamin turned to his shelf of scrolls; drew out one that had seen much handling; turned it rapidly to the passage he sought; and read, in a deep sonorous tone: '"—a man of sorrows—acquainted with grief——" This is the prophecy of Yeshayah. Proceed, please! Did he speak?'

'I did not hear him speak—not that day.'

'Ah!—so you saw him again!'

'When he was tried—at the Insula, a few days later—for treason.'
'You saw that?'

Demetrius nodded.

'What was his behavior there?' asked Benjamin. 'Did he plead for mercy?'

'No—he was quite composed. I could not understand what he said; but he accepted his sentence without protest.'

Benjamin excitedly spread open his ancient scroll.

'Listen, my friend! This, too, is from the prophecy of Yeshayah. "He was oppressed and afflicted, yet he opened not his mouth."'

'He did talk,' remembered Demetrius, 'but very calmly—and confidently. That was thought strange, too; for he had been cruelly whipped.'

Benjamin read again from the scroll in an agitated voice: '"He was wounded for our transgressions—and with his stripes we are healed."'

'Whose transgressions'—wondered Demetrius—'the Jews'?'

'Yeshayah was a Jewish prophet, my friend,' replied Benjamin. 'And he was foretelling the coming of a Jewish Messiah.'

'That means then that the Messiah's injuries would not be borne in the interest of any other people?' persisted Demetrius. 'If that is true, I do not think this Jesus was the Messiah! Before he died, he forgave the Roman legionaries who had nailed him to the cross!'

Benjamin glanced up with a start.

'How do you know that?' he demanded.

'So it was said by those who stood by,' declared Demetrius. 'It was heard by all.'

'This is a strange thing!' murmured Benjamin. Presently he roused from a long moment of deep meditation. 'Now—you may ask me questions, if you wish,' he said.

'I think you have answered my queries, sir. I thought you might tell me something more about the Messiah—and you have done so. According to the writings, he was to come as the champion of the Jewish people. The man I saw had no wish to be their champion. It made him unhappy when they urged kingship upon him. At his trial he said he had a kingdom—but it was not in the world.'

'Where then—if not in the world?' rasped Benjamin.

'You are much wiser than I, sir. If you do not know, it would be presumptuous for a pagan slave to attempt an explanation.'

'You are sarcastic, my young friend,' grumbled Benjamin.

'No, sir—I am entirely sincere—and bewildered. I think this Jesus was interested in *everybody!* I think he was *sorry for everybody!*' Demetrius paused, and murmured apologetically, 'Perhaps I have been talking too freely, sir.'

'You have a right to talk,' conceded Benjamin. 'I am a Jew—but I believe that our God is the father of mankind. Peradventure the

Messiah—when he comes to reign over the Jews—will establish justice for all.'

'I wish I could study these ancient prophecies,' said Demetrius.

'Well'—Benjamin shrugged—'and why not? Here they are. You have a good mind. If you have much time, and little to do, learn to read them.'

'How?'

'I might help you,' said Benjamin, amiably. He swung his thin legs over the edge of the table. 'You will excuse me now,' he added, abruptly. 'I must prepare my noonday meat.' Without further words of leave-taking, he moved slowly toward a door at the rear, and disappeared.

* * * * * *

Evidently Benjamin had finished his day's labor, for the sleek-topped worktable was unoccupied. A door in the far corner behind the largest loom, unnoticed by Marcellus on his previous visit, stood hospitably ajar. He walked toward it.

In pleasant contrast to the stifling confusion of the overcrowded shop, Benjamin's private quarters were simply but tastefully furnished. The orange-and-blue rug that covered the entire floor was of fine workmanship. There were three comfortable chairs and footstools, a couch with a pair of camel's-hair saddle-bags for a pillow, and a massive metal-bound chest. An open case of deep shelves, fitted around either side and below a large window, was filled to capacity with ancient scrolls.

A farther door opposite gave upon a shaded, stone-flagged court. Assuming that the old man expected him to proceed, Marcellus crossed the room. Benjamin, surprisingly tall in his long black robe and tasseled skull-cap, was laying a table in the center of his high-walled vine-thatched peristyle.

'I hope I am not intruding,' said Marcellus.

'It is never an intrusion,' said Benjamin, 'to pass through an open door in Athens. You are welcome.' He pointed to one of the rug-covered chairs by the table and put down the two silver goblets from his tray.

'I had not known that you lived here, at your shop,' remarked Marcellus, for something to say.

'For two reasons,' explained Benjamin, laying an antique knife beside the brown barley-loaf. 'It is more convenient, and it is prudent. One does not leave a shop unguarded in this city.'

'Or any other city of my acquaintance,' commented Marcellus.

'Such as—' Benjamin drew out his chair and sat.

'Well—such as Rome, for example. We are overrun with slaves. They are notorious thieves, with no regard for property rights.'

Benjamin laughed gutturally.

'The slave is indeed a predatory creature,' he remarked dryly. 'He makes off with your best sandals when the only thing you have stolen from him is his freedom.' He raised his cup and bowed to Marcellus. 'Shall we drink to the day when no man is another man's property?'

'Gladly!' Marcellus sipped his wine. It was of good vintage. 'My father,' he asserted, 'says the time will come when Rome must pay dearly for enslaving men.'

'He does not approve of it? Then I presume he owns no slaves.' Benjamin was intent upon evenly slicing the bread. Marcellus flushed a little at the insinuation.

'If slavery were abolished,' he said, defensively, 'my father would be among the first to applaud. Of course—as the matter stands—'

'Of course,' echoed Benjamin. 'Your father knows it is wrong, but other men of his social station practice it. In his opinion, it is better to be wrong than eccentric.'

'If I may venture to speak for my father,' said Marcellus, calmly, 'I do not think he has elaborated a theory of that nature. He is a man of integrity and generosity. His slaves are well treated. They probably have better food and shelter in our home—'

'I can readily believe that,' interrupted Benjamin. 'They have more to eat than they might have if they were free. Doubtless that is also true of your horses and dogs. The question is: Are men and beasts of the same category? Is there no essential difference between them in respect to the quality of their value? If a healthy, hard-working ass can be had for ten drachmas, and an able-bodied man can be had for two silver talents, the difference in their worth is purely quantitative. It is at that point that I find human slavery abhorrent. It is an offense to the majesty of the human spirit; for if any man deserves to be regarded as of the same quality as a beast of burden, then no man has any dignity left. I, Benjamin, believe that all men are created in the image of God.'

'Is that a Jewish conception?' asked Marcellus.

'Yes.'

'But wealthy Jews own slaves; do they not?' Marcellus raised the question casually as if it didn't matter much how or whether the old man answered it, but the charge stirred Benjamin to instant attention.

'Ah—there you have tapped one of the roots of our trouble!' he exclaimed. 'The Jew professes to believe that humanity was created in the image of God. Thus he affirms that God is his spiritual father. But that can be true only if he declares that all men are the children of God. Either they all are—or none! I, Benjamin, think they all are! Therefore, when I enslave another man, placing him at one with the cattle in the fields, I throw my whole case away.'

Marcellus broke his bread and amiably conceded that it didn't seem quite right for one man to own another. It was no way to regard a fellow human, he said, even if you treated him kindly. A man shouldn't be made to feel that he was just another animal.

'Oh—as for that'—Benjamin dismissed this idea with an indifferent wave of his thin arm—'you don't rob a slave of his divine character when you buy him and hitch him to a plow, between an ox and an ass. He has had no choice in the matter. It isn't he who has demoted mankind: it is *you!* He is still free to believe that God is his spiritual father. But *you* aren't! Now, you take the case of that handsome Greek who trails about after you. Slavery hasn't stopped *him* from being one of the sons of God, if he wants to consider himself so; but his slavery has made *you* a relative of the beasts, because that is your conception of man's value.'

'I am not much of a philosopher,' admitted Marcellus, carelessly. 'Perhaps, after I've been in Athens awhile, lounging on Mars' Hill, observing the spinning of sophistical cobwebs—'

'You'll be able to tie up sand with a rope,' assisted Benjamin, in the same temper. 'But what we're talking about is more than a pedantry. It is a practical matter. Here is your great Roman Empire, sending out its ruthless armies in all directions to pillage and persecute weak nations; bringing home the best of their children in stinking slave-ships, and setting the old ones at hard labor to pay an iniquitous tribute. Eventually the Roman Empire will collapse—'

'My father thinks that,' interposed Marcellus. 'He says that the Romans, with their slave labor, are getting softer and fatter and lazier, every day; and that the time will come—'

'Yes, yes—the time will come—but that won't be the reason!' declaimed Benjamin. 'The Romans will be crushed, but not because they are too fat. It will be because they have believed that all men are beasts. Enslaving other men, they have denied their own spiritual dignity. Not much wonder that your Roman gods are a jest and a mockery in the sight of all your intelligent people. What do *you* want with gods—you who think that men are like cattle, to be led by a halter? Why should *you* look to the gods, when your dog doesn't?'

Benjamin paused in his monologue to refill their goblets. He had been much stirred, and his old hand was trembling.

'I am a Jew,' he went on, 'but I am not unconversant with the religion of other races. Time was when your Roman deities were regarded with some respect. Jove meant something to your ancestors. Then the time came when Julius Caesar became a god, more important than Jove. Only the down-trodden any longer believed in the classic deities who controlled the sunrise and the rain, who dealt out rewards and punishments, who tempered the wind for the mariner, and filled the grape with goodness. And why—let me ask you—did Caesar make a mockery of the Roman religion? Ah—that was when the Romans had achieved enough military power to enslave other nations, buying and selling men, and driving them in herds. By that act they declared that all men—including themselves, of course—were of no relation to the gods! Vain and pompous Caesar was god enough when it became established that all men were animals!'

'I don't believe any sensible person ever thought that Julius was a god,' protested Marcellus.

'Down in his heart—no,' agreed Benjamin. 'Nor Caesar, himself, I dare say!'

'Is it your belief, then, that if the Romans abolished slavery they would think more highly of the old gods, and by their reverence make themselves more noble?'

Benjamin chuckled derisively.

'An "if" of such magnitude,' he growled, 'makes the rest of your question ridiculous.'

'Well—as for me'—Marcellus had tired of the subject, as his tone candidly announced—'I have no interest in the gods, be they classic or contemporary.'

'How do you account for the universe?' demanded Benjamin.

'I don't,' replied Marcellus. 'I didn't know that I was expected to.' And then, feeling that this rejoinder was more impolite than amusing, he added quickly: 'I should be glad to believe in a supernatural being, if one were proposed who seemed qualified for that office. It would clarify many a riddle. Yesterday you were saying that your people—the Samaritans—worshiped on the mountaintops. I can cheerfully do that too if I'm not required to personify the sunrise and the trees.'

'We do not personify the objects of nature,' explained Benjamin. 'We believe in one God—a Spirit—creator of all things.'

'Somewhere I have heard it said'—Marcellus' eyes were averted thoughtfully—'that the Jews anticipate the rise of a great leader, a champion, a king. He is to set them free and establish an enduring government. Do you Samaritans believe that?'

'We do!' declared Benjamin. 'All of our great prophets have foretold the coming of the Messiah.'

'How long have you been looking for him?'

'For many centuries.'

'And you are still hopeful?'

Benjamin stroked his long beard thoughtfully.

'The expectation ebbs and flows,' he said. 'In periods of national calamity there has been much talk of it. In times of great hardship and persecution, the Jews have been alert to discover among themselves some wise and brave man who might give evidence of messianic powers.'

'And never found one to qualify?' asked Marcellus.

'Not the real one—no.' Benjamin paused to meditate. 'It is a queer thing,' he went on. 'In a time of great need, when powerful leadership is demanded, the people—confused and excited—hear only the strident voices of the audacious, and refuse to listen to the voice of wisdom which, being wise, is temperate. Yes—we have had many zealous pretenders to messiahship. They have come and gone—like meteors.'

'But—in the face of all these disappointments, you sustain your faith that the Messiah will come?'

'He will come,' murmured Benjamin. 'Of course, every generation thinks its own problems are severe enough to warrant his coming. Ever since the Roman occupation, there has been a revival of interest in the ancient predictions. Even the Temple has pretended to yearn for the Messiah.'

'Pretended?' Marcellus raised his brows.

'The Temple is fairly well satisfied with things as they are,' grumbled Benjamin. 'The Roman Prefects grind the poor with vicious taxation, but they are careful about imposing too hard on the priests and the influential rich. The Temple would be embarrassed, I fear, if the Messiah put in an appearance. He might want to make some changes.' The old man seemed to be talking mostly to himself now, for he did not bother to explain what he meant.

'He might discharge the merchants, perhaps, who sell sacrificial beasts to the poor at exorbitant prices?' asked Marcellus, artlessly.

Benjamin rallied from his reminiscent torpor and slowly turned an inquiring gaze upon his pagan guest.

'How do you happen to know about that iniquity?' he asked slyly.

'Oh—I heard it discussed in Jerusalem.' Marcellus made it sound unimportant. 'It seems there had been a little protest.'

'A little protest?' Benjamin lifted an ironical eyebrow. 'It must have been quite an insistent protest to have come to the ears of a visiting Roman. What were you doing there—if I may venture to ask?'

'It was Empire business,' replied Marcellus, stiffly. He rose, readjusting the folds of his toga. 'I must not outstay my welcome,' he said, graciously. 'You have been most kind. I am indebted. May I have the Robe now?'

Benjamin withdrew, returning almost immediately. Marcellus examined the Robe in the waning light.

'It is well done,' he said. 'No one would know it had ever been torn.'

'But you,' said Benjamin, gravely. Marcellus shifted his position, uneasily, avoiding the old man's eyes. 'These stains'—added Benjamin—'I tried to remove them. They will not come out. You have not told me about this poor Jew. He was brave, you said; and died at the hands of his enemies. Was he a Galilean, perhaps?'

'I believe so,' replied Marcellus, restlessly. He folded the Robe over his arm, and extended his hand in farewell.

'Was his name Jesus?' Benjamin's insistent voice had dropped to a mere guttural whisper.

'Yes—that was his name,' admitted Marcellus, grudgingly. 'How did you know?'

'I learned of the incident from a long-time friend, one Popygos, a dealer in spices. He was in Jerusalem during this last Passover Week. Tell me'—Benjamin's tone was entreating—'how did you come by this Robe?'

'Does it matter?' countered Marcellus, suddenly haughty.

Benjamin bowed obsequiously, rubbing his thin hands.

'You must forgive me for being inquisitive,' he murmured. 'I am an old man, without family, and far from my native land. My scrolls— the history of my race, the words of our great prophets—they are my meat and drink, my young friend! They are a lamp unto my feet and a light upon my path. They are my heritage. My daily work—it is nothing! It busies my fingers and brings me my food; but my soul, my life— it is hidden and nourished in words so fitly spoken they are as apples of gold in pictures of silver!' Benjamin's voice had risen resonantly and his deep-lined face was enraptured.

'You are fortunate, sir,' said Marcellus. 'I, too, am fond of the classics bequeathed to us by men of great wisdom—Plato, Pythagoras, Parmenides—'

Benjamin smiled indulgently and wagged his head.

'Yes, yes—it was through their works that you were taught how to read—but not how to live! They who spoke the Hebrew tongue understood the words of life! Now—you see—my young friend—throughout these prophecies there runs a promise. One day, a Messiah shall arise and reign! His name shall be called Wonderful! And of his kingdom there shall be no end! No certain time is set for his coming—but he will come! Think you then that it is a mere idle curiosity in me to inquire diligently about this Jesus, whom so many have believed to be the Messiah?'

'I would hear more about these predictions,' said Marcellus, after a meditative pause.

'Why not?' Benjamin's deep set eyes lighted. 'I love to think of them. I shall gladly tell you; though it would be better if you could read them for yourself.'

'Is Hebrew difficult?' asked Marcellus.

Benjamin smiled and shrugged.

'Well—it is no more difficult than Greek, which you speak fluently. Naturally—it is more difficult than Latin.'

'Why—"naturally"?' snapped Marcellus, frowning.

'Forgive me,' retreated Benjamin. 'Perhaps the Greek asks more of the mind because the Greek writers—' The old man politely floundered to a stop.

'The Greek writers thought more deeply,' assisted Marcellus. 'Is that what you're trying to say? If so—I agree with you.'

'I meant no offense,' reiterated Benjamin. 'Rome has her poets, satirists, eulogists. There are many interesting little essays by your Cicero; rather childish. They pick flowers, but they do not sweep the sky!' Benjamin caught up a worn scroll from the table and deftly unrolled it with familiar hands. 'Listen, friend!—"When I consider thy heavens, the work of thy fingers, the moon and the stars which thou hast ordained, what is man that thou art mindful of him?"'

'Rather pessimistic, I'd say,' broke in Marcellus, 'albeit it sounds sensible enough.'

'But wait!' cried Benjamin. 'Let me go on, please!—"Thou hast made him a little lower than the angels, and hast crowned him with glory and honor." Ah—there is richness in the Hebrew wisdom! You should acquaint yourself with it!'

'For the present, I shall have to content myself with such choice bits of it as you may be good enough to offer me, from time to time,' said Marcellus. 'I am doing some sculpturing now, and it will claim my full attention.' He laid a small silk bag of silver on the table. 'Please accept this—for mending the Robe.'

'But I do not wish to be paid,' said Benjamin, firmly.

'Then give it to the poor,' said Marcellus, impatiently.

'Thank you.' Benjamin bowed. 'It has just occurred to me that if you would know something of this ancient Jewish lore—and are quite too busy to study it for yourself—you might permit your Greek slave to learn the language. I should be glad to instruct him. He is intelligent.'

'It is true that Demetrius is bright. May I ask how you discovered it?'

'He spent an hour here today.'

'Indeed! What was his errand?'

Benjamin shrugged the query away as of no consequence.

'He was sauntering about, and paid me a friendly call; brought me some figs; asked me some questions.'

'What manner of questions?'

'He may tell you if you ask him,' said Benjamin, dryly. 'He is your property; is he not?'

'I do not own his thoughts,' retorted Marcellus. 'Perhaps you have imputed to me a more brilliant talent for brutality than I possess.'

Old Benjamin smiled, almost benevolently, shook his head slowly, and laid a thin hand on Marcellus' broad shoulder.

'No—I do not think you are cruel, my son,' he declared, gently. 'But you are an unfortunate representative of a cruel system. Perhaps you cannot help yourself.'

'Perchance—when your Messiah comes,' rejoined Marcellus, crisply, still smarting under the old man's condescension, 'he may make some valuable suggestions.' He turned to go.

'By the say,' said Benjamin, following to the door, 'how long, after the crucifixion of Jesus, did you remain in Jerusalem?'

'I left the city before sunrise, the next morning,' replied Marcellus.

'Ah!' reflected Benjamin, stroking his white beard. 'Then you heard nothing further—about him?'

'What more was there to hear? He was dead.'

'Do you'—the old man hesitated—'do you know that—for a certainty?'

'Yes,' declared Marcellus. 'I am sure of it.'

'Were you there?' Benjamin's cavernous eyes insisted upon a direct answer. It was slow in coming.

'I saw him die,' admitted Marcellus. 'They pierced his heart, to make sure, before they took him down.'

To his amazement, Benjamin's seamed face lighted with a rapturous smile.

'Thank you, my friend!' he said, brightly. 'Thank you—for telling me!'

'I had not supposed my painful words would make you glad,' said Marcellus, in a tone of bewilderment. 'This Jesus was a brave man! He deserved to live! Yet you seem pleased to be assured that he was put to death!'

'There have been many rumors,' said Benjamin, 'many idle tales, reporting that the drunken legionaries left the scene before he died, and that the friends of the Galilean rescued and revived him.'

'Well—I happen to know that such tales are untrue!' said Marcellus, firmly. 'The executioners were drunk enough, but they killed the Galilean, and when they left—he was dead! This is not hearsay with me. *I know!*'

'You are speaking important words, my son!' Benjamin's voice was husky with emotion. 'I am glad you came today! I shall hope to see more of you, sir.' He raised his bony hand over Marcellus' head. His arm was trembling. 'The Lord bless you and keep you,' he intoned, reverently. 'The Lord make his face to shine upon you, and be gracious unto you. The Lord lift up his countenance upon you, and give you peace.'

There was a long moment of silence before Marcellus stirred. Much perplexed, and uncertain what was expected of him, he bowed respectfully to Benjamin; and, without further words, walked slowly through the shop and out into the twilight.

Chapter X

Now that Diana was expected back from Capri almost any day, the Gallio family felt that some explanation must be contrived to account for the sudden departure of Marcellus.

Unquestionably word had already reached Tiberius that *The Vestris* had arrived with Marcellus as her most important passenger. Diana would be eager to see him, and she had every reason to believe that he would be waiting impatiently for her return.

Lucia was for telling her that Marcellus had come home in such frail health that an immediate change of climate seemed imperative, though Diana would inquire about the nature of his malady, and wonder in what respect the climate of Athens was so highly esteemed.

Cornelia had weakly suggested that perhaps there were better physicians in Athens. Diana might be satisfied with that, she thought, or said she did; but this was nonsense, for everybody knew that most of the really good Athenian physicians had been imported to Rome.

'No,' Senator Gallio had observed judicially, 'you are both in error. When there is some serious explaining to be done, no contraption is as serviceable as the truth. Let her have it. If Diana and my son are in love, as you two seem to think, she has a right to know the story and it is our duty to tell her. It should not be difficult.' With everything thus sensibly settled, the Senator rose and was leaving his wife's boudoir when their daughter halted him.

'Assuming that I have it to do,' said Lucia, maturely, 'how much of the story is to be told?'

Her father made the query of no great importance with a negligent flick of his fingers.

'You can say that your brother was required to conduct the crucifixion of a Jewish revolutionist; that the experience was a shock; that it plunged him into a deep melancholy from which he has not yet fully recovered; that we thought it best for him to seek diversion.'

'Nothing, then,' mused Lucia, 'about those dreadful seizures of remorse—and the haunted look—and that odd question he insisted on asking, against his will?'

'Mmm—no,' decided the Senator. 'That will not be necessary. It should be sufficient to say that Marcellus is moody and depressed.'

'Diana will not be contented with that explanation,' declared Lucia. 'She is going to be disappointed, embarrassed, and indignant.

Quite aside from their fondness for each other, it was no small thing she did for Marcellus in having him recalled from exile. And she will think it very strange indeed that a Roman Tribune should be so seriously disturbed by the execution of a convict.'

'We are all agreed on that,' glumly conceded the Senator. 'I do not pretend to understand it. My son has never been lacking in courage. It is not like him to fall ill at the sight of blood.'

'Perhaps it would be better,' put in Cornelia, suddenly inspired, 'if we omit all reference to that dreadful crucifixion, and simply say that Marcellus wanted to do some sculpturing, and attend some lectures, and—'

'So urgently,' scoffed Lucia, 'that he couldn't wait a few days to see the girl who was responsible for bringing him home.'

Her mother sighed, took another stitch in her embroidery, and murmured that her suggestion did sound rather silly, an afterthought that her relatives accepted without controversy.

'He promised me he would write to her,' remembered Lucia.

'Well—we cannot wait for that,' said her father. 'It might be weeks. Diana will want to know—now! Better tell her everything, Lucia. She will get it out of you, in any case. A young woman bright enough to extort valuable favors from our crusty old Emperor will make her own deductions about this—no matter what you tell her.'

'If she really loves him,' cooed Cornelia, 'she will forgive him— anything!'

'Doubtless,' agreed her husband, dryly, moving toward the door.

'I'm afraid you do not know Diana very well,' cautioned Lucia. 'She has had no training that would fit her to understand. She idolizes her father, who would as lief kill a man as a mouse. I do not think she is experienced in forgiving people for being weak.'

'That doesn't sound like you, Lucia,' reproved her mother, gently, when the Senator was out of hearing. 'One would almost think you were not sympathetic with your brother. Surely—you do not think Marcellus weak; do you?'

'Oh—I don't know what to think,' muttered Lucia, dismally. 'What is there to think?' She put both her hands over her eyes and shook her head. 'We've lost Marcellus, Mother,' she cried. 'He was so manly! I loved him so much! It is breaking my heart.'

*   *   *   *   *   *

But if the problem of dealing out the bad news to Diana was perplexing, it was simple as compared with the dilemma that arose on the following afternoon when an impressively uniformed Centurion was shown in, bearing an ornate, official scroll addressed to Marcellus. It was from the Emperor. The Centurion said he was expected to wait for instructions, adding that the royal carriage would call early in the morning.

'But my son is not here,' said Gallio. 'He has sailed for Athens.'

'Indeed! That is most unfortunate!'

'I gather that you are acquainted with the nature of this message.'

'Yes, sir; it is no secret. The Emperor has appointed Tribune Marcellus to be the Commander of the Palace Guard. We are all much pleased, sir.'

'I sincerely regret my son's absence, Centurion. Perhaps I should send a message with you to the Emperor.' Gallio reflected for a moment. 'No—I shall go and explain to him in person.'

'Very good, sir. Will it be agreeable to start at dawn?'

So—they started at dawn, though it was not particularly agreeable, a swift drive from Rome to Neapolis being rated by the Senator as a doubtful pleasure. Moreover, he had no great relish for his errand. He was not unacquainted with the techniques of persuasive debate, but the impending interview with the Emperor would be unpleasant; for Tiberius had no patience and Gallio had no case. The horses galloped over the deep-rutted cobbles, the big carriage bounced, the painful hours dragged, the Senator's head ached. All things considered, it was not an enjoyable excursion, and by the time he reached the top of Capri, at midnight, there was nothing left in him but a strong desire to go to bed.

The Chamberlain showed him to a sumptuous apartment and Gallio sank into a chair utterly exhausted. Two well-trained Macedonians began unpacking his effects, laying out fresh linen. Another slave drew water for his bath while a big Nubian, on his knees, unlaced the Senator's sandals. A deferential Thracian came with a welcome flagon of chilled wine. Then the Chamberlain reappeared.

'The Emperor wishes to see you, sir,' he reported, in an apologetic tone.

'Now?' Gallio wrinkled his nose distastefully.

'If you please, sir. His majesty had left orders to have Tribune Marcellus shown into his presence immediately upon his arrival. When told that Senator Gallio had come instead, the Emperor said he would give him an audience at once.'

'Very well,' sighed Gallio. Signing to the Nubian to relace his sandals, the weary man rose stiffly and followed along to the Emperor's lavishly appointed suite.

The old man was sitting up in bed, bolstered about with pillows, his nightcap rakishly askew. A half-dozen attendants were fluttering about, inventing small errands.

'Out!' he yelled, as the Senator neared the imperial couch; and they backed nimbly away—all but the Chamberlain. 'You, too!' shrilled Tiberius—and the Chamberlain tiptoed to the door. Peering up into Gallio's face, the Emperor regarded him with a surly look of challenge.

'What is the meaning of this?' he squeaked. 'We confer a great honor upon your son, who has done nothing to deserve it, only to learn that—without so much as a by-your-leave—he has left the country. You, his father, have come to explain. Well!—be about it, then! High time somebody explained!'

'Your Majesty,' began Gallio, with a deep bow, 'my son will be very unhappy when he learns that he has unwittingly offended his Emperor, to whom he owes so much.'

'Never mind about that!' barked Tiberius, 'Get on with it! And make it short! I need my rest! They were a pack of fools to wake me up for no better cause—and you were a fool to let them! You, too, should be in bed. You have had a hard trip. You are tired. Sit down! Don't stand there like a sentry! I command you to sit down! You are an old, old man. Sit down—before you fall down!'

Gallio gratefully sank into the luxurious chair by the Emperor's massive golden bed, pleased to observe that the royal storm was subsiding somewhat.

'As Your Majesty has said, it is too late in the night for a lengthy explanation. My son Marcellus was appointed Legate of the Legion at Minoa—'

'Yes, yes—I know all about that!' spluttered Tiberius. 'We rescinded the order of that addlepated scamp in Rome and brought your son back. And then what?'

'From Minoa, sire, he was ordered to Jerusalem to help preserve the peace during the Jews' annual festival. A small but turbulent revolutionary party became active. Its leader was tried for treason and condemned to death by crucifixion.'

'Crucifixion, eh? Must have been a dangerous character.'

'I did not understand it so, Your Majesty. He was a young Jew of no great repute, a harmless, mild-mannered, peace-loving fellow from one of the outlying provinces—Galilee, I believe. It seems he had grossly offended the Temple authorities.'

'Indeed!' Tiberius leaned forward with sudden interest. 'What did he do?'

'It is their custom, sire, to sell sacrificial animals in the court of the Temple. The priests profit by it, demanding high prices from the poor. This Galilean was enraged over the fraud and the sacrilege; took up a drover's whip, and lashed the priests and the beasts out of the Temple and into the street, and—'

'Hi! Hi!' yelled Tiberius, so loudly that the Chamberlain put his head in at the door. 'Here—you! Worthless eavesdropper! Bring wine for Senator Gallio. We, ourself, shall have wine! Hi! Hi! Mild-mannered, peace-loving Galilean whipped the prating priests out into the street, eh? Not much wonder they crucified him! He was a reckless fellow, indeed! But when does your son appear in this story?'

'He was ordered to crucify the Jew—and it made him ill.' Gallio paused to sip his wine slowly, while the old man snuffled and bubbled into the huge goblet which the Chamberlain held to his lips.

'Ill?' Tiberius grinned sourly and belched. 'Sick at his stomach?'

'Sick in his head. If it is your pleasure, sire, I shall tell you about it,' said Gallio; and when Tiberius had nodded assent, he proceeded to an account of Marcellus' depression and strange behavior, and their decision to send him to Athens, where, they hoped, he might find mental diversion.

'Well!' grunted Tiberius. 'If your sensitive son cannot endure the scent of warm blood, we would not urge him to undertake the protection of our person. We had understood from the young daughter of Gallus that he was a brave man. In her sight he is highly esteemed, and it was to please her that we brought him home—and appointed him to command the Villa Guard. It is well for her that his weakness is made manifest before he has had an opportunity to bring disgrace upon her.'

This was too bitter a dose for Gallio to take without protest.

'Your Majesty places me in a difficult position,' he declared, riskily. 'It would be most unseemly in me to express a contrary opinion; yet the Emperor would surely consider me mean and cowardly did I not venture some defense of my own flesh and blood!'

Tiberius slobbered in the depths of his goblet for a moment that seemed very long to Gallio. At length he came up wheezing.

'Very—hic—well! Say on!' The old man scrubbed his wet chin with the back of a mottled hand. 'Defend your son!'

'Marcellus is not a weakling, sire. He is proud and brave; worthy of his Roman citizenship and his rank as a Tribune. I do not fully understand why he should have been so affected by the crucifixion of this Jew, except that—'

'Go on! Except what?'

'He thinks the Galilean was innocent of any crime deserving so severe a punishment. The Procurator himself declared the man innocent and tried to argue in his behalf.'

'And then condemned him to death? What manner of justice does the Empire administer in Jerusalem? Who is the Prefect now—this sleek and slimy fellow—what's his name—Herod?'

'They tried him before Herod, yes—but it was Pontius Pilate who sentenced him. Pilate is the Procurator.'

Tiberius laughed bitterly, coughed, and spat on the silk sleeve of his robe.

'Pontius Pilate,' he snarled reminiscently. 'He's the dizzy one who built that damned aqueduct. Wife wanted gardens. Had to have water. Robbed the Temple to build aqueduct. Fool! Had all the Jews in turmoil. Cost us thousands of legionaries to put down the riots. Had we to do it again, we would let Pilate settle his own account with the Jews! I never thought much of the fellow, letting his silly, spoiled wife lead him about by the nose.' The Emperor paused for breath. 'An impotent nobody,' he added, 'afraid of his wife.' Having grimly pondered this final observation, Tiberius startled his guest by breaking forth in a shrill, drunken guffaw. 'You are at liberty to laugh, too, Gallio,' he shouted. 'Afraid of his wife! Impotent nobody—'fraid of wife! Hi! Hi!'

Gallio grinned obligingly, but did not join in the Emperor's noisy hilarity over his self-debasing joke. Tiberius was drunk, but he would be sober again—and he might remember.

'And this serpent—Herod!' The Emperor rubbed his leaky old eyes with his fists, and rambled on, thickly. 'Well do we know of his perfidies. A loathsome leech, fattening on the blood of his countrymen. Gallio—I have waged war in many lands. I have enslaved many peoples. I have put their brave defenders to death. But—though I commanded their warriors to be slain, I had much respect for their valor. But—this Herod! This verminous vulture! This slinking jackal! —pretending to represent the interests of his conquered fellow Jews —while licking our sandal-straps for personal favors!—what a low creature he is! Yes, yes—I know—it is to the Empire's advantage to have such poltroons in high office throughout all our provinces— selling out their people—betraying them—' Exhausted by his long speech, Tiberius broke off suddenly, gulped another throatful of wine, dribbled a stream of it down his scrawny neck, explored his lips with a clumsy tongue, retched, and muttered, 'I hate a traitor!'

'I have sometimes wondered, sire,' remarked Gallio, thinking some rejoinder was expected, 'whether it really is to the advantage of the Empire when we allow treacherous scoundrels like Herod to administer the affairs of our subjugated provinces. Is it safe? Does it pay? Our subjects are defrauded, but they are not deceived. Their hatred smoulders, but it is not quenched.'

'Well—let them hate us, then,' growled Tiberius, tiring of the subject—'and much good may it do them! The Roman Empire does not ask to be loved. All she demands is obedience—prompt obedience— and plenty of it!' His voice shrilled, truculently. 'Let them hate us! Let the whole world hate us!' He clenched his gnarled old fists. The Chamberlain gently stroked his pillow to soothe his passion, and ducked as one of the bony elbows shot up unexpectedly in his direction.

Presently the heavy old head drooped. The Chamberlain ventured a beseeching glance at the Senator who half-rose from his chair, uncertain whether to take the initiative in a withdrawal. Tiberius roused and swallowed hard, making a wry face.

'We have gone far afield, Gallio,' he mumbled. 'We were discussing your frail son. He crucified a harmless Jew, and the injustice of it put him to bed, eh? And weeks afterward, he is still brooding. Very peculiar! How do you account for it?'

'The case is full of mystery, sire,' sighed Gallio. 'There is one small matter of which I have not spoken. It concerns this Jew's Robe.'

'Eh?' Tiberius leaned forward, spurred to curiosity. 'Robe? What about a robe?'

Gallio debated with himself, for a moment, how best to proceed, half-sorry he had alluded to the incident.

'My son was accompanied by his Greek slave, a quite intelligent fellow. It is from him that I have this feature of the story. It seems that when the Galilean was crucified, his discarded Robe lay on the ground, and my son and other officers—whiling the time—cast dice for it. Marcellus won it.'

Tiberius was sagging into his pillows, disappointed with so dull a tale.

'That night,' continued Gallio, 'there was a banquet at Pilate's Insula. According to the slave, my son was far from happy, but there was nothing peculiar in his behavior during or after the crucifixion. He had been drinking heavily, but otherwise was of normal mind. At the banquet, one of his staff officers from Minoa, far gone with wine, urged him to put on this Jew's Robe.' Gallio paused, and the old man's face showed a renewed interest.

'Well?' he queried, impatiently. 'Did he put it on?'

Gallio nodded.

'Yes—and he has never been the same since.'

'Ha!' exclaimed the Emperor, brightening. 'Now we are getting some place with this story! Does your son think the Jew laid a curse on his Robe?'

'It is hard to say what my son thinks, sire. He is very reticent.'

Suddenly a light shone in the old man's eyes.

'Ah—I see! That is why you sent him to Athens! He will consult the learned astrologers, soothsayers, and those who commune with the dead! But why Athens? There are better men at Rhodes. Or, you might have sent him here! There are no wiser men than my Rhodesian, Telemarchus!'

'No—Your Majesty; we did not send Marcellus to Athens to consult the diviners. We urged him to go away, for a time, so that he might not be embarrassed by meeting friends in his unhappy state of mind.'

'So—the dead Jew's Robe is haunted?' Tiberius smacked his lips. This tale was much to his liking. 'The Jews are a queer people; very religious; believe in one god. Evidently this Galilean was a religious fanatic, if he got himself into trouble with the Temple; had some new kind of religion, maybe.'

'Did your Majesty ever hear of the Messiah?' inquired Gallio.

The Emperor's jaw slowly dropped and his rheumy eyes widened.

'Yes,' he answered, in a hoarse whisper. 'He that is to come. They're always looking for him, Telemarchus says. They've been expecting him for a thousand years, Telemarchus says. He that is to come—and set up a kingdom.' The old man chuckled, mirthlessly. 'A kingdom, Telemarchus says; a kingdom that shall have no end; and the government shall be upon his shoulder. Telemarchus says it is written. I let him prattle. He is old. He says the Messiah will reign, one day, in Rome! Hi! Hi! I let Telemarchus prattle. Were he younger, by a century or two, I would have him whipped for his impudence. A Messiah—huh! A kingdom—pouf! Well'—Tiberius returned from his rumbling monologue—'what were you starting to say about the Messiah?'

'Nothing, sire—except that there was a strong feeling among the common people—my son's slave says—that this Galilean Jew was the promised Messiah.'

'What?' shouted Tiberius. 'You don't believe that, Gallio!'

'I am not religious, sire.'

'What do you mean—you're not religious? You believe in the gods; do you not?'

'I have no convictions on the subject, Your Majesty. The gods are remote from my field of study, sire.'

Tiberius scowled his stern disapproval.

'Perhaps Senator Gallio will presently be telling us that he does not believe his Emperor is divine!'

Gallio bowed his head and meditated a reply.

'How about it?' demanded the old man, hotly. 'Is the Emperor divine?'

'If the Emperor thought he was divine,' replied Gallio, recklessly, 'he would not need to ask one of his subjects to confirm it.'

This piece of impudence was so stunning that Tiberius was at a loss for appropriate words. After a long, staring silence he licked his dry lips.

'You are a man of imprudent speech, Gallio,' he muttered, 'but honest withal. It has been refreshing to talk with you. Leave us now. We will have further conversation in the morning. We are sorry your son cannot accept our appointment.'

'Good night, sire,' said Gallio. He retreated toward the door. Something in his weighted attitude stirred the old man's mellowed mind to sympathy.

'Stay!' he called. 'We shall find a place for the son of our excellent Gallio. Marcellus shall do his sculpture and attend the learned lectures. Let him dabble in the arts and drowse over the philosophies. Let him perfect himself in logic and metaphysics. By the gods!—there are other things needful at this court besides watching at keyholes and strutting with swords! Your son shall be our preceptor. He shall lecture to us. We are weary of old men's counsel. Marcellus shall give us a youthful view of the mysteries. Gallio—inform your son of our command!'

'Your Majesty is most kind,' murmured the Senator, gratefully. 'I shall advise my son of your generous words, sire. Perhaps this appointment may help to restore his ailing mind.'

'Well—if it doesn't'—the old man yawned mightily—'it won't matter. All philosophers are sick in the head.' He grinned, slowly sank back into his pillows, and the leathery lips puffed an exhausted breath. The Emperor of Rome was asleep.

*　　*　　*　　*　　*　　*

Informed by the Chamberlain that His Imperial Majesty was not yet awake, the Senator breakfasted in his room and set out for a walk. It had been many years since he had visited Capri; not since the formal opening of the Villa Jovis when the entire Senate had attended the festivities, memorable for their expensiveness rather than their impressiveness. Although fully informed about the enormously extravagant building operations on the island, he had not clearly pictured the magnitude of these undertakings. They had to be seen to be believed! Tiberius might be crazy, but he was an accomplished architect.

Walking briskly on the broad mosaic pavement to the east end of the mall, Gallio turned aside to a shaded arbor, sank into a comfortable chair, and dreamily watched the plume of blue smoke floating lazily above Vesuvius. Somehow the sinister old mountain seemed to symbolize the Empire; tremendous power under compression; occasionally spewing forth sulphurous fumes and molten metals. Its heat was not the kind that warmed and cheered, nor did its lava grow harvests. Vesuvius was competent only as a destroyer. They who dwelt in its shadow were afraid.

The same thing was true of the Empire, reflected Gallio. 'Let them hate us!' old Tiberius had growled. 'Let the whole world hate us!' Long before the Caesars, that surly boast had brought disaster to the Persians, the Egyptians, and the Greeks. Nemesis had laughed at their arrogance, and swept them—cursing impotently—into servitude.

Gallio wondered if he would be alive to witness the inevitable breakup of the Empire. What plans had Nemesis in mind for the disposal of Rome? What would be the shape of the new dynasty? Who would arise—and whence—to demolish the thing that the Caesars had built? Last night the disgusting old drunkard Tiberius had seemed almost frightened when he rehearsed the cryptic patter of the Jewish prophets. 'He that is to come.' Ah, yes—Tiberius saw the crisis nearing! Maybe the superstitious old fellow had never defined his exact reasons for being so deeply interested in the oracles and enchantments and ponderous nonsense of his avaricious soothsayers and stargazers; but that was *it!* Tiberius saw the Empire drifting toward the cataract! 'He that is to come.' Well—somebody would come—and the government would be upon his shoulder—but he wouldn't be a Jew! That was impossible! That was ridiculous!

Completely absorbed by his grim speculations, Gallio did not observe Diana's arrival until she stood directly before him, tall, slim, vital. She smiled and graciously held out her hand.

It was the first time he had had an opportunity for conversation with her, beyond the brief greetings they had exchanged when she came to visit Lucia. Until lately, Diana was only a little girl, shy and silent in his presence, but reputed to be high-spirited almost to the extent of rowdiness. In recent weeks, apprised of a growing attachment between his son and the daughter of Gallus, he had become somewhat more aware of her; but, this morning, it was almost as if he had never seen her before. Diana had grown up. She had taken on the supple grace and charming contours of a woman. She was beautiful! Gallio did not wonder that Marcellus had fallen in love with her.

He came to his feet, bowed deeply, and was warmed by her firm handclasp. Her steady eyes were set wide apart, framed in long, curling lashes, and arched by exquisitely modeled brows. The red silk bandeau accented the blue-blackness of her hair, the whiteness of her patrician forehead, the pink flush on her cheeks. Gallio looked into the level eyes with frank admiration. They were quite disturbingly feminine, but fearless and forthright as the eyes of a man; an inheritance from her father, perhaps. Gallus had a delightful personality, and an enviable poise, but—just underneath his amiability—there was the striking strength of a coiled spring in a baited trap. Diana's self-possessed smile and confident handclasp instantly won the Senator's respect, though the thought darted through his mind that the arrestingly lovely daughter of Gallus was equipped with all the implements for having her own way, and—if any attempt were made to thwart her—would prove to be a handful indeed.

'May I join you, Senator Gallio?' Diana's full lips were girlish, but her well-disciplined voice was surprisingly mature.

'Please sit down, my dear.' The Senator noted the easy grace of her posture as she took the chair opposite, artless but alert. 'I was hoping to have a talk with you,' he went on, resuming his seat.

Diana smiled encouragingly, but made no rejoinder; and Gallio, measuring his phrases, proceeded in a manner almost didactic:

'Marcellus came home from his long voyage, a few days ago, ill and depressed. He was grateful—we are all grateful, Diana—for your generous part in bringing him back to us. Marcellus will be eager to express his deep appreciation. But—he is not ready to resume his usual activities. We have sent him away—to Athens—hopeful that a change of environment may divert his gloomy mind.'

Gallio paused. He had anticipated an involuntary exclamation of surprise and regret, but Diana made no sound; just sat there, keenly attentive, alternately studying his eyes and his lips.

'You see'—he added—'Marcellus has had a severe shock!'

'Yes—I know,' she nodded, briefly.

'Indeed? How much do you know?'

'Everything you told the Emperor.'

'But—the Emperor is not yet awake.'

'I have not seen him,' said Diana. 'I had it from Nevius.'

'Nevius?'

'The Chamberlain.'

Gallio stroked his cheek thoughtfully. This Nevius must be quite a talkative fellow. Diana interpreted his dry smile.

'But you had intended to tell me, had you not?' she reminded him. 'Nevius is not a common chatterer, sir: I must say that for him. He is very close-mouthed. Sometimes,' she went on, ingenuously, 'it is difficult to make Nevius tell you everything that is going on at the Villa.'

The Senator's lips slowly puckered and his shoulders twitched with a silent chuckle. He was on the point of asking her if she had ever thought of taking up diplomacy as a profession; but the matter at issue was too serious for badinage. He grew suddenly grave.

'Now that you know—about Marcellus—I need not repeat the painful story.'

'It is all very strange.' Diana's averted eyes were troubled. 'According to Nevius, it was an execution that upset Marcellus.' Her expressive eyes slowly returned to search the Senator's sober face. 'There must be more to it than that, sir. Marcellus has seen cruel things done. Who has not? Is not the arena bloody enough? Why should Marcellus sink into grief and despair because he had to put a man to death?—no matter who—no matter how! He has seen men die!'

'This was a crucifixion, Diana,' said the Senator, quietly.

'And perfectly ghastly, no doubt,' she agreed, 'and Nevius says there was much talk of the man's innocence. Well—that wasn't Marcellus' fault. He didn't conduct the trial, nor choose the manner of execution. I can understand his not wanting to do it, but—surely no amount of brooding is going to bring this poor Jew back to life! There is a mystery behind it, I think. Nevius had a tale about a haunted Robe—and darkness in the middle of the afternoon—and a confused jumble about a predicted Messiah, or something like that. Does Marcellus think he has killed a person of great importance? Is that what's fretting him?'

'I shall tell you the very little that I know about it, Diana, and you may draw your own conclusions. As for me, it has been difficult to arrive at any sensible solution to the problem.' Gallio frowned studiously. 'For ages, the Jewish prophets have predicted the coming of a champion of their people's liberty. This fearless chieftain would restore the Jews' kingdom. Indeed, the traditional forecast—according to Emperor Tiberius, who is learned in all occult matters—is of

wider scope, prefiguring a king with a more extensive dominion than
the mere government of poor little Palestine.'

'Somebody the size of the Caesars?' wondered Diana.

'At least,' nodded Gallio, with a brief, contemptuous grin. 'Now
—it happens that a very considerable number of Jews thought they
had reason to believe that this Galilean, whom the Temple executives
and the Roman provincial government tried for treason and heresy,
was their promised Messiah—'

'But—surely'—broke in Diana—'Marcellus doesn't believe anything
like that! He's the last person in the world!'

'That is true,' agreed Gallio. 'He is not superstitious. But—according
to Demetrius, who was present throughout the whole affair, it was a
strange occasion. The Jew's demeanor at the trial was, to say the least,
unusual. Demetrius says everybody was on trial but the prisoner; says
the man's behavior on the cross was heroic. And Demetrius is a cold-
blooded fellow, not accustomed to inventing lies.'

'What do you think about the Robe?' queried Diana.

'I have no ideas,' confessed the Senator. 'Marcellus had had a hard
day. He was nervous, ashamed, overwrought. He may have been a
victim of his own imagination. But—when he put on that Robe—it
did something to him! We may not like the implications of this problem—but—well—there it is! You doubtless think it is silly to believe
that the Jew's Robe is haunted—and so do I. All such idiotic prattle
is detestable to me! I do not believe there is any energy resident in
an inanimate thing. As for the Messiah legend, I have no interest in
it. Whether the Galilean was justly accused, or not, is a closed incident, of no concern to me. But—after all of these considerations are
dismissed, either as foolish or finished—Marcellus is worrying himself into madness. That much, at least, we know—for a fact.' Gallio
rubbed his wrinkled brow and drew a hopeless sigh.

'Nevius says the Emperor wants Marcellus to come to Capri as a
teacher,' said Diana, after the brief silence between them. 'We don't
want him to do that; do we, sir?'

'I find it difficult to see Marcellus in that rôle,' agreed Gallio. 'He
has but scant respect for the kind of learning that engages the mind
of the Emperor.'

'Do you think he will consent?'

'Well'—Gallio made a helpless little gesture—'Marcellus may not
have much choice in the matter. He is, at present, able to remain
in Athens. But when he comes home, he will have to obey the Emperor's order, whether he enjoys it or not.'

Suddenly Diana leaned forward, her face clouded with anxiety.

'Tell him not to come home,' she whispered. 'He mustn't come
here!' She rose, and Gallio, mystified, came to his feet, regarding her
with serious interest. 'I must tell you something,' she went on,
nervously. She took him by the arm and pointed to a long row of

stakes, with little flags fluttering on them. 'This is where the Emperor is going to build the beautiful new villa. He is drawing the plans for it now. When it is finished, it is to be mine.'

Gallio stared.

'Yours?' he said, woodenly. 'Do you mean you want to live here —under the thumb of this cruel, crazy old man?'

Diana's eyes were full of tears. She shook her head, and turned her face away, still holding tightly to the Senator's arm.

'He suggested it, sir, when I was pleading with him to bring Marcellus home,' she confided, brokenly. 'It wasn't exactly a condition to his promise to send for Marcellus; but—he seems now to think it was. I thought he would forget about it. He forgets almost everything. But —I'm afraid he means to go through with it. That is why he wants Marcellus here. It is to be our villa.'

'Well,' soothed Gallio. 'Why not, then? Is it not true that Marcellus and you are in love?'

Diana nodded and bent her head.

'There will be much trouble if he comes to Capri,' she said, huskily. Then, dashing the tears from her eyes and facing Gallio squarely, she said: 'I must tell you all about it. Please don't try to do anything. Gaius has been here twice recently. He wants me to marry him. The Emperor will not let me go home. I have written to my mother and I know the letter was not delivered.'

'I shall tell her to come to you—at once!' declared Gallio, hotly.

'No, no—not yet—please!' Diana clutched his arm with both hands. 'Maybe there will be some other way out! I must not put my mother in danger!'

'But—Diana—you can't stay here—under these conditions!'

'Please! Don't say—or do—anything.' She was trembling.

'What are you afraid of, my dear?' demanded Gallio.

'I am afraid of Gaius!' she whispered.

Chapter XI

At sunrise on the seventh day of September a market gardener with fresh fruits and vegetables for the House of Eupolis reported that *The Vestris* had been sighted off Piraeus.

Feeling sure there must be letters for him on the ship, and unwilling to await their sluggish delivery through the Tetrarch's Insula in the city, Marcellus engaged a port-wagon and set off at once, accompanied by Demetrius.

Ordinarily the slave would have sat by the driver; but, of late, Demetrius and his master had been conducting all of their conversations in Aramaic. It was not an easy tongue, and when they spoke they enunciated carefully, watching each other's lips. This morning they sat side by side in the rear seat of the jolting wagon, and anyone casually observing them would not have guessed that one of these young men owned the other. Indeed—Demetrius was taking the lead in the conversation, occasionally criticizing his master's accent.

Every morning after breakfast, for several weeks, Demetrius had gone to Benjamin's shop for instruction, spending the day until late afternoon. The old weaver had not asked to be recompensed for his services as a pedagogue. It would be a pleasure to him, he had said. But as the days went by, Demetrius began to be useful in the shop, quickly picking up deftness in carding and spinning. In the evenings, he relayed his accumulated knowledge of Aramaic to Marcellus who, unwilling to be in Benjamin's debt, had presented him—over his protest—with two great bales of long-fibered Egyptian cotton and several bags of selected wools from the Cyprian Mountains where fleeces were appropriate to a severe climate.

Benjamin, who had no talent for flattery, had been moved to volunteer the statement—after a month had passed—that Demetrius was making surprising progress. If that were true, Demetrius had remarked, it was because he had received such clear instruction, to which Benjamin had replied that the best way to learn anything is to explain it to somebody else. Marcellus was receiving his Aramaic on the first bounce, but getting it thoroughly; for Demetrius was holding him to it with a tactful but relentless tyranny.

On the way to Piraeus, they were engaged in an animated discussion of the Ten Commandments, Marcellus approving of them, Demetrius complaining that they were unjust. On occasions, he became so enthusiastic in advocating his cause that he abandoned the Aramaic and took to the Greek, much to his master's amusement.

'Here, you!' shouted Marcellus. 'No talking about the Jewish Commandments in a heathen language!'

'But, sir, they are so unfair! "Thou shalt not steal." Very good; but there is no Commandment enjoining the man of property to deal generously with the poor, so they would have no wish to steal! "Thou shalt not covet!" Good advice; no doubt. But is it fair to tell the poor man he mustn't be envious of the rich man's goods—and then forget to admonish the rich man that he has no right to be so selfish?'

'Oh—you're just looking at it from the slave angle,' drawled Marcellus. 'You're prejudiced. The only fault I can find with the Commandments is their injunction against sculpture. This Jehovah was certainly no patron of the arts.'

'That was to keep them from making idols,' explained Demetrius.

'I know—but what's the matter with idols? They're usually quite artistic. The ordinary run of people are bound to worship something: it had better be something lovely! Old Zeus didn't raise a row when the Greek sculptors carved a flock of gods—all shapes and sizes—take your pick. There must be forty of them on Mars' Hill! They even have one up there in honor of "The Unknown God."'

'I wonder what Zeus thought of that one?' speculated Demetrius.

'He probably laughed,' said Marcellus. 'He does laugh, sometimes, you know. I think that's the main trouble with Jehovah. He doesn't laugh.'

'Maybe he doesn't think the world is very funny,' observed Demetrius.

'Well, that's his fault, then,' said Marcellus, negligently. 'If he created it, he should have made it a little funnier.'

Demetrius made no reply to that.

'I believe that's the silliest thing I ever said in my life!' reflected Marcellus, soberly.

'Oh—I wouldn't go so far as to say that, sir,' rejoined Demetrius, formally. They both laughed. This study of Aramaic was making their master-slave relationship very difficult to sustain.

*   *   *   *   *   *

Captain Fulvius, roaring orders to the sweating slaves, stared strangely at Marcellus as he came on deck; then beamed with sudden recognition and grasped him warmly by the hand.

'You are well again, sir!' he boomed. 'That is good! I hardly knew you. Many's the time I have thought about you. You were a very sick man!'

'I must have tried your patience, Captain,' said Marcellus. 'All is well now, thank you.'

'Ho! Demetrius!' Fulvius offered his hand, somewhat to Marcellus' surprise. 'I haven't forgotten that good turn you did me, son, on the voyage down from Joppa.'

'I hadn't heard about that,' said Marcellus, turning a questioning glance toward Demetrius.

'It was nothing, sir,' murmured Demetrius.

'Nothing!' shouted Fulvius. 'The fellow saves my life, and now declares it was nothing! Demetrius, you should be put in chains for that!' He turned to Marcellus. 'You were too ill to be interested in the story, sir; so we did not bother you with it. A mad slave—it gets quite hot, down in the bottom tier, sir—managed to slip his bracelet, one night, when we were standing off Alexandria; sneaked up on deck, and had a belaying-pin raised to dash my brains out. And your Demetrius got there just in time!'

'I am glad I happened to be standing by, sir,' said Demetrius.

'So am I!' declared the Captain, fervently. 'Well—it's good to see you both. There are letters for you, I notice, Legate. I asked the Tribune to take them to you when he went to deliver the message from the Emperor, but he is a haughty young fellow; said he was not a common errand-boy.'

'Message from the Emperor?' queried Marcellus, uneasily.

'You have not yet received it, then? Perhaps you passed the magnificent Tribune on the way. Will you stay and break bread with us?'

'It would be a pleasure, Captain Fulvius; but I should return without delay. This Tribune may be waiting.'

'Aye! He will be waiting and fuming; a restless fellow, who takes his duties hard; a very important fellow, too, who likes to give orders.' Fulvius sighed unhappily. 'And I shall have him on my hands for another threescore and five days, at least; for he is bearing a message also to Pontius Pilate in Jerusalem—and returns on *The Vestris*.'

'Can't you pitch him overboard?' suggested Marcellus.

'I can,' grinned Fulvius, 'but my wife is expecting me back in Ostia by early December. Legate, if you can spare Demetrius for the day, shall he not tarry with me?'

Marcellus was about to give his consent, but hesitated.

'He may come tomorrow, Fulvius, if you wish it. Perhaps he had best return with me now. This message from the Emperor might make some alterations in our plans.'

'Thank you, Captain Fulvius,' said Demetrius. 'I shall come if I can.'

Marcellus was more eager than the shambling horses to return to the city, but even at their plodding gait it was an uncomfortable ride, certainly not conducive to the pleasant perusal of letters, for the dusty, deep-rutted highway was crammed with lumbering wagons and over-burdened camel-trains, requiring frequent excursions to the ill-conditioned roadside.

He slit the seal of his father's bulky scroll, happy to note that it contained also messages from his mother and Lucia. Diana's letter

—he was surprised to find it addressed from Capri—might have been read first had the circumstances been more favorable. Marcellus revolved the scroll in his hands and decided he would enjoy it later in private.

'Evidently the daughter of Gallus had occasion to reopen her letter after sealing it,' he remarked, more to himself than Demetrius, who sat idly observant as his master inspected the scroll.

'The overlaid wax seems of a slightly different color, sir,' commented Demetrius.

More painstakingly, Marcellus examined the scroll again, picking at the second application of wax with the point of his dagger.

'You're right,' he muttered. 'The letter has been tampered with.'

'By a woman,' added Demetrius. 'There is her finger-mark.'

Frowning with annoyance, Marcellus tucked Diana's scroll into the breast of his tunic, and began silently reading his father's letter. He had just returned from Capri—he wrote—where he had explained his son's sudden departure.

'It was imperative that I should be entirely frank with the Emperor' —the letter went on—'because you had no more than reached open sea before a message arrived appointing you——'

'Demetrius—I bid you listen to this!' exclaimed Marcellus. 'The Emperor has appointed me Commander of the Guard—at Capri! Doubtless that is the import of the message I am receiving today. Commander of the Guard at Capri! What do you suppose the Commander of the Capri Guard has to do?'

The intimate tone meant that Demetrius was not only temporarily emancipated, but would probably be reproached if he failed to make prompt use of his privilege to speak on terms of equality.

'Taste soup, I should think,' he ventured. 'And sleep in his uniform —with one eye open.'

'While his slave sleeps with both eyes open,' remarked Marcellus in the same manner. 'I dare say you're right. The island is a hotbed of jealousy and conspiracy. One's life wouldn't be worth a punched denarius.' Resuming the letter, he read on for a time with a deepening scowl.

'I am not receiving that appointment,' he glanced up to say. 'My father advises me that the Emperor has something else in mind. Let me read you:—"He was much interested in what I felt obliged to tell him of your unpleasant experience in Jerusalem. And when I informed him that this crucified Jew was thought by some to have been the Messiah——"' Marcellus suddenly broke off and stared into Demetrius' face. 'How do you suppose my father found that out?' he demanded.

'I told him,' said Demetrius, with prompt candor. 'Senator Gallio insisted on a full account of what happened up there. I thought it

due you, sir, that an explanation be made—seeing you were in no
condition to make it yourself.'

'That's true enough,' admitted Marcellus, grimly. 'I hope you did
not feel required to tell the Senator about the Galilean's Robe.'

'Yes, sir. The Robe was responsible for your—your illness. The story
—without the Robe—would have been very confusing.'

'You mean—it was quite clear—with the Robe included?'

'No, sir. Perhaps that part of it will always be a mystery.'

'Well—let us get on with this.' Marcellus took up the scroll and
resumed his reading aloud:—' "The Emperor was stirred to an immense curiosity, for he is deeply learned in all of the religions. He
has heard much about the messianic prophecies of the Jews. He wishes
you to pursue your studies in Athens, especially concerning the religions, and return to Capri as a teacher." A *teacher!*' Marcellus
laughed, self-derisively; but Demetrius did not smile. 'Do you not
think this funny, Demetrius?' he insisted. 'Can you picture *me*—lectur-
ing to that menagerie?'

'No, sir,' replied Demetrius, soberly, 'I do not think this is funny.
I think it is a disaster!'

'You mean—I'll be bored?'

'Worse than bored!' exclaimed Demetrius, recklessly. 'It is a contemptible position, if you ask me, sir! The Emperor is said to have a
large contingent of astrologers, diviners of oracles, ghost-tenders,
dream-mechanics and all that sort of thing—clustered about him. It
would be a sorry business for my master to be engaged in!'

Marcellus had begun to share the Corinthian's seriousness.

'You think he wants me to teach a mess of superstitious nonsense?'

'Yes,' nodded Demetrius. 'He wants to hear some more about that
Robe.'

'But that isn't superstitious nonsense!' objected Marcellus.

'No—not to us—but it will be little else than that by the time
Emperor Tiberius and his soothsayers are through discussing it.'

'You feel deeply about this, Demetrius,' said Marcellus, gently.

'Well, sir—I don't want to see the Robe reviled by that loathsome
old man—and his crew of lunatics.'

Marcellus pretended to be indignant.

'Are you aware, Demetrius, that your references to the Emperor of
Rome might be considered bordering on disrespect?' They both
grinned, and Marcellus took up his father's letter again, reading aloud,
slowly:

> I doubt whether you would have any relish for this employment,
> my son. The Emperor is of strange, erratic mind. However—this is
> his command, and you have no choice but to obey. Fortunately, you
> are permitted to remain in Athens for a reasonable length of time,
> pursuing your studies. We are all eager to have you back in Rome, but
> I cannot counsel you to speed your return.

There was no reference to Diana. Marcellus thought this odd, for surely Diana must have been at the Villa Jovis while his father was there. He was anxious to read her letter. It disquieted him to know that she was a guest on that sinister island. Someone had opened her scroll. Someone was spying on her. It was not a safe place for Diana.

*   *   *   *   *   *

The House of Eupolis was apparently in a great state of excitement. It was not every day that a flashily uniformed Tribune arrived with a message from the Emperor of Rome; and the whole establishment—habitually reserved—was undeniably impressed by the occasion.

Dion, grave-faced and perspiring freely, was pacing up and down the driveway as the battered old port-wagon entered the gate.

'You must make haste, Marcellus!' he pleaded, in a frightened voice, as they pulled up beside him. 'There is a message from the Emperor! The Tribune has been waiting in a rage, shouting that if you did not soon arrive he would report our house to the Tetrarch!'

'Be at ease, Dion,' said Marcellus, calmly. 'You are not at fault.' Dismissing the carriage, he proceeded up the driveway, passing a huddle of scared garden-slaves who stared at him with awe and sympathy. Theodosia and her Aunt Ino hovered about her mother who sat stiffly apprehensive in the swing. The pompous figure of the Tribune strutted imperiously before the entrance to the house.

Instantly Marcellus recognized Quintus Lucian! So—that was why the fellow was showing off. Gaius' pet—Quintus! Doubtless the creature had had no stomach for his errand. That explained his obnoxious conduct on the ship. Gaius was probably in a red-hot fury because the old man at Capri had gone over his head with orders for Marcellus' return from Minoa; and now the Emperor had sent this detestable Quintus with a message—and there hadn't been anything that Quintus, or Gaius, either, could do about it.

'And how long shall the Emperor's envoy be kept waiting?' he snarled, as Marcellus drew nearer with Demetrius following at a few paces.

'I had not been advised to be on the alert for a message from His Majesty,' rejoined Marcellus, trying to keep his temper. 'But now that I am here, Tribune Quintus, I suggest that you perform your errand with the courtesy that a Roman expects from an officer of his own rank.'

Quintus grunted crossly and handed over the gaudily gilded imperial scroll.

'Are you to wait for a reply?' inquired Marcellus.

'Yes—but I advise you not to keep me waiting long! His Majesty's envoys are not accustomed to wasting their time at Greek inns.' The tone was so contemptuous that it could have only one meaning.

Demetrius moved forward a step and stood at attention. Marcellus, white with anger, made no retort.

'I shall read this in private, Quintus,' he said, crisply, 'and prepare a reply. You may wait—or you may return for it—as you prefer.' As he strode away, he muttered to Demetrius, 'You remain here.'

After Marcellus had disappeared, on his way to his suite, Quintus swaggered toward Demetrius and faced him with a surly grin.

'You his slave?' He nodded in the general direction Marcellus had taken.

'Yes, sir.'

'Who is the pretty one—by the swing?' demanded Quintus, out of the corner of his mouth.

'She is the daughter of Eupolis, sir,' replied Demetrius, stiffly.

'Indeed! We must make her acquaintance while we wait.' Shouldering past Demetrius, he stalked haughtily across the lawn, accenting each arrogant step with a sidewise jerk of his helmet. Dion, pale and flustered, scurried along toward the swing. Demetrius slowly followed.

With elegantly sandaled feet wide apart and arms akimbo, Quintus halted directly before Theodosia, ignoring the others, and looked her over with an appraising leer. He grinned, disrespectfully.

'What's your name?' he demanded, roughly.

'That is my daughter, sir!' expostulated Dion, rubbing his hands in helpless entreaty.

'You are fortunate, fellow, to have so fair a daughter. We must know her better.' Quintus reached for her hand, and Theodosia recoiled a step, her eyes full of fear. 'Timid; eh?' He laughed contemptuously. 'Since when was the daughter of a Greek innkeeper so frugal with her smiles?'

'But I implore you, Tribune!' Dion's voice was trembling. 'The House of Eupolis has ever been respectable. You must not offend my daughter!'

'Must not—indeed!' crowed Quintus. 'And who are you—to be advising the envoy of the Emperor what he must not do? Be gone, fellow!' He thrust out an arm toward Phoebe and Ino. 'You, too!' he barked. 'Leave us!'

Deathly white, Phoebe rose unsteadily and took a few steps, Ino supporting her. Dion held his ground for a moment, panting with impotent anger, but began edging out of range as their enemy fumbled for his dagger.

'What are you doing here, slave?' shouted Quintus, turning savagely to Demetrius.

'My master ordered me to remain, sir,' replied Demetrius; then, to Theodosia, 'You had better go with your father to the house.'

Purple with rage, Quintus whipped out his dagger and lunged forward. Demetrius sprang to meet the descending arm which he caught at the wrist with a tiger-claw grip of his right hand while his left crashed into the Tribune's face. It was a staggering blow that took Quintus by complete surprise. Before he could regain his balance, Demetrius had sent another full-weight drive of his left fist into the Tribune's mouth. The relentless finger-nails cut deep into his wrist and the dagger fell from his hand. The battle was proceeding too rapidly for Quintus. Dazed and disarmed, he struck wildly, blindly, while Demetrius, pressing forward step by step, continued to shoot stunning blows into the mutilated face.

Quintus was quite at his mercy now, and Demetrius knew it would be simple enough to administer the one decisive upper-cut to the jaw that would excuse the Emperor's envoy from any further participation in the fight; but a strong desire had laid hold on him to see how much damage could be inflicted on the Tribune's face before he finally put him away. It was becoming a quite sanguinary engagement. Both of Demetrius' fists were red with blood as they shot into the battered eyes and crashed against the broken nose. Quintus was making no defense now. Bewildered and blinded with blood, he yielded ground with staggering steps until he had been driven backwards to a huge pine where he put out a hand for support. He breathed with agonized, whistling sobs.

'You'll die for this!' he squeaked, through swollen lips.

'Very well!' panted Demetrius. 'If I'm to die for punishing you—!'

Grabbing Quintus by the throat-strap of his helmet, he completed the ruin of his shockingly mangled face. Then, satisfied with his work, he deliberately drew back his arm and put his full strength behind an ultimate drive at the point of the Tribune's jaw. The knees buckled and Quintus sank limply to the ground.

The Eupolis family had withdrawn some distance while the punishment was being administered. Now Dion came running up, ghastly pale.

'Have you killed him?' he asked, hoarsely.

Demetrius, breathing heavily, was examining his bruised and bleeding hands. He shook his head.

'We will all be thrown into prison,' moaned Dion.

'Don't think of trying to escape,' advised Demetrius. 'Stay where you are—all of you. You had nothing to do with it. That can be proved.' He started to walk away toward his master's suite.

'Shall I do anything for this fellow?' called Dion.

'Yes—bring a basin of water and towels. He will be coming around presently. And if he shows fight, send for me—and tell him that if I have to do this again, I shall kill him!'

Very much spent, Demetrius walked slowly to their quarters and proceeded through to the peristyle where Marcellus sat at the table writing, his face brightly animated. He did not look up from his letter.

'Demetrius! The Emperor commands me to go to Palestine and learn what is to be known—at first hand—about the Galilean!' Marcellus' voice was vibrant. 'Could anything have been more to my liking? Tiberius wants to know how much truth there is in the rumor that Jesus was believed to be the Messiah. As for me—I care naught about that! I want to know what manner of man he was! What a chance for us, Demetrius! We will pursue our Aramaic diligently with old Benjamin. Come early spring, we will journey into Galilee!' He signed his name to the letter, put down his stylus, pushed back his chair, looked up into Demetrius' pale face. 'Why—what on earth have you been doing?' he demanded.

'The Tribune,' said Demetrius, wearily.

Marcellus sprang to his feet.

'What? You haven't been fighting—with Quintus!'

'Not exactly fighting,' said Demetrius. 'He insulted the family—Theodosia in particular—and I rebuked him.'

'Well—from the look of your hands, I should say you had done a good job. But—Demetrius!—this is very serious! Greek slaves can't do that—not to Roman Tribunes—no matter how much it is needed!'

'Yes—I know, sir. I must run away. If I remain here, you will try to defend me—and get into trouble. Please—shall I not go—at once?'

'By all means!' insisted Marcellus. 'But—where will you go? Where can you go?'

'I don't know, sir. I shall try to get out into the country, into the mountains, before the news spreads.'

'How badly is Quintus hurt?' asked Marcellus, anxiously.

'He will recover,' said Demetrius. 'I used no weapons. His eyes are swollen shut—and his mouth is swollen open—and the last few times I hit him on the nose, it felt spongy.'

'Has he gone?'

'No—he was still there.'

Marcellus winced and ran his fingers through his hair.

'Go—wash your hands—and pack a few things for your journey.' Walking past Demetrius, he went to his bedroom and unlocking his strong-box filled a silk bag with gold and silver talents and other coins of smaller value. Returning, he sat down at the table, took up his stylus, wrote a page, stamped it with his heavy seal ring, rolled it, and thrust it into a scroll. 'Here you are,' he said, when Demetrius reappeared. 'This money will befriend you for the present—and this scroll contains your manumission. I shall remain here until spring; the ides of March, approximately. Then I shall go to Jerusalem. I cannot tell how long I may be touring about in the Palestinian provinces; all summer, certainly; perhaps longer. Then I am to return to Capri and report to the Emperor. For that I have no relish; but we will not borrow trouble.'

'Would I were going with you, sir!' exclaimed Demetrius.

'I shall miss you, Demetrius; but your first duty now is to put yourself quickly out of danger. Try to let me know, as soon as safety permits, where you are in hiding. Remember that I shall be burning with desire to learn that you have not been apprehended! Notify me of your needs. If you are captured, I shall leave no stone unturned to effect your deliverance.'

'I know that, sir.' Demetrius' voice was unsteady. 'You are very kind. I shall take the money. As for my freedom—not now.' He laid the scroll on the table. 'If I were caught with this on me, they might think you had rewarded me for punishing Quintus.' Drawing himself stiffly to attention, he saluted with his spear. 'Farewell, sir. I am sorry to go. We may never meet again.'

Marcellus reached out his hand.

'Good-bye, Demetrius,' he said, huskily. 'I shall miss you sorely. You have been a faithful friend. You will be much in my thoughts.'

'Please tell Theodosia why I did not tarry to bid her farewell,' said Demetrius.

'Anything between you two?' inquired Marcellus, with sudden interest.

'That much—at least,' admitted Demetrius.

They silently gripped each other's hands—and Demetrius sped away through the rose garden.

Marcellus moved slowly back into the house, relocked his strongbox, and went out by the front door. Dion was approaching, pale and agitated.

'You have heard, sir?' he asked, anxiously.

'How is he?' inquired Marcellus.

'Sitting up—but he is an unpleasant sight. He says he is going to have us all punished.' Dion was shaken with fear.

'Tell me—what really happened?'

'The Tribune showed much disrespect for Theodosia. Your slave remonstrated, and the Tribune lunged at him with his dagger. After that—well—your Demetrius disarmed him and began striking him in the face with his fists. It was a very brutal beating, sir. I had not thought your gentle-spoken slave could be so violent. The Tribune is unrecognizable! Has your slave hidden himself?'

'He is gone,' said Marcellus, much to Dion's relief.

Proceeding through the grove, they came upon the wretched Quintus, sitting slumped under the tall pine, dabbing at his mutilated face with a bloody towel. He looked up truculently and squinted through the slim red slit in a purpling eye.

'When I inform the Tetrarch,' he declaimed, thickly, 'there will be prison for you—and beheadings for the others.'

'What had you thought of telling the Tetrarch, Quintus?' inquired Marcellus, with a derisive grin. 'And what do you think they will say, at the Insula, when you report that after you had insulted a respectable young woman, and had tried to stab a slave who intervened, you let the

fellow disarm you and beat you with his bare hands until you couldn't
stand up? Go, Quintus, to the Insula!' went on Marcellus, mockingly.
'Let them all see how you look after having had a duel with a Greek
slave! The Tetrarch will probably tell you it was disgraceful enough for
a Roman Tribune to be engaged in a fight with a slave, even if he had
come out of it victorious! Come, then; let us go to the Insula, Quintus.
I shall accompany you. I wouldn't miss it for the world!'

Quintus patted his face gingerly.

'I shall not require your assistance,' he muttered.

'Let me put you up, sir,' wheedled Dion, 'until you feel better.'

'That is a good suggestion,' advised Marcellus. 'Dion certainly owes
you nothing for playing the scoundrel on his premises, but if he is
willing to give you shelter until you are fit to be seen, you would be
wise to accept his offer. I understand you are sailing on *The Vestris*,
the day after tomorrow. Better stay under cover here, and go directly
to the ship when she is ready to put off. Then none of your acquaintances at the Insula will have an amusing story to tell about you, next
time he visits Rome.'

'I shall have that slave of yours whipped to ribbons!' growled
Quintus.

'Perhaps you might like to do it yourself!' retorted Marcellus. 'Shall
I summon him?'

* * * * * *

The gray days were short, cold, and tiresome. Marcellus had discovered how heavily he had leaned on his Corinthian slave, not only
for personal service but friendship and entertainment. Demetrius had
become his alter ego. Marcellus was lost and restless without him.

Nothing interesting happened. The days were all alike. In the
morning he went early to old Benjamin's shop for his regular ration
of Aramaic, offered mostly in the form of conversation. At noon he
would return to the inn and spend the rest of the daylight in his
studio, hacking away without much enthusiasm or inspiration on a
marble head that resembled Diana Gallus less and less, every day. It
was still apparent that she was a girl, a Roman girl, a quite pretty
girl; but no one would have guessed that she was Diana.

And perhaps this was to be accounted for, surmised Marcellus, by
the increasing vagueness of Diana on the retina of his imagination.
She was very far away—and retreating. He had had two letters from
her. The first, from Capri, had been written in haste. She knew all
about the Emperor's orders that he was to continue his studies in
Athens and then proceed to Jerusalem and the northern provinces of
Palestine for authentic information about that mysterious young Jew.

As for herself, Diana said, the Emperor had insisted on her remaining at Capri for a few weeks; and, in view of his valued favors, she

had decided to do so. He had been very kind; he was lonesome; she must stay.

Her second letter had been written from home. It, too, sounded as if the carriage were waiting and someone were reading the words over her shoulder. The letter was friendly enough, solicitous of his welfare, but wanting in the little overtones of tenderness and yearning. It was as if their love had been adjourned to await further development in some undated future. Marcellus re-read this letter many times, weighing and balancing its phrases, trying to decide whether Diana had been taking extra precautions in case the scroll were read by a third party, or whether she was losing interest in their affection. It might be one or the other: it might indeed be both. Her words were not softly whispered. They were gentle—but clearly audible. And they made him very lonesome.

It was an important occasion, therefore, when the long letter arrived from Demetrius. A light snow had fallen in the night and the sky was heavily overcast. Marcellus had stood for a long time at the studio window debating whether to go to Benjamin's shop today. But the light was too poor for sculpturing. And the old man would be expecting him. With a mood to fit the sullen sky, he made his way to the shop where Benjamin greeted him with bright-eyed excitement.

'Here is a letter for you!'

'Indeed! Why was it sent here?'

'In my care. Addressed to me—but intended for you. It was brought by a slave attached to a caravan, and delivered here last night by Zenos, the noisy boy who runs errands for my friend Popygos. Demetrius, as you will see, is in Jerusalem. I read that much of it. Your slave is prudent. Fearing a letter addressed to you might be examined and reveal his whereabouts, he has sent it to me.' Benjamin laughed as he handed over the scroll. 'Now you will have an opportunity to put your Aramaic to practical use. It's very good Aramaic, too!' he added proudly.

Marcellus drew up a stool beside the worktable, unrolled the end of the long sheet of papyrus, and began reading aloud, with occasional hesitations and appeals to Benjamin who delightedly came to his rescue.

Esteemed Master (read Marcellus), I am writing this on the Jewish Sabbath in the upper chamber of an old house overlooking the Kidron, no great distance from the Temple area. I share this room with one Stephanos, a Greek of my own age, whom the Jews call Stephen. He is intelligent, well-informed, and friendly. At present he is absent, on some mysterious errand; possibly the same business that kept him out, last night, until shortly before dawn.

I arrived in Jerusalem but three days ago. You will be curious to learn the manner of my departure from Athens. Confident of Fulvius' friendship, I ran to Piraeus, boarded *The Vestris*, and confided my dilemma. Fulvius hid me in the hold. When the ship stood well out to sea, on the second day, I was brought on deck where I enjoyed full liberty. We had an important passenger who was recovering from an accident that had disfigured his face. He kept to his cabin until we had cleared from Alexandria. Recognizing me, he ordered Fulvius to put me in irons, which Fulvius refused to do, saying that I had paid my passage. This was untrue, though I had offered to pay. Fulvius told the distinguished passenger that if he wished he could have me apprehended at the next port.

We anchored at nightfall in the Bay of Gaza, and Fulvius secretly put me ashore in the small boat. Providing myself with a few necessities, I journeyed on foot over the same route taken by the Legion from Minoa to Jerusalem. In a desolate wady, some twelve parasangs northeast of Ascalon, I was captured and robbed by Bedouins, who did not otherwise harm me, and permitted my escape. The weather was extremely cold and I was lightly clad. That country is sparsely settled, as you may recall. The few inhabitants are poor, and hostile to strangers. I learned to relish warm goat-milk and frosted corn; and I was stoned while pillaging withered leeks from an ill-kept garden. I discovered that eggs, sucked from the shell, are delicious, and that a sleepy cow does not resent sharing her warmth with a wayfarer seeking shelter in her stall. The cattle of Judea are hospitable. On the last night of my journey, I was pleasantly surprised by being permitted to sleep in the stable of a tavern in the village of Bethlehem. In the morning the innkeeper sent his servant with a dish of hot broth and a small loaf of wheaten bread. The servant said it was a custom of the inn to befriend impoverished travelers. I observed that on the corner of the napkin, in which the bread was brought, there was embroidered the figure of a fish. It stirred my curiosity a little because a similar design had been burned with an iron into the timber of the stable-door. After leaving Bethlehem I noticed, at two road-crossings, the crude outline of a fish, drawn in the sand, and surmised that the device might indicate the direction taken by someone who wished to leave this cryptic advice for another person following. Not knowing what it meant—or caring very much—I dismissed the matter from my mind.

Arriving in Jerusalem, hungry and footsore, I decided to seek the house of a weaver, hoping I might be given some small tasks to provide me with food and shelter. In this I was most fortunate. At the shop of Benyosef I was kindly received by Stephanos, who works there. Learning that I am a Greek, and having been informed that I had done some carding and spinning for Benjamin in Athens, whose name Stephanos recognized, he commended me to Benyosef, and I was given employment. The wage is small, but consistent with the service I render, and is ample to sustain me for the present. Stephanos bade me lodge with him.

Of course, his interest in me is due, primarily, to the fact that I am a Greek. His people were long ago of Philippi, his great-grandparents having fled for refuge in Jerusalem when Macedonia was subjugated. It seems that there are hundreds of Greeks here, whose ancestors migrated to Jerusalem for the same reason. Not many of them are literate; and Stephanos, who is a student of the classics, longs for congenial company. He seemed pleased when, in response to his queries, I told him I was at least somewhat conversant with Greek literature.

On our first evening together, after we had eaten supper and were talking of many things relating to the unhappy Greeks, Stephanos idly drew the outline of a fish on the back of a papyrus tablet; and, pushing it across the table, raised his brows inquiringly.

I told him it signified nothing to me, though I had seen the symbol before. He then asked me if I had not heard of Jesus, the Galilean. I admitted that I had—but not very much—and would be interested in hearing more. He said that the people who believed in the teachings of Jesus were being so savagely persecuted that they met only in secret. This fish-emblem had been adopted as their method of identifying themselves to others of similar belief. He did not tell me how they came to use this device. Jesus was not a fisherman, but a carpenter.

Stephanos went on to say that Jesus advocated freedom for all men. 'Surely a slave should ally himself with such a cause,' he said. I told him I was deeply concerned, and he promised to tell me more about Jesus when there was an opportunity.

The house of Benyosef, I am discovering, is not only a weaver's shop, but a secret meeting-place for the men who were intimate friends of Jesus. My position here is so lowly and menial that my presence is unnoticed by the sober men who come neither to buy nor sell, but to slip in quietly and sit beside the old man, whispering while he whacks his ancient loom. (Benjamin would laugh at that loom.)

Yesterday a heavily bearded man of great strength and stature spent an hour in low-voiced conversation with Benyosef and two young fellows, in a far corner of the shop. Stephanos said they were Galileans. The huge man, he said, was called 'The Big Fisherman,' and the younger men, who were brothers, he referred to as 'The Sons of Thunder.' 'The Big Fisherman' seems a very forceful man. Perhaps he is the leader of the party, though why there should be a party at all, or so much secrecy, now that their Jesus is dead and his cause is lost, I do not pretend to understand. They all act as if they were suppressing some excitement. It does not resemble the excitement of fear; rather that of expectancy. They behave as if they had found something valuable and had hidden it.

This afternoon, a tall, well-favored man from the country came into the shop and was greeted with much warmth. I gathered that they had not seen him for some time. When the day's work was done, and Stephanos and I were on the way to our lodging, I remarked of this man that he seemed an amiable person whom every one liked, and he unexpectedly confided that the man was Barsabas Justus, of Sepphoris in Galilee. He then went on to say that Jesus had appointed twelve friends to serve as his accredited disciples. One of them, Judas of Kerioth, had betrayed Jesus' whereabouts to the priests. After his master's arrest, he was filled with remorse and hanged himself. The eleven disciples met later to elect a successor to this Judas, though why they felt the necessity to do that, after Jesus was dead, Stephanos did not explain.

They voted on two men who had followed Jesus about through the provinces, hearing him speak to the people and witnessing many strange deeds of which Stephanos may tell me when he is in a mood to speak more freely. I think he wants first to make sure that I will respect his confidence. One of these two men, Matthias by name, was elected to succeed the traitor Judas. The other man is this Barsabas Justus.

I venture to suggest, sir, that when you come to Jerusalem to make inquiries about Jesus' career, you could not do better than to contrive the acquaintance of a man like Barsabas Justus. This will not be easy to do. These friends of Jesus are watched closely for any indication that they are attempting to extend or preserve his influence. The Temple authorities evidently feel that the teachings of the Galilean contain the seeds of revolution against the established religion, and the Insula has probably been persuaded that the sooner everybody forgets about Jesus, the more likely it may be that this next Passover season can be celebrated without a political uprising.

During these past three days I have given much thought to a plan which might assist you in getting up into Galilee without exciting suspicion. You could appear in Jerusalem as a connoisseur of homespun fabrics, particularly interested in the products of Galilean household looms. Let it be known that such textiles are now highly esteemed in Rome. Inquire in the bazaars for such fabrics and pay generously for a few articles. They are not considered as of much value here, but might quickly become so if you permit yourself to be well cheated in two or three shops. Rumor spreads rapidly in this city.

In the course of your search for Galilean homespun you would naturally call at the house of Benyosef where you might let it be known that you contemplate a trip into the region around Capernaum to look for textiles. You could inquire whether it would be possible to employ, as a guide, some man well acquainted with that country.

Of the several Galileans who visit the shop, Barsabas Justus would be the most likely, I think, to accept such employment. The man they call 'The Big Fisherman' is too passionately absorbed in whatever he is doing in the city and 'The Sons of Thunder' appear to be weighted with duties, but Barsabas Justus seems to have fewer responsibilities. Unquestionably he is your man—if you can get him.

My belief is that they will scatter when Passover Week approaches, for the Insula will be on the alert, and these Galileans will want to avoid useless trouble. I suggest that you plan to arrive here about a month before the Passover. Spring will be approaching, and the country will be beautiful. It will be more prudent if you do not recognize me, even if we meet face to face; for, unless I am mistaken, Stephanos will—by that time—have taken me into his full confidence, and it would be most unfortunate if he suspected collusion between us. Stephanos does not know that I have ever been in Jerusalem before. If I can contrive a secret meeting when you come, I shall be overjoyed to talk with you, but I think you should ignore me completely. If a private conference is practical, I shall arrange for it and let you know—somehow.

Marcellus glanced up at Benjamin—and grinned.

'That boy should have been a Jew!' declared the old man. 'He has a keen mind—and is cunning.'

'Yes,' agreed Marcellus, dryly. 'I can see that a study of Aramaic has done wonders for him. He is crafty. However—this advice sounds sensible enough; don't you think?'

'I doubt it, my friend. This is a game that will have to be played with the utmost care,' warned Benjamin. 'The Jews have no reasons for trusting the Romans. Their confidence will not be easily won.'

'Do you think I might be able to pass myself off for a merchant?' inquired Marcellus, doubtfully.

'A good way to find out,' suggested Benjamin, with a twinkle, 'is to go over here to David Sholem's bazaar and buy something; and then go across the street and try to sell it to old Aaron Barjona.'

They both laughed.

'But—seriously,' said Marcellus. 'Do you think I might be able to get into Galilee by any such scheme as the one Demetrius suggests?'

'Not a chance!' scoffed Benjamin.

'Not if I offer the fellow a handsome wage?'

Benjamin shook his head decisively.

'No—not for a handsome wage. This Barsabas Justus may have much to give that you would like to know; but he will have nothing to sell.'

'You advise me not to attempt it?'

The old man laboriously threaded a needle, with many grotesque squints and grimaces. Having accomplished it, he grinned, triumphantly, and deftly rolled a tight knot into the end of the thread.

'It might be worth trying,' he grunted. 'These Galileans may be bigger fools than we think.'

Chapter XII

WITH almost no conversation they had eaten their lunch under an old fig tree, a little distance from the highway, and were now lounging in the shade.

Justus had stretched out his long frame on the grass, and with his fingers laced behind his shaggy head was staring up through the broad leaves into a bland April sky, his studious frown denoting perplexity.

Marcellus, reclining against the tree-trunk, moodily wished himself elsewhere. He was restless and bored. Old Benjamin's pessimistic forecast that this proposed expedition into Samaria and Galilee would be a disappointment had turned out to be correct.

Arriving in Jerusalem two weeks ago, Marcellus had acted fully upon Demetrius' written advice. Having engaged lodgings at the best inn, a commodious old house with a garden, halfway up the hill toward the suburb of Bethany, registering in the name of 'M. Lucan,' he had proceeded deliberately to bewilder the downtown bazaars with inquiries for homespun fabrics and garments—particularly articles of Galilean origin. He went from one shop to another, naïvely admiring the few things they showed him; recklessly purchasing robes and shawls at the first price quoted, professing to be immensely pleased to have them at any cost. And when the merchants confessed, with unfeigned lamentations, that their stock of Galilean textiles had run low, he upbraided them for their lack of enterprise.

Then he had laid up, for a few days, lounging in the garden of the inn, re-reading The Book of Yeshayah—old Benjamin's farewell gift—and waiting for the rumor of his business transactions to be whispered about among the clothing dealers. It was very trying to be so close to Demetrius and unable to communicate with him. One day he almost persuaded himself that this elaborate scheme for getting into Galilee was unnecessarily fantastic, and he half-resolved to go down to Benyosef's shop and explain, in the most forthright manner, that he had a desire to talk with men who had known Jesus in his own community. But, upon reflection, he saw that such a course might embarrass Demetrius; so he abandoned this impulsive procedure and impatiently bided his time.

At mid-afternoon on the fifth day of that second week, he went to the house of Benyosef, sauntering in casually to give the impression that he really wanted to do business; for he had observed that, in

Jerusalem, the serious customer with his mind set on something he intended to buy invariably tried to disguise his interest. The most ridiculous subterfuges were practiced. The customer would stroll in pretending he had come to meet a friend, or that he had lost his bearings and wanted to know how to find Straight Street. On the way out he would pause to finger some article of merchandise. Apparently these childish tricks deceived nobody. The more indifferent the customer was, the more attentively the merchant hovered about him. It was evident that all business in the Holy City was so full of mendacity that a man who gave evidence of an honest purpose was immediately suspected of rank imposture.

Pausing indecisively in the open doorway of Benyosef's shop, Marcellus glanced about in search of Demetrius. It was not going to be easy, after this long separation, to confront his loyal friend with the cool stare of a stranger. A survey of the cluttered shop failed to reveal the presence of Demetrius, but Marcellus was not sure whether he was disappointed or relieved; for he had dreaded this moment.

The clatter of the two antiquated looms slowed and ceased as he made his way toward the venerable weaver who, he felt, must be old Benyosef himself. If the aged Jew was alarmed at the presence of an urbane young Roman in his house, he gave no sign of it. He maintained his seat on the bench of his loom, methodically polite but not obsequious. Marcellus briefly stated his errand. Benyosef shook his long white beard. His weaving, he said, was all custom work. He had nothing made up to sell. If his client wished to order a coat, they would gladly make it for him, and it would be a good one. But as for homespun, it might be found in the bazaars; or, better, in the country. And with that laconic announcement, he deftly scooted a wooden shuttle through the open warp and gave the thread a whack with the beam that made the old loom shudder. It was apparent that so far as Benyosef was concerned the interview had terminated.

Four other men had been mildly interested—and a dark, handsome boy of twelve, who had stopped romping with a dog to listen. One of the men was a young Greek with a refined face, seated at a ramshackle loom adjacent to Benyosef's. Marcellus surmised that this might be Demetrius' friend Stephanos.

Near the wall, behind the looms, sat two men who bore a marked resemblance, one in his early thirties, the other considerably younger. They were deeply tanned, and simply dressed in country garb, their rustic, well-worn sandals indicating that they were accustomed to long journeys on foot. This pair, obviously brothers, might easily qualify as 'The Sons of Thunder,' though the appellation did seem rather incongruous, for they appeared benign enough, especially the younger whose expressive eyes had a marked spiritual quality. He would have passed more reasonably as a mystic than an agitator.

The fourth man, who sat in the corner on an inverted tub, was probably sixty. He, too, was an outlander, to judge by his homely dress and the shagginess of his gray-streaked hair and beard. Bronzed and bushy, he seemed out of place under a roof. During the brief colloquy, he had sat gently stroking his beard with the back of his hand, his brown eyes drifting lazily from old Benyosef to the eccentric Roman who, for some obscure reason, wanted to purchase articles of homespun.

At first sight of him, Marcellus thought this might be the man Demetrius had referred to as 'The Big Fisherman.' He was big enough. But another glance at the reposeful posture and the amiable smile assured Marcellus that if 'The Big Fisherman' was a man of energy and something of a party leader, the hairy one who lounged on the tub must be someone else, conceivably Barsabas Justus.

Now that the looms had gone into action again, Marcellus had begun to doubt whether this was the time or place to introduce his question about the possibility of finding a guide, but Benyosef had remarked that one might hope to buy homespun in the country; so the query would be natural enough. As if this were a fresh inspiration, Marcellus inquired, in his best Aramaic, and addressing them all impartially, whether they knew of a man—well acquainted in the northern provinces—who might be employed to accompany him on a leisurely tour.

Benyosef, ceasing his racket, scowled thoughtfully, but made no comment. The older brother shook his head. The younger calmly stared through and beyond the inquirer as if he had not heard. The Greek, who might be Stephanos, slowly turned about and faced the big man in the corner.

'You could go, Justus,' he said. 'You were intending to go home, anyhow; weren't you?'

'How long do you want to stay?' rumbled Justus, after some deliberation.

'Two weeks, perhaps, or three—or a month,' Marcellus tried not to sound too urgent. 'Once I am up there, and have found my way about,' he added, 'you could leave me—if you had other things to do.'

'When do you want to start?' inquired Justus, with a little more interest.

'Soon as possible. How about the day after tomorrow?'

'The day after tomorrow,' put in Benyosef, reproachfully, 'is the Sabbath of the Lord our God!'

'Sorry,' mumbled Marcellus. 'I had forgotten.'

'Don't you Romans ever observe a day of rest, young man?' demanded Benyosef, enjoying his right to be querulous.

'The Romans rest oftener than we do,' drawled Justus, encouraged to this audacity by the broad grin with which Marcellus had met the old man's impertinence.

'But not oftener than *you do!*' growled Benyosef, darting his bright little eyes at Justus.

This was good for a chuckle. Even the younger brother turned about and smiled a little. As if to prove himself a man of action, Justus rose and led the way to a wooden bench in front of the house. Marcellus, with a nod to the others, followed. So did the boy, who sat beside them, hugging his knees.

With more resourcefulness than Marcellus had expected, Justus led the conversation about necessary arrangements for the journey. They would need a small string of pack-asses, he said, to carry camp equipment; for some of the smaller villages offered very poor accommodations. Four asses would be sufficient, he thought, to pack everything including whatever might be purchased.

'Will you buy the asses for me, and the camping tackle?' asked Marcellus. 'Doubtless you could make better terms. How much money will it take?' He unstrapped his wallet.

'You are trusting me to buy these things?' inquired Justus.

'Why not? You look honest.' Noting that this comment had brought a little frown, he added, 'You would not be an acceptable visitor at old Benyosef's shop if you were unscrupulous.'

Justus gave him a long sidewise look without turning his head.

'What do you know about old Benyosef—and his shop?' he queried gruffly.

Marcellus shrugged.

'The place is of good repute,' he answered, negligently. 'Benyosef has been in business for a long time.'

'That means nothing,' retorted Justus. 'Plenty of rascals stay in business for a long time.' And when Marcellus had agreed to that with a nod, and an indifferent 'Doubtless,' Justus said: 'There will be no need to buy pack-asses. You can hire them—and a boy to drive them. Hire the tent, too, and everything else.'

'Will you see to it, then? Let us be on our way early on the first day of the week.' Marcellus rose. 'How much will you expect for your services?'

'I am willing to leave that to you, sir,' said Justus. 'As you heard Stephen say, I had intended going home in a few days to Sepphoris in Galilee. This journey will not inconvenience me. I have nothing to do at present. My time is of little value. You may provide me with food and shelter. And I could use a new pair of sandals.'

'Well—I mean to do better than that by you,' declared Marcellus.

'A new robe, then,' suggested Justus, holding up a frayed sleeve.

'With pleasure.' Marcellus lowered his tone and said, 'Pardon the question, but—but'—he hesitated—'you are a Jew; are you not?'

Justus chuckled and nodded, stroking his whiskers.

When they parted, a moment later, with a definite understanding to meet at the Damascus Gate soon after sunrise on the next morning after the Sabbath, Marcellus felt confident that the journey would be rewarding. Justus was a friendly old fellow who would tell him everything he wanted to know. He was just the type to enjoy reminiscence.

With his errand satisfactorily performed and nothing in particular to do, Marcellus strolled back toward the busy, ill-flavored market-place where he idled past the booths and stalls, pausing to listen, with amusement and disgust, to the violent rages of hucksters and shoppers over deals relating to one small pickled fish or a calf's foot. Vituperations rent the air. Unpleasant comments were made by customers reflecting on the merchants' ancestry. Insults were screamed, and ignored, and forgotten, which—had they been exchanged in a Roman barracks—would have demanded an immediate blood atonement. At one booth, where he stopped to witness an almost incredible scene involving the disputed price of a lamb kidney, Marcellus was a bit surprised to find, close beside him, the boy he had seen at Benyosef's shop.

Having had more than enough of the market-place, he decided to return to his inn. It was a long tramp. Turning about, at the top of the steps leading to the entrance, Marcellus looked down toward the city. The boy from Benyosef's was sauntering down the street. It was more amusing than annoying to have been followed. On second thought—these people were quite within their rights to investigate him as far as they could. Perhaps they wanted to know at what manner of place he was stopping. Had he been a guest at the Insula, they would have had nothing further to do with him.

That evening, as he sat in the walled garden of the inn, after supper, studying the ancient scroll that Benjamin had given him, Marcellus glanced up to find Stephanos standing before him.

'May I speak with you privately?' asked Stephanos, in Greek.

They walked to the far end of the garden, and Marcellus signed to him to sit down.

'You were surprised not to find Demetrius', began Stephanos. 'About a fortnight after he wrote to you, he had the misfortune to be recognized on the street by the Tribune with whom he had had trouble in Athens. No effort was made to apprehend him, but he believed that the Tribune might seek revenge. In that case his friends at Benyosef's shop might be involved—and we are in no position to defend ourselves.'

'Where did he go, Stephanos?' asked Marcellus, deeply concerned.

'I do not know, sir. He returned to our lodgings and awaited me. We sat up and talked nearly all through the night. Several of our men were in a secret meeting at Benyosef's shop. We joined them an hour before dawn. Demetrius, having bade us farewell, slipped away before the sun rose. He will return when it is safe; when the Tribune has left. You may leave a letter for him with me, if you like, or send it later in my care—should you find a messenger who can be trusted. He confided to me that you were coming and asked me to explain his absence. None of the others were told.' Stephanos lowered his voice, and continued, 'Demetrius also confided your reasons for wanting to visit Galilee.'

'Just how much did he tell you?' Marcellus studied the Greek's face.

'Everything,' replied Stephanos, soberly. 'You see, sir, he wanted to make sure that Justus would go along with you. He felt that I might be of some service in arranging this. And when he began to explain the nature of your interest in Jesus—with much hesitation, and many mysterious gaps in the story—I urged him to make a clean breast of the whole business; and he did. You can trust me to keep your secret.'

Marcellus had no rejoinder ready to meet this startling announcement. For a time he sat quietly deliberating.

'Are they suspicious of me, at Benyosef's shop?' he asked, at length. 'I was followed, this afternoon.'

'Young Philip is my nephew, sir,' explained Stephanos. 'I needed to know where you were lodging. You need have no anxiety about Philip. He will not talk. No one at the shop will learn of our meeting. I feared, for a moment, this morning, that John might recognize you, but apparently he did not. He is a dreamy fellow.'

'How could he have recognized me?' asked Marcellus.

'John was at the crucifixion, sir. Perhaps you may recall the young man who tried to comfort Jesus' mother.'

'His mother! She was there? How dreadful!' Marcellus bowed his head and dug his finger-tips into his temples.

'It was, indeed, sir,' muttered Stephanos. 'I was there. I recognized you instantly when you came into the shop, though of course I was expecting you. I think you may feel sure that John did not remember.'

'You have been very kind, Stephanos. Is there any way in which I can serve you?'

'Yes, sir.' The Greek lowered his voice to a whisper. 'Have you the Robe?'

Marcellus nodded.

'May I see it?' asked Stephanos.

'Yes,' said Marcellus. 'Come with me.'

* * * * * *

They had been on the road for three days now, and the name of Jesus had not been mentioned. For all his apparent ingenuousness, Justus was surprisingly profound. His ready smile promised a childish capitulation to your wishes. His deference to your rating as a well-to-do young Roman was graciously tendered. But your negligent prediction that Justus would be eager to talk about Jesus had turned out to be incorrect. You were learning that there were a few things which not even a wealthy, well-dressed Roman could acquire either by cajolery, command, or purchase; and one of these things was the story of Jesus.

It had never occurred to Marcellus that an occasion could arise when his Roman citizenship might be an inconvenience. If you were a Roman and had plenty of money, you could have what you wanted, anywhere in the world. Doors and gates were swung open, bars and bridges were let down, tables were set up, aliens climbed out of public vehicles to give you their seats, merchants made everybody else stand aside while they attended to your caprices. If you arrived late at the wharf, the boat waited. If there was only one commodious cabin, the rich Jew surrendered it without debate. When you said Come, people came; when you said Go, they went.

But if you had journeyed on foot into the improverished little provinces north of Jerusalem, ostensibly to purchase homespun, but actually to make inquiries concerning a certain penniless carpenter who had moved about in that region, your Roman citizenship was a nuisance and your money was of no aid.

The project—as Marcellus had originally conceived it—had presented no problems. Barsabas Justus, full of zeal for his new cause, would be bubbling with information about his hero. Perhaps he might even have designs on you as a possible convert. He would be eager to introduce you to the country people who had often met this strange Galilean face to face. You would be shown into their homes to see the outgivings of their household looms and, before you had a chance to sit down, they would be reciting stories of enchanted words and baffling deeds.

Well—it hadn't come out that way. True, the country people had welcomed you at their little wayside inns, had greeted you respectfully on the highway, had shown you their fabrics, had politely answered your random questions about their handicrafts; but they had had nothing to say about this Jesus. They were courteous, hospitable, friendly; but you, who had often been a stranger in strange places, had never felt quite so lonesome before. They all shared a secret; but not with you. Justus would present you to a household and tell them why you had come and they would make haste to bring out the best specimens of their weaving. And presently, the father of the family and Justus would exchange a covert glance of mutual understanding and quietly drift out of the room. After a while, your hostess would excuse herself, leaving you with auntie and the children; and you knew that she had slipped away to join her husband and Justus.

The very air of this country was full of mystery. For instance, there was this fish-emblem; figure of a fish, freshly cut into the bark of a sycamore, scrawled with a stick into the sand by the roadside, chalked on a stone fence, scratched into a bare table at a village inn. Demetrius had said it was the accepted token of the new movement to practice the teachings of Jesus.

On the second day out, Marcellus, hoping to make Justus talk, had asked casually:

'What's all this—about fish?'

And Justus had replied:

'That's what we live on—up here—fish.'

Marcellus had been miffed a little by this evasion. He resolved to ask no more questions.

*　*　*　*　*　*

Marcellus, lounging against the fig tree, studied the tanned face of old Justus, and wondered what he was thinking about; wondered, too, how long he was likely to lie there gazing wide-eyed at the sky. Justus gave no sign that he was aware of his client's restlessness.

After a while, Marcellus came slowly to his feet and sauntered over toward the pack-asses which the cloddish young driver—sound asleep under a tree—had staked out to graze.

Noticing with indignation that the lead donkey's bridle was buckled so short that the unhappy creature's mouth had been torn by the bit and was bleeding, he tugged the torturing harness off over the long ears; and, sitting down on the grass, proceeded to lengthen the straps by punching new holes with the point of his dagger. It was not an easy task, for the leather was old and stiff; and before he had put the bridle together again, the donkey-boy had roused and was watching him with dull curiosity.

'Come here, stupid one!' barked Marcellus. 'I shall not tolerate any cruelty to these beasts.' He reached into his wallet and drew out a copper coin. 'Go you to that house—or the next—or the next—and get some ointment—and don't come back here without it!'

After the dolt had set off, shambling down the road, Marcellus rose, carelessly patted the old donkey on the nose, and returned to find Justus sitting up, smilingly interested.

'You like animals,' he observed, cordially.

'Yes,' said Marcellus—'some animals. I can't say that I am particularly fond of donkeys; but it irritates me when I see them mistreated. We will have to keep an eye on that dunce!'

Justus nodded approvingly. Marcellus sat down beside him, aware that his guide was studying him with the air of having made a new acquaintance.

'Do you like flowers?' asked Justus, irrelevantly, after a lengthy, candid, and somewhat embarrasing inspection.

'Of course,' drawled Marcellus. 'Why not?'

'This country is full of wild flowers. It's the season for them. Later, it is very dry, and they wither. They are especially abundant this year.' Justus made a slow, sweeping gesture that covered the sloping hillside. 'Look, sir, what a wide variety.'

Marcellus followed the tanned finger as the gentle voice identified the blossoms with what seemed like confident knowledge; pink mustard, yellow mustard, blue borage, white sage, rayed umbel, plantain, bugle-weed, marigold, and three species of poppies.

'You must be an ardent lover of nature, Justus,' commented Marcellus.

'Only in the last couple of years, sir. I used to pass the flowers by without seeing them, as almost every man does. Of course I recognized the useful plants; flax and wheat, oats and barley and clover; but I never thought much about flowers until I made the close acquaintance of a man who knew all about them.'

Justus had again stretched out on the grass, and his tone had become so dreamily reminiscent that Marcellus, listening with suspended breath, wondered if—at last—the soft-voiced Galilean might be about to speak of his lost friend.

'He knew all about flowers,' reiterated Justus, with a little shake of his head, as if the recollection were inexpressibly precious. Marcellus thought of asking whether his friend had died or left the country, seeing that Justus' reference to him sounded as if it belonged to the past; but decided not to be too intrusive with his questions.

'You would have thought,' Justus was saying, half to himself, 'that the flowers were friends of his, the way he talked about them. One day he bade some of us, who were walking with him, to stop and observe a field of wild lilies. "See how richly they are clad!" he said. "They do no work. They do not spin. Yet even King Solomon did not have such raiment."'

'A lover of beauty,' commented Marcellus. 'But probably not a very practical fellow. Did he not believe in labor?'

'Oh, yes—he believed that people should be industrious,' Justus had been quick to declare, 'but he held that most of them spent too much time and thought on their bodies; on clothing—and food—and hoarding—and bigger barns—and the accumulation of things.'

'Sounds as if he wasn't very thrifty.' Marcellus grinned as he said it, so it wouldn't seem a contemptuous criticism; but Justus, staring at the sky, did not see the smile, and the comment brought a frown.

'He was not indolent,' said Justus, firmly. 'He could have had things, if he'd wanted them. He was a carpenter by occupation—and a skillful one too. It was a pleasure to see him handle keen-edged tools. When he mortised timbers they looked as if they had grown that way. There was always a fair-sized crowd about the shop, watching him work; children all over the place. He had a way with children—and animals—and birds.' Justus laughed softly, and exhaled a nostalgic sigh. 'Yes—he had a way with him. When he would leave the shop to go home, there was always a lot of children along—and dogs. Everything belonged to him; but he never owned anything. He often said that he pitied people who toiled and schemed and worried and cheated to possess a lot of things; and then had to stand guard over them to see that they weren't stolen or destroyed by moths and rust.'

'Must have been an eccentric person,' mused Marcellus, 'not to want anything for his own.'

'But he never thought he was poor!' Justus raised up on one elbow, suddenly animated. 'He had the spirit of truth. Not many people can afford that, you know.'

'What an odd thing to say!' Marcellus had stared into Justus' eyes, until the older man grinned a little.

'Not so odd, when you stop to think about it. A talent for truth is real property. If a man loves truth better than things, people like to be around where he is. Almost everybody wishes he could be honest, but you can't have the spirit of truth when your heart is set on dickering for *things*. That's why people hung about this carpenter and listened to everything he said: he had the spirit of truth. Nobody had to be on guard with him; didn't have to pretend; didn't have to lie. It made them happy and free as little children.'

'Did everybody respond to him—that way?' asked Marcellus, seriously.

'Almost everybody,' nodded Justus. 'Oh—sometimes people who didn't know him tried to deceive him about themselves, but'—he grinned broadly as if remembering an occasion—'but, you see, sir, he was so perfected in the truth that you couldn't lie to him, or pretend to be what you weren't. It simply couldn't be done, sir; either by word, tone, or manner! And as soon as people found that out, they dropped their weapons and defenses, and began to speak the truth, themselves! It was a new experience for some of them, and it gave them a sensation of freedom. That's why they liked him, sir. They couldn't lie to him, and so they told the truth—and—the truth set them free!'

'That's a new thought!' declared Marcellus. 'Your friend must have been a philosopher, Justus. Was he a student of the classics?'

Justus was briefly puzzled, and presently shook his head.

'I do not think so,' he replied. 'He just—*knew!*'

'I don't suppose he had very many admirers among the well-to-do,' ventured Marcellus—'if he discouraged the accumulation of property.'

'You would have been surprised, sir!' declared Justus. 'Plenty of rich men listened. I recall, one time a wealthy young nobleman followed him about for a whole afternoon; and before he left he came up closer and said, "How can I get that—what you have?"'

Justus paused so long and the look in his eyes grew so remote that Marcellus wondered whether he had drifted off to thinking about something else.

'And then—what did your carpenter say?'

'Told him he was too heavily weighted with *things*,' replied Justus. ' "Give your things away," he said, "and come along with me." '

'Did he?'

'No—but he said he wished he could. He went away quite depressed, and we were all sorry, for he was indeed a fine young fellow.' Justus shook his head, and smiled pensively. 'I suppose that was the first time he had ever really wanted something that he couldn't afford.'

'This carpenter must have been a very unusual man,' remarked Marcellus. 'He appears to have had the mind of a dreamer, a poet, an artist. Did he draw, perhaps—or carve?'

'Jews do not draw—or carve.'

'Indeed? How then do they express themselves?'

'They sing,' replied Justus—'and tell stories.'

'What manner of stories?'

'Oh—the legends of our people, mostly; the deeds of our great ones. Even the little children can recite the traditions and the prophecies.' Justus smiled benevolently, and seemed about to confide an incident. 'I have a grandson, sir. His name is Jonathan. We called him Jonathan because he was born with a crooked foot, like Jonathan of old—the son of King Saul. Our Jonathan is seven. You should hear him tell the story of the Creation, and the Great Flood, and the Exodus.'

'The Exodus?' Marcellus searched his memory.

'You do not know, sir?' Justus was tolerant but surprised.

'I know what the word means,' said Marcellus, defensively. 'Exodus is a going-away, or a road out; but I do not recall a story about it.'

'I thought everyone knew the history of our people's escape from bondage in Egypt,' said Justus.

'Oh—that!' recalled Marcellus. 'I didn't know that was an escape. Our history teachers insist that the Jews were expelled from Egypt.'

'That,' declared Justus, indignantly, 'is a vicious untruth! The Pharaoh tried to keep our fathers there—in slavery—to till their soil and build their monuments.'

'Well—no matter,' drawled Marcellus. 'There's nothing we can do about it now. I'll accept your version of the story, if you want to tell me.'

'Little Jonathan will recite it for you when we visit Sepphoris. He is a bright boy.' Justus' sudden anger had cooled.

'It is easy to see you are fond of him, Justus.'

'Yes—little Jonathan is all we have. My wife entered into her rest many years ago. My daughter Rebecca is a widow. Jonathan is a great comfort to us. Perhaps you know how it is, sir, in a home where a child is sick or crippled. He gets a little more care; a little more love, maybe, to make up for it. Jonathan still gets it, though he is all well now.'

'Well?' queried Marcellus. 'His foot—you mean?'

Justus nodded slowly, turning his face away.

'Is that not unusual?' persisted Marcellus.

The crow's-feet on Justus' temple deepened and his face was sober as he nodded again without looking up. It was plain now that he did not wish to be questioned further. Presently he tugged himself loose from his meditative mood, returned with a smile, stretched his long, bronzed arms, and rose to his feet.

'It is time we moved on, sir,' he declared, 'if we expect to reach Sychar by sunset. The town does not have a good inn. We will make camp this side, near Jacob's well. Ever hear of Jacob, sir?' He grinned, good-humoredly.

'I believe not, Justus,' confessed Marcellus. 'Is it such a good well?'

'No better than plenty of other wells, but a landmark; fifteen centuries old.'

They were on the highway again. The lout with the browsing donkeys had dragged his stubborn caravan out of the weeds. Justus turned about; and, shielding his eyes with his cupped hands, gazed intently down the road over which they had come. Marcellus' curiosity was rekindled. It was not the first time that Justus had stopped to look backward. And whenever they had come to a crossing, he had paused to look carefully in all directions. He did not seem to be apprehensive of danger. It was rather as if he had made an appointment to meet some one up here. Marcellus was on the point of asking if that were true, but discreetly decided it was none of his business.

For more than three hours they plodded along the dusty highway, not meeting many travelers, not making much conversation. It was late afternoon. A half-mile ahead, a cluster of sycamores was sighted and a few scattered dwellings.

'There are the outskirts of Sychar,' said Justus, lengthening his stride.

In a little while they reached the little suburb, a sleepy, shabby community of whitewashed, flat-roofed houses. In its center, by the roadside, was the historic well. Two women were walking away with water-jars on their shoulders. A third was arriving. Justus' steps lagged to give her time to draw up the huge bucket and fill her jar. She glanced apathetically in their direction, put down her jar, stared; and then proceeded vigorously with her task. Hurriedly filling the jar, and spilling much water about her feet, she shouldered her burden and made off toward one of the small houses.

'Have we alarmed her?' asked Marcellus, grinning. 'I had not thought we looked so fierce.'

'She is not frightened,' said Justus soberly.

It was a large well. The ancient stonework around it was of the height of a sheep, and broad enough to be sat upon comfortably. Justus, who had suddenly become preoccupied, sank wearily onto the ledge with his back toward the small group of dwellings. After standing about for some moments, wondering how long they were to linger here, Marcellus sat down on the opposite side to wait until Justus was ready to move on. His eyes idly followed the rapidly retreating figure of the woman until she entered one of the houses.

Almost immediately she reappeared without her water-jar and ran across the highway to a neighbor; entered, and came out in a moment accompanied by another younger and more attractive woman. They stood for a while looking toward the well; then advanced slowly, stopping frequently to parley, their faces full of perplexity.

'That woman is coming back, Justus, and bringing another along, and they are not coming for water,' drawled Marcellus.

Justus roused with a little jerk and turned his head. Then he rose and walked toward the woman who came quickly to meet him. They held a brief, low-voiced conversation, Justus solemnly shaking his head. The younger woman, her eyes—very pretty eyes, too—wide with curiosity, continued to press her queries, and Justus shook his head, as if saying, No—no—no. Finally he tipped his head slightly in Marcellus' direction, and the woman's eyes instantaneously followed the gesture. Justus was cautioning them not to pursue the matter, whatever it was.

Then the older woman left them and began slowly retracing her steps toward her house; and Justus, frowning heavily and nodding what seemed to be a reluctant consent, turned back toward the well. Yes—he would try to talk with her again, his manner plainly said. He would talk with her again, as soon as he could do so without arousing the curiosity of this Roman.

After Justus had unpacked their camping equipment and put up the sleeping-tent under a pair of rangy sycamores, he had mumbled something about having to go back to the village for bread, though Marcellus knew they had enough for their supper and suspected that his more urgent errand was to talk with that woman again; for his manner had made it plain that he wished to go alone.

Wearied by the long day's tramp and annoyed by his guide's secretiveness, he flung himself down on the rug that Justus had spread in front of the tent and moodily watched the sun going down over the tree-tops and house-roofs of the village.

Why did Justus want to have a private interview with this woman? What did they have to talk about? Something quite serious, apparently. Perhaps they would discuss this mystery. But why should there be a mystery? The Galilean was dead. Who was going to persecute these people for what the carpenter had said or done; or for their tender remembrance of him?

Marcellus was offended. Surely Justus had no reason to think that he had come up into this poverty-stricken land to harass the simple-hearted country-folk. There was no occasion for this fellow to treat him as if he were an ordinary eavesdropper!

Well—if Justus did not trust him, it was conceivable that he might secretly go through his belongings, looking for some evidence. If he did so—he would get a stunning surprise! There was one article of Galilean homespun, at the bottom of his gunny-bag, that Justus must not see!

Chapter XIII

It was well on toward sunset when they sighted Cana, after a fatiguing tramp from the village of Nain where Justus' insistence on observing the Sabbath had kept them off the road for a day—one of the most tedious and profitless days that Marcellus had ever experienced.

Justus had gone to the little synagogue in the morning. Had he been invited, Marcellus would have accompanied him, so hard up was he for diversion in an unkempt town where there was nothing of interest to see or do. But Justus had set off alone, after assuring Marcellus that there were ample provisions for his noonday meal.

About the middle of what threatened to an interminable afternoon, Marcellus, lounging on the ground in front of the tent, observed Justus returning in the company of an elderly woman and a tall, sober-faced young man. They walked slowly, preoccupied with serious conversation. When within a stadium of the camp, they came to a stop and continued their earnest talk for a long time. Then the woman and the young man who, Marcellus surmised, might have been her son, reluctantly turned back toward the village, arm in arm, while Justus came on wearing a studious frown.

Marcellus knew it was childish to feel any resentment over the quite obvious disinclination of Justus to acquaint him with his local friends. When there was trading in prospect, Justus was promptly polite with his introductions, but he was making it plain that their relationship was strictly on a business basis.

It wasn't that Marcellus had any considerable interest in meeting this gray-haired woman, or the thoughtful young man on whose arm she leaned affectionately; but he couldn't help feeling a bit chagrined over the snubbing. Of course, in all fairness to Justus, he reflected, the fellow had contracted only to take him into households where homespun might be purchased. He had not promised to introduce the young Roman merchant as his friend. Nor could Justus be expected to know—nor might he be permitted to suspect—that his patron had no interest whatsoever in this merchandising, but wanted only to meet and talk with persons who had known Jesus.

Returning to the tent, with an absent nod toward his idle client, Justus had sat silently staring at the distant hills. Occasionally Marcellus stole a glance in his direction, but he was completely oblivious. It could not be divined whether this retreat into silence was of a piece with Sabbath observance or whether some new reason accounted for his taciturnity.

Early the next morning, Justus had been suddenly animated with a desire to be on the highway. Breakfast was dispatched at top speed. The pack-asses and their socially inferior custodian were advised that there would be no nonsense on this day's journey. The sun was hot, but the determined guide led the little caravan with long, swinging strides. Marcellus was mightily relieved when, at high noon, Justus turned off the road and pointed to a near-by clump of olives.

'Shall we rest now, and eat?' he inquired.

'By all means!' panted Marcellus, mopping his brow. 'Is this Cana such an interesting city, then, that we must walk our legs off to get there today?'

'I am sorry to have pressed you,' said Justus. 'I did not explain because I wanted to give you a pleasant surprise at the end of the day. There is a young woman in Cana who sings every evening in the park.'

'Indeed!' muttered Marcellus, wearily. 'Well—she'd better be good!'

'She is good.' Justus began unpacking their lunch. 'The people of Cana have their supper early; and afterward a great many of them—both young and old—assemble about the fountain where this crippled girl sings the songs that our people love. Her family and the neighbors carry her there on her cot, and the people sit down and listen until dark.'

'Extraordinary!' commented Marcellus, rubbing his lame muscles. 'You say she's a cripple? I shall want to meet her. At the rate we're traveling, by the end of the day she and I may have a common cause.'

Justus acknowledged the raillery with a grin, broke a wheaten loaf, gave half of it to Marcellus, and seated himself on the grass.

'Miriam is a beautiful young woman,' he went on, munching his bread hungrily. 'She is about twenty-two now. Some seven years ago she was suddenly stricken with paralysis. That would have been a great misfortune in any case, but for Miriam it was a calamity. She had been very active in games, and a leader in the children's sports. Now she was unable to walk. Moreover, she added to her unhappiness by resenting her affliction, spending her days in such pitiful lamentations that her parents were beside themselves with grief, and their house was in mourning.'

'I take it that you knew them well,' contributed Marcellus, mildly interested.

'Not at that time,' admitted Justus, 'but the day came when that part of Miriam's story was quite widely discussed. For all of three years she lay on her bed, inconsolable, peevish, so embittered by her trouble that she rejected all the kindly efforts made to divert her mind. As time passed, she refused to admit her friends into her room; and sat alone, sullen and smouldering with rebellion.'

'And now she sings? What happened?'

'Now she sings,' nodded Justus; adding, after a meditative moment: 'I do not know the particulars, sir. I am not sure that anyone does. Miriam refuses to discuss it. Her parents profess not to know. When people have inquired of them, they have replied, "Ask Miriam." '

'Perhaps they are telling the truth when they say they do not know.' Marcellus was becoming concerned. 'Surely they could have no motive for refusing to explain the improvement in their daughter's disposition.'

Justus had nodded a few times, without comment.

'Maybe Miriam herself doesn't know,' speculated Marcellus, hopeful that the story had not come to an end. 'Maybe Miriam found that she had finally exhausted her resentment—and might as well make the best of it.' He paused to give Justus a chance to contradict this inexpert opinion; and, meeting no rejoinder, ventured another guess. 'Maybe she woke up one morning and said to herself, "I've been making everybody miserable. I'm going to pretend that I'm happy. I'll be cheerful—and sing!" Maybe she just reached that decision, after proving that the other course was futile.'

'Maybe,' murmured Justus, remotely.

'But you don't think so,' declared Marcellus, after a long interval of silence.

'I don't know.' Justus shook his head decisively. 'One of her girl friends, whom she hadn't seen for a couple of years, was to be married. They had urgently pleaded with Miriam to attend the wedding, but she would not go; and all that day she wept bitterly. But—that evening —when her parents returned from the wedding-feast—she met them with gladness; and sang!'

'Amazing!' exclaimed Marcellus. 'And has she a voice—really?'

'You may decide that for yourself, sir, when you hear her,' said Justus. 'And you may meet her in her home tomorrow. Naomi, her mother, does beautiful weaving. I shall take you there. She may have some things that might interest you. If you are rested now, sir, shall we be on our way?'

* * * * * *

They pitched their tent at the edge of little Cana, ate their supper quickly, and walked to the center of the village, overtaking many people headed in the same direction. Already fifty or more were seated on the ground in semicircular rows facing a natural fountain that gently welled up into the huge brick basin.

'I suppose this is Cana's drinking water,' said Marcellus, as they moved toward an unoccupied spot on the lawn.

'It is warm water,' said Justus. 'Hot springs abound in this region.' They seated themselves cross-legged on the ground.

'Is it thought to be a healing water?' asked Marcellus.

'Yes—but not by the people of Galilee. Travelers come from afar to bathe in the water from these springs.'

'Oh? Then Cana sees many strangers.'

'Not so many in Cana. They go mostly to Tiberias, on the Lake Gennesaret. It is a more important city, and possesses much wealth. It is only the rich who come to bathe in medicinal waters.'

'And why is that?' inquired Marcellus. 'Do not the poor believe in the virtue of these hot springs?'

Justus laughed. It was a deep, spontaneous laugh that he seemed to enjoy; an infectious laugh that evoked companionable chuckles in their vicinity, where many men and women had recognized the big, gentle-voiced neighbor from Sepphoris. Marcellus was discovering something new and interesting about Justus. He was naturally full of fun. You wouldn't have suspected it. He had been so serious; so weighted.

'The poor do not have the diseases, sir, that these springs are supposed to cure,' explained Justus. 'Only men accustomed to rich foods and an abundance of fine wines seek these healing waters. The Galileans do not suffer of ills arising from such causes.'

It was delicious irony, because so free of any bitterness. Marcellus admired the tone of the appreciative laughter that came from their candidly eavesdropping neighbors. His heart warmed toward them. He was going to feel at home with them.

'That's a new thought, Justus,' he replied, 'and a sound one. I never considered it before, but it is a fact that hot springs are intended for gluttons and winebibbers. Now that you speak of it, I recall having heard something about this city of Tiberias on Lake Gennesaret.'

'Often called the Sea of Galilee,' nodded Justus, 'but not by the Galileans.' The crowd seated about them had grown attentive, tilting its head at a favorable angle, frankly interested.

'Big lake?' wondered Marcellus.

'Big enough to be stormy. They have some rough gales.'

'Any fishing?'

Justus nodded indifferently, and a middle-aged man sitting in front of them turned his head, plainly wanting to say something. Marcellus caught his dancing eye, and raised his brows encouragingly.

'That's one of the diseases that poor people can afford, sir,' remarked the man, 'fishing!' Everybody laughed merrily at that.

'Do they catch them?' inquired Marcellus.

'Yes,' drawled Justus, 'they have caught them—all of them—a long time ago.' This sally was good, too; and the friendly hilarity increased the circle of listeners. Marcellus felt that they were showing quite an amiable attitude toward him; perhaps because he was sponsored by Justus who, it seemed, everyone knew; and, besides, Marcellus was doing fairly well with his Aramaic.

'But they still fish?' he inquired, artlessly.

A shrill childish voice unexpectedly broke in, from up the row a little way.

'Once they caught a great lot of them!' shouted the lad.

'Sh-sh!'—came a soft, concerted caution from his kin.

All eyes were now turning toward the fountain where a cot was being borne in from the street. The girl was sitting up, propped about with pillows. In her bare, shapely arms she hugged a small harp.

The sculptor in Marcellus instantly responded. It was a finely modeled, oval face, white with a pallor denoting much pain endured; but the wide-set, long-lashed eyes had not been hurt. Her abundant hair, parted in the middle, framed an intelligent brow. Her full lips were almost gay, as they surveyed the crowd.

Two men followed, carrying wooden trestles, and the cot was lifted up until everyone could see. A deep hush fell upon the people. Marcellus was much impressed by the unusual scene, and found himself wishing that the girl wouldn't try to sing. The picture was perfect. It was imprudent to risk spoiling it.

Miriam gently swept the strings of her harp with slim, white fingers. Then her face seemed to be transfigured. Its momentary gaiety had faded, and there had come an expression of deep yearning. It was clear that she had left them now, and was puttting out on an enchanted excursion. The luminous eyes looked upward, wide with far vision. Again she lightly touched the harp-strings.

The voice was a surprisingly deep, resonant contralto. That first tone, barely audible at its beginning, swelled steadily until it began to take on the pulsing vibration of a bell. Marcellus felt a quick tightening of his throat, a sudden suffusion of emotion that burned and dimmed his eyes. Now the song took wings!

'I *waited patiently for the Lord—and He inclined unto me—and heard my cry.*'

All around Marcellus heads were bent to meet upraised hands; and stifled sobs, with childish little catches of breath in them, were straining to be quiet. As for himself, he sat staring at the entranced girl through uncontrollable tears. He shook them out of his eyes—and stared!

'*And He hath put a new song in my mouth!*' exulted Miriam.

Justus slowly turned his head toward Marcellus. His seamed face was contorted and his eyes were swimming. Marcellus touched his sleeve and nodded soberly. Their gaze returned to the enraptured girl.

'*Then I said, "Lo—I come." In the volume of the Book it is written of me, "I delight to do Thy will, O God—and Thy law is in my heart!"*'

The song was ended and the close-packed crowd drew a deep sigh. Neighbors slowly turned their faces toward their best beloved, smiled wistfully with half-closed eyes, and shook their heads, lacking words to tell how deeply they had been moved. After an interval Miriam found her wings again. Marcellus reached for occasional phrases of her triumphant song, while rushing about in his heart to reacquaint himself with instinctive longings of his own. It was coming to an end now, even as the last rays of sunset filled the sky.

'*To give light to them that sit in darkness and in the shadow of death,*' sang Miriam, '*and to guide our feet in the way of peace.*'

Twilight was falling. The men bore Miriam away. The crowd silently scattered and took to the highway. It pleased Marcellus that Justus, trudging by his side in the darkness, did not ask him if he had liked Miriam's voice, or whether he had not been impressed by the unusual occasion.

* * * * * *

The home of Reuben and Naomi, at the northern extremity of the village, was more commodious and occupied a larger parcel of ground than most of the residences in Cana. The white-walled house, well back from the road, was shaded by tall sycamores. In the spacious front yard were many fruit trees, now gay and fragrant with blossoms; and on either side of this area there was an apparently prosperous vineyard.

It was with some difficulty that Marcellus had curbed his impatience to visit this home where he hoped to meet the crippled girl with the radiant face and the golden voice. Justus had seemed willfully tedious at the two places where they had called on their way; and had it not been imprudent, Marcellus would have dispatched these small transactions by purchasing whatever was offered.

'Let us first speak to Miriam,' said Justus, unlatching the gate. 'I see her sitting in the arbor.'

They crossed the neatly clipped grass-plot and sauntered toward the shaded arbor where Miriam sat alone. She wore a white himation trimmed with coral at the throat and flowing sleeves, but no jewelry except a slim silver chain about her neck with a tiny pendant —a fish—carved from a seashell. On the table beside her cot was the harp and a small case of scrolls. Her curly head was bent attentively over the lace medallion she was knitting. As they approached, she glanced up, recognizing Justus, and smiled a welcome.

'Oh—you needn't explain, Barsabas Justus,' she said when, after presenting Marcellus, he had added that the young man was interested in Galilean fabrics. 'Everybody in Cana knows about it.' She smiled into Marcellus' eyes. 'We are all excited, sir, over your visit; for it isn't often that anyone comes here to trade.'

There was a peculiar tone-quality in her low voice that Marcellus could not define, except that its warmth was entirely unself-conscious and sincere. Frequently he had observed, upon being introduced to young women, that they had a tendency to soar off into an impetuous animation, pitching their blithe remarks in a shrill key as if from a considerable distance. Miriam's voice was as unaffected and undefended as her smile.

'Naomi is at home?' asked Justus.

'In the house. Will you find her? I think she and Father are expecting you.'

Justus turned away, and Marcellus was uncertain whether to follow. Miriam helped him to a gratifying decision by pointing to a chair.

'I heard you sing,' he said. 'It was the most—' He paused to grope for an appropriate word.

'How do you happen to speak Aramaic?' she interposed gently.

'I don't—very well,' said Marcellus. 'However'—he went on more confidently—'even your own countrymen might find it difficult to describe your singing. I was deeply moved by it.'

'I am glad you wanted to tell me that.' Miriam pushed aside the pillow on which the lace medallion had been pinned, and faced him with candid eyes. 'I wondered a little what you might think. I saw you there with Justus. I had never sung for a Roman. It would not have surprised me if you had been amused; but would have hurt me.'

'I'm afraid we have a bad reputation in these provinces,' sighed Marcellus.

'Of course,' said Miriam. 'The only Romans we see in Cana are legionaries, marching down the street, so haughtily, so defiantly'— She straightened and swaggered her pretty shoulders, accenting her militant pantomime with little jerks of her head—'as if they were saying—' She paused and added, apologetically, 'But perhaps I should not tell you.'

'Oh—I know what we always seem to say when we strut,' assisted Marcellus. He protruded his lips with an exaggerated show of arrogance, and carried on with Miriam's march—' "Here—we come— your—lords—and—mas—ters!" '

They both laughed a little, and Miriam resumed her needlework. Bending over it attentively, she inquired:

'Are there many Romans like you, Marcellus Gallio?'

'Multitudes! I make no claim to any sort of uniqueness.'

'I never talked with a Roman before,' said Miriam. 'But I supposed they were all alike. They look alike.'

'In their uniforms, yes; but under their spiked helmets and shields, they are ordinary creatures with no relish for tramping the streets of foreign cities. They would much prefer to be at home with their families, hoeing in their gardens and tending their goats.'

'I am glad to know that,' said Miriam. 'It is so unpleasant to dislike people—and so hard not to think badly of the Romans. Now I shall say that great numbers of them wish they were at home with their gardens and goats; and I shall hope,' she went on, with a slow smile, 'that their desire may be fulfilled. Do you have a garden, sir?'

'Yes—we have a garden.'

'But no goats, I think.'

'There is no room for them. We live in the city.'

'Do you have horses?'

'Yes.'

'In Galilee,' drawled Miriam, 'horses require more room than goats. Would you like to tell me about your home?'

'Gladly. Our family consists of our parents and my sister Lucia and myself.'

'Does your father take care of the garden while you are abroad?'

'Well—not personally—no,' replied Marcellus, after a little hesitation; and when she glanced up from under her long lashes with an elder-sisterly grin, he asked, 'Are you having a good time?'

She nodded companionably.

'I might have known that you kept a gardener,' she said, 'and a maidservant too, no doubt.'

'Yes,' assented Marcellus, casually.

'Are they—slaves?' asked Miriam, in a tone that hoped not to give offense.

'Yes,' admitted Marcellus, uncomfortably, 'but I can assure you they are not mistreated.'

'I believe that,' she said, softly. 'You couldn't be cruel to anyone. How many slaves have you?'

'I never counted them. A dozen, perhaps. No—there must be more than that. Twenty—maybe.'

'It must seem odd to own other human beings,' reflected Miriam. 'Do you keep them locked up, when they're not working?'

'By no means!' Marcellus dismissed the query with a toss of his hand. 'They are free to go anywhere they please.'

'Indeed!' exclaimed Miriam. 'Don't they ever run away?'

'Not often. There's no place for them to go.'

'That's too bad.' Miriam sighed. 'They'd be better off in chains; wouldn't they? Then maybe they could break loose. As it is, the whole world is their prison.'

'I never thought about it before,' pondered Marcellus. 'But I suppose the whole world is a prison for everyone. Is anybody entirely free? What constitutes freedom?'

'The truth!' answered Miriam, quickly. 'The truth sets anyone free! If it weren't so, I might feel quite fettered myself, Marcellus Gallio. My country is owned by a foreign master. And, because of my lameness, I may seem to have very little liberty; but my spirit is free!'

'You are fortunate,' said Marcellus. 'I should give a great deal to experience a liberty independent of all physical conditions. Did you work out that philosophy for yourself? Was it a product of your illness, perhaps?'

'No, no!' She shook her head decisively. 'My illness made a wretched slave of me. I did not earn my freedom. It was a gift.'

Marcellus kept silent, when she paused. Perhaps she would explain. Suddenly her face lighted, and she turned toward him with an altered mood.

'Please forgive me for being inquisitive about you,' she said. 'I sit here all day with nothing new happening. It is refreshing to talk with someone from the outside world. Tell me about your sister Lucia. Is she younger than you?'

'Much.'

'Younger than I?'

'Six years younger,' ventured Marcellus, smiling into her suddenly widened eyes.

'Who told you my age?'

'Justus.'

'How did he happen to do that?'

'He was telling me, before we arrived in Cana, about your singing. He said that you never knew you could sing until—one day —you found that you had a voice—and sang. Justus said it came all unexpectedly. How do you account for it—if it isn't a secret?'

'It is a secret,' she said, softly.

They were coming around the corner of the house now—Naomi, first, with her arms full of robes and shawls, followed by Justus and Reuben. Marcellus came to his feet and was introduced. Reuben rather diffidently took the hand that Marcellus offered him. Naomi, apparently pleased by their guest's attitude, smiled cordially. It was easy to see the close resemblance of mother and daughter. Naomi had the same dimples in her cheeks.

'We have always gone to Jerusalem to attend the Passover at this season,' she said, spreading out her wares across the back of a chair. 'This year we shall not go. That is why I happen to have so many things on hand.'

Marcellus assumed his best business manner. Taking up a brown robe, he examined it with professional interest.

'This,' he said, expertly, 'is typically Galilean. A seamless robe. And excellent workmanship. Evidently you have had much practice in weaving this garment.'

Naomi's gratified expression encouraged him to speak freely. He felt he was making a good case for himself as a connoisseur of home-spun, and could risk an elaboration of his knowledge, particularly for Justus' information.

'A weaver of my acquaintance in Athens,' he went on, 'told me something about this robe. He was formerly of Samaria, I believe, and was quite familiar with Galilean products.' He glanced toward Justus, and met an inquisitive stare, as if he were searching his memory for some related fact. Now his eyes lighted a little.

'There was a young Greek working for Benyosef, a short time ago,' remarked Justus. 'I heard him say he had been with a weaver in Athens named Benjamin, from whom he had learned to speak Aramaic. Might this have been the same weaver?'

'Why—yes!' Marcellus tried to enjoy the coincidence. 'Benjamin is well respected in Athens. He is a good scholar, too.' He chuckled a little, 'Benjamin quite insists on speaking Aramaic with anyone whom he suspects of knowing the language.'

'He must have found you pleasant company, sir,' remarked Justus. 'I have noticed that you use many terms which are colloquial with the Samaritans.'

'Indeed!' said Marcellus, taking up a shawl, and returning his attention to Naomi. 'This is excellent wool,' he assured her. 'Is it grown here in Galilee?'

'In our own madbra,' replied Reuben, proudly.

'Madbra?' repeated Marcellus. 'In the desert?'

Justus laughed.

'See, Reuben?' he exclaimed. 'When the Samaritans say "madbra," they mean barren land.' He turned to Marcellus. 'When we say "madbra," we mean pasture. "Bara" is our word for desert.'

'Thanks, Justus,' said Marcellus. 'I'm learning something.' He dismissed this small episode by concentrating on the shawl. 'It is beautifully dyed,' he said.

'With our own mulberries,' boasted Naomi.

'Had I known you were acquainted with Benjamin,' persisted Justus, 'I should have told you about this young Greek, Demetrius; a most thoughtful fellow. He left suddenly, one day. He had been in some trouble—and was a fugitive.'

Marcellus politely raised his brows, but made it clear enough, by his manner, that they had other things to talk about.

'I shall want the shawl,' he said, 'and this robe. Now—let us see what else.' He began fumbling with the garments, hoping he had not seemed abrupt in disregarding the comments about Demetrius.

Presently Justus sauntered away toward the vineyard, and Reuben followed him.

'Why don't you show Marcellus Gallio those pretty bandeaus, Mother?' suggested Miriam.

'Oh—they're nothing,' said Naomi. 'He wouldn't bother with them.'

'May I see them?' asked Marcellus.

Naomi obligingly moved away, and Marcellus continued to inspect the textiles with exaggerated concern.

'Marcellus.' Miriam's tone was confidential.

He glanced up and met her level eyes inquiringly.

'Why did you lie to Justus?' she insisted, just above a whisper.

'Lie to him?' parried Marcellus, flushing.

'About that Greek. You did not want to talk about him. Perhaps you know him. Tell me, Marcellus. What are you? You're not a merchant. I know that. You have no real interest in my mother's weaving.' Miriam waited for a reply, but Marcellus had not recovered his self-possession. 'Tell me,' she coaxed, softly. 'What are you doing up here—in Galilee—if it isn't a secret?'

He met her challenging smile with an attempted casualness.

'It is a secret,' he said.

Chapter XIV

JUSTUS was coolly polite today, but remote. He was beginning to be skeptical about Marcellus. Yesterday at Reuben's house a few facts, unimportant when considered singly, had taken on size once they were strung together.

Marcellus, whose Aramaic was distinctly of the Samaritan variety, had recklessly volunteered that he knew old Benjamin, the weaver in Athens, who had derived from Samaria.

Demetrius, the handsome young Greek who had recently been in Benyosef's employ, also knew old Benjamin; had worked for him; and the Aramaic he spoke was loaded with Samaritan provincialisms. Clearly there was some sort of tieup between Marcellus and this fugitive slave, though the Roman had pretended not to have known him, and had shown no interest in the story of his hasty flight from Benyosef's shop. Doubtless Marcellus knew about it, and had reasons for wanting to evade any discussion of it. It all went to prove that you couldn't trust a Roman.

At sunset yesterday, Justus had strolled down the street by himself, making it clear that his Roman patron's company was not desired. For a little while Marcellus had debated the propriety of going alone to the fountain. His anxiety to hear Miriam sing again decided the matter.

The whole town was there and seated when he quietly joined the crowd at its shaded outskirts. No notice was taken of him, for Miriam had at that moment arrived and all eyes were occupied. Marcellus sat on the ground, a little way apart, and experienced the same surge of emotion that had swept through him on the previous evening. Now that he had talked with her, Miriam's songs meant even more. He had been strangely drawn to this girl. And he knew that she had been sincerely interested in him. It was not, in either case, a mere transient infatuation. There had been nothing coyly provocative in Miriam's attitude. She wanted only to be his friend, and had paid him the high compliment of assuming that he was bright enough to understand the nature of her unreserved cordiality.

As he sat there in the darkness, alternately stilled and stirred by her deep, vibrant, confident tones, he found himself consenting to the reality of her honest faith. His inherent, built-in skepticism yielded to a curious wistfulness as she sang, '*In the shadow of thy*

*wings will I make my refuge. . . . My heart is fixed. . . . Awake,
my glory! Awake, my harp!"* Miriam couldn't walk—but she could
fly.

Justus had briefly announced that they would be leaving early in
the morning for his home town, Sepphoris, where he must attend
to some errands.

'Will we be coming back through Cana?' Marcellus had asked.

'If it is your wish, yes,' Justus had replied, 'but we have seen everyone here who has weaving for sale.'

There wasn't much to be said after that. Marcellus could think
of no reasonable excuse for a return to Cana. He couldn't say, 'I
must have another private talk with Miriam.' No—he would have
to go, leaving her to wonder what manner of rôle he had been playing. Given one more day, one more confidential chat with Miriam,
he might have told her why he was here in Galilee.

When the last song was ended, he waited in the shadows for the
crowd to disperse. Justus, he observed, had moved forward to join
Reuben's party as it made its way to the street. It would be quite
possible to overtake this slow-moving group and say farewell to
Miriam. Perhaps she might be glad if he did. But on second thought
that seemed inadvisable. It might prove embarrassing to both of them.
Perhaps Reuben and Naomi shared the obvious suspicions of Justus
that there was something irregular about this Roman's tour of Galilee.
After lingering indecisively until the little park was cleared, Marcellus, deeply depressed and lonely, slowly retraced his way to the
little camp reproaching himself for having unnecessarily given them
cause to distrust him. He saw now that it would have been much
more sensible if he had told Justus, at the outset, why he wanted to
visit Galilee. Of course, Justus, in that event, might have refused to
conduct him; but the present situation was becoming intolerable.
Marcellus was very unhappy. He would have given much for a talk
with Demetrius tonight. Demetrius was resourceful. Had he been
along, by this time he would have found means for penetrating the
reticence of these Galileans.

*   *   *   *   *   *

It was nearing midday now. They had not exchanged a word for
more than an hour. Justus, who had been tramping on ahead,
paused to wait for Marcellus to come abreast of him. He pointed
to a house on a near-by shady knoll.

'We will stop there,' he said, 'though it is likely that Amasiah and
Deborah have gone to Jerusalem. They weave excellent saddlebags
and sell them to the bazaars when they attend the Passover.'

A stout, middle-aged woman came sauntering through the yard
to meet them as they turned in at the gate, her face suddenly beam-

ing as she recognized Justus. No—Amasiah was not at home. Yes—he had gone to Jerusalem.

'And why not you, Deborah?' asked Justus.

'Surely you know,' she sighed. 'I have no wish ever to see the Holy City again. Nor would Amasiah have gone but to sell the saddlebags.' She turned inquiring eyes toward Marcellus, and Justus introduced him with cool formality, explaining his mission. Deborah smiled briefly and murmured her regret that they had nothing to sell. No—everything had gone with Amasiah.

'All but a little saddleblanket I made for Jasper,' she added. 'I can show it to you.' They moved toward the house, and Deborah brought out the saddleblanket, a thick, well-woven trifle of gay colors. 'Jasper can get along without it, if you want it.' She nodded toward a diminutive, silver-gray donkey, browsing in the shade.

'I suppose Jasper is a little pet,' surmised Marcellus, lightly.

'Jasper is a little pest,' grumbled Deborah. 'I am too heavy to ride him any more, and Amasiah says he isn't worth his keep in a pack-train.'

'Would you like to sell him?' inquired Marcellus.

'You wouldn't have any use for him,' said Deborah, honestly.

'How much would you want?' persisted Marcellus.

'What's he worth, Justus?' asked Deborah, languidly.

Justus sauntered over to the donkey, pulled his shaggy head up out of the grass, and looked into his mouth.

'Well—if he's worth anything at all, which is doubtful, except maybe for a child to play with—he should bring twelve to fifteen shekels.'

'Has he any bad habits?' inquired Marcellus.

'Eating,' said Deborah, dryly.

'But he won't run away.'

'Oh, no; he won't run away. That would be too much of an effort.' They all laughed but Jasper, who sighed deeply.

'I'll give you fifteen shekels for the donkey and the blanket,' bargained Marcellus.

Deborah said that was fair enough, and added that there was quite a good saddle too, and a bridle that had been made especially for Jasper. She brought them. It was a well-made saddle, and the bridle was gaily ornamented with a red leather top-piece into which a little bell was set.

'How about twenty-five shekels for everything?' suggested Marcellus.

Deborah tossed the saddle across the donkey's back and began fastening the girths. Marcellus opened his wallet. Justus, watching the pantomime, chuckled. It relieved Marcellus to see him amused about something.

Jasper was reluctant to leave the grass-plot, but showed no distress when it came time to part with Deborah, who had led him as far as the gate. Marcellus took the reins and proceeded to the highway, Justus lingering for a private word with Deborah.

Late in the afternoon they reached the frowsy fringe of little Sepphoris, a typical Galilean village. Everybody waved a hand or called a greeting to Justus as the big fellow trudged on with lengthening strides. Soon they were nearing the inevitable public plaza. A small boy broke loose from a group of children playing about the brick-walled well and came running toward Justus with exultant shouts. He was a handsome lad with a sensitive face, a tousle of curly black hair, and an agile body. Justus quickened his steps and caught the little fellow up in his arms, hugging him hungrily. He stopped and turned about, his eyes brightly proud.

'This is my Jonathan!' he announced, unnecessarily.

The boy gave his grandfather another strangling embrace and wiggled out of his arms. He had sighted Jasper.

'Is this your donkey?' he cried.

'Perhaps you would like to ride him,' said Marcellus.

Jonathan climbed on, and Marcellus adjusted the stirrup-straps, a score of children gathering about with high-keyed exclamations. Justus stood by, stroking his beard, alternately smiling and frowning.

'What's his name?' asked Jonathan, as Marcellus put the reins in his hands. His small voice was shrill with excitement.

'His name is Jasper,' said Marcellus. 'You may have him, Jonathan. He is your donkey now.'

'Mine!' squeaked Jonathan. He gazed incredulously at his grandfather.

'This gentleman,' said Justus, 'is my friend, Marcellus Gallio. If he says the donkey is yours, it must be so.' He turned to Marcellus, and said, above the children's shouts of amazement at Jonathan's good fortune, 'That is most generous of you, sir!'

'Is he one of us, Grandfather?' Jonathan pointed a finger at his benefactor.

The two men exchanged quick glances; one frankly mystified, the other somewhat embarrassed.

'You *are* one of us,' declared Jonathan, 'or you wouldn't give your things away!'

Again Marcellus invaded Justus' eyes, but received no answer.

'Are you rich?' demanded Jonathan, immensely forthright.

'No one has ever said "yes" to that question, Jonathan,' laughed Marcellus, as Justus mumbled an unintelligible apology for his grandson's impertinence.

'But—you must be rich,' insisted Jonathan, 'to be giving your things away. Did Jesus tell you to do that?' He thrust his small face forward and studied Marcellus' eyes with childish candor. 'You knew

Jesus; didn't you? Did my grandfather tell you that Jesus straightened my foot—so I can walk and run?'

The children were quiet now. Marcellus found himself confronted with the necessity of making a public address, and was appropriately tongue-tied. After a difficult interval, he stammered:

'Y-yes—your grandfather told me—about your foot, Jonathan. I am very glad it got well. That is fine!'

'Let us go now,' muttered Justus, uneasily. 'My house is close by. Come! I want you to meet my daughter.'

Marcellus needed no urging. They proceeded up the street, their numbers increasing as they went. The news had traveled fast. People came out of their houses, wide-eyed with curiosity; children of all sizes ran to join the procession. One small boy on crutches, dangling a useless leg, waited for the parade, his pinched face alight with wonder. Justus stepped to the side of the road and gave him a friendly pat on the head as he passed.

Now they had arrived at the modest little home. The dooryard was scrupulously tidy. The narrow walk was bordered with tulips. Rebecca, a gentle-voiced, plain-featured matron of thirty-five, met them, considerably puzzled by all the excitement. Justus, on the doorstep, briefly explained; and, with a new cordiality, presented Marcellus.

'Oh—you shouldn't have done that, sir,' murmured Rebecca, though her shining eyes were full of appreciation. 'That is quite an expensive gift to make to a little boy.'

'I'm fully repaid,' smiled Marcellus. 'It is evident that the donkey is a success.'

'Look, Mother!' shouted Jonathan, waving his arm. 'It's *mine!*'

Rebecca nodded and smiled, and the noisy pack moved on in the wake of the town's young hero.

'This is a great day for Jonathan,' said Rebecca, as she led the way into their small, frugally furnished parlor.

'Yes, yes,' sighed Justus, sinking into a chair. He was frowning thoughtfully. 'It's a great day for the lad—but Jonathan's pretty young for a responsibility like that.'

'Oh—he's old enough,' remarked Marcellus. 'That lazy little donkey really should belong to a child. Jonathan will get along with him splendidly.'

'As for that—yes,' agreed Justus, soberly. He stroked his beard moodily, nodded his head several times and muttered to himself, 'Yes, yes; that's a good deal to expect of a little boy.' Then suddenly brightening he said to his daughter, 'Rebecca, we will pitch Marcellus Gallio's tent there beside the house. And he will have his meals with us.'

'Of course, Father,' responded Rebecca, promptly, giving their guest a hospitable smile. 'Is there anything you are enjoined not to eat, sir?' And when Marcellus looked puzzled, she hesitatingly explained, 'I am not acquainted with the Roman customs. I thought perhaps your religion—like ours—forbids your eating certain things.'

'Oh, no,' declared Marcellus, amiably. 'My religion has never inconvenienced anyone—not even me.' He quickly repented of this flippancy when he observed that his remark had drawn down the corners of his host's mouth.

'Do you mean that your people have no religion at all?' queried Justus, soberly.

'No religion!' protested Marcellus. 'Why—we have gods on every corner!'

'Idols—you mean,' corrected Justus, dourly.

'Statues,' amended Marcellus. 'Some of them quite well done, too. Imported from Greece, most of them. The Greeks have a talent for it.'

'And your people worship these—statues?' wondered Justus.

'They seem to, sir. I suppose some of them are really sincere about it.' Marcellus was tiring of this inquisition.

'But you, personally, do not worship these things,' persisted Justus.

'Oh—by no means!' Marcellus laughed.

'Then you do not believe in any Supreme Power?' Justus was shocked and troubled.

'I admit, Justus, that all the theories I have heard on this subject are unconvincing. I am open to conviction. I should be glad indeed to learn of a reliable religion.'

Rebecca, scenting a difficult discussion, moved restlessly to the edge of her chair, smiling nervously.

'I shall go and prepare your supper,' she said, rising. 'You men must be starving.'

'I didn't mean to be offensive, Justus,' regretted Marcellus, when Rebecca had left the room. 'You are a sincerely religious person, and it was thoughtless of me to speak negligently of these matters.'

'No harm done,' said Justus, gently. 'You wish you could believe. That is something. Is it not true, in our life, that they find who seek? You are a man of good intent. You are kind. You deserve to have a religion.'

Marcellus couldn't think of an appropriate rejoinder to that, so he sat silent, waiting for further directions. After a moment, Justus impulsively slapped his big brown hands down on his knees in a gesture of adjournment; and, rising, moved toward the door.

'Let us put up your tent, Marcellus,' he suggested kindly. It was the first time he had spoken Marcellus' name without the formal addition of 'Gallio.'

* * * * * *

Shortly after the family supper, which he had been too busy to attend, Jonathan appeared at the open front of the brown tent. He stood with his feet wide apart, his arms akimbo, and an expression of gravity on his sensitive lips. It was apparent that the day's experiences had aged him considerably.

Marcellus, writing at the small collapsible table, put down his stylus, regarded his caller with interest, and grinned. He mistakenly thought he knew what had been going on in Jonathan's mind. At the outset, his amazing windfall had dizzied him into a state of emotional instability that had made his voice squeaky and his postures jerky; but now that the crowd had gone home, and Jasper had been shown into the unoccupied stall beside the cow, and had been hand-fed with laboriously harvested clover, Jonathan's excitment had cooled. He was becoming aware of his new status as a man of affairs, a man of property, sole owner and proprietor of a donkey, the only man of his age in all Sepphoris who owned a donkey. Even his grandfather didn't own a donkey. Marcellus felt that Jonathan's behavior was approximately normal for a seven-year-old boy, in these circumstances.

'Well—did you put him up for the night?' he inquired, as one man to another.

Jonathan pursed his lips and nodded gravely.

'Will you come in and sit down?'

Jonathan came in and sat down, crossing his legs with mature deliberation.

'Did Jasper behave pretty well?'

Jonathan nodded several times, facing the ground.

Marcellus felt in need of some cooperation, but pursued his inquiries hopefully.

'Didn't bite anybody? Or kick anybody? Or lie down in his harness and go to sleep on the road?'

Jonathan shook his head slowly, without looking up, his tongue bulging his cheek.

Not having conversed with a small boy for many years, Marcellus began to realize that it wasn't as simple a matter as he had supposed.

'Well!' he exclaimed brightly. 'That's fine! Is there anything else you'd like to tell me about it?'

Jonathan glumly raised his head and faced Marcellus with troubled eyes. He swallowed noisily.

'Thomas asked me to let him ride,' he muttered, thickly.

'Something tells me that you refused,' ventured Marcellus.

Jonathan nodded remorsefully.

'I shouldn't fret about that,' went on Marcellus, comfortingly. 'You can let Thomas ride tomorrow. Perhaps he shouldn't have expected you to lend him your donkey on the very first day you had him. Is this Thomas a good friend of yours?'

'Did you see the boy with the crutches; the one with the limber leg?'

'The little boy your grandfather stopped to speak to?'

Jonathan nodded.

'Well—you can make it all up to Thomas,' cooed Marcellus, maternally. 'He'll have plenty of chances to ride. See here—if you feel so upset about this, why don't you run over to Thomas' house now and tell him he may ride Jasper, first thing in the morning.'

'They're going away tomorrow,' croaked Jonathan, dismally. 'Thomas and his mother. They don't live here. They live in Capernaum. They came here because his grandmother was sick. And she died. And now they're going back to Capernaum.'

'That's too bad,' said Marcellus. 'But it isn't your fault. If you're troubled about it, perhaps you'd better talk it over with your grandfather. Did you ever sleep in a tent, Jonathan?'

Jonathan shook his head, the gloom lifting a little.

'There's another cot we can set up,' said Marcellus. 'You go and talk to your grandfather about Thomas, and ask your mother if you may sleep in the tent.'

Jonathan grinned appreciatively and disappeared.

It was impossible not to overhear the conversation, for Justus was seated near the open window within an arm's reach of the tent. After a while, Marcellus became conscious of the deep, gentle voice of Justus and the rather plaintive treble of his troubled grandson. Immensely curious to learn how all this was coming out, he put down his stylus and listened.

'When Jesus told people to give their things away, he said that just to rich people; didn't he, Grandfather?'

'Yes—just to people who had things they could divide with others.'

'Is Marcellus rich?'

'Yes—and he is very kind.'

'Did Jesus tell him to give his things away?'

There was a long pause here that made Marcellus hold his breath. 'I do not know, Jonathan. It is possible.'

There was another long silence, broken at length by the little boy. 'Grandfather—why didn't Jesus heal Thomas' leg?'

'I don't know, son. Perhaps Jesus wasn't told about it.'

'That was too bad,' lamented Jonathan. 'I wish he had.'

'Yes,' sighed Justus. 'That would make things much easier for you; wouldn't it?'

'I'm glad he straightened my foot,' murmured Jonathan.

'Yes—that was wonderful!' rumbled Justus. 'Jesus was very good to you! I know that if you could do anything for Jesus, you would be glad to; wouldn't you?'

'I couldn't do anything for Jesus, Grandfather,' protested Jonathan. 'How could I?'

'Well—if you should find that there was something Jesus hadn't done, because they hadn't told him about it; something he would have wanted to do, if he had known; something he would want to do now, if he were still here—'

'You mean—something for Thomas?' Jonathan's voice was thin.

'Had you thought there was something you might do for Thomas?'

Little Jonathan was crying now; and from the sounds of shifting positions within the room, Marcellus surmised that Justus had taken his unhappy grandson in his arms. There was no more talk. After a half-hour or more, Jonathan appeared, red-eyed and fagged, at the door of the tent.

'I'm going to sleep with Grandfather,' he gulped. 'He wants me to.'

'That's right, Jonathan,' approved Marcellus. 'Your grandfather hasn't seen you for a long time. You may play in the tent tomorrow, if you like.'

Jonathan lingered, scowling thoughtfully and batting his eyes.

'Would it be all right with you if I gave Jasper away?' he asked, with an effort.

'To Thomas, maybe?' wondered Marcellus.

Jonathan nodded, without looking up.

'Are you sure you want to?'

'No—I don't want to.'

'Well—you're a pretty brave little boy, Jonathan! I'll say that for you!' declared Marcellus. This fervent praise, being altogether too much for Jonathan, led to his sudden disappearance. Marcellus untied his sandal-straps and lounged on his cot as the twilight deepened. This Jesus must have been a man of gigantic moral power. He had been dead and in his grave for a year now, but he had stamped himself so indelibly onto the house of Justus that even this child had been marked! The simile intrigued him for a moment. It was as if this Jesus had taken a die and a hammer—and had pounded the image of his spirit into this Galilean gold, converting it into the coins of his kingdom! The man should have lived! He should have been given a chance to impress more people! A spirit like that—if it contrived to get itself going—could make the world over into a fit habitation for men of good will! But Jesus was dead! A little handful of untutored country people in Galilee would remember for a few years —and the great light would be extinguished. It would be a pity! Little Jonathan would give up his donkey to a crippled boy, but only Sepphoris would ever know about it. Miriam would sing her inspired songs—but only for sequestered little Cana. Jesus' kingdom belonged to the world! But its coinage was good only in the shabby villages of Galilee. He would write that, tomorrow, to Demetrius.

* * * * * *

Marcellus ate his breakfast alone, Rebecca attentive but uncommunicative. He had ventured upon several commonplace remarks to which she had replied, amiably enough, in listless monosyllables. Yes—Jonathan and his grandfather had had their breakfast early. No—she didn't think they would be gone long.

After he had eaten, Marcellus returned to the tent and continued writing the letter he had begun to Demetrius; writing it in Greek; with no plans for its delivery. Everybody who was likely to be journeying to Jerusalem at this season had already gone.

Presently Justus appeared at the tent-door. Marcellus signed to him to come in, and he eased himself onto a camp-chair.

'Well,' began Marcellus, breaking a lengthy silence, 'I suppose little Jonathan has done a generous deed—and broken his heart. I am sorry to have caused him so much distress.'

'Do not reproach yourself, Marcellus. It may turn out well. True —the child is a bit young to be put to such a severe test. We can only wait and see how he behaves. This is a great day for Jonathan —if he can see it through.' Justus was proud—but troubled.

'See it through!' echoed Marcellus. 'But he has seen it through! Hasn't he given his donkey to the crippled lad? You don't think he may repent of his gallantry, and ask Thomas to give the donkey back; do you?'

'No, no—not that! But they're all down there on the corner telling Jonathan what a fine little fellow he is. You should have heard them— when Thomas and his mother set off—Thomas riding the donkey and his mother walking alongside, so happy she was crying. And all the women caressing Jonathan, and saying, "How sweet! How kind! How brave!"' Justus sighed deeply. 'It was too bad! But—of course—I couldn't rebuke them. I came away.'

'But—Justus!' exclaimed Marcellus. 'Surely it is only natural that the neighbors should praise Jonathan for what he did! It was no small sacrifice for a little boy! Isn't it right that the child should be commended?'

'Commended—yes,' agreed Justus, 'but not praised overmuch. As you have said, this thing has cost Jonathan a high price. He has a right to be rewarded for it—in his heart. It would be a great pity if all he gets out of it is smugness! There is no vanity so damaging to a man's character as pride over his good deeds! Let him be proud of his muscles, his fleetness, his strength, his face, his marksmanship, his craftsmanship, his endurance—these are the common frailties that beset us all. But when a man becomes vain of his goodness, it is a great tragedy! My boy is very young and inexperienced. He could be so easily ruined by self-righteousness, almost without realizing what ailed him.'

'I see what you mean!' declared Marcellus. 'I agree with you! This thing will either make Jonathan strong—beyond his years—or it will make a little prig of him! Justus—let's get out of here before the neighbors have had a chance to ruin him. We'll take him along with us! What do you say?'

Justus' eyes lighted. He nodded an enthusiastic approval.

'I shall speak with his mother,' he said. 'We will pack up and leave—at once!'

'That's sensible,' said Marcellus. 'I was afraid you might insist on Jonathan's remaining here—just to see how much of this punishment he could take.'

'No!' said Justus. 'It wouldn't be fair to overload the little fellow. He has done very well indeed. It is time now that we gave him a helping hand. We too have some obligations in this case, my friend!'

'You're right!' Marcellus began rolling up the letter he had just finished. 'I got Jonathan into this mess, and I'll do my best to help him through it without being damaged.'

Justus had no more than had time to enter the house until Jonathan put in an appearance at the door of the tent, wearing the wan, tremulous smile of a patient burden-bearer.

'Hi!—Jonathan,' greeted Marcellus, noisily. 'I hear you got young Thomas started on his way. That's good. What do you want with a donkey, anyhow? You have two of the best legs in town.' Busily preoccupied with the blankets he was folding up and stuffing into a pack-saddle, he absently chattered on, half to himself, 'A boy who was once a cripple—and then was cured—should be so glad he could walk that he would never want to ride!'

'But Jasper was such a nice donkey,' replied Jonathan, biting his lip. 'Everybody said they didn't know how I could give him up.'

'Well—never mind what everybody said!' barked Marcellus. 'Don't let them spoil it for you now! You're a stout little fellow—and that's the end of it! Here!—blow your nose—and give me a hand on this strap!'

Justus showed up in time to hear the last of it. He winced—and grinned.

'Jonathan,' he said, 'we are taking you with us on a few days' journey. Your mother is packing some things for you.'

'*Me?* I'm going along?' squealed Jonathan. 'Oh!' he raced around the corner of the tent, shouting gleefully.

Justus and Marcellus exchanged sober glances.

'That was a brutal thing I did just now!' muttered Marcellus.

' "Faithful are the wounds of a friend," ' said Justus. 'Jonathan will recover. He already has something new to think about—now that he is going with us.'

'By the way, Justus, where *are* we going?'

'I had thought of Capernaum next.'

'That can wait. We might overtake Thomas and Jasper. We don't want to see any more of them today. Let's go back to Cana. It will do little Jonathan good to have a look at Miriam.'

Justus tried to conceal a broad grin by tugging at his beard.

'Perhaps it would do you good too, Marcellus,' he ventured. 'But will you not be wasting your time? We have seen everything there is for sale—in Cana.'

Suddenly Marcellus, who had been tossing camp equipment into a wicker box, straightened and looked Justus squarely in the eyes.

'I think I have bought all the homespun I want,' he announced, bluntly. 'What I have been learning about this Jesus has made me curious to hear more. I wonder if you will help me meet a few people who knew him—people who might be willing to talk about him.'

'That would be difficult,' said Justus, frankly. 'Our people have no reasons for feeling that they can talk freely with Romans. They would find it hard to understand why a man of your nation should be making inquiries about Jesus. Perhaps you are not aware that the Romans put him to death. Maybe you do not know that the legionaries—especially in Jerusalem—are on the alert for any signs that the friends of Jesus are organized.'

'Do you suspect me of being a spy, Justus?' asked Marcellus, bluntly.

'No—I do not think you are a spy. I do not know what you are, Marcellus; but I am confident that you have no evil intent. I shall be willing to tell you some things about Jesus.'

'Thank you, Justus.' Marcellus drew from his tunic the letter he had written. 'Tell me: how may I send this to Jerusalem?'

Justus frowned, eyeing the scroll suspiciously.

'There is a Roman fort at Capernaum,' he muttered. 'Doubtless they have messengers going back and forth, every few days.'

Marcellus handed him the scroll and pointed to the address.

'I do not want this letter handled through the Capernaum fort,' he said, 'or the Insula at Jerusalem. It must be delivered by a trusted messenger into the care of the Greek, Stephanos, at Benyosef's shop.'

'So you do know that slave Demetrius,' commented Justus. 'I thought as much.'

'Yes—he is *my* slave.'

'I had wondered about that, too.'

'Indeed! Well—what else had you wondered about? Let's clean it all up, while we're at it.'

'I have wondered what your purpose was in making this trip into Galilee,' said Justus, brightening a little.

'Well—now you know; don't you?'

'I am not sure that I do.' Justus laid a hand on Marcellus' arm. 'Tell me this: did you ever see Jesus; ever hear him talk?'

'Yes,' admitted Marcellus, 'but I could not understand what he said. At that time I did not know the language.'

'Did you study Aramaic so you could learn something about him?'

'Yes—I had no other interest in it.'

'Let me ask one more question.' Justus lowered his voice. 'Are you one of us?'

'That's what I came up here to find out,' said Marcellus. 'Will you help me?'

'As much as I can,' agreed Justus, 'as much as you are able to comprehend.'

Marcellus looked puzzled.

'Do you mean that there are some mysteries here that I am not bright enough to understand?' he demanded, soberly.

'Bright enough—yes,' rejoined Justus. 'But an understanding of Jesus is not a mere matter of intelligence. Some of this story has to be accepted by faith.'

'Faith comes hard with me,' frowned Marcellus. 'I am not superstitious.'

'So much the better,' declared Justus. 'The higher the price you have to pay, the more you will cherish what you get.' Impulsively throwing aside his coat, he began pulling up tentstakes. 'We will talk more about this later,' he said. 'It is time we were on our way if we hope to reach Cana by sunset.' Suddenly he straightened with a new idea. 'I have it!' he exclaimed. 'We will go to Nazareth! It is much nearer than Cana. Nazareth was Jesus' home town. His mother lives there still. She will not hesitate to talk freely with you. When she learns that you—a Roman—saw her son, and were so impressed that you wanted to know more about him, she will tell you everything!'

'No—no!' exclaimed Marcellus, wincing. 'I have no wish to see her.' Noting the sudden perplexity on Justus' face, he added, 'I feel sure she would not want to talk about her son—to a Roman.'

* * * * * *

For the first three miles, Jonathan frolicked about the little caravan with all the aimless extravagance of a frisky pup, dashing on ahead, inexpertly throwing stones at the crows, and making many brief excursions into the fields. But as the sun rose higher, his wild enthusiasm came under better control. Now he was content to walk sedately beside his grandfather, taking long strides and feeling very manly. After a while he took his grandfather's hand and shortened his steps at the request of his aching legs.

Preoccupied with their conversation, which was weighty, Justus had been only vaguely aware of the little boy's weariness; but when he stumbled and nearly fell, they all drew up in the shade, unloaded the pack-train, and reapportioned their burdens so that the smallest donkey might be free for a rider. Jonathan made no protest when they lifted him up.

'I wish I had kept that nice saddle,' he repined.

'No, you don't,' drawled Marcellus. 'When you give anything away, make a good job of it. Don't skimp!'

'Our friend speaks truly, my boy,' said Justus. 'The donkey will carry you safely without a saddle. Let us move on, and when the sun is directly overhead, we will have something to eat.'

'I'm hungry now!' murmured Jonathan.

'The bread will taste better at noon,' advised Justus.

'I'm hungry too,' intervened Marcellus, mercifully. As he unstrapped the hamper, he added, out of the corner of his mouth, 'He's only a baby, Justus. Don't be too hard on him.'

Justus grumbled a little over the delay and the breakdown of discipline, but it was easy to see that he had been mellowed by Marcellus' gentle defense of the child. A token lunch was passed about, and presently they were on the highway again.

'You would have been delighted with the mind of Jesus,' said Justus, companionably. 'You have a generous heart, Marcellus. How often he talked about generosity! In his opinion there was nothing meaner than a mean gift. About the worst thing a man could do to himself or a fellow creature was to bestow a grudged gift. It was very hard on a man's character to *give* away something that should have been *thrown* away! That much of Jesus' teachings you could accept, my friend, without any difficulty.'

'That is a friendly comment, Justus, but you do me too much credit,' protested Marcellus. 'The fact is—I have never in my life given anything away that impoverished me in the least. I have never given anything away that I needed or wanted to keep. I suppose Jesus parted with everything he had.'

'Everything!' said Justus. 'He had nothing but the garments he wore. He held that if a man had two coats, he should give one away. During his last year with us he wore a good robe. Perhaps he would have given that away, too, if it hadn't been given to him in peculiar circumstances.'

'Would you like to tell me about it?' asked Marcellus.

'There was an ill-favored woman in Nazareth who was suspected of practicing witchcraft. She was a dwarfish person with an ugly countenance, and walked alone, friendless and bitter. The children cried after her on the road. And so a legend spread that Tamar had an evil eye. One Sabbath day the neighbors heard her loom banging, and warned her against this breaking of the law; for many of our people have more respect for the Sabbath than they have for one another. Tamar did not heed the warning and she was reported to the authorities who came in upon her, on a Sabbath morning, and destroyed her loom which was her living. Perhaps you can guess the rest of the story,' said Justus.

'It was fortunate for Tamar that Jesus was a good carpenter,' remarked Marcellus. 'But what did the authorities think of his coming to Tamar's aid? Did they accuse him of being sympathetic with Sabbath-breakers?'

'That they did!' declared Justus. 'It was at a time when the priests were on the alert to find him at fault. The people often urged him to speak in the village synagogues, and this displeased the rabbis. They were always haranguing the people about their tithes and sacrificial offerings. Jesus talked about friendship and hospitality to strangers and relief for the poor.'

'But—didn't the rabbis believe in friendship and charity?' wondered Marcellus.

'Oh, yes—of course. They took it for granted that everybody was agreed on that.'

'In theory, at least,' surmised Marcellus.

'Exactly! In theory. But securing funds to support the synagogue—that was practical! They had to talk constantly about money. It left them no time to talk about the things of the spirit.'

'Well—go on about Tamar,' interposed Marcellus. 'I suppose Jesus reconstructed her loom—and she wove him the Robe.'

'Right! And he wore it until he died.'

'Were you there—when he died?' asked Marcellus, uneasily.

'No—I was in prison.' Justus seemed disinclined to enlarge upon this matter; but, when questioned, told the story briefly. A few days before his trial for treason and disturbing the peace, Jesus had impulsively driven hucksters and bankers out of the Temple. Several of his friends had been arrested and thrown into prison on the charge of having gathered up some of the scattered coins from the pavement. The accusation was untrue, Justus insisted, but they were kept in prison for a fortnight. 'It was all over,' he said, sadly, 'when we were released. As for the Robe—the Roman soldiers gambled for it—and carried it away with them. We often wondered what became of it. It could have no value—for them.'

It was noon now, and a halt was made in a little grove where there was a spring and a green grass-plot for grazing. The donkeys were unburdened and tethered. The food was unpacked; a wineskin, a basket of bread, a parcel of smoked fish, an earthenware jar of cooked barley, a box of sun-cured figs. They spread a blanket on the ground for little Jonathan, who, stuffed to repletion and wearied by the journey, promptly tumbled down to sleep. Justus and Marcellus, lounging on the grass, pursued a low-voiced conversation.

'Sometimes thoughtless people misunderstood his attitude toward business,' Justus was saying. 'His critics noised it about that he had contempt for barter and trade; that he had no respect for thrift and honest husbandry.'

'I had wondered about that,' said Marcellus. 'There has been much talk about his urging people to give things away. It had occurred to me that this could be overdone. If men recklessly distributed their goods to all comers, how could they provide for their own dependents?'

'Let me give you an illustration,' said Justus. 'This subject came up, one day, and Jesus dealt with it in a story. He was forever contriving simple little fables. He said, a man with a vineyard wanted his grapes picked, for they were now ripe. Going down to the public market, he asked a group of idlers if they wanted a job. They said they would work all day for one denarius.'

'Rather high,' observed Marcellus.

'Rather! But the grapes had to be picked immediately, and the man wasn't in a position to argue; so he took them on. By noon, it was apparent that he would need more help. Again in the market-place he asked the unemployed what they would take to work that afternoon. And they said, "We will leave that up to you, sir." Well—when evening came, the men who had dickered with him for one denarius were paid off according to agreement. Then came the men who had worked shorter hours, leaving the wages to the owner's generosity.'

'So—what did he do?' wondered Marcellus, sincerely interested.

'Gave every man a denarius! All the way up and down the line— one denarius! He even gave a denarius to a few who hadn't worked more than an hour!'

'That might have started a row,' surmised Marcellus.

'And indeed it *did!* The men who had worked all day complained bitterly. But the owner said, "I paid you the price you had demanded. That was according to contract. These other men made no demands, but relied on my good will."'

'Excellent!' exclaimed Marcellus. 'If a man drives a hard bargain with you and you are forced to concede to it, you have no obligation to be generous. But if he lets *you* say how much he should have, that's likely to cost you something!'

'There you are!' nodded Justus. 'You have a right to weigh it out by the pennyworth, if the other fellow haggles. But if he leaves it up to you, the measure you give must be pressed down, shaken together, and running over!'

'Justus,' declared Marcellus, 'if it became a custom for people to deal with one another that way, the market-place wouldn't be quite so noisy; would it?'

'And all men would be better off,' said Justus. 'People wouldn't have to be taxed to employ patrols to keep the peace. And—as the idea spread,' he added, dreamily, 'all of the armies could be demobilized. That would lift a great weight off the shoulders of the people. And once they had experienced this more abundant life that Jesus proposed, it is not likely they would want to return to the old way.'

For some time they sat in silence, each busy with his own thoughts.

'Of course—it's utterly impractical,' declared Marcellus. 'Only a little handful would make the experiment, and at ruinous cost. The great majority would sneer and take advantage of them, considering them cowardly and feebleminded for not defending their rights. They would soon be stripped of everything!'

'That's true,' admitted Justus. 'Stripped of everything but *the great idea!* But, Marcellus, that idea is like a seed. It doesn't amount to much if you expect immediate returns. But if you're willing to plant it, and nourish it—'

'I suppose,' remarked Marcellus, 'it is as if some benefactor appeared in the world with a handful of new grain which, if men should feed on it, would give them peace and prosperity.'

'Very good,' approved Justus, 'but that handful of grain would not go very far unless it were sowed and reaped and sowed again and again. Jesus talked about that. Much of this seed, he said, would never come up. Some of it would lodge in the weeds and brambles. Some of it would fall upon stony ground. But a little of it would grow.'

'Justus—do you honestly believe there's any future for a theory like that—in this greedy world?' Marcellus was deeply in earnest.

'Yes—I do!' declared Justus. 'I believe it because he believed it! He said it would work like yeast in meal; slowly, silently; but—once it began—nothing could ever stop it. Nobody would ever be able to shut it off—or dig it up—or tear it out!'

'But—why did it begin—up here—in poor little Galilee—so remote from the main centers of world development?' wondered Marcellus.

'Well'—reflected Justus—'it had to begin *somewhere!*' After a moment of meditation, he faced Marcellus with a sly grin. 'Do you think this seed might have had a better chance to take root and grow, if it had fallen on the streets in Rome?'

'I think the question answers itself,' conceded Marcellus.

Justus reached over and patted the little boy's tanned cheek.

'On—now—to Cana,' he said, scrambling to his feet.

In a few minutes they were on the highway, Justus leading with long, swinging strides, indulging in a reminiscent monologue.

'How often we came over this road together!' he was recalling. 'Jesus loved Cana better than any other town in Galilee.'

'Better than Nazareth?' queried Marcellus.

'They never quite appreciated his spirit in Nazareth,' explained Justus. 'You know how it is. A prophet has no standing in his own community. The Nazarenes used to say, "How can this man have any wisdom? Don't *we* know him?" '

'Apparently they didn't rate very high in their own esteem,' laughed Marcellus.

'It was natural,' said Justus, sobering. 'He had grown up with them. He never held it against them that they did not respond to his teachings as they did in Cana and Capernaum. It was in Cana that he first exercised the peculiar powers you will be hearing about. I don't

THIS CLASSIC COMES TO YOU IN
The Rafael Palacios Binding

IN SEEKING a binding design suitable for encasing a group of modern American novels, the International Collectors Library commissioned the celebrated American artist and designer Rafael Palacios. You will recall seeing modern maps and other illustrative art in many of today's books from the brush and pen of this brilliant designer; and as a patron of the Collectors Library, you are aware that virtually all the magnifi-·cent replica bindings used in this program are in the nature of fine old bookbindings re-created by Mr. Palacios for modern readers' personal libraries.

The resulting design, which is used on your latest selection, is reproduced here. This design, with its interesting arrangement of lines and geometric forms and its almost palpable feeling of *movement,* reflects in a symbolic style the dynamic impact of twentieth-century literature upon the culture and thinking of our times.

Your handsome edition is bound in wine red, with a pronounced grain. The clean, uncluttered design is stamped in genuine 24K gold on cover and spine. The top edges of the pages are coated with gold, and a matching ribbon marker completes a volume you will be gratified to add to your collection of great classics in luxurious bindings.

THE INTERNATIONAL COLLECTORS LIBRARY is a publishing program dedicated to the preservation of the immortal masterworks of the past and the significant books of our own time...the great classics of fiction, history, biography, poetry, drama, travel, and adventure...clothed in bindings truly worthy of their imperishable contents.

INTERNATIONAL
COLLECTORS
LIBRARY Presents –

The Robe
by Lloyd C. Douglas

HE ROBE is a beautiful, disturbing, and infinitely understanding novel which has become a recognized classic of our time. It went through more than sixty printings, was translated into eighteen languages, and has been read by millions the world over. It was also made into a brilliant motion picture.

As a clergyman, Lloyd Douglas had written a number of essays on spiritual subjects, then decided that through the medium of fiction he could reach a vastly larger public with his ideas. His novel *Magnificent Obsession* (1929) remained for a long time at the top of the best seller list, and was followed by such books as *Green Light, White Banner,* THE ROBE and *The Big Fisherman,* an impressionistic biography of Simon Peter.

Who won the seamless robe of Christ when the Roman soldiers gambled for it at the foot of the Cross? Around this provocative theme the novelist weaves the story of THE ROBE. He creates an appealing character in Marcellus, the aristocratic young officer who wins the garment…and then finds that it inexorably changes his whole life and the lives of those who love him.

In its tremendous sweep, THE ROBE is reminiscent of such great historical novels of the past as *Ben Hur* and *Quo Vadis.* Its pages are filled with the panoply and splendor of imperial Rome, the turbulence and exaltation of the Holy Land in an era of ferment. But THE ROBE also has a quality of immediacy to our own times which is perforce lacking in the older works mentioned.

Your handsome edition comes in the Rafael Palacios binding of wine red, with an interesting geometric design stamped in gold.

(See other side)

THIS CLASSIC COMES TO YOU IN
The Rafael Palacios Binding

IN SEEKING a binding design suitable for encasing a group of modern American novels, the International Collectors Library commissioned the celebrated American artist and designer Rafael Palacios. You will recall seeing modern maps and other illustrative art in many of today's books from the brush and pen of this brilliant designer; and as a patron of the Collectors Library, you are aware that virtually all the magnificent replica bindings used in this program are in the nature of fine old bookbindings re-created by Mr. Palacios for modern readers' personal libraries.

The resulting design, which is used on your latest selection, is reproduced here. This design, with its interesting arrangement of lines and geometric forms and its almost palpable feeling of *movement*, reflects in a symbolic style the dynamic impact of twentieth-century literature upon the culture and thinking of our times.

Your handsome edition is bound in wine red, with a pronounced grain. The clean, uncluttered design is stamped in genuine 24K gold on cover and spine. The top edges of the pages are coated with gold, and a matching ribbon marker completes a volume you will be gratified to add to your collection of great classics in luxurious bindings.

THE INTERNATIONAL COLLECTORS LIBRARY is a publishing program dedicated to the preservation of the immortal masterworks of the past and the significant books of our own time...the great classics of fiction, history, biography, poetry, drama, travel, and adventure...clothed in bindings truly worthy of their imperishable contents.

Litho U.S.A.

INTERNATIONAL
COLLECTORS
LIBRARY Presents –

The Robe

by Lloyd C. Douglas

THE ROBE is a beautiful, disturbing, and infinitely understanding novel which has become a recognized classic of our time. It went through more than sixty printings, was translated into eighteen languages, and has been read by millions the world over. It was also made into a brilliant motion picture.

As a clergyman, Lloyd Douglas had written a number of essays on spiritual subjects, then decided that through the medium of fiction he could reach a vastly larger public with his ideas. His novel *Magnificent Obsession* (1929) remained for a long time at the top of the best seller list, and was followed by such books as *Green Light, White Banner,* THE ROBE and *The Big Fisherman,* an impressionistic biography of Simon Peter.

Who won the seamless robe of Christ when the Roman soldiers gambled for it at the foot of the Cross? Around this provocative theme the novelist weaves the story of THE ROBE. He creates an appealing character in Marcellus, the aristocratic young officer who wins the garment...and then finds that it inexorably changes his whole life and the lives of those who love him.

In its tremendous sweep, THE ROBE is reminiscent of such great historical novels of the past as *Ben Hur* and *Quo Vadis.* Its pages are filled with the panoply and splendor of imperial Rome, the turbulence and exaltation of the Holy Land in an era of ferment. But THE ROBE also has a quality of immediacy to our own times which is perforce lacking in the older works mentioned.

Your handsome edition comes in the Rafael Palacios binding of wine red, with an interesting geometric design stamped in gold.

(See other side)

suppose anyone has told you what happened there, one day, at a wedding.'

'No,' replied Marcellus, attentively. 'What happened?'

It was a story of some length, and Justus was so particular about the small details that Marcellus immediately surmised its importance. Anna, the daughter of Hariph and Rachel, was to be married. Hariph was a potter, an industrious fellow, but by no means prosperous, and the expense of the wedding dinner for Anna was not easy for them. However, Hariph was going to see his child properly honored. Anna was very popular, and Hariph and Rachel had a host of relatives. Everybody was invited and everybody came.

'Were you there, Justus?'

'No—that was before I knew Jesus. The story of what occurred, that day, quickly spread far and wide. I don't mind telling you that when I heard it, I doubted it.'

'Get on with it, please!' insisted Marcellus.

'Jesus arrived late. The wedding rites had been performed, and the guests had been at table for some time when he appeared. Poor Hariph was unhappy. He had not provided enough wine for so large a crowd. His predicament was whispered into Jesus' ear.'

Justus tramped on for half a stadium in moody silence.

'Maybe it is not the time yet to tell you this,' he muttered. 'You will not believe it. I did not believe it when they told me! Jesus slipped away from the table, and went to the small serving-room. He saw some of Hariph's earthenware jars in the little court outside, and told the servants to fill them with water. Then, having instructed them to serve it to the guests, he went back and resumed his place at the table. When the water was served, *it was wine!*'

'No—Justus—no!' exclaimed Marcellus. 'This spoils the story of Jesus!'

'I was afraid you weren't ready for it, my friend,' regretted Justus.

'Oh—but there must have been some better explanation of that wine,' insisted Marcellus. 'Jesus comes in with that radiant personality; everyone loving him. And even the water they drank in his presence tasted like wine! And so—this other utterly preposterous tale got bruited about.'

'Have it your own way, Marcellus,' consented Justus, kindly. 'It does not offend me that you doubt the story. You can believe in the wisdom and goodness of Jesus without that.'

They proceeded, without further conversation, up the long hill where, at the crest, Justus stopped, cupped his eyes with his big, brown hands, and gazed intently down the narrow road as far as he could see; a familiar, though unexplained, occurrence. The best Marcellus could make of these frequent long-range observations was his belief that Justus was expecting to meet someone by appointment. Today he thought of asking about it, but decided to wait until Justus wanted to tell him.

While they tarried, at the top of the hill, for the pack-train to overtake them, Marcellus broke the silence with a query.

'Did you not tell me, Justus, that Miriam discovered her matchless voice while her family was absent from home, attending a wedding-feast to which she had been invited—and had refused to go?'

'Yes,' assented Justus. 'It was Anna's wedding.'

'Jesus arrived late at the wedding,' remembered Marcellus.

'Yes.' Justus nodded and they exchanged a look of mutual understanding.

'I wonder what made him late,' reflected Marcellus.

'I, too, have often wondered about that,' said Justus, quietly.

'Do you suppose he might have asked Miriam not to tell?'

'It is possible.'

'So far as you know, Justus,' persisted Marcellus, 'did he ever confer a great gift upon someone—and request the beneficiary to keep it a secret?'

'Yes,' said Justus. 'There were many evidences of such events.'

'How do you explain that?' Marcellus wanted to know.

'Jesus found any public display of charity very offensive,' said Justus. 'Had it been possible, I think he would have preferred to do all of his generous deeds in secret. On one occasion he said to a great throng that had gathered on a hillside to hear him talk, "When you make gifts, do not let them be seen. Do not sound a trumpet that you may receive praise. When you do your almsgiving, let not your left hand know what your right hand is doing. No one but your Father will see. Only your Father will reward you."'

'What did he mean, Justus—about your Father rewarding you—if no one else knows? Take little Jonathan's case, for example: if nobody had learned about his giving his donkey to the crippled lad, would he have been secretly rewarded?'

'Of course!' declared Justus. 'If no one had known about the gift, Jonathan's heart would have overflowed with happiness. You wouldn't have heard him wishing that he had kept the saddle!'

'But the child had no way of keeping the matter quiet!' expostulated Marcellus.

'True,' nodded Justus. 'That was not Jonathan's fault, but his misfortune.'

'Do you think that peculiar radiance of Miriam's can be accounted for by her having kept her secret? In her case, she was not the donor. She was the recipient!'

'I know,' agreed Justus. 'If the recipient doesn't tell, then the donor is rewarded in his heart. It is thus that the recipient helps him to obtain his reward.'

'But now that Jesus is dead,' argued Marcellus, with a puzzled look, 'Miriam is free to tell her secret; is she not?'

Justus stroked his beard, thoughtfully.

'Probably not,' he murmured. 'If she were—she would tell.'

Chapter XV

THEY had reached Cana too late to hear Miriam sing, but Marcellus thought it was just as well, for Jonathan was so tired and sleepy that he could hardly hold his head up.

By the time they had pitched camp, washed off their dust, eaten a light supper, and put the little boy to bed, many voices could be heard; villagers strolling home in the moonlight from their customary rendezvous at the fountain.

Justus sauntered out to the street. Marcellus, wearily stretched at full length on his cot, heard him talking to a friend. After a while he returned to say he had been informed by Hariph the potter that Jesse, the son of Beoni, was leaving early in the morning for Jerusalem. Doubtless he would carry the letter to Demetrius.

'Very good!' Marcellus handed him the scroll and unstrapped his coin purse. 'How much will he expect?'

'Ten shekels should be enough.' There was an expression of satisfaction in Justus' face and tone, perhaps because the letter had been given up so casually. His look said that there could be nothing conspiratorial in this communication. 'Jesse will probably be over here presently,' he added. 'Hariph will tell him. He lives hard by the home of Beoni.'

'You can talk with him,' said Marcellus. 'I am going to sleep.'

And he did; but after a while the murmur of low-pitched voices roused him. He raised up on his elbow, and through the open tent-door the white moonlight showed Justus and a stocky, shaggy-haired man of thirty, seated cross-legged on the ground. Jesse, the son of Beoni, was rumbling gutturally about the business that was taking him to Jerusalem. He was going to attend the annual camel auction. They always had it at the end of Passover. Many caravans from afar, having disposed of their merchandise, offered their pack-animals for sale rather than trek them home without a pay-load. You could get a sound, three-year-old she-camel for as little as eighty shekels, Jesse said. He hoped to buy six, this time. He could easily sell them in Tiberias for a hundred or better. Yes—he made this trip every year. Yes—he would gladly carry Justus' letter to the Greek who worked for Benyosef. And when Justus asked him how much, Jesse said, 'Nothing at all. It's no bother.'

'But it isn't my letter,' explained Justus. 'It is sent by this Roman,

Marcellus Gallio, who is up here buying homespun. He's there in the tent, asleep.'

'Oh—that one! My mother told me about him. It is strange that he should want our simple weaving. No one ever thought it was valuable. Well—if it is his letter, and not yours, he should pay me eight shekels.'

'He will give you ten.' The coins were poured clinking into Jesse's hand.

'Eight is enough,' said Jesse. 'You keep the other two.'

'But I have done nothing to earn them,' protested Justus. 'They are yours. I think the Roman would prefer to give you ten.'

Jesse chuckled—not very pleasantly.

'Since when have the Romans turned soft-hearted?' he growled. 'I hope there is nothing queer about this scroll. They tell me the jail in Jerusalem is alive with vermin. How about it, Justus? You ought to know.' Jesse laughed at his own grim jest. 'You lodged there for a couple of weeks, last spring.'

Marcellus could not hear Justus' rejoinder. Perhaps he had merely grinned or scowled at Jesse's bucolic raillery.

'You can trust Marcellus,' said Justus, confidently. 'He is a man of good will. Not all Romans are crooked, Jesse. You know that.'

'Yes, yes,' consented Jesse. 'As the saying goes, "Every Jew has his Roman." Mine happens to be Hortensius.'

'You mean the Centurion, over in Capernaum, whose orderly Jesus cured of a palsy? Did you have dealings with him, Jesse?'

'I sold him four camels—shortly before that affair of his servant. Three for a hundred each. I told him he could have the other one for sixty because she was spavined. And he said, "She doesn't limp. What did you pay for her?" And I said, "Eighty—but I didn't know the spavin was bad until we were on the road two days." And he said, "She seems to be all right now." And I said, "She's rested. But she'll go lame on a long journey with anything of a load." And he said, "You needn't have told me." Then he said, "Do you know Jesus?" And I said, "Yes." And he said, "I thought so." And then he said, "Let's split the cost of the spavin. I'll give you seventy." And I said, "That's fair enough." And then I said, "Do you know Jesus, sir?" And he said, "No—but I heard him talk, one day." And then I asked him, just as if we were equals, "Are you one of us?" And he was busy counting out the money, and didn't answer that; but when he handed it to me he said—that was four years ago, and I looked younger than now—he said, "You keep on listening to Jesus, boy! You'll never be rich—but you'll never be poor!" '

'I'm glad you told me that, Jesse,' said Justus. 'You see what happened there? Hortensius heard Jesus talk about how people ought to treat one another. And maybe he wondered whether anybody was trying to practice it. And then you told him the truth about the spavined camel. And he began to believe that Jesus had great power.'

Jesse laughed.

'So you think the camel deal had something to do with his believing that Jesus could cure his sick orderly.'

'Why not?' It was Justus' turn to chuckle. 'I suppose the Centurion decided that any man who could influence a Jewish camel-drover to tell the truth about a spavin should be able to heal the sick. But'—Justus' tone was serious now—'however Hortensius came by his faith, he had plenty of it. I was there that day, Jesse. The Centurion came forward—a fine figure, too, in full uniform—and said, very deferentially, that his servant was sick unto death. Would Jesus heal him? "You need not trouble to come to my house, sir," he said. "If you will say that my servant is healed, that will be sufficient." Jesus was much pleased. Nothing like that had happened before. None of us had ever been that sure. He said to Hortensius, "You have great faith. Your wish is granted."'

'And then'—recollected Jesse—'they say that almost everyone in the crowd set off at top speed for Hortensius' house.'

'Yes,' said Justus, 'and they never did agree on a story. One report had it that the restored orderly met Hortensius at the gate. Some said the fellow was recovered and sitting up in bed. Others told that when the Centurion returned, the orderly was saddling a horse to ride to Capernaum. You know how these rumors get about. I suppose the fact is that none of these curious people was admitted to the Centurion's grounds.'

'But the man did recover, that day, from his sickness; didn't he?' Jesse insisted.

'He did, indeed!' declared Justus. 'I heard him say so. By the way—think you that Hortensius will be made Commander of the fort at Capernaum, now that old Julian has been promoted to suceed Pilate?'

'No such luck for Galilee!' grumbled Jesse. 'Everyone likes Hortensius. He is a just man, and he would be friendly to our cause. That old fox Herod will see to it that someone tougher than Hortensius gets the job. The thing that surprises me is the appointment of lazy old Julian to the Insula at Jerusalem.'

'Perhaps it's because Julian is lazy that the Temple crowd wanted him as their Procurator,' suggested Justus. 'The more indolent and indifferent he is, the more power will be exercised by the High Priest. He will let Caiaphas do anything he pleases. There are times, Jesse,' went on Justus, thoughtfully, 'when a weak, lazy, vacillating man—of good intent—is more to be feared than a crafty and cruel man. He shuts his eyes—and lets the injustices and persecutions proceed. In truth, our cause would have been better served if Pilate had remained.'

'Does anyone know what has become of Pilate?' asked Jesse.

'Sent back to Crete, I understand. Better climate. The rumor is that Pontius Pilate is a sick man. He hasn't made a public appearance for all of a year.'

'Why—that goes back to the crucifixion!' said Jesse. 'Do you mean that Pilate hasn't been seen in public since that day?'

'That's what they say. Benyosef thinks Pilate's sickness is mental.'

'Well—if that's the case, a change of climate will do him no good,' remarked Jesse. 'Hariph says he heard that there's talk of transferring the Commander of the fort at Minoa to Capernaum.'

'Impossible!' muttered Justus. 'They wouldn't dare! It was the legion from Minoa that put Jesus to death!'

'Yes—I know that,' said Jesse. 'I think, too, that it's just idle talk. Hariph didn't say where he'd picked it up. Someone told him that this Paulus from Minoa would probably be our next Commander. If so—we will have to be more careful than ever.'

Justus sighed deeply and rose to his feet.

'I must not keep you longer, Jesse. You have a long day ahead of you. Salute Benyosef for me, and any of the others who may have returned, now that the Passover is at an end. And'—he laid a hand on Jesse's shoulder—'keep watchful eyes on the roads, for no one knows the day—or the hour—' His deep voice throttled down to a whisper. They shook hands and Jesse drifted away.

With his face turned toward the tent-wall, Marcellus feigned sleep when Justus entered quietly. For a long time he lay wide awake, pondering the things he had overheard. So—it hadn't been so easy for Pilate. Pilate had washed his hands in the silver basin, but apparently the Galilean's blood was still there. So—Julian was in command at Jerusalem: Caiaphas could have his own way now. Julian wouldn't know; wouldn't care if he did know what persecutions were practiced on the little handful that wanted to keep the memory of Jesus alive. It wouldn't be long until old Benyosef and his secretive callers would have to give it all up. And perhaps Paulus was to be sent up here to keep Galilee in order. Well—maybe Paulus wouldn't be as hard on them as they feared. Paulus wasn't a bad fellow. Paulus had been forced to take part in the crucifixion of Jesus. That didn't mean he had approved of it. It was conceivable that Paulus might even take an interest in the Galilean friends of Jesus. But they would never accept his friendship. The very sight of him would be abhorrent. Justus' comments had made that clear. A man who had had anything to do with nailing their adored Jesus to the cross could never hope to win their good will, no matter how generously he treated them.

Marcellus realized now that he had been quite too sanguine in believing that his sincere interest in the story of Jesus might make it safe for him to confide in Miriam. He had been telling himself that Miriam—uncannily gifted with sympathetic understanding—would balance his present concern about Jesus against the stark facts of his part in the tragedy. Miriam, he felt, would be forgiving. That was her

nature; and, besides, she liked him, and would give him the benefit
of whatever doubts intruded. Perhaps he would not need to go the
whole way with his confession. It might be enough to say that he had
attended the trial of Jesus, and had seen him die. Whether he could
bring himself to be more specific about his own participation in this
shameful business would depend upon her reaction as he proceeded.

But he knew now that such a conversation with Miriam was un-
thinkable! Justus, too, was a fair-minded person to whom one might
safely confide almost anything; but Justus had revolted against the
shocking suggestion that an officer from *Minoa* might be sent to preserve the peace of Galilee. 'They wouldn't dare!' Justus had muttered
through locked teeth.

No—he couldn't tell Miriam. Perhaps it would be more prudent
if he made no effort to see her alone.

* * * * * *

Hariph the potter, upon whom Cana relied for most of its information on current events, had risen at daybreak with the remembrance that Reuben had mentioned his need of a few wine-jars.
Although it lacked some three months of the wine-pressing season,
this was as good a time as any to learn Reuben's wishes. Too, he
thought Reuben might be glad to learn that Barsabas Justus had
arrived in Cana, last evening, with his small grandson—the one who,
crippled from birth, had been made sound as any boy ever was—and
the handsome young Roman who for some obscure reason, was buying up homespun at better than market prices. To this might be
added the knowledge that Jesse, the son of Beoni, had been engaged
by this Marcellus to carry an important letter to Jerusalem. After these
items had been dealt out to Reuben, piecemeal, he could be told
that Justus would be taking his grandson to see Miriam.

And so it happened that when the three callers sauntered across
Reuben's well-kept lawn, at mid-forenoon, instead of taking the
family by surprise they discovered that their visit was awaited.

Feeling that little Jonathan might enjoy a playmate, Miriam had
sent for her nine-year-old cousin Andrew, who lived a mile farther
out in the country. And Andrew's widowed mother, Aunt Martha,
had been invited too, which had made her happy, for she had not
seen Justus in recent months. There were many questions she wanted
to ask him

They were all in the arbor, grouped about Miriam who was busy
with the inevitable embroidery. She was very lovely, this morning,
with a translucent happiness that made her even prettier than Marcellus had remembered. After greetings and introductions had been
attended to—the artless sincerity of Miriam's welcome speeding Marcellus' pulse—they all found seats. Miriam held out a slim hand to

Jonathan and gave him a brooding smile that brought him shyly to her side.

'You must be a very strong boy, Jonathan,' she told him, 'keeping up with these big men on a journey, all the way from Sepphoris.'

'I rode a donkey—most of the time,' he mumbled, self-consciously; then, with more confidence, 'I had a nicer donkey—of my own. His name was Jasper.' He pointed a finger vaguely in Marcellus' direction without looking at him. 'He gave Jasper to me. And I gave him to Thomas, because Thomas is lame.'

'Why—what a lovely thing to do!' exclaimed Miriam. Her shining eyes drifted past Jonathan and gave Marcellus a heart-warming glance, and then darted to Justus, whose lips were drawn down to a warning frown. 'I suppose Thomas really needs a donkey,' she went on, accepting Justus' hint. 'It must have made you very happy to do that for him.'

Jonathan smiled wanly, put one brown bare foot on top of the other, and seemed to be meditating a dolorous reply. Divining his mood, Miriam intercepted with a promising diversion.

'Andrew,' she called, 'why don't you take Jonathan to see the conies. There are some little ones, Jonathan, that haven't opened their eyes yet.'

This suggestion was acted upon with alacrity. When the children had scampered away, Naomi turned to Marcellus.

'What's all this about the donkey?' she inquired, smiling.

Marcellus recrossed his long legs and wished that he had been included in the expedition to inspect the conies.

'I think Jonathan has told it all,' he replied, negligently. 'I found a lazy little donkey that nobody wanted and gave him to Jonathan. There was a lame lad in the neighborhood and Jonathan generously presented him with the donkey. We thought that was pretty good—for a seven-year-old.'

'But we don't want his good-heartedness to go to his head,' put in Justus, firmly. 'He's already much impressed.'

'But Jonathan is only a child, Barsabas Justus,' protested Miriam.

'Of course!' murmured Martha.

'I know,' mumbled Justus, stroking his beard. 'But we can't have him spoiled, Miriam. If you have an opportunity, speak to him about it. . . . Well, Reuben, what's the prospect for the vineyard?'

'Better than usual, Justus.' Reuben slowly rose from his chair. 'Want to walk out and have a look at the vines?'

They ambled away. Presently Naomi remembered something she had to do in the kitchen. Aunt Martha, with a little nod and a smile, thought she might help. Miriam bent over her work attentively as they disappeared around the corner of the house.

'You have been much in my thoughts, Marcellus,' she said softly, after a silence which they both had been reluctant to invade with some casual banality.

'You can see that I wanted to come back.' Marcellus drew his chair closer.

'And now that you're here'—Miriam smiled into his eyes companionably—'what shall we talk about first?'

'I am much interested in the story of that carpenter who did so many things for your people.'

Miriam's eyes widened happily.

'I knew it!' she cried.

'How could you have known it?' wondered Marcellus.

'Oh'—archly—'by lots of little things—strung together. You knew nothing about textiles, nor does good old Justus, for that matter. You have had no experience in bargaining. It was clear that you were in Galilee on some other errand.'

'True—but what made you think I was interested in Jesus?'

'Your choosing Justus to conduct you. He saw as much of Jesus as anyone except Simon and the Zebedee boys who were with him constantly. But you had me quite mystified.' She shook her head and laughed softly. 'Romans are under suspicion. I couldn't understand why Justus had consented to come up here with you. Then it came out that you knew the Greek who works for Benyosef. He must have planned your meeting with Justus, for surely that was no accident! The men who frequent Benyosef's shop are friends of Jesus. So—I added it all up—and—'

'And concluded that I had employed Justus to inform me about Jesus,' interposed Marcellus. 'Well—your deduction is correct, though I must say that Justus seems to know a great deal that he isn't confiding to me.'

'Have you told him why you are interested in Jesus?' Miriam studied his eyes as she waited for his reply.

'Not fully,' admitted Marcellus, after some hesitation. 'But he is not suspicious of my motive.'

'Perhaps if you would tell Justus exactly how you happened to become interested in Jesus, he might be more free to talk,' suggested Miriam; and when Marcellus failed to respond promptly, she added, 'I am full of curiosity about that, myself.'

'That's a long story, Miriam,' muttered Marcellus, soberly.

'I have plenty of time,' she said. 'Tell me, Marcellus.'

'A year ago, I was in Jerusalem—on business—' he began, rather uncertainly.

'But not buying homespun,' she interjected, when he paused.

'It was government business,' Marcellus went on. 'I was there only a few days. During that time, there was a considerable stir over the arrest of this Galilean on a charge of treason. I was present at the trial where he was sentenced to death. It seemed clear that the man was innocent. The Procurator himself said so. I had much difficulty putting the matter out of my mind. Everything indicated that Jesus was a remarkable character. So—when I had occasion to come to Jerusalem again, this spring, I decided to spend a few days in Galilee, and learn something more about him.'

'What was it—about Jesus—that so deeply impressed you?' Miriam's tone entreated full confidence.

'His apparently effortless courage, I think,' said Marcellus. 'They were all arrayed against him—the Government, the Temple, the merchants, the bankers, the influential voices, the money. Not a man spoke in his behalf. His friends deserted him. And yet—in the face of cruel abuse—with a lost cause—and certain death confronting him— he was utterly fearless.' There was a thoughtful pause. 'It was impossible not to have a deep respect for a person of that fiber. I have had an immense curiosity to know what manner of man he was.' Marcellus made a little gesture to signify that he had ended his explanation.

'That wasn't such a very long story, after all, Marcellus,' remarked Miriam, intent upon her work. 'I wonder that you were so reluctant to tell it. Did you, perhaps, omit to tell Justus some of the things you have just told me?'

'No,' said Marcellus. 'I told him substantially the same thing.'

'But I thought you said you had not told him fully!'

'Well—what I have told you and Justus is sufficient, I think, to assure you that my interest is sincere,' declared Marcellus. 'At least, Justus appears to be satisfied. There are some stories about Jesus which he hints at—but refuses to tell—because, he says, I am not ready to be told. Yesterday he was lamenting that he had talked about that wedding-feast where the guests thought the water tasted like wine.'

'You didn't believe it.' Miriam smiled briefly. 'I do not wonder. Perhaps Justus is right. You weren't prepared for such a story.' A slow flush crept up her cheeks, as she added, 'And how did he happen to be talking of Anna's wedding?'

'We had been hoping to reach Cana in time to hear you sing,' said Marcellus, brightly, glad to have the conversation diverted. 'Naturally that led to comments about your sudden discovery of your inspiring voice. Justus had told me previously that it had occurred on the day of a wedding-feast. I pressed the subject, and he admitted that your strange experience had happened on the same day.'

'The changing of water into wine—that was too much for you,' laughed Miriam, sympathetically. 'I'm not surprised. However'—she went on, seriously—'you seem to have had no trouble believing in my discovery that I could sing. It has completely transformed my life—my singing. It instantly made me over into another kind of person, Marcellus. I was morbid, helpless, heart-sick, self-piteous, fretful, unreasonable. And now—as you see—I am happy and contented.' She stirred him with a radiant smile, and asked, softly, 'Is that so much easier to understand than the transformation of water into wine?'

'Shall I infer, then, that there was a miracle performed in your case, Miriam?' asked Marcellus.

'As you like,' she murmured, after some hesitation.

'I know you prefer not to discuss it,' he said, 'and I shall not pursue you with queries. But—assuming that Jesus spoke a word that made you sing—why did he not add a word that would give you power to walk? He straightened little Jonathan's foot, they say.'

Miriam pushed her embroidery aside, folded her arms, and faced Marcellus with a thoughtful frown.

'I cannot tell you how I came by my gift,' she said, 'but I do not regret my lameness. Perhaps the people of Cana are more helped by the songs I sing—from my cot—than they might be if I were physically well. They all have their worries, agonies, defeats. If I had been made whole, perhaps they would say, "Oh—it's easy enough for Miriam to sing and rejoice. Miriam has no trouble. Why indeed shouldn't she sing?"'

'You're a brave girl!' declared Marcellus.

She shook her head.

'I do not feel that I merit much praise, Marcellus. There was a time when my lameness was a great affliction—because I made it an affliction. It afflicted not only me but my parents and all my friends. Now that it is not an affliction, it has become a means of blessing. People are very tender in their attitude toward me. They come to visit me. They bring me little gifts. And, as Jesus said so frequently, it is more blessed to give than to receive. I am fortunate, my friend. I live in an atmosphere of love. The people of Cana frequently quarrel—but not with me. They are all at their best—with me.' She flashed him a sudden smile. 'Am I not rich?'

Marcellus made no response, but impulsively laid an open hand on the edge of the cot, and she gave him hers with the undeliberated trust of a little child.

'Shall I tell you another strange story, Marcellus?' she asked, quietly. 'Of course Justus must have told you that after Jesus had done some amazing things in our Galilean villages, the news spread throughout the country, and great crowds followed him wherever he went; hundreds, thousands; followed along for miles and miles and days and days! Men in the fields would drop their hoes and run to the road as the long procession passed; and then they too would join the throng, maybe to be gone from home for a week or more, sleeping in the open, cold and hungry, completely carried away! Nothing mattered—but to be close to Jesus! Well—one day—he was entering Jericho. You haven't been to Jericho, have you? No—you came up through Samaria. Jericho is one of the larger towns of Judea. As usual, a big crowd followed him and the whole city rushed to the main thoroughfare as the word spread that he had come. At that time, the Chief Revenue Officer of Jericho was a man named Zacchaeus—'

'A Greek?' broke in Marcellus.

'No—he was an Israelite. His name was Zaccai, really; but being in the employ of the Roman Government—' Miriam hesitated, colored a little, and Marcellus eased her embarrassment with an understanding grin.

'You needn't explain. These provincial officers usually alter their names as soon as they begin to curry favor with their foreign masters. It's fashionable now to have a Greek name; much smarter and safer than to have a Roman name. I think I know something about this Zaccai—alias Zacchaeus—without meeting him. He is a common type of rascally tax-collector; disloyal to everybody—to the Government—and his own countrymen. We have them in all of our provinces throughout the Empire. You can't have an empire, Miriam, without scoundrels in the provincial seats of government. Think you that Tiberius could govern faraway Hispania and Aquitania unless certain of their men betrayed their own people? By no means! When the provincials officers go straight, the Empire goes to pieces! . . . But —pardon the interruption, Miriam, and the long speech. Tell me about Zacchaeus.'

'He was very wealthy. The people of Jericho feared and hated him. He had spies at every keyhole listening for some rebellious whisper. Anyone suspected of grumbling about the Government was assessed higher taxes, and if he protested, he was charged with treason. Zacchaeus had built a beautiful home on a knoll at the southern boundary of Jericho and lived like a prince. There were landscaped gardens and lagoons—and scores of servants.'

'But no friends,' surmised Marcellus.

'Neither among the rich nor poor; but Zacchaeus did not care. He had contempt for their hatred. Well—on this day—having heard that Jesus was proceeding toward Jericho, Zacchaeus came down into the city for a glimpse of him. The waiting crowd was so dense that he abandoned his carriage and struggled through the multitude to reach a spot where he might see. A legionary, recognizing him, assisted him to climb up into the fork of a tree, though this was forbidden to anyone else. Presently Jesus came down the street with his large company, and stopped by the tree. He called to Zacchaeus, addressing him by his name, though they had never met, saying, "May I dine with you today?"'

'And what did the people of Jericho think of that?' wondered Marcellus.

'They were indignant, of course,' said Miriam. 'And Jesus' closest friends were very unhappy. Zacchaeus had been so mean—and now Jesus had singled him out for special attention. Many said, "This Galilean is no better than the priests, who are ever truckling to the rich."'

'I suppose Zacchaeus made the most of their discomfiture,' commented Marcellus.

'He was much flattered; hurried down from the tree and swaggered proudly at Jesus' side as the procession moved on. And when they arrived at his beautiful estate, he gave orders that the multitude might enter the grounds and wait—'

'While he and his guest had dinner,' assisted Marcellus. 'They must not have liked that.'

'No—they were deeply offended; but they waited. And saw Jesus enter the great marble house of Zacchaeus. After they had sat waiting for almost an hour, Zacchaeus came out and beckoned to the people. They scrambled to their feet and ran to hear what he might say. He was much disturbed. They could see that something had happened to him. The haughtiness and arrogance was gone from his face. Jesus stood a little way apart from him, sober and silent. The great multitude stood waiting, every man holding his breath and staring at this unfamiliar face of Zacchaeus. And then he spoke, humbly, brokenly. He had decided, he said, to give half of all he owned to feed the poor. To those whom he had defrauded, he would make abundant restitution.'

'But—what had happened?' demanded Marcellus. 'What had Jesus said to him?'

Miriam shook her head.

'Nobody knows,' she murmured; then, with averted, reminiscent eyes, she added, half to herself: 'Maybe he didn't say anything at all. Perhaps he looked Zacchaeus squarely in the eyes until the man saw —reflected there—the image of the person he was meant to be.'

'That is a strange thing to say,' remarked Marcellus. 'I'm afraid I don't understand.'

'Many people had that experience,' said Miriam, softly. 'When Jesus looked directly into your eyes—' She broke off suddenly, and leaned far forward to face him at close range. 'Marcellus,' she went on, in an impressive tone lowered almost to a whisper, 'if you had ever met Jesus—face to face—and he had looked into your eyes until— until you couldn't get away—you would have no trouble believing that he could do *anything—anything he pleased!* If he said, "Put down your crutches!" you would put them down. If he said, "Pay back the money you have stolen!" you would pay it back.'

She closed her eyes and relaxed against the cushions. Her hand, still in his, was trembling a little.

'And if he said, "Now you may sing for joy!" ' ventured Marcellus, 'you would sing?'

Miriam did not open her eyes, but a wisp of a smile curved her lips. After a moment, she sat up with suddenly altered mood, reclaimed her hand, patted her curls, and indicated that she was ready to talk of something far afield.

'Tell me more about this Greek who worked for Benyosef,' she suggested. 'Evidently he too is interested in Jesus, or he wouldn't have had the confidence of the men who meet one another there.'

'It will be easy to talk about Demetrius,' replied Marcellus, 'for he is my closest friend. In appearance he is tall, athletic, handsome. In mind, he is widely informed, with a sound knowledge of the classics. At heart, he is loyal and courageous. As to his conduct, I have never known him to do an unworthy thing.' Marcellus paused for a moment, and went on resolutely. 'When I was seventeen, my father presented Demetrius to me—a birthday gift.'

'But—you said he is your closest friend!' exclaimed Miriam. 'How can that be? Does he not resent being enslaved?'

'No man can be expected to like slavery, Miriam; but, once you have been a slave, there is not very much you could do with your freedom if you achieved it. I have offered Demetrius his liberty. He is free to come and go as he likes.'

'You must have been a good master, Marcellus,' said Miriam, gently.

'Not always. At times—especially during the past year—I have made Demetrius very unhappy. I was moody, restless, wretched, sick.'

'And why was that?' she asked. 'Would you like to tell me?'

'Not on this fair day,' rejoined Marcellus, soberly. 'Besides—I am well now. I need not burden you with it.'

'As you please,' she consented. 'But—how did Demetrius happen to be working in Benyosef's shop?'

'That is a long story, Miriam.'

'You—and your long stories,' she put in, dryly.

Marcellus feigned a wince—and smiled.

'Briefly, then—we were in Athens. Through no fault of his, and in defense of some helpless people, Demetrius engaged in combat with a man who held a position of authority, but had not been advised that a blow delivered by this Greek slave would stun an ox. It was a well-justified battle, albeit one-sided and of short duration. But we thought it prudent for Demetrius to lose no time increasing the distance between himself and the Athenian jail. So—he drifted to Jerusalem, and because he had some knowledge of carding and spinning—'

'And how had he picked that up?' asked Miriam, busy again with her precise stitches.

'At a weaver's shop in Athens. He was studying Aramaic under the weaver's instruction—and made himself useful.'

'Was that where you got your Aramaic, Marcellus?'

'Yes.'

'Did you learn carding and spinning, too?'

'No,' laughed Marcellus. 'Just Aramaic—such as it is.'

'That was in preparation for this tour of Galilee, I think,' ventured Miriam. 'And when you have learned all you wish to know about Jesus—what then?'

'My plans are uncertain.' Marcellus frowned his perplexity. 'I must go back to Rome, though my return is not urgent. Naturally I want to rejoin my family and friends, but—'

Miriam took several little stitches before she looked up to ask, almost inaudibly—'But what?'

'Something tells me I am going to feel quite out of place in Rome,' he confessed. 'I have been much impressed by what I have heard of your brave Galilean's teachings about human relations. They seem so reasonable, so sensible. If they became popular, we could have a new world. And, Miriam, we must have a new world! Things can't go on this way! Not very much longer!'

Miriam put down her work and gave him her full attention. She had not seen him in such a serious mood before.

'During these past few days,' he went on, 'I have had a chance to look at the world from a different angle. It wasn't that I had never stopped to think about its injustice, its waste, its tragic unhappiness. But—out here in this quiet country—I lie at night, looking up at the stars, and suddenly I recall Rome!—its greed and gluttony at the top; its poverty and degradation growing more and more desperate all the way down to the bottom of damp dungeons and galleys and quarries. And Rome rules the world! The Emperor is a lunatic. The Prince Regent is a scoundrel. They rule the world! Their armies control the wretched lives of millions of people!' He paused, patted a damp brow, and muttered, 'Forgive me, my friend, for haranguing you.'

'Would it not be wonderful,' exclaimed Miriam, 'if Jesus were on the throne?'

'Impossible!' expostulated Marcellus.

'Maybe not,' said Miriam, quietly.

He studied her eyes, wondering if she were really serious, and was amazed at her sober sincerity.

'You can't be in earnest!' he said. 'Besides—Jesus is dead.'

'Are you sure of that?' she asked, without looking up.

'I agree that his teachings are not dead, and something should be done to carry them to as many people as can be reached!'

'Do you intend to tell your friends about him—when you go home?' Marcellus sighed.

'They would think me crazy.'

'Would your father think you were crazy?'

'He would, indeed! My father is a just man of generous heart, but he has contempt for people who interest themselves in religion. He would be embarrassed—and annoyed, too—if I were to discuss these things with our friends.'

'Might he not think it brave of you?'

'Brave? Not at all! He would think it was in very bad taste!'

Justus and Reuben were sauntering in from the vineyard, much occupied with their low-voiced conversation.

'How long will you be here, Marcellus?' asked Miriam, with un-disguised concern. 'Will I see you again; tomorrow, maybe?'

'Not tomorrow. We go to Capernaum tomorrow, Justus says. He wants me to meet an old man named Nathaniel. Ever hear of him?'

'Of course! You will like him. But you are coming back to Cana, aren't you, before you return to Jerusalem?'

'I'd like to.'

'Please. Now you let me have a word with Justus, alone; will you?'

'Justus,' said Marcellus, as the men approached, 'I shall go back to the village, and meet you there at your convenience.'

He offered his hand to Reuben, who clasped it cordially. Evidently Justus had given Reuben a friendly account of him.

'Good-bye, Miriam,' he said, taking her hand. 'I shall see you next week.'

'Good-bye, Marcellus,' she said. 'I shall be looking for you.' The bearded Galilean stood by and watched them exchange a lingering look. Reuben frowned a little, as if the situation perplexed him. The frown said that Reuben didn't want his girl hurt. This Roman would go away and forget all about her, but Miriam would remember.

'You're coming back this way, then,' said Reuben to Justus, as Marcellus moved away.

'It seems so.' Justus grinned.

'Let me tell Naomi that you will tarry and break bread with us,' said Reuben.

When they were alone, Miriam motioned to Justus to sit down beside her.

'Why don't you tell Marcellus everything?' she asked. 'He is deeply concerned. It seems he knows so little. He was in Jerusalem and attended the trial at the Insula, heard Jesus sentenced to death, and knows that he was crucified. And that is all. So far as he is aware, the story of Jesus ended that day. Why haven't you told him?'

'I intend to, Miriam, when he is prepared to hear it. He would not believe it if I were to tell him now.' Justus moved closer and lowered his voice. 'I thought perhaps you would tell him.'

'I almost did. Then I wondered if you might not have some reason—unknown to me—for keeping it a secret. I think Marcellus has a right to know everything now. He thinks it such a pity that no plans have been made to interest people in Jesus' teachings. Can't you tell him about the work they are doing in Jerusalem—and Joppa—and Cae-sarea? He hasn't the faintest idea of what is going on!'

'Very well,' nodded Justus. 'I shall tell him—everything.'

'Today!' urged Miriam.

'Tell me truly, daughter,' said Justus, soberly. 'Are you losing your heart to this foreigner?'

Miriam took several small, even stitches before she looked up into his brooding eyes.

'Marcellus doesn't seem a bit foreign to me,' she said, softly.

* * * * * *

Aimlessly sauntering back to the tent Marcellus began sorting over the homespun he had accumulated, wondering what he should do with it. Now that there was no longer any reason for pretending an interest in such merchandise, the articles already purchased were of no value to him. The thought occurred—and gave him pleasure—that he might take them to Miriam. She would be glad to see that they were distributed among the poor.

He took up a black robe and held it against the light. It was of good wool and well woven. He had paid twenty shekels for it. Fifteen would have been enough, but the woman was poor. Besides, he had been trying to make a favorable impression on Justus by dealing generously with his fellow countrymen.

With nothing better to entertain him, Marcellus sat down on the edge of his cot, with the robe in his hands, and indulged in some leisurely theorizing on the indeterminate value of this garment. If you computed the amount of skilled labor invested by the woman who wove it, on a basis of an adequate wage per hour for such experienced workmanship, the robe was easily worth thirty shekels. But not in Sepphoris, where she lived; for the local market was not active. In Sepphoris it was worth twelve shekels. A stranger would have been asked fifteen. Marcellus had made it worth twenty. Now it wasn't worth anything!

He would give it to Miriam, who had no use for it, and it still wouldn't be worth anything until she had donated it to someone who needed it. At that juncture, the robe would begin to take on some value again, though just how much would be difficult to estimate. If the man who received this excellent robe should be inspired by it to wash his hands and face and mend his torn sandals—thereby increasing public confidence in his character, and enabling him to find employment at a better wage—the robe might eventually turn out to be worth more than its original cost. If the man who received it was a lazy scalawag, he might sell it for whatever it would fetch, which wouldn't be much; for no person of any substance would want—at any price—a garment that had been in the possession of this probably verminous tramp. You could amuse yourself all day with speculations concerning the shifting values of material things.

Marcellus had been doing an unusual amount of new thinking, these past few days, on the subject of property. According to Justus, Jesus had had much to say about a man's responsibility as a possessor of material things. Hoarded things might easily became a menace; a mere fire-and-theft risk; a breeding-ground for destructive insects; a source of worry. Men would have plenty of anxieties, but there was no sense in accumulating worries over *things!* That kind of worry destroyed your character. Even an unused coat, hanging in your closet; it wasn't merely a useless thing that did nobody any good; it was an active agent of destruction to your life. And your *life* must be saved, at all costs. What would it advantage a man—Jesus had demanded—if he were to gain the whole world—and lose his own life?

A bit bewildered by this statement, Marcellus had inquired:

'What did he mean, Justus, about the importance of saving your own life? He didn't seem to be much worried about losing his! He could have saved it if he had promised Pilate and the priests that he would go home and say nothing more to the people about his beliefs.'

'Well, sir'—Justus had tried to explain—'Jesus didn't mean quite the same thing that you have in mind when he talked about a man's life. You see—Jesus wasn't losing his life when they crucified him, but he would have lost it if he had recanted and gone home. Do you understand what I mean, Marcellus?'

'No—I can't say that I do. To speak that way about life is simply trifling with the accepted definition of the word. I believe that when a man is dead, he has lost his life; perhaps lost it in a good cause; perhaps still living—for a little while—in the memory of those who believed in him and cherished his friendship. But if our human speech is of any use at all, a man who is dead has lost his life.'

'Not necessarily,' protested Justus. 'Not if his soul is still alive. Jesus said we need have no fear of the things that kill the body. We should fear only the things that kill the soul.' And when Marcellus had shrugged impatiently, Justus had continued, 'The body isn't very important; just a vehicle; just a kit of tools—to serve the soul.' He had chuckled over Marcellus' expression of disgust. 'You think that sounds crazy; don't you?' he added, gently.

'Of course!' Marcellus had shrugged. 'And so do you!'

'I admit it's not easy to believe,' conceded Justus.

And then Marcellus had stopped in the road—they were on their way from Sepphoris to Cana—and had delivered what for him was a long speech.

'Justus,' he began, 'I must tell you candidly that while I am much interested in the sensible philosophy of your dead friend Jesus, I hope you will not want to report any more statements of that nature. I have a sincere respect for this man's mind, and I don't wish to lose it.'

He had half-expected Justus to be glum over this rebuke, but the big fellow had only grinned and nodded indulgently.

'I didn't mean to be offensive,' said Marcellus.

'I am not troubled,' said Justus, cordially. 'It was my fault. I was going too fast for you; offering you meat when you should have milk.'

*   *   *   *   *   *

He tossed the black robe aside and examined a white shawl with a fringe. He couldn't imagine his mother wearing it, but the woman who had made it had been proud of her handiwork. He remembered how reluctant she was to see it go out of her little house, down on the Samaritan border somewhere. She should have been permitted to keep the shawl. It meant more to her than it could possibly mean to anyone else. Such things should never be sold; or bought, either. Marcellus recalled the feeling of self-reproach he had often experienced at lavish banquets in Rome where the wines were cooled with ice that had been brought from the northern mountains by relays of runners who sometimes died of exhaustion. No honest man could afford such wine. It had cost too much.

Well—he would give all of these garments to Miriam. She would put them to good use. But—wouldn't it be rather ungracious to let Miriam know that these things, fabricated with great care by her own fellow countrymen, weren't worth carrying away?

'But they are gifts,' he would say to Miriam. 'The people who receive them will be advantaged.'

And then Miriam would have a right to say, though she probably wouldn't, 'How can they be gifts, Marcellus, when they are only useless things that you don't want to be bothered with?'

And then, assuming that Miriam had said that, he could reply: 'But so far as the people are concerned who get these things, they would be gifts; wouldn't you say?'

'No,' he thought she might reply, 'they would never be gifts. You see, Marcellus—' And then she would go on to explain again how Jesus had felt about gifts.

He pitched the heavy white shawl back onto the pile of homespun and glanced up to see a tall, lean, rugged-faced fellow standing at the door of the tent. The visitor grinned amiably and Marcellus invited him to come in. He eased himself down on a campstool, crossed his long legs, and said his name was Hariph.

'Doubtless you came to see Justus,' said Marcellus, cordially. 'He is at Reuben's house. If you call this afternoon, I think he will be here.'

Hariph nodded, but made no move to go; sat slowly swinging his pendent foot and nursing his elbows on his knee while he candidly surveyed the furniture of the tent, the heap of homespun, and the urbane stranger from Rome.

'I think I have heard Justus speak of you,' said Marcellus, feeling that if Hariph meant to stay awhile some conversation might be appropriate. 'You are a potter, I believe. You make water-jars and wine-jars—and things like that.'

Hariph nodded and the grin widened a little.

'Tell me,' went on Marcellus, hopefully, 'is it customary to use the same sort of jar either for wine or water?'

'Oh, yes, sir,' replied Hariph, with deliberate professional dignity. 'Many do that. Water or wine—it's all the same. Oil, too. Same pot.'

'But I suppose that after you've had oil in a pot, you wouldn't want to put wine in it,' observed Marcellus, sensibly enough, he thought.

'No—that wouldn't be so good,' agreed Hariph. 'The wine would taste of oil.'

'The same thing might be true, I daresay, of water in a jar that had held wine,' pursued Marcellus. 'The water might taste like wine.'

Hariph stopped swinging his foot and gazed squintingly toward the street, the fine lines on his temple deepening. Marcellus surmised that the town gossip was trying to decide whether it would be prudent to discuss the matter. After some delay, he turned to his young host and gratified him by saying:

'Did Justus tell you?'

'Yes.'

'Did you believe it?' asked Hariph.

'No,' replied Marcellus, firmly. 'I should be much interested in hearing what you think about it.'

'Well, sir,' rejoined Hariph, 'we ran out of wine at the wedding of my daughter Anna, and when Jesus came he made wine—out of water. I don't know how. I just know that he did it.'

'Did you taste it?'

'Yes, sir. I never tasted wine like that—before or since.'

'What was it—a heavy, potent wine?'

'N-no, sir.' Hariph screwed up his face indecisively. 'It was of a delicate flavor.'

'Red?' queried Marcellus.

'White,' remembered Hariph.

'White as water?'

'Yes, sir.' Hariph's eyes collided briefly with Marcellus' dry smile, and drifted away. Nothing further was said for a long moment.

'I am told that everyone was very fond of Jesus,' remarked Marcellus.

'Indeed they were, sir!' responded Hariph. 'He came late, that day. You should have seen them when he appeared; the shouts of greeting; many leaving their places to crowd about him. It was so, wherever he went, sir. Nobody had eyes for anyone else.'

'Had you ever kept wine in those jars, Hariph?' asked Marcellus.

'Yes, sir,' admitted Hariph.

Marcellus nodded his head slowly and grinned.

'Well—thank you for telling me,' he said. 'I was almost sure there must be an explanation.' He rose, significantly. 'I am glad you called, Hariph. Shall I tell Justus you will be back later?'

Hariph had not risen. His face was perplexed.

'If it was only that one thing, sir,' he said, quite unaffected by his dismissal—'if it had been only that one time—'

Marcellus sat down again and gave respectful attention.

'But—from that day on, sir,' continued Hariph, deliberately, 'there were many strange happenings.'

'So I have heard,' admitted Marcellus. 'Let me ask you: did you see any of these mysterious things done, or did you just learn about them from others? Strange stories always grow in the telling, you know.'

'Has anyone told you,' asked Hariph, 'how Jesus fed a crowd of five thousand people when he had nothing but a little basketful of bread and a couple of smoked fish?'

'No,' said Marcellus, eagerly. 'Tell me, please.'

'Perhaps Justus will tell you, if you ask him. He was there. He was closer to it—when it happened.'

'Were you there, Hariph?'

'Yes—but I was rather far back in the crowd.'

'Well, tell me what you saw. I shall be much interested in your view of it. Where did all this happen?'

'It wasn't so very long after our wedding. Jesus had begun going about through the villages, talking with the people, and large crowds were following him'

'Because of what he said?' interposed Marcellus.

'Partly—but mostly because of the reports that he was healing all manner of diseases, and giving blind men their sight, and—'

'Do you believe that—about the blind men?'

'Yes, sir!' declared Hariph. 'I saw one man who could see as well as you can, sir.'

'Had you known him before?'

'No, sir,' confessed Hariph. 'But his neighbors said he had been blind for years.'

'Did you know them—his neighbors?'

'No, sir. They were from down around Sychar.'

'That kind of testimony,' observed Marcellus, judicially, 'wouldn't get very far in a court of law; but you must have some good reason for believing it. . . . Well—go on, please, about the strange feast.'

'Always there were big crowds following him,' continued Hariph, undismayed by the Roman's incredulity. 'And sometimes they weren't easy to handle. Everybody wanted to be close enough to see these wonderful things happen; and you never could tell when it would be. It's no small matter, sir'—Hariph interrupted himself to comment— 'when one of your own neighbors, as you might say, who had grown up with the other youngsters of his village, and had worked at a carpenter's bench, takes to talking as nobody else had ever talked; and stopping in the middle of a speech to point his finger at some old man who might be standing in the front row, with his mouth open and both hands cupped behind his ears, trying to hear—and suddenly the old man yells "Ahhh!"—and begins dancing up and down, shouting, "I can hear! I can hear! I can hear!" And Jesus wouldn't have stopped talking: he would just point at the man—and he could hear!'

'Did you ever see Jesus do that, Hariph?' demanded Marcellus.

'No, sir—but there were plenty who did; people whose word you could trust, too!'

'Very well,' consented Marcellus, indulgently. 'Now tell me about the feeding of the five thousand people. You say you saw that?'

'It was this way, sir. It all began over in Capernaum. A lot of strange things had happened, and the news had spread abroad until a great crowd had collected, a disorderly crowd it was; for nobody was trying to keep them from pushing and jostling and tramping on one another.'

'It's a wonder they didn't call out the legionaries,' said Marcellus. 'There's a fort at Capernaum.'

'Yes—and many of the soldiers were there; but I don't think the priests and elders of the city wanted the crowd to be kept in order. They probably hoped something would happen, a bad accident, maybe, so that Jesus could be arrested for disturbing the peace.'

'But didn't he have a few close friends who might have demanded the people to cease this confusion?'

'Yes, sir—Jesus had many close friends. He named twelve of them to be known as his disciples. But they had no authority to give orders to that big crowd. They were really beside themselves to know what to do. Reuben and I had gone over to Capernaum—like everybody else—to see what was going on. When we arrived, the people were milling about in the central plaza. I never was in such a press, sir! Men and women with sick children in their arms, being pushed roughly in the swaying pack. Blind men. Half-dead people on cots, carried by their friends. There were even lepers in the crowd.' Hariph chuckled grimly. 'Nobody jostled *them!*'

'It's a wonder they weren't arrested,' put in Marcellus.

'Well, sir,' drawled Hariph, 'when a leper is out on his own, not even a legionary is anxious to lay hands on him. And you couldn't blame the poor lepers, sir. They hoped to be healed, too.'

'Is Jesus supposed to have healed lepers, Hariph?' Marcellus' tone was loaded with doubt.

'Yes, sir. . . . Well, when the crowd became unmanageable, Jesus began retreating down toward the shore. Several of his disciples had run on ahead and engaged a boat. And before the people realized what was happening, Jesus and his twelve closest friends were pulling away from the beach.'

'Wasn't that a rather heartless thing to do?' queried Marcellus.

'He had tried to talk to them, sir, but there was too much confusion. You see—the people who crowded in about him hadn't come to hear him talk, but to witness some strange thing. They wouldn't even give way to the cripples or the blind or the very sick ones borne on cots. And then, too, Jesus had just received bad news. One of his best friends, whom old Herod Antipas had thrown into prison, had just been beheaded. Word of it came to Jesus while he was trying to deal with that unruly mob. You can't blame him, sir, for wanting to get away.'

'Quite to the contrary, Hariph!' declared Marcellus. 'It's gratifying to hear that he could be puzzled about something. It was lucky that there was a boat available. Was the crowd enraged?'

'Oh—they behaved each according to his own temper,' remembered Hariph. 'Some shook their fists and shouted imprecations. Some shook their heads and turned away. Some wept. Some stood still and said nothing, as they watched the boat growing smaller.'

'And what did you and Reuben do?'

'Well, sir—we decided to go home. And then somebody noticed that the boat was veering toward the north. A great shout went up, and the people began racing toward the beach. It seemed likely that the party in the boat was making for some place up in the neighborhood of Bethsaida.'

'How far was that?' inquired Marcellus.

'For the boat—about six miles. For the crowd—nearly nine. It was a hot day and rough going. That country up there is mostly desert. But everybody went, or so it seemed. It was a singular sight, sir, that long procession stumbling over the stones and through the dried weeds. It was far past midday when we found them.'

'Did Jesus seem annoyed when the crowd arrived?'

'No—just sorry,' murmured Hariph. 'His face was sad. The people were so very tired. They weren't pushing one another—not after that trip!' He laughed a little at the recollection.

'Did he chide them for the way they behaved in Capernaum?'

'No, sir. He didn't say anything for a long time. The people flung themselves down to rest. Justus told me afterward that Simon urged Jesus to talk to them, but he wanted to wait until all of them had arrived; for some were carrying their sick, and were far behind. He didn't speak a word until they were all there. And then he stood up and began to talk. He did not reprove us for trailing him to this place, nor did he have aught to say of the people's rudeness. He talked about all of us being neighbors. We were all one family. Everyone was very quiet. There wasn't a sound—but the voice of Jesus. And remember, sir; there were five thousand people in that crowd!' Hariph's chin twitched involuntarily. He cleared his throat. Marcellus studied his face soberly.

'I am not one to weep easily, sir,' he went on, huskily. 'But there was something about those words that brought the tears. There we were—nothing but a great crowd of little children—tired and worn out—and here was a man—the only man there—and all the rest of us nothing but quarrelsome, stingy, greedy, little children. His voice was very calm, but—if you can believe me, sir—his words were as ointment on our wounds. While he talked, I was saying to myself, "I have never lived! I have never known how to live! This man has the words of life!" It was as if God Himself were speaking, sir! Everybody was much moved. Men's faces were strained and their tears were flowing.' Hariph wiped his eyes with the backs of his hands.

'After a while,' he continued, brokenly, 'Jesus stopped talking and motioned to some who had carried a sick man all that long way, and they brought their burden and put it down at Jesus' feet. He said something to the sick man. I could not hear what it was. And the sick man got up! And so did everybody else—as if Jesus had suddenly pulled us all to our feet. And everyone drew a gasp of wonder!' Hariph grinned pensively and faced Marcellus directly with childishly entreating eyes. 'Do you believe what I am telling you, sir?'

'It is difficult, Hariph,' said Marcellus, gently. 'But I think you believe what you are saying. Perhaps there is some explanation.'

'That may be, sir,' said Hariph, politely. 'And then there were many, many others who went to Jesus to be healed of their diseases; not jostling to be first, but waiting their turn.' He hesitated for a moment, embarrassed. 'But I shall not weary you with that,' he went on, 'seeing you do not believe.'

'You were going to tell me how he fed them,' prompted Marcellus.

'Yes, sir. It was growing late in the afternoon. I had been so moved by the things I had heard and seen that I had not thought of being hungry. Reuben and I, knowing there would be nothing out there to eat, had stopped at a market-booth in Capernaum and had bought some bread and cured fish. In any other kind of crowd, we would have eaten our luncheon. But now that we had begun to feel hungry, I was ashamed to eat what I had before the faces of the men about me; for, as I have said, Jesus had been talking about us all being of one family, and how we ought to share what we had with one another. I should have been willing to divide with the man next to me; but I didn't have much more than enough for myself. So—I didn't eat; nor did Reuben.'

'I daresay there were plenty of men in the crowd who faced the same dilemma,' surmised Marcellus.

'Well—the disciples were around Jesus telling him he had better dismiss the people, so they could go to the little villages and buy food. Justus told me afterward that Jesus only shook his head and told them that the people would be fed. They were much bewildered and worried. There was a small boy, sitting very close and overhearing this talk. He had a little basket, his own lunch, not very much; just enough to feed a boy. He went to Jesus with his basket and said he was willing to share what he had.'

Marcellus' eyes lighted, and he leaned forward attentively.

'Go on!' he demanded. 'This is wonderful.'

'Yes—it really was wonderful, sir. Jesus took the basket and held it up for the people to see. And then he told how the boy wanted to share his food with all of the people. And he looked up and thanked God for the little boy's gift. It was very, very quiet, sir. Then he began breaking the small loaves into bits, and the fish he tore into little shreds; and he gave these fragments to his disciples and told them to feed the people.'

'Did the crowd laugh?' asked Marcellus.

'Well—no, sir. We didn't laugh, though almost everyone smiled over such a big crowd being fed on almost nothing, as you might say. As I told you, I had been ashamed to bring out the food I had, and now I was ashamed not to; so I unwrapped my bread and fish, and broke off a piece, and offered it to the man next to me.'

'Wonderful!' shouted Marcellus. 'Was he glad to get it?'

'He had some of his own,' said Hariph, adding, quickly, 'But there were plenty of people who did not have any food along with them, sir. And everyone was fed, that day! After it was over, they gathered up a dozen basketfuls of fragments, left over.'

'It sounds as if some other people, besides you and Reuben, had had the forethought to bring some provisions along,' speculated Marcellus. 'They probably wouldn't have gone out into the desert with empty baskets. This is really a marvelous story, Hariph!'

'You believe it, sir?' Hariph was happily surprised.

'Indeed I do! And I believe it was a miracle! Jesus had inspired those stingy, selfish people to be decent to one another! It takes a truly great man to make one harmonious family out of a crowd like that! I can't understand the healing, Hariph; but I believe in the feeding! And I'm glad you wanted to tell me!'

Chapter XVI

THEY were on the way from Cana to Capernaum. All day their narrow road had been gaining altitude, not without occasional dips into shallow valleys, but tending upward toward a lofty plateau where the olive-green terrain met an azure sky set with masses of motionless white clouds.

It had been a fatiguing journey, with many pauses for rest, and as the shadows slanted farther to the east, the two men trudged the steepening grade in silence, leaving the little pack-train far behind. They were nearing the top now. Justus had promised that they would make camp in the lee of the great rock they had sighted two hours ago. There was a cool spring, he said, and plenty of forage. He hoped they would find the spot untenanted. Yes—he knew the place well. He had camped there many times. There was a splendid view. Jesus had loved it.

Throughout this tour of Galilee, Marcellus had paid very little attention to the physical characteristics of the province. Until now, the landscape had been unremarkable, and he had been fully preoccupied by the strange business that had brought him here. Marcellus had but one interest in this otherwise undistinguished land of rock-strewn fields, tiny vineyards, and apathetic villages drowsing in the dust around an ancient well. He was concerned only about a mysterious man who had walked these winding roads, a little while ago, with crowds of thousands surging about him.

It was not easy today, on this sleepy old highway, to picture either the number or the temper of that multitude. The people must have come from long distances, most of them, for this country was not thickly populated. Nor was it easy to imagine the confusion, the jostling, the shouting. Such Galileans as Marcellus had seen were not emotional, not responsive; a bit stolid, indeed.

That weary, weather-beaten woman, leaning on her hoe, in the frowsy little garden they had just passed—had she, too, bounded out of her kitchen, leaving their noonday pottage on the fire, to join in that curious throng? This bearded man in the meadow—her husband, obviously; now sluggishly mowing wisps of grass with his great-grandfather's scythe—had he run panting to the edge of the crowd, trying to scramble through the sweating pack for a glimpse of the face of Jesus?

It was almost incredible that this silent, solemn, stodgy province could ever have been haled out of its age-long lethargy and stirred to such a pitch of excitement. Even Justus, looking back upon it all, could only shake his shaggy head and mutter that the whole affair was quite beyond comprehension. You could think what you liked about the miracles, reflected Justus, soberly: many of the people were hysterical and had reported all manner of strange occurrences, some of which had never been satisfactorily confirmed. The air had been full of wild rumors, Justus said. A few Nazarenes had been quoted as remembering that when Jesus was a lad, at play with them, he had fashioned birds of clay, and the birds had come to life and had flown away. You could hear such tales by the score, and they had confused the public's estimate of Jesus, making him seem a mountebank in the opinion of many intelligent people.

But these passionate throngs of thousands who followed, day after day, indifferent to their hunger and discomfort—all Galilee knew that this was true because all Galilee had participated. You might have good reasons for doubting the validity of some of these miracle stories, but you couldn't doubt this one! Obscure little Galilee, so slow and stupid that its bucolic habits and uncouth dialect were stock jokes in Judea, had suddenly come alive! Its dull work was abandoned. Everybody talking at once! Everybody shouting questions which nobody tried to answer! Camels were left standing in their harness, hitched to water-wheels. Shuttles were left, midway of the open warp. Tools lay scattered on the floor of the carpenter shop. Plows stopped in the furrow. Fires burned out in the brickkiln. Everybody took to the road, on foot, on donkeys, on carts, on crutches. Helpless invalids who couldn't be left were bundled up on stretchers and carried along. Nothing mattered but to follow the young man who looked into your eyes and made you well—or ashamed—or tightened your throat with longing for his calm strength and floral purity.

Now the bright light had gone out. The great crowds had scattered. The inspired young man was dead. Galilee had gone back to sleep. It was a lonesome land. Perhaps the Galileans themselves were now conscious of its loneliness, after having briefly experienced this unprecedented activity.

Marcellus wished he knew how much of Jesus' influence still remained alive. Of course, you could depend upon a few of them—those who had known him best and owed him much—to remember and remember until they died; people like Miriam. Or were there any more like Miriam? Justus had said that some of these Galileans had been completely transformed, almost as if they had been born again. Certain men of low estate had learned new occupations. Certain beggars had become productive. A few publicans had become respected citizens. Women who had been known as common scolds were going about doing deeds of kindness. But perhaps the majority had been unable to hold on to their resolutions. He must press Justus for some more information about that.

Now they had arrived at the top of the terrain, every step adding depth to the view. Far to the north lay a range of snow-capped mountains. A few steps farther on, and the distant turrets and domes of a modern city glistened in the declining sun. There was no need to inquire its name: it had to be Tiberias. Marcellus lengthened his stride to keep pace with Justus who was moving swiftly toward the northern rim, turning his head from side to side, and peering intently in all directions, as if he had expected to meet a friend up here.

Suddenly the whole breath-taking panorama was spread before them and Marcellus had his first sight of the deep-blue lake that had figured so much in his guide's conversation. It had been around this little sea that Jesus had spent most of his days. Justus dropped wearily to the ground, folded his arms, and sat in silent contemplation of the scene. Marcellus, a little way apart, reclined on his elbows. Far in the distance was a slanting sail. All along the shore-line, flat-roofed villages straggled down to the water's edge.

After a long interval, Marcellus stirred.

'So—this is the Sea of Galilee!' he said, half to himself.

Justus nodded slowly. Presently he pointed to the farthest settlement that could be seen.

'Capernaum,' he said. 'Eight miles.'

'I daresay this lake has some tender memories for you, Justus,' remarked Marcellus. 'Tell me,' he went on, with a slow gesture that swept the landscape, 'has the general behavior of those people been greatly altered by the career of Jesus?'

'It is hard to say,' replied Justus. 'They do not talk much about it. They are afraid. The Roman fort is close by. One could easily get into trouble by asking questions. One only knows what has happened in the lives of one's friends. I expect to visit some of them while we are here.'

'Will I see them?' inquired Marcellus, doubtfully.

'Not many,' said Justus, frankly. 'You will see old Bartholomew, as I told you. He has a story I want you to hear. Bartholomew will not be afraid to talk to you, after I assure him it will be safe.' He turned about and faced Marcellus with a reminiscent smile. 'You might be interested in knowing how Jesus and Bartholomew first met. The old man was sitting out in his little fig orchard, one morning, when Jesus and Philip passed the house. And Jesus cheerily waved a hand and said, "Peace be upon you, Nathanael!" '

'I thought his name was Bartholomew,' put in Marcellus.

'That's the amusing part of it,' chuckled Justus. 'It is not customary with us to call venerable men by their given names. I don't suppose old Bartholomew had heard himself called Nathanael for at least two-score years. And here was this young stranger taking an immense liberty with him.'

'Was he offended?' asked Marcellus, with a grin.

'Well—perhaps not seriously offended, but certainly astonished. He called Jesus to come to him, perhaps intending to take him to task for what looked like a bit of impudence. Philip told me the story. He said that old Bartholomew was looking stern as he waited for Jesus to approach. Then his eyes widened and softened; and he smiled and said, "You know my name." "Yes," replied Jesus, "and because it means 'Godgiven' it is fitting, for you are an Israelite of high integrity."'

'That should have pleased the old man,' observed Marcellus.

'It did,' said Justus, soberly. 'It made him a disciple.'

'You mean—he came along—and followed after Jesus?'

'Yes. There was something strange about that. The old man had long since taken to his chair in the garden, thinking his active days were ended. But he got up and went along with Jesus—and he rarely left his side for nearly three years.'

'His vigor was restored?' Marcellus' face showed disbelief.

'No—he was still an old man. It was hard work for him to keep up with the others. He got very weary indeed, and he wheezed and panted like any other hard-pressed old man—'

'But he came along,' assisted Marcellus.

'Yes—Bartholomew came along. No one else would have ventured to call him Nathanael—but Jesus did, invariably. And Bartholomew liked it.'

'Perhaps Jesus did that to keep the old man going,' suggested Marcellus. 'Maybe it made him feel younger.'

'Well—it wasn't only Bartholomew who felt young and immature in the company of Jesus.' Justus frowned and stroked his beard, his habit when groping for an elusive memory. 'With the exception of John, all of the close friends and disciples of Jesus were older than he—but he was our senior—by years and years. Sometimes, after we had slipped away for an hour's rest, he would say, "Come, children: we must be on our way." But no one smiled—or thought it peculiar.'

'He seemed remote?' asked Marcellus.

Justus deliberately pondered a reply, then shook his head.

'No—not remote. He was companionable. You wanted to get closer to him—as if for protection. I think that's why the people were always crowding about him—until he hardly had room to move.'

'That must have put him under a great strain,' said Marcellus. 'Didn't he ever seem weary?'

'Very, very weary!' remarked Justus. 'But he never protested. Sometimes men would brace a shoulder against the crowd and push their way in, knocking others off their footing, but I can't recall that he ever rebuked anyone for it. . . . Marcellus, did you ever see a flock of little chickens climbing over one another to get under the hen's wings? Well—the hen doesn't seem to notice; just holds out her feathers, and lets them scramble in. That was his attitude. And that was our relation to him.'

'Very strange!' murmured Marcellus, abstractedly. 'But I think—I understand—what you mean,' he added, as from a distance.

'You couldn't!' declared Justus. 'You think you understand—but—you would have had to know Jesus to comprehend what I am saying. Some of us were old enough to have been his father—but we were just—just little chickens! Take Simon, for example. Simon was always the leader among the disciples. I hope you meet him when you go back to Jerusalem. Simon is a very forceful, capable man. Whenever Jesus happened to be absent from us, for an hour, Simon was far and away the big man of the company, everyone deferring to him. But—when Jesus would rejoin us'—Justus grinned, pursed his lips, and slowly shook his head—'Simon was just a little boy; just a humble, helpless little boy! A little chicken!'

'And Bartholomew—he was a little chicken, too?'

'Well,' deliberated Justus, 'not quite in the same way, perhaps. Bartholomew never expressed his opinions so freely as Simon when Jesus was away from us. He didn't have quite so far to drop—as Simon. It was amazing how much fatigue the old fellow could endure. He attended the last supper they had together on the night Jesus was betrayed. But when the news came in that the Master had been arrested, it was too much for Bartholomew. He was very sick. They put him to bed. By the time he recovered—it was all over.' Justus closed his eyes, sighed deeply, and an expression of pain swept his face. 'It was all over,' his lips repeated, soundlessly.

'He must be quite infirm, by this time,' said Marcellus, anxious to lift the gloom.

'About the same,' said Justus. 'Not much older. Not much weaker.' He grinned a little. 'Bartholomew has a queer idea now. He thinks he may never die. He sits all day in the fig orchard, when the weather is fair.'

'Looking up the road, perhaps,' speculated Marcellus—'and wishing he might see Jesus again, coming to visit him.'

Justus had been gazing down at the lake. Now he turned his eyes quickly toward Marcellus and stared into his face. After a rather tense moment, which left Marcellus somewhat bewildered, Justus returned his gaze to the lake.

'That is exactly what old Bartholomew does,' he murmured. 'All day long. He sits—watching the road.'

'Old men get strange fancies,' commented Marcellus.

'You don't have to be old,' said Justus, 'to get strange fancies.'

The little caravan, which had lagged on the last steep climb, now shuffled over the shoulder of the hill. Jonathan came running across, and snuggled down beside Justus.

'When do we have supper, Grandfather?' he wheedled.

'Quite soon, son,' answered Justus, gently. 'Go and help the boy unload. We will join you presently.' Little Jonathan scampered away.

'The lad seems in quite good spirits today,' observed Marcellus.

'That's Miriam's work,' declared Justus. 'She had a long talk with Jonathan yesterday. I think we need not worry about him now.'

'That conversation must have been worth hearing,' said Marcellus.

'Jonathan didn't seem inclined to talk about it,' said Justus, 'but he was deeply impressed. You noticed how quiet he was, last night.'

'I doubt whether there is another young woman—of Miriam's sort —in the whole world!' announced Marcellus, soberly.

'There is a widow in Capernaum,' said Justus. 'Perhaps you may have an opportunity to meet her. She spends all of her time with the very poor who have sickness in their houses. He name is Lydia. You might be interested in her story.'

'Tell me, please.' Marcellus sat up and gave attention.

'Lydia lost her husband, Ahira, while still quite a young woman. I do not know how it is in your country, but with us the predicament of a young widow is serious. She goes into retirement. Lydia was one of the most beautiful girls in Capernaum so everyone said. Ahira had been a man of considerable wealth, and their home was in keeping with his fortune. Shortly after his death, Lydia became grievously afflicted with an ailment peculiar to women, and gradually declined until her beauty faded. Her family was most sympathetic. At great expense, they summoned the best physicians. They carried her to many healing springs. But nothing availed to check her wasting disease. The time came when it was with great difficulty that she could move about in her room. And now the whole country began to be stirred by reports of strange things that Jesus had done for many sick people.' Justus hesitated, seemingly in doubt as to his procedure with the story. Marcellus waited with mounting curiosity.

'I think I had better tell you,' continued Justus, 'that it wasn't always easy for substantial people to have an interview with Jesus. As for the poor, they had no caste to lose. Most of them were in the habit of begging favors, and were not reticent about crowding in wherever they thought it might be to their advantage. But men and women in better circumstances—no matter how much they wanted to see Jesus—found it very hard to put down their natural pride and push into that clamorous multitude. Jesus regretted this matter. Often and often, he consented to talk alone with important men, late in the night, when he sorely needed his rest.'

'Men who wanted to be privately cured of something?' asked Marcellus.

'Doubtless—but I know of some cases in which very influential men, who had no malady at all, invited Jesus into their homes for a long conference. Once we waited at the gate of Nicodemus ben

Gorion, the most widely known lawyer of this region, until the cocks crew in the early morning. And there was nothing the matter with Nicodemus; at least, nothing physical.'

'Do you suppose he was warning Jesus to cease his work?' wondered Marcellus.

'No. Nicodemus came out with him, that night, as far as the gate. Jesus was talking earnestly to him. When they parted, each man laid a hand on the other's shoulder. We only do that with social equals. Well—as I had meant to say—it would have taken a lot of courage for a gently bred woman of means to have invaded the crowd that thronged about Jesus.'

'That's quite understandable,' agreed Marcellus.

'One day, when Jesus was speaking in the public plaza in Capernaum, a well-to-do man named Jairus pushed his way through the crowd. The people made way for him when someone spoke his name. It was plain to see that he was greatly excited. He went directly to Jesus and said that his little daughter was sick unto death. Would Jesus come at once? Without asking any questions, Jesus consented, and they started down the principal street, the crowd growing larger as they went. When they passed Lydia's house, she watched them from the window, and saw Jairus, whom she knew, walking at Jesus' side.'

'Where were you, Justus?' asked Marcellus. 'You seem quite familiar with these details.'

'As it happened, it was in the neighborhood of Lydia's house that I joined the crowd. I had come with a message for Simon, who had serious illness at home. His wife's mother was sick, and had become suddenly worse. I was as close to Jesus as I am to you when this thing happened. I don't suppose Lydia would have attempted it if she hadn't seen Jairus in the throng. That must have given her confidence. Summoning all her poor strength, she ran down the steps and into that crowd, desperately forced her way through, and struggled on until she was almost at Jesus' side. Then, her courage must have failed her; for, instead of trying to speak to him, she reached out and touched his Robe. I think she was frightened at her own audacity. She turned quickly and began forcing her way out.'

'Why didn't some of you call Jesus' attention to her?' asked Marcellus.

'Well'—defended Justus—'there was a great deal of confusion—and it all happened so quickly—and then she was gone. But, instantly, Jesus stopped and turned about. "Who touched me?" he demanded.'

'You mean—he felt that contact—through his Robe?' exclaimed Marcellus.

Justus nodded—and went on.

'Simon and Philip reminded him that there were so many crowding about. Almost any of them might have brushed against him. But he wasn't satisfied with that. And while he stood there, questioning them, we heard this woman's shrill cry. They opened the way for her to come to him. It must have been a very trying moment for Lydia. She had lived such a sheltered life. The crowd grew suddenly quiet.'

Justus' voice was husky as he recovered the scene.

'I saw many pathetic sights, through those days,' he continued, 'but none more moving. Lydia came slowly, with her head bowed and her hands over her eyes. She knelt on the ground before Jesus and confessed that she was the one who had touched him. Then she lifted her eyes, with the tears running down her cheeks, and cried, "Master! I have been healed of my affliction!"'

Overcome by his emotions, Justus stopped to wipe his eyes on his sleeve. Steadying his voice with an effort, he went on:

'Everyone was deeply touched. The people were all in tears. Jairus was weeping like a child. Even Jesus, who was always well controlled, was so moved that his eyes were swimming as he looked down into Lydia's face. Marcellus—that woman gazed up at him as if she were staring into a blinding sunshine. Her body was shaking with sobs, but her face was enraptured! It was beautiful!'

'Please go on,' insisted Marcellus, when Justus fell silent.

'It was a very tender moment,' he said, thickly. 'Jesus gave her both of his hands and drew her gently to her feet; and then, as if he were speaking to a tearful little child, he said, "Be comforted, my daughter, and go in peace. Your faith has made you whole."'

'That is the most beautiful story I ever heard, Justus,' said Marcellus, soberly.

'I hardly know why I told you,' muttered Justus. 'I've no reason to think you could believe that Lydia was cured of her malady merely by touching Jesus' Robe.'

He sat waiting, with an almost wistful interest, for a further comment from Marcellus. It was one thing to say of a narrative that it was a beautiful story; it was quite another thing to concede its veracity. Marcellus had been adept in contriving common-sense explanations of these Galilean mysteries. The story of Lydia's healing had obviously moved him, but doubtless he would come forward presently with an attempt to solve the problem on natural grounds. His anticipated argument was so long in coming that Justus searched his face intently, astonished at its gravity. He was still more astounded when Marcellus replied, in a tone of deep sincerity:

'Justus—I believe every word of it!'

* * * * * *

Notwithstanding his weariness, Marcellus had much difficulty in going to sleep that night. Justus' story about Lydia had revived the memory of his own strange experiences with the Robe. It had been a long time since he had examined his mind in respect to these occurrences.

He had invented reasons for the amazing effects the Robe had wrought in his own case. His explanation was by no means conclusive or satisfying, but he had adopted it as less troublesome than a forthright admission that the Robe was haunted.

The case, viewed rationally, began with the fact that he had had a very serious emotional shock. The sight of a crucifixion was enough to leave scars on any decent man's soul. To have actually conducted a crucifixion was immeasurably worse. And to have crucified an innocent man made the whole affair a shameful crime. The memory of it would be an interminable torture, painful as a physical wound. Not much wonder that he had been so depressed that all his mental processes had been thrown into disarray.

There was that night at the Insula when he had drunkenly consented to put on the blood-stained Robe. Apparently his weighted remorse over the day's tragedy had reached a stage where it could not endure this one more perfidy. A wave of sickening revulsion had swept through him, as if some punitive power—resident in the Robe—had avenged the outrage.

For a long time Marcellus had suffered of that obsession. The Robe was possessed! He shuddered when he thought of it. The Robe had become the symbol of his crime and shame.

Then had come his remarkable recovery, that afternoon in Athens. His mental affliction had reached a moment of crisis. He could bear it no longer. The only way out was by suicide. And at that critical juncture, the Robe had stayed his hand.

For a few hours thereafter, Marcellus had been completely mystified. When he tried to analyze the uncanny thing that had happened to him, his mind refused to work on it. Indeed, he had been so ecstatic over his release from the bondage of his melancholia that he was in no mood to examine the nature of his redemption. Such brief and shallow reasoning as he put upon it was as futile as an attempt to evaluate some fantastic, half-forgotten dream.

The time came when he could explain his recovery even as he had explained his collapse. The Robe had been a focal point of interest on both occasions. But—did the Robe actually have anything to do with it? Wasn't it all subjective?

The explanation seemed sound and practical. His mind had been deeply wounded, but now it had healed. Evidently the hour had arrived, that afternoon in the cottage at the inn, when his harassed mind determined to overthrow the torturing obsession. It was a reasonable deduction, he felt. Nature was always in revolt against things that thwarted her blind but orderly processes. For many years a tree might wage a slow and silent warfare against an encumbering wall, without making any visible progress. One day the wall would topple; not because the tree had suddenly laid hold upon some supernormal energy, but because its patient work of self-defense and self-release had reached fulfillment. The long-imprisoned tree had freed itself. Nature had had her way.

Marcellus had contented himself with this explanation. He had liked the analogy of the tree and the wall; had liked it so well that he had set it to work on other phases of his problem. You had had a peculiar experience that had forced you to a belief in the supernatural. But your mind—given a chance to resume its orderly functions—would begin to resist that untenable thought. It wasn't natural for a healthy mind to be stultified by alleged supernatural forces. No matter how convincing the evidences of supernatural power, one's mind would proceed—automatically, involuntarily—to push this intrusive concept away, as a tree-root pushes against an offending wall.

Until long after midnight, Marcellus lay on his cot, wide awake, re-examining his own rationalizings about the Robe in the light of Lydia's experience, and getting nowhere with it. He had impulsively told Justus that he believed the story. There was no reason to doubt the good man's integrity; but, surely, somewhere along the line there must be an explanation. Maybe Lydia's malady had run its course, that day, needing only this moment of high emotional stress to effect her release. He silently repeated this over and over, trying to make it sound reasonable; trying to make it stick. Then he agreed with himself that his theory was nonsense, and drifted off to sleep.

Rousing with a start, Marcellus cautiously raised up on one elbow and peered out through the open tent-door. In the gray-blue, pre-dawn twilight he dimly saw the figure of a tall, powerfully built, bearded man. It was quite too dark to discern the intruder's features.

His attitude did not denote furtiveness. He stood erect, apparently attempting to identify the occupants of the tent, and probably finding it impossible. Presently he moved away.

As soon as he had disappeared, Marcellus arose, quietly strapped his sandals, buckled his belt, and slipped out. There had been nothing sinister in this unexpected visitation. Obviously the man was neither a thief nor an ordinary prowler. He had not acted as if he had plans to molest the camp. It was quite conceivable that he had arranged to meet Justus up here and had been delayed. Finding the campers still asleep, he had probably decided to wait awhile before making himself known.

This seemed a reasonable surmise, for upon their arrival at the hilltop yesterday afternoon Justus had scrutinized the terrain as if expecting to be joined here by some acquaintance; though that was a habit of his; always scanning the landscape whenever an elevation presented a farther view; always peering down cross-roads; always turning about with a start whenever a door opened behind him.

It was still too dark to explore the terrain in quest of the mysterious visitor. Marcellus walked slowly toward the northern rim of the narrow plateau where he and Justus had sat. Low in the east, beyond the impenetrable darkness that mapped the lake, the blue was beginning to fade out of the gray. Now the gray was dissolving on the horizon and a long, slim ribbon of gleaming white appeared. Outspread lambent fingers reached up high, higher, higher into the dome from beyond a dazzling, snow-crowned mountain. Now the snow was touched with streaks of gold. Marcellus sat down to watch the dawn arrive.

At not more than a stadium's distance, also facing the sunrise, sat the unidentified wayfarer, not yet aware that he was observed. Apparently absorbed by the pageant in the east, he sat motionless with his long arms hugging his knees. As the light increased, Marcellus noted that the man was shabbily dressed and had no pack; undoubtedly a local resident; a fisherman, perhaps, for the uncouth knitted cap, drawn far down over his ears, was an identifying headgear affected by sailors.

With no wish to spy on the fellow, Marcellus noisily cleared his throat. The stranger slowly turned his head; then arose nimbly and approached. Halting, he waited for the Roman to speak first.

'Who are you?' asked Marcellus. 'And what do you want?'

The newcomer ran his fingers through his beard, and smiled broadly. Then he tugged off the wretched cap from a swirl of tousled hair.

'This disguise,' he chuckled, 'is better than I had thought.'

'Demetrius!' Marcellus leaped to his feet and they grasped each other's hands. 'Demetrius!—how did you find me? Have you been in trouble? Are you being pursued? Where did you come by such shabby clothes? Are you hungry?'

'I learned yesterday afternoon in Cana that you were on the way to Capernaum. I have not been in much trouble, and am not now pursued. The clothes'—Demetrius held up his patched sleeves, and grinned—'are they not befitting to a vagrant? I had plenty to eat, last night. Your donkey-boy helped me to my supper and lent me a rug.'

'Why didn't you make yourself known?' asked Marcellus, reproachfully.

'I wanted to see you alone, sir, before encountering Justus.'

'Proceed, then,' urged Marcellus, 'and tell me as much as you can. He will be waking presently.'

'Stephanos told you of my flight from Jerusalem—'

'Have you been back there?' interrupted Marcellus.

'No, sir; but I contrived to send Stephanos a message, and he wrote me fully about your meeting.' Demetrius surveyed his master from head to foot. 'You are looking fit, sir, though you've lost a pound or two.'

'Walking,' explained Marcellus. 'Good for the torso; bad for the feet. Keep on with your story now. We haven't much time.'

Demetrius tried to make it brief. He had fled to Joppa, hoping to see his master when his ship came in. He had been hungry and shelterless for a few days, vainly seeking work on the docks.

'One morning I saw an old man dragging a huge parcel of green hides along the wharf,' he went on. 'I was so desperate for employment that I shouldered the reeking pelts and carried them to the street. The old Jew trotted alongside protesting. When I put the loathsome burden down, he offered me two farthings. I refused, saying he had not engaged me. He then asked what I would take to carry the hides to his tannery, a half-mile up the street that fronted the beach. I said I would do it for my dinner.'

'No details, Demetrius!' insisted Marcellus, impatiently. 'Get on with it!'

'These details are important, sir. The old man wanted to know what part of Samaria I had come from. Perhaps you have discovered that our Aramaic is loaded with Samaritan dialect. His people had lived in Samaria. His name was Simon. He talked freely and cordially, asking many questions. I told him I had worked for old Benjamin in Athens, which pleased him, for he knew about Benjamin. Then I confided that I had worked for Benyosef in Jerusalem. He was delighted. At his house, hard by the tannery, he bade me bathe and provided me with clean clothing.' Demetrius grinned at his patches. 'This is it,' he said.

'You shall have something better,' said Marcellus. 'I am a clothing merchant. I have everything. Too, too much of everything. So—what about this old Simon?'

'He became interested in me because I had worked for Benyosef, and asked me if I were one of them, and I said I was.' Demetrius studied Marcellus' face. 'Do you understand what I mean, sir?' he asked, wistfully.

Marcellus nodded, rather uncertainly.

'Are you, really—one of them?' he inquired.

'I am trying to be, sir,' responded Demetrius. 'It isn't easy. One is not allowed to fight, you know. You just have to take it—the way he did.'

'You're permitted to defend yourself; aren't you?' protested Marcellus.

'*He* didn't,' replied Demetrius, quietly.

Marcellus winced and shook his head. They fell silent for a moment.

'That part of it,' went on Demetrius, 'is always going to be difficult; too difficult, I fear. I promised Stephanos, that morning when I left Jerusalem, that I would do my best to obey the injunctions—and in less than an hour I had broken my word. Simon Peter—he

is the chief of the disciples—the one they call "The Big Fisherman"—
he baptized me, just before dawn, in the presence of all the others
in Benyosef's shop, and, sir—'

'Baptized you?' Marcellus' perplexity was so amusing that Demetrius was forced to smile, in spite of his seriousness.

'Water,' he explained. 'They pour it on you, or put you in it, which-
ever is more convenient—and announce that you are now clean, in
Jesus' name. That means you're one of them, and you're expected
to follow Jesus' teachings.' Demetrius' eyes clouded and he shook
his head self-reproachfully as he added, 'I was in a fight before my
hair was dry.'

Marcellus tried to match his slave's remorseful mood, but his grin
was already out of control.

'What happened?' he asked, suppressing a chuckle.

Demetrius glumly confessed his misdemeanor. The legionaries had
a habit of stopping unarmed citizens along the road, compelling them
to shoulder their packs. A great hulk of a soldier had demanded this
service of Demetrius and he had refused to obey. Then there was
the savage thrust of a lance. Demetrius had stepped out of the way,
and the legionary had drawn up for another onslaught.

'In taking the lance from him,' continued Demetrius, 'I broke it.'

'Over his head, I suspect,' accused Marcellus.

'It wasn't a very good lance, sir,' commented Demetrius. 'I am
surprised that the army doesn't furnish these men with better equipment.'

Marcellus laughed aloud. 'And then what?' he urged.

'That was all. I did not tarry. Now that I have broken my promise'
—Demetrius' tone was repentant—'do you think I can still consider
myself a Christian? Do you suppose I'll have to be baptized again?'

'I wouldn't know,' mumbled Marcellus, busy with his own
thoughts. 'What do you mean—"a Christian"?'

'That's the new name for people who believe in Jesus. They're
calling Jesus "The Christos"—meaning "The anointed." '

'But that's Greek! All of these people are Jews; aren't they?'

'By no means, sir! This movement is traveling fast—and far. Simon
the tanner says there are at least three hundred banded together down
in Antioch.'

'Amazing!' exclaimed Marcellus. 'Do you suppose Justus knows?'

'Of course.'

'This is astounding news, Demetrius! I had considered the whole
thing a lost cause! How could it stay alive—after Jesus was dead?'

Demetrius stared into his master's bewildered eyes.

'Don't you—haven't you heard about that, sir?' he inquired,
soberly. 'Hasn't Justus told you?'

Both men turned at the sound of a shrill shout.

'Who is the child?' asked Demetrius, as Jonathan came running toward them. Marcellus explained briefly. The little boy's pace slowed as he neared them, inquisitively eyeing the stranger.

'Grandfather says you are to come and eat now,' he said moving close to Marcellus, but giving full attention to the unexplained man in the shabby tunic.

'Do you catch fish?' he asked. 'Have you a boat? Can I ride in it?'

'This man's name is Demetrius,' said Marcellus. 'He is not a fisherman, and he does not own a boat. He borrowed the cap.'

Demetrius smiled and fell in behind them as Marcellus, with the little boy's hand in his, walked toward the tent. Jonathan turned around, occasionally, to study the newcomer who followed with measured steps.

Justus, busily occupied at the fire, a few yards from the tent, glanced up with a warm smile of recognition and a word of greeting, apparently not much surprised at the arrival of their guest.

'May I take over, sir?' asked Demetrius.

'It is all ready; thank you,' said Justus. 'You sit down with Marcellus, and I shall serve you.'

Demetrius bowed and stepped aside. Presently Justus came to the low table he had improvised by drawing a couple of packing-cases together, and served Marcellus and Jonathan with the broiled fish and honey cakes. Jonathan motioned with his head toward Demetrius and looked up anxiously into Marcellus' face.

'Why doesn't he come and eat with us?' he inquired.

Marcellus was at a loss for a prompt and satisfactory reply.

'You needn't worry about Demetrius, son,' he remarked, casually. 'He likes to stand up when he eats.'

Instantly he divined that he had taken the wrong turn. Justus, who was sitting down opposite them, with his own dish, frowned darkly. He had some deep convictions on the subject of slavery. It was bad enough, his glum expression said, that Demetrius should be Marcellus' slave. It was intolerable that this relationship should be viewed so casually.

Jonathan pointed over his shoulder with his half-eaten cake in the direction of Demetrius who was standing before the fire, dish in hand, apparently enjoying his breakfast.

'That man stands up when he eats, Grandfather!' he remarked in a high treble. 'Isn't that funny?'

'No,' muttered Justus, 'it is not funny.' With that, he left the table, and went over to stand beside the slave.

Marcellus decided not to make an issue of it and proceeded to some lively banter with Jonathan, hoping to distract the child's attention.

Demetrius surveyed Justus' grim face and smiled.

'You mustn't let this slave business distress you, sir,' he said, quietly. 'My master is most kind and considerate. He would gladly give his life for me, as I would for him. But—slaves do not sit at table with their masters. It is a rule.'

'A bad rule!' grumbled Justus, deep in his throat. 'A rule that deserves to be broken! I had thought better of Marcellus Gallio.'

'It is a small matter,' said Demetrius, calmly. 'If you wish to make my slavery easier, please think no more of it, sir.'

At that, Justus' face cleared a little. There was no use making a scene over a situation that was none of his business. If Demetrius was contented, there wasn't much more to be said.

After they had eaten, Justus carried a dish of food out to the donkey-boy, Jonathan trotting along, still perplexed about the little episode.

'Grandfather,' he shrilled, 'Marcellus Gallio treats Demetrius no better than we treat our donkey-boy.'

Justus frowned, but made no attempt to explain. His grandson had given him something new to think about. In the meantime, Demetrius had joined Marcellus, his bearded lips puckered as he tried to dicipline a grin.

'Perhaps it will clear the air for everybody, sir,' he said, 'if I go on by myself to Capernaum. Let me meet you, late this afternoon.'

'Very well,' consented Marcellus. 'Ask Justus where he proposes to stop. But—are you sure it is prudent for you to go down to Capernaum? We have a fort there, you know.'

'I shall be watchful, sir,' promised Demetrius.

'Take this!' Marcellus poured a handful of coins into his palm. 'And keep your distance from that fort!'

* * * * * *

Demetrius, unencumbered, made good progress down the serpentine road to the valley floor. The air was hot. He carried his shabby coat and the disreputable cap under his arm. The lake-shore on this side was barren and unpopulated. Tossing off his clothing, he waded out and swam joyously, tumbled about like a dolphin, floated on his back, churned the water with long overhand strokes, luxuriating in his aquatics, and the thorough cleansing. He came out shaking his mop of hair through his fingers, the blazing sun drying him before he reached the little pile of patched and faded garments.

Tiberias gleamed white in the mid-forenoon sun. The marble palace of Herod Antipas, halfway up the hill, appropriately set apart from the less noble but surprisingly lavish residences, glistened dazzlingly. Demetrius imagined he could see a sinuous shimmer of heat enveloping the proud structure, and was glad he did not have to live there. He was not envious of Herod's privilege to spend the summer here. However, he reflected, the family had probably sought a more congenial altitude for the hot season, leaving a small army of servants to sweat and steal and quarrel until the weather eased with the coming of autumn.

He had reached the little city now, and proceeded on through it, keeping close to the beach, where many fishing-boats had been drawn up on the sand, and the adjacent market-booths reeked of their merchandise. Occasionally he was viewed with a momentary curiosity by small groups of apathetic loungers, sitting cross-legged in the shade of dirty foodshops. The air was heavy with decaying fruit and the stench of rancid oil sizzling in tarnished pans. It had been a long time since breakfast, and Demetrius had had an unusual amount of exercise.

He tarried before one of the unpleasant foodstalls. The swarthy cook scowled, and waved his wooden spoon at the shabby traveler with the uncouth cap—and no pack.

'Be on your way, fellow!' he commanded. 'We have nothing to give you.'

Demetrius jingled his money, and made a wry face.

'Nor have you anything to sell that a dog would eat,' he retorted.

The greasy fellow instantly beamed with a wheedling smile, lifting his shoulders and elbows into a posture of servitude. It was this type of Jew that Demetrius had always despised, the Jew who was arrogant, noisy, and abusive until he heard a couple of coins clink. Immediately you were his friend, his brother, his master. You could pour out a torrent of invective on him now, if you liked. He would be weather-proofed and his smile undiminished. He had heard the pennies.

'Oh—not so bad as that, sir!' exclaimed the cook. 'The evil smell' —he wagged a confidential thumb toward the neighboring booth— 'it is that one who defiles the air with his stale perch and wretched oil.' Tipping a grimy kettle forward, he stirred its steaming contents, appreciatively sucking his lips. 'Delicious!' he murmured.

A tousled, red-eyed legionary sauntered up from the waterfront, rested an elbow on the end of the high table, and sourly sniffed the heavy scent of burning fat. His uniform was dirty. Apparently he had slept where he fell. Doubtless he was ready for food now. He gave Demetrius a surly stare.

'Have a bowl of this fine pottage, Centurion,' coaxed the cook. 'Choice lamb—with many costly spices. A great helping for only two farthings.'

Demetrius repressed a grin. 'Centurion'—eh? Why hadn't the Jew gone the whole way and addressed the debauched legionary as 'Legate'? But perhaps he knew where to stop when dishing up flattery. The unkempt Roman snarled a curse, and rubbed his clammy forehead with his dirty brown bandeau. The cook took up an empty bowl and smiled encouragingly at Demetrius, who scowled and shook his head.

'None for me,' he muttered, turning away.

'I'll have some!' declared the legionary, truculently, slapping an empty wallet.

The cook's eager face collapsed, but he was not in a position to refuse the penniless soldier. With a self-piteous shrug, he half-filled the bowl and put it down on the filthy table.

'Business is so bad,' he whined.

'So is your pottage,' mumbled the legionary, nursing a hot mouthful. 'Even that slave would have none of it.'

'Slave, sir?' The cook leaned over the high table to have another look at the tall Greek, who was moving leisurely up the street. 'He has a wallet full of money. Good money, too—from the sound of it! A thief, no doubt!'

The legionary put down his spoon. His lip curled in a crafty grin. If an overdue soldier could reappear at the fort with a prisoner in tow, he might make a better case for his absence all night.

'Hi—you!' he shouted. 'Come back here!'

Demetrius hesitated, turned, held a brief parley with himself, and retraced his steps. It would do no good to attempt an escape in the neighborhood of a fort.

'Did you call me, sir?' he asked quietly.

'How do you happen to be in Tiberias alone, fellow?' The legionary wiped his stubbled chin. 'Where is your master? Don't pretend you're not a slave—with that ear.'

'My master is on the way to Capernaum, sir. He sent me on to seek out a desirable camping-place.'

This sounded reasonable. The legionary untidily helped himself to another large spoonful of the pottage.

'Who is your master, fellow? And what is he doing in Capernaum?'

'A Roman citizen, sir; a merchant.'

'A likely tale!' snorted the legionary. 'What manner of merchandise does a Roman find in Capernaum?'

'Homespun, sir,' said Demetrius. 'Galilean rugs and robes.'

The legionary chuckled scornfully and scraped the bottom of his bowl with a shaky spoon.

'Greek slaves are usually better liars than that,' he growled. 'You must think me a fool. A slave in rags and patches, seeking a campsite for a Roman who comes all the way to little Capernaum to buy clothing!'

'And with much money on him!' shrilled the cook. 'A robber he is!'

'Shut up, pig!' bellowed the legionary. 'I should take you along, were you not so filthy.' Setting his soiled bandeau at a jaunty angle, he rose, tightened his belt, belched noisily, and motioned to Demetrius to fall in behind him.

'But why am I apprehended, sir?' demanded Demetrius.

'Never mind about that!' snarled the legionary. 'You can tell your story at the fort.' With an exaggerated swagger, he marched stiffly up the street without turning to see whether his captive was following.

Demetrius hesitated for a moment, but decided that it would be foolhardy to attempt an escape in a vicinity so well patrolled. He would go along to the fort and try to send a message to Marcellus.

Beyond the limits of Tiberias the grim old sand-colored barracks loomed up on the arid hillside. Above the center of the quadrangle reared the parapets of the inevitable praetorium. The legionary strutted on toward the massive wooden gate. A sentry sluggishly unbarred the heavy barricade. They passed into the treeless, sun-blistered drill-ground and on between orderly rows of brown tents, unoccupied now, for it was noon and the legion would be in the mess-hall. Presently they brought up before the relatively impressive entrance to the praetorium. A gray-haired guard made way for them.

'Take this slave below and lock him up,' barked the legionary.

'What's your name, fellow?' demanded the guard.

Demetrius told him.

'And your master's name?'

'Lucan—a Roman citizen.'

'Where does he live?'

'In Rome.'

The guard gave the disheveled legionary an appraising glance. Demetrius thought he saw some hesitancy on the part of the older man.

'What's the charge?' asked the guard.

'Suspicion of theft,' said the legionary. 'Lock him up, and let him explain later how he happens to be wandering about, away from his master, dressed like a fisherman—and with a wallet full of money.'

'Write his name on the slate, then,' said the guard. 'The Centurion is at mess.'

The legionary fumbled with the chalk, and handed it to Demetrius.

'Can you write your name, slave?' he inquired gruffly.

In spite of his predicament, Demetrius was amused. It was obvious that neither of these Romans could write. If they couldn't write, they couldn't read. He took the chalk and wrote:

'Demetrius, Greek slave of Lucan, a Roman encamped in Capernaum.'

'Long name—for a slave,' remarked the legionary. 'If you have written anything else—'

'My master's name, sir.'

'Put him away, then,' said the legionary, turning to go. The old guard tapped on the floor with his lance and a younger guard appeared. He signed with a jerk of his head that Demetrius should follow, and strode off down the corridor to a narrow stairway. They descended to the prison. Bearded faces appeared at the small square apertures in the cell-doors; Jewish faces, mostly, and a few tough-looking Bedouins.

Demetrius was pushed into an open cell at the far end of the narrow corridor. A perpendicular slit, high in the outer wall, admitted a frugal light. The only furniture was a wide wooden bench. Anchored to the masonry lay a heavy chain with a rusty manacle. The guard ignored the chain, retreated into the corridor, banged the heavy door shut and pushed the bolt.

Slumping down on the bench, Demetrius surveyed his cramped quarters, and wondered how long he would have to wait for some official action in his case. It suddenly occurred to him that if the dissipated legionary suspected the entry on the slate he might have thought it safer to rub it out. In that event, the new prisoner stood a good chance of being forgotten. Perhaps he should have made a dash for it when he had an opportunity. Assuming a speedy trial, how much should he tell? It would difficult to explain Marcellus' business in Galilee. Without doubt, old Julian the Legate was under orders to make short work of this Christian movement. There was no telling what attitude he might take if he learned that Marcellus had been consorting with these disciples of Jesus.

As his eyes became accustomed to the gloom, Demetrius noticed a shelf in the corner bearing an earthenware food-basin and a small water-bowl. He had been hungry an hour ago. Now he was thirsty. Moving to the door he crouched—for the barred port was not placed for a tenant of his height—and looked across the narrow corridor into a pair of inquisitive Roman eyes framed in the opposite cell-door. The eyes were about the same age as his own, and seemed amused.

'When do we get food and water?' asked Demetrius, in circus Latin.

'Twice,' replied the Roman, amiably. 'At mid-morning—you should have arrived earlier—and again at sunset. Praise the gods—I shan't be here for the next feeding. I'm getting out this afternoon. My week is up.'

'I can't wait until sunset for water,' muttered Demetrius.

'I'll wager you ten sesterces you'll wait until they bring it to you,' drawled the Roman. He straightened to relieve his cramped position, revealing a metal identification tablet on the chain around his neck.

'What is your legion?' inquired Demetrius, seeing his neighbor was disposed to be talkative.

'Seventeenth: this one.'

'Why aren't you in the legion's guardhouse,' ventured Demetrius, 'instead of down in this hole with the civilians?'

'The guardhouse is full,' chuckled the legionary.

'Was there a mutiny?' inquired Demetrius.

Not a mutiny, the legionary explained. They had had a celebration. Julian the Legate had been transferred to Jerusalem. The new

Legate had brought a detachment of fifty along with him from his old command, to guard him on the journey. During the festivities, much good wine had flowed; much good blood, too, for the detachment from Minoa was made up of quarrelsome legionaries—

'From Minoa!' exclaimed Demetrius. 'Is Tribune Paulus your new Legate?'

'Indeed he is!' retorted the legionary. 'And plenty hard! Old Julian was easy-going. This fellow has no mercy. As for the fighting, it was nothing; a few dagger cuts, a couple of bloody noses. One man from Minoa lost a slice off his ear.' He grinned reminiscently. 'I sliced it off,' he added, modestly. 'It didn't hurt him much. And he knew it was accidental.' After a little pause, 'I see somebody nicked you on the ear.'

'That wasn't accidental,' grinned Demetrius, willing to humor the legionary, who laughed appreciatively, as if it were a good joke on the Greek that he had been enslaved.

'Did you run away?' asked the Roman.

'No—I was to have joined my master in Capernaum.'

'He'll get you out. You needn't worry. He's a Roman, of course.'

'Yes,' said Demetrius, 'but he doesn't know I'm here.' He lowered his voice. 'I wonder if you could get a message to him. I'd gladly give you something for your trouble.'

The legionary laughed derisively.

'Big talk—for a slave,' he scoffed. 'How much? Two denarii, maybe?'

'I'll give you ten shekels.'

'That you won't!' muttered the legionary. 'I don't want any of that kind of money, fellow!'

'I didn't steal it,' declared Demetrius. 'My master gave it to me.'

'Well—you can keep it!' The legionary scowled and moved back from the door.

Demetrius sat down dejectedly on the bench. He was very thirsty.

Chapter XVII

OF COURSE it was sheer nonsense to say that you had full confidence in Nathanael Bartholomew's integrity but disbelieved his eye-witness account of the storm.

Nor could you clarify this confusion by assuming that the old man had been a victim of hallucination. Bartholomew wasn't that type of person. He was neither a liar nor a fool.

According to his story, told at great length as they sat together in his little fig orchard, Jesus had rebuked a tempest on the Sea of Galilee; had commanded the gale to cease, and it had obeyed his voice—instantly! Jesus had spoken and the storm had stopped! Bartholomew had snapped his dry old fingers. Like *that!*

And the story wasn't hearsay. Bartholomew hadn't heard it from a neighbor who had got it from his cousin. No, sir! The old man had been in the boat that night. He had heard and seen it all! If you couldn't believe it, Bartholomew would not be offended; but it was *truth!*

The tale was finished now. The aged disciple sat calmly fanning his wrinkled neck, drawing his long, white beard aside and loosening the collar of his robe. Marcellus, with no further comments to offer and no more questions to ask, frowned studiously at his own interlaced fingers, conscious of Justus' inquisitive eyes. He knew they expected him to express an opinion; and, after a silence that was becoming somewhat constrained, he obliged them by muttering to himself, 'Very strange! Very strange indeed!'

The dramatic story had been told with fervor, told with an old man's verbosity, but without excitement. Bartholomew wasn't trying to persuade you; nor was he trying to convert you. He had nothing to sell. Justus had asked him to tell about that storm, and he had done so. Perhaps it was his first opportunity for so complete a recital of all its incidents. Certainly it was the first time he had ever told the story to someone who hadn't heard it.

Shortly after Demetrius had set off alone, that morning, the little caravan had proceeded slowly down the winding road to the valley; had skirted the sparsely populated lake-shore to Tiberias where the ostentatious Roman palaces on the hills accented the squalor of the waterfront; had followed the beach street through the city; had passed the frowning old fort, and entered the sprawling suburbs of Capernaum.

Jonathan had been promised a brief visit with Thomas—and the donkey; so they had turned off into a side street where, after many inquiries, they had found the little house and an enthusiastic welcome. Upon the urgent persuasion of Thomas and his mother, Jonathan was left with them, to be picked up on the morrow. Everybody agreed that the donkey recognized Jonathan, though the elders privately suspected that the sugar which had been melting in the little boy's warm hand for the past two hours might have accounted for Jasper's flattering feat of memory.

Regaining the principal thoroughfare, they had moved on toward the business center of the town which had figured so prominently in Justus' recollections of Jesus. They had halted for a moment in front of Lydia's home, and Justus was for making a brief call, but Marcellus dissuaded him as it was nearing midday and a visit might be inopportune.

The central plaza had seemed familiar. The synagogue—ironically more Roman than Jewish in its architecture, which was understandable because Centurion Hortensius had furnished the money—spread its marble steps fanwise into the northern boundary of the spacious square, exactly as Marcellus had pictured it; for it was from these steps that Jesus had addressed massed multitudes of thousands. It was almost deserted now, except for the beggars, tapping on the pavement with their empty bowls; for everybody who had a home to go to was at his noonday meal.

Marcellus felt he had been here many times before. Indeed he was so preoccupied with identifying the cherished landmarks that he almost forgot they were to have met Demetrius here. Justus had reminded him, and Marcellus had looked about apprehensively. It would be a very awkward situation if Demetrius had been arrested. He had no relish for an interview with old Julian; not while on his present mission. Justus relieved his anxiety somewhat by saying he had told Demetrius where they would make camp, on the grounds of the old Shalum Inn; but what could be detaining Demetrius in the meantime?

'Perhaps he misunderstood me,' suggested Justus.

'It's possible,' agreed Marcellus, 'but unlikely. Demetrius has a good ear for instructions.'

They had sauntered down to the beach, strewn with fishing-boats drawn up on the shingle, leaving the donkey-boy to keep an eye out for Demetrius. Justus had suggested that they eat their lunch on the shore. After waiting a half-hour for the Greek to show up, they had packed their lunch kit and proceeded northward, Marcellus anxious but still hopeful of meeting his loyal slave at the inn. It was a quiet spot—the Inn of Ben-Shalum—with spacious grounds for travelers carrying their own camping equipment. No one had seen anything of a tall Greek slave. Hastily unpacking, they put up the tent in the shade of two tall sycamores, and made off toward the home of Bartholomew, a little way up the surburban street.

And now the old man had ended the story they had come to hear. In its preliminary phases, episodes had been introduced which bore no closer relation to the eventful storm than that they had occurred on the same day. Jesus had been very weary that night; so weary that he had slept at the height of the gale and had had to be awakened when it became clear that the little ship was foundering. Such deep fatigue had to be accounted for; so Bartholomew had elaborated the day's activities.

Sometimes, for a considerable period, the husky old voice would settle deep in the sparse white beard and rumble on in an almost inaudible monotone, and you knew that Bartholomew had deserted you and Justus for the great crowd that sat transfixed on a barren coast—a weary, wistful, hungry multitude of self-contained people who, in the melting warmth of Jesus' presence, had congealed into one sympathetic family, for the sharing of their food.

'A clean, bright lad,' Bartholomew was mumbling to himself; 'a nephew of Lydia's, who had none of her own; he spent most of his time at her house. She had packed his little basket.'

And then, suddenly remembering his guests, Bartholomew had roused from his reverie to tell Marcellus all about Lydia's strange healing; and Justus had not intervened with a hint that their young Roman friend had already heard of her experience. Having finished with Lydia—and Jairus, too, whose little daughter had been marvelously restored that day—the old man had drifted back to his memories of the remarkable feast in the desert.

'The boy must have been sitting at the Master's feet,' he soliloquized, with averted eyes. 'He must have been sitting there all the time; for when Jesus said we would now eat our supper, there he was —as if he had popped up from nowhere—holding out his little basket.'

It had taken Bartholomew a long time to tell of that strange supper; the sharing of bread, the new acquaintances, the breaking down of reserve among strangers, the tenderness toward the old ones and the little ones. . . . And then the tempo of the tale speeded. Wisps of chill wind lashed the parched reeds. Dark clouds rolled up from the northeast. The old man swept them on with a beckoning arm; black clouds that had suddenly darkened the sky. There was a low muttering of thunder. The crowd grew apprehensive. The people were scrambling to their feet, gathering up their families, breaking into a run. The long procession was on its way home.

Darkness came on fast, the lowering black clouds lanced by slim, jagged, red-hot spears that spilled torrents splashing onto the sun-parched sand. Philip was for rushing to shelter in the little village of

Bethsaida, two miles east. Peter was for beaching the big boat and using the mainsail for cover. And when they were all through making suggestions, Jesus said they would embark at once and return to Capernaum.

'He said we had nothing to fear,' went on Bartholomew, 'but we were afraid, nevertheless. Some of them tried to reason with him. I said nothing, myself. Old men are timid,' he paused to interpolate, directly to Marcellus. 'When there are dangers to be faced, old men should keep still, for there's little they can do, in any case.'

'I should have thought,' commented Marcellus, graciously, 'that an elderly man's experience would make him a wise counselor—on any occasion.'

'Not in a storm, young man!' declared Bartholomew. 'An old man may give you good advice, under the shade of a fig tree, on a sunny afternoon; but—not in a storm!'

The boat had been anchored in the lee of a bit of a cove, but it was with great difficulty that they had struggled through the waves and over the side. Unutterably weary, Jesus had dropped down on the bare bench near the tiller and they had covered him up with a length of drenched sail-cloth.

Manning the oars, they had maneuvered into open water, had put out a little jib and promptly hauled it in, the tempest suddenly mounting in fury. No one of them, Bartholomew said, had ever been out in such a storm. Now the boat was tossed high on the crest, now it was swallowed up, gigantic waves broke over their heads, the flood pounded them off their seats and twisted the oars out of their hands. The tortured little ship was filling rapidly. All but four oars had been abandoned now. The rest of the crew were bailing frantically. But the water was gaining on them. And Jesus slept!

Justus broke into the narrative here as Bartholomew—whose vivid memory of that night's hard work with a bailing-bucket brought big beads of perspiration out on his deep-lined forehead—had paused to wield his palm-leaf fan.

'You thought Jesus should get up and help; didn't you?' Justus was grinning broadly.

The old man's lips twitched with a self-reproachful smile.

'Well,' he admitted, 'perhaps we did think that after getting us into this trouble he might take a hand at one of the buckets. Of course'—he hastened to explain—'we weren't quite ourselves. We were badly shaken. It was getting to be a matter of life or death. And we were completely exhausted—the kind of exhaustion that makes every breath whistle and burn.'

'And so—you shouted to him,' prodded Justus.

'Yes! We shouted to him!' Bartholomew turned to address Marcellus. 'I shouted to him! "Master!" I called. "We are going to drown! The boat is sinking! Don't you care?"' The old man dropped his

head and winced at the memory. 'Yes'—he muttered, contritely. '*I*
said that—to my Master.'

After a moment's silence, Bartholomew drew a deep sigh, and continued. Jesus had stirred, had sat up, had stretched out his long, strong
arms, had rubbed his fingers through his drenched hair.

'Not alarmed?' inquired Marcellus.

'Jesus was never alarmed!' retorted Bartholomew, indignantly. 'He
rose to his feet and started forward, wading through the water, hands
reaching up to steady him as he made for the housing of the main-
mast. Climbing up on the heavy planking, he stood for a moment
with one arm around the mast, looking out upon the towering waves.
Then he raised both arms high. We gasped, expecting him to be
pitched overboard. He held both hands outstretched—and spoke! It
was not a shrill shout. It was rather as one might soothe a frightened
animal. "Peace!" he said. "Peace! Be still!"'

The climax of the story had been built up to such intensity that
Marcellus found his heart speeding. He leaned forward and stared
wide-eyed into the old man's face.

'Then what?' he demanded.

'The storm was over,' declared Bartholomew.

'Not *immediately!*' protested Marcellus.

Bartholomew deliberately raised his arm and snapped his brittle
old fingers.

'Like *that!*' he exclaimed.

'And the stars came out,' added Justus.

'I don't remember,' murmured Bartholomew.

'Philip said the stars came out,' persisted Justus, quietly.

'That may be,' nodded Bartholomew. 'I don't remember.'

'Some have said that the boat was immediately dry,' murmured
Justus, with a little twinkle in his eyes as if anticipating the old man's
contradiction.

'That was a mistake,' sniffed Bartholomew. 'Some of us bailed out
water all the way back to Capernaum. Whoever reported that should
have helped.'

'How did you all feel about this strange thing?' asked Marcellus.

'We hadn't much to say,' remembered Bartholomew. 'I think we
were stunned. There had been so much confusion—and now everything was quiet. The water, still coated with foam, was calm as a pond.
As for me, I experienced a peculiar sensation of peace. Perhaps the
words that Jesus spoke to the storm had stilled us too—in our hearts.'

'And what did *he* do?' asked Marcellus.

'He went back to the bench by the tiller and sat down,' replied
Bartholomew. 'He gathered his Robe about him, for he was wet
and chilled. After a while he turned to us, smiled reproachfully, and
said, as if speaking to little children, "Why were you so frightened?"
Nobody ventured to answer that. Perhaps he didn't expect us to

say anything. Presently he reclined, with his arm for a pillow, and went to sleep again.'

'Are you sure he was asleep?' asked Justus.

'No—but he was very quiet and his eyes were closed. Perhaps he was thinking. Everyone thought he was asleep. There was very little talk. We moved to the center of the boat and looked into each other's faces. I remember Philip's whispering, "What manner of man is this—that even the winds and waves obey him?"'

The story was finished. Marcellus, for whose benefit the tale had been told, knew they were waiting for him to say whether he believed it. He sat bowed far forward in his chair, staring into the little basket he had made of his interlaced fingers. Bartholomew wasn't willfully lying. Bartholomew was perfectly sane. But—by all the gods!—you couldn't believe a story like *that!* A man—speaking to a storm! Speaking to a storm as he might to a stampeded horse! And the storm obeying his command! No!—you couldn't have any of *that!* He felt Justus' friendly eyes inquiring. Presently he straightened a little, and shook his head.

'Very strange!' he muttered, without looking up. 'Very strange indeed!'

* * * * * *

The afternoon was well advanced when the gray-haired captain of the guard came down to free the legionary who had sliced off the ear of a visiting fellow-in-arms from Minoa.

Demetrius listened attentively at the little port in his door as his neighbor's bolt was drawn, hoping to overhear some formal conversation relative to the prisoner's release; but was disappointed. Neither man had spoken. The heavy door was swung back and the legionary had emerged. The captain of the guard had preceded him down the dusky corridor. The sound of their sandals, scraping on the stone floor, died away.

Shortly afterward there was a general stir throughout the prison; guttural voices; unbolting of doors and rattling of heavy earthenware bowls and basins; the welcome sound of splashing water. Feeding time had arrived and was being greeted with the equivalent of pawing hoofs, clanking chains, and nostril-fluttering whimpers in a stable. Demetrius' mouth and throat were dry; his tongue a clumsy wooden stick. His head throbbed. He couldn't remember ever having been that thirsty; not even in the loathsome prison-ship on the way from Corinth to Rome, long years ago.

It seemed they would never reach his end of the corridor. He hoped the water would hold out until they came to his cell. That was all he wanted—water! As for food, it didn't matter; but he had to have water —*now!*

At length they shuffled up to his door, unbolted it, and swung it wide open. Two burly, brutish, ear-slit Syrian slaves appeared in the doorway. The short, stocky one, with the spade beard, deep pock-marks, and greasy hands, plunged his gourd-dipper into an almost empty bucket of malodorous pottage and pointed angrily to the food-basin on the shelf. Demetrius, with nothing on his mind but his consuming thirst, had been waiting with his water-bowl in hand. He reached up for the food-basin, and the surly Syrian dumped the gourdful of reeking hot garbage into it. Then he rummaged in the bottom of a filthy bag and came up with a small loaf of black bread which he tossed onto the bare bench. It bounced and clattered like a stone.

Retreating to make room for his companion, the stocky one edged out into the corridor and the tall one entered with a large water-jar on his shoulder. Half-crazed with thirst, Demetrius held his water-bowl high. The Syrian, with a crooked grin, as if it amused him to see a Greek in such a predicament, tipped the jar, and from its con-siderable height poured a stream that overflowed the bowl, drenching the prisoner's clothing. There was hardly more than a spoonful left. The Syrian was backing toward the door.

'Give me water!' demanded Demetrius, huskily.

The fellow sneered, tipped the jar again, and poured the remain-der of the water over Demetrius' feet. Chuckling, but vigilant, he moved back into the doorway.

Though the bowl was not large, it was heavy and sturdy pottery, and in the hand of a man as recklessly thirsty and angry as Demetrius it was capable of doing no small amount of damage. But for the thick mop of kinky hair that covered his forehead, the bowl might have cracked the Syrian's skull, for it was delivered with all the earnest-ness that Demetrius could put into it.

Dropping the water-jar, which broke into jagged fragments, the dizzied Syrian, spluttering with rage, whipped out a long dagger from his dirty sash, and lunged forward. Hot pottage would not have been Demetrius' choice of weapons, but it was all he had to fight with; so he threw it into his assailant's face. Momentarily detained by this unexpected onslaught, the Syrian received another more serious blow. Raising the heavy food-basin in both hands, Demetrius brought it down savagely on the fellow's forearm, knocking the dagger from his hand.

Unarmed, the Syrian reeled back into the corridor where the stocky one, unable to force his way into the cell, was waiting the outcome of the battle. Demetrius took advantage of this moment to pick up the dagger. With the way cleared, the stocky one—dagger in hand—was about to plunge in; but when he saw that the prisoner had armed himself, he backed out and began swinging the door shut.

Unwilling to be trapped and probably killed with a lance thrust through the port, Demetrius threw his weight against the closing door and forced his way out into the corridor. Excited by the confusion, the prisoners set up a clamor of encouraging shouts that brought the elderly Captain of the guard and three others scurrying down the stone stairway. They paused, a few feet from the engagement. One of the younger guards was for rushing in to separate them, but the Captain put out an arm and barred the way. It wasn't every day that you could see a determined fight waged with daggers. When angry men met at close range with daggers, it was rough sport.

Cautious in their cramped quarters, the contestants were weaving about, taking each other's measure. The Syrian, four inches shorter but considerably outweighing the Greek, crouched for a spring. One of the younger guards emptied his flat wallet into his hand.

'Two shekels and nine denarii on the Syrian pig,' he wagered. The others shook their heads. The Greek was at a disadvantage. The dagger was the favorite weapon with the Syrians—a dagger with a long, curving blade. The Syrian considered it good strategy to slip up behind an enemy in the dark and let him have it between the ribs a little below and to the right of the left shoulder. On such occasions one needed a long knife. Demetrius was not unfamiliar with daggers, but had never practiced with one that had been especially contrived for stabbing a man in the back.

He was finding his borrowed weapon unwieldy in this narrow corridor. It was close-in fighting and decidedly dangerous business. The tall Syrian lurked far back in the darkness behind his companion. The stocky one, facing an appreciative audience of guards, seemed eager to bring the event to an early conclusion. They were sparring actively now, their clashing blades striking sparks in the gloom. Demetrius was gradually retreating, quite definitely on the defensive. The guards backed away to give them a chance. The pace of the fighting increased, the Syrian forcing the action.

'Ha!' he shouted; and a dark, red streak showed up on the Greek's right sleeve, above the elbow. An instant later, a long gash appeared across the back of the Syrian's hand. He gave a quick fling of his arm to shake off the blood, but not quick enough. A cut had opened over his collar-bone, dangerously close to his throat. He retreated a step. Demetrius pursued his advantage, and added another gash to his antagonist's hand.

'On guard—Greek!' shouted the Captain. The tall Syrian in the rear had drawn back his arm to hurl a chunk of the broken water-jar. Demetrius dodged, at the warning, and the murderous missile grazed the side of his head.

'Enough!' yelled the Captain. Grasping Demetrius' shoulder, he pushed him aside, the younger guards followed with lances poised to strike.

'Come out of there, vermin!' the Captain ordered. The Syrians sullenly obeyed, the stocky one yielding his bloody dagger as he squeezed by the guards. The procession started down the corridor and up the stairs. Arriving on the main floor, the Captain led the way along the spacious hall, and out into the courtyard. Water was brought, wounds were laved and crudely bandaged. Demetrius grabbed a water-jar, and drank greedily. The cut on his arm was deep and painful, and the wide abrasion on his temple burned, but now that he had had a drink, nothing else mattered much.

The Captain gave a command to proceed and they re-entered the praetorium, turned to the left at a broad marble staircase, and ascended to the second floor. A sentry informed the guard at an imposing door that Captain Namius wished to see the Legate. The guard disappeared, returning presently with a curt nod. They advanced through the open door and filed into the sumptuous courtroom, brightly lighted with great lamps suspended from beautifully wrought chains.

Demetrius' wounds were throbbing, but he was not too badly hurt to be amused. Paulus, rattling a leather dice-cup, was facing Sextus across the ornately carved table that dominated the dais at the far end of the room. So—Paulus, transferred to the command of the fort at Capernaum, had brought his old gambling companion along. The guards and their quarry, preceded by two sentries in gay uniforms, marched forward. Legate Paulus glanced disinterestedly in their direction and returned his attention to the more important business in hand. Shaking the cup, he poured out the dice on the polished table, and shrugged. Sextus grinned, took the cup, shook it languidly, poured it out—and scowled. Paulus laughed, and sat down in the huge chair behind the table. Centurion Sextus came to attention.

'What is it, Namius?' yawned Paulus.

'The Syrians were fighting this Greek prisoner, sir.'

'What about?' asked Paulus, impatiently.

Captain Namius didn't know. The Syrian slaves were feeding the prisoners, and 'somehow got mixed up with this Greek.'

'Step nearer, Greek.' Paulus' eyes had narrowed. He was searching his memory. Demetrius stepped forward, scowling to keep from smiling. Sextus leaned over and mumbled something. Paulus' eyes lighted. He nodded and grinned dryly.

'Take the Syrians away for the present, Captain,' he said. 'I would talk with this Greek.' He waited until the guards and the Syrians had left the room.

'Are you badly hurt, Demetrius?' asked Paulus, kindly.

'No, sir.' Demetrius was becoming aware that the room was slowly revolving and growing dark. The Legate's ruddy face was blurred. He heard Paulus bark an order and felt the edge of a chair pushed up behind him. He slumped down in it weakly. A sentry handed him a glass of wine. He gulped it. Presently the vertigo cleared. 'I am sorry, sir,' he said.

'How do you happen to be here, Demetrius?' inquired Paulus. 'But no—that can wait. Where is your master?'

Demetrius told him.

'Here?—in Capernaum!' exclaimed Paulus. 'And whatever brings the excellent Tribune Marcellus to this sadly pious city?'

'My master has taken a fancy to Galilean homespun, sir. He has been touring about, looking for—such things.'

Paulus frowned darkly and stared into Demetrius' face.

'Is he well—in his head, I mean?'

'Oh, yes, sir,' said Demetrius, 'quite so, sir.'

'There was a rumor—' Paulus did not finish the sentence, but it was evident that he expected a rejoinder. Demetrius, unaccustomed to sitting in the presence of his betters, came unsteadily to his feet.

'The Tribune was ill, sir, for several months. He was deeply depressed. He went to Athens—and recovered.'

'What was he so depressed about, Demetrius?' asked Paulus; and when the reply was not immediately forthcoming, he added, 'Do I know?'

'Yes, sir,' said Demetrius.

'Something cracked—when he put on that Robe—at the Procurator's banquet.'

'Yes, sir. It did something to him.'

'I remember. It affected him strangely.' Paulus shook himself loose from an unpleasant recollection. 'Now—for your case. Why are you here?'

Demetrius explained in a few words, and when Paulus inquired about the fight, he replied that he had wanted water and the Syrian wouldn't give it to him.

'Bring Captain Namius in!' commanded Paulus. A sentry went out and returned almost immediately with the guards and the Syrians. The examination proceeded swiftly. Namius gave an account of the duel in the corridor.

'We stopped it,' he concluded, 'when this Syrian picked up a shard of the broken water-jar and threw it at the Greek.'

'Take him out and give him thirty-nine lashes with a bull-whip!' shouted Paulus. 'Lock the other pig up—and don't try to fatten him. That will be all, Captain.'

'And the Greek, sir?' asked Namius.

'Put him to bed, and have the physician attend to his cuts.'

Namius gave an order. The guards made off with the Syrians.

'Shall I go now, sir?' asked Demetrius.

'Yes—with the Captain. No—wait. You may go, Namius. I shall summon you.' Paulus watched the retreating figure of the old guard until he reached the door; then, glancing about the room, he said

quietly, 'You may all go.' He looked up over his shoulder. 'You, too,
Sextus. I want a word alone with Demetrius.'

*   *   *   *   *   *

They had almost nothing to say to each other on the way back to
the inn. Justus, preoccupied and somehow elevated, as if the afternoon
with Bartholomew had reinvigorated his spirit, strode along with confident steps.

As for Marcellus, the old disciple's story had impressed and disturbed him. Had he never known of Jesus until today, and Bartholomew had said, 'I heard this man speak to a storm—and the storm
ceased,' he could have dismissed that statement as utterly preposterous. But the testimony about Jesus' peculiar powers had been cu-
mulative. It had been coming at him from all directions.

Marcellus' footsteps lagged as his thoughts became more involved.
Justus, appreciating his dilemma, gave him an understanding smile,
lengthened his stride, and moved on alone, leaving his bewildered
patron to follow at his leisure.

The trouble was: once you began to concede that there might
be an element of truth in some of these stories, it was unreasonable
to draw an arbitrary line beyond which your credulity would not go.
It was childish to say, 'Yes—I believe Jesus could have done *this*
extraordinary thing, but I don't believe he could have done *that!*'

Some of the stories permitted a common-sense explanation. Take
Hariph's naïve account of the wedding-feast, for example. That
wasn't hard to see through. The porous water-jars had previously held
wine. Of course you had to concede the astounding effect of Jesus'
personality on the wedding-guests who loved, admired, and trusted
him. Not everybody could have made that water taste like wine. You
were willing to grant that. Mean and frugal fare could be made
pleasantly palatable when shared with a well-loved friend. If the water-
into-wine episode had been the only example of Jesus' inexplicable
power, it would present no problem at all. But there was Miriam's
sudden realization that she possessed an inspired voice; had made
this amazing discovery on the same day that the other thing had
happened in the home of Hariph. If you consented to Miriam's story
—and its truth was self-evident—you might as well accept Hariph's.
And there was the strange feeding of the five thousand. You could
explain that without difficulty. Under Jesus' persuasive words about
human brotherhood, they had shared their food. You had to concede
nothing here but the tremendous strength of Jesus' personality, which
you were glad enough to do because you believed in it yourself. De-
mosthenes had wrought wonders with his impassioned appeals to the
Greeks. Such infusions of courage and honesty required no miracle.

But there was little Jonathan. The whole town of Sepphoris knew
that Jonathan had been born a cripple. Of course you could main-

tain that Jesus could have manipulated that crooked little foot and reduced its dislocation; and if that were the only story of Jesus' surprising deeds, your explanation might suffice. To be sure, that leaves the entire population of Sepphoris believing something that wasn't true; but even that was possible. There was no limit to the credulity of unsophisticated people. Indeed, they rather liked to believe in the uncanny.

There was Lydia, healed of a long-time disease by touching Jesus' Robe. Well—you couldn't say that was impossible in the face of your own experience. You had impulsively told Justus that you believed it, and Justus felt that you were ready to hear about the storm. If you believed that Jesus' supernormal power could heal the physical and mental sickness of those who merely touched his Robe, by what reasoning do you disbelieve that he could still a storm? Once you impute to him supernormal power, what kind of impertinence consents to your drawing up an itemized list of the peculiar things he can and cannot do? Yet this storm story was too, too much! Here you have no human multitude yielding to the entreating voice. This is an inanimate, insensible tempest! No human being—however persuasive—could still a storm! Concede Jesus *that* power, and you admit that he was *divine!*

'I have taken the liberty of asking Shalum to bake us a fish,' announced Justus, as Marcellus slowly sauntered toward the tent. 'We will have supper at the inn. It will be a relief from my poor cooking.'

'Very well,' agreed Marcellus, absently. 'Haven't seen anything of Demetrius?'

'No—and I inquired at the inn.'

'I had almost forgotten about the poor fellow,' confessed Marcellus. 'There has been much to think about, this afternoon.'

'If Demetrius has been arrested, he will give an account of himself,' said Justus, reassuringly. 'You will learn his whereabouts promptly, I think. They will surrender him—for a price—no matter what the indictment is. Valuable slaves don't stay long in jail. Shall we go to supper now, sir?'

The dining-hall had accommodations for only a score of guests, but it was tastefully appointed. Because the lighting facilities in small town hostelries were not good, travelers dined early. The three dignified Pharisees, whose commodious tent had been pitched in the sycamore grove during the afternoon, occupied a table in the center of the room. Two centurions from the fort were enjoying their wine at a table by a western window while they waited to be served. Shalum—grizzled, bow-legged, obsequious—led the way to a corner table, bowing deeply when Justus introduced his friend.

'Is he a Christian?' asked Marcellus, as Shalum waddled away.

Justus blinked with surprise, and Marcellus grinned.

'Yes,' said Justus, in a barely audible tone that strongly counseled caution.

'You didn't think I knew that word; did you?' murmured Marcellus.

Justus did not reply; sat with arms folded, staring out into the garden.

'Demetrius picked it up in Joppa,' explained Marcellus, quietly.

'We must be careful,' admonished Justus. 'Pharisees have small hearts, but big ears.'

'Is that a saying?' Marcellus chuckled.

'Yes—but not a loud saying,' warned Justus, breaking one of the small brown loaves. He raised his voice a little and said, casually, 'Shalum bakes good bread. Have some.'

'You come here frequently?'

'This is the first time for a year and a half,' confided Justus. 'Last time I was in this room, it was full. Shalum gave a dinner for Jesus. All of the disciples and a few others were here; and there must have been a hundred outside. Shalum fed them too.'

'Nothing secret about it then.'

'No—not then. The priests were already plotting how they might destroy his influence with the people, but they were not yet openly hostile.'

'That's strange,' said Marcellus. 'When Jesus was alive and an active menace to the priests' business, no effort was made to keep his doings a secret. Now that he is dead and gone—you must talk about him in whispers.'

Justus looked Marcellus squarely in the eyes—and smiled. He seemed about to make some rejoinder, but refrained. An old servitor came with their supper; the baked fish on a large platter, lentils in cream, stewed figs, and a pitcher of wine. It was an attractive meal and they were hungry.

'Did you sit close to Jesus at that dinner?' asked Marcellus, after some moments devoted to their food.

'No—I sat with Matthias, over yonder by the door.'

'Where did Jesus sit?' inquired Marcellus.

'There,' nodded Justus, 'where you're sitting.'

Marcellus started.

'No one should ever sit here!' he declared.

Justus' eyes mellowed, and he approved Marcellus' sentiment with a comradely smile.

'You talk like a Christian yourself, my friend,' he murmured; adding, after a moment, 'Did you enjoy Bartholomew's story?'

'It wasn't meant to be enjoyed!' retorted Marcellus. 'I confess I'm thoroughly bewildered by it. Bartholomew is a fine old man. I'm convinced that he believes his story true.'

'But you don't believe it,' said Justus.

'Bartholomew made one statement, Justus, that may throw a little light on the matter. Do you remember his saying that he felt at peace, that he felt calmed, when Jesus spoke to the storm? Maybe that's where the storm was stilled, the storm in these men's minds! Jesus spoke to their fears, and they were reassured.'

'Does that explanation content you?' asked Justus, soberly.

'Of course not!' admitted Marcellus. 'But—see here, Justus! You can't have Jesus stopping a storm!'

'Why not?' asked Justus, gently.

'Why not! Don't you realize that he has to be superhuman to do that? Can't you see that such an act makes him *a god?*'

'Well—and if it does—'

'Then you're left with a lot more explaining to do. Suppose you say that Jesus is divine; a god! Would he permit himself to be placed under arrest, and dragged about in the night from one court to another, whipped and reviled? Would he—this god!—consent to be put to death on a cross? A god, indeed! Crucified—dead—and buried!'

Justus sat for a moment, saying nothing, staring steadily into Marcellus' troubled eyes. Then he leaned far forward, grasped his sleeve, and drew him close. He whispered something into Marcellus' ear.

'No, Justus!' declared Marcellus, gruffly. 'I'm not a fool! I don't believe that—and neither do you!'

'But—*I saw him!*' persisted Justus, unruffled.

Marcellus swallowed convulsively, and shook his head.

'Why do you want to say a thing like that to me?' he demanded, testily. 'I happen to know it isn't true! You might make some people believe it—but not me! I hadn't intended to tell you this painful thing, Justus, but—*I saw him die!* I saw a lance thrust deep into his heart! I saw them take his limp body down—dead as ever a dead man was!'

'Everybody knows that,' agreed Justus, calmly. 'He was put to death and laid away in a tomb. And on the morning of the third day, he came alive, and was seen walking about in the garden.'

'You're mad, Justus! Such things don't happen!'

'Careful!' warned Justus. 'We mustn't be overheard.'

Pushing his plate away, Marcellus folded his arms on the table. His hands were trembling.

'If you think Jesus is alive,' he muttered, 'where is he?'

Justus shook his head, made a hopeless little gesture with both hands, and drew a long sigh.

'I don't know,' he said, dreamily, 'but I do know he is alive.' After a quiet moment, Justus brightened a little. 'I am always looking for him,' he went on. 'Every time a door opens. At every turn of the road. At every street-corner. At every hillcrest.'

Marcellus' eyes had widened, and he nodded understandingly.

'I knew you were always expecting to meet someone,' he said. 'If you persist in that habit, you'll lose your mind.' Neither man spoke for some moments. Marcellus looked toward the door. 'Do you mean to say,' he asked cautiously, 'that you wouldn't be surprised if Jesus came in here now—and asked Shalum to serve him his supper?'

Justus repressed a smile at the sight of Marcellus' almost boyish expression of complete bafflement.

'No,' he replied, confidently. 'I shouldn't be surprised, at all. I confess I was badly shaken the first time I saw him. As you say, such things don't happen. They're quite impossible. Had I been alone, I should have doubted my senses—and my sanity, too.'

'Where was this?' demanded Marcellus, as seriously as if he expected to believe the story.

'At Benyosef's house; quite a little company of us; ten days after Jesus had been put to death. We had had a simple supper together. The sun had set, but the lamps had not yet been lighted. There had been much talk about Jesus' reappearance. Several of the disciples claimed to have seen him. I, for one, didn't believe it; though I kept still. There had been a lot of confusing reports. On the morning of the third day, some women had gone to the sepulcher and found it empty. One of them said she had seen Jesus, walking in the garden; said he had spoken to her.'

'Hysterical, I dare say,' put in Marcellus.

'That's what I made of it,' admitted Justus. 'And then there was a story that two men had seen him on the highway and asked him to have supper with them at an inn.'

'Reliable people?'

'I didn't know them. One was a man named Cleopas, a cousin of Alphaeus. I never heard the other man's name.'

'Sounds like poor testimony.'

'It occurred that way to me,' said Justus. 'Several of the disciples declared he had come into the room where they were sitting, that same night. But—they were terribly wrought up, and I thought they might have imagined seeing him, what with so many strange reports flying about—'

'Naturally!' agreed Marcellus. 'Once the stories started, the hallucinations multiplied. Well—go on. You were at Benyosef's house—'

'John had been telling how he looked and what he said—'

'He's that dreamy young fellow, eh?'

'Yes—that's the one,' Justus went on, undisturbed by the implications of Marcellus' query. 'And when John had finished his story, Thomas stood up and spoke his mind—and my mind, too. "I don't believe a word of it!" he shouted. "And I don't intend to believe it until I have seen him with my own eyes—and touched his wounds with my hands!"'

'He was a bold fellow,' remarked Marcellus. 'Was John offended?'

'I don't know,' said Justus, absently. 'He didn't have much time to be offended. Jesus was standing there—at Thomas' elbow.'

'No—Justus!'

'Yes—with the same compassionate smile we all knew so well.'

'A specter?'

'Not at all! He was a little thinner. You could see the effects of the bad treatment he had suffered. There were long scratches on his forehead. He held his hands out to Thomas—'

'Did you all gather about him?' asked Marcellus, with a dry throat.

'No—I think we were stunned. I'm sure I was. I couldn't have moved if I had tried. There was complete silence. Jesus stood there, holding out his hands and smiling into Thomas' eyes. You could see the deep wounds in his palms. "Touch them," he said, gently. This was too much for Thomas. He covered his face with his hands and cried like a child.'

The dining-room had cleared. Twilight was settling. Shalum came over to inquire if there was anything else he could do for them. Marcellus glanced up bewilderedly at this summons back to reality.

'I have been telling my friend some things about Jesus,' said Justus.

'Yes, yes,' nodded Shalum. 'Once, when he honored my poor house, he was seated there, sir, where you are sitting.'

'Did he rise and speak—at the dinner?' asked Marcellus.

'He did not rise to speak,' remembered Justus.

'He told a story,' said Shalum. 'It seems someone had asked him to explain what was meant by "my neighbor" as it is written in our law. And Jesus told a fable about a man who was traveling from Jerusalem to Jericho—a dangerous road—and beset by Bedouins who stripped, robbed, and wounded him, leaving him half-dead. A priest came along and saw him, but passed on. A Levite, too, paused—but went his way. Then a Samaritan came—we do not care much for Samaritans up here, sir—and tied up the man's wounds—and took him to an inn. "Which of these men," he asked, "was a neighbor to him who fell among thieves?" '

'That was easily answered, I think,' observed Marcellus. 'Had I been here, I should have asked another question. I am told that Jesus did not believe in fighting—regardless of the circumstances. Now, if the brave Samaritan had arrived while the Bedouins were beating the life out of this unfortunate fellow, what was he supposed to do; join in the defense, or wait until the robbers had completed their work—and fled?'

Shalum and Justus exchanged looks of inquiry, each inviting the other to reply.

'Jesus was interested in binding up wounds,' said Justus, solemnly; 'not in inflicting them.'

'Does that answer your question, sir?' inquired Shalum.

'No,' said Marcellus. 'Perhaps we should go, Justus. It is growing dark.' They rose. 'The fish was good, Shalum. Let us have another for breakfast.'

Taking up the little lantern that Shalum had provided, Justus led the way across the well-kept grounds to the tent where he lighted their larger one and hung it to the center pole. Marcellus unlaced his sandal-thongs, took off his belt, and lounged on his cot, his eyes following Justus as he made his bed.

'And then what happened,' asked Marcellus, 'after Thomas looked at the wounds?'

'Benyosef filled a supper-plate, and offered it to Jesus,' said Justus, sitting down on the edge of his cot. 'There was a piece of broiled fish, a small loaf, and some honey in the comb. And Jesus took it—and ate.'

'Not just a spirit then,' commented Marcellus.

'I don't know,' mumbled Justus, uncertainly. 'He ate it—or some of it. The day was fading fast. Philip suggested that the lamps be lighted. Andrew, who was near the door to an adjoining room, went out and returned with a taper. Old Benyosef held up a lamp and Andrew lighted it. Jesus was not there.'

'Vanished?' Marcellus sat up.

'I don't know. It was getting dark in there. He might have gone out through the door. But nobody heard it open or close.'

'Had he come in through the door?'

'I don't know. I didn't hear it. The first I knew, he was standing there beside Thomas. And then—when the lamp was lighted—he wasn't there.'

'What do you suppose became of him?'

'I don't know.' Justus shook his head.

There was a long silence.

'Ever see him again?' asked Marcellus.

Justus nodded.

'Once more,' he said, 'about a month afterward. But in the meantime, he was seen up here in Galilee. A very unfortunate thing happened on the night Jesus was tried. When they had him before old Annas, Simon was waiting in the courtyard where the legionaries had built a fire. A servant-girl said to Simon, "Aren't you a friend of this Galilean?" And Simon said, "No—I don't know him." '

'But I thought Simon was a leader among the disciples,' remarked Marcellus.

'That's what made it so bad,' sighed Justus. 'Ordinarily, Simon is a bold fellow, with plenty of courage. But he certainly did himself no credit that night. He followed along, at a distance, when they took Jesus to the Insula, and waited, across the street, while the trial was held. I don't know where he went after the procession started out toward the place of execution, or where he spent the night and the next day. I heard him confess it all. He was sick with remorse, and hurried back home.'

'So—Simon wasn't present on that first occasion when the disciples thought they saw Jesus.'

'No—but Jesus told them to be sure and tell Simon.'

'Did Jesus know that Simon had denied his friendship?'

'Oh, yes—he knew. You see that's why he was so anxious to have Simon know that everything was all right again. Well—the next morning, the Zebedee brothers and Thomas decided to take old Bartholomew home. He had been sick. They put him on a donkey and set out for Galilee where they found Peter, restless and heartsore, and told him what had happened. He was for rushing back to Jerusalem, but they counseled him to wait; for the news of Jesus' return was being noised about, and the priests were asking questions. And Benyosef's shop was being watched. So—that night, they all went fishing. In the early morning, at sunrise, they left off and sailed toward the east shore. Bartholomew said that when they were within about two hundred cubits of the beach—chilled and drowsy from their long night on the water—they were suddenly roused by a loud shout and a splash. Simon had jumped overboard and was swimming. They all leaped up to see what had come over Simon. And they saw Jesus standing at the water's edge, waiting. It was a very tender meeting, he said, for Simon had been quite broken-hearted.'

'And then'—Marcellus' voice was impatient—'did he vanish—as before?'

'Not at once. They broiled fish for breakfast on the beach. He sat and talked with them for above an hour, showing special attention to Simon.'

'What did he talk about?'

'Their future duties,' replied Justus, 'to remember and tell the things he had taught. He would come back, he said, though he could not tell them the day or the hour. They were to be on the alert for his coming. After they had eaten, someone suggested that they return to Capernaum. They had beached the boat, and all hands—except Jesus—fell to work, pushing off into the water. Bartholomew was up in the bow, rigging a sail. The others scrambled over the side and shipped the oars. When they looked about for Jesus, he was nowhere to be seen.'

'But he appeared again—another time?'

'The last time he was seen,' said Justus, 'I was present. It was on a hill top in Judea, a few miles north of Jerusalem. Perhaps I should tell you that the disciples and other friends of Jesus were closely watched, through those days. Such meetings as we had were late in the night and held in obscure places. In Jerusalem, the Temple people had the legionaries of the Insula patrolling the streets in search of us. Up here in Galilee, Herod Antipas and Julian the Legate had threatened death to anyone who so much as spoke Jesus' name.'

'They too believed that he had returned to life?' inquired Marcellus.

'Perhaps not. I don't know. But they knew they had failed to dispose of him. They thought the people would soon forget and settle down to their old ways; but it soon appeared that Jesus had set some forces in motion—'

'I don't understand,' broke in Marcellus. 'What forces?'

'Well—for one thing—the Temple revenues were falling off. Hundreds of people, accustomed to paying tithes, stayed away from the synagogues whose priests had persecuted Jesus. There was no violence; but in the market-places throughout all Judea, Samaria and Galilee, merchants who had thought to win favor with the authorities by denouncing Jesus found that their business was failing. The Christians were patronizing one another. It was apparent that they were in collusion and had a secret understanding. An edict was published prohibiting any assembly of Jews' adherents. We agreed among ourselves to hold no more meetings until such time as it might be more prudent.'

'How many Christians were there in Jerusalem, at that time?' asked Marcellus. 'A score, perhaps?'

'About five hundred that had declared themselves. One afternoon, about five weeks after the crucifixion, Alphaeus came to my house saying that Simon had called a meeting. A week hence, we were to assemble shortly after sunrise on a hill, quite off the highway, where we had often spent a day of rest when Jesus was with us. Knowing it was dangerous to be seen on the roads in company with others of our belief, we journeyed singly. It was a beautiful morning. As I came to the well-remembered footpath that led across the fields toward the hills, I saw—in the early dawn-light—several men preceding me; though I could identify none but Simon, who is a tall man. As the grade grew steeper, I overtook old Bartholomew leaning on his staff, already tired and laboring for breath.'

'He had walked all that way from Capernaum?' asked Marcellus.

'And had spent the whole week at it,' said Justus. 'But it seemed that the hill would be too much for him. I counseled him not to try; that his heart might fail him; but he wouldn't listen. So I gave him an arm and we trudged along slowly up the winding path that became more difficult with every turn. Occasionally we had glimpses of the others, widely separated, as they climbed the rugged grade. We were about halfway up when Bartholomew stopped, pointed with his staff, and hoarsely shouted, "Look you! On the rock!" I looked up—and there he was! He was wearing a white robe. The sunshine made it appear dazzling. He was standing on the big white rock—at the summit—waiting.'

'Were you amazed?'

'No—not amazed; but eager to press on. Bartholomew urged me to leave him. He would make it alone, he said. But the good old man was half-dead with weariness, so I supported him the rest of the way. When we came out at length on the little plateau in a shady grove, we saw him. Jesus was standing, with both arms outstretched in a gesture of blessing. The disciples were kneeling about his feet. Simon, with his great hands covering his face, had bowed over until his head nearly touched the ground. Poor old Bartholomew, much moved and thoroughly spent, couldn't take another step. He fell to his knees. So did I, though we were at least a hundred cubits from the others. We bowed our heads.' Justus' voice broke, and for a moment he was overcome with emotion. Marcellus waited silently for him to regain his self-control.

'After a while,' continued Justus, thickly, 'we heard the murmuring of voices. We raised our eyes. He was gone.'

'Where, Justus? Where do you think he went?' asked Marcellus, huskily.

'I don't know, my friend. I only know that he is alive—and I am always expecting to see him. Sometimes I feel aware of him, as if he were close by.' Justus smiled faintly, his eyes wet with tears. 'It keeps you honest,' he went on. 'You have no temptation to cheat anyone, or lie to anyone, or hurt anyone—when, for all you know, Jesus is standing beside you.'

'I'm afraid I should feel very uncomfortable,' remarked Marcellus, 'being perpetually watched by some invisible presence.'

'Not if that presence helped you defend yourself against yourself, Marcellus. It is a great satisfaction to have someone standing by—to keep you at your best.' Justus suddenly came to his feet, and went to the door of the tent. A lantern was bobbing through the trees.

'Someone coming?' inquired Marcellus, sitting up.

'A legionary,' muttered Justus.

'News of Demetrius, perhaps.' Marcellus joined Justus at the tent-door. A tall legionary stood before them.

'I bear a message,' he announced, 'from Legate Paulus to Tribune Marcellus Lucan Gallio.'

'*Tribune!*' murmured Justus—in an agitated voice.

'The Legate presents his compliments,' continued the legionary, in formal tones, 'and desires his excellent friend, Tribune Marcellus, to be his guest tonight at the fort. If it is your wish, you may accompany me, sir, and I shall light your way.'

'Very good,' said Marcellus. 'I shall be ready in a moment. Tarry for me at the gate.'

The legionary brought up his spear in a salute and marched away.

'Apparently Demetrius is safe!' exclaimed Marcellus, brightly.

'And I have betrayed my people!' moaned Justus, sinking down on his cot. 'I have delivered my friends into the hands of their enemies!'

'No—Justus—no!' Marcellus laid a hand on his shoulder. 'All this may seem disquieting to you, but I assure you I am not a spy! It is possible I may befriend you and your people. Wait for me here. I shall return by midday tomorrow.'

Justus made no response; sat dejectedly, with his face in his hands, until Marcellus' footsteps faded away. It was a long night of agony and remorse. When the first pale blue light appeared, the heavyhearted Galilean gathered up his few belongings; made his way to the silent street, and trudged along, past the old fort, to the plaza. For a long time, he sat on the marble steps of the synagogue, and when the sun had risen he proceeded to the little house where he had left Jonathan.

Thomas' mother was in the kitchen, preparing breakfast.

'You are early,' she said. 'I was not expecting you so soon. I hope all is well with you,' she added, searching his troubled face.

'I wish to be on the road as soon as may be,' he replied.

'But where is your young Roman—and your little pack-train?'

'They are remaining here,' said Justus. 'Jonathan and I are going home.'

Chapter XVIII

PAULUS had been in command of the fort at Capernaum only a week, but he already knew he wasn't going to like it here.

For a dozen years he had been hoping to get out of Minoa. It was a disgrace to be stationed there, and the Empire meant you to realize that an appointment to this fort was a degradation.

The buildings were ugly and shabby, the equipment bad, the climate abominable. No provision had ever been made for an adequate water-supply. On the sun-blistered grounds there wasn't a tree, a flower, or a blade of grass; not even a weed. The air was always foul with yellow, abrasive dust. You couldn't keep clean if you wanted to, and after a few months at Minoa you didn't care.

The garrison was lazy, surly, dirty, and tough. With little to do, except occasional brief and savage raids on the Bedouins, discipline was loose and erratic. There were no decent diversions; no entertainment. When you couldn't bear the boredom and discomfort another minute, you went down to Gaza and got drunk, and were lucky if you didn't get into a bloody brawl.

As for that vicious old city, was not Gaza known throughout the world for the squalor of its stinking kennels where the elderly riff-raff of a half-dozen quarrelsome races screamed imprecations, and the younger scum swapped unpleasant maladies, and the hapless stranger was stripped and robbed in broad daylight? Gaza had her little imperfections; there was no doubt about that. But she had docks and wharves and a spacious harbor. Little costal ships tied up to her piers; bigger ships lay at anchor in her bay. You strolled down to watch them come and go, and felt you were still in contact with the outside world. Sometimes ships' officers would come out to the fort for a roistering evening; sometimes military men you had known in Rome would visit you while their vessel took on cargo.

Paulus' unexpected appointment to Capernaum had been received with hilarious joy. He had never been there, but he had heard something about its quiet charm. Old Julian had been envied his post.

For one thing—the fort was within a half-hour's ride of Tiberias, that ostentatious seat of the enormously wealthy sycophant, Herod Antipas. Paulus had no notion he was going to like this toad: he had nothing but contempt for these provincial lickspittles who would sell their own sisters for a smile from some influential Roman; but Herod frequently entertained interesting guests who, though they might despise him, must make a show of honoring his position as Tetrarch of Galilee and Peraea.

And Capernaum, everyone said, was beautiful; ringed by green hills, with snow-capped mountains in the distance. There was a lovely inland sea. The people were docile. They were reputed to be melancholy over the execution of their Jesus, but they were not violently resentful. Doubtless that problem would solve itself if you gave it time. Old Julian's tactics—listening at the keyholes of cottages for revolutionary talk, the posting of harsh edicts, floggings and imprisonments—what did they accomplish but to band these simple, harmless people together for mutual sympathy? Of course, if the foolhardy fishermen persisted in making a nuisance of their cult, you would have to punish them, or get yourself into trouble with Herod. That's what you would be there for—to keep the peace.

Now that you were here, you had much more peace than you had bargained for. Had the gods ever ordained such quiet nights? Paulus had not fully appreciated this oppressive silence for the first day or two. There was the novelty of settling into his immeasurably better quarters. He proudly inspected the trim pleasure-craft that Herod had placed at the disposal of the Legate. He luxuriated in the well-equipped baths, thinking kindly of old Julian whom he had never had any use for.

The fort buzzed with activity. A fairly large contingent from Minoa had accompanied Paulus. There had been the usual festivities at the Insula in Jerusalem during Passover Week—though Paulus had been moody and taciturn, anxious to have it over with, and move on. His retinue had come along to Capernaum, for defense on the journey as well as to dignify his inauguration. A generous dinner had been served after the ceremonies to which Herod—represented by a deputy —had contributed lavish supplies of potent wine. It was a noisy night. Heads had been cracked, noses flattened, more urgent arguments had been settled with knives. Paulus had filled the courtrooms with battered celebrants; had crowded the guardhouse; had stormed and shouted oaths new to the local legionaries; and, well pleased with his first day's duties, had gone to bed tight as a drum.

Next day, the Minoa contingent had left for home—all but Sextus. At the last minute, Paulus—with a premonition of loneliness—had told Sextus to remain, at least for a time. And when the last of them had disappeared, a strange quietness settled over the fort. That night, after Sextus had ambled off early to bed, Paulus sat by his window watching the moonlight on the lake. Except for Sextus' snoring, the silence was profound. Perhaps it had been a mistake to retain Sextus. He wasn't very good company, after all.

What did one do for diversion in Capernaum? This little town was sound asleep. The Herod family was away. Tiberias was dead as a doornail. If this was a sample of life at Capernaum, you had been better off at Minoa.

The days trudged along, scraping their sandal-heels; sitting down, now and then, for a couple of hours, while Time remained standing. Paulus, strolling in the courtyard, paused before the sundial, read its laconic warning,'Tempus fugit,' and sourly remarked to Sextus, 'It's apparent that old Virgil never visited Capernaum.'

After a week, Paulus was so restless that he even thought of contriving some errand to Jerusalem, though his recent visit there had been lacking in interest. Perhaps that was because the insufferable young Quintus, who had been sent by the Crown to reshuffle the Palestinian commands, was too, too much in evidence. Paulus, who was a good hater, had never despised anybody so quickly, so earnestly. Quintus was a vain, overbearing, patronizing, strutting peacock; he was an insolent, ill-mannered puppy; he was a pompous ass! In short, Paulus didn't like him at all. But Quintus would have sailed for home by now. Maybe Quintus was what had ailed Jerusalem, this time.

* * * * * *

It was late afternoon. The sun was setting. Paulus and Sextus had been apathetically shaking the old leather dice-cup on the long table in the courtroom. Sextus yawned cavernously and wiped his eyes.

'If it's bedtime,' drawled Paulus, 'perhaps we'd better light the lamps.' He clapped his hands. A guard scurried up. Paulus pointed to the lamps. The guard saluted and made haste to obey. 'Nine,' mumbled the Legate, handing the dice-cup to his drowsy friend.

At this juncture, old Namius had come in with three disheveled slaves. Somewhere, Paulus felt, he had seen that tall Greek. Sextus jogged his memory. Ah—Demetrius! He had always liked Demetrius, in spite of his cool superiority. Demetrius was a haughty fellow, but you had respect for him. Paulus suddenly recalled having seen an announcement, posted at the Insula in Jerusalem, offering a reward for the capture of a Greek slave belonging to Tribune Marcellus Gallio. The bulletin said that the Greek had assaulted a Roman citizen in Athens, and was thought to be in hiding in Jerusalem. So—here he was. Somebody had gathered him in. But no—a brief examination revealed that Demetrius had been arrested on suspicion. He had been loitering; he was shabby; he had money. In prison he had fought the rascally Syrians who denied him water. So much for that. Then Paulus had wanted to know about Marcellus, who had been reported crazy— or the next thing to it—and was delighted to learn that his friend was in the neighborhood.

But before he could release Demetrius, he must learn something about this charge against him. If it were true that he had struck a Roman, and run away, you couldn't dismiss him so easily. Paulus put them all out, including Sextus, who didn't like it.

'Demetrius'—Paulus frowned judiciously—'what have you to say about this report that you are a fugitive; that you struck a Roman citizen in Athens? That is very serious, you know!'

'It is true, sir,' replied Demetrius, without hesitation. 'I found it necessary to punish Tribune Quintus severely.'

'Quintus!' shouted the Legate. 'You mean to say you struck Quintus?' He leaned forward over the desk, eyes beaming. 'Tell me all about it!'

'Well, sir—the Tribune came to the Inn of Eupolis with a message for my master. While waiting for the reply, he made himself grossly offensive to the daughter of the innkeeper. They are a highly respected family, sir, and the young woman was not accustomed to being treated like a common trollop. Her father was present, but feared to intervene lest they all be thrown into prison.'

'So—you came to the damsel's rescue, eh?'

'Yes, sir.'

'Don't you know you can be put to death for so much as touching a Roman Tribune?' demanded Paulus, sternly; and when Demetrius had slowly and remorsefully nodded his head, the Legate's frown relaxed, and he asked, in a confidential tone, 'What did you do to him?'

'I struck him in the face with my fist, sir,' confessed Demetrius. 'And—once I had struck him—I knew I had committed a crime punishable by death, and couldn't make my position any worse, so—'

'So—you hit him again, I think,' surmised Paulus, with mounting interest. 'Did he fight back?'

'No, sir. The Tribune was not expecting that first blow, and was unprepared for the next one.'

'In the face?' Paulus' eyes were wide and bright.

'Many times, sir,' admitted Demetrius.

'Knock him down?'

'Oh, yes, sir; and held him up by his helmet-strap, and beat his eyes shut. I was very angry, sir.'

'Yes—I can see that you were.' Paulus put both hands over his suddenly puffed cheeks and stifled something like a hiccough. 'And then you ran off?'

'Without a moment's delay, sir. There was a ship sailing. The Captain befriended me. Tribune Quintus was on board, and would have had me apprehended, but the Captain let me escape in the small boat at Gaza. From there I walked to Jerusalem.'

'Didn't the Captain know he could be punished for that?' growled Paulus. 'What was his name?'

'I cannot remember, sir,' regretted Demetrius, after some hesitation.

'That is undoubtedly a lie,' said Paulus, 'but you are to be commended for your loyalty. So, then, you went to Jerusalem. Why?'

'My master expected to come shortly.'

'What did you do there?'

Demetrius told him of the weaver's shop. Paulus grew interested again.

'I understand there is a weaver's shop where the leaders of the Jesus-people meet. What was the name of your weaver?'

'Benyosef, sir.'

'That was the name! And how did you happen to be in that company, Demetrius? Are you, perhaps, one of these—these—what do they call them—Christians?'

'Yes, sir,' confessed Demetrius, tardily. 'Not a very good one; but I believe as they do.'

'You can't!' shouted Paulus. 'You have a good mind! You don't mean to tell me that you believe all this nonsense—about Jesus returning to life, and being seen on various occasions!'

'Yes, sir,' said Demetrius. 'I am sure that is true.'

'But—see here!' Paulus stood up. 'You were out there, that day, and saw him die!'

'Yes, sir. I am sure he died; and I am sure he is alive.'

'Have you seen him?' Paulus' voice was unsteady.

Demetrius shook his head and the Legate grinned.

'I hadn't thought,' he said, dryly, 'that you could be taken in by such a story. Men who die do not return. Only fools think so!' Paulus sat down again, relaxing in his chair. 'But you are not a fool. What makes you believe that?'

'I heard the story from a man who did see him; a man of sound mind; a man who does not lie.' Demetrius broke off, though it was evident he would have said more.

'Very well; go on!' commanded the Legate.

'It did not surprise me very much,' continued Demetrius. 'There never was a person like that before. Surely—you, sir, must have noticed that. He had something nobody else ever had! I don't believe he was an ordinary man, sir.'

'How do you mean—not ordinary? Are you trying to say that you think he was something else than a man? You don't think he was a god?'

'Yes, sir,' said Demetrius, firmly. 'I think he was—and is—a god!'

'Nonsense! Don't you know we are locking up people for saying things like that about this dead Galilean?' Paulus rose impetuously and paced back and forth behind the long table. 'I mean to let you go—for your master's sake; but'—he stopped suddenly and shook a warning finger—'you are to clear out of Galilee—and there's to be no more talk about this Jesus. And if you ever tell anyone that you told me about your assault on Quintus—and I learn of it—I'll have you flogged! Do you understand? I'll have you stripped and lashed with a bull-whip!'

'Thank you, sir,' said Demetrius, gratefully. 'I am very sorry that I struck him.'

'Then you don't deserve your freedom,' growled Paulus. 'That's why I am turning you loose—and now you're sorry you did it. And you believe that dead men come to life. You're crazy!' He clapped his hands, and a guard stalked in. 'Make this Greek comfortable,' he barked. 'Have the physician attend to his cuts. Give him a good supper and a bed. He is to be released from prison.'

Demetrius wincingly brought his arm up in a salute, and turned to follow.

'One more thing!' rasped Paulus, to the guard. 'When you have finished with the Greek, return here. I want you to carry a message to Shalum's Inn. Make haste!'

* * * * * *

Marcellus was pleased to observe that Paulus' promotion had not altered his manner. The easy informality of their friendship was effortlessly resumed.

A small table had been laid in the Legate's handsomely furnished suite; a silver cake-tray, a bowl of fresh fruit, a tall flagon of wine. Paulus, clean-shaven, wearing an expensive white toga and a red silk bandeau that accented the whiteness of his close-cropped hair, was a distinguished figure. He met his guest in the doorway and embraced him warmly.

'Welcome, good Marcellus!' he exclaimed. 'And welcome to Galilee; though, if you have been touring about up here, you may be better acquainted with this province than I.'

'It is a delight to see you again, Paulus!' rejoined Marcellus. 'All my good wishes for the success and happiness of your new command! It was most generous of you to send for me.'

With his arm around Marcellus' shoulders, Paulus guided his friend to a chair by the table, and sauntered to its mate on the other side.

'Come; sit down.' He filled their goblets. 'Let us drink to this happy meeting. Now you must tell me what brings you into my quiet little Galilee.'

Marcellus smiled, raised the goblet to the level of his eyes, and bowed to his host.

'It would take an hour to explain my errand, Paulus,' he replied, sipping his wine. 'A long story—and a somewhat fantastic one, too. In short, the Emperor ordered me to learn something more about the Galilean whom we put to death.'

'A painful business for you, I think,' frowned Paulus. 'I still reproach myself for placing you in such an unhappy position that night at the Procurator's banquet. I did not see you again, or I should have tried to make amends. If it is not too late to say so I am sorry it happened. I was drunk.'

'We all were,' remembered Marcellus. 'I bore you no ill-will.'

'But it wasn't drunkenness that ailed you, sir, when you groped your way out of that banquet-hall. When you put on the dead man's Robe, something happened to you. Even I, drunk as I was, could see that. By the gods!—I thought you must have sighted a ghost!' Raising his goblet, Paulus drank deeply; then, shrugging his dour mood aside, he brightened. 'But why revive unpleasant memories? You were a long time ill. I heard of it and was sad. But now you are quite recovered. That is well. You are the picture of health, Marcellus. Drink—my friend! You have hardly tasted your wine; and it is good.'

'Native?' Marcellus took another sip.

Paulus grinned; then suddenly stiffened to pantomime an attitude of cool hauteur.

'My eminent patron,' he declaimed, with elaborate mockery, 'my exalted lord, the ineffable Herod Antipas—Tetrarch of Galilee and Peraea, robber of the poor, foot-washer to any titled Roman that comes within reach—he sent the wine. And though Herod himself may be a low form of life, his wine is noble.' Slipping easily out of his august rôle, Paulus added, casually, 'I have had no native wine yet. By the way—the country people have a story that our Jesus once supplied a wedding-party with a rare vintage that he made by doing some incantations over a water-pot. There are innumerable yarns of this order. Perhaps you have heard them.'

Marcellus nodded, but did not share the Legate's cynical amusement.

'Yes,' he said, soberly. 'I have heard them. They are very hard to understand.'

'Understand!' echoed Paulus. 'Don't tell me you have tried to understand them! Have we not plenty of such legends in Rome— tales that no one in his right senses gives a second thought to?'

'Yes—I know, Paulus,' agreed Marcellus, quietly, 'and I should want to be among the last to believe them; but—'

At the significant pause, Paulus stood up, busying himself with refilling their goblets. He offered the silver cake-tray, which Marcellus declined, and sat down again with a little gesture of impatience.

'I hope you aren't going to say that these Galilean stories are credible, Marcellus,' he remarked, coolly.

'This Jesus was a strange man, Paulus.'

'Granted! By no means an ordinary man! He had a peculiar kind of courage, and a sort of majesty—all his own. But I hope you don't believe that he changed water into wine!'

'I do not know, Paulus,' replied Marcellus, slowly. 'I saw a child who had been born with a crippled foot; now as active as any other little boy.'

'How do you know he was born with a crippled foot?' demanded Paulus.

'The whole village knew. There was no reason why they should have invented the story for my benefit. They were suspicious of me. In fact, the boy's grandfather, my guide, was reluctant to talk about it.'

'Well—you can be sure there is some reasonable explanation,' rasped Paulus. 'These people are as superstitious as our Thracian slaves. Why—they even believe that this man came to life—and has been seen!'

Marcellus nodded thoughtfully.

'I heard that story for the first time about an hour ago, Paulus. It is amazing!'

'It is preposterous!' shouted Paulus. 'These fools should have contented themselves with tales of water changed to wine—and the magical healing of the sick.' Paulus drank again, noisily. His ruddy face showed annoyance as he watched Marcellus absently toying with the stem of his goblet, his eyes averted. 'You know well enough that the Galilean was dead!' he stormed, angrily. 'No one can tell you or me that he came to life!' Drawing up the sleeve of his toga, Paulus tapped his muscular forearm with measuring fingers, and shrilled, 'I thrust my spear into his chest that deep!'

Marcellus glanced up, nodded, and dropped his eyes again, without comment. Paulus suddenly leaned forward over the table, and brought his fist down with a thump.

'By the gods! Marcellus'—he shouted—'*you believe it!*'

There was a tense silence for a long moment. Marcellus stirred and slowly raised his eyes, quite unruffled by the Legate's outburst.

'I don't know what to believe, Paulus,' he said, quietly, 'Of course my natural reaction is the same as yours; but—there is a great mystery here, my friend. If this story is a trumped-up lie, the men who have been telling it at the risk of their lives are quite mad; yet they do not talk like madmen. They have nothing to gain—and everything to lose —by reporting that they saw him.'

'Oh—I'll concede that,' declared Paulus, loftily. 'It's no uncommon thing for a fanatic to be reckless with his life; but—look you, Marcellus! —however difficult that is to understand—you can't have a dead man coming back from his grave! Why—a man who could overcome death, could—'

'Exactly!' broke in Marcellus. 'He could do anything! He could defy any power on earth! If he cared to, he might have the whole world for his kingdom!'

Paulus drank greedily, spilling some of it on the table.

'Odd thing to say,' he muttered, thickly. 'There was some talk at his trial—about his kingdom: remember? Pilate asked him—absurdly enough, I thought—if he were a king.' Paulus chuckled mirthlessly.

'He said he was—and it shook Pilate a little, too. Indeed—it stunned everybody, for a minute; just the cool audacity of it. I was talking with Vinitius, that night at the banquet, and he said the Galilean explained that his kingdom was not in the world; but—that doesn't mean anything. Or does it?'

'Well—it certainly wouldn't mean anything if *I* said it,' replied Marcellus. 'But if a man who had been out of this life were able to return from—from wherever he had been—he might conceivably have a kingdom elsewhere.'

'You're talking rubbish, Marcellus,' scoffed Paulus. 'I'll assist you,' he went on, drunkenly. 'You are my guest, and I must be polite. If it's so—that a dead man—with some kind of elsewhere-kingdom—has come back to life:—mind you, now, I know it isn't so—but if it's so—I'd rather it were this Jesus than Quintus or Julian or Pilate—or the half-witted Gaius that old Julia whelped.' He laughed boisterously at his own absurdity. 'Or old Tiberius! By the gods!—when crazy old Tiberius dies, I'll wager he stays dead! By the way—do you mean to go back and tell the old fool this story? He'll believe it, you know, and it will scare the very liver out of him!'

Marcellus grinned tolerantly, reflecting that the Legate—albeit pretty drunk—had said something worth thinking about.

'Good idea, Paulus,' he remarked. 'If we're going to have a king who knows how to outlive all the other kings, it might be a great thing for the world if he were a person of good deeds and not evil ones.'

The Legate's face sobered, and Marcellus, noting his serious interest, enlarged upon his impromptu idea.

'Consider these tales about Jesus, Paulus. He is reputed to have made blind men see: there is no story that he made any man blind. He is said to have changed water into wine; not wine into water. He made a crippled child walk; he never made any child a cripple.'

'Excellent!' applauded Paulus. 'The kings have been destroyers, despoilers. They have made men blind, crippled, broken.' He paused, and went on, muttering half to himself, 'Wouldn't the world be surprised if once it should have a government that came to the rescue of the blind and sick and lame? By the gods!—I wish this absurd tale about the Galilean were true!'

'Do you mean that, Paulus, or are you jesting?' demanded Marcellus, earnestly.

'Well'—compromised the Legate—'I'm as serious as the matter warrants, seeing it hasn't a leg to stand on.' His forehead wrinkled in a judicial frown. 'But—see here, Marcellus, aren't you going in for this Jesus business a little too far for your own good?'

Marcellus made no reply, other than an enigmatic pursing of the lips. Paulus grinned, shrugged, and replenished his goblet. His manner said they would drop that phase of the subject.

'What else do they say about him, up here in the country?' he asked negligently. 'You seem to have been making inquiries.'

'They have a story in Cana,' replied Marcellus, casually, 'about a young woman who discovered she could sing. The people think Jesus was responsible for it.'

'Taught her to sing?'

"No. One day she found that she could sing. They believe he had something to do with it. I heard her, Paulus. There hasn't been anything quite like it—so far as I know.'

'Indeed!' enthused Paulus. 'I must tell the Tetrarch. It's part of my business, you know, to please the old rascal. He may invite her to entertain one of his banquets.'

'No, Paulus, please!' protested Marcellus. 'This girl has been gently bred. Moreover, she is a cripple; can't stand up; never leaves the neighborhood.'

'He gave her a voice, and left her a cripple; eh?' Paulus grinned. 'How do you explain that?'

'I don't explain it; I just report it. But—I sincerely hope you will say nothing about her to Herod. She would feel very much out of place in his palace, if what I have heard about him is correct.'

'If what you've heard is revolting,' commented Paulus, bitterly, 'it's correct. But if you are so concerned about these Christians, it might be to their advantage if one of their daughters sang acceptably for the lecherous old fox.'

'No!' snapped Marcellus, hotly. 'She and her family are friends of mine. I beg of you not to degrade her with an invitation to meet Herod Antipas or any member of his household!'

Paulus agreed that they were a precious lot of scoundrels, including Herod's incorrigible daughter Salome. A dangerous little vixen, he declared, responsible for a couple of assassinations, and notoriously unchaste. He chuckled unpleasantly, and added that she had come by her talents honestly enough, seeing that her father—if he was her father—hadn't even the respect of the Sanhedrin, and her mother was as promiscuous as a cat. He snorted contemptuously, and drank to take the taste of them out of his mouth. Marcellus scowled, but made no comment. Presently he became aware that Paulus was regarding him with a friendly but reproachful inspection.

'I wonder if you realize, Marcellus,' Paulus was saying, 'that your keen concern for these Christians might sometime embarrass you. May I talk to you about that, without giving offense?'

'Why not, Paulus?' replied Marcellus, graciously.

'Why not? Because it may sound impertinent. We are of the same rank. It does not behoove me to give you advice—much less injunctions.'

'Injunctions?' Marcellus' brows lifted a little. 'I'm afraid I don't understand.'

'Let me explain, then. I assume you know what has been happening in Palestine during the past year. For a few weeks, after the execution of the Galilean, his movement appeared to be a closed incident. The leaders of his party scattered, most of them returning to this neighborhood. The influential men of Jerusalem were satisfied. There were sporadic rumors that Jesus had been seen in various places after his death, but nobody with any sense took these tales seriously. It was expected that the whole affair would presently be forgotten.'

'And then it revived,' remarked Marcellus, as Paulus paused to take another drink.

'Revived is not the word. It hadn't died. Undercover groups had been meeting in many cities. For a few months there were very few outward signs of it. The authorities had contempt for it, feeling that it was a thing of no importance, either as to size or quality. Then— one day—it began to dawn on the priests that their synagogues were not being patronized; the tithes were not paid. Then the merchants observed that their business was increasingly bad. In Jericho, more than half of the population now make no secret of their affiliations. In Antioch, the Christians are quite outspoken; adding daily to their numbers. Nor is interest in this party limited to the poor and helpless, as was at first supposed. Nobody knows how many there are in Jerusalem, but the Temple is beside itself with anxiety and anger, prodding the Insula to do something drastic. Old Julian is being harassed by the priests and merchants, who are making it plain that he must act—or resign.'

'What does he think of doing about it?' inquired Marcellus.

'Well'—Paulus flicked his hands in a baffled gesture—'it's obvious that the movement cannot be tolerated. It may look innocuous to a casual visitor like yourself; but, to the solid respectables of Jerusalem, it is treason, mutiny, blasphemy, and a general disintegration of their established ways. Julian doesn't want a bloody riot on his hands, and has been playing for time; but the city fathers are at the end of their patience.'

'But—surely they can't find much fault with the things Jesus taught,' interposed Marcellus. 'He urged kindness, fair dealing, good will. Don't the influential men of Palestine believe in letting the people treat one another decently?'

'That isn't the point, Marcellus, and you know it,' argued Paulus, impatiently. 'These Christians are refusing to do business on the old basis. More and more they are patronizing one another. Why—right here in little Capernaum—if you don't have the outline of a fish scrawled on the door of your shop, it doesn't pay to open up.' He studied his friend's interested face—and grinned. 'I suppose you know what that fish stands for.'

Marcellus nodded—and smiled broadly.

'No—it isn't a bit funny!' warned Paulus, grimly. 'And I must strongly counsel you that the less you see of these Christians, the better it will be for'—he checked himself, and finished lamely in a tone almost inaudible—'for all of us.'

'But—for me—in particular, I think you mean,' said Marcellus.

'Have it your own way.' Paulus waved his arm. 'I'm not having a good time—saying these things to you. But—I don't want to see you get into trouble. And you easily could, you know! When the pressure is put on, it's going to get rough! The fact that you're a Roman Tribune will not count for much—once the stampede begins! We are going to make war on the Christians, Marcellus, no matter who they are! Why don't you clear out before you are apprehended? Take your slave —and go!'

'I do not know where he is,' admitted Marcellus.

'Well—I do,' grinned Paulus. 'He is in bed, somewhere here in the fort.'

'A prisoner?'

'No—but he ought to be.' The Legate laughingly recounted the afternoon's revelations. 'By the way,' he ended, 'did you see him destroy Quintus?'

Marcellus, who had been much amused by the recital, shook his head.

'I saw the Tribune shortly afterward,' he said. 'The work had been well done, I assure you.'

'It gratified me to hear about it,' said Paulus, 'as I have no respect for Quintus and his misfortunes do not annoy me; but'—he grew suddenly serious—'this was no light offense, and may yet have to be settled for. Your Demetrius is free to go, but I hope he will not linger in this country; at least, not in my jurisdiction. Nor you, Marcellus! Consider your predicament: your slave is wanted for assaulting a Tribune; moreover, he is known to have been in close association with the Christian party in Jerusalem. He can be apprehended on either count. Now—it may be assumed that you know all this. In short, you have been harboring a criminal and a Christian; and your own position as a friend of the Christians is of no advantage to you. What do you intend to do about it?'

'I had thought of remaining in Palestine for a few weeks, before proceeding to Rome,' said Marcellus. 'I have no definite plans.'

'Better have some plans!' advised Paulus, sternly. 'Your situation is more hazardous than you think. It will do your pious Galilean friends no good to have you championing their cause. I tell you candidly that they are all in imminent danger of arrest. I advise you to pack your travel equipment early in the morning, go quietly across country to Joppa, and take the first ship that heads for home.'

'Thanks for the counsel, Paulus,' replied Marcellus, noncommittally. 'May I have a word with Demetrius now?'

Paulus frowned darkly and dismissed the request with a gesture of exasperation.

'The fact that your Greek slave is a superior fellow and your friend,' he said, crisply, 'does not alter his status in the opinion of my own retinue. I suggest that you wait until morning to see him.'

'As you like,' said Marcellus, unruffled.

Paulus rose unsteadily.

'Let us retire now,' he said, more cordially, 'and meet for breakfast at sunrise. Then'—he smiled meaningly—'if you will insist upon leaving at once, I shall speed you on your way. I shall do better than that: I shall order a small detachment of legionaries, acquainted with the less traveled roads, to see you safely to Joppa.'

'But I am not going to Joppa, Paulus,' declared Marcellus, firmly. 'I am not leaving Palestine until I have fully satisfied myself about this story of the Galilean's return to life.'

'And how are you to do that?' demanded Paulus. 'By interviewing a few deluded fishermen, perhaps?'

'That's one way of putting it,' rejoined Marcellus, unwilling to take offense. 'I want to talk with some of the leaders.'

'They are not here now,' said Paulus. 'The foremost of them are in Jerusalem.'

'Then I am going to Jerusalem!'

For a moment, Paulus, with tight lips, deliberated a reply. A sardonic grin slowly twisted his mouth.

'If you start tomorrow for Jerusalem,' he predicted ominously, 'you should arrive about the right time to find them all in prison. Then—unless you are more prudent than you appear to be at present—you will get into a lot of trouble.' He clapped his hands for the guard. 'Show the Tribune to his room,' he ordered. Offering his hand, with his accustomed geniality, he smiled and said, 'I hope you rest well. We will see each other in the morning.'

Chapter XIX

THEY entered the city unchallenged two hours before sunset. The sentries at the Damascus Gate did not so much as bother to ask Marcellus his name or what manner of cargo was strapped to the tired little donkeys. It was evident that Jerusalem was not on the alert.

The journey from Capernaum had been made with dispatch, considering the travelers were on foot. By rising before dawn and keeping steadily at it—even through the sultry valleys, where all prudent rested in the shade while the sun was high—the trip had been accomplished in three days.

Warned by Paulus' grim forecast of drastic action about to be taken against the Christians, Marcellus had expected to encounter arrogant troops and frightened people, but the roads were quiet and the natives were going about their small affairs with no apparent feeling of insecurity. If it were true that a concerted attack on them had been planned, it was still a well-guarded secret.

Their leave-taking of Capernaum had been almost without incident. Arriving early at the tent, they found that Justus had disappeared. Shalum had no explanation to offer. The mother of little Thomas, when they stopped at her home to make inquiries, had no more to say than that Justus and Jonathan had left for Sepphoris an hour ago. Marcellus had a momentary impulse to follow them and reassure Justus; but, remembering Paulus' injunction that the Galileans would now be better served if he gave them no further attention, he proceeded on his way with many misgivings. It was no small matter to have lost Justus' friendship. He wanted to stop in Cana and have a farewell word with Miriam, but decided against it.

After supper that first night out—they had camped in a meadow five miles southeast of Cana—Marcellus had insisted on hearing all about Demetrius' experiences with the Christians in Jerusalem, especially with reference to their belief in the reappearance of Jesus. The Greek was more than willing to tell everything he knew. There was no uncertainty in his mind about the truth of the resurrection story.

'But—Demetrius—that is impossible, you know!' Marcellus had declared firmly when his slave had finished.

'Yes, I know, sir,' Demetrius had admitted.

'But you believe it!'

'Yes, sir.'

'Well—there's no sense to be made out of that!' grumbled Marcellus, impatiently. 'To admit a thing's impossible, and in the next breath confess your belief in it, leaves your argument in very bad shape.'

'If you will pardon me, sir,' ventured Demetrius, 'I was not arguing. You asked me: I told you. I am not trying to persuade you to believe in it. And I agree that what I have been saying doesn't make sense.'

'Then the story is nonsense!' reasoned Marcellus; and after he had given his slave ample time to reply, he added crisply, 'Isn't it?'

'No, sir,' reiterated Demetrius, 'the story is true. The thing couldn't happen; but it did.'

Feeling that this sort of conversation didn't have much to recommend it, Marcellus had mumbled good night and pretended to sleep.

On the next day and the day thereafter, the subject had been discussed on the road, as profitlessly. Jesus had been seen after his death. Such things didn't happen; couldn't happen. Nevertheless, he had been seen; not once, but many times; not by one man only, but by a score. Demetrius was advised that he was losing his mind. He conceded the point without debate and offered to change the subject. He was told that he had been duped and deluded, to which accusation he responded with an indulgent nod and a smile. Marcellus was thoroughly exasperated. He wanted to talk about it; wanted Demetrius to plead his case, if he had one, with an air of deep conviction. You couldn't get anywhere with a man who, when you called him a fool, calmly admitted it.

'I never would have thought, Demetrius,' Marcellus had said, taking pains to make it sound derisive, 'that a man with as sound a mind as yours would turn out to be so childishly superstitious!'

'To tell you the truth, sir,' Demetrius had replied, 'I am surprised at it myself.'

They had been trudging along, with Marcellus a little in advance, stormily vaunting his indignation over his slave's stubborn imbecility, when it suddenly occurred to him that he wasn't having it out with Demetrius—but with himself. He swung about, in the middle of an angry sentence, and read—in his companion's comradely grin—a confirmation of his discovery. Falling into step, he walked along in silence for a while.

'Forgive me, Demetrius,' he said, self-reproachfully. 'I have been very inconsiderate.'

Demetrius smiled broadly.

'I understand fully, sir,' he said. 'I went through all that, hour after hour, day after day. It is not easy to accept as the truth something that one's instinct rejects.'

'Well, then'—deliberated Marcellus—'let us, just for sake of argument, batter our instincts into silence and accept this, for the moment, as the truth. Consider the possibilities of a man with a divine personality who, if he wants to, can walk up to Emperor Tiberius, without fear, and demand his throne!'

'He will not want to,' rejoined Demetrius. 'If he were that sort of person, he would have demanded Pilate's seat. No—he expects to come into power another way; not by demoting the Emperor, but by inspiring the people. His rule will not begin at the top. It will begin at the bottom—with the common people.'

'Bah!' scoffed Marcellus. 'The common people, indeed! What makes you think they have it in them to set up a just government? Take this weak-spined little handful of pious fishermen, for example: how much courage is to be expected of them? Why—even when their Jesus was on trial for his life, they were afraid to speak out in his defense. Except for two or three of them, they let him go to his death alone!'

'True, sir,' said Demetrius, 'but that was before they knew he could overcome death.'

'Yes, but Jesus' ability to overcome death wouldn't make their lives any more secure than they were before.'

'Oh—yes, sir!' exclaimed Demetrius. 'He promised them that they too would live forever. He said that he had overcome death—not only for himself—but for all who had faith in him.'

Marcellus slowed to a stop, thrust his thumbs under his belt, and surveyed his slave with a frown of utter mystification.

'Do you mean to say that these crazy fishermen think they are going to live forever?' he demanded.

'Yes, sir—forever—with him,' said Demetrius, quietly.

'Ridiculous!' snorted Marcellus.

'It seems so, sir,' agreed Demetrius. 'But if they sincerely believe that—whether it is true or not will have no bearing on their behavior. If a man considers himself stronger than death, he has nothing to fear.'

'Then why are these people in hiding?' asked Marcellus, reasonably enough, he thought.

'They have their work to do, sir. They cannot be too reckless with their lives. It is their duty to tell the story of Jesus to as many as can be reached. Every man of them expects to be killed, sooner or later, but—it won't matter. They will live on—somewhere else.'

'Demetrius—do you believe all this nonsense yourself?' asked Marcellus, pityingly.

'Sometimes,' mumbled Demetrius. 'When I'm with them, I believe it.' He tramped on moodily through the dust, his eyes on the road. 'It isn't easy,' he added, half to himself.

'I should say not!' commented Marcellus.

'But, sir,' declared Demetrius, 'the fact that an idea is not easy to understand need not disparage it. Are we not surrounded with facts quite beyond our comprehension?' He stretched a long arm toward the hillside, gay with flowers. 'We can't account for all that diversity of color and form—and we don't have to. But they are facts.'

'Well—that's beside the point,' protested Marcellus. 'Stick to your business, now, and don't let your mind wander. We'll agree that all life's a mystery. Proceed with your argument.'

'Thank you, sir,' grinned Demetrius. 'Now—these disciples of Jesus honestly believe that the world will eventually be ruled by faith in his teachings. There is to be a universal government founded on good will among men. Whoever believes and practices this has the assurance that he will live forever. It isn't easy to believe that one may live forever. I grant you that, sir.'

'And not much easier to believe that the world could be governed by good will,' put in Marcellus.

'Now—the Emperor,' went on Demetrius, 'rules the world by force. That is not easy. Thousands of men have to lose their lives to support this form of government. Germanicus leads an expedition into Aquitania, promising his Legates riches in captured goods and slaves if they follow and obey him at the risk of their lives. They take that chance. Many of them are killed and have nothing to show for their courage. Jesus promises everlasting life as a reward for those who follow and obey him in his effort to bring peace to the world. His disciples believe him, and—'

'And take that chance,' interposed Marcellus.

'Well, sir; it isn't a more hazardous chance than the legions take who follow Germanicus,' insisted Demetrius. 'This faith in Jesus is not easy, but that doesn't make it nonsense—if you will pardon my speaking so freely'

'Say on, Demetrius!' approved Marcellus. 'You are doing well, considering what kind of material you have to work with. Tell me—do you, personally, expect to live on here forever—in some spectral form?'

'No.' Demetrius shook his head. 'Somewhere else. He has a kingdom—somewhere else.'

'And you truly believe that!' Marcellus studied his slave's sober face as if he had never seen it before.

'Sometimes,' replied Demetrius.

Neither had anything to say for a while. Then, coming to an abrupt halt, the Greek faced his master with an expression of self-confidence.

'This faith,' he declared deliberately, 'is not like a deed to a house in which one may live with full rights of possession. It is more like a kit of tools with which a man may build him a house. The tools will be worth just what he does with them. When he lays them down, they will have no value until he takes them up again.'

*   *   *   *   *   *

It was nearly sundown when Demetrius arrived at the shop of Benyosef, for much time had been consumed in the congested streets

on the way to the inn where Marcellus had stopped on his previous
visit to Jerusalem. The travel equipment and Galilean purchases had
to be unloaded and stored. The man who owned the donkeys had to
be paid off. Marcellus was eager for a bath and fresh clothing. Having
made his master comfortable and having attended to his own recondi-
tioning, Demetrius had set off to find Stephanos.

Since his course led directly past Benyosef's, he decided to look in;
for it was possible that his friend was still at work. The front door
was closed and bolted. Going around to the side door which admitted
to the family quarters, he knocked; but there was no response. This
seemed odd, for the aged Sarah never went anywhere, and would
surely be here at suppertime.

Perplexed, Demetrius hastened on to the shabby old house where
he had lodged with Stephanos. Here, too, the doors were locked and
apparently everyone was gone. A short distance up the street, a person-
able young Jew, John Mark, lived with his widowed mother and an
attractive young cousin, Rhoda. He decided to call there and inquire,
for Stephanos and Mark were close friends, though he had often wondered whether it wasn't the girl that Stephanos went to see.

He found Rhoda locking the high wicket-gate and preparing to
leave with a well-filled basket on her arm. She greeted him warmly,
and Demetrius noted that she was prettier than ever. She seemed to
have matured considerably in his absence.

'Where is everybody?' he inquired, after a brief account of the closed
houses he had visited.

'Oh—don't you know?' Rhoda handed him the basket and they
moved toward the gate. 'We all have supper together now. You must
come with me.'

'Who have supper together?' wondered Demetrius.

'The Christians. Simon began it many weeks ago. They leased the
old building where Nathan had his bazaar. We all bring food every
evening, and share it. That is,' she added, with an impatient little
shrug, 'some of us bring food—and all of us share.'

'It doesn't sound as if it was much fun,' observed Demetrius.

'Well'—Rhoda tossed her curly head—'it hasn't turned out as Simon
had expected.'

They were walking rapidly, Demetrius taking long strides to keep
pace with the clipped steps that seemed to be beating time for some
very vigorous reflections. He decided not to be too inquisitive.

'How is Stephanos?' he asked, with a sly smile that Rhoda tried
unsuccessfully to dodge.

'You will see him presently,' she replied, archly. 'Then you may
judge for yourself.'

'Rhoda'—Demetrius sounded at least sixty—'those pink cheeks tell
me that something has been going on here since I left. If this means
what I think, I am happy for both of you.'

'You know too much, Uncle Demetrius,' she retorted, with a prim smile. 'Can't Stephen and I be friends—without—'

'No—I don't think so,' interjected Demetrius. 'When is it going to be, Rhoda? Will I have time to weave a tablecloth for you?'

'A little one.' She flashed him a bright smile.

Promising that he would borrow a loom and begin work early in the morning, if his master could spare him the time, Demetrius found his curiosity mounting in regard to these daily suppers.

'How many people come?' he asked.

'You will be surprised! Three hundred or more. Many have disposed of their property in the country and are living here now; quite a colony of them. At least a hundred take all of their meals at the Ecclesia.'

'The Ecclesia,' repeated Demetrius. 'Is that what you call it? That's Greek, you know. Most of you are Jews; are you not? How did you happen to call your headquarters the Ecclesia?'

'Stephen,' said Rhoda, proudly. 'He said it was a suitable name for such an assembly. Besides—fully a third of the Christians are Greeks.'

'Well—it's a comfort to see the Jews and Greeks getting together on something,' remarked Demetrius. 'Just one big, happy family; eh?' he added, with some private misgivings.

'It's big enough: no question about that!' murmured Rhoda; and then, making hasty amends for this comment, she continued, 'Most of them are deeply in earnest, Demetrius. But there are enough of the other kind to spoil it.'

'Quarreling; are they? I'm afraid they won't get very far with this new idea that what the world needs is good will.'

'That's what Stephen says,' approved Rhoda. 'He is quite disappointed. He thinks this whole business—of having all the Christians live together—is a mistake. He believes they should have stayed at home and kept on with their daily work.'

'What's the rumpus about?' Demetrius couldn't help asking.

'Oh—the same old story,' sighed Rhoda. 'You Greeks are stingy and suspicious and oversensitive about your rights, and—'

'And you Jews are greedy and tricky,' broke in Demetrius, with a grin.

'We're *not* greedy!' exclaimed Rhoda.

'And we Greeks are not stingy!' retorted Demetrius. They both laughed.

'That's a good little picture of the rumpus,' said Rhoda. 'Poor Simon. He had such high hopes for the Ecclesia. I was so sorry for him, last night, I could have cried. After supper he made us a serious talk, repeating some of the words of Jesus about loving one another, even those who mistreat us; and how we were all the children of God, equal in his sight, regardless of our race. And—if you'll believe it—right while Simon was speaking, an old man from the country, named Ananias, got up and stamped out!'

Demetrius could think of no appropriate comment. It gave him a sickish feeling to learn that so lofty an ideal had fallen into such disrepute in the hands of weak people. Rhoda sensed his disappointment.

'But please don't think that Simon is held lightly,' she went on. 'He has great influence! The people believe in him! When he walks down the street, old men and women sitting at their windows beg him to stop and talk with them. Stephen says they even bring out their sick ones on cots so that he may touch their foreheads as he passes. And—Demetrius—it's wonderful how they all feel toward Stephen, too. Sometimes I think that if anything ever happened to Simon—' Rhoda hesitated.

'Stephen might be the leader?' asked Demetrius.

'He is big enough for it!' she declared. 'But don't tell him I said that,' she added. 'He would think it a great misfortune if anything happened to Simon.'

They were nearing the rangy old bazaar now. Several women were entering with baskets. A few men loitered about the open door. No legionaries were to be seen. Apparently the Christians were free to go and come as they pleased.

Rhoda led the way into the large, bare, poorly lighted room, crowded with men, women, and children, waiting beside the long tables on which food was being spread. Stephanos advanced with a welcoming smile.

'Adelphos Demetrius!' he exclaimed, extending both hands. 'Where did you find him, Rhoda?'

'He was looking for you.' Her tone was tenderly possessive.

'Come, then,' he said. 'Simon will want to see you. You're thin, my friend. What have they been doing to you?'

Demetrius flinched involuntarily as Stephanos squeezed his arm.

'A little accident,' he explained. 'It's not quite healed.'

'How did you do it?' asked Rhoda. 'You've a cut on your wrist too; a bad one!'

Demetrius was spared the necessity of replying, Stephanos coming to his rescue with a little pantomime of pursed lips and a slight shake of his head for Rhoda's benefit.

'You were fighting, I think,' she whispered, with a reproving grin. 'Christians don't fight, you know.' Impishly puckering a meaningful little smile at Stephanos, she added, 'They don't even fret about things.' Preoccupied, Stephanos missed this sally, and beckoned to Demetrius to follow him.

*   *   *   *   *   *

Conversation on the way back was forced and fragmentary. John Mark and his mother walked on ahead. The tall Greeks followed on either side of Rhoda, who felt dwarfed and unimportant, for it was evident, by their taciturnity, that they wanted to be alone with each other. She did not resent this. She was so deeply in love with Stephanos that anything he did was exactly right, even when he so plainly excluded her from his comradeship with Demetrius.

After a hasty good night at Mark's gate, the Greeks sauntered down the street toward their lodgings, silently at first, each waiting for the other to speak. Stephanos' steps slowed.

'Well—what did you think of it?' he demanded, bluntly. 'Tell me truly.'

'I'm not quite sure,' temporized Demetrius.

'But you are!' snapped Stephanos. 'You have seen our Christian Ecclesia in action. If you are not quite sure, that means you think we have taken the wrong road!'

'Very well,' consented Demetrius, with an indulgent chuckle. 'If that's what I think, why not go on and tell me what you think? You've had a better chance to form an opinion. I haven't seen your Ecclesia do anything yet—but eat. What else is it good for? I'm bound to say, Stephanos, that if I were selecting a company of people to engage in some dangerous tasks requiring endless faith and courage, I might have skipped a few who were present tonight.'

'There you are!' lamented Stephanos. 'That's what ails it. Jesus commands us to carry on his work, no matter at what cost in privation, pain, and hazard of life; and all we've accomplished is a free boarding-house and loafing-place for anybody who will say, "I believe." '

'Doubtless Simon's intentions were good,' observed Demetrius, feeling that he was expected to make some comment.

'Excellent!' agreed Stephanos. 'If everybody connected with the Ecclesia had the bravery and goodness of Simon Peter, the institution might develop great power. You see—at the beginning, what he wanted was a close-knit body of men who would devote their full time to this work. He thought they could inspire one another if they lived together. You remember how it was at the shop, Demetrius, the disciples spending hours in conference. Simon wanted to increase this circle, draw in other devoted men, and weld them together in spirit and purpose.'

'And made the circle a little too large?' suggested Demetrius.

Stephanos came to a halt, and moodily shook his head.

'The whole plan was unsound,' he said, disconsolately. 'Simon announced that any Christian might sell his property and bring the proceeds to the Ecclesia with the promise that his living would be provided for.'

'No matter how much or how little he had?' queried Demetrius.

'Right! If you owned a farm or a vineyard, you sold it—probably at a sacrifice—and brought Simon the money. If you had nothing but a few chickens, a milk-goat, and a donkey, you came with the money you'd got from that. And all would live together in brotherly love.'

Gloomily Stephanos recited the misadventures of this unhappy experiment. The word had quickly spread that any Christian family could insure its living by joining the Ecclesia. There was no lack of applicants. Simon had rejoiced to see the large number of people who professed to be Christians. At an all-night conference in Benyosef's shop, Simon had been almost beside himself with happiness. The kingdom was growing!

'That night,' continued Stephanos, 'It was decided that Simon should remain to oversee our Ecclesia. The others were to see how nearly ready the Christians were to attempt similar projects in Joppa, Caesarea, Antioch, and other good-sized cities. So—they scattered; John, James, Philip, Alphaeus, Matthew—' Stephanos made an encircling gesture that included all the rest of them. 'Simon is impetuous, you know. When he captures an idea, he saddles and bridles it and rides away at a gallop!'

'And the Ecclesia grew!' assisted Demetrius.

'In numbers—yes! Large families, with next to nothing, moved in to live in idleness, lustily singing hymns and fervent in prayer, but hardly knowing what it was all about, except that they had three meals a day and plenty of good company.'

'And how did the other people like it, the ones who had owned considerable property?'

'Well—that was another problem. These people began to feel their superiority over the indigents. The more money you had contributed to the Ecclesia, the more right you thought you had to dictate the policies of the institution.' Stephanos drew an unhappy smile. 'Only this morning, one arrogant old fellow, who had been impudent and cross over something Simon had said, was discovered to have cheated in his dealings with the Ecclesia, and when Simon confronted him with it, he went into such a mad rage that he had a stroke. Died of it! And Simon will probably get the blame for it.'

'It must be very discouraging,' said Demetrius.

'That isn't all!' sighed Stephanos. 'This daily supper! Many merchants are coming to these meetings now—bringing their food along; I must give them credit for that—but quite clearly patronizing the Ecclesia to make friends for business reasons. In short—the Ecclesia is becoming too, too popular!'

'What's to be done about it?' Demetrius wanted to know.

Stephanos moved on slowly, shaking his head.

'Demetrius—until this Ecclesia began to take in boarders, the Christian community in Jerusalem was a reckonable force. Men continued their gainful occupations, careful to deal honestly and charitably, eager to live according to Jesus' commandments, and talking of his way of life to all who would give heed. And in the evening they would assemble to hearten one another. Simon would stand up and challenge them to greater efforts. He would repeat the words of Jesus, and renew their strength. He was magnificent!' Stephanos stopped again and faced his friend sadly. 'You heard him tonight—squandering his splendid energies in wheedling a lot of selfish, bickering people to forget their little squabbles and stop nagging one another. Did you notice that weak, solicitous smile on his face as he entreated them to be more generous with their gifts to the Ecclesia? Well—that wasn't Simon! That wasn't the Simon who fired the hearts of the men who used to meet in the night to repledge their all to the cause of our Christos! It is a disgrace!' Stephanos clenched both hands in his tousled hair and shook his head hopelessly. 'Is it for this,' he cried, 'that Jesus suffered on the cross—and died—and rose again?'

'Have you talked with Simon about it?' asked Demetrius, after a discreet interval.

'Not lately. A couple of weeks ago, when it became evident there was going to be an open ruction between the Jews and Greeks, several of us inquired whether we could do anything to help him, and he appointed seven of us to oversee the fair apportioning of food and clothing; but—Demetrius—my feeling for Jesus and his worth to the world is a sort of exalted passion that can't bring itself down to the low level of listening patiently to ill-mannered quarrels over whether Bennie Issacher was given a better coat than little Nicolas Timonodes.'

Demetrius snorted his sympathetic disgust and suggested that his friend would do well to keep away from such annoyances.

'I mean to do just that!' declared Stephanos. 'I made a decision tonight. I'm not going back there, any more!'

'It is possible,' said Demetrius, 'that Julian may soon solve the Ecclesia's difficulties. Had you heard anything about an attack? My master thinks the Christians are presently to be set upon by the Insula.'

Stephanos laughed bitterly.

'If the Procurator waits a little while, the Ecclesia will destroy itself, and save him the bother. But—tell me—how does your Roman master feel about Jesus, now that he has been in Galilee?'

'Much impressed, Stephanos. He finds it difficult to believe that Jesus came alive, but he considers him the greatest man who ever lived. He wants to talk with you. He was deeply touched when you asked to see the Robe, and were so moved by the sight of it.'

'He still has it, I suppose,' murmured Stephanos. 'Do you think he would let me see it again, Demetrius? So much has happened, lately, to depress me. Do you know—my friend—that when I touched the Robe, that night, it—it did something for me! I can't explain it—but—'

'Let us go to the inn!' said Demetrius, impetuously. 'Now! He will still be up, and glad to see you. I think you need to have a talk with each other.'

'Are you sure he won't think it an intrusion?' asked Stephanos, anxiously.

'No—he will welcome you. It will be good for you both.'

Once the decision was made, Stephanos set the pace with long, determined strides.

'Are you going to tell the Tribune about the Ecclesia?' he asked.

'By no means!' declared Demetrius. 'I believe that Marcellus is on the way to becoming a Christian. He is infatuated with the story of Jesus, and talks of nothing else. If he decides to be a Christian, he will be a good one and a brave one; you can depend on that! But we mustn't expose him to things that might disgust him. If he knew that some of his companions in this cause were mere quarrelsome idlers, he might not want to debase himself.'

'Those are hard words, my friend,' said Stephanos.

'It gave me no pleasure to say them,' rejoined Demetrius. 'But I know the Tribune very well. It is true he has been brought up as a pagan, but he is particular about the company he keeps.'

* * * * * *

They found Marcellus alone and reading. He greeted them warmly, showing an instant interest in Stephanos, who was ready with an apology for the untimely call.

'There is no one I would rather see, Stephanos,' he said, cordially, offering him a chair. 'You sit down too, Demetrius. You men have had a pleasant reunion, I think.'

'Did you have an interesting journey in Galilee, sir?' asked Stephanos, rather shyly.

'Interesting—and bewildering,' replied Marcellus. 'Justus was a good guide. I heard many strange stories. It is difficult to believe them and difficult not to believe them.' He paused, his expression inviting a rejoinder; but Stephanos, at a disadvantage in the presence of this urbane Roman, merely nodded, with averted eyes.

'I was greatly attracted by old Nathanael Bartholomew,' went on Marcellus.

'Yes,' said Stephanos, after a tongue-tied interval.

Demetrius, growing restless, thought he would come to his timid compatriot's rescue.

'I think Stephanos would like to see the Robe, sir,' he suggested.

'Gladly!' agreed Marcellus. 'Will you find it for him, Demetrius?'

After some moments in the adjoining room, during which time Marcellus and Stephanos sat silent, Demetrius returned and laid the folded Robe across his friend's knees. Stephanos gently smoothed it with his finger-tips. His lips were trembling.

'Would you like to be alone—for a little while?' asked Marcellus, softly. 'Demetrius and I can take a walk in the garden.'

Stephanos gave no sign that he had heard. Gathering the Robe up into his arms, he glanced at Marcellus and then at Demetrius, with a new light of assurance in his eyes.

'This was my Master's Robe!' he announced, in confident tones, as if delivering a public address. 'He wore it when he healed the sick and comforted the sorrowing. He wore it when he spoke to the multitudes

as no man has ever spoken. He wore it when he went to the cross to die
—for *me*—a humble weaver!' Stephanos boldly searched Marcellus'
astonished face. 'And for *you*—a wealthy Tribune!' He turned toward
Demetrius. 'And for *you*—a slave!'

Marcellus leaned forward on the arms of his chair, baffled by the
suddenly altered manner of the Greek who had thrown aside his reticence to declare his faith in such resonant tones.

'You killed my Lord, Tribune Marcellus!' went on Stephanos,
boldly.

'Stephanos! Please!' entreated Demetrius.

Marcellus held up a cautioning hand toward his slave.

'Proceed, Stephanos!' he commanded.

'It was forgivable,' went on Stephanos, rising to his feet, 'for you
did not know what you were doing. And you are sorry. The Temple
and the Insula killed him! And they did not know what they were
doing. But they are not sorry—and they would do it again—tomorrow!'
He took a step toward Marcellus, who rose from his chair, and stood,
as one receiving an order. 'You—Tribune Marcellus Gallio—can make
amends for what you have done! He forgave you! I was there! I heard
him forgive you! Make friends with him! He is alive! I have seen him!'

Demetrius was at his elbow now, murmuring half-articulate entreaties. Gently taking the Robe from him, he tugged him back to
his chair. They all sat down, and there was a long moment when no
one spoke.

'Forgive me, sir,' said Stephanos, contritely. He clumsily rubbed the
back of a nervous hand across his brow. 'I have been talking too freely.'

'You need not reproach yourself, Stephanos,' replied Marcellus,
huskily. 'You have not offended me.'

There was a long, constrained silence which no one seemed disposed to break. Stephanos rose.

'It is late,' he said. 'We should go.'

Marcellus held out his hand.

'I am glad you came, Stephanos,' he said, soberly. 'You are welcome to come again. . . . Demetrius—I shall see you here in the
morning.'

*   *   *   *   *   *

Badly shaken and perplexed, Marcellus sat for an hour staring at the
wall. At length, he was overcome by the day's fatigue. Stretching out
on his bed, he fell asleep. Shortly before dawn he was roused by hoarse
cries and shrill screams accompanied by savage commands and thudding blows. It was not unusual, at an inn, to be annoyed at almost any
hour of the day by loud lamentations signifying that some hapless
kitchen-slave was being flogged; but this pandemonium, which seemed
to emanate from the courtyard below, sounded as if the whole establishment was in trouble.

Marcellus pushed his long legs over the edge of his bed, walked to the window, and looked down. Instantly he knew what was happening. Julian's threatened day of wrath had arrived. A dozen legionaries, in full battle equipment, were clubbing the household slaves into a corner of the courtyard. Evidently other troops were inside, chasing their quarry out. The entire lower floor was in confusion. There were blows and protestations, scuffling of feet, splintering of door-panels. Presently there was a scurry of sandals on the stairs. Marcellus' door was thrown open.

'Who are you?' bawled a brutish voice.

'I am a Roman citizen,' replied Marcellus coolly. 'And you would do well, fellow, to show better manners when you enter the room of a Tribune.'

'We have no manners today, sir,' retorted the legionary, with a brief grin. 'We are searching for Christians.'

'Indeed!' growled Marcellus. 'And does Legate Julian think these poor, harmless people are important enough to warrant all this racket at daybreak?'

'The Legate does not tell me what he thinks, sir,' scored the legionary, 'and it is not customary for ordinary troops to ask him. I am obeying orders, sir. We are rounding up all the Christians in the city. You are not a Christian, and I am sorry I have disturbed you.' He was retreating into the hall.

'Stay!' shouted Marcellus. 'How do you know I am not a Christian? Can't a Roman Tribune be a Christian?'

The legionary chuckled, shrugged, tugged off his heavy metal helmet, and wiped his dripping forehead with a swipe of his rough sleeve.

'I've no time for jesting, sir, if the Tribune will excuse me.' He resumed his helmet, saluted with his spear, and stamped down the hall.

The cries outside were subsiding now. Apparently the evacuation had been completed. A terrified group of slaves had huddled against the area wall, nursing their bruises. Apart from them a little way stood a few shabbily clad, frightened guests. The aging wife of Levi, the innkeeper, hovered close to them. She was pale, and her head kept jerking up involuntarily with some nervous quirk. Marcellus wondered whether she did that all the time or only when she was badly scared.

The tall, handsome Centurion marched forward, faced the victims, shouted for silence, drew out an impressive scroll to its full length, and in a dry crackle read an edict. It was pompously phrased. There was to be no further assembling of the blasphemers who called themselves Christians. There was to be no further mention, in public or private, of the name of Jesus the Galilean, who had been found guilty of treason, blasphemy, and offenses against the peace of Jerusalem. This edict was to be considered the first and last official warning. Disobedience would be punishable by death.

Rolling up the scroll, the Centurion barked an order, the detachment stiffened, he stalked toward the street, they fell in behind him.

After a moment, one old retainer, with blood oozing through the sparse white hair on his temple and trickling down over his bare shoulder, quietly crumpled into a shapeless heap. A slave-girl of twenty stooped over him and cried aloud. A bearded Greek bent down and listened with his ear against the old man's chest. He raised up and shook his head. Four of them picked up the limp body and moved off slowly toward the servants' quarters, most of the others trudging dejectedly after them. The innkeeper's wife turned slowly about. Her head was bobbing violently. She pointed to a fallen broom. A limping slave with a crooked back took up the broom and began ineffectively sweeping the tiled pavement. Except for him, the courtyard was empty now. Marcellus turned away from the window, scowling.

'Brave old Julian!' he muttered. 'Brave old Roman Empire!'

He finished his dressing and went below. Levi met him at the foot of the stairs with much bowing and fumbling of hands. He hoped the Tribune had not been disturbed by all the commotion. And would he have his breakfast served at once? Marcellus nodded.

'We will have less trouble with these Christians now,' declared Levi, to assure his Roman guest that his sympathies were with the Insula.

'Had they been causing you trouble?' asked Marcellus, negligently.

Levi hunched his shoulders, spread out his upturned fingers, and smirked.

'It is enough that their sect is in disfavor with the Government,' he parried, discreetly.

'That wasn't what I asked you,' growled Marcellus. 'Have these Christians, who were being knocked about here this morning, given you any cause for complaint? Do they steal, lie, fight? Do they get drunk? Are they brawlers? Tell me—what sort of people are they?'

'In truth, sir,' admitted Levi, 'I cannot complain of them. They are quiet, honest, and faithful. But, sir, as the Insula has decreed, we cannot tolerate blasphemy!'

'Blasphemy? Rubbish!' snarled Marcellus. 'What does the Insula know or care about blasphemy? What is it that these people blaspheme, Levi?'

'They have no respect for the Temple, sir.'

'How could they, when the Temple has no respect for itself?'

Levi shrugged a polite disapproval, though he still smiled weakly.

'The religion of our people must be protected, sir,' he murmured, piously.

Marcellus made a little grimace and sauntered out into the sunny arcade where he found, laying his breakfast table, the slave-girl who had been so deeply grieved over the old man's death in the courtyard. Her eyes were red with weeping, but she was going about her duties competently. She did not look up when Marcellus took his seat.

'Was that old man related to you?' he asked, kindly.

She did not reply. Sudden tears overflowed her eyes and ran down her cheeks. In a moment she moved away, obviously to return to the kitchen for his breakfast. Levi strolled toward his table.

'How was this girl related to the old man they killed?' asked Marcellus.

'He was her father,' said Levi, reluctantly.

'And you are making her serve the table?'

Levi's shoulders, elbows, eyebrows, and palms came up in a defensive gesture.

'Well—it is her regular task, sir. It is not my fault that her father was killed.'

Marcellus rose, and regarded his host with cool contempt.

'And you prate about your religion! What a mean fellow you are, Levi!' He strode toward the door.

'But, please, sir!' begged Levi. 'I myself shall serve you! I am sorry to have given offense!' He toddled off toward the kitchen. Marcellus, angrily returning to his table, wondered if the loathsome creature would slap the girl for unwittingly creating an awkward incident.

* * * * * *

Demetrius had risen at daybreak so that he might have time to do an errand at the Ecclesia before going on to attend his master at the inn. He had tried to dress without waking his friend who, he knew, had spent a restless night; but Stephanos roused and sat up, rubbing his eyes.

'I'll see you this evening,' whispered Demetrius, as if his companion were still asleep and shouldn't be wakened. 'Shall I meet you here?'

'At the Ecclesia,' mumbled Stephanos.

'Thought you weren't going there any more.'

'I can't let good old Simon down, Demetrius. He is alone, now that the other disciples are away on missions.'

Tiptoeing out of the house, Demetrius walked rapidly toward the Ecclesia, where he hoped to have a private word with Simon. It had seemed almost disloyal not to counsel with Stephanos about this, but Marcellus had insisted upon secrecy. He wanted an interview with Simon. Demetrius was to arrange for it, if he could. There had been no opportunity to ask Simon, last night. Perhaps he would have a better chance to see him alone this morning before the day's activities began.

The Ecclesia was already astir. Cots were being folded up and put away to make room for tables. Tousled, half-dressed children of all sizes were racing about, babies were crying, old men were crouching in out-of-the-way corners, scowling meditatively as they stroked their patriarchal beards. The women were bustling back and forth between the kitchen at the rear and the breakfast-tables which their men were setting up. Demetrius approached the nearest group and inquired for Simon. One of them glanced about, and pointed. Simon was standing by a window, quite apart from the others, brooding over a tattered scroll. Even in this relaxed posture there was something majestic about this huge Galilean. If only he had a suitable setting and a courageous constituency, thought Demetrius, Simon would have great weight. The man was of immense vitality and arresting personality, a natural leader. Not much wonder the people wanted him to lay his hands upon their sick.

Approaching, Demetrius waited to be recognized. Simon glanced up, nodded soberly, and beckoned to him.

"Sir, my master—Marcellus Gallio—earnestly desires a conversation with you, at your convenience,' said Demetrius.

'He that went into Galilee with Justus?' queried Simon. 'To look for homespun—or so he said.'

'My master did acquire a large quantity of homespun, sir,' said Demetrius.

'And what else?' asked Simon, in his deep voice.

'He became much interested in the life of Jesus, sir.'

'I think he had that before he went,' rumbled Simon, studying Demetrius' eyes. 'I think that was why he went.'

'Yes, sir,' conceded Demetrius. 'That was his real object in going to Galilee. He is deeply concerned—but full of questions. At present he is at Levi's inn. May I tell him you will talk with him—in private?'

'I will talk with him—on the morrow—at mid-afternoon,' said Simon. 'And as he desires privacy, let him come to me in the refuse-field, north of the city, the place they call Golgotha. There is a path through the field which leads to a knoll in the center of it.'

'I know where it is, sir.'

'Then show him the way. Bid him come alone.' Simon rolled up the scroll; and, inattentive to Demetrius' murmured thanks, walked toward the tables. There was a whispered demand for silence, and the confusion ceased, except for the crying of a baby. Those who were seated rose. In a powerful, resonant voice, Simon began to read.

> The people that walked in darkness have seen a great light. They that dwell in the shadow of death, upon them the light shines. For unto us a child is born. Unto us a son is given. The government shall be upon his shoulder.

There was a clamor at the entrance, and all eyes turned apprehensively. Crisp commands were being shouted. The frightened people did not have long to wait in anxiety. The doors burst open, and a whole company of legionaries marched in, deploying fanwise as they advanced. With their spears held horizontally, breast-high, they moved rapidly forward, pushing the terrified Christians before them. Some of the older ones fell down in their excitement. They were ruthlessly prodded to their feet and shoved on in the wake of the scurrying pack that was massing against the rear wall.

Demetrius, who had remained near the window quite apart from
the residents, found himself in the position of a spectator. The troops
swept on relentlessly. Simon, a towering figure, stood his ground. He
was alone, now, all the others having huddled at the wall. The Centurion shouted an order, and the company halted. He strode arrogantly
toward Simon and faced him with a sardonic grin. They were of the
same height, both magnificent specimens of manhood.

'Are you, then, the one they call The Fisherman?' demanded the
Centurion.

'I am!' answered Simon, boldly. 'And why are you here to break up
a peaceful assembly? Has any one of us committed a crime? If so—
let him be taken for trial.'

'As you wish,' snapped the Centurion. 'If you want to be tried for
blasphemy and treasonable utterances, the Procurator will accom-
modate you. . . . Take him away!'

Simon turned about and faced his desperate people.

'Be of good cheer!' he shouted. 'Make no resistance! I shall come
back to you!'

'That you will not!' broke in the Centurion. In obedience to a
sharp command and a sweep of his sword, two burly legionaries leaped
forward, caught Simon by the arms, whirled him about, and started
for the door. The company pressed forward toward the defenseless
crowd. The Centurion called for silence. Palefaced women nervously
cupped their hands over the mouths of their screaming children. An
edict was read. By order of the Procurator, there was to be no further
assembling of the blasphemers who called themselves Christians.

Demetrius began slowly edging his way along the wall in the direction of the front door. He caught fragments of the Centurion's announcement. This building was to be vacated immediately. Anyone
found on the premises hereafter would be taken into custody. The
name of Jesus, the blasphemer and traitor, was never again to be
spoken.

'Away with you now!' yelled the Centurion. 'Back to your homes!
And do not inquire for your Fisherman! You will not see him any
more!'

As he neared the door, realizing that the speech had ended and the
troops would be promptly moving out, Demetrius speeded his going,
ran to the street and crossed it, dodged into a narrow alley, pursued it
to the next street, slowed to a brisk walk, and proceeded to Levi's
inn. Everything was quiet there. He entered and moved toward the
stairway leading to Marcellus' quarters. Levi, observant, called him
back.

'Your master is out,' he said.

'Do you know where he went, sir?' inquired Demetrius, anxiously.

'How should I?' retorted Levi.

Thinking that Marcellus might have left instructions in his room,

Demetrius asked and was granted permission to go upstairs. A Greek slave-girl was putting the room to rights. She recognized him and smiled shyly. Informed of his errand, she joined in the search for a message.

'Did you see my master this morning?' asked Demetrius.

She shook her head.

'We had much trouble here, a little while ago,' she said.

Demetrius pressed her for particulars, and she told him what had occurred. He went to the window and stood for a long moment, looking out, trying to imagine what might be Marcellus' reaction to this cruel business. He would be very angry, no doubt. He would want to do something about it, perhaps. It was not inconceivable that Marcellus might go to Julian and remonstrate. The more Demetrius deliberated on this possibility, the more reasonable it seemed. It would be an audacious thing to do, but Marcellus was impetuous enough to attempt it. After all—the word of a Tribune should have some weight.

He turned about and met the Greek girl's eyes. They were friendly but serious. Glancing cautiously toward the open door, she moved closer to him and whispered, 'Are you one of us?'

Demetrius nodded soberly, and she gave him an approving smile. With a sudden burst of interest in her duties, she began folding and patting the blankets on the bed, as if suspicious that she might be found idling.

'Better stay off the streets today,' she said, softly, out of the corner of a pretty mouth. 'Go down to the kitchen. You'll be safe there.'

'Thanks,' said Demetrius. 'That's not a bad idea. Besides—I'm hungry.' He was crossing the room. The girl laid her hand on his sleeve as he passed her.

'Does your master know you are one of us?' she whispered.

Demetrius was not sure how this question should be answered, so he gave her an enigmatic smile which she was free to interpret as she chose, and left the room. The ever-present Levi met him at the foot of the stairs and unexpectedly informed him that it was a fine morning.

'Beautiful!' agreed Demetrius, aware that the Jew was sparring for news.

'Had your master left instructions for you?' asked Levi, amiably.

'I am to have my breakfast, sir, and await his return.'

'Very good,' said Levi. 'Go to the kitchen. They will serve you.' He tagged along as far as the door. 'I suppose everything was quiet on the streets this morning.'

'It was still quite early, sir, when I left my lodgings,' replied Demetrius, unhelpfully.

After his breakfast of bread, milk, and sun-cured figs, he paced restlessly up and down the small area bounded by the servants' quarters. Nobody seemed inclined to talk. The girl who had served him was crying. He resolved to stroll over to the Insula and wait outside.

Something told him that Marcellus was there. Where else could he be?

* * * * * *

Having finished his breakfast, which Levi himself had served with a disgusting show of servility, Marcellus began to be apprehensive about the safety of Demetrius, who, he felt, should have arrived by this time unless he had encountered some trouble.

He did not know where Stephanos lived, but they could tell him at Benyosef's shop. Then it occurred to him that Benyosef's might have been visited by the legionaries. Doubtless they knew it was a meeting-place of the disciples of Jesus, and might be expected to deal severely with anyone found there. Prudence suggested that he keep out of that storm-center. If Demetrius had been arrested, it would be sensible to wait until order had been restored. Then he could learn where his slave was, and make an effort to have him released.

The obsequious Levi helped him to a decision. Marcellus was stalking up and down in the courtyard, feverishly debating what to do, when the Jew appeared in the doorway, obviously much interested in his guest's perturbation. Levi did not say anything; just stood there slowly blinking his brightly inquisitive eyes. Then he retreated into the little foyer and emerged a moment later carrying a chair, as to say that if the Tribune knew what was good for him today, he would stay where he was and avoid getting into trouble. Marcellus scowled, lengthened his stride; and, without a backward glance, marched down the steps to the street.

To reach Benyosef's shop, it was necessary to traverse a few blocks on the rim of the congested market district where the shabby hovels of the very poor huddled close to the reeking alleys. Here there was much excitement, frantic chatter, and gesticulations. Marcellus slowed his steps near one vociferous group of slatternly people and learned that the Christians' meeting-place had been invaded, emptied, and locked up. The leaders had been dragged off to prison. Simon the Fisherman was to be beheaded.

Marcellus quickened his pace. A little way down the street, in the vicinity of Benyosef's shop, a crowd had gathered. At the edge of it, apparently waiting for orders, ranged a company of legionaries, negligently leaning on their spears. Someone in the middle of the crowd was making an impassioned speech. In a moment Marcellus had drawn close enough to recognize the voice.

It was Stephanos. Bareheaded, and in the brown tunic he wore at his loom, he had evidently been dragged out for questioning; and from the sullen silence of the throng, it was to be inferred that these people were willing to wait patiently until the reckless Greek had incriminated himself.

Taller than most, Marcellus surveyed the spectators with curiosity to discover what manner of men they were. Instantly he divined the nature of this audience. They were well dressed, for the most part, representing the more substantial element from the business district. There was a sprinkling of younger priests, too. The face of the crowd was surly, but everybody was listening in a tense silence.

Stephanos was not mincing his words. He stood there boldly, in the open circle they had formed about him, his long arms stretched out in an appeal to reason—but by no means an appeal for mercy. He was not defiant, but he was unafraid.

It was no rabble-rousing speech addressed to the emotions of ignorant men, but a scathing indictment of Jerusalem's leaders who, Stephanos declared, had been unwilling to recognize a cure for the city's distresses.

'You have considered yourselves the Chosen People!' he went on, audaciously. 'Your ancestors struggled out of one bondage into another, century after century, ever looking for a Deliverer, and never heeding your great teachers when they appeared with words of wisdom! Again and again, inspired leaders have risen among your people, only to be thwarted and reviled—not by the poor and needy—but by such as you!'

A concerted growl rumbled through the angry crowd.

'Which of the prophets,' demanded Stephanos, 'did your fathers not persecute? And now you have become the betrayers—and murderers—of the Just One!'

'Blasphemer!' shouted an imperious voice.

'You!' exclaimed Stephanos, sweeping the throng with an accusing hand—'you—who claim to have received your law at the hands of angels—how have you kept it?'

There was an infuriated roar, but no one moved to attack him. Marcellus wondered how much longer the suppressed fury of these maddened men would tolerate this rash excoriation.

From far back on the fringe of the crowd, someone hurled a cobblestone. It was accurately thrown and struck Stephanos on the cheekbone, staggering him. Instinctively he reached up a hand to wipe away the blood. Another stone, savagely hurled by a practiced hand, crashed against his elbow. A loud clamor rose. For an instant, Marcellus hoped it might be a protest against this lawless violence, but it was quickly evident that the hoarse shouts were in denunciation of the speech, and not the stoning. A vengeful yell gave sinister applause to the good aim of another stone as it struck the Greek full in the face. Two more, not so well thrown, went over Stephanos' head and drove into the crowd. Trampling upon one another, the dignitaries on the other side of the open circle scurried for cover against the walls and fences. Stephanos, shielding his bleeding head with his arms, backed away slowly from the hostile throng, but the stones kept coming.

The Centurion barked an order now and the legionaries sprang into action, plowing roughly through the pack, tossing men right and left, with utter disregard of their importance. Marcellus, who had been standing beside a tall soldier, followed him through, and was surprised to see him jab his elbow into the face of a stocky priest whose ponderous dignity hadn't permitted him to move swiftly enough. Now the legionaries were lined up inside the semicircle of spectators. They had made a fence of their spears. The stones were coming faster now, and with telling effect. Marcellus began to realize that this was no impulsive, impromptu incident. The better citizens were not throwing stones, but without doubt they had planned that the stones should be thrown. The men who were doing it were expert.

Stephanos was down now, on his elbows and knees, trying to protect his head with one bleeding hand. The other arm hung limp. The crowd roared. Marcellus recognized that bestial cry. He had heard it many a time in the Circus Maximus. He pushed his way on to the side of the tall legionary who, after a glance in his direction, made room for him.

Several of the younger men in the shouting multitude now decided to take a hand in the punishment. The Centurion pretended not to notice when they dodged under the barricade of spears. Their faces were deeply flushed and contorted with rage. There was nothing more they could do to Stephanos, who had crumpled on the ground, but perhaps the stones they threw were to be merely tokens of their willingness to share the responsibility for this crime.

Marcellus' heart ached. There had been nothing he could do. Had Julian been there, he might have protested, but to have denounced the Centurion would have done no good. The fellow was obeying his orders. Poor Stephanos lay dead, or at least unconscious, but the dignitaries continued to stone him.

Immediately in front of Marcellus—on the other side of the barrier —stood a young, bookish man, wearing a distinctive skullcap with a tassel, evidently a student. He was of diminutive stature, but sturdily built. His hands were clenched and his rugged face was twisted with anger. Every thudding stone that beat upon the limp body had his approval. Marcellus studied his livid face, amazed that a man of his seeming intelligence could be so viciously pleased by such an exhibition of inhuman brutality.

Presently a fat man, in an expensive black robe, ducked through the line, took off his robe, and tossed it to the short one, bidding him hold it. Another man of lofty dignity followed his friend in; and, handing his robe also to the bow-legged scholar, began clawing up a stone from the pavement.

Marcellus, towering over the short-legged fellow, leaned forward and demanded, sternly, 'What harm had he done to *you?*'

The little man turned about and glanced up impudently into Marcellus's eyes. He was a malicious creature, but no fool. It was a face to be remembered.

'He is a blasphemer!' he shouted.

'How does the crime of blasphemy compare with murder?' growled Marcellus. 'You seem to be a learned man. Perhaps you know.'

'If you will come to the Rabbinical School tomorrow, my friend,' replied the little man, suddenly cooled by the prospect of airing his theology, 'I shall enlighten you. Ask for Saul—of Tarsus,' he added, proudly. 'I am a Roman citizen—like yourself, sir.'

There were no stones flying now. The crowd was growing restless. The young theologian had handed back the robes he had held and was shouldering out through the loosening throng. The legionaries were still maintaining their barricade, but were shifting their weight uneasily as if impatient to be off. The Centurion was soberly talking, out of the corner of his mouth, to a long-bearded Jew in an impressive black robe. The multitude was rapidly disintegrating.

Marcellus, with brooding eyes fixed on the broken body of the gallant Greek, thought he saw a feeble movement there. Stephanos was slowly rising up on one elbow. A hush fell over the people as they watched him rise to his knees. The blood-smeared face looked up, and the bruised lips were parted in a rapturous smile. Suddenly Stephanos raised his arm aloft as if to clutch a friendly hand.

'I see him!' he shouted, triumphantly. 'I see him! My Lord Jesus— take me!' The eyes closed, the head dropped, and Stephanos crumpled down among the stones.

The spectators, momentarily stunned, turned to go. Men did not pause to ask questions. They scurried away as if frightened. Marcellus' heart was pounding and his mouth was dry. But he found himself possessed of a curious exaltation. His eyes were swimming, but his face trembled with an involuntary smile.

He turned about and looked into the bewildered eyes of the tall legionary.

'That was a strange thing, sir!' muttered the soldier.

'More strange than you think!' exclaimed Marcellus.

'I would have sworn the Greek was dead! He thought he saw someone coming to rescue him!'

'He *did* see someone coming to rescue him!' shouted Marcellus, ecstatically.

'That dead Galilean, maybe?' queried the legionary, nervously.

'That Galilean is not dead, my friend!' declared Marcellus. 'He is more alive than any man here!'

Thoroughly shaken, his lips twitching with emotion, Marcellus moved away with the scattering crowd. His mind was in a tumult. At the first corner, he turned abruptly and retraced his steps. Nobody was interested in Stephanos now. The troops from the Insula, four abreast, were disappearing down the street. None of the friends of the intrepid Greek had yet ventured to put in an appearance. It was quite too soon to expect that any of them would take the risk.

Dropping to one knee beside the battered corpse, Marcellus gently drew aside the matted hair and gazed into the impassive face. The lips were still parted in a smile.

After a long time, old Benyosef hobbled out of the shop. His eyes were red and swollen with weeping. He approached diffidently, halting a few steps away. Marcellus looked up and beckoned to him and he came, pale with fright. Stooping over, with his wrinkled hands bracing his feeble knees, he peered into the quiet face. Then he searched Marcellus' eyes inquisitively, but without recognition.

'It was a cruel death, sir,' he whimpered.

'Stephanos is not dead!' declared Marcellus. 'He went away with Jesus!'

'I beg of you—do not mock our faith, sir!' pleaded Benyosef. 'This has been a sad day for us who believe in Jesus!'

'But did he not promise you that if you believe in him, you will never die?'

Benyosef slowly nodded his head, staring into Marcellus' eyes incredulously.

'Yes—but *you* do not believe that, sir!' he mumbled.

Marcellus rose and laid his hand on the old man's thin arm.

'Jesus may never come for me, Benyosef,' he said, quietly, 'and he may never come for you—but he came for Stephanos! Go, now, and find a younger man to help me. We will carry the body into your shop.'

Still pale with fright, the neighbors gathered about the mangled form of Stephanos as it lay on the long table in Benyosef's workroom. They were all crying. Rhoda's grief was inconsolable. Some of the men regarded Marcellus with suspicion that he might be there to spy upon them. It was no time to explain that he felt himself one of them. Presently he was aware of Demetrius at his elbow, and importuned him to stay and be of service.

Taking Benyosef by the arm, he led the tearful old man into the corner back of his loom.

'There is nothing I can do here,' he said, laying some gold coins in the weaver's hand. 'But I have a request of you. When Justus comes again to Jerusalem, tell him I saw Stephanos welcomed into Jesus' kingdom, and am persuaded that everything he told me—in Galilee— is the truth.'

* * * * * *

It had been a long day for Simon, sitting there heavily manacled in the darkness. At noon they had brought him some mouldy bread and a pitcher of water, but he had not eaten; he was too heartsick for that.

For the first hour after his incarceration, derisive voices from adjoining cells had demanded to know his name, his crime, and when he was to die. With noisy bravado, they jested obscenely about their impending executions, and taunted him for being too scared to speak. He had not answered them, and at length they had wearied of reviling him.

The wooden bench on which he sat served also as a bed. It was wider than the seat of a chair, and Simon could not rest his back against the wall. This unsupported posture was fatiguing. Sometimes he stretched his huge frame out on the bench, but with little ease. The wall was damp, as was the floor. Huge rats nibbled at his sandals. The heavy handcuffs cut his wrists.

He thought that he could have borne these discomforts and the threat of a death sentence with a better fortitude had he been able to leave behind him a determined organization to carry on the work that had been entrusted to him. Obviously he had blundered. Perhaps it had been a mistake to establish the Ecclesia. Maybe the time had not come for such a movement. He had been too impatient. He should have let it grow, quietly, unobtrusively, like yeast in meal, as Jesus had said.

What, he wondered, would become of the Christian cause now, with all of them scattered and in hiding? Who would rise up as their leader? Philip? No—Philip was a brave and loyal fellow, but—he lacked boldness. The leader would have to be audacious. John? No. James? No. They had the heart for it, but not the voice. There was Stephen. Stephen might do it—but not in Jerusalem. The Jews would insist on an Israelite, as perhaps they should; for the Christian heritage was of the Hebrew people.

Why had the Master permitted this dreadful catastrophe? Had he changed his plans for the prosecution of his work? Had he lost confidence in the leader he had appointed? Simon's memory reconstructed the eventful day when Jesus had said to him, 'Simon—I shall call you Peter; Peter the Rock! I shall build on this Rock!' Simon closed his eyes and shook his head as he compared the exultation of that moment with the utter hopelessness of his present plight.

When night fell, a guard with a flickering torch noisily unlocked each cell in turn and another replenished the water-pitcher. Noting that his bread had not been eaten, the guard did not give him any more; nor did he offer any comment. Perhaps it was not unusual for men, awaiting death, to take but little interest in food.

At feeding time there had been much rattling of chains and scuffling of feet, but everything was quiet now. Simon grew drowsy, slumped back uncomfortably with his head and shoulders against the old wall, and slept. After a while, he found himself experiencing a peculiar dream; peculiar in that it didn't seem like a dream, though he knew it was, for it couldn't be real. In his dream, he roused, amazed to find that the manacles had slipped from his hands and were lying open on the bench. He lifted his foot. The weight was gone. He drew himself up and listened. Everything was quiet but the rhythmic breathing of his fellow prisoners. He had never had a dream of such keen vividness.

Simon stood up and stretched his long arms. He took three or four

short steps toward the cell-door, slipping his sandals along the stone
floor as he felt his way in the darkness. There was no sound of the
scuffling of his sandals on the flagging. Except for this, the dream was
incredibly real. He put out his hand and touched the heavy, nail-
studded door. It noiselessly retreated. He advanced his hand to touch
the door again. It moved forward. He took another step—and another.
There had never been such a dream! Simon was awake and could
feel his heart pounding, and the rapid pulse-beat in his neck; but he
knew he was still asleep on the bench.

He put his hand against the damp wall and moved on with cautious
steps that made no sound. At the end of the long corridor, a feeble
light showed through the iron bars of a door. As he neared it the door
swung open so slowly and noiselessly that Simon knew the thing was
unreal! He walked through with firmer steps. In the dim light he saw
two guards sitting on the floor, with their arms around their knees
and their heads bent forward in sleep. They did not stir. He proceeded
toward the massive entrance gates, recognizing the ponderous lock
that united them. He expected his dream to swing them open, but
they had not moved. He put his hand on the cold metal, and pushed,
but the heavy gates remained firm.

By this he knew that the dream was over, and he would rouse to
find himself manacled in his cell. He was chilly. He wrapped his
robe more tightly about him, surprised that he still had the unim-
peded use of his hands. He glanced about, completely bewildered over
his strange mental condition. Suddenly his eye lighted on a narrow
gate, set within one of the greater gates. It was open. Simon stepped
through, and it closed behind him without a sound. He was on the
street. He started to walk briskly. At a crossing, he stumbled against
a curbing in the darkness. Surely this rough jar would waken him.
Simon stood still, looked up at the stars, and laughed softly for joy. He
was awake! He had been delivered from prison!

What to do now? Where to go? With lengthened steps, he made
his way to Benyosef's, where all was dark. He moved on to the home
of John Mark. A frail light showed from an upstairs window. He
tapped at the high wicket gate. After a little delay, the small port
in the gate was opened and he saw the frightened face of Rhoda.

She screamed and fled to the open house-door.

'It is Simon!' he heard her shout. 'Simon has returned from the
dead!'

Rushing back to the gate, she unbolted it and drew it open. Her
eyes were swollen with weeping, but her face was enraptured. She
threw her arms around Simon, hugging him fiercely.

'Simon!' she cried. 'Jesus has brought you back from death! Did
you see Stephen? Is he coming too?'

'Is Stephen dead, Rhoda?' asked Simon, sadly.

Her grip relaxed, and she slumped down into a dejected little figure of hopeless grief. Simon raised her up tenderly and handed her over to Mark's mother.

'We heard they had killed you,' said Mark.

'No,' said Simon. 'I was delivered from prison.'

They moved slowly into the house, Rhoda weeping inconsolably. The place was crowded with Christians. Their grieving eyes widened and their drawn faces paled as Simon entered, for they had thought him dead. They made way for him in silence. He paused in the midst of them. Some great experience had come to Simon. He had taken on a new dignity, a new power. Slowly he raised his hand and they bowed their heads.

'Let us pray,' said Peter the Rock.

'Blessed be God who has revived our hope. Though in great heaviness for a season, let us rejoice that this trial of our faith—more precious than gold—will make us worthy of honor when our Lord returns.'

* * * * * *

After walking up and down on the other side of the street facing the Insula for an hour or more, Demetrius' anxiety overwhelmed his patience. He must have been mistaken in his surmise that Marcellus would visit Julian himself on behalf of the persecuted Christians.

Abandoning his vigil, he made off rapidly for Benyosef's shop. While still a long way off, he began meeting well-dressed, sullen-faced men, apparently returning from some annoying experience. When he saw the sunshine glinting on the shields of an approaching military force, Demetrius dodged into an alley, and continued the journey by a circuitous route.

In spite of the edict prohibiting any further assembly of Christians, fully a score were crowded into the shop, silently gathered about a dead body. To his amazement, Demetrius saw his master in the midst of the people, almost as if he were in charge. He shouldered his way through the sorrowing group. Rhoda was down on her knees before the body, sobbing piteously. It seemed very unreal to find Stephanos, with whom he had talked only a few hours ago, lying here broken and dead.

Marcellus had taken him aside, when he had regained his composure.

'You remain with them, Demetrius,' he had said. 'Assist them with the burial. My presence here is an embarrassment. They cannot account for my interest, and are suspicious. I am going back to the inn.'

'Did you see this happen, sir?' Demetrius had asked.

'Yes.' Marcellus drew closer and said confidentially, 'And much more happened than appears here! I shall tell you—later.'

After they had put poor Stephanos away—and no one had molested them while on their errand—Demetrius had returned home with John Mark, thinking he would be free presently to rejoin Marcellus at the inn. But Mark's mother, Mary, and Rhoda too, had insisted so urgently on his remaining with them that he dared not refuse. When their unwanted supper had been disposed of and darkness had fallen, friends of the family began to arrive singly and by twos and threes until the lower rooms were filled. No one acted as a spokesman for the pensive party. There was much low-voiced conversation about a vision that appeared to Stephen before he died, but none of them had been close enough to know exactly what had happened. Demetrius had not attached much significance to the rumors. The only one who felt confident was Rhoda.

And then, to the utter amazement of everyone, Simon had arrived; a more important, more impressive figure than he had been before. He seemed reluctant to tell the details of his release from prison; but, by whatever process that had come to pass, the experience had built Simon up. He even seemed taller. They all felt it, and were shy about initiating conversation with him; hesitant about asking questions. Oddly enough, he had quietly announced that henceforth they should call him Peter.

Beckoning John Mark apart, Demetrius had suggested that they ask Simon Peter to lodge there. As for himself, he would cheerfully surrender his room and return to the inn. So—it had been arranged that way and Demetrius had slipped out unobtrusively. It was nearing midnight when he tapped at Marcellus' door, finding him awake and reading. They had talked in whispers until daybreak, their master-slave relationship completely ignored in their earnest discussion of the day's bewildering experiences.

'I too am a Christian!' Marcellus had declared, when he had finished his account of the stoning of Stephanos, and it seemed to Demetrius that the assertion had been made with more pride than he had ever put into 'I am a Roman!' It was very strange, indeed, this complete capitulation of Marcellus Gallio to a way of belief and behavior so foreign from his training and temperament.

Early in the afternoon, Demetrius accompanied him to the edge of the disreputable field that was called Golgotha. They were quiet as they approached it. Acrid smoke curled lazily from winnows of charred refuse. In the distance a grass-covered knoll appeared as a green oasis in a desert.

'Do you remember the place, sir?' asked Demetrius, halting.

'Vaguely,' murmured Marcellus. 'I'm sure I couldn't have found it. Is it clear in your memory, Demetrius?'

'Quite so. I came late. I could see the crosses from here, and the crowd.'

'What was I doing when you arrived?' asked Marcellus.

'You and the other officers were casting dice.'

'For the Robe?'

'Yes, sir.'

Neither spoke for a little while.

'I did not see the nailing, Demetrius,' said Marcellus, thickly. 'Paulus pushed me away. I was glad enough to escape the sight. I walked to the other side of the knoll. It has been a bitter memory, I can tell you.'

'Well, sir,' said Demetrius, 'here is the path. I shall wait for you at the inn. I hope you will not be disappointed, but it seems unlikely that Simon Peter would try to keep his appointment.'

'He will come, I think,' predicted Marcellus. 'Simon Peter is safer from arrest today than he was yesterday. Both the Insula and the Temple have tried to convince the public that the Christians have no legal or moral sanction for their beliefs. Having captured their leader, with the expectation of making a tragic example of him, they are now stunned by the discovery that their victim has walked out of prison. Neither Julian nor Herod will want to undertake an explanation of that event. I think they will decide that the less said or done now, in the case of The Big Fisherman, the better it will be for everybody concerned. I fully expect Simon Peter will meet me here—unless, in all the confusion, he has forgotten about it.'

* * * * * *

Peter had not forgotten. Marcellus saw him coming, a long way off, marching militantly with head up and a swinging stride that betokened a confident mind. The man had leadership, reflected the admiring watcher.

As The Big Fisherman neared the grassy knoll, however, his steps slowed and his shoulders slumped. He stopped and passed an unsteady hand over his massive forehead. Marcellus rose and advanced to meet him as he mounted the slight elevation with plodding feet. Peter extended his huge hand, but did not speak. They sat down on the grass near the deep pits where the crosses had stood, and for a long time they remained in silence.

At length, Peter roused from his painful meditation and glanced at Marcellus with heavy eyes, which drifted back to the ground.

'I was not here that day,' rumbled the deep, throaty voice. 'I did not stand by him in the hour of his anguish.' Peter drew a deep sigh.

Marcellus did not know what to say, or whether he was expected to say anything. The big Galilean sat ruefully studying the palms of his hands with a dejection so profound that any attempt to relieve it would have been an impertinence. Now he regarded Marcellus with critical interest, as if noting him for the first time.

'Your Greek slave told me you were interested in the story of Jesus,' he said, soberly. 'And it has come to me that you were of friendly service, yesterday, when our brave Stephen was taken away. Benyosef thought he heard you profess the faith of a Christian. Is that true, Marcellus Gallio?'

'I am convinced, sir,' said Marcellus, 'that Jesus is divine. I believe that he is alive, and of great power. But I have much to learn about him.'

'You have already gone far with your faith, my friend!' said Peter, warmly. 'As a Roman, your manner of living has been quite remote from the way of life that Jesus taught. Doubtless you have done much evil, for which you should repent if you would know the fullness of his grace. But I could not ask you to repent until I had told you of the wrongs which I have done. Whatever sins you may have committed, they cannot compare to the disloyalty for which I have been forgiven. He was my dearest friend—and, on the day that he needed me, I swore that I had never known him.'

Peter put his huge hands over his eyes and bowed his head. After a long moment he looked up.

'Now'—he said—'tell me how much you know about Jesus.'

Marcellus did not immediately reply, and when he did so, his words were barely audible. He heard himself saying, as if someone else were speaking:

'I crucified him.'

* * * * * *

The sun was low when they rose to return to the city. In those two hours, Marcellus had heard the stirring details of a story that had come to him previously in fragments and on occasions when his mind was unprepared to appreciate them.

They had found a strange kinship in their remorse, but Peter— fired by his inspiring recollections of the Master-man—had declared it was the future that must concern them now. He had daring plans for his own activities. He was going to Caesarea—to Joppa—perhaps to Rome!

'And what will you do, Marcellus?' he asked, in a tone of challenge.

'I am going home, sir.'

'To make your report to the Emperor?'

'Yes, sir.'

Peter laid his big hand heavily on Marcellus' knee and earnestly studied his eyes.

'How much are you going to tell him—about Jesus?' he demanded.

'I am going to tell the Emperor that Jesus, whom we thought dead, is alive—and that he is here to establish a new kingdom.'

'It will take courage to do that, my young brother! The Emperor will not like to hear that a new kingdom is coming. You may be punished for your boldness.'

'Be that as it may,' said Marcellus, 'I shall have told him the truth.'

'He will ask you how you know that Jesus lives. What will you say?'

'I shall tell him of the death of Stephanos—and the vision that he had. I am convinced that he saw Jesus!'

'Emperor Tiberius will want better proof than that.'

Marcellus was silently thoughtful. It was true, as Peter had said, such testimony would have very little weight with anyone disinclined to believe. Tiberius would scoff at such evidence, as who would not? Senator Gallio would say, 'You saw a dying man looking at Jesus. How do you know that is what he saw? Is this your best ground of belief that your Galilean is alive? You say he worked miracles: but you, personally, didn't see any.'

'Come,' said Peter, getting to his feet. 'Let us go back to the city.' They strode along with very little to say, each immersed in his thoughts. Presently they were in the thick of city traffic. Peter had said he was going back to John Mark's house. Marcellus would return to the inn. Now they were passing the Temple. The sun was setting and the marble steps—throughout the day swarming with beggars— were almost deserted.

One pitiful cripple, his limbs twisted and shrunken, sat dejectedly on the lowest step, waggling his basin and hoarsely croaking for alms. Peter slowed to a stop. Marcellus had moved on, a little way, but drifted back when he observed that Peter and the begger were talking.

'How long have you been this way, friend?' Peter was saying.

'Since my birth, sir,' whined the beggar. 'For God's sake—an alms!'

'I have no money,' confessed Peter; then, impulsively, he went on— 'but such as I have I give you!' Stretching out both hands to the bewildered cripple, he commanded, 'In the name of Jesus—stand up— and walk!' Grasping his thin arms, he tugged the beggar to his feet —and he stood! Amazed—and with pathetic little whimpers—half-laughing, half-crying, he slipped his sandals along the pavement; short, uncertain, experimental steps—but he was walking. Now he was shouting!

A crowd began to gather. Men of the neighborhood who recognized the beggar were pushing in to ask excited questions. Peter took Marcellus by the arm and they moved on, walking for some distance in silence. At length Marcellus found his voice, but it was shaky.

'Peter! How did you do that?'

'By the power of Jesus' spirit.'

'But—the thing's impossible! The fellow was born crippled! He had never taken a step in his life!'

'Well—he will walk now,' said Peter, solemnly.

'Tell me, Peter!' entreated Marcellus. 'Did you know you had this power? Have you ever done anything like this before?'

'No—not like this,' said Peter. 'I am more and more conscious of his presence. He dwells in me. This power—it is not mine, Marcellus. It is his spirit.'

'Perhaps he will not appear again—except in men's hearts,' said Marcellus.

'Yes!' declared Peter. 'He will dwell in men's hearts—and give them the power of his spirit. But—that is not all! *He will come again!*'

Chapter XX

It was common knowledge that Rome had the noisiest nights of any city in the world, but one needed a quiet year abroad to appreciate this fully.

Except for the two celebrated avenues intersecting at the Forum —the Via Sacra and the Via Nova—which were grandly laid with smooth block of Numidian marble, all of the principal thoroughfares were paved with cobblestones ranging in size from plums to pomegranates.

To relieve the congestion in these cramped, crooked streets and their still narrower tributaries, an ordinance—a century old—prohibited the movements of market-carts, delivery wagons, or any other vehicular traffic from sunrise to sunset, except imperial equipages and officially sanctioned parades on festal occasions.

Throughout the daylight hours, the business streets were gorged with milling crowds on foot, into which the more privileged ruthlessly rode their horses or were borne on litters and portable chairs; but when twilight fell, the harsh rasp and clatter of heavy iron wheels grinding the cobblestones set up a nerve-racking cacophony accompanied by the agonized squawk of dry axles, the cracking of whips, and the shrill quarrels of contenders for the right of way; nor did this maddening racket cease until another day had dawned. This was every night, the whole year round.

But the time to see and hear Rome at her utmost was during the full of a summer moon when much building construction was in progress, and everybody who had anything to haul took advantage of the light. Unable to sleep, thousands turned out in the middle of the hideous night to add their jostling and clamor to the other jams and confusions. Shopkeepers opened up to serve the meandering insomniacs with sweets and beverages. Hawkers barked their catchpenny wares; minstrels twanged their lyres and banged their drums; bulging camel-trains doggedly plodded through the protesting throng, trampling toes and tearing tunics; great wagons loaded with lumber and hewn stone plowed up the multitude, pitching the furrows against the walls and into open doorways. All nights in Rome were dreadful, and the more beautiful nights were dangerous.

Long before their galley from Ostia had rounded the bend that brought the city into full view on that bright June midnight of their homecoming, Marcellus heard the infernal din as he had never heard it before; heard it as no one could hear it without the preparation of a month's sailing on a placid summer sea.

The noise had a new significance. It symbolized the confounded outcry of a competitive world that had always done everything the hard way, the mean way, and had very little to show for its sweat and passion. It knew no peace, had never known peace, and apparently didn't want any peace.

Expertly the galley slipped into its snug berth to be met by a swarm of yelling porters. Demetrius, one of the first passengers over the rail, returned in a moment with a half-dozen swarthy Thracians who made off with their abundant luggage. Engaging another port-wagon for themselves, the travelers were soon swallowed up in a bedlam of tangled traffic through which they inched along until Marcellus, weary of the delay, suggested that they pay off the driver and continue on foot.

He had forgotten how insufferably rude and cruel the public could be. Massed into a solid pack, it had no intelligence. It had no capacity to understand how, if everyone calmly took his turn, some progress might be made. Even the wild animals around a water-hole in the jungle had more sense than this surly, selfish, shoving mob.

Marcellus' own words, spoken with such bland assurance to the cynical Paulus, flashed across his mind and mocked him. The kingdom of good will, he had declared, would not come into being at the top of society. It would not be handed down from a throne. It would begin with the common people. Well—here were your common people! Climb up on a cart, Marcellus, and tell the common people about good will. Admonish them to love one another, aid one another, defer to one another; and so fulfill the law of Christ. But—look out!—or they will pelt you with filth from the gutters; for the common people are in no mood to be trifled with.

*   *   *   *   *   *

The reunion of the Gallio family, an hour later, was one of the happiest experiences of their lives. When Marcellus had left home a year ago, shaky, emaciated, and mentally upset, the three who remained mourned for him almost as if he were dead. True, there had been occasional brief letters assuring them that he was well, but there was a conspicuous absence of details concerning his experiences and only vague intimations of a desire to come home. Between the lines they read, with forebodings, that Marcellus was still in a state of mental upheaval. He had seemed very far away, not only in miles but in mind. The last letter they had received from him, a month ago, had said, in closing, 'I am trailing an elusive mystery for the Emperor. Mysteries are his recreation. This one may turn out to be something more serious than a mere pastime.' The Senator had sighed and shaken his head as he slowly rolled up the scroll.

But now Marcellus had come back as physically fit as a gladiator, mentally alert, free of his despondency, in possession of his natural zest and enthusiasm.

And something else had been added, something not easy to define, a curious radiance of personality. There was a new strength in Marcellus, a contagious energy that vitalized the house. It was in his voice, in his eyes, in his hands. His family did not at first ask him what this new thing was, nor did they let him know that it was noticeable; neither did they discuss it immediately with one another. But Marcellus had acquired something that gave him distinction.

The Senator had been working late in his library. He had finished his task, had put away his writing materials, and had risen from his desk-chair when he heard confident footsteps.

Leaving Demetrius in the driveway to await the arrival of their luggage, Marcellus—joyfully recognized by the two old slaves on guard at the front door—had walked swiftly through to the spacious atrium. His father's door was partly open. Bursting in on him unceremoniously, he threw his arms around him and hugged him breathless. Although the Senator was tall and remarkably virile for his years, the Tribune's overwhelming vitality completely engulfed him.

'My son! My son!' Gallio quavered, fervently. 'You are well again! Strong again! Alive again! The gods be praised!'

Marcellus pressed his cheek against his father's and patted him on the back.

'Yes, sir!' he exclaimed. 'More alive than ever! And you, sir, grow more handsome every day! How proud I am to be your son!'

Lucia, in her room, suddenly stirred in her sleep, sat up wide-awake, listened, tossed aside the silk covers, listened again with an open mouth and a pounding heart.

'Oh!' she called. 'Tertia! My robe! Tertia! Wake up! Hurry! My sandals! Marcellus is here!' Racing down to the library, she threw herself into her brother's arms, and when he had lifted her off her feet and kissed her, she cried, 'Dear Marcellus—you are well!'

'And you—my sweet—are beautiful! You have grown up; haven't you?' He lightly touched her high coronet of glossy black hair with caressing fingers. 'Lovely!'

The Senator put his arms around both of them, to their happy surprise, for it was not his custom to be demonstrative with his affection.

'Come,' he said gently. 'Let us go to your mother.'

'It is very late,' said Marcellus. 'Should we waken her?'

'Of course!' insisted Lucia.

They crowded through the doorway, arm in arm. In the dimly lit atrium, a little group of the older servants had assembled, tousled and sleepy, their anxious eyes wondering what to expect of the son and heir who, on his last visit home, had been in such a distressing state of mind.

'Ho!—Marcipor!' shouted Marcellus, grasping the outstretched hand. 'Hi!—Decimus!' It wasn't often that the stiff and taciturn butler unbent, but he beamed with smiles as he thrust out his hand. 'How are you, Tertia!' called Marcellus to the tall, graceful girl descending the stairs. They all drew in closer. Old Servius was patted on the shoulder, and the wrinkled, toothless mouth chopped tremulously while the tears ran unchecked.

'Welcome! Welcome!' the old man shrilled. 'The gods bless you, sir!'

'Ah—Lentius!' hailed Marcellus. 'How are my horses?' And when Lentius had made bold to reply that Ishtar had a filly, three months old—which made them all laugh merrily as if this were a good joke on somebody—Marcellus sent them into another gale of laughter by demanding, 'Bring in the filly, Lentius! I must see her at once!'

There were more than a score of slaves gathered in the atrium now, all of them full of happy excitement. There had never been such an utter collapse of discipline in the Gallio household. Long-time servants, accustomed to moving about soberly and on tiptoe, heard themselves laughing hilariously—laughing here in the atrium!—laughing in the presence of the Senator! And the Senator was smiling, too!

Marcellus was brightening their eyes with his ready recognition, calling most of them by name. A pair of pretty Macedonian twins arrived, hand in hand, dressed exactly alike; practically indistinguishable. He remembered having had a glimpse of them, two years ago, but had forgotten their names. He looked their way, and so did everyone else, to their considerable embarrassment.

'Are you girls sisters?' he inquired.

This was by far the merriest thing that anyone had said, and the atrium resounded with full-throated appreciation.

'Decimus!' shouted the Senator, and the laughter ceased. 'You will serve supper! In an hour! In the banquet-room! With the gold service! Marcipor!—let all the lamps be lighted! Throughout the villa! And the gardens!'

Marcellus brushed through the scattering crowd and bounded up the stairs. Cornelia met him in the corridor, outside her door, and he gathered her hungrily into his arms. They had no adequate words for each other; just stood there, clinging together, Cornelia smoothing his close-cropped hair with her soft palm and sobbing like a child, while the Senator, with misty eyes, waited a little way apart, fumbling with the silk tassels on his broad sash.

Her intuition suggesting that Marcellus and their emotional mother might need a quiet moment alone together, Lucia had tarried at the foot of the staircase for a word with Decimus about the supper. All the other servants had scurried away to their duties, their very sandal-straps confiding in excited whispers that this was a happy night and a good place to be.

'Not too much food, Decimus,' Lucia was saying. 'Some fresh fruit and cold meats and wine—and a nut-cake if there is one. But don't cook anything. It is late, and the Senator will be tired and sleepy before you have time to prepare an elaborate dinner. Serve it in the big dining-room, as he said, and use the gold plate. And tell Rhesus to cut an armful of roses—red ones. And let the twins serve my brother. And—'

With suddenly widened eyes, she sighted Demetrius—tall, tanned, serious, and handsome—entering the atrium. Dismissing the butler with a brief nod, Lucia held her arm high and waved a welcome, her flowing sleeve baring a shapely elbow. Decimus, keenly observant, scowled his displeasure and stalked stiffly away.

Advancing with long strides, Demetrius came to a military halt before her, bowed deferentially, and was slowly bringing up his spear-shaft to his forehead in the conventional salute when Lucia stepped forward impulsively, laying both hands on his bronzed arms.

'All thanks, good Demetrius,' she said, softly. 'You have brought Marcellus home—well and strong as ever. Better than ever!'

'No thanks are due me for that,' he rejoined. 'The Tribune needed no one to bring him home. He is fully master of himself now.' Demetrius raised his eyes and regarded her with frank admiration. 'May I tell the Tribune's sister how very—how very well she is looking?'

'Why not—if you think so?' Lucia, toying with her amber beads, gave him a smile that meant to be non-committal. 'There is no need asking you how you are, Demetrius. Have you and the Tribune had some exciting experiences?' Her eyes were wincingly exploring a long, new scar on his upper arm. He glanced down at it with a droll grin. 'How did you get that awful cut?' she asked, squeamishly.

'I met a Syrian,' said Demetrius. 'They are not a very polite people.'

'I hope you taught him some of the gentle manners of the Greeks,' drawled Lucia. 'Tell me—did you kill him?'

'You can't kill a Syrian,' said Demetrius, lightly. 'They die only of old age.'

Lucia's little shrug said they had had enough of this banter and her face slowly sobered to a thoughtful frown.

'What has happened to my brother?' she asked. 'He seems in such extraordinarily high spirits.'

'He may want to tell you—if you give him time.'

'You're different, too, Demetrius.'

'For the better, I hope,' he parried.

'Something has expanded you both,' declared Lucia. 'What is it? Has Marcellus been elevated to a more responsible command?'

Demetrius nodded enthusiastically.

'Will his new assignment take him into danger?' she asked, suddenly apprehensive.

'Oh, yes, indeed!' he answered, proudly.

'He doesn't appear to be worrying much about it. I never saw him so happy. He has already turned the whole villa upside-down with his gaiety.'

'I know. I heard them.' Demetrius grinned.

'I hope it won't spoil them,' she said, with dignity. 'They aren't used to taking such liberties; though perhaps it will not hurt—to have it happen—this once.'

'Perhaps not,' said Demetrius, dryly. 'It may not hurt them—to be really happy—this once.'

Lucia raised her brows.

'I am afraid you don't understand,' she remarked, coolly.

'I'm afraid I do,' he sighed. 'Had you forgotten that I too am a slave?'

'No.' She gave a little toss of her head. 'But I think you have.'

'I did not mean to be impudent,' he said, contritely. 'But what we are talking about is very serious, you know; discipline, slavery, mastery, human relations—and who has a right to tell others when they may be happy.'

Lucia searched his face with a frown.

'Well—I hope my brother's genial attitude towards our servants is not going to make us lose our control of this house!' she snapped, indignantly.

'It need not,' said Demetrius. 'He believes in a little different kind of control; that is all. It is much more effective, I think, than controlling by sharp commands. More pleasant for everybody; and, besides, you get better service.'

Marcellus was calling to her from the head of the stairs.

'I am sorry I spoke impatiently, Demetrius,' she said, as she moved away. 'We are so glad you are home again.'

He met her level eyes and they smiled. He raised his spear-shaft to salute. She pursed her lips, shook her head, and made a negligent gesture.

'Never mind the salute,' she said—'this once.'

Marcipor, who had been lingering impatiently in the alcove, waiting for this conversation to end, came forward as Lucia disappeared up the stairway. He fell into step with Demetrius and they strolled out through the peristyle into the moonlight.

'It is amazing—how he has recovered!' said Marcipor. 'What happened to him?'

'I shall tell you fully when there is an opportunity; later tonight, if possible. Marcellus has become an ardent believer. He toured through Galilee—'

'And you?' asked Marcipor. 'Were you not with him?'

'Only part of the time. I spent many weeks in Jerusalem. I have much to tell you about that. Marcipor—the Galilean is alive!'

'Yes—we have heard that.'

' "We"?—and who are "we"?' Demetrius took hold of Marcipor's arm and drew him to a sudden halt.

'The Christians in Rome,' replied Marcipor, smiling at his friend's astonishment.

'Has it then come to Rome—so soon?'

'Many months ago—brought by merchants from Antioch.'

'And how did you find out?'

'It was being whispered about in the markets. Decimus, who is forever deriding the Greeks, was pleased to inform me that certain superstitious traders from Antioch had brought the report of a Jewish carpenter who had risen from the dead. Remembering what you had told me about this man, I was devoured with curiosity to hear more of it.'

'And you found the men from Antioch?' encouraged Demetrius.

'The next day. They were quite free to talk, and their story sounded convincing. They had had it from an eye-witness of many astounding miracles—one Philip. Seeking to confirm it, several of them went to Jerusalem where they talked with other men who had seen this Jesus after his death—men whose word they trusted. All that—added to what you had reported—gave me cause to believe.'

'So—you are a Christian!' Demetrius' eyes shone. 'You must tell the Tribune. He will be delighted!'

Marcipor's face grew suddenly grave.

'Not yet—Demetrius. My course is not clear. Decimus made it his business to inform the Senator of this new movement, describing it as a revolution against lawful authority.'

'Has the Senator done anything about it?'

'Not that I know of, but is it not natural that his feeling toward the Christians should be far from complacent? He associates all this with his son's misfortunes. Now—if Marcellus is told that we have a large body of believers here in Rome, he might impetuously throw himself into it. That would be dangerous. The Christians are keeping under cover. Already the patrols are beginning to make inquiries about their secret meetings. We must not cause a breach between Marcellus and his father.'

'Very well, Marcipor,' agreed Demetrius. 'We will not tell the Tribune, but he will find it out; you may be sure of that. And as for estrangement, it is inevitable. Marcellus will not give up his belief, and it is quite unlikely that the Senator could be persuaded of its truth. Old men do not readily change their opinions. However—this new cause cannot wait, Marcipor, until all the opinionated old men have approved of it. This story of Jesus is our only hope that freedom and justice may come. And if it is to come—at all—it must begin now!'

'I believe that,' said Marcipor—'but still—I shouldn't like to see Marcellus offend his father. The Senator is not going to live long.'

'There was just such a case reported to Jesus,' said Demetrius. 'I had this from a Galilean who heard the conversation. A young man, very much impressed that it was his duty to come out openly for this new way of life, said to Jesus, "My father is an old man, sir, with old views. This new religion is an offense to him. Let me first bury my father, and then I shall come—and follow." '

'That sounds reasonable,' put in Marcipor, who was sixty-seven.

'Jesus didn't think so,' went on Demetrius. 'It was high time for a drastic change in men's belief and behavior. The new message couldn't wait for the departure of old men with old views. Indeed, these old men were already dead. Let them be buried by other dead ones.'

'Did he say that?' queried Marcipor.

'Well—something like that.'

'Sounds rather rough—to me—coming from so gentle a person.'

Demetrius slipped his hand affectionately through the older Corinthian's arm.

'Marcipor—let us not make the mistake of thinking that, because this message of Jesus concerns peace and good will, it is a soft and timid thing that will wait on every man's convenience, and scurry off the road, to hide in the bushes, until all other things go by! The people who carry this torch are going to get into plenty of trouble. They are already being whipped and imprisoned! Many have been slain!'

'I know, I know,' murmured Marcipor. 'One of the traders from Antioch told me of seeing a young Greek stoned to death by a mob in Jerusalem. Stephanos was his name. Did you—by any chance—know him?'

'Stephanos,' said Demetrius, sadly, 'was my closest friend.'

* * * * * *

Marcellus had not finished his breakfast when Marcipor came in to say that Senator Gallio was in his library and would be pleased to have a talk with the Tribune at his early convenience.

'You may tell the Senator that I shall be down in a few minutes,' said Marcellus.

He would have preferred to postpone, for a few days, this serious interview with his father. It would be very difficult for the Senator to listen to his strange story with patience or respect. For some moments Marcellus sat staring out the open window, while he absently peeled an orange that he didn't intend to eat, and tried to decide how best to present the case of Jesus the Galilean; for, in this instance, he would be more than an advocate. Marcellus would be on trial, too.

Marcus Lucan Gallio was not a contentious man. His renown as a debater in the Senate had been earned by diplomacy; by his knowing when and how much to concede, where and whom to appease, and the

fine art of conciliation. He never doggedly pursued an argument for
vanity's sake. But he was proud of his mental morality.

If, for example, he became firmly convinced that at all times and
everywhere water seeks a level, there would be no use in coming to
him with the tale that on a certain day, in a certain country, at the
behest of a certain man, water was observed to run uphill. He had no
time for reports of events which disregarded natural laws. As for
'miracles,' the very word was offensive. He had no tolerance for such
stories and not much more tolerance for persons who believed in them.
And because, in his opinion, all religions were built on faith in supernatural beings and supernatural doings, the Senator was not only contemptuous of religion, but admitted a candid distaste for religious
people. Anybody who went in for such beliefs was either ignorant or
unscrupulous. If a man, who had any sense at all, became a religious
propagandist, he needed watching; for, obviously, he meant to take
advantage of the feebleminded who would trust him because of his
piety. Some people—according to Senator Gallio—seemed to think
that a pious man was inevitably honest, whereas the facts would show
that piety and integrity were categorically irrelevant. It was quite
proper for old Servius to importune his gods. One could even forgive
old Tiberius for his consuming interest in religion, seeing that he was
out of his head. But there was no excuse for such nonsense in a healthy,
educated man.

Marcellus had been treated with deep sympathy when he had come
home a year ago. He had suffered a great shock and his mind was
temporarily unbalanced. He couldn't have said anything too preposterous for his father's patience. But now he was sound in body and
mind. He would tell the Senator this morning an amazing story of a
man who had healed all manner of diseases; a man who, having been
put to death on a cross, rose from his grave to be seen of many witnesses. And this would undoubtedly make the Senator very angry—and
disgusted. 'Bah!' he would shout. 'Nonsense!'

*   *   *   *   *   *

This forecast of his father's probable attitude had been appallingly
accurate. It turned out to be a very unhappy interview. From almost
the first moment, Marcellus sensed strong opposition. He had decided
to begin his narrative with Jesus' unjust trials and crucifixion, hoping
thus to enlist the Senator's sympathy for the persecuted Galilean, but
he was not permitted to build up his case from that point.

'I have heard all that, my son,' said Gallio, crisply. 'You need not
review it. Tell me of the journey you made into the country where
this man lived.'

So—Marcellus had told of his tour with Justus; of little Jonathan,
whose crippled foot had been made strong; of Miriam, who had been
given a voice; of Lydia, who had found healing by a touch of his Robe;

of old Nathanael Bartholomew, and the storm at sea—while his father gazed steadily at him from under shaggy frowning brows, offering no comments and asking no questions.

At length he had arrived at the phase of the story where he must talk of Jesus' return to life. With dramatic earnestness he repeated everything that they had told him of these reappearances, while the lines about the Senator's mouth deepened into a scowl.

'It all sounds incredible, sir,' he conceded, 'but I am convinced that it is true.' For a moment, he debated the advisability of telling his father about the miracle he had seen with his own eyes—Peter's healing of the cripple. But no—that would be too much. His father would tell him he had been imposed upon by these miracle stories reported to him by other men. But there would be nothing left for the Senator to say except. 'You lie!' if he told him that he himself had seen one of these wonders wrought.

'On the testimony of a few superstitious fishermen!' growled Gallio, derisively.

'It was not easy for me to accept, sir,' admitted Marcellus, 'and I am not trying to persuade you of it. You asked me to tell you what I had learned about Jesus, and I have told you truly. It is my belief that this Galilean is still alive. I think he is an eternal person, a divine person with powers that no king or emperor has ever possessed, and I further believe that he will eventually rule the world!'

Gallio chuckled bitterly.

'Had you thought of telling Tiberius that this Jesus intends to rule the world?'

'I may not need to say that to Tiberius. I shall tell him that Jesus, who was put to death, is alive again. The Emperor can draw his own conclusions.'

'You had better be careful what you say to that crazy old man,' warned Gallio. 'He is insane enough to believe you, and this will not be pleasant news. Don't you know he is quite capable of having you punished for bringing him a tale like that?'

'He can do no more than kill me,' said Marcellus, quietly.

'Perhaps not,' drawled Gallio; 'but even so light a punishment as death—for an aspiring young man—might be quite an inconvenience.'

Marcellus humored his father's grim jest with a smile.

'In sober truth, sir, I do not fear death. There is a life to come.'

'Well—that is an ancient hope, my son,' conceded Gallio, with a vague gesture. 'Men have been scrawling that on their tombs for three thousand years. The only trouble with that dream is that it lacks proof. Nobody has ever signaled us from out there. Nobody has ever come back to report.'

'Jesus did!' declared Marcellus.

Gallio sighed deeply and shook his head. After a moody silence, he pushed back his chair and walked slowly around the big desk, as Marcellus rose to meet his approach.

'My son,' he said, entreatingly, laying his hands on the broad shoulders, 'go to the Emperor and tell him what you have learned of this Galilean prophet. Quote Jesus' words of wisdom. They are sensible and should do Tiberius much good if he would heed them. Tell him— if you must—about the feats of magic. The old man will believe them, and the more improbable they are the better they—and you—will please him. That, in my opinion, should be sufficient.'

'Nothing about Jesus' return to life?' inquired Marcellus, respectfully.

'Why should you?' demanded Gallio. 'Take a common-sense view of your predicament. Through no fault of yours, you have had an unusual experience, and are now obliged to report on it to the Emperor. He has been mad for a dozen years or more and everybody in Rome knows it. He has surrounded himself with scores of scatter-brained philosophers, astrologers, soothsayers, and diviners of oracles. Some of them are downright impostors and the rest of them are mentally unhinged. If you tell Tiberius what you have told me, you will be just one more monkey added to his menagerie.'

It was strong medicine, but Marcellus grinned; and his father, feeling that his argument was gaining ground, went on, pleadingly.

'You have a bright future before you, my son, if you will it so; but not if you pursue this course. I wonder if you realize what a tragedy may be in the making for you—for all of us! It will be a bitter experience for your mother, and your sister, and your father, to know that our friends are telling one another you have lost your mind; that you are one of the Emperor's wise fools. And what will Diana say?' he continued, earnestly. 'That beautiful creature is in love with you! Don't you care?'

'I do care, sir!' exclaimed Marcellus. 'And I realize that she may be sadly disappointed in me, but I have no alternative. I have put my hand to this plow—and I am not turning back!'

Gallio retreated a step and lounged against his desk, with a sly smile.

'Wait until you see her before you decide to give her up.'

'I am indeed anxious to see her, sir.'

'Will you try to meet her, down there, before you talk to Tiberius?'

'If possible, yes, sir.'

'You have made your arrangements for the voyage?'

'Yes, sir. Demetrius has seen to it. We leave this evening. Galley to Ostia. To Capri on *The Cleo.*'

'Very good,' approved Gallio, much encouraged. He slapped Marcellus on the back. 'Let us take a walk in the gardens. And you haven't been to the stables yet.'

'A moment, please, sir—before we go.' Marcellus' face was serious.

'I know you have a feeling that everything is settled now, according to your wish, and I would be happy to follow your counsel if I were free to do so.'

'Free?' Gallio stared into his son's eyes. 'What do you mean?'

'I feel obliged, sir, to tell the Emperor of Jesus' return to life.'

'Well, well, then,' consented Gallio, brusquely, 'if you must talk about that, let it be as a local rumor among the country people. You don't have to tell Tiberius that *you* believe it! If you want to say that a few fishermen thought they saw him, that should discharge your obligation. You have no personal knowledge of it. *You* didn't see him!'

'But I saw a man who did see him, sir!' declared Marcellus. '*I saw this man looking at him!*'

'And that constitutes proof—in your opinion?' scoffed Gallio.

'In this instance—yes, sir! I saw a Greek stoned for his Christian belief. He was a brave man, ready to risk his life for his faith. I knew him, and trusted him. When everyone thought him dead, he raised up, smiled, and shouted, "*I see him!*" And—*I know that he saw him!*'

'But you don't have to tell that to Tiberius!' said Gallio, testily.

'Yes, sir! Having heard and seen that, I should be a coward if I did not testify to it! For I, too, am a Christian, sir! I cannot do otherwise!'

Gallio made no reply. With bent head, he turned away slowly and left the room, without a backward glance.

Lamenting his father's disappointment, Marcellus sauntered out to the pergola, feeling sure that Lucia would be waiting for him. She saw him coming and ran to meet him. Linking their arms, she tugged him along gaily toward their favorite rendezvous.

'What's the matter?' she insisted, shaking his arm. 'Have a row with the Senator?'

'I hurt his feelings,' muttered Marcellus.

'I hope you weren't talking to him about that awful business up there in Jerusalem that made you sick!'

'No, dear; but I was telling him about that man—and I would be glad to tell you, too.'

'Thanks, my little brother!' chaffed Lucia. 'I don't want to hear a word of it! High time you forgot all about it! . . . Here, Bambo! . . . Make a fuss over him, Marcellus. He hardly knows you.' Her lips pouted. 'Neither do I,' she murmured. 'Aren't you ever going to be happy any more? Last night we all thought you were well again. I was so glad I lay awake for hours, hugging myself for joy! Now you're blue and moody.' Big tears stood in her eyes. 'Please, Marcellus!'

'Sorry, sister.' He put his arm around her. 'Let us go look at the roses. . . . Here, Bambo!'

Bambo strolled up and consented to have his head patted.

* * * * * *

The Emperor had not been well for many weeks. Early in April, while rashly demonstrating how tough he was, the old man had ambled down to the uncompleted villa on the easternmost end of the mall in a drenching rain and had taken a severe cold, the effects of which had depleted his not too abundant vitality.

In normal circumstances Tiberius, customarily careful of his health, would have taken no such risk; or, having taken it, would have gone at once to bed, fuming and snorting, to be packed in hot fomentations and doctored with everything that the court physicians could devise.

But on this occasion the Emperor, having renewed his youth—or at least having attained his second childhood—had sat about with Diana in the dampness of the new villa, wet to the skin, after which he had sauntered back to the Jovis pretending to have enjoyed the rain and refusing to permit anyone to aid him, though it was clear enough that he was having a hard chill: he had sneezed sloppily in the Chamberlain's face while hoarsely protesting that he was sound as a nut.

That the young daughter of Gallus had been innocently but unmistakably responsible for this dangerous imprudence—and many another hazardous folly on the part of the aging Emperor—was now the unanimous opinion of the household staff.

The beauteous Diana was getting to be a problem. For the first few weeks after her arrival, more than a year ago, the entire population of Capri—with the exception of the Empress Julia, whose jealousy of her was deep and desperate—had rejoiced in the girl's invigorating influence on Tiberius. His infatuation for Diana had done wonders for him. Boyishly eager to please her, he was living more temperately, not only in what he ate and drank, but in what he said and did. Not often now was the Emperor noticeably intoxicated. His notorious tantrums were staged less frequently and with less violence. When annoyed, he still threw things at his ministers, but it had been a long time since he had barked at or bitten anyone. And whereas he had frequently humiliated them all by slogging about the grounds looking like the veriest ragamuffin, now he insisted on being shaved almost every morning and was keenly interested in his costumes.

This had met the enthusiastic approval of everybody whose tenure of office was in any way related to his own—and that included almost everyone on Capri, ministers, minstrels, physicians, dancers, gardeners, vintners, tailors, astrologers, historians, poets, cooks, guards, carpenters, stonemasons, sculptors, priests, and at least three hundred servants, bond and free. The longer they could keep the Emperor alive, the better for their own careers; and the more contented he was, the less arduous their task of caring for him.

It was quite natural, therefore, that Diana should be popular. The poets in residence composed extravagant odes appropriately extolling her beauty, and—with somewhat less warrant—her sweet and gentle disposition, for she was of uncertain temper and not at all reticent about expressing her feelings when displeased.

But, as time went on, it began to be whispered about that the infirm Emperor, in trying to show off for Diana, was wearing himself out. He was at her nimble heels from sunrise to sunset, in all weathers, fiercely gouging the graveled paths with his cane as they toured the island, and wheezing up and down stairs in her lavish new villa which seemed almost as far from completion as it had been six months previously, though a hundred skilled workmen had been hard at it every day. Nothing was ever quite fine enough. Mantels had to be taken down and rebuilt, again and again. Mosaic floors and walls were ripped out and done over. One day the old man had testily remarked that he didn't believe the villa would ever be completed, an impromptu forecast which, albeit spoken lightly, turned out to be a sound prediction.

For some time considerable sympathy was felt for Diana. Though no one knew certainly—for she was far too wise to confide fully in anyone connected with this university of gossip, intrigue, and treachery—it was generally believed that the brilliant and beautiful girl was being detained at Capri against her personal wishes. This seemed to be confirmed by the fact that on the occasions of her mother's visits, every few weeks, Diana would weep piteously when the time came for Paula's departure. There might be certain advantages in being the sole object of the Emperor's devotion; but, considered as a permanent occupation, it left a good deal to be desired.

A legend had gradually taken form and size concerning Diana's prospects. The Chamberlain, in his cups, had confided to the Captain of the Guard that the comely daughter of Legate Gallus was in love with the son of Senator Gallio, a probably hopeless attachment, seeing that the young Tribune was sick in the head and had been spirited out of the country. This information was soon common knowledge.

No one was more interested in Diana's aspirations than old Julia, who contrived to inspect every letter she sent and received. And it was believed that Julia relayed copies of all such correspondence to Gaius; for, on each occasion of having spied upon Diana's letters, she had dispatched a scroll to the Prince by special messenger.

During the winter, Gaius had not visited Capri; but, advised of the Emperor's indisposition, he had come in latter April, attended by a foppish retinue, and had spent a week, pretending to be much concerned over the old man's ill-health, but fully enjoying the nightly banquets which Tiberius had ordered.

On these occasions the Emperor—barely able to hold his weary head up—drowsed and roused and grinned like a skull and drowsed again, a ludicrous caricature of imperial power. On his right, but paying no attention to him, reclined old Julia, wigged, painted, ablaze with jewels and shockingly cadaverous, smirking and fawning over Gaius who lounged beside her.

None of the fifty dissolute sycophants, who sprawled about the over-loaded tables, dared risk exchanging a wink or a smile, but it was an amusing pantomime, with the Emperor half-asleep and the Empress disgustingly pawing at the gold-embroidered sleeve of the Prince while he, disdainfully indifferent to her caresses, leaned far forward to make amorous grimaces at Diana, on the other side of Tiberius, stripping her with his experienced, froglike eyes, while she regarded him with the cool detachment of one reading an epitaph on an ancient monument.

This had been privately enjoyed by almost everybody but Celia, the beautiful but feather-headed wife of Quintus and niece of Sejanus, long-time friend and adviser of Tiberius. Celia was beside herself with an anxiety she could not disguise. She would have been ready to kill Diana had the girl shown Gaius the slightest encouragement, but she was also much annoyed over Diana's frosty disinterest in the Prince's attentions. Who indeed did this young Gallus think she was—to be so haughty? She had better mend her manners! The crazy old man she was leading about—like a dog on a leash—would be dying one of these fine days; and then where would she be?

It had been a depressing week for Celia. Ever since Quintus had been sent abroad on some state mission of high importance, she had been the center of interest at the Prince's social functions, serving as hostess and enjoying his candid and clumsy preferment. At first it had been believed that Gaius was showing her special favors to ingratiate himself with old Sejanus, who held a strong hand on the imperial purse-strings. But as time went on, and the Prince's visits at Celia's villa were of daily occurrence, this flattery had gone to her head and she had made the mistake of snubbing many friends who, though they had endured her snobberies for diplomacy's sake, were carefully preparing to avenge themselves when an opportune moment arrived. It had been Celia's hope that the Prince would find further business for her husband in foreign parts, but now it had been announced that Quintus was returning presently. As if that were not dismaying enough, Gaius was giving his full attention to Diana.

On the last day of this visit to the Emperor, Celia had arranged what she thought was a private moment with the Prince—though there were few conversations on Capri which the whole island didn't know by nightfall—and tearfully took him to task for his recent indifference.

'I thought you liked me,' she whimpered.

'Not when your nose is red,' he grumbled. 'You'd better stop making yourself ridiculous.'

'Can't you send Quintus away again?' she wheedled.

'That braying ass?' retorted Gaius. 'We trust him with an ambassadorial errand, and he gets himself slapped all over the campus of a Greek inn by an unarmed slave!'

'I don't believe it!' shrilled Celia. 'It's a story someone invented to discredit him! I thought you were Quintus' friend.'

'Bah! Quintus' only friend is his mirror! Had I cared for your husband, would I have made a cuckold of him?'

Celia had wept hysterically.

'You liked me well enough,' she cried, 'until you came here and noticed this Gallus girl's curves! And it's plain to see she despises you! What an impudent creature she is!'

'Mind you don't plan to do her some injury!' growled Gaius, clutching her arm roughly. 'You would better forget all about her now, and be contented with your husband when he comes.' He chuckled infuriatingly. 'You and Quintus are admirably suited to each other.'

'You can't do this to me!' she shouted, reckless with rage. 'Where will you stand with Sejanus when I tell him you have treated me like an ordinary trollop?'

Gaius shrugged.

'Where will *you* stand—when you tell him that?' he sneered.

Whereupon Celia had sought comfort in a call on the Empress, suddenly remembering a social duty which most of the rest forgot in the confusion of departure.

Julia had been surprisingly effusive; and Celia, red-eyed and outraged, was a ready victim to the Empress' sympathetic queries.

'Poor Gaius!' sighed old Julia. 'So impressionable! So lonesome! And so beset with cares! You must make allowances for him, my dear. And he really is in love, I think, with the daughter of Gallus. It would not be a bad alliance. Gallus is a great favorite with the army, at home and abroad. Indeed—Gallus *is* the army! And if my son is to succeed to the throne, he needs the good will of our legions. Futhermore—as you have seen for yourself, the Emperor is so foolishly fond of Diana that her marriage with Gaius would practically insure my son's future.'

'But Diana hates him!' cried Celia. 'Anyone can see that!'

'Well—that is because she thinks she is in love with the half-crazy son of Gallio.' Julia's thin lips puckered in an omniscient smile. 'She will get over that. Perhaps—if you would like to square accounts with the luscious Diana, you might give yourself no bother to deny the reports that Marcellus is insane.' And with that, the Empress had kissed Celia and waved her out.

Wiping her lips vigorously, Celia returned to the Jovis where the party was assembling for conveyance down the mountain to the imperial barge. She was still hopeful that Gaius, on the return trip, would repent of his discourtesies and restore her to his favor.

'Where is the Prince?' she inquired, with forced brightness, of her cousin Lavilla Sejanus, as the slave-borne chairs were being filled.

'He isn't going back to the city with us,' Lavilla had had malicious pleasure in replying. 'I daresay he wants to have a quiet visit with Diana.'

'Well—he can have her!' retorted Celia, hotly.

'Don't be too sure of that!' shrilled Minia, Lavilla's younger sister, who was thought to have been wholly occupied with the conversation she was having with Olivia Varus, in the chair beside her.

'Diana is waiting for Marcellus Gallio to come back,' put in Olivia.

'Much good that will do her,' sniffed Celia. 'Marcellus has lost his mind. That's why they sent him away.'

'Nonsense!' scoffed Lavilla. 'The Emperor sent him away to make some sort of investigation—in Athens—or somewhere. Think he would have sent a crazy man?'

'Why not?' giggled Minia.

'Who told you that, Celia?' demanded Olivia.

'The Empress!' declared Celia, impressively. 'I don't think it's a secret.'

'Neither do I,' drawled Lavilla. 'It may have been—but it isn't now.'

'Why should you care?' inquired Minia, languidly.

'Well—I rather like Marcellus,' said Lavilla, 'and Diana, too. It's unfortunate to have such a story strewn about. Besides—I don't believe it!'

'But the Empress told me!' snapped Celia, indignantly.

Lavilla arched her brows, pursed her lips, and shrugged.

'I wonder why,' she said.

* * * * * *

It was mid-afternoon when *The Cleo* sighted the island and another hour had passed before she tied up at the wharf. It had been a perfect day. Marcellus had never seen the Bay of Neapolis so blue. Demetrius was left at the docks to oversee the conveyance of their luggage to the Villa Jovis.

Engaging a waiting chair, Marcellus was borne up the long flight of marble steps, and the sinuous path, and more steps, and another path, luxuriating in the ruinously expensive beauty with which the Emperor had surrounded himself. The old man might be crazy, but he was an artist.

Now that they had come up to the plateau, Tiberius' wonder city —dominated by the massive Jovis—gleamed white in the June sunshine. Lean old philosophers and fat old priests lounged in the arbors, and on the graveled paths that bounded the pools other wise men strolled with their heads bent and their hands clasped behind them. Were all of the Emperor's counselors old men? Naturally they would be. It aged Marcellus to face the prospect of joining forces with these doddering ancients.

It surprised and gratified him that he had so little explaining to do in accounting for his presence. He spoke his name to the patrol and

they passed him without examination. He told the porter who he was
and the porter sent another with a message to the Captain of the
Guard, who came without delay and led him through the vasty peristyle into the cool, high-ceilinged atrium where, presently, the Chamberlain entered to greet him with much deference.

The Emperor, who was resting, would be made aware of Tribune
Marcellus' arrival. Meantime—would the Tribune be pleased to go to
the apartment which had been prepared for him?

'I was expected, then?' asked Marcellus.

'Oh, yes, sir,' replied Nevius. 'His Majesty had learned of Tribune
Marcellus' arrival in Rome.'

It was a sumptuous suite that they showed him, with a small, exquisitely appointed peristyle of its own, looking out upon a colorful
garden. A half-dozen Nubians were preparing his bath. A tall Macedonian slave came with a flagon of wine, followed by another bearing
a silver salver filled with choice fruits.

Marcellus stepped out into the peristyle, frowning thoughtfully. It
was an unexpectedly lavish reception he was having at the hands of
the Emperor. His rank entitled him to certain courtesies, but the attention he was receiving needed a better explanation. It was flattering
enough, but perplexing. Demetrius had arrived now, and the porters
had brought the luggage. The Chamberlain came out to announce
that the Tribune's bath was ready.

'And at your convenience, sir,' added Nevius, 'the daughter of
Gallus will receive you—in the garden—at her villa.'

*   *   *   *   *   *

They had offered to conduct him, but Marcellus preferred to go
alone after receiving general directions. Diana's villa! And what did
Diana want with a villa—at Capri? Or did she want a villa? Or was it
the old man's idea?

He was approaching it now, involuntarily slowing his steps as he
marveled at its grace and symmetry. It was a large house, but conveyed no impression of massiveness. The Doric columns of the portico
were not ponderous; the carving on the lintel was light and lacy. It
was an immense doll's house, suggestive of something an ingenious
confectioner might have made of white sugar.

A guard met him on the tessellated pavement and led the way in
and through the unfurnished atrium, ceiled with blue in which gold
stars were set; and on to the peristyle where many workmen glanced
down from the scaffoldings with casual interest in the guest. Beyond
lay the intentions of a terraced garden. Pointing to the pergola that
was on the southern rim of the plateau, the guard retraced his steps
and Marcellus proceeded with lengthened stride, full of happy anticipation.

Diana was leaning against the marble balustrade, looking out upon the sea. Sensitive to his coming, perhaps hearing his footsteps, she slowly turned about; and, resting her elbows on the broad stone railing, waited his approach with a sober, wide-eyed stare which Marcellus easily interpreted. She was wondering—and with deep apprehension —whether he had fully recovered from his mental sickness; whether there would be constraint in their meeting. Her eyes were a little frightened, and she involuntarily pressed the back of her hand against her lips.

Marcellus had no time to regard the attractive costume she wore, the gracefully draped white silk stola with the deep crimson border at the throat, the slashed sleeves loosely clasped with gold buttons, the wide, tightly bound girdle about the hips, the pearl-beaded crimson coronet that left a fringe of black curls on her white forehead; but Diana was an enchanting picture. She had developed into a mature woman in his absence. In his recollections of her, Diana was a beautiful girl. Sometimes he had wondered, when abroad, whether he might have idealized her too extravagantly; but now she was far more lovely than he had remembered. His happiness shone in his face.

Slowly she advanced to meet him, tall and regal in the caressing lines of the while stola, her full lips parting in a tentative smile that was gaining confidence with every step. She extended her hands, as he neared her, still studying him with a yearning hope.

'Diana!' he exclaimed hopefully. 'Dearest Diana!' Grasping her hands, he smiled ecstatically into her uplifted eyes.

'Have you really come back to me, Marcellus?' she murmured.

He drew her closer and she came confidently into his arms, reached up her hand and laid her palm gently on his cheek. Her long lashes slowly closed and Marcellus tenderly kissed her eyes. Her hand moved softly around his neck, suddenly tightening, almost fiercely, as his lips touched hers. She drew a quick, involuntary breath, and raced his heart with her unrestrained answer to his kiss. For a long moment they clung to each other, deeply stirred.

'You are adorable!' whispered Marcellus, fervently.

With a contented sigh, Diana childishly snuggled her face against his breast while he held her tightly to him. She was trembling. Then, slowly disengaging herself from his arms, she looked up into his face with misty, smiling eyes.

'Come—let us sit down,' she said softly. 'We have much to talk about.' The timbre of her voice had altered too. It had deepened and matured.

Marcellus followed her graceful figure to the marble lectus that gave an entrancing view of the sea, and they sat, Diana facing him with a brooding concern.

'Have you seen the Emperor?' she asked; and when he shook his head absently—as if seeing the Emperor was a matter of small importance—she said, soberly, 'Somehow I wish you didn't have to talk with him. You know how eccentric he has been; his curiosity about magic and miracles and stars and spirits—and such things. Lately he has been completely obsessed. His health is failing. He doesn't want to talk about anything else but metaphysical things.'

'That's not surprising,' commented Marcellus, reaching for her hand.

'Sometimes—all day long and far into the night,' she went on, in that new, deep register that made every word sound confidential, 'he tortures his poor old head with these matters, while his queer sages sit in a circle about his bed, delivering long harangues to which he tries to listen—as if it were his duty.'

'Perhaps he is preparing his mind for death,' surmised Marcellus.

Diana nodded with cloudy eyes.

'He has been impatient for your return, Marcellus. He seems to think that you may tell him something new. These old men!' She flung them away with a scornful gesture. 'They exhaust him; they exasperate him; and they impose upon him—cruelly! That horrible old Dodinius, who reads oracles, is the worst of the lot. Always, at the Feast of the New Moon, he slaughters a sheep, and performs some silly ceremonies, and pretends he has had a revelation. I don't know how.'

'They count the warts on the sheep's underpinning, I think,' recalled Marcellus, 'and they examine the entrails. If a certain kink in an intestine points east, the answer is "Yes"—and the fee is five hundred sesterces.'

'Well'—Diana dismissed the details with a slim hand—'however it is accomplished, dirty old Dodinius does it; and they say that he has occasionally made a true prediction. If the weather is going to be stormy, he always knows it before anyone else.'

'Perhaps he feels the change in his creaking hinges,' suggested Marcellus.

'You're a confirmed skeptic, Marcellus.' She gave him a sidelong glance that played at rebuking him. 'There should be no frivolous comments about these holy men. Dodinius' best forecast was when he discovered that Annaeus Seneca was still living, next day after the report had come that the old poet was dead. How he divined that, the gods only know; but it was true that Seneca had drifted into a death-like coma from which he recovered—as you know.'

'You don't suppose he hired Seneca to play dead,' ventured Marcellus, with a chuckle.

'My dear—if Annaeus Seneca wanted to connive with somebody, it wouldn't be an old dolt like Dodinius,' Diana felt sure. Dropping the badinage, she grew serious. 'About ten days ago, it was revealed to him —so he insists—that the Emperor is going to live forever. He hasn't found it easy to convince the Emperor, for there is quite a lot of precedent to overcome; but you will find His Majesty immensely curious about this subject. He wants to believe Dodinius; sends for him, first thing in the morning, to come and tell him again all about the revelation; and Dodinius, the unscrupulous old reptile, reassures him that there can be no doubt of it. Isn't that a dreadful way to torment the Emperor in his last days when he should be allowed to die in peace?'

Marcellus, with eyes averted, nodded non-committally.

'Sometimes, my dear'—Diana impulsively leaned forward, shaking her head in despair—'it makes me hot with shame and loathing that I have to live here surrounded by these tiresome men who fatten on frauds! All one ever hears, on this mad island, is a jumble of atrocious nonsense that no healthy person, in his right mind, would give a second thought to! And now—as if the poor old Emperor hadn't heard enough of such stupid prattle—Dodinius is trying to persuade him to live forever.'

Marcellus made no comment on that; sat frowningly gazing out on the sea. Presently he stirred, returned, and put his arm about her shoulders.

'I don't know what you have come to tell the Emperor, Marcellus,' continued Diana, yielding to his caress, 'but I do know it will be honest. He will want to know what you think of this crazy notion that Dodinius has put into his head. This may call for some tact.'

'Have you a suggestion?' asked Marcellus.

'You will know what to say, I think. Tiberius is a worn-out old man. And he certainly doesn't look very heroic. But there was a time when he was brave and strong. Perhaps—if you remind him—he will be able to remember. He wasn't afraid to die when he was vigorous and had something to live for.' Diana lightly traced a pattern on Marcellus' forearm with her finger-tips. 'Why should that weary old man want to live forever? One would think he should be glad enough to put his burden down—and leave all these scheming courtiers and half-witted prophets—and find his peace in oblivion.'

Marcellus bent over her and kissed her lips, and was thrilled by her warm response.

'I love you, dear!' he declared, passionately.

'Then—take me away from here,' she whispered. 'Take me some place where nobody is insane—and nobody talks metaphysical rubbish —and nobody cares about the future—or the past—or anything but just now!' She hugged him closer to her. 'Will you, Marcellus? The Emperor wants us to live here. That's what this horrible villa is about.' Diana's voice trembled. 'I can't stay here! I can't! I shall go mad!' She put her lips close to his ear. 'Let us try to slip away. Can't we bribe a boat?'

'No, darling,' protested Marcellus. 'I shall take you away, but not as a fugitive. We must bide our time. We don't want to be exiles.'

'Why not?' demanded Diana. 'Let us go some place—far, far away—

and have a little house—and a little garden—close by a stream—and live in peace.'

'It is a beautiful picture, dear,' he consented, 'but you would soon be lonely and restless; and besides—I have some important work to do that can't be done—in a peaceful garden. And then, too—there are our families to consider.'

Diana relaxed in his arms, earnestly thinking.

'I'll be patient,' she promised, 'but don't let it be too long. I am not safe here.'

'Not safe!' exclaimed Marcellus. 'What are you afraid of?'

Before she could reply, they both started—and drew apart—at the sound of footsteps. Glancing toward the villa, Marcellus saw the guard approaching who had directed him to the pergola.

'Tiberius is too feeble and preoccupied to be of any protection to me,' said Diana, in a low voice. 'The Empress is having more and more to say about our life here on this dreadful island. Gaius comes frequently to confer with her—'

'Has that swine been annoying you?' broke in Marcellus.

'I have managed to avoid being alone with him,' said Diana, 'but old Julia is doing her utmost to—'

The guard had halted, a little distance away.

'Yes—Atreus?' inquired Diana, turning toward him.

'The Emperor is ready to receive Tribune Marcellus Gallio,' said the guard deferentially.

'Very well,' nodded Marcellus. 'I shall come at once.'

The guard saluted and marched stiffly away.

'When and where do we meet, dear?' asked Marcellus, rising reluctantly. 'At dinner, perhaps?'

'Not likely. The Emperor will want to have you all to himself this evening. Send me a message—to my suite at the Jovis—when you are at liberty. If it is not too late, I may join you in the atrium. Otherwise, let us meet here in the pergola, early in the morning.' Diana held out her hand and Marcellus kissed it tenderly.

'Does this Atreus belong to you?' he asked.

Diana shook her head.

'I brought only two maids from home,' she said. 'All the others who attend me belong here. Atreus is a member of the guard at the Jovis. He follows me about wherever I go.'

'Is he to be trusted?' asked Marcellus, anxiously.

Diana shrugged—and drew a doubtful smile.

'How can one tell who is to be trusted in this hotbed of conspiracy? Atreus is respectful and obliging. Whether he would take any risks in my behalf—I don't know. Whether he is now on his way to tell old Julia that he saw you kiss me—I don't know. I shouldn't care to bet much on it—either way.' Diana rose, and slipped her arm through his. 'Go, now,' she whispered. 'The poor old man will be waiting—and he is not patient. Come to me—when you can.'

Marcellus took her in his arms and kissed her.

'I shall be thinking of nothing else,' he murmured—'but you!'

* * * * * *

The last time Marcellus had seen the Emperor—and that at a considerable distance—was on the opening day of the Ludi Florales, eleven years ago. Indeed, it was the last time that anyone had seen him at a public celebration.

His recollection was of an austere, graying man, of rugged features and massive frame, who paid but scant attention to the notables surrounding him in the imperial box, and even less to the spectacles in the arena.

Marcellus had not been surprised at the glum detachment of this dour-faced man; for it was generally known that Tiberius, who had always detested crowds and the extravagance of festivals, was growing alarmingly morose. Elderly men—like Senator Gallio—who could remember the wanton profligacy of Augustus, and had rejoiced in the Tiberian economies which had brought an unprecedented prosperity to Rome, viewed the Emperor's increasing moodiness with sympathetic regret. The younger generation, not quite so appreciative of the monarch's solid virtues, had begun to think him a sour and stingy old spoil-sport, and earnestly wished he would die.

Tiberius had not fully accommodated them in this respect, but he had done the next thing to it; for, not long afterward, he had taken up his residence on Capri; where his subsequent remoteness from the active affairs of government was almost equivalent to an abdication.

That had been a long time ago; and as Marcellus—in full uniform—sat in the spacious, gloomy atrium, waiting to be summoned into the imperial bedchamber, he prepared his mind for the sight of a very old man. But nobody could prepare himself for an interview with this old man who, on first sight, seemed to have so little of life left in him; but, when stirred, was able to mobilize some surprisingly powerful reserves of mental and physical vigor.

The Emperor was propped up in his pillows, an indistinct figure, for the sun was setting and the huge room was full of shadows. Nothing appeared to be alive in the massive bed but the cavernous eyes that had met Marcellus at the door and accompanied him through the room to the straight-backed chair. The face in the pillows was a scaffolding of bulging bones thinly covered with wrinkled parchment. The neck was scrawny and yellow. Under the sparse white hair at Tiberius' sunken temple a dogged artery beat slow but hard, like the tug of an exhausted oar at the finish of a long race. The bony hand that pointed to the chair—which had been drawn up uncomfortably close to the bedside—resembled the claw of an old eagle.

'Your Majesty!' murmured Marcellus, bowing deeply.

'Sit down!' rumbled Tiberius, testily. 'We hope you have learned something about that haunted Robe!' He paused to wheeze asthmatically. 'You have been gone long enough to have found the river Styx —and the Jews' Garden of Eden! Perhaps you rode home on the Trojan Horse—with the Golden Fleece for a saddle-blanket!'

The old man turned his head to note the effects of his acidulous drollery, and Marcellus—thinking that the Emperor might want his dry humor appreciated—risked a smile.

'Funny; is it?' grumped Tiberius.

'Not if Your Majesty is serious,' replied Marcellus, soberly.

'We are always serious, young man!' Digging a sharp elbow into his pillow, the Emperor drew himself closer to the edge of the bed. 'Your father had a long tale about the crucifixion of a mad Galilean in Jerusalem. That fellow Pilate—who forever gets himself into trouble with the Jews—ordered you to crucify this fanatic, and it went to your head.' The old man licked his dry lips. 'By the way—how is your head now?'

'Quite well, Your Majesty,' responded Marcellus, brightly.

'Humph! That's what every crazy man thinks. The crazier he is, the better he feels.' Tiberius grinned unpleasantly, as one fool to another, and added, 'Perhaps you think your Emperor is crazy.'

'Crazy men do not jest, sire,' parried Marcellus.

Tiberius screwed up a mouth that looked like the neck of an old, empty coin-purse, and frowningly cogitated on this comforting thought.

'How do you know they don't?' he demanded. 'You haven't seen all of them—and there are no two alike. But'—suddenly irritable— 'why do you waste the Emperor's time with such prattle? Be on with your story! But wait! It has come to our ears that your Greek slave assaulted the son of old Tuscus with his bare hands. Is this true?'

'Yes—Your Majesty,' admitted Marcellus, 'it is true. There was great provocation; but that does not exonerate my slave, and I deeply regret the incident.'

'You're a liar!' muttered Tiberius. 'Now we shall believe nothing you say! But—tell us that story first.'

The malicious old eyes grew brighter as Marcellus obediently reported the extraordinary episode under the trees at the House of Eupolis, and by the time Quintus had been unrecognizably disfigured by the Greek's infuriated fists the Emperor was up on one elbow, his face beaming.

'And you still have this slave?' barked Tiberius. 'He should have been put to death! What will you take for him?'

'I should not like to sell him, sire; but I shall gladly lend him to Your Majesty—for as long as—'

'Long as we live; eh?' rasped the old man. 'A few weeks; eh? Perhaps we may live longer! Perhaps your Emperor may never die!' The lean chin jutted forward challengingly. 'Is that silly?'

'It is possible for a man to live forever,' declared Marcellus.

'Rubbish!' grunted Tiberius. 'What do you know about it?'

'This Galilean, sire,' said Marcellus, quietly. 'He will live forever.'

'The man you killed? He will live forever? How do you make that out?'

'The Galilean came to life, sire.'

'Nonsense! You probably bungled the crucifixion. Your father said you were drunk. Did you stay until it was over—or can you remember?'

Yes—Marcellus had stayed. A Centurion had driven his spear deep into the dead man's heart—to make doubly sure. There was no question about his death. The third day afterward, he had come to life, and had been seen on many occasions by different groups of people.

'Impossible!' yelled Tiberius. 'Where is he now?'

Marcellus didn't know. But he did know that this Jesus was alive; had eaten breakfast with friends on a lake-shore in Galilee; had appeared in people's houses. Tiberius propped himself up on both elbows and stared, his chin working convulsively.

'Leaves footprints when he walks,' resumed Marcellus. 'Turns up unexpectedly. Talks, eats, shows his wounds which—for some curious reason—do not heal. Doesn't bother to open the door when he enters. People have a queer feeling of a presence beside them; they look about, and there he is.'

Tiberius glanced toward the door and clapped his dry old hands. The Chamberlain slipped in noiselessly and instantly, as if—upon being summoned—he hadn't had far to come.

'Lights—stupid one!' shouted the old man, shrilly. He snuggled down, shivered, and drew the covers up over his emaciated shoulder. 'Proceed,' he muttered. 'Doesn't open the door; eh?'

'Two men are walking along the highway, late afternoon, discussing him,' went on Marcellus, relentlessly. 'Presently he falls into step with them. They invite him to supper at an inn, some twelve miles from Jerusalem.'

'Not a ghost, then!' put in Tiberius.

'Not a ghost; but this time he does not eat. Breaks the bread, murmurs thanks to his God, and disappears. Enters a house in Jerusalem, a few minutes later; finds friends at supper—and eats.'

'Might show up almost anywhere; eh?' speculated Tiberius, adding, half to himself, 'Probably not if the place were well guarded.' And when Marcellus had let this observation pass without hazarding an opinion, the old man growled, 'What do you think?'

'I think it wouldn't make any difference,' ventured Marcellus. 'He will go where he pleases. He opens the eyes of the blind and the ears of the deaf; heals lepers, paralytics; lunatics. I did not believe any of these things, Your Majesty, until it was impossible not to believe them. He can do anything!'

'Why, then, did he let them put him to death?' demanded Tiberius.

'Your Majesty, well versed in the various religions, will remember that among the Jews it is customary to make a blood offering for crimes. It is believed that the Galilean offered himself as an atonement gift.'

'What crimes had *he* committed?' asked Tiberius.

'None, sire! He was atoning for the sins of the world.'

'Humph! That's an ingenious idea.' Tiberius pondered it gravely, his eyes on the ceiling. 'All the sins; everybody's sins! And, having attended to that, he comes alive again, and goes about. Well—if he can make atonement for the sins of the whole world, it's presumable that he knows what they are and who has committed them. Cosmic person; eh? Knows all about the whole world; eh? Are you fool enough to believe all that?'

'I believe—Your Majesty'—Marcellus was proceeding carefully, spacing his words—'that this Jesus—can do whatever he wills to do—whenever—wherever—and to whomever he pleases.'

'Including the Emperor of Rome?' Tiberius' tone recommended prudence.

'It is conceivable, sire, that Jesus might visit the Emperor, at any time; but, if he did, it would surely be in kindness. Your Majesty might be greatly comforted.'

There was a long, thoughtful moment before Tiberius wanted more information about the strange appearances and disappearances. 'Quite absurd—making himself visible or invisible—at will. What became of him, while invisible? Did he—did he blot himself out?'

'The stars do not blot themselves out, sire,' said Marcellus.

'Your reasoning is, then, that this person might be in the room *now*, and we unable to see him.'

'But Your Majesty would have nothing to fear,' said Marcellus. 'Jesus would have no interest in the Emperor's throne.'

'Well—that's a cool way to put it, young man!' growled Tiberius. 'No interest in the throne; eh? Who does this fellow think he is?'

'He thinks he is the Son of God!' said Marcellus, quietly.

'And you!' Tiberius stared into his eyes. 'What do you think?'

'I think, sire, that he is divine; that he will eventually claim the whole world for his kingdom; and that this kingdom will have no end.'

'Fool!—Do you think he will demolish the Roman Empire?' shouted the old man.

'There will be no Roman Empire, Your Majesty, when Jesus takes command. The empires will have destroyed one another—and themselves. He has predicted it. When the world has arrived at complete exhaustion, by wars and slaveries, hatreds and betrayals, he will establish his kindgom of good will.'

'Nonsense!' yelled Tiberius. 'The world can't be ruled by good will!'

'Has it ever been tried, Your Majesty?" asked Marcellus.

'Of course not! You're crazy! And you're too young to be that crazy!' The Emperor forced a laugh. 'Never has so much drivel been spoken in our presence. We are surrounded by wise old fools who spend their days inventing strange tales; but you have outdone them all. We will hear no more of it!'

'Shall I go, then, Your Majesty?' inquired Marcellus, coming to the edge of his chair. The Emperor put out a detaining hand.

'Have you seen the daughter of Gallus?' he asked.

'Yes, Your Majesty.'

'You are aware that she loves you, and has waited these past two years for your return?'

'Yes, Your Majesty.'

'She was deeply grieved when you came back to Rome, a year ago, and were ashamed to see her because of the sickness in your head. But —hopeful of your recovery—she has had eyes for no one else. And now—you return to her polluted with preposterous nonsense! You, who are so infatuated with kindness and good will—what does Diana think of you now? Or have you informed her how cracked you are?'

'We have not talked about the Galilean, sire,' said Marcellus, moodily.

'This young woman's happiness may mean nothing to you—but it means everything to us!' The Emperor's tone was almost tender. 'It is high time, we think, that you take some steps to deal fairly with her. Let there be no more of this folly!'

Marcellus sat with clouded eyes, making no reply when Tiberius paused to search his face.

'We now offer you your choice!' The old voice was shrill with anger. 'You will give up all this Jesus talk, and take your rightful place as a Roman Tribune and the son of an honored Roman Senator—or you will give up the daughter of Gallus! We will not consent to her marriage with a fool! What say you?'

'Will Your Majesty permit me to consider?' asked Marcellus, in an unsteady voice.

'For how long?' demanded Tiberius.

'Until noon tomorrow.'

'So be it, then! Noon tomorrow! Meantime—you are not to see Diana. A woman in love has no mind. You might glibly persuade her to marry you. She would repent of it later. This decision is not for the daughter of Gallus to make. It is all yours, young man! . . . That will do! You may go!'

Stunned by the sudden turn of affairs and the peremptory dismissal,

Marcellus rose slowly, bowed, and moved toward the door where the old man testily halted him.

'Stay! You have talked of everything but the haunted Robe. Let us hear about that before you go. We may not see you again.'

Returning to his chair, Marcellus deliberately reported his own strange restoration, traceable to the Robe; told also of Lydia's marvelous recovery. Having secured the Emperor's attention, he recited tales of other mysterious occurrences in and about Capernaum; spoke of the aged Nathanael Bartholomew; and Tiberius—with an old man's interest in another old man's story—showed enough curiosity about the storm on the lake to warrant the telling of it—all of it. When they wakened Jesus at the crest of the tempest, Tiberius sat up. When Jesus, wading through the flooded boat, mounted the little deck and stilled the storm as a man soothes a frightened horse—

'That's a lie!' yelled the Emperor, sinking back into his pillows; and when Marcellus had no more to say, the old man snorted: 'Well!—go on! Go on! It's a lie—but a new lie! We will say that for it! Plenty of gods know how to stir up storms: this one knows how to stop them! . . . By the way—what became of that haunted Robe?'

'I still have it, sire.'

'You have it here with you? We would like to see it.'

'I shall send for it, Your Majesty.'

The Chamberlain was instructed to send for Demetrius. In a few moments, he appeared; tall, handsome, grave. Marcellus was proud of him; a bit apprehensive, too, for it was easy to see that the Emperor was instantly interested in him.

'Is this the Greek who slaughters Roman Tribunes with his bare hands?' growled Tiberius. 'Nay—let him answer for himself!' he warned Marcellus, who had begun to stammer a reply.

'I prefer to fight with weapons, Your Majesty,' said Demetrius, soberly.

'And what is your favorite weapon?' barked Tiberius. 'The broadsword? The dagger?'

'The truth, Your Majesty,' replied Demetrius.

The Emperor frowned, grinned, and turned to Marcellus.

'Why—this fellow's as crazy as you are!' he drawled; then, to Demetrius, 'We had thought of keeping you as one of our bodyguard, but—' He chuckled. 'Not a bad idea! The truth; eh? Nobody else on this island knows how to use that weapon. You shall stay!'

Demetrius' expression did not change. Tiberius nodded to Marcellus, who said, 'Go—and fetch the Galilean Robe.' Demetrius saluted deeply and made off.

'What manner of miracle will be wrought upon the Emperor, do you think?' inquired Tiberius, with an intimation of dry bravado.

'I do not know, sire,' replied Marcellus, gravely.

'Perhaps you think we would better not experiment with it.'

Tiberius' tone made a brave show of indifference, but he cleared his throat huskily after he had spoken.

'I should not presume to advise Your Majesty,' said Marcellus.

'If you were in our place—' Tiberius' voice was troubled.

'I should hesitate,' said Marcellus.

'You're a superstitious fool!' growled the Emperor.

Demetrius was re-entering with the brown Robe folded over his arm. Tiberius' sunken eyes narrowed. Marcellus rose; and, taking the Robe from Demetrius, offered it to the old man.

The Emperor reached out his hand, tentatively. Then, slowly recoiling, he thrust his hand under the covers. He swallowed noisily.

'Take it away!' he muttered.

Chapter XXI

MANY a Roman of high distinction would have been overwhelmed with joy and pride by a summons to have breakfast at the bedside of the Emperor, but Diana's invitation distressed her.

Since late yesterday afternoon she had been dreamily counting the hours until she could keep her early morning engagement with Marcellus. She was so deeply in love with him that nothing else mattered. Now the happy meeting would have to be postponed; perhaps abandoned altogether if last night's prolonged interview in the imperial bedchamber had turned out badly.

Until after midnight, Diana—disinterestedly jabbing uneven stitches into an embroidery pattern—had listened to every footfall in the corridors, alert for a message. At length she had persuaded herself that Marcellus thought it too late to disturb her. After a restless night, she had welcomed the dawn; had stood at the window, impatient, ecstatic, waiting for the moment when—with any degree of prudence —she might slip out of the Villa Jovis and speed to her enchanted pergola.

And now the message had come from the Emperor. Concealing her disappointment from the servants, Diana made ready to obey the summons. While her maids fluttered about, helping her into gay colors— which usually brightened the old man's dour mood—she tried to imagine what might have happened. Perhaps Tiberius had proposed some project for Marcellus which would amount to his imprisonment on this wretched island. Knowing how anxious she was to leave Capri, Marcellus might have tried to decline such an offer. In that case, Diana—deeply obligated to the Emperor—would be asked to use her influence. Her intuition warned her that this breakfast with Tiberius might be a very unhappy occasion.

Dispatching Acteus to inform Marcellus that she could not keep her engagement, Diana practiced a few bright smiles before her mirror; and, resolutely holding on to one of them, marched into the imperial presence.

'How very good of Your Majesty!' she exclaimed. 'I hope I have not kept you waiting. Are you famished?'

'We have had our breakfast,' sulked Tiberius, 'an hour ago.' He jabbed a sharp, brown thumbnail into the ribs of the Chamberlain who was fussing with the pillows. 'Pour a goblet of orange juice for the daughter of Gallus—and then get out! All of you!'

'Not feeling so well?' purred Diana.

'Don't try to joke with us, young woman!' snorted the old man. 'That will do now!' he yelled, at the Chamberlain. 'Stop pottering—and be gone! And close the door!'

'I wish I could do something,' sympathized Diana, when they were alone.

'Well—perhaps you can! That's why we sent for you!'

'I'll do my best, Your Majesty.' Diana held her big goblet in both hands to keep it from trembling.

'We had a long talk with your handsome fool.' Tiberius boosted his tired bones over to the edge of the big bed, and scowled into Diana's anxious eyes. 'You said that old Dodinius was crazy. Compared to this Marcellus, Dodinius is a ray of light!'

'I'm sorry,' murmured Diana. 'I was with him for an hour, yesterday afternoon, and he talked sensibly enough.'

'Perhaps you did not discuss the one thing that touches him off. Do you know he has become convinced that this Jesus is divine—and has intentions to rule the whole world?'

'Oh, no—please!' entreated Diana, suddenly sickened.

'You ask him! You won't have to ask him! You just say, "Jesus"—and see what happens to you!'

'But—naturally'—stammered Diana, loyally—'Marcellus would want to tell Your Majesty everything about this poor dead Jew, seeing that's why he was sent abroad.'

'Poor dead Jew—indeed!' shrilled Tiberius. 'This Galilean came to life again! Went about the country! Walked, talked, ate with people! Still going about, they think! Likely to turn up anywhere!'

'Perhaps they didn't kill him,' suggested Diana.

'Of course they killed him!' snarled Tiberius.

'And Marcellus thinks he came to life: did he see him?'

'No—but he believes it. And he has it that this Jesus is a god, who will take command of the world and rule it without armies.'

Diana winced and shook her head.

'I thought he was fully recovered,' she said, dismally. 'This sounds as if he were worse off than ever. What are we to do?'

'Well—if there is anything to be done, you will have to do it yourself. May we remind you that our interest in this mad young Tribune is solely on your account? It was for your sake that we brought him back from that fort at Minoa. For your sake, again, we found an errand for him outside the country to give him time to recover his mind. We see now that we sent him to the wrong place—but it is too late to correct that mistake. He knows that he is under a heavy obligation to you. Besides—he loves you. Perhaps you can prevail upon him to abandon his interest in this Galilean.' The old man paused, shook his head slowly, and added, 'We doubt whether you can do anything. You see, my child, he really believes it!'

'Then—why not let him believe it?' insisted Diana. 'I love him—no

matter what he believes about that—or anything! He won't pester me
with this crazy idea; not if I tell him I have no interest in it.'

'Ah—but there's more to it than that, young woman!' declared
Tiberius, sternly. 'It isn't as if Marcellus, as a casual traveler in Galilee,
had happened upon this strange story and had become convinced of its
truth. In that case, he might regard it as a seven-day wonder—and let
it go at that. As the matter stands, he probably considers himself bound
to do something about it. He crucified this Jesus! He has a debt to
pay! It's a bigger debt—by far—than the one he owes you!'

'Did he say that, Your Majesty?' asked Diana, deeply hurt.

'No—he did not say that. But your Marcellus, unfortunately, is a
young man of strong will and high integrity. This is going to cause
him a great deal of trouble—and you, too, we surmise. He will feel
obligated to take part in this Jesus movement.'

'Movement?' echoed Diana, mystifiedly.

'Nothing less—and it has in it the seeds of revolution. Already,
throughout our Palestinian provinces, thousands are professing that
this Jesus is the Christos—the Anointed One—and are calling themselves Christians. The thing is moving rapidly, up through Macedonia,
down through Mesopotamia; moving quietly, but gathering strength.

Diana listened with wide, incredulous eyes.

'You mean—they might try to overthrow the Empire?'

'Not by force. If some foolhardy fellow were to stand up on a cart
and yell at these captive people to take up arms against their masters,
they would know that was hopeless. But—here comes a man without
an army; doesn't want an army; has no political aspirations; doesn't
want a throne; has no offices to distribute; never fought a battle; never
owned a sword; hasn't a thing to recommend him as a leader—except'
—Tiberius lowered his voice to a throaty rumble—'except that he
knows how to make blind men see, and cripples walk; and, having
been killed for creating so much excitement, returns from the dead,
saying, "Follow me—and I will set you free!" Well—why shouldn't
they follow him—if they believe all that?' The old man chuckled mirthlessly. 'There's more than one kind of courage, my child,' he soliloquized, 'and the most potent of all is the reckless bravery of people
who have nothing to lose.'

'And you think Marcellus is one of these Christians?' queried Diana.

'Of course he is! Makes no bones about it! He had the audacity to
tell us—to our face—that the Roman Empire is doomed!'

'Why—what an awful thing to say!' exclaimed Diana.

'Well—at least it's a dangerous thing to say,' mumbled Tiberius; 'and
if he is fool enough to blurt that out in the presence of the Emperor, he
is not likely to be prudent in his remarks to other people.'

'He might be tried for treason!' feared Diana.

'Yes—but he wouldn't care. That's the trouble with this new
Galilean idea. The people who believe it are utterly possessed! This

Jesus was tried for treason—and convicted—and crucified. But he rose from the dead—and he will take care of all who give up their lives as his followers. They have no fear. Now—you set a thing like that in motion—and there'd be no end to it!'

'But what has Marcellus to gain by predicting doom for the Empire?' wondered Diana. 'That's quite absurd, I think.'

'Had you thought the Roman Empire might last forever?' rasped Tiberius.

'I never thought much about it,' admitted Diana.

'No—probably not,' mumbled the old man, absently. He lay for some time staring at the high-vaulted ceiling. 'It might be interesting,' he went on, talking to himself—'it might be interesting to watch this strange thing develop. If it could go on—the way it seems to be going now—nothing could stop it. But—it won't go on—that way. It will collapse—after a while. Soon as it gets into a strong position. Soon as it gets strong enough to dictate terms. Then it will squabble over its offices and spoils—and grow heady with power and territory. The Christian afoot is a formidable fellow—but—when he becomes prosperous enough to ride a horse—' Tiberius suddenly broke out in a startling guffaw. 'He! he! he!—when he gets a horse! Ho! ho! ho!—a Christian on horseback will be just like any other man on horseback! This Jesus army will have to travel on foot—if it expects to accomplish anything!'

Diana's eyes widened as she listened, with mingled pity and revulsion, to the mad old Emperor's prattle. He had talked quite rationally for a while. Now he was off again. By experience she knew that his grim amusement would promptly be followed by an unreasonable irascibleness. She moved to the edge of her chair, as to inquire whether she might go now. The old man motioned her back.

'Your Marcellus has another audience with us at noon,' he said, soberly. 'We told him we had no intention of permitting you to throw yourself away by marrying a man who has anything to do with this dangerous Jesus business. If he goes in for it seriously—and we have no doubt he intends to—he will lose his friends—and his life, too. Let him do it if he likes; but he shall not drag you along! We told him he must choose. We told him if he did not abandon this Christian party at once, we would give you in marriage to Gaius.'

'Oh—please—no!' begged Diana.

'We admit,' chuckled Tiberius, 'that Gaius has his little faults; but he can make a Princess of you! You may not think it an ideal alliance, but you will be happier as a Princess than as the wife of a crazy man in love with a ghost!'

'What did he say,' Diana whispered, 'when you told him you would give me to Gaius?'

'He wanted until noon—today—to consider.' The old man raised up on his elbow to note the effect of this shocking announcement.

His grin slowly faded when he saw how painfully she had been wounded.

'He had to have time to consider,' she reflected, brokenly—'to consider—whether he would let me be handed over—to Gaius!'

'Yes—and our opinion is that he will let that happen! Regardless of his love for you, my child, he will not give up his Jesus!' Tiberius shook a long bony finger directly in her face. 'That's what we meant when we told you that this Christian movement is no small thing! Men who believe in it will give up everything! With Marcellus, nothing else matters. *Not even you!*'

'Then—perhaps there is no reason why I should talk to him,' said Diana, hopelessly. 'It would only hurt us both.'

'Oh—it's worth a trial. We pledged him not to talk with you until he had come to a decision, but we shall send him word that he is released from his promise. Perhaps you can help him decide.'

Diana rose and moved toward the door.

'Better not confront him with our threat to give you to Gaius,' called the old man. 'You are not supposed to know that.'

* * * * * *

They sat close together on the marble lectus in the sequestered pergola, silently gazing out upon a calm summer sea. It lacked less than a half-hour of noon now and Marcellus would have to be going; for he had an urgent appointment with an old man, and old men—whatever their faults—had a high regard for punctuality.

Everything, it seemed, had been said. Diana, emotionally exhausted, leaned her head against Marcellus' shoulder. Sometimes an involuntary sob tore into her breathing, and his arm would tighten about her protectingly.

When they had met here, three hours ago, Diana thought she had reason to hope that their love would solve the problem. Marcellus, strong but tender, had disclosed a depth of passion that had shaken them both. Nothing could tear them apart now; nothing! Diana was ecstatic. There could be no trouble for them now. So long as they had each other, let the world do what it liked. Let the Empire stand or fall! Let this Jesus go about forever doing good and ruling men by good will, or let him fail of it, and the world go on fighting and starving as it had always been fighting and starving: they had each other, and nothing could separate them! She hungrily raised her face to meet his kisses. He felt her heart pounding. They were one!

'Come, now,' Diana had whispered, breathlessly, 'let us sit down—and make some plans.'

They sat, very close together, and very much aware of each other, until Diana drew a little apart and shook her head. Her eyes were radiant, but her lips were trying to be resolute.

'Please—Marcellus!' she murmured, unsteadily. 'Talk to me! Let us decide what we will say to the Emperor. He wants me to be happy, and he knows I love you. Why not ask him to give you something to do in Rome?'

'But he expects you to live here,' Marcellus reminded her.

'Perhaps we can talk him out of that,' hoped Diana. 'My villa is not finished. Ill as he is, Tiberius knows he cannot supervise it. I think it worries him. He may be glad enough to have done with it. Let us tell him we want to go back to Rome—at least for a while—and visit our people—and be married. Maybe he will consent.'

'He might,' agreed Marcellus, from a considerable distance. 'There's no telling what the Emperor will think—about anything.'

'And then'—went on Diana, with girlish enthusiasm—'you could do all the things you liked to do, and renew your old friendships—and go to the Tribunes' Club—'

Marcellus frowned.

'Well—what's the matter with the Tribunes' Club?' demanded Diana. 'You used to spend half your time there—in the gymnasium and the baths.'

Marcellus leaned forward with his elbows on his knees and stared moodily at his interlaced fingers.

'That was before I knew what it had cost to erect that marble club-house,' he said, soberly.

'Oh, my dear—why can't you leave off fretting over things you can't help?' implored Diana. 'It distresses you that the marble was quarried by slaves. Well—and so was this marble we're sitting on—and the marble that went into your villa at home. Let's agree it's too bad that some people are slaves; but—what are you going to do about it—all by yourself?'

Marcellus sighed deeply and shook his head. Then, suddenly straightening, he faced her with a surprisingly altered mood, his eyes alight.

'Diana—I am bursting to tell you a story—about a man—about a remarkable man!'

'If he's the man I think you mean'—Diana's face had lost its animation—'I'd really rather you didn't. He has caused you so much unhappiness, and I think it is time you put him out of your mind. I don't believe he has been good for you.'

'Very well,' consented Marcellus, the smile fading from his eyes. 'As you like.' He fell silent.

Impetuously, Diana moved closer to him, repentant.

'I shouldn't have said that,' she whispered. 'Tell me about him.'

Marcellus was well prepared for this opportunity. He had given much thought to what he would say when the time came for him to tell Diana about Jesus. It would not be easy to make her understand. All of her instincts would be in revolt. She would be deeply prejudiced against the story. He had carefully planned the speech he would make to her, in which he must explain Jesus as a divine liberator of the world's oppressed. But now—with Diana's warm and supple contours snuggled close against him, he decided to abandon this larger appraisal and deal more simply with his story. He began by telling her about Jonathan and the donkey.

'Why—what a perfectly mean thing to do to that little boy!' she exclaimed, when Jonathan sorrowfully gave up his donkey to Thomas.

'It was a severe test,' admitted Marcellus, 'but it made a little man of Jonathan.'

'And why did they want Jonathan to be a little man?' queried Diana, making it clear that if she were obliged to listen to this Galilean story, she reserved the right to make comments and ask questions. 'I should have thought,' she went on, innocently, 'that Jonathan would have been ever so much more attractive as a little boy.'

Conceding that the phrase, 'little man,' had not been skillfully chosen, Marcellus thought he should tell her how children felt toward Jesus; how—according to Justus—they swarmed about him in his carpenter shop; how, when Jesus went home in the evening, a crowd of little ones accompanied him. And dogs.

'Well—I'm glad about the dogs,' drawled Diana. 'From what I had heard of his goodness, I had supposed that dogs might feel rather embarrassed in his company.' Instantly she realized that this flippancy had stung. Marcellus recoiled as if she had slapped him.

'His goodness was not negative, Diana, and it was not smug, and it was not weak,' declared Marcellus. 'May I reconstruct your picture of him?'

'Please do,' murmured Diana, absently. She caressingly retied the heavy silk cord at the throat of his tunic, and smiled into his sober eyes from under her long lashes, her full lips offering a forthright invitation. Marcellus swallowed hard, and gave her a fraternal pat on the cheek. She sighed and shouldered back under his arm.

Then he told her all about Miriam; all about the wedding-feast—and Miriam's voice.

'And she never could sing before?'

'No—she had never wanted to sing before.'

'And you talked with her—and heard her sing? You liked her, I think. Was she pretty?'

'Very!'

'Jewess?'

'Yes.'

'They are very pretty, sometimes,' conceded Diana. 'It's too bad she was a cripple.'

'She didn't mind being lame. This other gift was so very important.'

'Why didn't Jesus let her walk?'

'Sounds as if you thought he could,' commented Marcellus, encouraged.

'Well'—replied Diana, defensively—'you think he could; don't you?
I'm taking your word for it.'

'Miriam thinks she can do more good to the unfortunate in her
town if she, too, has a disability—'

'And can sing—in spite of her affliction,' interposed Diana. 'She
must be a fine person.'

'She hadn't been a fine person,' said Marcellus—'not until this
strange thing happened to her.'

'Was she in love with Jesus?'

'Yes—everybody was.'

'You know what I mean.'

'No—I don't think she was. Not that way.'

Diana thoughtfully rubbed her cheek against Marcellus' sleeve.

'Wasn't Jesus in love with anyone?' she murmured.

'Everyone,' said Marcellus.

'Perhaps he thought it was wrong—to love just one person—above
all others.'

'I think that might have been wrong—for him. You see, Diana, Jesus
was not an ordinary person. He had unusual powers, and felt that his
life belonged to the public.'

'What other things did he do?' Diana's curiosity seemed to be more
serious. 'There was little Jonathan's foot, and Miriam's voice—'

'I must tell you about Lydia.'

But—before he went into the story of Lydia's touching the Robe,
Marcellus thought he should review his own peculiar experiences with
it. Diana grew indignant as he relived that tragic night at the Insula
in Jerusalem when Paulus had forced him to put on the Galilean's
Robe.

'This poor Jesus had suffered enough!' she exclaimed. 'They had no
right to make a mockery of his clothes! And he had been so brave—
and had done no wrong!'

Heartened by her sympathy, Marcellus had gone on to tell her all
about that afternoon in Athens when—desperate over his mental condition—he had decided to destroy himself.

'You may find it hard to understand, dear, how a person could come
to a decision to take his own life.'

'Oh, no!' Diana shook her head. 'I can understand that, Marcellus.
I could easily come to that decision—in certain circumstances.'

'It is a lonely business—suicide,' muttered Marcellus.

'Perhaps that is why I can understand it,' said Diana. 'I am well
acquainted with loneliness.'

Then Marcellus proceeded to tell her about his finding of the Robe,
and the peculiar effect it had on him. Diana looked up into his face,
her eyes swimming with tears.

'There's no use trying to explain,' he went on. 'I gathered up the
Robe in my hands—and it healed my mind.'

'Maybe that was because you knew it had belonged to another lonely man,' suggested Diana.

'Curiously enough,' said Marcellus, 'that was the sensation I had when I held the Robe in my arms. Some strange friendship—a new, invigorating friendship—had come to my rescue. The painful tension was relaxed. Life was again worth living.' He gravely studied her brooding eyes. 'I wonder if you believe what I am saying.'

'Yes, dear—I believe it; and, considering your earlier experience with his Robe, I am not very much surprised.' She was silent for a moment, and then said, 'Tell me now about this Lydia.'

It was quite a lengthy story, with many unforeseen excursions. Diana had remarked that it must almost have killed Lydia when she had to force her way into that huge crowd of strangers in the street. And that had led Marcellus to interrupt himself long enough to describe those crowds; how the poor people had dropped their sickles and left their looms and followed for days, sleeping on the ground, going hungry and footsore—if only they might stay close to Jesus.

Diana listened with rapt attention, narrowed eyes, parted lips, as the Galilean story went on—and on—toward its close.

'And you honestly think he is alive—now?' she asked, earnestly.

Marcellus nodded his head, and after a moment continued with an account of the reappearances.

'And you really think Stephanos saw him?' asked Diana, in an awed voice.

'Do you find that so hard to believe, dear, after the other things I have told you?'

'I want to believe what you believe, Marcellus.'

He had drawn her into his arms and kissed her.

'It means much to me, my darling, to have shared this story with you,' he said, tenderly. 'Knowing how you felt about the supernatural, I hardly expected you to be so understanding.'

'Well—this is different!' Diana suddenly released herself and sat up to face him. 'What I feared was that it might somehow affect your life—and mine, too. It is a beautiful story, Marcellus, a beautiful mystery. Let it remain so. We don't have to understand it. And we don't have to do anything about it; do we? Let us plan to live—each for the other—just as if this hadn't happened.'

She waited a long time for his reply. His face was drawn, and his eyes were transfixed to the far horizon. Diana's slim fingers traced a light pattern on the back of his hand.

'But it *has* affected my life, darling!' said Marcellus, firmly. 'I *can't* go on as if it hadn't happened.'

'What had you thought of doing?' Diana's voice was unsteady.

'I don't know—yet,' he replied, half to himself. 'But I know I have a duty to perform. It is not clear—what I am to do. But I couldn't go back to living as I did—not even if I tried. I *couldn't!*'

Then, with a depth of earnestness that stilled her breathing, Marcellus poured out his pent-up convictions about this strange thing that had come to pass. It wasn't just a brief phenomenon that had mystified the country people of little Galilee. It was nothing less than a world-shaking event! For thousands of years, the common people of the whole earth had lived without hope of anything better than drudgery, slavery, and starvation. Always the rapacious rulers of some empire were murdering and pillaging the helpless.

'Look at our record!' he exclaimed, with mounting indignation. 'The Roman Empire has enslaved half the population of the world! And we have thought it brave to subdue these little, undefended states! Look at the heroic sculpture and the bronze tablets dedicated to Emperors and Princes, Knights and Prefects, Legates and Tribunes, who have butchered thousands whose only crime was their inability to protect themselves and their lands! This, we thought, was a great credit to the Empire; a gallant thing to do! "I sing of men and of arms!" chants old Publius Vergilius. Sounds brave; doesn't it?

'Diana, dear,' he went on, gravely, 'while on the ship coming home I fell to thinking about the Roman splendors, the monuments in the Forum, the marble palaces; and then I remembered that all of these beautiful and impressive things have either been stolen from other people of better talents than our own, or built with tribute money extorted from the ragged and hungry! And I hated these things! And I hated what we had called Heroism!'

'But you can't do anything about that, Marcellus,' protested Diana, weakly.

Marcellus' storm was subsiding to a mutter. With bitter irony he growled: 'Invincible old Rome—that lives in sloth and luxury—paid for by people up in Aquitania, Anglia, Hispania, Gaul—and down in Crete—and over in Cappadocia, Pontus, and Thrace—where little children cry for food! Ah, yes—our brave ones will sneer, no doubt, at the unarmed Jesus. They will revile him as a weakling, because the only blood he ever shed was his own! But the time will come, my dear, when this *Jesus will have his own way!*'

'So—then—what will you do?' Diana asked, with a weary sigh.

'For the present, I'm sure only of what I will *not* do!' declared Marcellus, passionately. 'I shall not be going back to lounge about in the Tribunes' Club, pretending to have forgotten I know a man who can save the world! I am done with this iniquity! I am free of this shame!'

'But—do you mean to cut yourself off from all your old friends—and—and go about with these poor slaves?' asked Diana.

'It is *we* who are the poor slaves, my dear,' deplored Marcellus. 'These ragged ones, who follow the divine Galilean, are on their way to freedom!'

'You mean—they will band together—and revolt?'

'They may still wear chains on their wrists, Diana, but not on their souls!'

'You're not thinking of joining them!' Diana's cheeks were pale.

'I *have* joined them!' muttered Marcellus.

Impetuously springing to her feet, Diana gave way to a surprising outburst of desperate disappointment.

'Then you can leave me out of it!' she cried. Burying her face in her arms, and weeping inconsolably, she went on, half-incoherently, 'If you're going to ruin yourself—and make an outcast of yourself— and become an object of ridicule—that's for you to decide—but—'

As impulsively as she had torn away from him, Diana slumped down dejectedly on the lectus, and threw her arms tightly around his neck.

'You are dreaming, Marcellus!' she sobbed. 'You are making a new world out of people and things that don't exist! And you know it! *If* men would stop fighting—*if* men would live as your Jesus wants them to—*if* men would be honest and merciful—then there would be a new world! Nobody would be killed! Little children would have enough to eat! Yes—but men are not made that way. Maybe there will come a time when people will stop mistreating one another—and weeds will stop growing—and lions will stop biting—but not in our time! Why shall we make ourselves wretched? Why not accept things as they are? Why throw your life away?' Diana pressed her wet face hard against his shoulder. 'Marcellus,' she moaned piteously, 'don't you know you are breaking my heart? Don't you care?'

'My darling,' said Marcellus, huskily, 'I care—so much—that I would rather die than see you in sorrow. I am not choosing—which way I shall go. I am not permitted a choice.'

There seemed nothing to say, after that. It was nearing noon and Marcellus would have to go to the Emperor. Diana raised her face and glanced at the sundial. Her eyes were heavy with weeping and the tight little curls on her forehead were damp. Marcellus' throat ached in pity as he looked down into her flushed face. She smiled pensively.

'I must be a dreadful sight,' she sighed.

Marcellus kissed her eyes.

'You must not keep him waiting,' she murmured, lifelessly. 'Come back to me—this afternoon—soon as you can—and tell me about it.'

He drew her tightly to him. Her lips trembled as he kissed her.

'Our happiness was too sweet to last, Marcellus. Go, now, dear, I shall try to understand. I know this has been as hard for you as for me. I shall always love you.' Her voice fell to a whisper, 'I hope your Jesus will take care of you.'

'Do you believe what I told you about him?' asked Marcellus, gently.

'Yes, dear—I believe it.'

'Then—I think he will take care of you, too.'

* * * * * *

The Chamberlain was waiting for him in the atrium and led him directly to the imperial suite. Opening the door, he stood aside deferentially, and when Marcellus had passed in, he noiselessly closed the door behind him.

Tiberius, propped up high in his pillows, regarded him with a penetrating scowl as he crossed the room and approached the massive bed. Marcellus, bowing deeply, came to attention and waited the Emperor's pleasure. For a long time the old man stared silently into his grave face.

'It is plain to see,' he said, soberly, 'that you have decided to cast your lot with your Jesus. We were sure you would take that course.'

Marcellus inclined his head—but made no audible reply.

There was another long, strained silence.

'That will be all, then,' growled Tiberius. 'You may go!'

Marcellus hesitated for a moment.

'Go!' shouted the Emperor. 'You are a fool!' The shrill old voice rose to a scream. 'You are a fool!'

Dazed and speechless in the face of the old man's clamorous anger, Marcellus retreated unsteadily toward the door, which had swung open.

'You are a fool!' shrieked Tiberius. 'You will die for your folly!' The cracked voice deepened to a hoarse bellow. '*You are a brave, brave fool!*'

* * * * * *

Stunned by the encounter, Marcellus walked slowly and indecisively into the atrium where the Chamberlain, bowing obsequiously, pointed him out toward the high-vaulted peristyle.

'If you are ready, sir,' he said, 'the chair is waiting to take you down to the wharf. Your luggage has preceded you, and is on the barge.'

'I am not ready to go,' declared Marcellus, crisply. 'I have another appointment here before I leave.'

The Chamberlain drew a frosty smile and shook his head.

'It is His Majesty's command, sir. You are to go—immediately.'

'May I not have a word with my slave?' protested Marcellus. 'Where is he?'

'Your Greek, sir, is temporarily in confinement. He objected so violently to seeing your effects packed and carried off that it was necessary to restrain him.'

'He fought?'

'One of the Nubians, sir, was slow about regaining consciousness. Your slave is rough—very rough. But—the Nubians will teach him better manners.' The Chamberlain bowed again, with exaggerated deference, and pointed toward the luxurious chair. Four brawny Thracians stood at attention beside it, waiting for their passenger. He hesitated. A file of palace guards quietly drew up behind him.

'Farewell, sir,' said the Chamberlain. 'A pleasant voyage to you.'

Chapter XXII

Apparently the word had been circulated on the spacious deck that as soon as this belated passenger arrived the barge would put off, for much interest was shown at the rail when the chair drew up beside the gangway. There was some annoyance, too, especially on the patrician faces of a group of Senators unaccustomed to waiting the convenience of a tardy Tribune.

The beautiful barge moved quietly away from the wharf, and the passengers—a score or more—disposed themselves in the luxurious chairs grouped under the gay awning. A light and lazy breeze ruffled the blue bay. The two banks of long oars swung rhythmically, gracefully, to the metallic beat of the boatswain's hammers. Click! Clack! A crimson sail slowly climbed the forward mast; and, after a few indecisive flutters, resolved to aid the slaves below.

Marcellus found a seat quite apart from the others and moodily surveyed the distant wharves of Puteoli, on the mainland. After a while, a dozen sleek and nearly naked Nubians came up from the hold, bearing silver trays high above their shaved brown heads, and spread fanwise among the passengers. The Emperor's midday hospitality was generous, but Marcellus was not hungry.

The Augusta, at her present speed, should be able to reach Rome by late afternoon of the day after tomorrow. For the first time in his life, Marcellus had no desire to go home. There would be endless explanations to make. His father would be disappointed, hurt, exasperated; his mother would resort to tears; Lucia would try to be sympathetic, but it would be sheer pity. He attempted to imagine a conversation with Tullus. They had been very close and confidential. What had they to talk about, were they to meet now? Tullus would inquire, rather gingerly, what all he had been up to, these past two years. Was there any conceivable answer to that question?

As the afternoon wore on, Marcellus' disinclination to return to Rome was crystallizing to a definite decision, and he began to consider alternatives. At sunset, he sauntered to the Captain's quarters and inquired casually whether *The Augusta* was calling at any of the coast ports before reaching Ostia, and was advised that she was making no stops; not even at Ostia.

He was hungry at dinner-time. A smart breeze had risen, as the twilight came on, and the deck was abandoned. Marcellus went to his cabin, opened his largest bag, and took out the Galilean Robe, folding it as compactly as possible. Wrapping it around his leather wallet, he secured it with a strap. The wallet was heavy.

On the evening he had left home, his father had sent Marcipor down to the galley with a parting gift. Distraught, Marcellus had not opened it until he and Demetrius were on board *The Cleo*. He was amazed. As if to make amends for his part in their estrangement, the Senator had provided him with a very large sum of money. It was all in gold pieces of high denomination. Marcellus had been touched by his father's lavish generosity; saddened, too, for it was almost as if the Senator had said that his son would now be free to go his own way.

Removing his toga, Marcellus rolled it up and stuffed it into the big bag to replace the Robe. Then, having refastened the bag, he stretched out on his berth and waited for the time to pass. Most of his thoughts were about Diana, and his loss of her. Occasionally he glanced at the hourglass on his bedside table. Four times he reversed it. If his computation was correct, *The Augusta* would round the promontory off Capua about midnight.

There was only one sentry patrolling the afterdeck when Marcellus strolled aimlessly toward the stern with his package buckled to the back of his heavy tunic-sash. The sentry paid him but little attention as he stood at the rail. Doubtless the restless passenger had come out to look at the stars. Perhaps a gratuity might be forthcoming if a little service were offered.

A light blinked in the darkness a mile away.

'That is the lighthouse at Capua, sir,' volunteered the sentry.

'Yes,' said Marcellus, indifferently.

'May I bring you a chair, sir?'

'Yes.'

The water was not uncomfortably cold. Marcellus had let himself into it feet-first, without a splash. It was a gratifyingly long time before the sentry gave the alarm. Evidently he had made quite a business of finding a comfortable chair for the Tribune. Now there were other shouts. The boatswain had stopped beating on his anvil. *The Augusta* could not be more than two stadia away, but she was only a row of dim lights, her black hull already blended into the darkness.

Marcellus turned his face toward the shore and proceeded with long, overarm strokes to pull Capua nearer. After a while, flipping over on his back, he looked for *The Augusta*. Only the lamp at the masthead was visible. Doubtless the barge had resumed her journey.

It was the longest swim that Marcellus had ever undertaken. His clothing weighted him. The packet of gold was heavy. Once he thought seriously of tugging off the heavy silk tunic that dragged at his arms, but the threat of arriving at Capua clad only in trunks and a sheer subucula induced him to struggle on. He tried to unfasten his sandal-straps, but found it impossible. The beacon in the light-house seemed to be growing brighter. He hoped he was not imagining this, for he was getting very tired.

At length the choppy waves began to smooth out into long combers. Lower lights shone feebly along the shore. The surf grew rougher. Marcellus could hear it crash against the seawall. He shifted his course leftward to avoid the lighthouse escarpment and the huddle of docks. It was hard going, across the rip-tide. His lungs were beginning to hurt. A great wave carried him forward; and, retreating, left him a temporary footing. Bracing against the weight of its undertow, he held his ground until it had run out. All but spent, he staggered toward the beach and flung himself down in the lee of a fishing-dory, his teeth chattering with the cold. It occurred to him that he should feel immensely gratified over the success of his difficult adventure, but found himself indifferent.

Wringing the water out of his clothes, Marcellus vigorously swung his arms to warm himself, and plodded up wearily through the deepening sand until he found a dry spot that still retained something of its daytime heat. There he spent the rest of the night, sleeping lightly, and anxious for the dawn. When the sun rose, he spread out the Robe on the sand. It dried quickly and he put it on over his damp tunic, comforted by its warmth. He was in better spirits now, glad to be alive.

At a fisherman's hut he asked for something to eat, but he was eyed with suspicion by the surly old couple, who told him they had no food. Up farther in the town, at a sailor's inn, he was crudely served with black bread and a greasy pottage. Disheveled loungers gathered about him to ask questions which he made no effort to answer satisfactorily. When he opened his wallet to pay, they drew in closer about him, eyes wide with avaricious interest; but as he over-topped them all and appeared unalarmed by their curiosity, no one made a move to detain him.

Proceeding through the dirty little town, he turned eastward on a dusty, deserted highway. His sandals were drying now, and felt more comfortable, though they had begun to look quite disreputable. Marcellus was bareheaded, having lost his bandeau in the sea. Nobody could have mistaken him for a Tribune.

The expensive leather wallet was inappropriate, and he concealed it in the breast of his tunic. At the first village, three miles inland, he spent a few coppers for a well-worn goatskin bag, of considerable capacity, emptied his wallet into it; and, later, dropped the wallet into an abandoned cistern.

Before reaching the next village, he took off his tunic, wrapped it around the package of gold that had nearly drowned him last night, and bought another off the washline of a vintner's cottage paying the owner ten sesterces, for which he was so well satisfied that he and his wife chuckled behind Marcellus' back as he moved away. The brown tunic was coarsely woven and had seen hard service, but it was clean.

The sun was high now, and Marcellus carried the Galilean Robe folded over his arm. He frequently paused to rest in the shade beside the descending stream that grew more and more active as the grade stiffened toward the foothills of the distant, snow-capped Apennines. He had no plans, but he was not depressed; nor was he lonesome. Indeed, he had a curious sense of well-being. The country was beautiful. The trees were in full leaf, the nesting birds were busy and happy, the wild-flowers along the bank of the lively stream were exquisite in their fragile beauty. Marcellus drew deep sighs of contentment, gratified but surprised that he could feel so free of any care. He regarded his own appearance with amusement. He had never looked like this before. He stroked his stubbly jaw and wondered whether a razor could be found in one of the villages. If not, no matter. That night, with the Robe for a cover, he slept in the open, remembering— as he drifted off—something Justus had said of Jesus' homelessness: 'The foxes had holes, the birds had nests; but Jesus had no bed, no pillow.' Marcellus drew the Robe closer about him. It was not heavy, but it was warm and comforting. He fell asleep thinking of Diana, but not hopelessly. In the morning he rose refreshed, bathed in the cold stream, and breakfasted on wild strawberries.

The stone mileposts had been announcing, with increasing optimism, that travelers on this uphill road were nearing Arpino. Marcellus cudgeled his memory. What did he know about Arpino? Delicious little melons! Arpino melons! And exactly the right time for them, too.

The road was wider now and showed better care. The fences were well-kept. On either side of the highway, vineyards—the plentiful grapes still green—were being cultivated and irrigated. The traffic on the road was increasing. Here were the melon fields; acres and acres of ripening melons; a procession of high-boxed carts laden with melons; dozens and scores of men, women, and children, scattered through the fields, all bent to the task of gathering melons.

Near a busy open gate, Marcellus sat down on the stone fence and viewed the scene. The little town at the top of the rise seemed to be built on a comparatively level terrain, sheltered on the east by a sheer wall of rock that based one of the loftiest peaks of the range. The village itself—or as much as could be seen of it—was composed of small square cottages crowded closely together. North of this cramped huddle of houses and on slightly higher ground the red-tile roofs of a quite imposing villa shone through the trees surrounding it, doubtless the home of the big man who owned the melon business.

After a while, Marcellus decided to move on up to the village. The swarthy overseer at the open gate, importantly checking the emerging carts on a slate held in the crook of his hand, hailed him. Was he looking for work?

'What kind of work?' Marcellus wanted to know.

The overseer jabbed a thumb toward the melon field.

'Two sesterces,' he said, gruffly—'and a cot—and food.'

'But the day is nearly half gone, sir,' said Marcellus. 'Perhaps one sesterce would be sufficient. I have had no experience in picking melons.'

The bewildered overseer rested the heavy slate on his hip, spat thoughtfully, and stared at the newcomer, apparently lacking a formula for dealing with this unprecedented situation. While he deliberated, Marcellus picked up one of the big willow baskets from a heaped pile beside the gate and was moving off toward his new occupation.

'Wait, fellow!' called the overseer. 'Can you read and write?'

Marcellus admitted that he could.

'And compute?'

Yes—Marcellus could compute.

'Kaeso has discharged his scrivener.'

'Who is Kaeso?' inquired Marcellus, so unimpressed that the overseer drew himself to full height before declaiming—with a sweep of his arm embracing the fields and the town—that Appius Kaeso owned everything in sight. He pointed toward the villa.

'Go up there,' he said, 'and ask for Kaeso. Tell him Vobiscus sent you. If he does not hire you, come back and work on the melons.'

'I'd much rather work on the melons,' said Marcellus.

The overseer blinked a few times, uncertainly.

'A scrivener is better paid and has better food,' he said, slightly nettled by the traveler's stupidity.

'I suppose so,' nodded Marcellus, adding, with cool obstinacy, 'I should prefer to pick melons.'

'Doesn't it make any difference to you, fellow,' snapped the overseer, 'whether you make two sesterces or ten?'

'Not much,' confessed Marcellus. 'I am not specially interested in money—and it's quite beautiful out here in the open, with that majestic mountain in sight.'

Vobiscus, shielding his eyes, gazed up at the towering peak beyond Arpino, frowned, looked up again, grinned a little, and rubbed his chin.

'You aren't crazy; are you?' he asked, soberly, and when Marcellus had said he didn't think so, the overseer told him to go on up to the villa.

* * * * * *

Kaeso had the traditional arrogance of a short-statured man of wealth and authority. He was of a pugnacious stockiness, fifty, smooth-shaven, expensively dressed, with carefully groomed, grizzled hair and amazingly well-preserved teeth. It was immediately evident that he was accustomed to barking impatient questions and drowning timorous replies in a deluge of belittling sarcasm.

Marcellus had stood quietly waiting while the restless, bumptious fellow marched heavily up and down the length of the cool atrium, shouting his unfavorable opinions of scriveners in general and his most recent one in particular. They were all alike; dishonest, lazy, incompetent. None of them was worth his salt. Every time Kaeso passed the applicant, he paused to glare at him belligerently.

At first, Marcellus had regarded this noisy exhibition with an impassive face, but as it continued, he found himself unable any longer to repress a broad grin. Kaeso stopped in his tracks and scowled. Marcellus chuckled good-humoredly.

'It is to laugh—is it?' snarled Kaeso, jutting his chin.

'Yes,' drawled Marcellus, 'it is to laugh. Maybe it wouldn't be funny if I were hungry—and in dire need of work. I suppose that's the way you talk to everybody who can't afford to talk back.'

Kaeso's mouth hung open and his eyes narrowed with unbelief.

'But—go right on.' Marcellus waved a hand negligently. 'Don't mind me: I'll listen. Do you care if I sit down? I've been walking all morning, and I'm tired.' He eased into a luxurious chair and sighed. Kaeso stalked toward him and stood with feet wide apart.

'Who are you, fellow?' he demanded.

'Well, sir,' replied Marcellus, with a smile, 'while your question, asked in that tone, deserves no answer at all, I am an unemployed wayfarer. Your man Vobiscus insisted that I offer my services as a scrivener. Realizing that this is your busiest season, I thought I might do you a good turn by helping out for a few days.'

Kaeso ran his stubby fingers through his graying hair and sat down on the edge of an adjacent lectus.

'And you, sir,' went on Marcellus, 'instead of giving me an opportunity to explain my call, began to pour forth.' His eyes drifted about through the well-appointed atrium. 'If I may venture to say so, you probably do not deserve to live in such a beautiful villa. Your manner of treating strangers doesn't seem to belong here. In these lovely surroundings, there should be nothing but quiet courtesy—and good will.'

Kaeso, stunned by the stranger's impudence, had listened with amazement. Now he came to his feet, his face contorted with anger.

'You can't say things like that to me!' he shouted. 'Who do you think you are? You insult me in my house—yet you look like a common vagrant—a beggar!'

'I am not a beggar, sir,' said Marcellus, quietly.

'Get out!' snapped Kaeso.

Marcellus rose, smiled, bowed, walked slowly toward the open peristyle, and down the broad marble steps, Kaeso following him as far as the portico. Sauntering through the village, he went back to the melon field, aware that he was being trailed at a little distance by a tall Macedonian. Vobiscus viewed his return with much interest.

'Kaeso didn't want you?' he inquired.

Marcellus shook his head, picked up a basket, and walked through the field until he came to the first little group of laborers. They glanced up with sour curiosity. One old man straightened, with a painful grimace, and looked him over with the utmost frankness.

It was a fine day, observed Marcellus, pleasantly. For a backache, retorted the old man. This drew a sullen chortle from the neighbors, one of whom—a scowling old woman of twenty—bitterly admonished him that he'd better work awhile, and then tell them how fine a day it was.

Conceding this point so cheerfully that the sulky girl gave him a reluctant but pathetically childish smile, Marcellus doffed his robe —folding it carefully and laying it on the ground beside the goat-skin bag—and fell to work with enthusiasm.

'Not so fast, not so fast,' cautioned the old man. 'Kaeso won't pay you any better for killing yourself.'

'And Vobiscus will be bawling at us for shirking,' added a cloddish fellow, up the line a little way.

'These are the finest melons in the world!' remarked Marcellus, stopping to wipe his dripping forehead. 'It's a pleasure to work with the finest—of something. Not many people have a chance to do that. Sunshine, blue sky, beautiful mountains—and the finest—'

'Oh—shut up!' yelled the clod.

'Shut up yourself!' put in the old woman of twenty. 'Let him talk! They *are* good melons!'

For some unknown reason everybody laughed at that, in various keys and tempers, and the mood of the sweating toilers brightened a little. Presently the overseer strolled over from the gate and the melon-pickers applied themselves with ostentatious diligence. He paused beside Marcellus, who looked up inquiringly. Vobiscus jerked his head toward the villa.

'He wants to see you,' he said, gruffly.

Marcellus nodded, picked up his laden basket in his arms, and poured out a few into the old man's basket. Then he gave some to the worn-out girl who raised her eyes in a smile that was almost pretty. On up the line of workers, he distributed his melons, emptying the last dozen of them into the basket of the oaf who had derided him. The sullen fellow pulled an embarrassed grin.

'Will you be coming back?' squeaked the old man.

'I hope so, sir,' said Marcellus. 'It is pleasant work—and good company.'

'Oh—it's *sir* you are now, old one?' teased the oaf. Much boisterous laughter rewarded this sally. The girl with the scowl did not join in the applause.

'What's paining you, Metella?' yelled the witty one.

She turned on him angrily.

'It's a pity that a stranger can't show us a little decent respect without being cackled at!'

As Marcellus turned to go, he gave her an approving wink that smoothed out the scowl and sent a flush through the tan. A dozen pairs of eyes followed him as he moved away at the side of Vobiscus, who had been an impatient spectator.

'They're not out here to joke—and play,' mumbled Vobiscus.

'You'd get more melons picked,' advised Marcellus. 'People work better when they're happy. Don't you think so?'

'I don't know,' said Vobiscus. 'I never saw anybody working who was happy.' He lengthened his steps. 'You'd better stretch your legs, fellow. Kaeso isn't good at waiting.'

'He's probably as good at waiting as I am at hurrying,' replied Marcellus, dryly.

'You don't know Kaeso,' muttered Vobiscus, with an ominous chuckle. 'He doesn't coddle people; only horses.'

'I can believe that,' said Marcellus. Throwing the old bag over his shoulder, he strolled out to the highway, tarried for another look at the mountain, and sauntered up the hill.

* * * * * *

Kaeso was at his desk when Marcellus was shown in. He was making a showy pretense of being busily engaged and did not glance up. After Marcellus had stood waiting before the desk for what seemed to him a long time, without receiving any attention, he turned away and walked over to a window that looked out upon a flower-garden.

'You say you are a scrivener?' called Kaeso, sharply.

'No, sir.' Marcellus slowly retraced his steps. 'Your man asked me if I could read, write, and compute. I can do that—but I am not a scrivener by profession.'

'Humph! How much do you want?'

'You will know, sir, how much my services are worth to you. I shall accept what you think is just.'

'I gave the last man ten sesterces—and his keep.'

'It seems a trifling wage,' observed Marcellus, 'but if you cannot afford to pay more—'

'It's not a question of what I can afford!' retorted Kaeso, pompously. 'It's a question of what you will take!'

'I shouldn't have thought that a proud and successful man like you, sir, would want a stranger to donate part of his time to serving you. You called me a beggar, an hour ago, in a tone indicating that you had no respect for beggars. Perhaps I misunderstood you.'

Kaeso pushed his folded arms halfway across the desk and glared up into Marcellus' complacent eyes. He appeared to be contemplating a savage rejoinder; but impulsively changed his tactics.

'I'll give you twenty,' he grumbled—'and let me tell you something!' 'his voice was rising to an angry pitch. 'There's to be no shirking—and no mistakes—and no—'

'Just a moment!' broke in Marcellus, coolly. 'Let me tell *you* something! You have a bad habit of screaming at people. I can't believe that you get any pleasure out of terrorizing others who can't help themselves. It's just a habit—but it's a hateful habit—and I don't like it—and you're not to indulge in it when you're addressing *me!*'

Kaeso rubbed his jaw with the back of his hand.

'Nobody ever dared to talk to me like that!' he smouldered. 'I don't know why I let you do it.'

'I'll gladly tell you.' Marcellus laid his hands flat on the desk and leaned far forward with a confidential smile. 'You have accumulated a great deal of property and power—but you are not contented. There is something you lack—something you would like to have. You are not sure what it is—but you think *I* know. That is why you sent for me to come back, Kaeso.'

'I sent for you, fellow'—Kaeso was wagging his head truculently —'because I need a scrivener!'

'Well—I'm not a scrivener,' drawled Marcellus, turning away, 'and you're shouting again. If you will excuse me, I'll go back to the melon field. I found some very companionable people out there.'

'What? Companionable? Those melon-pickers?' rasped Kaeso. 'They're a pack of dirty, lazy thieves!'

'Not naturally, I think,' said Marcellus, judicially. 'But for their extreme poverty and drudgery, they might be quite decent and industrious and honest—just as you, sir, might be a very charming person if you had no opportunity to be a bully.'

'See here, fellow!' snarled Kaeso. 'Are you going out there to gabble with these idlers—and try to make them believe they're unjustly treated?'

'No—any man who works from dawn to dusk at hard labor—for three sesterces—will not need to be told that he's getting bad treatment.'

'So!—they've been complaining; eh?'

'Not to me, sir. When I left them, I thought they were in quite a merry mood.'

'Humph! What have they got to be merry about?' Kaeso pushed back his chair, rose; and, opening a tall cabinet in the corner, drew out a large sheaf of papyrus sheets and an armful of scrolls. Dumping the correspondence on his desk, he pointed to it significantly.

'Sit down!' he commanded. 'Take up that stylus, and I'll tell you how to reply to these letters. They are orders from markets and great houses in Rome—for melons—and grapes—and pears. You will read them to me and I shall tell you what to say. And have a care! I do not read—but I will know what they are saying!'

Disinclined to argue, and alive with curiosity to see what might come of this unfamiliar business, Marcellus sat down and began to read the letters aloud. Kaeso seemed childishly pleased. He was selling melons! Cartloads and cartloads of choice Arpino melons! And getting a top price for them! And advance orders for grapes in August. Presently Marcellus came upon a letter written in Greek, and started to read it in that language.

'Ah—that Greek!' snorted Kaeso. 'I do not understand. What does it say?' And when Marcellus had translated it, he inquired, with something like respect, 'You write Greek, too? That is good.' He rubbed his hands with satisfaction. It would be pleasant to let these great ones know that he could afford to have a scholar for a scrivener. When the letter was ended, he remarked, irrelevantly, 'We will find you a better tunic.'

'I have a better tunic, thank you,' said Marcellus, without looking up.

'Is it that you like flowers?' asked Kaeso, after they had finished for the day; and when Marcellus had nodded, he said, condescendingly, 'The scrivener is permitted to walk in the gardens of the villa. If you like horses, you may visit my stables.'

'Very gracious of you, sir,' said Marcellus, absently.

*　*　*　*　*　*

Antonia Kaeso was at least a dozen years younger than her husband. But for her tightly pursed mouth and unlighted eyes she might have been considered attractive, for her features were nicely moulded, her figure was shapely, and her tone was refined. Marcellus, encountering her among the roses with garden shears and a basket, had reasons for surmising that she was a victim of repression.

She greeted him casually, unsmilingly, remarking in a flat monotone that she supposed he must be her husband's new scrivener. Marcellus admitted this, adding that he was pleased to find employment in such a pleasant environment, which drew a sidelong, bitter smile from her eyes, a smile in which her lips had no share.

'You mean the flowers—and the mountain,' she said.

'Yes—they are beautiful.' He was for sauntering on, seeing that his permission to walk in the garden had not included the right to a leisurely chat with the mistress of the villa; but the enigmatic wife of Kaeso detained him.

'What is your name, scrivener? My husband did not say.'

'Marcellus Gallio.'

'There is a Senator of that name—Gallio.' She was cutting the half-opened roses with long stems and tossing them at random toward the basket. Marcellus stooped and began arranging them in orderly fashion.

'Yes—that is true,' he said.

'Are you related?' she asked, much occupied with her task.

Marcellus laughed, self-deprecatingly.

'Would a humble scrivener be related to a Senator?' he countered.

'Probably not,' she agreed, coolly. 'But you are not a humble scrivener. You are patrician.' She straightened up and faced him with level eyes. 'It's in your voice, in your face, in your carriage.' The short upper lip showed a row of pretty teeth, as she pointed with her shears. 'Look at your hands! They're not accustomed to work—of any kind! Don't be alarmed,' she went on, with a little shrug, 'I won't give you away, though that silk tunic may. Weren't you rather indiscreet to put it on? I saw you in the other one, this morning, from my window. Wherever did you find it?' She was stooping low, busy with her shears. 'How do you like masquerading as a scrivener, Marcellus Gallio? Are you sure you aren't related to the Senator?'

'He is my father,' said Marcellus.

'I believe that,' she replied, turning her face toward him with an honest smile. 'But why do you tell me?'

'Because you seem to like frankness—and because I prefer to tell you the truth. I have not tried to deceive your husband. He did not ask my name.'

'But I think you would be pleased if he did not know.'

'Yes—I should prefer that he does not know.'

'That is unfortunate,' she said, ironically. 'You are robbing Appius Kaeso of much pleasure. Were he able to say that he had the son of a Senator for his scrivener, he would be unbearably exalted.'

'Perhaps you don't understand Kaeso,' soothed Marcellus.

'I don't understand Kaeso!' she exclaimed. 'By all the gods! That is my occupation—understanding Kaeso!'

'He requires special handling, my friend,' declared Marcellus. 'Kaeso is immensely proud of his power over all these people in Arpino. They obey him because they fear him. He could have even more power over them if they obeyed because they liked him.'

'Imagine Kaeso doing anything to make them like him!' she scoffed.

'I can imagine it,' rejoined Marcellus, quietly. 'And if we can induce him to make the experiment, it will greatly improve the atmosphere of this place. Would you like to cooperate with me?'

'It's much too late,' she objected. 'Kaeso could never win their friendship—no matter what he might do for them. And you must remember that the common laborers of Arpino are a dirty, ignorant lot!'

'They *are* dirty!' agreed Marcellus. 'And you can't expect dirty people to be decent. They antagonize one another because each man despises himself—and no wonder. I was thinking about that, this morning. These people should have bathing facilities. There's not much temptation to get into this ice-cold mountain stream. It should not be much of a task to build a large swimming-pool, and let the hot sun warm the water. There is a quarry hard by. The people could construct the pool themselves in the idle interval between the melons and the grapes—if they had any encouragement.'

'Ah—you don't know the Arpinos!' protested the wife of Kaeso.

'If they are worse than other people, there must be a reason,' said Marcellus. 'I wonder what it is.'

'Why should you care, Marcellus Gallio?'

A handsome youth in his early teens was strolling toward them. There was no question about his identity. His resemblance to his mother was so striking as to bring a smile.

'Your son, I think,' said Marcellus.

'Antony,' she murmured, with an ecstatic little sigh. 'He is my life. He wants to be a sculptor. His father does not approve, and will not consent to his having instruction. He is such a lonely, unhappy child. . . . Come here, Antony, and meet the new scrivener, Marcellus Gallio.'

'Your mother tells me you are fond of modeling,' said Marcellus, when Antony had mumbled an indifferent greeting. 'Would you like to let me see what you are doing?'

Antony screwed up a sensitive mouth.

'Would you know anything about it?' he asked, with his mother's disconcerting candor.

'Enough to make a few suggestions, perhaps.'

*   *   *   *   *   *

Antony couldn't wait until morning, but went to the scrivener's quarters after dinner, carrying the model he had been working on —two gladiators poised for action. He put it down on Marcellus' table and backed off from it shyly, murmuring that he knew it wasn't much.

'It's not at all bad, Antony,' commended Marcellus. 'The composition is good. The man on this side is a foolhardy fellow, though, to take that stance. What are their names?'

Suspecting that he was being teased, Antony grinned and said he hadn't named them.

'To do your best work on them,' said Marcellus, seriously, 'they must have personality. You should consider them as real people, and know all about them. Let us attend to that first; shall we?' He drew up a chair for Antony and they sat, facing the model.

'Now—the man on this side is Cyprius. The legionaries captured him down in Crete, burned his house down, drove off his cattle, murdered his wife and son—a boy about your age—and took him to Rome in a prison-ship He was an excellent swordsman, so they gave him his choice of dueling in the arena or pulling an oar in a galley.

So, he chose the arena, and now he is fighting for his life, hoping to kill this other man whom he never saw before.'

'Oh—you're just making that up,' accused Antony, glumly.

'Yes—but that's the way these duels are staged in the arena, Antony, between men who must kill or be killed. Now—your other man is a Thracian. His name is Galenzo. He had a little farm, and a vineyard, and some goats, and three small children. His wife tried to hide him in the hay when the legionaries came, but they struck her down before the children's eyes and dragged Galenzo away on a chain. He fought so hard that they sold him to a praetor who needed gladiators for the games at the Feast of Isis. Now Cyprius and Galenzo are fighting, so the people may have a chance to lay wagers on which one will kill the other. How were you betting, Antony? I shall risk a hundred sesterces on Galenzo. I don't like the way Cyprius stands.'

'I hadn't thought of betting,' said Antony, dispiritedly. He turned to Marcellus with pouting lips. 'You don't like fighting; do you?'

'Not that kind.'

'Maybe you never fought,' challenged Antony. 'Maybe you would be afraid to fight.'

'Maybe,' rejoined Marcellus, undisturbed by the boy's impudence.

'I'll take that back!' sputtered Antony. 'I don't think you'd be afraid to fight. I'll bet you could. Did you ever?'

'Not in the arena.'

'Did you ever kill anyone, sir?'

Marcellus postponed his reply so long that Antony knew his question could have but one answer. His eyes were bright with anticipation of an exciting story.

'Did he put up a good fight, sir?'

'It is not a pleasant recollection,' said Marcellus. There was an interval of silence. 'I wish you had chosen some other subject for your model, Antony. I'm not much interested in this one'—he suddenly invaded Antony's moody eyes—'nor are you, my boy! You're not the type that goes in for slaughter. You don't believe in it; you don't like it; and if you had it to do, it would turn your stomach. Isn't that so?'

Antony explored the inside of his cheek with a defenseless tongue, and slowly nodded his head.

'It's worse than that,' he confessed. 'I would be afraid to fight. Maybe that's why I draw pictures of fighting—and make models of gladiators. Just trying to pretend.' He hung his head, morosely. 'I haven't a scrap of courage,' he went on. 'It makes me ashamed.'

'Well—I'm not so sure about that,' consoled Marcellus. 'There are many different kinds of courage, Antony. You've just come through with the best kind there is—the courage to tell the truth! It required much more bravery to say what you've just said than it takes to black another man's eye.'

Antony raised his head and brightened a little.

'Let's start another model,' he suggested.

'Very well—I shall try to think of something that we both might enjoy. Come back early in the morning. If you will lend me some clay, perhaps I may have a rough sketch to show you when you come.'

*   *   *   *   *   *

Antony laughed merrily. Marcellus had made a rectangular swimming-pool. Seated on the stone ledge, at intervals, were figures of bathers—men, women, and children. One thin old man had an absurdly long beard tossed over his shoulder. A tiny baby on all fours was about to tumble in. Its mother was coming at full gallop. The large feet and bony legs of a diver protruded from the immobile water.

'You didn't do all that this morning!' said Antony.

'No—I worked on it most of the night. It's just a beginning, you see. We need many more people sitting around the pool, and diving and swimming. Would you like to complete it?'

'It would be fun, I think,' said Antony.

'You can give it a lot of detail. Move it to a much larger modeling-board and you will have room to do some landscaping. Remember that big white rock, down by the bridge, where there is a natural basin? You might put in the bridge and the rock and the acacia trees. Then everybody would know where the pool is.'

'I say, sir, it wouldn't be a bad idea to *have* a pool like that!'

*   *   *   *   *   *

After a week's acquaintance with his new duties, Marcellus was able to complete his day's work by mid-afternoon. Antony would be loitering in the atrium, restlessly passing and repassing the open door to the library. Kaeso had observed this growing attachment, not without some satisfaction.

'They tell me you are helping to amuse my son,' he remarked. 'Don't feel that you must, if it's a burden. You have plenty of work to do.'

Marcellus had assured him that he enjoyed Antony's company; that the boy had artistic talent; that he needed encouragement; and when Kaeso had derided art as a profession, an argument arose.

'I can't think that a real man would want to waste his time playing with mud,' said Kaeso, scornfully.

'Clay,' corrected Marcellus, unruffled. 'Modeling-clay. There's as much difference between mud and clay as there is between Arpino melons and—ordinary melons. It is not unnatural, sir, a man's desire to create something beautiful. Antony may become an able sculptor.'

'Sculptor!' sneered Kaeso. 'And of what use is a sculptor?'

Marcellus had made no reply to that. He continued putting away his accounts and desk implements, with a private smile that stirred Kaeso's curiosity, and when queried, remarked that Antony probably came by it naturally.

'You, sir,' he explained, 'have created a successful business. Your son can hardly hope to improve upon it. It is complete. He, too, wants to create something. You have bequeathed him this ambition. And now you resent his having a desire that he inherited from you.'

Kaeso, purring with self-satisfaction, twirled his thumbs and grinned for more. Marcellus obliged him. Many sculptors starved to death before they were well enough known to earn a living by their art. Antony would not have to starve. His father was rich, and should take pride in his son's ability. Appius Kaeso had made his name important in commerce. Antony Kaeso might make his name mean as much in the field of art.

'You don't want Antony to be unhappy and unsuccessful when he might easily make you proud of him. Show him a little attention, sir, and you'll discover you have a loyal and affectionate son.'

'Ah—the boy has always been cold and disdainful,' complained Kaeso—'like his mother.'

'If I may venture to contradict you,' said Marcellus, 'Antony is a very warm-hearted youngster. You could have his love if you wanted it. Why not come along with me now, sir, and have a look at something he is making?'

Grumbling that he had no interest in such nonsense, Kaeso had accompanied him to Antony's room. They stood before the model in silence, Antony visibly nervous and expectant of derision.

Kaeso studied the elaborate scene, rubbed his jaw, chuckled a little, and shook his head. Antony, watching his father with pathetic wistfulness, sighed dejectedly.

'It's in the wrong place,' declared Kaeso. 'When the snow melts, the spring freshets come plunging through that hollow. It would tear your masonry out. You must build it on higher ground.'

With that, Marcellus said he had an errand, if they would excuse him, and left the room. He sauntered down the hall and out through the peristyle, wearing a smile of such dimensions that when he encountered Antonia she insisted on knowing what had happened. Her eyes widened with unbelief as he told her briefly that her husband and her son were conferring about the best place to build a swimming-pool.

'Shall I join them?' she asked, childishly.

'No—not this time,' said Marcellus.

*   *   *   *   *   *

It was mid-July now. At sunset, every day, Marcellus went down to the nearest melon field and sat by the gate where the workers from all the fields received their wages. For a while the people merely waved a hand and smiled as they passed him. Then some of them ventured to tarry and talk. The scrivener, they all agreed, was indeed a queer one, but there was something about him that inclined them to him. They had a feeling that he was on their side.

For one thing, there was this rumor that they were to have a swimming-pool. When the last of the melons were harvested, anyone who wished to work on the community pool could do so. Nobody knew how much would be paid for this labor, but they were to be paid. Everybody felt that the scrivener had been responsible for this project. Some of the bolder ones asked him about it and he professed not to know much of the plan, which, he said, was Appius Kaeso's idea; and they would be told all about it, when the time came.

One afternoon, when fully a score of workers had gathered about him, Marcellus told them a story about a man he knew in a faraway country, who had important things to say to poor people with heavy burdens, and how he believed that a man's life did not consist of the things he owned, and how much unhappiness could be avoided if men did not covet other men's possessions. If you want to be happy, make other people happy. He paused—and found himself looking squarely into Metella's eyes, pleased to see them so softly responsive.

'And what did this Jesus do to make other people happy?' asked an old man.

Well—in the case of Jesus, Marcellus had explained, he wasn't just an ordinary man; for he performed remarkable deeds of healing. He could make blind men see. People had but to touch him, and they were cured of their diseases. It was dark that evening before the melon-workers trudged up the hill. Reproaching himself for having detained them so long, Marcellus had said, 'If you want to hear more stories about Jesus, let us meet tomorrow in the village, after you have your supper.'

And so it had become a daily event for Marcellus to meet the people of Arpino on the grassy knoll at the foot of the mountain. He told them of the great, surging crowds that had followed Jesus; told them, with much detail, about the miracles, about little Jonathan's foot—and the story of the donkey that the lad gave to his crippled friend. He told them about Miriam's voice, and the broken loom that Jesus had mended, and how the woman had woven him a robe.

They had sat motionless, hardly breathing, until darkness fell. All Arpino looked forward to these evening stories, and discussed them in the fields next day. Even Vobiscus came and listened. One evening, Antonia and Antony appeared at the edge of the crowd while Marcellus was telling them about the feeding of five thousand people from a small boy's lunch-basket. It was a story of many moods, and the Arpinos laughed and wept over it. And then there was the great storm that Jesus had stilled with a soothing word.

'I hear you've been entertaining the people with strange stories,' remarked Kaeso, next day.

'About a great teacher, sir,' explained Marcellus, 'and his deeds for the relief of the people in the provinces of Palestine.'

'What kind of deeds?' pursued Kaeso; and when Marcellus had told him a few of the miracle-stories he said, 'Did this Jesus deal only with the poor?'

'By no means!' said Marcellus. 'He had friends among the rich, and was frequently invited to their houses. You might be interested, sir, in something that happened at the home of a wealthy man named Zacchaeus.'

'Divided half of his money among the poor; eh?' remarked Kaeso, when the story was finished. 'Much thanks he got for that, I suppose.'

'I don't know,' said Marcellus. 'I daresay the only way you could find out how people would act, in such a case—'

'Divide your money with them—and see; eh?' grumbled Kaeso.

'Well—you might make a little experiment that wouldn't cost quite so much,' said Marcellus, soberly. 'For example, have Vobiscus pay everybody four sesterces, instead of three, from now to the end of the melon season.'

'Then they'd raise a row if we went back to the old wage!' protested Kaeso.

'Very likely,' agreed Marcellus. 'Maybe it isn't worth doing. It would probably just stir up trouble.'

'Vobiscus would think I had gone crazy!' exclaimed Kaeso.

'Not if you increased his wages too. Vobiscus is a valuable man, sir, and very loyal. He isn't paid enough.'

'Did he say so?' snapped Kaeso.

'No—Vobiscus wouldn't complain to me.'

'He has never asked for more.'

'That does not mean he is getting enough.'

'Perhaps you will be wanting better wages too.' Kaeso chuckled unpleasantly.

'Vobiscus gets six sesterces. Let us pay him ten, and I will be content with sixteen instead of twenty.'

'Very well,' said Kaeso. 'You're a fool—but if that's the way you want it—'

'With one stipulation, sir. Vobiscus is not to know how his raise in wages came about. Let him think you did it—and see what happens.'

* * * * * *

Kaeso took much pride in the pool, and admitted that he was glad the idea had occurred to him to build it. The people didn't know what had come over Kaeso, but they believed the same thing was happening to him that had happened to them. He even conceded to Marcellus that the sesterces he had added to the workers' wage might have had something to do with the gratifying fact that there had been a surprisingly small loss lately on melons bruised by careless handling. Marcellus did not tell him that he had made them a speech, the next morning after their pay was increased, in which he had suggested that they show their appreciation by being more faithful to their employer's interests.

The grapes were ripening now, and Kaeso enjoyed strolling through the vineyards. Sometimes the older ones ventured to turn their heads in his direction, and smile, rather shyly. One afternoon, he heard them singing, as he came down the road. When he appeared at the gate, the song stopped. He asked Vobiscus.

'They thought it might annoy you, sir,' stammered Vobiscus.

'Let them sing! Let them sing!' shouted Kaeso, indignantly. 'What makes them think I don't want to hear them sing?'

Vobiscus was clean-shaven today, and carrying himself with an air. Yesterday the wife of Kaeso had called at his house to show his wife a tapestry pattern and ask her how she had dyed the shawl she wore last night.

Near the end of a day when Marcellus had said he was going to stroll down to the vineyards, Antony asked if he might go along. At the gate, Marcellus picked up a couple of baskets and handed one to Antony.

'Want to do me a little favor?' he asked. 'Come along—and we'll gather some grapes.'

'Why should we?' inquired Antony. 'What will they think of us?'

'They will think no less of us,' said Marcellus, 'and it will make them think better of themselves—and their work.'

Presently they came upon an old woman who was straining hard to lift her heavy basket up to the platform of a cart. The driver, lounging against the wheel, watched her lazily.

'Give her a hand, Antony,' said Marcellus, quietly.

Everybody in that vicinity stopped work for a moment to witness this strange sight. The elegant son of Kaeso, who, they all had thought, considered the people of Arpino as dirt under his dainty feet, had volunteered to share a laborer's burden. There was a spontaneous murmur of approval as Marcellus and Antony moved on.

'Thank you, Antony,' said Marcellus, in a low tone.

'I didn't mind giving her a lift,' said Antony, flushing as he noted the appreciative smiles of the workers.

'You gave *everybody* a lift,' said Marcellus, 'including yourself, I think.'

* * * * * *

When August was more than half gone and the orders for fruit had dwindled until the scrivener's duties for the season were of small importance, Marcellus told Kaeso that he would like to be on his way.

'How about staying on for a while to help Antony with his modeling?' suggested Kaeso.

'I have shown him almost everything I know,' said Marcellus.

'Nonsense!' scoffed Kaeso. 'He can learn much from you. Besides—

you are good for him. Antony's a different boy. You're making a man of him.'

'That's your doing, Kaeso,' said Marcellus, gently. 'Can't you see the way Antony hangs on your words? He admires you greatly, sir. It should be your own privilege to make a man of him.'

'Will you come back to Arpino next summer?' asked Kaeso, almost entreatingly.

Marcellus expressed his gratitude for the invitation, but did not know where he might be, next summer. Finishing his work at the desk, he was more painstaking than usual in filing things away, Kaeso moodily watching him.

'When are you leaving?' he asked.

'Early in the morning, sir. I am going to Rome.'

Kaeso followed him out into the garden where they met Antonia. In her presence he invited Marcellus to dine with the family. Antonia smiled her approval.

'He is leaving us,' said Kaeso. 'Where is Antony? I shall tell him.' He turned back toward the house.

'Aren't you contented here, Marcellus?' asked Antonia, gently, after a little silence between them. 'Haven't we done everything you wished?'

'Yes—that's why I'm going.'

She nodded understandingly and gave him a pensive smile.

'Marcellus—do you remember the story you told us about the people's belief—in Cana, was it?—that Jesus had changed water into wine?'

'You found that hard to believe, I think,' he said.

'No,' she murmured; 'I can believe that story. It's no more mysterious than the changes you have made—in Arpino.'

* * * * * *

That evening, according to their recent custom, all the villagers assembled on the knoll to wait for Marcellus to appear and tell them a story. When he came, Kaeso and Antonia and Antony were with him. Sitting down in the open circle the people had left for him, Marcellus hesitated for a long moment before beginning to speak.

'You have all been very kind to me,' he said, 'and you will be much in my thoughts, wherever I may go.'

A disappointed little sigh went over the crowd.

'I have told you many stories about this strange man of Galilee, who befriended the poor and helpless. Tonight, I shall tell you one more story about him—the strangest story of them all. Let that be my parting gift to you.'

It was a sad story, of a misunderstood man, forsaken at the last, even by his frightened friends; a dismaying story of an unfair trial and a cruel death, and Marcellus told it so impressively that most of his audience was in tears.

'Now, there was nothing so strange about that,' he went on, in a suddenly altered mood, 'for wise men have always been misunderstood and persecuted—and many of them have been slain—as Jesus was. But Jesus came to life again!'

'What? No!' shouted an old man, in a quavering voice. They hushed him down, and waited for Marcellus to go on.

In the tense silence, the amazing story proceeded. Jesus was in the world—alive—to remain until his kingdom of kindness should rule all men—everywhere.

'You need not weep for him!' declared Marcellus. 'He asks no pity! If you want to do something to aid him, be helpful to one another—and await his coming.'

'Where is he now, sir?' called the old man, shrilly.

'No one knows,' said Marcellus. 'He might appear—anywhere—any time. We must not be found doing anything that would grieve him if he should come upon us suddenly—at an hour when we were not expecting him. Will you keep that in your remembrance?'

The twilight was falling fast now and so was the dew. It was time they dispersed. Marcellus drew a folded, much-handled sheet of papyrus from the breast of his tunic, and held it up in the fading light.

'One day,' he said, 'when a great company of Galileans had assembled about him on a hilltop, Jesus talked to them quietly about what he called "the blessed life." My friend Justus remembered these words and recited them for me. I wrote them down. Let me read them to you—and then we will part.'

The Arpinos leaned forward to listen; all but Metella, who sat hugging her knees, with her face buried in her folded arms. A deep hush fell over them as Marcellus read:

'Blessed are the poor in spirit, for theirs is the kingdom of heaven. Blessed are they that mourn, for they shall be comforted. Blessed are the meek, for they shall inherit the earth. Blessed are they who hunger and thirst after righteousness, for they shall be filled. Blessed are the merciful, for they shall obtain mercy. Blessed are the pure in heart, for they shall see God. Blessed are the peacemakers, for they shall be called the children of God. Blessed are they who are persecuted for righteousness' sake, for theirs is the kingdom of heaven. Rejoice and be glad, for great will be your reward.'

* * * * * *

Rising before dawn, Marcellus slipped quietly out of the villa, meeting no one—except Metella, who startled him by stepping out of the shrubbery near the gate to say farewell in a tremulous little voice. Then she had started to scamper away. He spoke her name softly.

Taking her toil-roughened hands, he said tenderly, 'Metella, you are indeed a faithful friend. I shall always remember you.'

'Please'—she sobbed—'take good care of yourself—Marcellus!' And then, abruptly tearing loose from him, she had disappeared in the dark.

It was with a strange sense of elation that he strode along the foot-hill road in the shadow of the mountain as a pink sunrise lighted the sky. Last night, after taking leave of the Kaeso family—who had made an earnest effort to dissuade him—he had gone to bed with misgivings. He was happy in Arpino. He knew he had been sent there on a mission. Lately, something kept telling him his work was done; telling him he must go to Rome. All night, with the entreaties of young Antony still sounding in his ears, he kept asking himself, 'Why *am* I going to Rome?'

This morning, his anxieties had been put aside. He did not know why he was headed toward Rome, but the reason would appear in due time. He had never been able to explain to himself why, when he had been washed up by the tide on the Capua beach, he had turned his face toward Arpino; or why, tarrying at Kaeso's melon field, he had accepted employment. It was almost as if he were being led about by an invisible hand.

By mid-afternoon, the winding road had angled away from the mountain range and was being joined and widened by many tributaries. It was becoming a busy highway now, drawing in all manner of laden carts and wagons from the gates and lanes of the fertile valley. The day was hot and the air was heavy with dust. Scowling drivers lashed their donkeys cruelly and yelled obscenities as they contended for the right of way. Every added mile increased the confusion and sharpened the ostentatious brutality of the men who pressed toward Rome.

It was as if the Imperial City had reached out her malevolent arms in all directions to clutch and pollute her victims as they moved into the orbit of her fetid breath; and they, ashamed of their rustic simplicities, had sought to appear urbane by cursing one another. Marcellus, making his way past this ill-tempered cavalcade, wondered whether many people could be found in Rome who would care to hear about the man of Galilee.

Arriving in the good-sized town of Alatri at sundown, Marcellus found the only tavern buzzing with excitement. An agitated crowd milled about in the stableyard. Inside, there was barely standing room. He made his way in and asked the tall man wedged beside him what was going on. The news had just come from Rome that Prince Gaius was dead.

At this juncture, the tavern-keeper stood up on a chair and announced importantly that all who did not wish to be served should get out and make way for his guests. Most of the shabby ones sullenly withdrew. In the center of the room, three flashily dressed wool-buyers from Rome sat at a table, laving the day's dust with a flagon of wine. Crowded about them was an attentive audience, eager for further details concerning the tragedy. Marcellus pressed close and listened.

Last night there had been a banquet at the palatial home of Tribune Quintus and his wife Celia, the niece of Sejanus, in honor of young Caligula, the son of Germanicus, who had just arrived from Gaul. Prince Gaius had been taken suddenly ill at dinner and had died within the hour.

The wool-merchants, conscious of their attentive auditors, and growing less discreet as they replenished their cups from the second flagon, continued to discuss the event with a knowledgeable air, almost as if they had been present at the fateful banquet. It was evident that they were well informed on court gossip, as indeed anyone in Rome could be if he made friends with servants.

There was little doubt, declared the wool-men, that the Prince had been poisoned. He had been in the best of health. The sickness had been swift and savage. Suspicion had not centered definitely on anyone. Tribune Tullus, who in the afternoon had married the young daughter of Senator Gallio—sister of Tribune Marcellus, the one who drowned himself in the sea, a few weeks ago—had spoken some hot words to the Prince, earlier in the evening; but they had both been so drunk that little importance had been attached to the argument.

Old Sejanus had sat opposite the Prince at dinner, and everybody knew that Sejanus had no use for Gaius. But it was agreed that if the crafty old man had wanted to assassinate the Prince he had too much sense to risk it in such circumstances.

'How does it happen that Quintus can live in a palace and give expensive dinners?' inquired the tavern-keeper, anxious to show that he knew a thing or two about the great ones. 'Old Tuscus, his father, is not rich. What did Quintus ever do to make a fortune? He has led no expeditions.'

The wool-merchants exchanged knowing glances and shrugged superiorly.

'Quintus and the Prince are great friends,' said the fat one who presided over the flagon.

'You mean the Prince and Quintus' wife are great friends,' recklessly chuckled the one with the silver trinkets on his bandeau.

'Oh, ho!' divined the tavern-keeper. 'Maybe that's how it happened!'

'Not so fast, wise man,' admonished the eldest of the three, thickly. 'Quintus was not present at the banquet. He had been sent, at the last minute, to Capri.'

'Who did it, then?' persisted the tavern-keeper.

'Well—that's what everybody wants to know,' said the fat one, holding up the empty flagon. 'Here! Fill that up—and don't ask so many questions.' He glanced about over the silent group, his eyes tarrying for a moment as they passed Marcellus. 'We're all talking too freely,' he muttered.

Marcellus turned away, followed by the tavern-keeper, and inquired for a bath and a room for the night. A servant showed him to his cramped and cheerless quarters, and he began tossing off his clothes. So—Diana need not be worried about Gaius' attentions any more. That was a great relief. Who would rule Rome now? Perhaps the Emperor would appoint tight-pursed old Sejanus to the regency for the present.

So—Gaius had been poisoned; eh? Perhaps Celia had done it. Maybe Gaius had mistreated her. He couldn't be loyal to anyone; not for very long. But, no—Celia wouldn't have done it. More likely that Quintus had left instructions with a servant, and had contrived some urgent business at Capri to provide an alibi. Quintus could dispose of the servant easily enough. Marcellus wondered if Quintus had encountered Demetrius at Capri. Well—if he had, Demetrius could take care of himself very nicely.

So—Lucia was married. That was good. She had always been in love with Tullus. Marcellus fell to speculating on the possibility that Lucia might have confided to her husband the story of Gaius' crude attempts to make love to her when she was little more than a child. If she had—and if Tullus were drunk enough to be foolhardy—but no, no—Tullus wouldn't get drunk enough to do a thing like that. Tullus would have used a dagger.

Marcellus reverted to Celia, trying to remember everything he could about her; the restless, sultry eyes; the sly, preoccupied smile that always made her manner seem older than her slim, girlish body. Yes—Celia might have done it. She was a deep one, like her Uncle Sejanus.

Well—whatever had caused the Prince's indigestion, the dangerous reptile was dead. That was a comfort. Perhaps Rome might now hope for a little better government. It was inconceivable that the Empire could acquire a worse ruler than Gaius Drusus Agrippa.

Chapter XXIII

WHEN the hard-riding couriers brought the report to Capri that Gaius was dead, the Emperor—in the firm opinion of old Julia—was much too ill to be confronted with such shocking news. That, of course, was nonsense, as the Empress well knew; for her son had long been Tiberius' favorite aversion, and these tidings, far from doing the sick old man any damage, might have temporarily revived him.

But, assuming that the tragic death of a Prince Regent should be viewed as an event too calamitous to be announced at the bedside of a seriously ailing Emperor, everybody conceded that Julia was within her rights in commanding that no mention be made of it to her enfeebled husband, though it was something of an innovation for the Empress to display so much solicitude in his behalf.

With less mercy, Julia had immediately thrust a letter into the hands of the exhausted Centurion who had brought the bad news, bidding him return to Rome at top speed. The Centurion, resentful at being pushed off the island without so much as an hour's respite and a flagon of wine, had no compunctions about showing the address of the Empresss' urgent message to his long-time friend the Chamberlain who had accompanied him and his aides to the wharf. The letter was going to Caligula.

'Little Boots,' growled the Centurion, contemptuously.

'Little brat!' muttered the Chamberlain, who had seen something of Germanicus' son when he was ten.

Old Julia, for whom Fate seemed always contriving fortuitous events, was feverish to see her grandson at this critical juncture. She had not felt so urgent a need of him, the day before yesterday, when Quintus had suddenly appeared with the suggestion—phrased as diplomatically as possible—that the Empress immediately invite the youngster to Capri. Julia had laughed almost merrily.

'He's a handful for Gaius; eh?' she snapped. 'Well—let Gaius bear his burden the best he can, for a month or two.'

'The Prince thought Your Majesty would be impatient to see Little Boots,' wheedled Quintus, 'and wanted me to say that he would not detain him in Rome if Your Majesty—'

'We can wait,' chuckled Julia.

But today the situation had changed. Julia wanted very much to see

Little Boots. How lucky for him that he should have happened to be available at this important hour!

Bearing her bereavement with fortitude, as became a Roman and an Empress, Julia nervously counted the dragging hours; watched and waited at her northern windows; grew almost frantic at the sight of a large deputation of Senators being borne up the hill to the Villa Jovis; and strained her old eyes for a certain black-hulled ferry—her own ferry —plying across the bay from Puteoli.

Nobody on Capri thought, when young Caligula arrived, that his ambitious grandmother had anything larger in mind for the puny youth than a brief interim regency, probably under the guidance of Sejanus—as a little child might hold the dangling ends of the reins and pretend he was driving. Perhaps Julia herself had not ventured to dream of the amazing thing that came to pass.

Caligula, at sixteen, was wizened and frail. He jerked when he walked. His pasty-white, foxish face was perpetually in motion with involuntary grimaces and his restless fingers were always busily picking and scratching like a monkey. He was no fool, though. Back of the darting, close-set eyes a malicious imagination tirelessly invented ingenious pursuits to compensate for his infirmities.

Because of his child's defects, Germanicus had insisted on having him under his eye, even in the heat of military campaigns. The officers had petted and flattered him until he was abominably impudent and outrageously cruel. His bestial pranks were supposed to be amusing. Someone had made a pair of little boots for him, like those worn by the staff officers, and the legend spread that Germanicus' sick boy frequently waddled out in front of a legion on review and barked shrill orders. The whimsical nickname 'Caligula' ('Little Boots') stuck to him until nobody remembered that he had been named for his Uncle Gaius. As a lad, everything Caligula did was cute, including the most shocking vandalisms and brutalities. By the time he was sixteen, it wasn't thought so clever when 'Little Boots' would jerkily propel himself up to a Centurion and slap him in the face; and even Germanicus, noting that his heir was becoming an intolerable pest, thought it time he was given another change of scenery. So—he was sent back to Rome again to visit his Uncle Gaius, who, it was hoped, would make something of him. What manner of miracle the Prince might have wrought was to remain forever a matter of conjecture. It was rumored that Germanicus' staff officers, upon learning of the death of Gaius, agreed that he could hardly have timed his departure more opportunely.

Caligula arrived on Capri in the late afternoon and old Julia took him at once—duly instructed as to his behavior—into the deeply shadowed bedchamber of the Emperor, where a dozen or more Senators stood about in the gloom, obviously waiting for Tiberius to take notice of them.

The old man dazedly roused to find a weeping youth kneeling beside his pillow. In a grieving voice the Empress explained that poor Gaius was dead, and Caligula was inconsolable.

Tiberius pulled his scattered wits together, and feebly patted Caligula on the head.

'Germanicus' boy?' he mumbled, thickly.

Caligula nodded, wept noisily, and gently stroked the emaciated hand.

'Is there anything I can do for you, sire?' he asked, brokenly.

'Yes—my son.' Tiberius' tired old voice was barely audible.

'You mean—the Empire?' demanded Julia, in much agitation.

The attentive Senators moved in closer about the bed.

'Yes—the Empire,' breathed Tiberius, weakly.

'Have you heard that?' Julia's tone was shrill and challenging as she threw back her head to face the stunned group at the bedside. 'Caligula is to be the Emperor! Is it not so, Your Majesty?'

'Yes,' whispered Tiberius.

*   *   *   *   *   *

It was late in the night. The Emperor lay dying. He had been close to it on several occasions. There was no doubt about it this time.

The learned physicians, having made all their motions, took turns holding the thin wrist. The priests, who had spent the day cooling their heels in the atrium, were admitted to do their solemn exercises. The Senators, who had been invited to withdraw after the incredible announcement had been made at sunset, were permitted to enter, now that it was reasonably sure the old man would have nothing more to say. They were still dazed by the blow he had delivered and were wondering how they would tell the Senate that Germanicus' deficient son was to rule the Empire. Of course the Senate, if it courageously took the bit in its teeth, could annul Tiberius' action; but it was unlikely that the solons would risk offending Germanicus and the army. No—their new Emperor—for good or ill—would be Little Boots.

Diana Gallus had not seen Tiberius for a fortnight. Old Julia had given orders that she was not to be admitted. Every morning and evening Diana had appeared at the door of the imperial bedchamber to inquire, and had been advised that the Emperor was too ill to be disturbed.

Shortly after Demetrius' arrival on Capri, he had been assigned to serve as Diana's bodyguard. Strangely enough, this had been done at the suggestion of Tiberius, who, perhaps with some premonition that he might not long be able to insist upon her adequate security, had felt that Marcellus' intrepid slave would protect her.

As the Emperor grew more frail, and the Empress' influence became more pressing throughout the island, Demetrius' anxiety about Diana's welfare increased; though he was careful not to let her know the full extent of his worry. He began making private plans for her rescue, in case her insecurity should become serious.

At the enforced departure of Marcellus, Diana had become restless, moody, and secluded. There was no one on the island in whom she could confide. Most of her daylight hours were spent in her pergola, reading without interest and indifferently toying with trifles of needle-work. Sometimes she would bring one of her maids along for company. As often she came alone, with Demetrius trailing her at a respectful distance and always within call. Her admiration for the Greek had always been deep and sincere. Now she began to lean on him as a close and understanding friend.

When the rumor had drifted back to Capri that Marcellus had been drowned, Demetrius knew it wasn't true, and comforted Diana with his reasons. Marcellus had no cause to commit suicide. He had become aware of a new and serious obligation. The story that Marcellus had drowned himself as *The Augusta* was rounding the promontory off Capua, only a mile off shore, amused Demetrius, so confident was he that his master had taken that favorable occasion to disappear. Diana believed this too, but Demetrius had to reassure her again and again when her loneliness was oppressive.

Their conversation became less formal as the days passed. Demetrius would sit on the side steps of the pergola answering Diana's persistent questions about their life in Athens, the House of Eupolis, Theodosia, and the escape after the affair with Quintus, for whom she had a bitter contempt.

'Why don't you go back to Theodosia when you are free?' she asked one day. 'Maybe she is waiting for you. Have you ever heard from her?'

Yes—Demetrius had written and he had heard from her, though not for a long time. One could never tell what might happen. Yes—if he were free, and Marcellus had no need of him, yes—he would go back to Athens.

The afternoons would pass quickly, Diana insatiable with her queries, Demetrius telling his interminable stories of old Benyosef's shop, and Stephanos, and the Galileans who came to talk in low voices about the mysterious carpenter who had come alive to live evermore.

Diana would listen attentively as she bent over her small tapestries and lace medallions. Demetrius' hands would be busy too, twisting and braiding short lengths of hemp that he had picked up on the wharves, and splicing them expertly into long, thick cords. Under the sea side of the pergola floor he had secreted his supplies, much to Diana's amusement.

'You are like a squirrel, Demetrius,' she had remarked, teasingly. 'Why do you hide your things, if they're worth nothing, as you say?' One day she bent over his shoulder and watched him deftly working the twisted hempen cords with his wooden awl. 'Why—you're making a rope!' she exclaimed. 'Whatever are you doing that for?' Following it around to the corner of the pergola, she was amazed to find a huge coil secreted. 'I think this is more than play!' she declared, soberly.

'It keeps my hands employed,' drawled Demetrius. 'You have your tapestry. I have my rope.'

After his daily duties had been discharged, and he had seen Diana safely to her suite, it was his custom to take long walks in the night. The sentries on the grounds became acquainted with his strange nocturnal habits, and attached no significance to them. Striding along the winding paths, pausing for a leisurely chat with lonesome guards, he would descend the long stairways to the wharves where the boatmen and dock employees came to know him. Sometimes he lent a hand for an hour or two, darning rents in a sailcloth, splicing ropes, and caulking leaks with pitch and tow. Not infrequently, having urged Diana to order more than she wanted for dinner, he would appear at the docks with confections and other delicacies.

'You seem immensely fond of those men down there,' Diana had remarked; and Demetrius had explained that they did not have many good things to eat; and, besides, he enjoyed their friendship.

Every night when he left the docks he would carry off as large a bundle of hemp as could be stowed under his tunic. Nobody cared. He was well liked and could do as he pleased. Sometimes he would take one of the idle dories and row up along the rocky rim of the island for an hour, explaining that he needed exercise. The lazy boatmen thought him peculiar, but were willing to humor him.

Early every morning, a freight barge went across to Puteoli to meet the farmers and fruit-growers and butchers who came with their products for the island. One night when Demetrius appeared at the wharf he found the dock hands especially interested in his arrival. A large consignment of Arpino melons had come over in the forenoon, and one of the melons—if he would believe it—had been sent expressly to Demetrius. They gave it to him, and stood about, wide-eyed with curiosity, as he opened the small, slatted box.

'Know somebody at Arpino?' they inquired.

'He's got a girl in Arpino!' guffawed a boatman.

Demetrius couldn't think of anyone who would be sending him a melon from Arpino—or anywhere else. He turned it over slowly in his hand. On one side, there had been lightly scratched with a knife-point a small, crude drawing.

'Somebody's name, is it?' one asked. They all crowded in close to contribute the flavor of garlic to this mystery.

'Probably just a joke,' muttered an old boatman, turning away. 'That silly Umbrian that skippers the barge has been playing a little trick on you.'

Demetrius chuckled and said he'd get even; but he could hardly conceal his excitement. It wasn't a bargeman's hoax. The scrawl on the

melon was an irregular, almost unrecognizable outline of a fish! So
—Marcellus was in the melon business!

Next morning, as they sat chatting in the pergola, Demetrius asked
Diana if she had ever heard of Arpino melons, and she promptly
remembered how much they had liked them at home.

'Yesterday,' said Demetrius, 'when the freight barge came over from
the mainland with melons, there was one sent specially to me.' He rose
and handed it to her. Diana inspected it with interest.

'How odd! Do you know anyone there? What is this device? It looks
like a fish. Does it mean anything?'

'When the Christians in Judea and Galilee,' explained Demetrius,
sauntering back to his seat on the steps, 'wanted to inform one another
of their whereabouts, or the road they had taken, they drew a rough
picture of a fish, in the sand by the roadside, on a rock at a crossing,
or over a doorway. If two strangers met at a tavern table, and one of
them wanted to know whether the other was a Christian, he idly traced
the figure of a fish with his finger.'

'Why a fish?' inquired Diana.

'The Greek word for fish is made up of initials for the words
which mean, "Jesus Christ Son of God Savior." '

'How interesting!' exclaimed Diana. 'But do you suppose there are
any Christians at Arpino?'

Demetrius looked into her eyes and smiled mysteriously.

'There is at least one Christian in Arpino,' he said, 'and I think
we both know who he is.'

'Marcellus!' whispered Diana, breathlessly.

* * * * * *

This afternoon, all Capri had been excited over the arrival of young
Caligula. Demetrius had caught sight of him, kicking himself along at
the side of the Empress as they entered the Villa Jovis. An hour later,
the island had fairly rocked with the news that this repulsive youth
would presently wear the crown. Coupled with this shocking rumor
came the report that the Emperor had sunk into a deep coma from
which his emergence was most unlikely.

Now that Tiberius was no longer to be reckoned with, and Julia's
insufferable grandson was all but on the throne, the Empress would
be capable of any atrocity that her caprice might suggest. She could
even be vile enough, thought Demetrius, to insist on Diana's showing
favors to Caligula.

By the time twilight fell, that evening, there was a confirmation of
these forebodings. Diana had been invited to a quiet dinner with the
Empress and her now eminent grandson. Despite the fact that the
Emperor was snoring the tag end of his life away, young Caligula must
have some pleasant diversion.

Reluctantly, Diana accepted the invitation, realizing that it was nothing less than a command, Demetrius accompanying her to the Villa Dionysus, where, for two anxious hours, he paced to and fro on the frescoed pavement, waiting for her to reappear. When, at length, she came out through the peristyle into the bright moonlight, it was evident from her manner that something had happened. In an agitated voice she confided that the loathsome Caligula had paid her such impudent attentions that even Julia had muttered a stern word of caution.

'That settles it!' declared Demetrius, firmly. 'You can't stay here! I am going to try to take you off the island—tonight!'

'But—it's impossible, Demetrius!' she protested.

'We shall see. It will be dangerous. But it is worth trying.' Briefly he instructed her what to do. Diana shuddered. 'You won't be afraid; will you?' he demanded, searching her eyes.

'Yes!' she confessed. 'Of course I'll be afraid! I don't see how I can do it! But—I'll try! I'd rather drown than have that slimy idiot put his hands on me again.'

'Slip out of the Jovis, then, and go alone to your pergola, an hour before midnight!'

Leaving Diana at her door, Demetrius set out on his usual nightly excursion, going first to the pergola, where he dragged the long rope from its hiding-place, secured one end to a small pine tree, and tossed the length of it down the almost perpendicular precipice. For a moment he stood there looking down over the face of the slightly slanting rock to the dashing surf far below, and winced as he pictured Diana's sensations when she confronted this hazardous adventure. Surely it would demand a great deal of courage. He wouldn't have wanted to do it himself.

Returning swiftly to his own quarters, he picked up the compact bundle of clothing he had assembled for Diana—a stonemason's coarse smock and heavy leggings, and a knitted cap such as the wharfmen wore.

Everywhere the inquisitive sentries detained him to chatter about the amazing events of the day, and he was obliged to tarry. Time was precious, but he must not arouse suspicion by an appearance of haste or stress. At the wharf he unchained the best dory available, shipped the oars, waved a hand to the boatmen, and made off slowly in the moonlight. As soon as it was discreet, he began to lengthen his strokes. It was a long, hard pull around the eastern point of the massive island. The waves grew suddenly rougher as he came out into the wind of the open sea.

Demetrius' heart pounded fiercely. It was not only the grueling exertion, but his fear that Diana might be overtaken. On an ordinary occasion it would have been next to impossible for her to go to her pergola so late at night without being questioned. But nothing was quite normal on Capri tonight. The Emperor was dying. Nobody's behavior would be scrutinized. People would be scurrying about on unfamiliar errands. Maybe Diana would have no trouble in keeping her engagement; but, even if she were lucky enough to do that, it was a perilous risk she still had to face.

At length he recognized, in the moonlight, the tall cliff and the overhanging eaves of the pergola. Maneuvering the heavy dory as close as he dared to the foot of the towering rock, Demetrius strained his eyes toward the summit. The boat was almost unmanageable in the insistent swells of a high tide. The agonizing minutes dragged along, as he scanned the ledge a full hundred and fifty feet above the waves.

Now his heart gave a great bound! A little way from the top, a gray-clad figure began slipping down. Diana seemed very small and insecure. Demetrius wished she would take it more slowly. He had cautioned her about that. She would burn her hands; perhaps lose her grip. When a little more than halfway down, she slipped several feet before checking herself by twining her legs more tightly about the rope.

Demetrius' eyes widened at the amazing thing that was happening. Diana's descent had slowed to a stop. Now she was actually moving up! He lifted his eyes to the top of the cliff. Two figures on the ledge above were toiling at the rope. Demetrius dropped the oars and funneled his hands about his mouth.

'Let go!' he shouted.

There was a tense moment of indecision in which Diana was tugged up another foot.

'Jump, Diana!' called Demetrius.

The uncontrolled dory was carried broadside on a wave that almost dashed it against the rock. Suddenly Diana leaped free of the rope and came hurtling down into a huge comber. Its retreat swept her far out. For a long moment, she was not to be seen. Bending to his oars, Demetrius tugged the dory away from the cliff, desperately searching the water. Now her head appeared on the curve of a great swell. Diana was swimming. Demetrius pulled alongside and threw an arm about her. She was badly frightened and her breath was coming in gasps and sobs. He bent far over the side of the boat. Diana put her arms around his neck, and he tugged her in over the rail. She crumpled up in a heap at his feet, drenched and exhausted.

Demetrius dragged the cumbersome dory about, and began the laborious trip around the curve of the island, keeping close in the shadow of the rock. It was hard going. Sometimes they seemed to be making no progress at all. Neither spoke until they were in the quiet water on the bay side. Thoroughly spent, Demetrius pulled the dory into the dark mouth of a grotto, and slumped over with his elbows on his knees and his head in his hands.

'You are a brave girl, Diana!' he said, huskily.

'I don't feel very brave,' she said, in a weak voice, 'but I am terribly cold.'

'There is some dry clothing for you in the locker at the bow.' He took her hand and steadied her as she climbed over his seat. 'Lift up the trap,' he said, 'and you will find it.'

'Is this supposed to be a disguise?' she inquired, presently.

'No—it's intended to keep you warm.'

'Why didn't Acteus and that other guard shoot at me?' asked Diana.

'Because they might have hit you,' said Demetrius. 'You need not be afraid of an arrow. Acteus was told to keep you on the island; not to harm you. Did you know he was following you?'

'Not until I was almost at the pergola. I heard them behind me, and recognized the voice of Acteus when he called. It was an awful feeling when I found myself being drawn up.' Diana shuddered. 'It was hard to let go of that rope.'

'I should think it might have been. Are you getting warm now?' Demetrius was taking up the oars. 'Did you find the cap?'

'Yes—it's dreadful. Where are we going now, Demetrius?'

'Over off the mainland—and up the coast to some open beach.'

'And then what—and where?'

'Hide for the day—and row all night tomorrow—and leave the boat somewhere near Formia. But—don't worry. You are off this dangerous island. Nothing else matters.'

Diana was quiet for a long time. Demetrius had settled to his heavy task. The oars swept steadily, powerfully, as the dory drove into a rapidly rising breeze. An occasional wave splashed against the rail and showered them with spray.

'Demetrius!' called Diana. 'How far is it from Formia to Arpino?'

'Fifty miles—northeast,' shouted Demetrius, between strokes.

'Were you ever there? You seem to be acquainted with that country.'

'No—never there—looked it up—on the map.'

'Are we going to Arpino?'

'Want to?'

Diana did not reply. The breeze was growing stronger and Demetrius was laboring hard. A wave broke over the side.

'You'll find—leather bailing bucket—up there,' called Demetrius. 'You aren't frightened—are you?'

'No—not now,' she sang out cheerfully.

'Keep me headed for that row of lights at Puteoli.'

'A little to the right, then. Demetrius—it seems almost as if someone were looking after us tonight.'

'Yes, Diana.'

'Do you believe that—truly?'

'Yes.'

'Think he will take care of us—if a storm blows up?'

Demetrius tugged the unwieldy old tub out of the trough, and for an interval rowed hard. Then he replied, in detached phrases, measured by the sweep of the long oars.

'He has been known—to take care—of his friends—in a storm.'

* * * * * *

So impatient was Caligula to occupy his exalted office that the state funeral of Tiberius—which he did not attend because of some slight indisposition—was practically eclipsed by lavish preparations for the coronation; and, as for Uncle Gaius' obsequies, not many Princes had been put away with less pomp or at so modest an expense.

Perhaps, had Emperor Tiberius been a more popular hero, public sentiment might have demanded a better show of respect for the old man's departure, but so little had been heard of him for the past dozen years that nobody really cared whether he lived or died. Even in the Senate, where the most eloquent of the Romans were skilled in saying things they did not mean, the orations extolling Tiberius were of an appalling dullness.

There was no decent interval of perfunctory mourning. All night, workmen were busy tearing down the funereal trappings along the Corso and the Via Sacra through which the Emperor had taken his last ride that afternoon. The older patricians were shocked by this irreverence; not that they any longer cared a fig about Tiberius, who, for the Empire's sake, should have had the goodness to die years ago; but it boded ill for Rome, they felt, to be crowning a youth so impudently defiant of the proprieties. But the traditions meant as little to Caligula as the counsel of his dismayed ministers. The stories of his insane egotism, his fits and rages, and his utter irresponsibility swept through the city like a fire.

The coronation festivities lasted for a week and were conducted with an extravagance that knew no precedent in the experience of any nation's capital. Hundreds of thousands were fed and wined and welcomed to the games, which for wanton brutality and reckless bloodshed quite surpassed anything that Rome had ever seen. The substantial citizenship of the Empire stood aghast, stunned to silence. As for the habitually empty-bellied rabble, Little Boots was their man. So long as he dished out bread and circuses it was no concern of theirs how or whether the bill was settled. Indeed, Little Boots led them to believe that it was by his personal generosity that they were fed and entertained, and was forthright in his denunciation of the wealthy, who, he shouted, were responsible for the people's poverty.

Old Sejanus, frightened and desperate, came before the Senate to remonstrate and plead for immediate action; but nothing was done, and that night Sejanus was assassinated. Crafty old Julia, who had come to Rome expecting to be glorified as the Empress dowager, was hustled onto the imperial barge without ceremony and shipped back to Capri.

The palace reeked of dissolute parties that continued for days and nights and days. All the common decencies were abandoned. Uninvited hundreds crowded into the banquets. Priceless art objects were overturned and broken on the mosaic floors. Riotous guests slipped and rolled down the slimy marble stairways. Never had so many been so drunk.

Triumphal processions, hastily improvised in celebration of some half-forgotten holiday, would move out unannounced into the avenue, bearing in the foremost golden chariot the garishly arrayed, drunken, disheveled, grimacing, twitching Emperor, sowing handfuls of sesterces into the hysterical street-crowds from a grain-bag that Quintus held in his arms, while the greedy rabble fought in the filthy gutters like dogs, and the pompous Quintus—Little Boots' favorite—laughed merrily at the sport, his lips still cut and swollen from the brutal slapping he had received from the bejeweled hands of old Julia's whimsical grandson.

The patricians kept to their villas, inarticulate and numb with cold anger and despair. There was nothing they could do. They did not protest when Caligula ordered the heads knocked off the venerated busts of the great in the Forum, and marble models of his own installed with impressive ceremonies. They did not protest when he fitted up a gold-and-ivory stall in the palace for his horse Incitatus, nor did they protest when he elevated Incitatus to the rank of Consul.

The populace laughed inopportunely when Little Boots announced that Incitatus was divine; and, annoyed that this declaration should have been taken lightly, he brought forth an edict demanding that his distinguished horse must henceforth be worshiped in the temples, to the considerable embarrassment of the priests, whose dignity—by reason of other eccentric orders from the throne—was already somewhat in need of repair.

Almost every day the Emperor savagely inquired of Quintus whether any progress had been made in his search for the haughty and beautiful daughter of Gallus, and would be freshly enraged to learn that no trace of her had been discovered. A guard had been set about the absent Legate Gallus' villa. Paula's movements—if the unhappy woman could be said to move at all—were carefully watched. Her servants were questioned, threatened, tortured. On Capri, the guard Acteus and three wharf attendants had been put to death. And Quintus had been advised that he had better contrive some more favorable news of his far-flung investigation if he knew what was good for him.

But Quintus' failure to find Diana was for no lack of personal interest in this quest. For one thing, when they found Diana they would probably find Demetrius too. He had a score to settle there. It fretted him that he had not been told of the Greek's presence on the island when he had visited the Empress, at Gaius' behest, to implore her to take Caligula off his hands.

Of course it was possible that Diana and Demetrius might have been drowned. Their dory had been found adrift. The weather had been stormy. Nobody along the coast, all the way up from Formia to Capua, had seen anything of the fugitives.

Little Boots fumed and shouted. Diana was the only person he knew who had regarded him with undisguised contempt. Moreover, according to the story of her escape from Capri, she had plenty of courage. It would be a pleasure to break her, he muttered. Quintus' mobile lips still smiled obsequiously, but his brows contracted in a cautioning frown.

'The slave Demetrius, Your Majesty, who contrived her flight, should be disposed of before the daughter of Gallus is taken.'

'Why?' barked Caligula. 'Is the slave in love with her? You said she was in love with that mad Tribune who crucified the Jew, and lost his head over thinking he had killed a god.'

Quintus' eyes had lighted with surprise that Little Boots remembered what he had told him about the Galilean, and the large following he had attracted. Caligula had been so very drunk, and had seemed to pay no attention. Apparently the story had impressed him.

'True, Your Majesty,' said Quintus. 'This Demetrius was the slave of Marcellus, the son of old Gallio. Doubtless he has sworn to protect Diana.'

'If he can!' sneered Caligula.

'If he cannot, sire—and Diana is captured—this Greek would not hesitate to risk his life in avenging her.'

'Pouf! What could he do? You are a timid fool, Quintus! Do you think this slave would force a violent entrance into our presence?'

'The Greek is a dangerous man, Your Majesty,' warned Quintus. 'He was once reckless enough to attack a Tribune with his bare hands!'

'And lived?' shouted Caligula.

'Quite openly! And became a member of the Emperor's guard at the Villa Jovis!'

'Did Tiberius know of the slave's crime?'

'Doubtless. The Empress knew—for I told her.'

'Who was the Tribune that the Greek attacked?'

Quintus fidgeted, and Caligula—eyeing him sharply—burst into laughter. Quintus flushed, and grinned sheepishly.

'Emperor Tiberius never liked me, sire,' he mumbled.

'Perhaps the old man appointed the slave a member of his guard to reward him,' chuckled Caligula. 'Well—here is your chance to settle with this savage. Find him—and run him through!' he advised, with an appropriate gesture.

Quintus pursed his lips and slowly elevated a prudent shoulder.

'I should not enjoy fighting a duel with a slave, Your Majesty.'

Little Boots rocked with laughter.

'Not with this one—in any case!' He suddenly sobered and scowled. 'You make haste to find that Greek! If you are afraid to meet him, let a braver man attend to it! We do not like the idea of his being at large. But—tell me more of this Marcellus, who threw himself into the sea. He became a follower of the Jew; eh? Does the daughter of Gallus entertain such notions?'

Quintus said he didn't know, but that he had reasons to believe the Greek slave was a Christian, as he had consorted with these people in Jerusalem.

'But he fights; eh?' commented Caligula. 'It was our understanding that this crazy Jesus-cult does not permit fighting.'

'Well—that may be so, Your Majesty,' conceded Quintus, 'but if this Greek is enraged, he will not ask anybody's permission to fight. He is a wild animal!'

Little Boots nervously picked at his pimples.

'What do you think of the strength of our palace guard, Quintus?'

'They are awake, sire, and loyal.'

'It would be quite impossible for an assassin to enter our bed-chamber; eh?'

'From without, yes, Your Majesty. But if the Greek decided to kill the Emperor, he might not try to enter the palace. He would probably leap up over the Emperor's chariot-wheel with a dagger.'

'And be instantly bludgeoned to death by the people,' declared Caligula, his chin working convulsively.

'Of course, Your Majesty,' assented Quintus, not displeased to note Little Boots' agitation. 'But the bludgeoning might come too late to be of service to the Emperor. As for the Greek, if he decided to get revenge, he would not haggle at the price.'

Caligula held up a shaky goblet and Quintus made haste to re-plenish it.

'Hereafter, there must be better protection of our person when we are before the people. There must be a strong double guard marching on either side of the imperial chariot, Quintus. You shall see to it!'

'Your Majesty's order will be obeyed. But if I may venture to say so, this danger could be avoided, sire. Let the daughter of Gallus—if she still lives—go her way unmolested. The Emperor would have no comfort with her; and to keep her in chains might provoke much unrest in the army where Legate Gallus is held in high esteem.'

Little Boots drank deeply, hiccoughed, and drew a surly grin.

'When we need your advice, Quintus, we will ask for it. The Emperor of the Roman Empire does not inquire whether his decisions are approved by every legionary in the army.' Little Boots' voice rose shrilly. 'Nor are we concerned over the mutterings of the fat old men in the Senate! We have the people with us!'

Quintus smiled obediently, but offered no comment.

'Speak up, fool!' screamed Little Boots. 'The people are with us!'

'As long as they are fed, Your Majesty,' ventured Quintus.

'We shall feed them when we like,' snarled Little Boots, thickly.

Quintus did not reply to that. Observing that the large silver goblet was empty again, he refilled it.

'And when we stop feeding them—then what?' challenged Little Boots, truculently. 'Is there to be disorder—and do we have to lash them back to their kennels?'

'Hungry people, sire,' said Quintus, quietly, 'can make themselves very annoying.'

'By petty pillaging? Let them steal! The owners of the markets are rich. Why should we concern ourself about that? But we will tolerate no mobs, no meetings!'

'It is not difficult, Your Majesty, to deal with mobs,' remarked Quintus. 'They can be quickly dispersed after the spokesmen are apprehended. It is not so easy to break up the secret meetings.'

Caligula set down his goblet—and scowled darkly.

'What kind of people are they who dare to hold secret meetings?'

Quintus deliberated a reply, frowning thoughtfully.

'I have not mentioned this to Your Majesty, because the Emperor is already burdened with cares; but it is believed that there are many followers of this new Galilean cult.'

'Ah—the people who are forbidden to fight. Let them meet! Let them whisper! How many are there?'

'Nobody knows, sire. But we have word that the party is growing. Several houses, where numbers of men were seen to enter nightly, have been watched. In a few cases the patrol has entered, finding no disorder, no arms, and apparently no heated talk. In each instance, no more meetings were held in the house that had been investigated. That probably means they resolved to meet elsewhere. Prince Gaius had been investigating them for months, but without much success.'

'It's a small matter,' mumbled Caligula, drowsily. 'Let them meet and prattle. If they want to think their dead Jew is divine, what of it? Incitatus is divine'—he giggled, drunkenly—'but nobody cares much.'

'But these Christians claim that the Galilean is not dead, sire,' rejoined Quintus. 'According to their belief, he has been seen on many occasions since his crucifixion. They consider him their King.'

'King!' Little Boots suddenly stirred from his torpor. 'We will see to that! Let them believe what else they please about this Jew—but we will have no nonsense about his kingship! Arrest these fools, wherever you find them, and we will break this thing up before it starts!'

'It has started, Your Majesty,' said Quintus, soberly. 'All Palestine is full of it. Recently the party has become strong enough to come out openly in Corinth, Athens, and other Grecian cities.'

'Where are the authorities?' demanded Caligula. 'Are they asleep?'

'No, Your Majesty. The leaders have been imprisoned and some have been put to death; but these people are fanatically brave. They think that if they die for this cause they shall live again.'

'Bah!' shouted Caligula. 'Not many will be found believing in such rubbish! And the few who do believe it will be helpless nobodies!'

Quintus sat silently for a while with his eyes averted.

'Cornelius Capito is anxious about it, sire. He estimates that there are more than four thousand of these Christians in Rome at the present hour.'

'And what is he doing about this treason?' demanded Caligula.

Quintus shook his head.

'It is a strange movement, sire. It has only one weapon; its belief that there is no death. Cornelius Capito is not equipped to crush something that refuses to die when it is killed.'

'You are talking like a fool, Quintus!' mumbled Caligula. 'Command this cowardly old dotard to come here tomorrow, and give an account of himself! And—see you to it that the Greek slave is arrested before many days have passed. Bring him here alive, if possible.' The imperial voice was becoming incoherent. 'Call the Chamberlain. We would retire.'

* * * * * *

If, on his faraway travels, some chance acquaintance had asked Marcellus Gallio whether he knew his way about in Rome, he would have replied that he surely ought to know Rome, seeing he had lived there all his life.

He was now discovering that it was one thing to know Rome from the comfortable altitude of a wealthy young Tribune, son of an influential Senator, and quite another thing to form one's estimates of Rome from the viewpoint of an unemployed, humbly dressed wayfarer with temporary lodging at a drovers' tavern hard by the public markets that crawled up the bank of the busy Tiber to front a cobbled, crowded, littered street, a street that clamored and quarreled and stank—all day and all night.

It had not yet been disclosed to Marcellus why he had felt impelled to return to Rome. He had been here ten days now, jostled by the street crowds, amazed and disgusted by the shameless greed, filth, and downright indecency of the unprivileged thousands who lived no better than the rats that overran the wharf district. The Arpinos had been poor and dirty too, and ragged and rude; but they were promptly responsive to opportunities for improvement. Surely these underdogs of Rome were not of a different species. Marcellus tried to analyze the problem. Perhaps this general degradation was the result of too much crowding, too little privacy, too much noise. You couldn't be decent if you weren't intelligent; you couldn't be intelligent if you couldn't think—and who could think in all this racket? Add the stench to the confusion of cramped quarters, and who could be self-respecting? Marcellus felt himself deteriorating; hadn't shaved for three days. He had a good excuse. The facilities at Apuleius' tavern were not conducive to keeping oneself fit. Nobody shaved; nobody was clean; nobody cared.

On the day of the Emperor's funeral, Marcellus was in the sweating, highly flavored throng that packed the plaza in front of the Forum Julium as the solemn procession arrived for the ceremonies. He was shocked to see how his father had aged in these recent weeks. Of course he had had much to worry about. There was a haunted expression on the faces of all these eminent men, and no wonder; for the Empire was in a shameful plight indeed! Marcellus winced at the sight of Senator Gallio, who had ever borne himself with such stately dignity, and had now surrendered to despair. It made his heart ache.

Day after day, for another fortnight, he wandered about the streets, pausing now and then to listen to a hot dispute, or ask a friendly question of a neighbor; but usually men turned away when he tried to engage them in conversation. By his tone and manner, he was not their sort, and they distrusted him. And always the memory of his father's melancholy face and feeble step haunted him.

One evening, intolerably depressed, he dispatched a message to Marcipor, stating briefly where he was living, and requesting a private interview at such a time and place as Marcipor might suggest; preferably not at the tavern of Apuleius. Two hours later the messenger returned with a letter directing Marcellus to go out, the next day, along the Via Appia, until he came to the old Jewish cemetery. Marcipor would meet him there about mid-afternoon.

Marcellus remembered the place. There was an interesting story about it. Two centuries ago, when Antiochus had conquered Palestine, life had been made so wretched for the Jews that thousands of them had migrated, and Rome had got more than her share.

Alarmed by the volume of this immigration, laws were passed to restrict the liberties of these refugees. They were banished to the wrong side of the Tiber, limited as to the occupations they might pursue, denied Roman citizenship, and—as the animosity against them increased—ruthlessly persecuted.

Traditionally respectful to their dead, the Jews were greatly distressed when Rome assigned them a burial ground far south of the city where only a shallow deposit of soil covered a massive tufa rock fully a hundred feet deep. Passionate patriots made it a practice to go out there by night and desecrate the graves.

At a prodigious cost of labor, the afflicted Jews proceeded to carve an oblique tunnel into the solid stone. On the lower level, they made long, labyrinthine corridors in the walls of which they dug crypts for their dead, and rooms where hard-pressed fugitives might hide.

As time passed, the persecutions eased. Many wealthy Jews, having contributed generously to the erection of state buildings and monuments, were admitted to citizenship; and by their influence the burdens laid upon their less lucky kindred were lightened. The old burial ground fell into disuse. Few persons visited 'The Catacombs' now except students of antiquities. Marcellus wondered why Marcipor, who was getting to be an old man, had selected this place for their meeting. It was a long walk.

He arrived somewhat earlier than the appointed time, but Marcipor was already there, waiting for him in the cypress grove that extended from the busy highway a full quarter-mile to the abandoned subterranean tombs.

Marcipor, who had been sitting on the ground, scrambled to his feet and hurried forward with outstretched hands, his deep-lined face contorted with emotion. Deeply moved by the old servitor's attitude, Marcellus grasped his hands hungrily. He was not a Tribune now. Time swung backward for both of them. The little boy, who had so often come running to the calm and resourceful Corinthian when there was a cut finger or a broken toy, now put his arms around the old man, and held him close.

'We feared you were dead,' said Marcipor, brokenly. 'The family has mourned for you. Tell me'—he held Marcellus at arm's length and studied his face—'why did you afflict them so? It was not like you to do that, my son. . . . Come—let us sit down. I am very weary.'

'Good Marcipor, I was forced to an unhappy choice of afflictions for my family. If they thought me dead, they would grieve; but they would remember me with affection. Had I come home, sworn to spend my life in the service of a cause which demands the complete breaking away from the manner of life expected of Senator Gallio's son, I should have caused them all a greater sorrow. As it stands, they are bereaved; but not humiliated.'

'And why have you told *me*?' asked Marcipor. 'This is indeed a weighty secret to confide to one who would be loyal to his master.'

'I saw my father on the day of the Emperor's funeral, Marcipor. His handsome face was haggard, his eyes were dulled with despair, his shoulders slumped, the proud, statesmanly bearing was gone. The light was out. I tried to forget that harrowing glimpse of my father, but it tortured me. That is why I have sought your counsel. Shall I return? Is there anything I can do?'

With bowed head and downcast eyes, Marcipor meditated a reply.

'Of course you will say,' continued Marcellus, 'that I should renounce the work I have undertaken and resume my former place in my father's house. I cannot expect you to understand the obligation that is laid on me, for you have had no opportunity to—'

'No—my son!' broke in Marcipor. 'You could not renounce your new calling; not even if you tried! I am not as ignorant of this matter as you think. Once a man has become convinced that Jesus is the living Son of God, who is here to set up a kingdom of justice and good will for all people, he does not surrender that faith! If—for any reason—he turns away from it, that means he never had it!'

Marcellus leaned forward to listen, with widening eyes.

'Marcipor!' he exclaimed. 'You are a Christian?'

'When you were at home, the last time, Demetrius thought I should tell you of my belief, and my association with the other Christians in Rome—'

'Other Christians?' repeated Marcellus, amazed.

'Yes, my son—and they are in grave danger. I knew that if you were told of a growing Christian party in Rome, you would join it. These men—for the most part obscure—can assemble secretly, in small groups, without attracting much attention. A Tribune could not do that. I thought it more prudent that you keep away from these meetings. Now—in the past few days—the new Emperor has published an edict threatening death to anyone found in an assembly of Christians. What will happen to our cause in Rome remains to be seen. Young Caligula is cruel and headstrong, they say.'

'Young Caligula is insane!' muttered Marcellus.

'It would seem so,' went on Marcipor, calmly, 'but he is bright enough to carry out his design for slaughter. I knew, when you wrote me you were here, that you would presently locate some Christians and associate with them. You should think twice before you take that risk. We who are unimportant can hide. You cannot; not for long. The Emperor would welcome the opportunity to make an example of you!'

'But you would not counsel me to run away!' challenged Marcellus.

'No one who knows you as well as I do, my son, would use those words. But—your life is valuable. While this threat is active, there is little you can do for frightened people in hiding. If you leave the city, until the Emperor's diseased mind turns toward some other cruel pastime, you could return—and be of service. There's no use throwing your life away!'

Marcellus reached out a hand and affectionately patted the old man's knee.

'Marcipor,' he said, gently, 'you have been speaking as my father's trusted servant, concerned for the welfare of his son. For that I am grateful. But this is not the kind of advice that one Christian gives another. Has Demetrius—or anyone—told you of Jesus' last journey to Jerusalem, when his disciples—knowing how dangerous it would be for him to appear there during the Passover—tried to dissuade him from going? They pointed out that his life was precious; that it mustn't be wasted; that he must be saved for service to the people.'

'What did he say?' wondered Marcipor.

'He told them it was poor advice; told them that no man should caution his friend against going into danger for duty's sake; told them that sometimes a man had to lose his life to save it, and that those who tried to save themselves would surely lose themselves. No—you mean it well enough, Marcipor; but I'm remaining in Rome! Can't you realize that our cause might be lost if we who believe in it are frugal of our blood?'

Marcipor slowly nodded his head, and laboriously came to his feet. 'Come, then,' he said. 'Let us go—and join them.'

'Where?' asked Marcellus.

'In the tombs,' said Marcipor, pointing through the trees. 'About thirty men are meeting there to seek counsel about future plans.'

'Are there so many as thirty Christians in Rome?' Marcellus was surprised and pleased.

'My son,' said Marcipor, 'there are nearly four thousand Christians in Rome! These men are their appointed leaders.'

Marcellus stood speechless for a long moment, pondering this almost incredible announcement. At length he found his voice.

'His kingdom is coming, Marcipor! It is gaining strength, faster than I had thought!'

'Patience, my son!' murmured Marcipor, as he led the way toward the tombs. 'It has still a long, hard road to travel.'

The narrow, uneven steps down into the tunnel were dark as night. As they reached the lower level, a feeble glow outlined the entrance to a corridor at the left. Marcipor proceeded into it with the confidence of one who knew his way. A tall man, in a laborer's tunic, stepped forward; and, holding a dim lantern high above his head, peered into Marcellus' face.

'Who is this, Marcipor?' he demanded.

'Tribune Marcellus Gallio. He is one of us, Laeto.'

'And what have we to do with Tribunes?' asked Laeto, gruffly.

'Marcellus has given up much for his faith, Laeto,' said Marcipor, gently. 'He knows more about the Galilean than any of us—save one.'

'Very well,' consented Laeto, reluctantly—'if you vouch for him.'

They proceeded through the long corridor, groping their way, Marcellus wondering at its vast extent. Marcipor lagged and took his arm.

'Laeto views our new cause as a banding together of the poor,' he confided, softly. 'You will find a good deal of that sentiment among the Christians. They can't be blamed much, for they have been long oppressed. But it would be unfortunate if Jesus' kingdom turned out to be a poor man's exclusive haven.'

'Perhaps it would have been better if my identify had remained a secret,' said Marcellus.

'No—it will be good for the Christians in Rome to know that a man with a few coins in his purse can be a worthy follower. We have been hearing too much about the virtues of poverty.'

They turned an abrupt corner to the right and faced another narrower passage that continued on and on, the walls studded with stone slabs bearing names and dates of Jews long dead. A small light flickered, revealing a heavy wooden door at the end of the corridor. Another sentinel moved out of the shadows and confronted them. Marcipor again explained Marcellus. The sentinel pointed with his torch to a small drawing on the lintel.

'Do you know what that sign means?' he inquired.

'It is the Christian's secret symbol, sir,' replied Marcellus.

'Did someone tell you that—or have you seen it before?'

'I have seen it in many places—in Galilee—and Jerusalem.'

'Let me ask you then,' said the sentinel, 'why is the symbol a fish? Is there anything sacred about a fish?'

Marcellus explained respectfully. The sentinel listened with keen attention.

'You may enter,' he said, stepping aside.

It was a large rectangular room with accommodations for many more people than sat in the semicircular rows in the far corner, huddled closely about a huge, bearded man who was talking to them in a deep guttural tone.

They moved quietly forward, in the dim light, Marcipor leading, until the speaker's earnest voice became plainly audible. Marcellus recognized it, and plucked at the good old Corinthian's sleeve.

'Know him?' whispered Marcipor, with a pleased smile.

'Of course!' said Marcellus, excitedly.

It was the Big Fisherman!

Chapter XXIV

It was early morning but already promising to be another hot day. The swarthy overseer of the vineyard, temporarily at ease, lounged against the gatepost and yawningly watched the laborers—four score or more of men, women, and grown-up children—as they cut the huge purple clusters; carefully, for this fruit was going to a select market.

Some distance down the highway a little wisp of dust was rising from the lazy feet of a shaggy gray donkey attached to a decrepit high-wheeled cart filled with hay. A slim youth walked ahead, impatiently tugging at a long lead-strap. At intervals the donkey stopped and the tall boy in the knitted cap would brace his feet and pull with all his weight, his manner suggesting complete exasperation.

Vobiscus, the overseer, watched and grinned. The young fellow didn't know much about donkeys or he would walk alongside with a stout thornbush in hand. Who was he? Vobiscus was acquainted with all the donkeys, carts, and farmer-boys likely to be plodding along the road in the vicinity of Arpino, but this forlorn outfit lacked identification. He studied it with increasing interest as it crept forward. Nobody would be hauling hay to market in such a cart, and this youngster hadn't come from a hayfield. He wore a long, coarse tunic and the sort of leggings that quarrymen used for protection against flying chips of stone. The bulging old cap might have belonged to a boatman. It was much too heavy for this weather. Vobiscus wondered why he didn't take it off.

Directly in front of the open gate, the donkey took root again, and the slim youth—without a glance at Vobiscus, who was sauntering out into the road—jerked so furiously at the lead-strap that the old bridle broke. Finding himself at liberty, the donkey ambled off to the roadside and began nibbling at the grass, while the angry boy trailed along, pausing to pick up the dragging bridle which he examined with distaste. Then he threw it down and scrubbed his dusty hands up and down on the skirt of his ill-fitting tunic. They were delicate hands, with long, tapering fingers. He glanced about now, gave the overseer a brief and not very cordial inspection, and walked with short, clipped steps to the donkey's head.

Vobiscus, thoughtfully stroking his jaw, made a thorough, item by item, head to foot appraisal of the unhappy young stranger. Then his cheek began to bulge with a surmising tongue and an informed smile wrinkled his face. He picked up the brittle old harness and unbuckled the broken straps.

'I thought you were a boy,' he said, kindly. 'I'll fix the bridle for you, daughter. Go over there and sit down in the shade—and help yourself to some grapes from that basket. You look worn out.'

The tall girl gave him a long, cool stare. Then her lips parted in a smile that made Vobiscus' heart skip a beat. She rubbed her forehead wearily, and tugged off the outlandish old woolen cap, releasing a cascade of blue-black hair that came tumbling down over her shoulders. Vobiscus laughed discreetly, appreciatively. The girl laughed too, a tired little whimpering laugh that was almost crying.

'You are kind,' she murmured. 'I will do that. I am so warm— and thirsty.'

The intolerable donkey had now jammed a wheel against the stone fence and was straining to free himself. Vobiscus went around to the tail of the cart for an armful of hay to entertain him until the bridle was put in order.

'Oh, no, please!' called the girl, sharply. 'He mustn't have any of the hay. It—it isn't good for him!' Her eyes were frightened.

Vobiscus turned his head toward her and scowled.

'What have you in this cart, young woman?' he demanded, roughly, thrusting his arm deep into the hay.

'Please!—it's my brother! He is ill! Don't disturb him!'

'Your brother is ill; eh?' scoffed Vobiscus. 'So—you load him into a cart and cover him up with hay! A likely tale!' He began tossing the hay out onto the road. 'Ah—so you're the sick brother!'

The girl came swiftly to Vobiscus' side and laid her hand on his arm as Demetrius sat up, frowning darkly.

'We are in trouble,' she confided. 'We came here hoping to find a man named Marcellus Gallio, knowing he would aid us.'

'Marcellus has been gone for a week.' The scowl on Vobiscus' face relaxed a little. 'Are you friends of his?'

They both nodded. Vobiscus looked from one to the other, suspiciously.

'You are a slave, fellow!' he said, pointing at Demetrius' ear. A sudden illumination widened his eyes. 'Ah-ha!' he exclaimed. 'I have it! You're wanted! Both of you! Only yesterday legionaries from Capri were at the villa searching for the daughter of Gallus and a Greek slave who were thought to be on the way to Rome.'

'You are right, sir,' confessed Demetrius. 'This young woman is the daughter of Legate Gallus, and engaged to marry Marcellus Gallio who is my master. My name is Demetrius.' Vobiscus started.

'That's sounds like the name,' he mumbled to himself. 'Tell me— did Marcellus send you a message, some weeks ago?'

'Yes, sir—a small melon, in a box.'

'Any writing?'

'A picture—of a fish.'

Demetrius gazed anxiously up and down the road and stepped out of the cart. Deep in the vineyard a lumbering load of fruit was slowly moving toward the gate.

'Before this fellow sees you,' cautioned Vobiscus, 'busy yourself with that donkey, and keep out of sight. You had better stay here for the present.' He turned to Diana. 'You will be safe, I think, to go up to the villa. Don't hurry. Inquire for Antonia, the wife of Appius Kaeso. Tell her who you are. You two must not be seen together. Everybody in Arpino knows about the search for you.'

'Perhaps they will be afraid to give me shelter,' said Diana.

'Well—they will tell you—if they are,' replied Vobiscus. 'You can't stay here! That's sure!'

* * * * * *

The tall Macedonian by the villa gate gave her a disapproving look.

'And why do you want to see the wife of Kaeso?' he demanded, sharply. 'Perhaps you had better talk to Appius Kaeso, young fellow.'

'No—his wife,' insisted Diana. 'But I am not a beggar,' she added.

The Macedonian cocked his head thoughtfully and grinned.

'Come with me,' he said, in the soft voice of a conspirator. Leading the way to the garden, and sighting his mistress, he signed to the newcomer to proceed, and turned back toward the gate.

Antonia, girlishly pretty in gay colors and a broad-brimmed reed hat, was supervising a slave as he wielded a pruning-knife in the rose arbor. Hearing footsteps she glanced about and studied the approaching stranger.

'You may go!' she said to the slave. He turned to stare at the visitor. 'At once!' commanded Antonia.

'Please forgive my intrusion,' began Diana—'and my dreadful appearance. It has been necessary for me to look like a boy.'

Antonia showed a row of pretty teeth.

'Well—maybe it has been necessary,' she laughed—'but you don't look like a boy.'

'I've tried to,' insisted Diana. 'What is it that gives me away?'

'Everything,' murmured Antonia. She drifted to the stone lectus beside the path. 'Come—sit down—and tell me what this is all about. They are hunting for you: is that not so?'

Briefly but clearly, the words tumbling over one another, Diana poured out her story with a feeling of confidence that she would not be betrayed.

'I musn't get you into trouble,' she went on—'but—oh—if I might bathe—if you would hide me away until I had a night's sleep—I could go on.' Diana's weary eyes were swimming.

'We can take some chances for anyone who loves Marcellus,' said Antonia. 'Come—let us go into the house.' She led the way to the atrium where they encountered Kaeso emerging from his library. He stopped and blinked a few times, incredulously. Antonia said, 'Appius, this is the daughter of Legate Gallus whom the soldiers were inquiring about. . . . Diana, this is my husband.'

'I shall go away, sir, if you wish.' Diana's voice was plaintive.

'What have you done, that they want to arrest you?' inquired Kaeso, facing her soberly.

'She ran away from Capri,' volunteered Antonia, 'because she was afraid of the boy Emperor. Now he is determined to find her.'

'Ugh!' growled Kaeso. 'Little Boots! *Little skunk!*'

'Hush!' warned Antonia. 'You'll have us all in prison yet! Now— what shall we do with Diana? Appius, she is engaged to marry Marcellus!'

Kaeso exclaimed joyfully and grasped her hands.

'You're going to stay here with us,' he declared. 'Whoever takes you away will have to fight! Are you alone? The legionaries said they were looking also for a Greek slave who had escaped with you.'

'He is down at the vineyard with Vobiscus,' said Antonia. 'And you'd better do something about it, Appius.'

'How about the servants? How much do they know?'

'Let us not try to make a secret of it,' suggested Antonia. 'We will tell them the truth. When they know that Diana is to marry Marcellus —and that the Greek is his slave—there is no one in Arpino who would—'

'Don't be too sure of that!' said Kaeso. 'There's a reward posted, you know.' He pointed toward the peristyle. 'That Macedonian out there could have quite a merry fling with a thousand sesterces. I shall tell him—and all of them—that if anyone gives out information he will be flogged! Or worse!'

'Do as you think best, dear,' consented Antonia, gently. 'But I believe that trusting them will be safer than threatening them. I think that would be Marcellus' advice if he were here.'

'Marcellus is always giving people credit for being bigger than they are,' remembered Kaeso. He gave Diana an inquiring smile. 'Are you one of these Christians too?'

'I'm afraid not,' sighed Diana. 'It's too hard for me to understand. . . . Did he'—she glanced toward Antonia—'did he talk much about it while he was here?'

'Turned the village upside-down with it!' chuckled Kaeso. 'Antonia will tell you. She has gone Christian too!'

'Marcellus was good for us all,' murmured Antonia. She gave Appius a sidelong smile, and added, 'including the master of Arpino.'

* * * * * *

Young Antony had been so absorbed in his modeling that he had remained in his studio all day, unaware that they were housing a fugitive. Breezing into the dining-room, that evening, spluttering apologies for his tardiness, he stopped suddenly just inside the doorway and looked into the smiling eyes of the most beautiful creature he had ever seen, wearing the most beautiful pink silk stola he had ever seen, failing to recognize it as his mother's.

On three different occasions, Antony had gone with his parents to Rome for a few days' attendance at great national festivals. There had been fleeting glimpses of lovely patrician girls in their gay litters and—at a distance—in their boxes at the circus; but never before had he been this close to a young woman of Diana's social caste. He faced her now with such spontaneous and unreserved admiration that Kaeso, glancing up over his shoulder, chuckled softly.

'Our son, Antony,' said his mother, tenderly. 'Our guest is Diana, dear, the daughter of Legate Gallus.'

'Oh!' Antony swallowed hard. 'They are after you!' He eased into his seat across from her, still gazing intently into her face. 'How did you get here?'

'Diana hoped to find Marcellus,' explained Antonia.

'Do you know Marcellus?' asked Antony, happily.

'She is his girl,' announced the elder Kaeso, adding, in the little silence that followed, 'And he is a lucky fellow!'

'Y-e-s,' agreed Antony, so fervently that his parents laughed.

Diana smiled appreciatively into Antony's enraptured eyes, but refused to be merry over his honest adoration. It was no joke.

'I am glad you all like Marcellus so well,' she said, softly. 'He must have had a good time here. You are a sculptor; aren't you? Your mother told me.' And when Antony had hitched about, protesting that he hadn't done anything very important, she said, 'Perhaps you will let me see.' Her voice was unusually deep-toned for a girl, he thought. Girls were always screaming what they had to say. Diana's throaty voice made you feel that you had known her a long time. Antony nodded, with a defensive smile and a little shrug that hoped she wouldn't be expecting to see something really good.

'Marcellus taught him about all he knows,' Antonia remarked, gratefully, as if Diana should be thanked too for this favor.

'He should have been a sculptor,' said Diana, 'instead of a soldier.'

'Right!' declared Antony. 'He detests fighting!'

'But not because he doesn't know how to fight,' Diana hastened to say. 'Marcellus is known to be one of the most expert swordsmen in Rome.'

'Indeed!' exclaimed Kaeso. 'I wouldn't have thought he had any interest in dangerous sports. He never discussed such things with us.'

'Once I asked him if he had ever killed anybody,' put in Antony, 'and it made him awfully unhappy. He said he didn't want to talk about it.'

Diana's face had suddenly lost its animation, and Antony knew he had blundered upon a painful subject. His embarrassment increased when his father said to her, 'Perhaps you know.'

Without raising her eyes, Diana nodded and gave a little sigh.

'Do you like horses?' asked Kaeso, sensing the need of a new topic.

'Yes, sir,' replied Diana, obviously preoccupied. Glancing from one to another, she went on: 'Perhaps we should not leave it—just that way. It wouldn't be quite fair to Marcellus. A couple of years ago he was ordered to put a man to death—and it turned out that the man was innocent of any crime, and had been held in high esteem by many people. He has grieved over it.'

'He would!' sympathized Antonia. 'There never was a more gentle or generous person; always trying to do things for other people.'

Appius Kaeso, eager to lift Diana's depression, seemed anxious to talk about Marcellus' popularity in Arpino. Soon he was pleased to observe that she was listening attentively, her eyes misty as he elaborated on the many kindnesses Marcellus had done, even giving him full credit for the new swimming-pool.

'He was a crafty fellow,' chuckled Kaeso. 'He would trap you into doing things like that, and then pretend it was your own idea. Of course—that was to make you feel good, so you would want to do something else for the people—on your own hook.'

Antony, amazed by his father's admissions, covertly sought the surprised eyes of his pretty mother, and gave her a slow wink that tightened her lips in a warning not to risk a comment.

'Marcellus certainly was an unusual fellow,' continued Kaeso. 'It was easy to see that he had had every advantage and had lived well, but he used to go down into the melon fields and work alongside those people as if they were his own sort: and how they loved it! Every evening, out here on the green, they would gather about him and he would tell them stories about this man Jesus—from up in the Jews' country somewhere—who went about performing all manner of strange miracles. But he must have told you about this man, Diana.'

'Yes,' she nodded, soberly. 'He told me.'

'They put him to death,' said Antonia.

'And Marcellus insists he came to life again,' said Kaeso, 'though I'm sure there was some mistake about that.'

Antony, who had dropped out of the conversation, and apparently wasn't hearing a word of it—to judge from his wide-eyed, vacant stare —had attracted his mother's attention. Kaeso and Diana instinctively followed her perplexed eyes.

'What are you thinking about, boy?' Kaeso wanted his question to sound playful.

Ignoring his father's inquiry, Antony turned to Diana.

'Do you know who crucified that Galilean?' he asked, earnestly.

'Yes,' admitted Diana.

'Do I know?'

Diana nodded, and Antony brought his fist down hard on the table. 'Now it all makes sense!' he declared. 'Marcellus killed this man who had spent his life doing kind things for needy people—and the only way he can square up for it is to spend *his* life that way!' Antony's voice was unsteady. 'He can't help himself! He has to make things right with this Jesus!'

Appius and Antonia speechlessly regarded their son with a new interest.

'Yes—but that isn't quite all, Antony,' said Diana. 'Marcellus thinks this man is in the world to remain forever; believes there is to be a new government ruled by men of good will; no more fighting; no more stealing—'

'That's a noble thought, Diana,' interposed Kaeso. 'Who doesn't long for peace? Who wouldn't be glad to see good men rule? Nothing new about that wish. Indeed—any kind of government would be better than ours! But it's absurd to hope for such a thing, and a man as bright as Marcellus ought to know it! He is throwing his life away!'

'Maybe not!' protested Antony. 'Maybe this Jesus didn't throw his life away! If we're ever to have a better world—well—it has to begin *sometime—somewhere*—hasn't it? Maybe it has begun now! What do you think, Diana?'

'I—don't—know, Antony.' Diana put both hands over her eyes and shook her head. 'All I know is—I wish it hadn't happened.'

* * * * * *

When three weeks had passed uneventfully, Diana began to wonder whether it might not now be safe for her to proceed to Rome. Perhaps the young Emperor had forgotten his grievance and had given up searching for her. Kaeso was not so optimistic.

'Little Boots has been much occupied,' he said. 'What with the funeral of old Tiberius, his own coronation, and the festal week, he hasn't had much time to think about anything else. Moreover, his legionaries have all been on duty in the processions and at the games. But he will not forget you. Better wait a little while longer.'

Antonia had slipped an arm around Diana affectionately.

'You can see that Appius wants to keep you here, dear, as long as possible—and so do Antony and I.'

Diana knew that. Their hospitality had been boundless. She had come to love Antonia, and young Antony's attitude toward her had been but little short of worship.

'You have all been so kind,' she said. 'But my mother will be dreadfully worried. Naturally they would go first to her seeking information about me. All she knows is that I escaped from Capri in a little boat. I can't even send her a message, for the guards would trace it back to Arpino.'

Sometimes in the evening Demetrius, who was working in the vine-yard and lodging with Vobiscus, would come to inquire. Diana would tell him to be patient, but she knew he was consumed with restlessness and anxious to rejoin Marcellus.

One night at dinner, Kaeso had seemed so preoccupied that Diana felt something had happened. When they returned to the atrium, Vobiscus was found waiting with a note for her. It had been hastily written—in Greek. Demetrius was just leaving for Rome, hoping to find his master.

'My presence here only adds to your danger,' he wrote. 'Kaeso approves my going. He has been most generous. Follow his advice. Do not try to communicate with your home. I shall see your mother if possible.'

Vobiscus had tarried near the open doorway to the peristyle, and Diana went to him. Had Demetrius left on foot—or was he driving the donkey?

'He rode one of the master's fast horses,' said Vobiscus, 'and wore an outfit of the master's clothing.'

Diana rejoined the family seated about the fountain. Their voices were low. She felt they had been discussing her problem.

'You were very kind to Demetrius,' she said, softly. 'I hope you know how deeply I appreciate what you have done for him—and for me—and Marcellus.'

Kaeso flipped a negligent gesture, but his eyes were troubled.

'The Greek was not safe here,' he said, soberly. 'Indeed, nobody is any longer safe anywhere! Two of our carters returned this afternoon from Rome. The city is in disorder. Drunken mobs of vandals have been looting the shops and assaulting respectable citizens. The Emperor pretends to believe that the Christians have a hand in it, and they are being thrown into prison and whipped.'

The color left Diana's cheeks.

'I wonder how Marcellus is faring,' she said. 'He would do so little to protect himself.'

'Our men say that the search for your Greek has become active again,' said Kaeso—'and for you too, Diana. It appears that Demetrius is wanted on an old charge of having assaulted a Tribune. He is to be taken, dead or alive. As for you, the Emperor pretends to be concerned about your safety. The rumor is that the Greek slave made off with you, and Caligula wants you to be found.'

'Poor Demetrius!' murmured Diana. 'What chance will he have, with so many looking for him?'

'Well—he knows his life is worth nothing if they catch him,' said Kaeso, grimly. 'He will make them earn their reward: you may be sure of that!'

'Was he armed?' wondered Diana.

'Nothing but a dagger,' said Kaeso.

'Appius is posting sentries at elevated points on our two highways,' said Antonia. 'The sight of legionaries approaching will be their signal to speed back here and report.'

'When they were here before,' said Kaeso, 'they searched the villa thoroughly, but never so much as turned their heads to inquire among the laborers. They would not expect to find the daughter of Legate Gallus working in a vineyard.'

'Why—that is just the place for me, then!' exclaimed Diana.

Antonia and Appius exchanged glances.

'Appius hesitated to suggest it,' said Antonia.

'It might be fun,' said Diana.

'Early in the morning, then,' said Kaeso, relieved. 'Antonia will find you suitable clothing. I wish there were some other way to hide you, Diana—but you are not safe here in the villa. It is possible that if they found you they might treat you with every consideration; but it's the Emperor's doings—and everything he does is evil!'

*   *   *   *   *   *

About two hours after midnight, old Lentius—dead asleep on his pallet of straw in the corner of a vacant box-stall—came suddenly awake and rose up on both elbows to listen. Bambo, who always slept beside him, was listening sharply too—and growling ominously.

From outside in the stable-yard came the sound of sandals and hoofs. Someone was leading a horse. Lentius took down his dim lantern from its peg and unfastened the door. Bambo scurried out with savage threats, but in an instant was barking joyfully. Lentius trudged after him, holding the lantern high.

'No, no—Bambo!' came a weary voice. 'Make him shut up, Lentius. He'll rouse the house.'

'Demetrius!' The bent old man peered up into a haggard face.

'Rub this horse down, Lentius. I've abused him. Careful about the water. He's very hot.' Demetrius patted the sagging head sympathetically.

'Bring him in here.' Lentius led the way into his bedchamber. 'They've been hunting you!' he said, in a husky whisper, as he closed the door. 'See here! This horse has been hurt! There's blood all over his shoulder and down his leg!'

'That's mine,' mumbled Demetrius, stripping his shoulder bare. 'I was being pursued by three cavalrymen—out on the Via Appia —about five miles. I outdistanced two of them, but one overtook me, and nicked me with his sword while I was dragging him out of his saddle. Find me some water, Lentius, and a bandage.'

The old slave examined the deep cut and drew a hissing breath through his lips.

'That's a bad one!' he muttered. 'You've lost a lot of blood. Your tunic is soaked. Look at your sandal! You'd better lie down over there!'

'I believe I will,' said Demetrius, weakly, tumbling down on the pallet. Lentius was hovering over him with a basin of water and a sponge. Bambo sniffed inquisitively and turned away to lick the horse's foreleg. 'Lentius—has Tribune Marcellus been here lately?'

Lentius stopped laving the wound—and stared.

'The Tribune! Hadn't you heard? He's been dead—these three months or more! Drowned himself in the sea—poor young master!'

'Lentius, you were fond of the young master, and he liked you. I'm going to trust you with a secret. Now—you're not to repeat this to anybody! Understand? The Tribune is alive—here in Rome.'

'No!' exulted the old man. 'Why doesn't he come home?'

'He will—some day. Lentius—I wonder if you could wake up Marcipor without tearing the house down.'

'It would be easier to waken Decimus. He is on the first floor.'

'I don't want Decimus. Here—let me up. I'll go myself.' Demetrius made an effort to rise, but slumped down again. 'I'm weaker than I thought,' he admitted. 'See if you can get Marcipor. Throw something into his room, and when he comes to the window tell him you want him. Don't speak my name. And ask him to bring some bandages. This isn't going to do any good. Give that horse another drink of water now. Go away—Bambo!'

Marcipor arrived presently, much excited and out of breath, trailed by old Lentius.

'You're badly hurt, my son!' he murmured. 'We must send for the physician.'

'No, Marcipor,' objected Demetrius. 'I'd rather take my chances with this sword-wound than risk having my head cut off. . . . Lentius, if you have another vacant stall, take this friendly horse away and clean him up. And you might take the dog too. Marcipor will look after me.'

Reluctantly, old Lentius led out the tired horse, Bambo following dutifully. Marcipor fastened the door and knelt down in the straw close to Demetrius. He began bandaging the cut.

'You're in danger!' he said, in a trembling voice.

'Not for the moment. Tell me, Marcipor—what's the news? Have you seen anything of Marcellus?'

'He is in the Catacombs.'

'Weird place to hide!'

'Not so bad as you'd think. The Christians have been stocking it with provisions for months. More than a hundred men down there now; the ones who have been identified and are being hunted.'

'They'll be caught like hares in a trap—when the patrols discover where they are.'

'No—it won't be so easy as that,' said Marcipor. 'There are miles of confusing tunnels in that old hideout. The legionaries will not be anxious to go down single-file into that dark hole. They know the old stories about searching parties who went into the Catacombs to hunt fugitive Jews—and never found their way out. . . . How does it feel, Demetrius? Is that too tight?'

There was no answer. Marcipor laid his ear against Demetrius' bared chest, listened, shook him gently, called him in a frightened voice, splashed water in his face; but without response. For an instant he stood irresolute, desperate; then ran panting toward the house, wondering whom he should call for help. Gallio, in his nightclothes, was descending the stairs as Marcipor rushed through the atrium.

'What is the commotion about, Marcipor?' he demanded.

'It's Demetrius, sir!' cried Marcipor. 'He is wounded—dying—out here in the stable!'

'Have you sent for the physician?' asked Gallio, leading the way with long strides.

'No, sir—he did not want a physician. He is in hiding.'

'Put one of the servants on a horse—instantly—and summon Sarpedon. And find help to carry Demetrius into the house. He shall not die in a stable—like a dog!'

Lentius was holding up the lantern for him as Gallio hurried into the stall. 'Demetrius!' he called. 'Demetrius!'

The sunken eyes slowly opened and Demetrius drew a painful sigh.

'At—your—service, sir.' His white lips moved clumsily.

'Attention!' barked Gallio, surveying the wide-eyed group that had crowded about the door. 'Take him up carefully and bring him to the house. Put him in Marcellus' room, Marcipor. Get him out of these soiled garments and wrap him in heated blankets.'

There was a little excitement in the stable-yard as one of the younger slaves made off at a gallop for Sarpedon. A half-dozen grooms and gardeners gathered about the straw pallet and raised it gently.

'You should have called me at once, Marcipor!' said Gallio, sternly, as they followed toward the house. 'Am I then known among you to be so heartless I must not be told when a loyal servant is sick unto death?'

'It was difficult to know what to do,' stammered Marcipor. 'He is being hunted down. He would not have come here, sir, but he wanted to inquire about his master.'

'Meaning me?' Gallio halted abruptly in Marcipor's path.

'Meaning Marcellus, sir.'

'But—had he not heard?'

'He thinks Marcellus is still alive, sir.' Marcipor's voice was weak. 'Demetrius believes that his master is here—in Rome.' They moved past the slaves, shuffling along with their burden, and mounted the steps.

'You told him the truth?' asked Gallio, dejectedly.

'That is the truth, sir,' confessed Marcipor. He put out a hand to steady Gallio, whose face was working convulsively.

'Why have I not been told this?' he demanded, hoarsely.

'Marcellus is a Christian, sir. They are being closely watched. He did not want to endanger the family by coming home.'

'Where is he, Marcipor?' Gallio was climbing the stairs, slowly, a very old man clutching at the balustrade.

'In the Catacombs, sir,' whispered Marcipor.

'What? My son? Down in those old caves with a rabble of brawlers and looters?'

'Not rabble, sir!' disputed Marcipor, recklessly. 'Not brawlers! Not looters! They are honest men of peace—hiding from a cruel idiot who calls himself an Emperor!'

'Quiet, Marcipor!' commanded Gallio, in a husky whisper, as they passed the apartment of Lucia—at home for a few days while Tullus was on special duty. 'How can we get word to my son?'

'It will jeopardize the household, sir, if Marcellus is trailed here.'

'Never mind that! Send for him!'

The slaves had deposited Demetrius on his bed now and were filing out of the room.

'Hold your tongues—about this!' warned Marcipor. He was closing the door on them when Tertia appeared, much frightened.

'What has happened, Marcipor?' She glanced into the room, gave a smothered cry, and dashed through the doorway, throwing herself down on her knees beside the bed. 'Oh—what have they done to you?' she moaned. 'Demetrius!'

Marcipor laid his hand on her shoulder.

'Come,' he said, gently. 'You must help. Go and find more blankets—and heat them.'

'I cannot send for Marcellus, sir.' Marcipor was tugging off his friend's blood-soaked tunic. 'There is no one in this house—except myself—who would be admitted to the Catacombs.'

'And why should they admit *you?*' challenged Gallio sharply. 'You are not one of them; are you?'

Marcipor nodded gravely and busied himself unstrapping Demetrius' sandals.

'Then—saddle a couple of horses—and go!' commanded Gallio. 'Here!—let me do that!' He turned back his sleeves and attacked the stiffened sandal-straps.

Presently Tertia returned with additional blankets, followed by Lucia with a cup of mulled wine. Gallio took the spoon from her hand and poured a few drops of the hot stimulant between Demetrius' parted lips. He swallowed unconsciously. Gallio raised him up a little and put the cup to his mouth, but he did not respond to it. Tertia was sobbing. Lucia gave her a gentle push and pointed to the door.

'Your brother is alive!' said Gallio, when they were alone.

Lucia started, put both hands to her face, and opened her mouth in amazement—but no words came. She clutched at her father's sleeve.

'Marcipor has gone for him,' murmured Gallio, continuing to administer the hot wine with the spoon. 'I hope he gets here—in time.'

'Marcellus—alive!' whispered Lucia, incredulously. 'Where is he?'

Gallio frowned darkly.

'In the Catacombs!' he muttered.

'Oh—but he can't!' exclaimed Lucia. 'He mustn't! Those people are all to be killed! Father!' she moaned. 'That's where Tullus is! He has been ordered to raid the Catacombs!'

Gallio passed his hand over his forehead as to rub away the stunning blow. Tertia pushed the door open to admit Sarpedon, who walked to the bed without speaking, and pushed up Demetrius' eyelids with a practiced thumb. He pressed the back of his hand against the feeble beating in the throat, shook his head, laid his palm against his patient's heart.

'Hot water,' he ordered. 'Fomentations. It may be useless—but— we can try.'

* * * * * *

No explanations were needed to account for Diana's employment in the vineyard. Everybody in Arpino knew her story; had known it and discussed it for nearly three weeks. The villa had not tried to make a secret of her presence there; and the villagers, pleased at being trusted, had felt a partnership in her protection.

Kaeso was proud of his town. It was no small thing, he thought, for all Arpino to hold its tongue in the face of the reward offered for information leading to Diana's discovery. There were, however, a couple of good reasons for this unanimous fidelity.

In the first place, a reward promised by the Emperor was a doubtful claim, even if you had earned it honorably. When had the officials ever kept their promises to the people? In the opinion of Arpino, the fewer dealings you had with the Government, the better you were off. It was crammed with deceit and subterfuge, all the way from the Emperor and the other great ones on down to the lazy drunkard who rode over from Alatri once a year to collect the poll-tax. The Arpinos hadn't a scrap of respect for the Government, either local or national, believing it to be operated by fools and rascals. Even if you were mean enough to disclose the whereabouts of Marcellus' girl, you could be sure that whoever got the reward it wouldn't be you. So reasoned the younger men, lounging of an evening on the green, after arguing idly for an hour on what one might do with a thousand sesterces.

But—according to Antonia—there was a better reason than that why Arpino had kept its secret. Marcellus was gratefully remembered for the many benefits he had contrived. He was already in a fair way to become a legendary character. They had never known anyone like him. It was generally believed—for Arpino was amenable to superstitions—that Marcellus was under the special protectorate of this new Galilean god, who, albeit devoted to peace and good will, had been known to enter people's houses without knocking; and you didn't care to risk having him appear at your bedside, some dark night, to shake you awake, and inquire why you had sold his friend Marcellus' promised bride to Caligula.

Early in the morning of Diana's first day in the vineyard, Vobiscus halted a few of the older men and women as they entered, informing them that she would presently arrive for work—and why. They were to spread the word among the others that the daughter of Legate Gallus was to be treated as they treated one another. She was not to be favored or queried or stared at; nor was she to be shunned. If the legionaries should appear in the vineyard, everyone was to attend to his own business and make no effort to protect Diana, which might only draw attention to her.

When Metella came in, Vobiscus detained her at the gate, explaining that she was to wait until Diana arrived. Then she was to conduct her to a section of the vineyard farthest from the highway, and show her what to do.

'She needn't really work, you know,' grinned Vobiscus, 'but she ought to know how, in case—'

'I don't see why you picked on me,' complained Metella. 'Will I be expected to carry her basket, so she won't soil her lily-white hands?'

'She will not impose on you,' said Vobiscus. 'I should think you would like to get acquainted with someone of her sort. You liked Marcellus; didn't you?'

'Get acquainted; eh?' sniffed Metella. 'I can just see her getting acquainted with anybody like me!'

'Don't be so touchy!' said Vobiscus. 'Here she comes now. Take her with you. Don't be embarrassed. Treat her as if she was—a nobody.'

'A nobody—like me; eh?' commented Metella, bitterly.

'Here I am, Vobiscus,' announced Diana. 'Tell me where I am to go, please.'

'Metella will look after you.' Vobiscus pointed his thumb at the girl, who stood by, scowling. She handed Diana a basket and stiffly led the way, Diana quickly coming abreast of her.

'I hope I'm not going to be a nuisance, Metella. Maybe—if you show me how you do it—'

'You won't need any showing,' said Metella, crisply, staring straight ahead as they passed between rows of curious eyes. 'You'll be just pretending to work.'

'Oh—I shall want to do better than that,' protested Diana, in the low voice that made everything she said sound like a secret.

'It will spoil your hands,' said Metella, sourly—after a long delay.
'Come, now!' coaxed Diana. 'If you'll tell me what I'm doing or
saying that makes me seem a snob, I'll try to stop it.'

Metella drew a slow, reluctant smile that lighted her face a little.
Then the scowl returned, as she plodded along doggedly.

'You had decided you weren't going to like me,' said Diana, 'and I
don't think that's fair. That isn't the way one girl should treat another.'

'But we aren't just two girls together,' objected Metella. 'You're
somebody—and I'm nobody.'

'That's partly true,' agreed Diana, soberly. 'I *am* somebody—and I
thought you were, too. You certainly don't look like a nobody, but
you ought to know.'

Metella gave her a quick glance out of the tail of her eye, shrugged
and grinned.

'You're funny,' she said, half to herself.

'I don't feel very funny,' confided Diana. 'I'm frightened, and I
want to go home to my mother.'

Metella's steps slowed, and she regarded Diana with an almost
sympathetic interest.

'They will not look for you in the vineyard,' she said. 'But they
might find you in the night, at the villa.'

'I have thought of that,' said Diana, 'but there's no place else for
me to sleep.'

Metella mumbled 'That's so,' and put down her basket. She handed
Diana a pair of short, heavy shears. 'All you have to do,' she demonstrated, 'is to clip off the bunch close to the branch, and be careful
not to bruise it.' For some time they worked side by side in silence.

'Have you any room to spare in your house, Metella?' asked Diana.

'I'm sorry,' said Metella. 'It's only a little house, with two small
bedrooms. One for my father and mother.' There was a long pause.
'You wouldn't want to share my kennel.'

'Why not?' said Diana. 'Would you let me?'

'It would make me very happy,' said Metella, wistfully.

'I would pay you, of course.'

'Please!' murmured Metella. 'Don't spoil it.'

Diana laid her hand gently on the girl's thin shoulder, and looked
squarely into her face.

'You told me you were a nobody,' she murmured. 'Aren't you
ashamed?'

Metella gave an embarrassed little chuckle and rubbed the corner
of her eye with a tanned finger.

'You're funny, Diana,' she whispered.

* * * * * *

Marcipor rode swiftly, for his errand was urgent. The night air was
chilly. The horses were lively, especially the Senator's black gelding,

capering alongside. Old Marcipor, who in recent years was not often in the saddle, wished he had chosen to ride Gallio's mount. He could have controlled him better.

Crossing the river on the imposing stone bridge that Julius had built to serve the Via Appia, Marcipor left the celebrated highway and turned off to the right on a rutted road that angled southerly toward the extensive tufa quarries.

It was quite too hazardous an adventure, he felt, to approach the Catacombs by the usual entrance. If the tunnel in the cypress grove were being watched, even from a distance, a man with two horses in charge would most certainly be challenged.

He had never used the secret entrance when alone, and was far from sure that he would be able to find it, for it was skillfully concealed in one of the long-abandoned quarries. He knew he would recognize the quarry, when he came to it, for it was the next one beyond an old toolhouse beside the road. Arriving there, he tied the horses and made his way slowly down the precipitous grade to the floor of the quarry. Feeling his way carefully along the wall in the feeble light of a quarter-moon, the old man came upon a shallow pool—and remembered having waded through it. Beyond the pool there was a cleft in the jutting rock. He entered the narrow aperture and was moving cautiously into its deeper darkness when a gruff voice halted him. Marcipor gave his name, and the sentry—whom he recognized—told him to proceed.

'I came for Marcellus Gallio,' he said. 'His Greek slave, also one of us, lies dying of wounds. It is a hard trip for an old man, Thrason. Will you go and find Marcellus, giving him this message?'

'If you will stand guard, Marcipor.'

It seemed a long time, waiting in the stifling darkness, hearing no sound but the dull thump of his own aging heart. He strained to listen for the scrape of sandals on the rough tufa. At length he saw the frail glow of a taper, far down the slanting tunnel. As it approached, Marcipor saw that two men were following Thrason; Marcellus first, and—the Big Fisherman!

There was a brief, low-voiced colloquy. It was agreed that Marcellus and Peter were to take the horses. Marcipor would spend the night in the Catacombs.

'You told my father I was out here?' asked Marcellus.

'Yes—but he is so rejoiced to know you are alive, sir, that he was not disturbed by your being with the Christians. You may be sure he will keep your secret. Go now, sir. Demetrius had not long to live!'

*   *   *   *   *   *

Lentius led the hot horses away. Lucia, waiting on the portico, ran down the steps and threw herself into her brother's arms, weeping softly and clutching his sleeves in her trembling fingers.

'Is Demetrius still alive?' asked Marcellus, urgently.

'He is still breathing,' said Lucia—'but Sarpedon says he is losing ground very fast and can't live more than another hour.'

Marcellus turned and beckoned to his companion.

'This is Simon Peter, Lucia. He is lately come from Galilee. He, too, knows Demetrius.'

The huge, heavily bearded outlander bowed to her.

'Your servant, my sister!' he said, in a rich, deep voice.

'Welcome,' said Lucia, tearfully. 'Come—let us lose no time.'

Gallio, aged and weary, met them at the top of the stairs, embracing his son in silence. Cornelia, much shaken by the night's events, swayed weakly into his arms, whimpering incoherent endearments. Peter stood waiting on the stairway. The Senator turned toward him with a challenging stare. Lucia indifferently supplied the introduction.

'A friend of Marcellus,' she said. 'What is your name, please?'

'Peter,' he said, in his deep guttural voice.

The Senator nodded coolly, his attitude signifying that the ungroomed stranger was out of his proper environment. But now Peter, who had grown impatient over the delay, had a surprise for Senator Gallio. Advancing, the huge Galilean confronted his haughty Roman host with the authoritative air of one accustomed to giving commands.

'Take me to Demetrius!' he demanded.

At the sound of this strange, insistent voice, Cornelia released Marcellus and gazed at the big foreigner with open-mouthed curiosity. Gallio, dwarfed by the towering figure, obediently led the way to Demetrius' room. They all followed, and ranged themselves about the bedside, Marcellus laying his hand gently on the tousled head. At a sign from Gallio, who was obviously impressed by the determined manner of their mysterious guest, Sarpedon rose from his chair by the bed and made way for the newcomer. With calm self-assurance, Peter took up Demetrius' limp hands in his great, brown fists and shook them.

'Demetrius!' he called, as if he were shouting to him at a vast distance; as if the dying Greek were miles and leagues away. There was no response; not so much as the flicker of an eyelid. Peter called again —in a booming voice that could easily have been heard over on the avenue. '*Demetrius! Return!*'

Nobody breathed. The company about the bed stood statuesque, waiting. Suddenly Peter straightened to his full height and faced them with extended arms and dismissing hands.

'Go!' he commanded. 'Leave us—alone—together!'

They silently obeyed, filing out into the corridor; all but Marcellus, who lagged to ask if he should go too. Peter nodded. He was stripping off his homespun robe as Marcellus closed the door. They all drifted along the corridor to the head of the stairway where, for some time, they stood silently listening for further loud calls from the big Galilean who had taken possession of their house. Marcellus expected to hear some whispers of protest, but no one spoke. A tense silence prevailed. No sound came from Demetrius' room.

After a while the Senator broke the tension by turning toward the stairs. With the cautious tread of a frail old man he slowly descended. Sarpedon sullenly followed, and eased himself into a chair in the atrium. Cornelia took Marcellus by the arm and led him into her bedchamber, Lucia following. No one was left in the corridor now but Tertia, who tiptoed back to Demetrius' door. Crouching down beside it, she waited and listened, hearing nothing but her own stifled sobs.

A half-hour later, Marcellus came out of his mother's room, and queried Tertia with a whisper. She shook her head sadly. He went down to the library and found his father seated at his desk, with no occupation. The haggard old Senator pointed to a chair. After a long moment, he cleared his throat and drew a cynical smile.

'Does your unkempt friend think he is a miracle-worker?'

'Peter is strangely gifted, sir,' said Marcellus, feeling himself at a serious disadvantage.

'Very unusual procedure, I must say! He takes command of the case, discharges our physician, dismisses us from the room. Do you expect him to perform some supernatural feat up there?'

'It would not surprise me,' said Marcellus. 'I admit, sir, Peter has no polish, but he is thoroughly honest. Perhaps we should withhold judgment until we see what happens.'

'Well—the thing that will happen is the death of Demetrius,' said Gallio. 'However—it would have happened, in any event. I should have protested against this nonsense, if there had been the shadow of a hope that Demetrius might recover with proper treatment. I wonder how long we will have to wait for this Jew to finish his incantations—or whatever he is doing.'

'I don't know, sir,' confessed Marcellus. After a considerable pause, he asked, 'Have you learned any of the particulars about Demetrius' injuries?'

Gallio shook his head.

'You will have heard, of course, that he helped Diana escape from Capri? It is said that he is wanted on an old charge of assaulting a Tribune.'

Marcellus came to his feet and leaned over his father's desk.

'She escaped! I haven't heard a word of it. Where is she now?'

'No one seems to know. She is not at home. The Emperor pretends to be much concerned about her welfare, and has had searching parties looking for her.'

'And why is *he* so interested?' asked Marcellus, indignantly; and when his father made no reply, he added, 'Perhaps Demetrius knows where she is. Maybe he got into trouble on her account.'

Gallio made a weary, hopeless gesture.

'If Demetrius knows,' he said, 'he will take his secret along with him, my son.'

Restless and distraught, Marcellus returned to his mother's room and found her sleeping. Lucia was curled up on a couch. He sat down beside her and held her hand. The gray-blue light of dawn had begun to invade the dark corners.

'Is that man still in there?' whispered Lucia.

Marcellus nodded dejectedly, walked to the door, opened it and looked down the corridor. Tertia had left her post. He closed the door, and resumed his seat on the couch beside his sister.

* * * * * *

Tertia started at the sound of the door-latch. The bearded face of the massive Galilean peered out into the corridor.

'Go—quietly,' whispered Peter—'and prepare some hot broth.'

'Oh—is he going to live?' breathed Tertia.

Peter closed the door softly, without replying. Sensing that the family was not yet to be summoned, Tertia slipped down the rear stairway. When she returned, she tapped gently on the door and Peter opened it only far enough to admit her, and closed it again. Demetrius, very white, was propped up in the pillows, awake, but seemingly dazed. He regarded her with a listless glance.

'Do not talk to him yet,' advised Peter, kindly. 'He has come a long way, and is still bewildered.' He took up his robe and put it on. 'You may feed him the broth, as much or as little as he wants. You remain with him. Do not call his master until he asks for him. Admit no others until he is stronger. I am going now.'

'But, sir,' protested Tertia, 'are you leaving without seeing the family? They will want to thank you.'

'I do not want to answer questions,' said Peter, huskily; and Tertia could see that the big man was fatigued. 'I do not want to talk. I am spent.'

At the door, he turned to look again at Demetrius.

'Courage!' he said, in a low tone of command. 'Remember the promise I have made—for you to keep! You are to return to your own countrymen—and testify for our Christos who has made you whole!'

Demetrius' white forehead wrinkled a little, but he made no reply.

After the door had closed, Tertia held a spoonful of the hot broth to his lips. He took it apathetically, studying her face for recognition. She gave him more broth and smiled into his perplexed eyes.

'Know me now?' she whispered, wistfully.

'Tertia,' he answered, with an effort; then, 'Call Marcellus.'

She put down the cup and hastened to find the Tribune. The others crowded about her, asking insistent questions, but she was resolute that only his master might see him now. Marcellus went swiftly, his heart beating hard. He took Demetrius' hands.

'Peter has brought you back!' he said, in an awed voice.

Demetrius moistened his lips with a sluggish tongue.

'A long journey,' he mumbled.

'Do you remember anything?'

'A little.'

'See anyone?'

'Not clearly—but there were many voices.'

'Did you want to return?'

Demetrius sighed and shook his head.

'Where is Peter?' asked Marcellus.

'Gone,' said Demetrius.

Tertia, suspecting that his laconic replies meant he wished to talk to Marcellus privately, slipped out of the room. Demetrius brightened perceptibly.

'Diana is at Arpino—at the villa of Kaeso—in good hands—but —you had better go to her. The Emperor wants her. She is in danger.'

'Are you well enough, Demetrius,' asked Marcellus, nervously—'to let me go—at once?'

'Yes, sir. I shall be leaving, too. Peter made a vow. I am to return to Greece.'

'For the new Kingdom!' Marcellus regarded him with an expression of deference. 'You have been given a great responsibility—full of danger. I shall make out your certificate of manumission—today.'

'I shall be sorry to leave you, sir,' sighed Demetrius.

'Nor do I want you to go,' declared Marcellus. 'But if your life has been saved with a vow, you must fulfill it—at any cost!'

Tertia had opened the door a little way, her anxious frown hinting that there had been enough talk. Marcellus nodded for her to come in. She brought the bowl of broth to the bedside. Demetrius took it hungrily.

'That's good!' said Marcellus. 'You're gaining fast.'

Feeling that the other members of the family should be notified without further delay, he went to his mother's room, finding them all there. He blurted out the news that Demetrius had recovered and was having his breakfast.

'Impossible!' said Gallio, starting toward the door.

Marcellus intercepted him.

'Wait a little, sir,' he advised. 'He's not very strong yet. It is an effort for him to talk.'

'But I want to speak to this Galilean!' said Gallio. 'This is no small thing that has happened. Demetrius was dying! Sarpedon said so!'

'Peter has left, sir. Tertia says he was very weary and didn't want to see anyone.'

'How do you think he did all this?' inquired Cornelia.

'He is a Christian,' replied Marcellus. 'Some of these men who lived close to Jesus have developed peculiar powers. It was no great surprise to me, mother, that Demetrius recovered. He, too, is a Christian. He says that Peter made a vow for him to keep. He is to go back to Greece and work among his own countrymen—'

'What kind of work?' Lucia wanted to know.

'Enlisting people to support the new Kingdom,' said her brother.

'Won't he get into trouble—talking about a new Kingdom?' she asked.

'Doubtless,' agreed Marcellus. 'But Demetrius will not let that detain him.'

'Perhaps he may be glad to return to Greece,' said Lucia. 'Didn't you tell me he was fond of a girl in Athens? What was her name—Theodosia?'

The Senator said he was going down to have his breakfast in the library, and asked Marcellus to join him. Cornelia said she was going back to sleep.

Lucia went to her suite; and, a few minutes later, tapped softly on Demetrius' door. Tertia admitted her, and left the room.

'We are so glad you are better,' said Lucia. 'Marcellus says you are going home to Greece.' She laid a ring in his hand. 'I have kept it safely for you. Now you should have it back.'

Demetrius regarded the ring with brooding eyes, and rubbed it caressingly between his palms. Lucia gave him a sly smile.

'Perhaps you will give it to Theodosia,' she said.

He smiled—but sobered instantly.

'She may find it a costly gift,' he said. 'It might not be fair—to ask Theodosia to share my dangers.'

Sarpedon came in now and stood at the foot of the bed, silently viewing his patient with baffled eyes. It was plain to see that Demetrius was surprised to see him.

'The physician,' said Lucia. 'Do you remember his being here in the night?'

'No,' said Demetrius. 'I don't remember.'

'What did he do—that big fellow from Galilee?' queried Sarpedon, moving around to the other side of the bed.

'He prayed,' said Demetrius.

'What god does he pray to?' asked Sarpedon.

'There is only one,' replied Demetrius.

'A Jewish god?'

'No—not Jewish. God is the father of all men—everywhere. Anyone may pray to him in the name of Jesus who has come to establish a Kingdom in justice and peace.'

'Ah—this new Christian heresy!' said Sarpedon. 'Is your friend from Palestine aware that he can be arrested for pretending to heal diseases by such practices?'

'Pretending?' exclaimed Lucia. 'He wasn't pretending when he healed Demetrius!'

'He should be reported to the authorities,' said Sarpedon, walking stiffly toward the door.

'One would think that a physician would rejoice to see his patient get well,' remarked Lucia, 'no matter how he was healed.'

Sarpedon made no comment. Closing the door emphatically, he proceeded downstairs and entered the library where the Senator and Marcellus were at breakfast. Abandoning his customary suavity, he voiced an indignant protest.

'Come, Sarpedon, sit down,' said the Senator, amiably, 'and have breakfast with us. We do not blame you for feeling as you do. But this is an unusual occurence. You did the best you could. Doubtless you are pleased that the Greek is recovering, even if the treatment was—what shall we say?—irregular?'

Sarpedon refused the fruit that Decimus obsequiously offered him, and remained standing, flushed with anger.

'It might be unfortunate,' he said, frostily, 'if it were known that Senator Gallio had called in one of the Christian seditionists to treat an illness in his household.'

Marcellus leaped from his chair and confronted Sarpedon, face to face.

'You—and your Hippocratic oath!' he shouted. 'You are supposed to be interested in healing! Has it come to pass that your profession is so jealous—and wretched of heart—that it is enraged when a man's life is restored by some other means than your futile remedies?'

Sarpedon backed toward the door.

'You will regret that speech, Tribune Marcellus!' he declared, as he stamped out of the room.

For a few minutes, neither the Senator now Marcellus spoke, as they resumed their places at the table.

'I had hoped we might conciliate him,' said Gallio. 'His pride has been wounded. He can cause us much trouble. If he lets it be known that we are harboring Demetrius—'

'True—we must get Demetrius out of here!'

'Will he be able to travel—today?'

'He must! I am riding to Arpino. He shall go with me.'

'Nonsense!' scoffed the Senator. 'He cannot sit a horse today! I have it! We will send him in a carriage to Pescara. They will hardly be looking for him at an Adrian port.' He rose and paced the room. 'I shall go with him. My presence in the carriage may help him to evade too close scrutiny. Besides—I may be of some service in securing his passage. If there is no ship sailing at once, I may be able to charter one that would see him as far as Brundisium. He should have no difficulty finding a ship there, bound for Corinth.'

'This is most generous of you, sir,' declared Marcellus. 'If every man treated his slaves—'

'Well—as for that'—the Senator chuckled a little—'it has not been my custom to turn out my carriage and personally escort my slaves when they embark for foreign lands. Demetrius' case is different. He has had his life handed back to him in an extraordinary manner and he must keep the pledge that was made for him. Otherwise—he has no right to live!'

'You would make a good Christian, sir,' said Marcellus, realizing at once—by his father's sudden scowl—that the remark was untimely.

'Honorable men were keeping their word, my son, long before this Christian religion was proposed. . . . Come—let us arrange to be on our way. This is not a bad day for it. Rome will not be looking for fugitives this morning. The Ludi Romani will be the city's only concern. Tell Lentius to get out the carriage.'

Chapter XXV

SKIRTING the rim of the city by a circuitous route, and avoiding the congested highways until they were a dozen miles to the east, the carriage, and the horsemen who followed at a little distance, had proceeded without being challenged. Sometimes they had been detained at intersections by the heavy traffic pouring in from the country, but no one had questioned them.

The Senator's belief that this might be safely accomplished had proved correct. If a man wished to leave Rome inconspicuously, this was the day for it. The Ludi Romani—most venerable and popular of all the festivals—was at hand. Though still three days in the offing, the annual celebration in honor of Jupiter was casting a pleasant shadow before it.

Already the populace was in a carnival mood, the streets crowded with riotous merrymakers. Residents were decorating their houses with gay banners and bunting. Their guests were arriving from afar. The noise and confusion increased hourly as every avenue of approach to the capital was jammed with tourists, homecomers, minstrels, magicians, hawkers, dancers, acrobats, pickpockets, and traveling menageries of screeching monkeys and trained bears.

Everyone had caught the contagion of hilarity. All serious work had been abandoned; all discipline relaxed. The word had spread that this year's Ludi Romani would be notable for its gaiety. The new Emperor was not stingy. Glum old Tiberius, who frowned on amusements, was dead and buried. Tight-pursed old Sejanus, who had doled out the sesterces—a few at a time—to Prince Gaius, was also dead. So was Gaius—and good riddance it was, too. This season's Ludi Romani would be worth attending! Little Boots would see to it that everybody had a good time. Even the harried Christians could count upon a ten-day respite from persecution, for the authorities would be too drunk to bother with them.

At Avezzano, the Senator's carriage halted in the shade near a fork in the road. Marcellus, reining up alongside, dismounted to bid farewell to the occupants, for their ways parted here. Thrusting his arm through the open window, he shook hands with his father, assuring him that they would meet soon; and then with Demetrius, who, still weak, was much moved by their parting. Marcellus tried bravely to keep his own voice under control.

'Safe journey, Demetrius!' he said. 'And success to all your undertakings! It may be a long time before we meet—'

'Perhaps not, sir,' murmured Demetrius, smiling wanly.

'Well—be the time long or short, my friend, we shall meet! You
believe that; don't you?'

'With all my heart!'

Remounting the mettlesome Ishtar, Marcellus galloped away, waving a hand as he turned south on the road to Arpino. Here the traffic
was lighter and better time could be made. As the grade stiffened,
Ishtar's enthusiasm cooled somewhat, and she settled to an easy canter.

Now that he had seen Demetrius safely started on his journey,
Marcellus found his spirits reviving. He was on the way to Diana!
Nothing else mattered now. At Alatri, he fed Ishtar in the stableyard
of the inn, while a slave—to whom he had tossed a few coppers—
rubbed her down. Leaving the town, Marcellus led the mare for a mile;
then, remounting, pressed on. The peaks of the Apennines glistened
in the afternoon sunshine.

It was deep in the night when he reached Arpino and was recognized by the guard at the villa gate.

'Do not rouse anyone,' he said. 'I shall stable the mare and find
some place to sleep.'

Not content to trust even Kaeso's competent hostlers with the care
of Ishtar, Marcellus supervised her drinking, talking to her all the
while in a fraternal tone that made the stable-boys laugh. Learning
that his former quarters were unoccupied, he went to bed utterly
exhausted by his experiences during the past twenty-four hours.

*   *   *   *   *   *

Appius Kaeso had felt it an unnecessary precaution for Diana to
work in the vineyard through these days immediately preceding and
during the Ludi Romani which, he knew, would be occupying the
full attention of all who were interested in taking her to the Emperor.

Last night they had brought her back to the villa; and as this was
the first morning, for some time, that Diana could feel comparatively
safe and at leisure, Antonia had insisted upon her sleeping undisturbed until she was thoroughly rested.

Coming out to the stables shortly after dawn, Kaeso learned of Marcellus' arrival and went to his room, finding him awake. In the ensuing
half-hour of serious talk, they informed each other of everything that
had occurred since they parted. Kaeso, Marcellus observed, had lost
much of his impetuous bluster, but could still be identified by his willingness to offer prompt advice.

'Why don't you marry Diana at once?' queried Kaeso. 'As you are
supposed to be dead, Caligula thinks he has a right to pretend an
interest in her welfare. When she becomes your wife, he has no further
justification for concerning himself about her.'

Marcellus, sitting half-dressed on the edge of his bed, spent so long a moment of meditation that Kaeso added, impatiently, 'You two are in love with each other: aren't you?'

'Yes—but the fact is, Kaeso,' said Marcellus, disconsolately, 'Diana is not at all sure that she wants to marry me.'

'Isn't sure?' retorted Kaeso. 'Of course she's sure! Why else would she say she was engaged to you?'

'Did she say that?' Marcellus sat up attentively.

'Nothing less! Isn't it true?'

'Last time I saw her, Kaeso, she insisted that our marriage would be a mistake, because of my being a Christian.'

'Pouf! Diana is as good a Christian as you are! If being a Christian means showing sympathy and friendliness for people who are beneath you, Diana is entitled to a prize! You should have seen her in the vineyard! For a week or more she has been living in a small cottage, rooming with the girl Metella, to whom she has become much attached; and, as for Metella, it has made her over into another kind of person! You wouldn't know her!'

'I'm glad,' said Marcellus. 'I'm glad Diana has had this experience.' His eyes clouded. 'But there is a great deal of difference between Diana's willingness to practice Christian principles and my own obligation to associate myself with a movement that the Government has outlawed—and spend my time with men whose lives are in constant danger. That is what Diana objects to.'

'Well—you can't blame her for that!' snorted Kaeso.

'Nor me,' declared Marcellus. 'I have no choice in this matter.'

*　　*　　*　　*　　*　　*

They met alone in the cool atrium. Antonia, who had been seated beside him, suddenly broke off in the midst of what she was saying, and sped away. Diana was slowly descending the marble stairway. Coming quickly to his feet, Marcellus crossed the room to meet her. She hesitated for a moment at first sight of him; then, with an ecstatic smile, came swiftly into his arms.

'My beloved!' murmured Marcellus, holding her tightly to him. For a long moment they stood locked in their embrace, hungrily sharing the kiss she had offered him. With closed eyes, and tiny breaths like a child's sobs, Diana relaxed in his arms.

'You came for me,' she whispered.

'I wish I could have you—always—darling.'

She nodded slowly, without opening her eyes.

'It was meant to be,' she breathed, softly.

'Diana!' He laid his cheek against hers, gently. 'Do you mean that? Are you mine—in spite of everything?'

Reaching up both arms, she wrapped them tightly around his neck and gave him her lips passionately.

'Today?' whispered Marcellus, deeply stirred.

She drew back to face him with wide eyes, bright with tears.

'Why not?' she murmured. Slipping out of his arms, she took him by the hand. 'Come!' she said, happily. 'Let us tell them!' Her voice was tender. 'Marcellus—they have been so very good to me. This will please them.'

Antonia had joined Appius in the garden. Their faces beamed as Marcellus and Diana came down the path, arm in arm, and they rose to meet them. Antonia surprised Marcellus with a kiss that was by no means a mere performance of a social duty, and Diana kissed Appius, to his immense gratification. Then she hugged Antonia, joyfully.

'Appius,' she said, 'as the master of Arpino, you can marry us. Is that not so?'

'It's the very best thing I do!' boasted Appius, thumping his chest.

'Today?' asked Marcellus.

'Of course!' assured Appius.

'Let us sit down,' suggested Antonia, 'and make some plans. Now— we can have a quiet little wedding in the atrium, with nobody but the family—By the way—where is Antony?'

'Not up yet,' said Marcellus. 'I've inquired for him.'

'Or'—went on Antonia—'we can invite everybody! These people in Arpino love you both. It would be wonderful for them if—'

'Let's have it out on the green,' urged Diana.

'Where Marcellus used to talk to them,' said Appius.

'At sunset,' said Antonia.

'If we are agreed on that,' said Appius, 'I shall send word to Vobiscus that they are to have a holiday. It will give them a chance to clean up, and be presentable.'

'That's very kind,' said Marcellus.

'Here comes Antony now—the sluggard,' said his mother, tenderly. Antony was sauntering along with his head bent, apparently in a profound study. Presently he glanced up, paused momentarily, and then came running. Marcellus embraced him affectionately.

'Why hasn't someone called me?' complained Antony. 'How long can you stay with us, Marcellus?'

'We are going to keep them as long as we can, dear,' said his mother. 'Diana and Marcellus are to be married—tonight.'

Antony, stunned a little by the announcement, solemnly offered Marcellus his hand. Then he turned to Diana, hardly knowing how to felicitate her.

'She's supposed to be kissed,' advised his father.

Antony flushed and appeared at a great disadvantage until Diana came to his rescue with a kiss so frankly given that his composure was restored.

Saying that he must dispatch a servant to the vineyard, Kaeso turned away. Antonia announced that if they were to have a party tonight, she would have to do something about it without delay. Antony, surmising that he too was expected to contrive an errand, remembered that he hadn't had his breakfast. Marcellus and Diana sat down on the lectus, their fingers intertwined.

'Now you must tell me how Demetrius found you,' said Diana.

It was a long story, a moving story that brought the tears to her eyes. Poor Demetrius—so loyal and so brave! And his restoration—so mysterious! How happy to be free—and going home! And back to Theodosia!

'He hasn't much to offer her,' said Marcellus. 'The life of an active Christian, my dear, is lightly held. Demetrius is not a man to shun danger. However—Theodosia will love him no less on that account. If he goes to her, she will take him—for good or ill.'

'I think you meant a little of that for me,' murmured Diana. 'Very well, Marcellus—I shall accept you that way.'

He drew her close and kissed her.

'Kaeso believes,' he said, after a long silence, 'and I agree with him, that it may be fairly safe now for me to take you home to your mother. There is no charge against you. There will be no point to Caligula's pretense of rescuing you, after we are married.'

'But how about *you*, dear?' asked Diana, anxiously. 'There will be much talk about your return, after you were thought to be drowned. Will it come to the Emperor's ears that you are a Christian?'

'Very likely—but we must take that risk. Caligula is erratic. His attention may be diverted from the Christians. The fact that my father is an influential Senator might make the youngster think twice before arresting me. In any case—you can't remain in seclusion indefinitely. Let's have it done with—and see what comes of it.'

'When shall we go?'

'The Kaesos will be hurt if we rush away. Let us wait until the day after tomorrow. The Ludi Romani will have begun. Perhaps we can make the trip safely.'

'Without any attempt to avoid the patrols?'

'Yes, darling. If we were to disguise ourselves—and be apprehended —we would have thrown our case away.'

Diana snuggled into his arms.

'I shall not be afraid,' she murmured, 'if you are with me.'

* * * * * *

All afternoon the men of Arpino raked the grass on the village green. Vobiscus superintended the building of a little arbor which the girls decorated with ferns and flowers. All day long, the kitchens of the villa were busy. The ovens turned out honey cakes. The air was heavy with the appetizing aroma of lambs and ducks roasting on spits before hot charcoal fires. Kaeso's vintner thought his master had gone mad when he learned that wine was to be served to all Arpino!

The hum of voices on the green was hushed when the wedding-party appeared at the villa gate. Then there arose a concerted shout! Cheers for Diana! Cheers for Marcellus! Cheers, too, for the Kaesos!

They took their places under the little, impromptu portico, and a silence fell as Kaeso—never so dignified—joined their hands and demanded them to say that they wished to be husband and wife. In orotund tones, he announced their marriage.

The wedded pair turned about to face the Arpinos. Another happy shout went up! The Kaeso family offered affectionate wishes and caresses. For a moment, the village wasn't sure what to do. An old man ventured to come forward and take their hands, bobbing his head violently. Vobiscus came strutting a little, as became the overseer, followed by his wife, who wore the gayest shawl present. More women came up, trailed by their husbands who shouldered themselves along, grinning awkwardly and scratching an ear. Marcellus knew most of them by name. Diana hugged Metella, and Metella cried. She was going to put Marcellus off with a stiff little curtsy, but he caught her to him and kissed her, which was by far the most noteworthy incident of the occasion. There were cheers for Metella—who was so embarrassed she didn't know where to go or what to do when she got there. Presently Appius Kaeso signaled Vobiscus that he wanted to make an announcement, and Vobiscus gave a stentorian growl that produced a profound silence. The master, he declaimed, had something to say. Kaeso bade them to the feast. Already the villa slaves were coming out through the gate in an imposing procession, weighted by their pleasant burdens.

'Well'—said Kaeso—'shall we return to the villa?'

'Oh, please, no!' said Diana. 'Let us have our dinner here—with them.'

'You surely are a precious darling!' murmured Marcellus.

'But we have ices!' protested Kaeso.

Diana slipped her arm through his, affectionately.

'They can wait,' she whispered.

Kaeso smiled down into her eyes, and nodded indulgently.

'Will you look at Antony?' laughed his mother. Antony, behind a table, wearing an apron, was slicing lamb for the common people of Arpino.

*   *   *   *   *   *

Sarpedon told. With his professional pride deeply wounded, and nothing left to lose in the regard of the Gallio household, he decided to make good his threat to Marcellus.

But it was something more than an impulsive desire to avenge his humiliation that led the physician to betray the family whose lucrative patronage he had inherited from his noted father.

Had the unhappy incident occurred a few weeks earlier, Sarpedon would have pocketed his indignation; but times had changed. Nothing was now to be had by currying favor with the conservatives. Indeed, under the present dynasty one had far better cut loose from such dead weight and not risk going down with it. Young Caligula had no patience with the elder statesmen who believed in national economy and viewed his reckless extravagances with stern disapproval. It was common knowledge that Little Boots intended to break the gray-haired obstructionists at the earliest opportunity.

Sarpedon knew Quintus, though he had seen nothing of him since his sudden elevation to a place of prominence in Caligula's court. Fortunately for himself, old Tuscus had died in the spring; and Sarpedon, who had ministered to the aged poet-statesman's infirmities, had had no occasion to see anything more of their household. He did not know whether he was to be retained as the family physician, now that the old man was gone. Doubtless it would be greatly to his advantage if he could show Quintus which side he was on in the struggle between Little Boots and the Senate.

Hot and eager though he was, Sarpedon had too much sense to go plunging into Quintus' august presence with his betrayal of the Gallios. He dignifiedly asked for an appointment, and restlessly waited the three days which elapsed before the high and mighty Quintus could give him an audience. This delay, however, had enabled Sarpedon to improve his story; for, in the meantime, his butler had learned from Decimus that the Senator and Marcellus had made off with the convalescent Greek on some secret journey.

Having fought his way through the swirling crowds, and arriving at the Imperial Palace disheveled and perspiring, Sarpedon was left standing—for there was no place to sit down—in the great gold and marble and ivory foyer swarming with provincial potentates waiting their turn for favors. Though it was still early in the forenoon, the garishly arrayed dignitaries represented every known state of intoxication, ranging from rude clownishness on through to repulsively noisy nausea.

At length the physician was permitted a brief interview with Quintus, who was prepared to make short work of him until he said he had information about Gallio's Greek slave Demetrius. At that, Quintus gave attention. A Jewish Christian had been invited into the Gallio villa to perform mummeries over the Greek, who had been slightly wounded. Tribune Marcellus—far from dead—had brought the Christian quack to the villa, and had made it plain enough that he too was thoroughly in sympathy with these Christian revolutionists. The Senator and Marcellus had spirited the Greek out of the house and set off with him, doubtless to hide him somewhere.

Quintus was deeply interested, but all the thanks Sarpedon received was a savage denunciation for waiting so long before bringing the news.

'You always were a bungler, Sarpedon!' yelled Quintus. 'Had you not been the son of your wise father, no one would trust you to purge a dog of his worms!'

Having thus learned where he stood in the esteem of the Emperor's favorite, Sarpedon bowed deeply and backed himself out of the room and into the stinking foyer. One hardly knew, these days, how to conduct oneself with any hope of favor at Caligula's hands. One thing was sure, the Empire was on the way toward ruin; but, long before Caligula crashed, he would have seen to it that everybody who believed in any decencies at all was battered into silent submission.

Quintus did not immediately notify Little Boots of Sarpedon's disclosures, thinking it better to capture his quarry. Perhaps he might learn something that would please the Emperor. Marcellus was alive. Without question, he would know the whereabouts of Diana.

A small contingent of seasoned Palace Guards was detailed to put the Gallio villa under surveillance and report all movements there.

Next day they brought back word that the Senator had returned alone in his carriage; but so great was the confusion at the Palace that Quintus decided to wait a more convenient season for action. The court festivities were at such a pitch that there was no room for anything more. The Senator's case would have to wait. Meantime—he told the guards—they should continue their watch at the villa. If Tribune Marcellus showed up, they were to place him under arrest.

This affair was likely to cause the haughty Tullus some embarrassment before they had done with it; but—Quintus shrugged—let Tullus take his medicine and like it. He had no more use for Tullus than he had for Marcellus. It pleased him now to reflect that he had suggested Tullus for the dirty job of cleaning the Christians out of the Catacombs. Quintus chuckled. It would be droll, indeed, if Tullus found himself obliged to arrest his long-time friend: his brother-in-law, too! Very well—let them take it!

* * * * * *

Late in the night of the third day of the Ludi Romani, the news was brought to Quintus that Diana had just arrived at her mother's home, accompanied by Marcellus.

Little Boots, who had been drinking heavily all day, was in a truculent mood, cursing and slapping his attendants as they tried to get him to bed. Ordinarily, after a whole day's drunkenness, His Majesty could be put away quietly; but such was the infernal din on the streets below and throughout the Palace that the Emperor was wide awake with a bursting head.

Even Quintus was coming in for his share of abuse. He found himself responsible for the noise of the celebrants and the shocking condition of the palace. Furthermore, declared the thick-tongued Emperor, the ceremonies today in the Forum Julium had been a disgrace;

and whose fault was that; if not Quintus'? Never had there been anything so tiresome as that interminable Ode to Jupiter! Never had
there been anything so dull as those solemn choruses!

'Yes—but—Your Majesty, were we not obliged to follow the ancient
ritual?' Quintus had asked in honeyed tones. Immediately he repented
of having tried to defend himself. It was the wrong time to answer
Little Boots with a 'yes—but,' no matter what justification warranted
it. His Majesty went into a shrieking, slobbering rage! He was aweary
of being served by fools. High time, he felt, to give some better man
a chance to do his bidding. In nothing—in *nothing* had Quintus
proved himself an able minister!

At that point, Quintus, needing to improve his standing in the
Emperor's regard, had motioned them all out of the imperial bedchamber.

'The daughter of Gallus has been found, Your Majesty,' he announced.

'Ha!' shouted Little Boots. 'So—at last—your snails caught up with
her; eh? And where did they find this beautiful icicle?'

'At home, sire. She arrived there but an hour ago.'

'Did your favorite Greek bring her back?'

'No, sire—the Greek has been hidden by Senator Gallio. Diana was
brought back by Tribune Marcellus, who was thought to have
drowned himself.'

'Oh?—so he turned up; eh? The lover! And what has he been doing
since he was supposed to have drowned?'

'In seclusion somewhere, sire. It is reported that he is a Christian.'

'What?' screamed Little Boots. 'A Christian! And why should a
Tribune consort with such rabble? Does the fool think he can lead a
revolution? Let him be arrested for sedition! Bring him here at once!
Now!'

'It is very late, Your Majesty, and tomorrow is a crowded day.'

'We are weary unto death, Quintus, with these tiresome ceremonies.
What manner of torture does old Jupiter inflict on us tomorrow?'

'Your Majesty attends the games in the forenoon. Then there is
the reception to the Praetorian Guard and the Senate, followed by
the banquet for them—and their women.'

'Speeches—no doubt,' groaned Little Boots.

'It is the custom, sire, and after the banquet there is a procession
to the Temple of Jupiter where the Senate does its homage at twilight.'

'A dull occasion, Quintus. Has it occurred to you that this banquet
for the sullen old dotards might be enlivened with something besides
oratory?'

'Your Majesty will have diverting company at table—the daughter
of Herod Antipas, sire, who is the Tetrarch of Galilee and Peraea.'

'That scrawny, jingling wench—Salome?' yelled Little Boots. 'We
have seen quite enough of her!'

'But I thought Your Majesty had found her very entertaining,' said Quintus, risking a sly smile. 'Was she not eager to please Your Majesty?'

Little Boots made a wry face. Suddenly his heavy eyes lighted.

'Invite the daughter of Gallus! Let her be seated at our right, and Salome at our left. We will encourage Salome to repeat some of her best stories.' He laughed painfully, holding his head.

'Would not Legate Gallus consider that a grave offense to his daughter, sire?'

'It will serve her right,' mumbled Little Boots, 'for bestowing her precious smiles upon a Tribune who hopes to see another government. Send for him without delay, and let him be confined in the Palace prison!'

Quintus made a fluttering gesture of protest.

'Imprisoned—as a Tribune—of course,' Little Boots hastened to add. 'Make him comfortable. And let Diana be bidden to this banquet. You, personally, may extend the invitation, Quintus, early tomorrow. If she is reluctant to accept, suggest that the Emperor might be more disposed to deal leniently with her Christian friend should she be pleased to honor this occasion with her presence.'

'But I thought Your Majesty had been attracted to Diana, and had hoped to win her favor. Would it serve Your Majesty best to threaten her? Perhaps—if she were made much of by the Emperor, the daughter of Gallus might forget her fondness for Marcellus.'

'No!' barked Little Boots. 'What that haughty creature needs is not flattery, but a flick of the whip! And as for her lover'—he cocked his head and grinned bitterly—'we have other plans for him.'

'He is the son of Senator Gallio, sire!' said Quintus.

'All the worse for him!' shouted Little Boots. 'We'll give the old man a lesson too—and the Senate can draw its own conclusions!'

* * * * * *

No less a personage than Quintus himself, attended by a handsomely uniformed contingent of Equestrian Knights, delivered the banquet invitation to Diana. Summoned early from her rooms, she met him in the atrium. She was pale and her eyes were swollen with weeping, but she bore herself proudly. Paula, dazed and frightened, stood by her side.

Quintus deferentially handed her the ornate scroll; and while Diana helplessly fumbled with the gaudy seals, he thought to save a little precious time—for the forenoon was well advanced and the day was loaded with duties. He explained the message. Diana gasped involuntarily.

'Will you say to His Majesty,' spoke up Paula, trying to steady her trembling voice, 'that the daughter of Legate Gallus is far too heartsick to be a suitable dinner companion for the Emperor?'

'Madame'—Quintus bowed stiffly—'this imperial summons is not addressed to the wife of the Legate Gallus, but to his daughter. As she is present, she shall answer for herself.

'My mother has spoken the truth, sir,' said Diana, weakly. 'Please tell the Emperor that I must be excused. I am too ill.'

'Perhaps you should be told,' said Quintus, coldly, 'that your friend Tribune Marcellus, now resting in a dungeon at the Palace, will be arraigned tomorrow on a charge of sedition. The Emperor's judgment in this case may be tempered somewhat if the daughter of the Legate Gallus is disposed to be gracious to His Majesty.'

'Very well.' Diana's voice was barely audible. 'I shall come.'

'If my husband were here,' announced Paula, throwing all prudence aside, 'some blood would flow before this cruel thing came to pass!'

'Madame—you are overwrought,' observed Quintus. 'May I suggest that it is not to your advantage to make such statements? I shall not report this to His Majesty—but I advise you to be more discreet.' Bowing deeply, he turned and marched out through the peristyle, followed stiffly by his retinue.

* * * * * *

Marcellus was surprised at the consideration he was shown by the Palace Guards who arrested him and by the officials at the prison. Perhaps it was due to his rank. Roused from a deep sleep, at the Gallus villa, he had gone down to the atrium to face a Centurion attended by a deputation of twenty legionaries.

Aware that it was useless to resist so formidable a party, he had asked permission to return to his room for his personal belongings, and the request was courteously granted. It was a sorry parting. Diana clung to him, weeping piteously.

'Be brave, darling,' he had entreated. 'Perhaps this is only to humiliate me. The Emperor will probably rebuke me—and set me free—with an admonition. Let us not despair.'

Tearing himself away, he had obediently followed the Centurion. They had offered him a horse; had put him in the midst of them; no one of the drunken merrymakers on the streets could have suspected that he was under arrest.

At the Palace he was taken to the prison. It was subterranean, but well lighted and ventilated, and the room they gave him was comfortably furnished. The Centurion informed him that he was free to notify his friends of his whereabouts: his messages would be dispatched forthwith, and any visitors would be admitted.

Marcellus sat down at once before the desk and wrote a letter.

Marcipor: I am in the Palace prison, held on a charge of treason. Inform my family. You will be permitted to visit me, but perhaps it would be better if the Senator does not subject himself to such a painful errand. I am well treated. Bring me the Robe.—Marcellus.

Shortly after dawn, Marcipor appeared. He bore himself with the gravity and weariness of a very old man. The guards retired after admitting him, their demeanor indicating that no effort would be made to listen to their conversation. Marcipor's hands were cold and shaky. His eyes were full of trouble.

'I would rather die, my son,' he quavered, 'than see you subjected to this grievous persecution.'

'Marcipor—it has sometimes been found necessary for a man to give up his life in defense of a great cause. I am sorely troubled, but not for myself. I sorrow for those who love me.'

'Let me send for Peter!' entreated Marcipor. 'He has great power. He might even be able to deliver you from prison.'

Marcellus shook his head.

'No—Marcipor; Peter's life is too valuable to be put in jeopardy.'

'But the Christos! Might he not come to your rescue—and Peter's?' asked the old man, tearfully.

'It is not right to put the Christos to a test, Marcipor.'

'Here is the Robe, sir.' Marcipor unlaced his tunic and drew out the seamless garment.

Marcellus held it in his arms.

'Let not your heart be troubled, Marcipor,' he said, gently, laying his hand on the old slave's bowed shoulder. 'Come again, tomorrow. There may be better tidings.'

* * * * * *

What hurt Diana most, as she sat at the high table beside the drunken Emperor, was the baffled look of disappointment in Senator Gallio's eyes. He had come alone to the banquet, and only because he must. They had seated him at a distant table, but he and Diana had exchanged glances, and it was plain to see that he believed she had forsaken his son in his hour of peril. She longed to go to him and explain her predicament, but it was quite impossible. Their situation was already much too precarious.

Caligula was giving most of his attention to Salome. He had tried, without success, to have her repeat some of her ribald stories; but Salome, suspecting that she was being used as a catspaw, had assumed an air of virtue. Little Boots, not having seen her in this rôle, was at a loss to know what to do with her. His plan for his entertainment at this boresome banquet was getting quite out of hand. With Diana on his right, coldly dignified and taciturn, and Salome on his left, refusing to conspire with him for Diana's discomfiture, the Emperor— who had arrived at the surly stage of his drunkenness—decided to better his position.

Turning to Salome, he remarked, with intention that Diana should overhear:

'We have captured one of these Christians who seem bent on overturning the government. His case is of special interest because he is a Tribune. Would it amuse you, sweet Salome, to see a Christian Tribune recant—in the presence of the Praetorian Guard and the Senate?'

Salome gave him an enigmatic smile, over her shoulder.

'Unless the Emperor means to see it through,' she drawled, 'it is risky. These Christians do not recant, Your Majesty. My father once undertook to humiliate a Christian before our court; and the fellow—instead of recanting—delivered an address that practically ruined the reputation of the whole family! Me—especially! You should have heard the things he said about me! It was intolerable! We had to punish him.'

Caligula's malicious little, close-set eyes sparkled.

'Whip him?' he asked—making sure Diana heard.

'We beheaded him!' rasped Salome.

'Well—' responded Caligula. 'You *did* punish him; didn't you? What do you do to people, up there in Galilee, when they say something *false* about you?' He laughed loudly, punching Salome in the ribs with his elbow. Then he turned about to see how Diana was liking the conversation. She was deathly white.

Quintus, acting as Praetor, arose to announce Cornelius Capito, who proceeded to make the worst speech of his life; for it was inevitable that it should be a eulogy of Caligula, and old Capito was an honest man. A chorus choir filed in and sang an ode. An Egyptian Prince delivered an address which all but put Caligula to sleep. He beckoned to Quintus, and Quintus whispered to an aide.

'Now,' said Little Boots to Salome, 'we will look into the loyalty of our Christian Tribune. They have gone to fetch him.'

'Remember what I said, sire! These people have no fear.'

'Would you like to lay a little wager?'

'Anything you say, Your Majesty,' she shrugged.

Caligula unclasped an emerald bracelet from his wrist and laid it on the table.

Salome unfastened a gold locket from the chain about her neck and opened it.

'Humph!' grunted Caligula. 'What is it—a lock of hair; eh?'

'From the head of the only honest man I ever met,' declared Salome. 'He was also the bravest.'

Caligula struggled to his feet and the entire assembly of Roman dignitaries rose and bowed. With a benevolent sweep of his arm, he bade them resume their seats. He was moved, he said, by the many expressions of fidelity to the Crown. It was apparent, he went on, thickly, that the Praetorian Guard and the Senate appreciated the value of a united loyalty to the Emperor and the Empire. They cheered him, briefly.

It had lately come to the Emperor's notice, he said, that a secret party of seditionists, calling themselves Christians, had been giving

themselves to vain talk about a King—one Jesus, a Jewish brawler—
who for treason and disturbance of the peace had been put to death
in Jerusalem. His disciples—a small company of ignorant and superstitious fishermen—had spread the word that their dead chieftain had
come alive and intended to set up a Kingdom.

'This foolishness,' continued Caligula, 'would hardly deserve our
recognition were it confined to the feeble-minded fanatics and the
brawlers who fan the flame of such superstitions in hope of gain. But
it now comes to our attention that one of our Tribunes—Marcellus
Gallio—'

Slowly the eyes of the banquet guests moved toward Senator Gallio.
He did not change countenance; sat staring, gray-faced, at Caligula;
his mouth firm-set, his deep eyes steady.

'We are reluctant to believe,' went on Caligula, 'that these reports
concerning Tribune Marcellus are true. It is his right, under our law,
to stand up before you—and make his defense!'

* * * * * * *

Diana was so very proud of him; so very, very proud of him as he
marched, head erect, in the hollow square of Palace Guards as they
stalked into the banquet hall and came to a halt before the Emperor's
high table. The guards were all fine specimens of manhood, in their
late twenties and early thirties; athletes, square-jawed, broad-shoul-
dered, bronzed; yet—in every way—Marcellus, thought Diana, was the
fittest of them all; and if ever this Jesus, whose own heroism had inspired her beloved Marcellus to endure this trial—if ever this Jesus was
to have a champion worthy of him—surely he could ask for none more
perfect than her Marcellus!

She had been so, so afraid he might not understand her being here
beside this sick and drunk and loathsome little wretch, with the pasty
skin and beady eyes and cruel mouth. But no—but no!—Marcellus
understood. Their eyes met, his lighting in an endearing smile. His
lips pantomimed a kiss! Diana's heart beat hard—and her eyes were
swimming.

Marcellus was asked to stand forth—and he stepped forward to face
the Emperor. Everybody stood. The silence in the hall was oppressive.
Outside in the Palace plaza the procession was forming that would
convey Rome's lawgivers to the Temple of Jupiter. The triumphal
music was blaring discordantly from a dozen gaudily decorated equipages in the waiting cavalcade, and the sweating crowds that had
massed in the avenue were shouting drunkenly; but, within the spacious banquet-hall, the silence was tense.

'Tribune Marcellus Gallio,' began Caligula, with attempted dignity,
'you have been accused of consorting with a party of revolutionists
known as Christians. It is said that these promoters of sedition—for
the most part slaves and vandals—have proclaimed the kingship of one

Jesus, a Palestinian Jew, who was put to death for treason, blasphemy, and disturbances of the public peace. What have you to say?'

Diana searched her beloved's impassive face. There was not a trace of fear. Indeed, to judge by his demeanor, the Emperor might have been bestowing an honor. How handsome he was in his Tribune's uniform! What was that brown garment that he held tightly in his folded arms? Diana's throat tightened as she identified the Robe. A hot tear rolled down her cheek. Oh—please—Christos! Marcellus is carrying your Robe! Please—Christos—Marcellus loves you so! He has given up so much for you! He is trying so hard to atone for what he did to you! Please—Christos! Do something for my Marcellus!

'It is true, Your Majesty,' Marcellus was replying, in a steady voice that could be heard through the banquet-hall, 'I am a Christian. But I am not a seditionist. I am not engaged in a plot to overthrow the Government. This Jesus, whom I put to death on a cross, is indeed a King; but his Kingdom is not of this world. He does not seek an earthly throne. His Kingdom is a state of mind and heart that strives for peace and justice and good will among all men.'

'You say you put this Jew to death?' barked Caligula. 'Why, then, are you risking your life to serve as his ambassador?'

'It is a fair question, sire. This Jesus was innocent of any crime. At his trial, the Procurator, who sat in judgment, entreated the prosecutors to release him. He had gone about among the country people advising them to be kind to one another, to be honest and truthful, merciful and forbearing. He had healed their sick, opened the eyes of the blind, and had spoken simple words of consolation to the distressed. They followed him—thousands of them—from place to place—day by day —hanging on his words and crowding close to him for comfort. They forsook their synagogues, where their priests had been interested in them only for their tithes and lambs, and banded themselves together to barter only with men who weighed with honest scales.' Marcellus paused, in his lengthy speech.

'Proceed!' commanded the Emperor. 'You are an able advocate!' He smiled contemptuously. 'You are almost persuading us to be a Christian.'

'Your Majesty,' went on Marcellus, in a remorseful tone, 'I was ordered to conduct the execution. The trial had been held in a language I did not understand; and not until my crime had been committed did I realize the enormity of it.'

'Crime—you say?' shouted Caligula, truculently. 'And was it a crime, then, to obey the command of the Empire?'

'The Empire, Your Majesty, is composed of fallible men who sometimes make mistakes. And this, sire, was the greatest mistake that was ever made!'

'So!—the Empire makes mistakes, then!' growled Caligula. 'Perhaps you will be foolhardy enough to say that the Emperor himself might make a mistake!'

'It is I, Your Majesty, who am on trial; not the Emperor,' said Marcellus, bowing.

Caligula was not quite prepared to deal with that comment. He flushed darkly. A throaty little chuckle came up from Salome's direction, spurring his anger.

'What is that brown thing you have clutched in your arms?' he demanded, pointing his finger.

'It is his Robe, Your Majesty.' Marcellus held it up for inspection. 'He wore it to the cross.'

'And you have the impudence to bring it along to your trial; eh? Hand it to the Commander of the Guard.'

Marcellus obeyed. The Centurion reached out a hand, rather reluctantly, and in effecting the transfer, the Robe fell to the floor. The Centurion haughtily waited for the prisoner to pick it up, but Marcellus made no move to do so.

'Hand that garment to the Commander!' ordered Caligula.

Marcellus stooped, picked up the Robe, and offered it to the Commander who motioned to the guard beside him to receive it. The guard took it—and dropped it. All breathing was suspended in the banquet-hall.

'Bring that thing here!' shouted Caligula, bravely. He extended his hand with fingers outspread. Marcellus moved to obey. Salome glanced up suddenly, caught Caligula's eye, and ventured a warning frown. 'Hand it to the daughter of Legate Gallus,' he commanded. 'She will keep it for you—as a memento.'

It was a most impressive moment. Marcellus reached up and handed the Robe to Diana, who leaned forward eagerly to receive it. They exchanged an intimate, lingering smile quite as if they were alone together. Marcellus stepped back to his place beside the Commander, and all eyes were fixed on Diana's enraptured face as she gathered the Robe to her bosom, regarding it with a tenderness that was almost maternal.

Little Boots was not easily embarrassed, but it was plain to see that the situation was becoming somewhat complicated. He had intended it as a drama to impress the Senate. These great ones needed to learn that their new Emperor expected unqualified loyalty and obedience, and plenty of it, whether the subject be a penniless nobody or a person of high rank. The play hadn't gone well. The other actors were neglecting to furnish cues for the imperial speeches. His face was twisted with a mounting rage. He glared at Marcellus.

'You seem to attach a great deal of significance to this old coat!'

'Yes, Your Majesty,' replied Marcellus, quietly.

'Are you fool enough to believe that there is some magic in it?'

'It does possess a peculiar power, Your Majesty, for those who believe that it was worn by the Son of God.'

There was a concerted stir throughout the great room; sound of a quick, involuntary intake of breath; throaty sound of incredulous murmurs; metallic sound of sidearms suddenly jostled in their scabbards as men turned about to dart inquiring glances at their neighbors.

'Blasphemer!' bellowed Caligula. 'Have you the effrontery to stand there—at this sacred feast in honor of Jupiter—and calmly announce that your crucified Jew is divine?'

'It is not in disrespect to Jupiter, Your Majesty. Many generations of our people have said their prayers to Jupiter, and my King is not jealous of that homage. He has compassion upon every man's longing to abide under the shadow of some sheltering wing. Jesus did not come into the world to denounce that aspiration, but to invite all who love truth and mercy to listen to his voice—and walk in his way.'

Diana was so proud; so very proud of Marcellus! Really—it wasn't Marcellus who was on trial! Everybody in the great room was on trial —all but Marcellus! Caligula was storming—but he had no case! Oh— she thought—what an Emperor Marcellus would have made! She wanted to shout, 'Senators! Give Marcellus the crown! Let him make our Empire great!'

The stirring music from the plaza was growing in volume. The shouts of the multitude were strident, impatient. It was time for the procession to start.

'Tribune Marcellus Gallio'—said Caligula, sternly—'it is not our wish to condemn you to death in the presence of your aged father and the honorable men who, with him, serve the Empire in the Senate. Deliberate well, therefore, when you reply to this final question, Do you now recant—and forever renounce—your misguided allegiance to this Galilean Jew—who called himself a King?'

Again a portentous hush fell over the banquet-hall. Salome was observed to glance up with an arch smile and a little shrug, as she picked up the Emperor's emerald bracelet and clasped it on her arm.

'Your Majesty,' replied Marcellus, 'if the Empire desires peace and justice and good will among all men, my King will be on the side of the Empire and her Emperor. If the Empire and the Emperor desire to pursue the slavery and slaughter that have brought agony and terror and despair to the world'—Marcellus' voice had risen to a clarion tone —'if there is then nothing further for men to hope for but chains and hunger at the hands of our Empire—my King will march forward to right this wrong! Not tomorrow, sire! Your Majesty may not be so fortunate as to witness the establishment of this Kingdom—but it is coming!'

'And that is your final word?' asked Caligula.

'Yes, Your Majesty,' said Marcellus.

Caligula drew himself up erectly.

'Tribune Marcellus Gallio,' he announced, 'it is our decree that you be taken immediately to the Palace Archery Field—and put to death— for high treason.'

Even while the sentence was being passed, a fresh sensation stirred the audience. Diana had left her place at the Emperor's table and was walking proudly, confidently, down the steps of the dais, to take her stand beside Marcellus. He slipped his arm about her, tenderly.

'No, darling—no!' he entreated, as if no one heard. 'Listen to me, my sweetheart! You mustn't do this! I am willing to die—but there is no reason why you should risk your life! Bid me farewell—and leave me!'

Diana smiled into his eyes, and faced the Emperor. When she spoke, her voice was uncommonly deep, for a girl, but clearly audible to the silent spectators of this strange drama.

'Your Majesty,' she said, calmly, 'I, too, am a Christian. Marcellus is my husband. May I go with him?'

There was an inarticulate murmur of protest through the banquet-hall. Caligula nervously fumbled with his fingers and shook his head.

'The daughter of Gallus is brave,' he said, patronizingly. 'But we have no charge against her. Nor have we any wish to punish her. You love your husband—but your love will do him no good—when he is dead.'

'It will, sire, if I go with him,' persisted Diana, 'for then we will never part. And we will live together—always—in a Kingdom of love— and peace.'

'In a Kingdom; eh?' chuckled Caligula, bitterly. 'So—you too be-lieve in this nonsense about a Kingdom. Well'—he flicked a negligent gesture—'you may stand aside. You are not being tried. There is no indictment.'

'If it please Your Majesty,' said Diana, boldly, 'may I then provide evidence to warrant a conviction? I have no wish to live another hour in an Empire so far along on the road to ruin that it would consent to be governed by one who has no interest in the welfare of his people.'

There was a spontaneous gasp from the audience. Caligula, stunned to speechlessness, listened with his mouth open.

'I think I speak the thoughts of everyone present, sire,' went on Diana, firmly. 'These wise men all know that the Empire is headed for destruction—and they know why! As for me—I have another King —and I desire to go with my husband—into that Kingdom!'

Little Boots' face was livid.

'By the gods—you shall!' he screamed. 'Go—both of you—into your Kingdom!'

He jerked a gesture toward the Commander of the Guards. There was an order barked. A bugle sounded a strident blast. The drums rattled a prolonged roll. The tall soldiers, marking time, waited the crisp command. The word was given. Marcellus and Diana, hand in hand, marched in the hollow square, as it moved down the broad aisle toward the imposing archway. Old Gallio, trembling, pushed forward through the crowd, but was detained by friendly hands and warning murmurs.

As the procession of guards, and the condemned, disappeared through the great marble arch, the audience was startled by the harsh, drunken laughter of Little Boots.

Amid loud, hysterical guffaws, he shrieked, 'They are going into a better Kingdom! Ha! Ha! They are going now to meet their King!'

But nobody—except Little Boots—thought it was an occasion for derisive laughter. There was not a smile on any face. They all stood there, grim and silent. And when Little Boots observed that his merriment was not shared, he suddenly grew surly, and without a dismissing word, stumbled toward the steps of the dais where Quintus took his arm. Outside—the metal music blared for Jupiter.

Hand in hand, Diana and Marcellus kept step with the Guards. They were both pale—but smiling. With measured tread the procession marched briskly the length of the corridor, and down the marble steps into the congested plaza. The massed multitude, not knowing what was afoot, but assuming that this was the first contingent of the notables who would join the gaudy parade to the Temple of Jupiter, raised a mighty shout.

Old Marcipor strode forward from the edge of the crowd, tears streaming down his face. Marcellus whispered something into Diana's ear. She smiled—and nodded.

Slipping between two of the guards, she tossed the Robe into the old man's arms.

'For the Big Fisherman!' she said.

THE END